FIRST IMPRESSIONS

A Selection of Recent Titles by Margaret Thornton

ABOVE THE BRIGHT BLUE SKY
DOWN AN ENGLISH LANE
A TRUE LOVE OF MINE
REMEMBER ME
UNTIL WE MEET AGAIN
TIME GOES BY
CAST THE FIRST STONE *
FAMILIES AND FRIENDSHIPS *
OLD FRIENDS, NEW FRIENDS *
FIRST IMPRESSIONS *

* *available from Severn House*

FIRST IMPRESSIONS

Margaret Thornton

This first world edition published 2014
in Great Britain and 2015 in the USA by
SEVERN HOUSE PUBLISHERS LTD of
19 Cedar Road, Sutton, Surrey, England, SM2 5DA.
Trade paperback edition first published
in Great Britain and the USA 2015 by
SEVERN HOUSE PUBLISHERS LTD.

British Library Cataloguing in Publication Data

Thornton, Margaret, 1934- author.
First Impressions.
1. Widows–Fiction. 2. Vacations–Germany–Black
Forest–Fiction. 3. Bus travel–Fiction. 4. Love stories.
I. Title
823.9'14-dc23

ISBN-13: 978-0-7278-8472-5 (cased)
ISBN-13: 978-1-84751-575-9 (trade paper)
ISBN-13: 978-1-78010-621-2 (e-book)

Typeset by Palimpsest Book Production Ltd.,
Falkirk, Stirlingshire, Scotland.

One

Jane Redfern leaned back in her seat as the coach pulled away from the depot just outside Preston. The seat next to her was empty at the moment, and she couldn't help hoping that it would remain so. She knew, however, that that was not very likely. Most probably every seat would be booked for this popular coach tour to the Black Forest in Germany.

Don't be so faint-hearted! Jane rebuked herself. She had come on this holiday for a change of scenery and a well-earned rest, and, so her friends had assured her, for a chance to meet interesting people. As they headed south along the motorway the driver broke into her wandering thoughts.

'Good morning, everyone. My name is Mike, and I'm your driver for the next ten days. So let's start by saying hello, shall we? Good morning, everyone . . .'

There was a feeble reply from the passengers. 'Good morning . . .'

Some added, '. . . Mike.'

'Now, that won't do at all, will it?' the driver rejoined. 'Let's sound as though we mean it. Good morning, everyone . . .' His voice was louder this time.

The reply from the passengers was louder too, and Jane made herself join in the greeting. She was hoping, though, that Mike wouldn't turn out to be one of those larger than life chaps, forcing everyone to join in and have a jolly good time. It wasn't that she was averse to mixing with people, but she liked it to be on her own terms.

'That's much better!' said Mike. 'Now, I'll leave you alone for a while to catch up on your sleep if you like, or to have a natter. We'll be picking up the rest of our passengers at our depot in the Midlands, that'll be in a couple of hours, so I'll leave you in peace till then.'

Jane tried to relax. She opened her copy of *Woman's Own* but her mind would not settle to reading a romantic story or details of people's problems. She had problems of her own, but nothing like the lurid tales that were to be found here; stories of infidelity and double-dealing and wayward children. And some even more personal than those, if you could believe the half of it!

She turned to the fashion page. For the summer of 2005 skirts were still short, but if you had worn a miniskirt back in the nineteen seventies maybe you were too old to wear one again. Jane had been a teenager then and had worn miniskirts when she was not in school uniform. Now, at the age of forty-five, she felt she was unable to wear very short skirts, but she had bought a couple of new dresses for her holiday, with hemlines that were rather more modest, just above the knee. Most of the time, though, she wore trousers and jumpers, or what they now called 'tops', which covered a wide variety of garments: blouses, sweaters, T-shirts, tunics – they were all known as tops. Colours were vibrant again this year: raspberry pink, acid yellow, lime green . . . Jane favoured bright colours as a rule as her complexion was pale, and her dark hair and brown eyes were enhanced by more glowing shades, or so her friends had told her. Left to herself she was not inclined to be an avid follower of fashion. Not any more . . .

She closed her magazine. Her thoughts kept straying to her mother whom she had left behind the previous day in a retirement home on the outskirts of the town. It had taken a great deal of persuasion for her mother to agree to this measure. Indeed, Jane herself had been loath to take such a step, but her friends had insisted that she was badly in need of a break, and surely her mother would not object, 'just for a week or ten days?'

Jane had agreed that she did need a rest and a break from routine. She had suffered from a nasty attack of flu during the winter and had never really regained her strength. She was working almost full time as well as running her home and caring for her mother. When she had first broached the subject of the rest home her mother had been adamant that she would not go into what she called 'one of those old folks' homes'.

'Not on your life!' Alice Rigby had retorted. 'I'm not going to one of those places where they sit around like zombies all day, staring at the telly. I may be getting on a bit, Jane, but I've still got all my marbles.'

'But it isn't like that at the place I've found, Mother.' Jane had visited the few homes that had been recommended to her and had found one that she considered very suitable. 'It's called 'Evergreen', and it's more like a hotel than a rest home. You'd have your own private room – en suite – and your own TV, although there's a large one in the lounge as well that the residents like to watch together. They all seemed very nice and friendly.'

'And why are they there, eh? Tell me that. Because their children can't be bothered to look after them, that's why.'

'I don't know, Mother! I don't know their life histories, do I?'

Jane couldn't help feeling a little exasperated. Her mother was enough to try the patience of a saint at times. And Jane knew that she wasn't a saint although she did do her best. She and her mother had never got along all that well. Even as a child Jane had felt that her mother was overcritical of her, unwilling to give her too much praise for her achievements. She always felt that Mother would have preferred to have had a son, but her parents had been blessed with just the one child.

Jane's father, Joe Rigby, had adored his little girl and had done his best to ease the tension that often built up between his two womenfolk. When Joe had died, some eight years ago, Jane had felt as though she had lost a friend and ally as well as a father. Fortunately, though, she was happily married by that time to Tom Redfern. They had both been in their early thirties when they married and they had had no children. They would have liked to have had a family, but no children had come along. Rather than having tests to discover why, they had decided they were very happy as they were. And adoption had never been considered. When Alice had started to suffer with osteoarthritis a year after her husband's death, Jane had persuaded her, eventually, to sell her home and go to live with them.

It was lucky that Tom was easy-going and bore with the often difficult elderly lady. But it was a devastating blow to Jane when, two years ago, Tom died after an attack of bronchitis that had turned to pneumonia. The two women were left alone together and had to get along as well as they could. It was far from easy at times, and Jane knew that her mother would benefit from a change of company just as much as she would.

'It would only be for ten days, Mother,' Jane had told her, 'while I have a holiday, and I'm sure you'd enjoy it. It's a big old house that's been modernized, and there's a lovely garden at the back where you can sit and relax. And a games room . . .'

'I can't see myself playing ping-pong!' retorted Alice.

'Not those sort of games, Mother! They were playing cards, and dominoes, and some of them were doing a big jigsaw puzzle.'

'Huh! Jigsaws! Those are for kids.'

Jane sighed. 'Well, I've done my best. You said yourself that I needed a break, didn't you? And it would be a nice change for you as well.'

Alice didn't answer for a moment. Then, 'Well, I suppose I might give it a try,' she admitted. 'And where are you thinking of gadding off to on this holiday?'

Jane had already made a provisional booking with the travel company, crossing her fingers that her mother would eventually see reason. 'It's a little trip abroad, Mother, with the Galaxy Travel company; to France and then on to Germany.'

'Germany!' Alice stared at her in amazement. 'Why in heaven's name do you want to go to Germany? They were our enemies not so long ago. Don't you remember?'

'That was years ago, Mother. And of course I don't remember. How could I? I wasn't even born then. And people don't think like that any more. We're all in the EU now, aren't we?'

'And the least said about that the better,' Alice muttered.

Jane went on as though she hadn't heard her. 'Well, that's where I intend to go. From what I've heard Germany is a beautiful country. The hotel is in a village in the Black Forest, and we'll be travelling through the Rhine valley as well.'

But Alice was still way back in the past. 'Your father did his best for King and Country in the war. He was in the D-Day landings. I didn't know him then, of course, but he told me enough about it. He never had any time for the Germans. I'm sure I don't know what he would have thought about it, you going hobnobbing with the folks he was fighting against.'

Jane felt that her father would have told her to go and enjoy herself. Like many of the men who had served in the Second World War, Joe Rigby had not wished to relive his experiences. There were many who did so, looking back with pride and nostalgia to their glory days, and going off each year to reunions. But Joe had taken up a new career on leaving the army, looking to the future and not back to the past. Jane believed his policy had been to live and let live, despite what his widow was saying.

'It's all history, Mother,' Jane had told her. 'So . . . are you willing to give it a try in this place I've found? I want you to be very sure about it,' she added.

'I'm as sure as I'll ever be,' said Alice, with an exaggerated sigh. 'You go ahead and do as you please. I know I'll have no peace if I don't agree.'

'Thank you, Mother,' Jane said quietly. She had confirmed the reservation the next day, and for the last two months had been looking forward to her trip abroad.

She had been abroad before, but only twice. The first time had been on a school trip to France when she was fifteen years old. The group of twelve fifth-formers had stayed at the homes of their penfriends in the town of Rouen. It had been Jane's father who had persuaded her mother that it would be good for Jane to go, and because her dad had been keen she had gone along with the idea. She had been homesick, though, for some of the time and had found everything very strange. She and her penfriend, Adele, had got on reasonably well, though, and Jane had learnt to speak French quite fluently after furthering her study of the language when she got back to school.

She and her husband, Tom, had spent their honeymoon in Paris; a wonderful five days that she looked back on with poignant nostalgia. Since that one time they had holidayed in the UK, touring Scotland, the Yorkshire Dales or the Cotswolds in their own car. They had both been drivers, and Jane still used the car for work and for ferrying her mother around. She had never wanted to go touring alone, and although she had several friends, some of them close ones, they were all happily married.

After a couple of hours the coach pulled up at the depot in the Midlands.

'We'll stop here for forty minutes,' said Mike. 'It's a comfort stop, so make use of the facilities, and have a quick cup of tea or coffee, if you wish. We'll be picking up the rest of our passengers here. Then we have one more stop for lunch in another two hours or so, and after that it's full steam ahead for Dover. OK, ladies and gents, see you in a little while . . .'

Jane made use of the facilities, as suggested. There was a toilet at the back of the coach, which seemed to be obligatory now, but the majority of passengers preferred not to use it. Jane had a fear of opening the wrong door and ending up on the motorway! She paid an exorbitant price for a polystyrene beaker of coffee, had a look round WH Smith's, then it was time to return to the coach.

She noticed as soon as she stepped aboard that there was now someone sitting in the seat next to hers, halfway down the coach. And it was a man! She felt her heart plummet to the soles of her new summer shoes. She had been hoping that it might be a woman of around her own age, with whom she could form a friendship, if only for the duration of the holiday.

It wasn't that she disliked men. She had been happily married, and she got along well enough with the men she met in the course of her work and with her friends' husbands. But she found herself ill at ease and a little tongue-tied when she was with men she didn't know. For the past year, by which time her friends had thought she might be glad of some male company, she had been subjected to various attempts at match-making. Several times she had been asked to go to supper parties, and had found herself sitting next to a man who, also, was without a current partner. To her friends' disappointment, nothing had come of these attempts. They did not seem to realize that she was content on her own, for the time being at least. She still missed Tom very much and had never felt the need for exclusive male friendship. She could never feel for anyone else what she had felt for Tom.

At first glance she saw a man whom she guessed to be around her own age, very spruce and efficient-looking with sleek dark hair. She could not judge his height as he was sitting down, but he stood as he saw her approaching, rather diffidently, although she was trying to summon up her courage. He was of medium height, as she was, and of a slim athletic build.

She smiled, unsurely, and he nodded at her, his lips curving just a little. He stood to one side to allow her to pass. 'Yours is the window seat, I believe,' he said.

'Er . . . yes; I think so,' she faltered. 'That's where I was sitting, but I don't mind. You can sit by the window if you like.'

He smiled then, as though he was amused. 'Well, we're not going to fall out about it, are we? I only booked a couple of weeks ago, so I'm sure the seat is yours. I thought I was lucky to get a place at all as I'd left it so late.'

They both sat down, then Jane decided she would take off her jacket. The weather was improving now, it had been cloudy in the early morning when she had left home and it had looked as though it might rain. It had been an unsettled month so far, but now, by mid-June, everyone was hoping that the summer would eventually arrive. The clouds had dispersed and the sun was shining now.

'Shall I put that up on the rack for you?' her travelling companion asked as she shuffled out of her jacket.

'Oh, thank you, that's very kind,' she replied. It was more of a cupboard than a rack over each seat where smaller belongings could be stored.

They had not yet introduced themselves, and Jane was wondering whether to make the first move when the driver came down the coach counting heads.

'All present and correct,' Mike said as he sat down behind the wheel. 'Thanks for getting back on time. If you continue to do that it will make life much easier for us drivers. I've got my mate with me now to assist with the driving. This is Bill . . .'

A cheerful-looking man of a somewhat corpulent build stood

up and said, 'How do, everyone,' to the passengers. It would be easy to remember which was which driver as they were dissimilar in looks. Bill was ginger-haired, whereas Mike was dark and slimmer than his colleague.

'How do, Bill,' most of them replied, not quite so timidly now.

'We won't be travelling enormous distances,' said Mike. 'It's a pretty easy tour, lots of time for looking around, not a whistle-stop tour like some of them are. But Galaxy Travel have been surprisingly generous in allowing us two drivers, and I'm sure we're all going to have a very pleasant time together. So, ladies and gents, off we go again . . .'

It was Bill who addressed them as Mike drove away. He stood facing them at the front of the coach. 'I'm obliged to draw your attention to the emergency exits,' he said, pointing to the windows at the front and rear. 'And there's a first aid box above the driver's seat. So now that's out of the way it's time to get to know one another. I dare say most of you know the person sitting next to you, your hubby or the wife, or your best friend or partner, eh? But if you don't know them, then say hello to them now. Or else say 'how do' to the people sitting across from you. It's good to make new friends, isn't it?'

Jane and her travelling companion turned to look at one another, then, to her relief, he laughed and held out his hand. 'Hello, or should I say how do? I'm David Falconer, usually known as Dave.'

He held her hand in a firm grasp, and as he smiled at her in a friendly way she noticed that his eyes were a luminous grey, candid and clear. She began to feel more at ease. Perhaps it was going to turn out all right.

'How do you do?' she said politely. She had been told it was not correct to say 'Pleased to meet you', although lots of people did. 'I'm Jane Redfern, always known as Jane! That's the only name I've got,' she added. 'I've often wished my parents had given me a second one.'

He smiled. 'Not always a good thing, believe me! My second name is Archibald – after my father, but I hate it! He was always called Archie – I guess he didn't like it either – so I can't imagine what possessed my parents to saddle me with it.

But there's nothing wrong with Jane; a good old English name, isn't it?'

'Yes, I suppose so . . .'

'So . . . what brings you here, Jane, travelling to Germany with Galaxy? And on your own? I assume you're on your own?'

'Yes, I am,' she replied. 'It took quite a lot of courage for me to make the booking. But my friends tried to assure me that I'd nothing to worry about, and Galaxy Travel was highly recommended. I would have preferred to come with a friend, but it just wasn't possible. They're all married, you see . . . and my husband died two years ago.'

'Oh . . . I see; I'm sorry,' Dave said quietly. 'I'm in the same position myself, as a matter of fact. I lost my wife four years ago and I've never been able to find anyone to come away with me. Actually, I'm not bothered, I suppose I'm a bit of a loner. I don't mind my own company, but it's usually a friendly crowd on these Galaxy tours.'

'You've been with them before, then?'

'Yes, this is my third time. The first time I did a five-day tour to the bulb fields in Holland, and last year I went to Belgium – to Brussels and Bruges. So I thought I'd go a little further afield this time. What about you? Why did you choose Germany?'

'I liked the sound of it in the brochure, and it's a leisurely tour – a night in Calais, then a night in the Rhine valley, then six nights in the Black Forest. I like to see nice scenery and interesting places, rather than sea and sand. My mother threw up her hands in horror, though, at the idea of me going to Germany.'

Dave smiled. 'Yes, elderly folk have long memories. But we're never likely to forget, are we, while they're still showing war films on the TV? My father loved to watch them even though he'd served in the war. He came through it unscathed, though, he was one of the lucky ones.'

'Yes, so was my father,' said Jane. 'He never talked about it, though. It's Mother who still thinks of the Germans as our enemies.'

'You still have both your parents, have you, Jane?'

She told him briefly of her circumstances; about her father's death and how, as she was the only child, she now lived with and cared for her mother. 'I hope she's settled down in the home,' she said, 'and isn't finding fault with everything.'

'Try not to worry,' said Dave. 'It's not for very long and the majority of homes are very comfortable. I do know how you feel, though. My mother is in a retirement home, permanently, I'm afraid. But she loves it and she's made lots of new friends. It was a hard decision for me and my sister to make, but in the end it was Mother who decided for us. She chose the place she wanted to go to and she's very happy there. She would have felt isolated living with me – out in the wilds, she said – and my sister lives down in the south of England.

'Do you live in the country, then, Dave?' asked Jane. To her surprise she found it quite easy to use his Christian name.

'Yes, I have a farm in Shropshire, a few miles from Shrewsbury, on the way to Welshpool. It's not all that far from the Welsh border. Mother finds it lonely after living in Shrewsbury all her life.'

'You mean . . . you're a farmer?' Jane looked at him in some surprise. Dressed, as he was, in a smart sports jacket, with a modern striped shirt and a toning tie he looked the picture of elegance. The last thing she would have expected him to be was a farmer. He looked more like a bank manager.

He laughed. 'Yes, that's what I am. What did you expect? A pork pie hat and corduroy breeches, and a straw between my teeth?'

'No, of course not,' said Jane hurriedly, fearful that she might have offended him. 'I was just . . . rather surprised, that's all.'

'Yes, I know I don't look much like a farmer when I'm not working. I seldom get a chance to dress smartly, so I make the most of it when I can. I'm not able to get away from the farm all that often.'

'You've left someone in charge this week?'

'My son. He works there along with me. I expect he'll take it over . . . one of these days. And we have a couple of farm hands, and casual labour when we need it.'

'So it's a family business, is it, passed from one generation to the next?'

'Sort of . . . It belonged to my grandfather, then my uncle

took it over. My father wasn't interested in farming – just the opposite, he became a solicitor – but the love of the land was passed on to me. I started working with my uncle when I left school. Then I did a college course to learn more about it, and so . . . there I am. A real live farmer, though I may not fit the image!'

Jane couldn't help thinking that he looked more like a gentleman farmer, but she didn't say so. Maybe, despite his immaculate appearance now, he would not be afraid of mucking in with the rest of his fellow workers.

'What sort of a farm is it?' she asked. 'Arable, sheep, cows . . .?' She laughed. 'I'm afraid I'm very ignorant when it comes to farming.'

'Mainly arable,' he replied. 'It's good fertile soil in Shropshire. But we have a small herd of cows as well, and pigs and poultry. No sheep. We're quite near to Wales but the land is fairly flat where we are; ideal for growing crops . . . And I think that's quite enough about me. What about you, Jane? I should imagine you have a job, as well as running a home? I know most women do nowadays.'

'Yes, I have a job,' she replied. 'I work for the GPO. I've been with them ever since I left school.'

'You work on the counter?'

'Yes, I trained as a counter clerk. I was sent all over the place when I was training – to Yorkshire and Manchester and Liverpool. Then I was fortunate in getting a post at the main office in Preston, which is where I live. That's where I met my husband, when he was transferred there from the office in Coventry. It was his first job as a supervisor after being a postman.' She stopped, aware that she might be rambling on about things that were irrelevant. 'Anyway, I'm in charge of a sub post office now, near to where I live. It's convenient because it means I'm able to get home at lunchtime to see to Mother.'

'A lot of sub post offices have closed down, haven't they?' said Dave.

'Yes, I'm afraid so. More and more are disappearing, even some of the larger ones. Fingers crossed, though, we're still open. It's a thriving little business, part of a newsagent's and general store so we think it might be safe for a while.'

The couple of hours to the lunch stop had flown by, and Jane was surprised when Bill announced that they would be stopping in five minutes' time. 'I know some of you will have brought your own sandwiches,' he said, and you can stop on the coach to eat them if you wish. Or there are some tables and wooden benches outside the service place. OK, ladies and gents, see you in forty-five minutes.'

'I expect you've brought your own lunch, haven't you?' asked Dave. Jane agreed that she had done so.

'I'm afraid I'm not so well organized,' he told her. 'I'll go and stretch my legs and have a spot of lunch. I know it'll cost me an arm and a leg!' He grinned. 'But never mind, eh? We're on holiday, aren't we? See you later, Jane . . .'

She was relieved that he had gone. She was enjoying his company, but she would have felt embarrassed if they had left the coach together, as though they were a couple. She wouldn't have known what to do. Stay with him? Or wander off on her own? Luckily the decision had been made for her. She stayed where she was for a few moments, then she decided that as it was a pleasant day she would eat her ham sandwiches outside, and perhaps buy a carton of orange juice at the shop.

Then she would phone her mother, as she had promised to do. It might be the last chance she had before leaving the shores of England.

Two

'Phone call for you, Alice . . .' Nancy, one of the care assistants popped her head round the door of the lounge where several of the residents were watching the television. 'I expect it'll be your daughter.'

'Yes, no doubt it will.' Alice Rigby eased herself out of the armchair, then, with the aid of her stick she made her way slowly to the hallway where the telephone was situated. She took her time about it. She was unable to walk quickly anyway, but it wouldn't do any harm to keep her daughter waiting a moment or two. She'd be on that mobile phone, of course, a newfangled idea that Alice had no time for.

She sat down on the chair by the telephone table and picked up the receiver. 'Hello . . .' she said.

'Hello, Mother; it's me.' Jane sounded bright and cheerful, as well she might, setting off on a Continental holiday.

'Well, of course it's you!' answered Alice. 'Who else would be ringing me? Hardly anyone knows I'm here, and if they do they're not likely to ring.'

'No . . . well, I just wanted to make sure that you've settled in and that everything's as it should be. You're all right, are you, Mother?'

'As right as I'll ever be, I suppose,' Alice replied grudgingly. 'I was just watching that antique programme, *Bargain Hunt* or whatever it's called, where they go round flea markets and car boot sales, so I won't talk for long or I'll miss it. Anyway, it'll be running up your bill on that mobile phone.'

'That's all right, I told you I got a good deal for the mobile . . . I'm glad you're enjoying your TV. It's a good set in your room, is it?'

'It's OK, but I was in the lounge, watching on the big set. Nearly as big as the Odeon screen it is! There's a few of them like to watch the antiques, like I do.'

'Well, that's great, isn't it? I told you that you'd meet some nice people and make new friends, didn't I?'

'Yes, I suppose so. They're not so bad, some of them seem nice enough. I don't know about friends, mind, but I dare say I can put up with 'em for ten days.'

'What's the food like? Have you had a good dinner . . . or lunch, whatever they call it?'

'Can't grumble. It was lamb casserole today, quite tasty, and apple crumble for afters. They have the main meal at midday, lunch, they call it, but it's a substantial meal. I've no complaints there, not so far. Then they have what they call high tea at half past five. It was ham salad last night, then there's a supper time drink if you want one.'

'Sounds like a four-star hotel, Mother! I'm pleased you're enjoying it.'

'I didn't say that, did I? I'm putting up with it 'cause I know it won't be for long.' Alice knew, though, that she was enjoying it far more than she had thought she would, but she was determined not to let Jane get away with it so easily. She was aware, however, that she might have sounded a little abrupt. It had become second nature to her now to appear so. She relented a little.

'Anyway, you go and have a good holiday, Jane. Don't worry about me; I'll be OK. I'll still be here when you get back, God willing.'

'Of course you will, Mother. I'll try to phone you from France or Germany, but I don't know what the signal will be like for the mobile. There'll be phones at the hotels, of course.'

'Don't bother. I've said I'll be all right. Just . . . just have a good time, and take care of yourself in those foreign lands. Bye for now . . .'

Bye, Mother. You take care as well . . .'

Alice was surprised to find that her eyes were a little moist as she put down the phone. She blinked hastily. She really had no time for that sort of sentimental nonsense. Jane was a good girl, though, and Alice knew that she deserved a holiday. She really didn't know how she would manage without Jane to look after her nowadays, but it worked both ways, of course. Jane was glad of the financial help that Alice was able to provide for bills and the upkeep of their home.

It was, in truth, Jane's house. It had been Jane's and Tom's until he had died two years ago. Alice had fought against the idea of giving up her own home, but after Joe had died it had become increasingly difficult for her to manage alone. She had arthritis in her knees and hips but, so far, had refused to undergo an operation despite the advice of the doctors. She was very stubborn, always insisting that she could manage well enough. She had been very grateful, though, to Jane and Tom for sharing their home with her. Then Tom had died, unexpectedly, two years ago, and she and her daughter had been left alone together.

That was the trouble. They saw too much of one another and tended to get on one another's nerves. Alice loved her daughter far more than she let on. She had been forty when Jane was born, and her husband five years older. She had always been very much a 'daddy's girl', and Alice had never been a maternal sort of person. She had found it hard to show her feelings although she loved their little girl just as much as Joe did. The child was a great blessing to them. Alice had been thirty-six when she and Joe married, and they had given up hope of having children. Then when Jane had been born four years after their marriage it had seemed like a miracle. She had loved her then, and she loved her now. The sad thing was that Jane did not know how much.

Alice limped back into the lounge where the antiques programme was just finishing.

'The red team won,' said Flora, the woman with whom she had struck up a sort of friendship. 'They got a lot for that Doulton jug, but the blue team came a cropper with that figurine – it wasn't Chelsea, just a reproduction.'

'Sorry I missed it,' said Alice, 'but I had to chat to my daughter, seeing that she'd taken the trouble to ring me.'

'You told her you were settling in nicely, did you?'

'I told her I was OK.' Alice grinned. 'I must admit I'm pleasantly surprised, but it wouldn't do to sound too keen.'

'You're a crafty one, Alice,' said Flora with a chuckle. 'Never give too much away, do you? I thought as soon as I met you, there's more to this one than meets the eye!'

'Yes, maybe so. But you don't start telling people your life story till you get to know them, do you?' Alice felt, though, that she would like to get to know Flora better as the week went on.

'As far as my daughter's concerned, I'm not going to tell her that everything's fine and dandy, not so soon. She knows I've always had an aversion to these places. It took a good deal of persuasion, I can tell you, to get me to agree to come here. So I'm not going to tell her that I'm . . . well, that I might be changing my mind about old folks' homes.'

'Come on now,' said Flora. 'You can't really call this an old folks' home, can you? I must admit that I wasn't too keen on the idea myself, not at first. I'd seen some dreadful programmes on the TV about the neglect – even ill treatment – in some homes, and I wondered how anyone could let their loved ones live in such places.'

'Yes, I know what you mean,' said Alice. 'But even the places where the staff are kind and caring – like they are here, of course – I didn't fancy the idea of that either. I'm not keen on jolly sing-songs, or playing Bingo, or acting daft, all that sort of thing. And some of the folk that they show on the telly! Honestly! Dribbling and snuffling, or else just staring into space. They look about a hundred years old, some of them. I know I'm no spring chicken myself, but God forbid that I should ever get like that. "No thanks," I said to Jane. "You'll not get me into one of those places, not even for a week."'

'But you changed your mind?' Flora's beady brown eyes twinkled behind her spectacles.

'Well . . . I had to, didn't I? The lass deserves a holiday. I gave the place a once over, though, before I committed myself, and I decided it didn't seem so bad. Of course, it's not for folk who are seriously ill, is it, or those that are . . . well, past it, if you know what I mean?'

'No, it's more for rest and recuperation. They get a lot of people who are recovering from an operation – that's why I came here the first time – or staying for a short time, like you are. There are several, though, who are here on a more permanent basis, like I am now. We don't know how permanent, though, do we?' Flora gave a wry grin. 'But it's best not to think about that, eh?'

'Definitely not!' said Alice. 'I intend to keep going for many more years . . . God willing. This arthritis is a blessed nuisance, but it's not going to kill me. It's your heart that keeps you going, isn't it? And I've never had any problems there, thank the Lord.'

Flora nodded. 'It's the same with me.' She, too, suffered from arthritis. 'I should imagine we're about the same age, Alice, you and me, aren't we?'

Alice did not readily admit to being eighty-five. She knew she didn't look her age, so she tried to keep it a secret from 'nosy parkers'. However, she didn't put Flora into that category. She had only known the woman for a day, but she had decided that she liked her. She would be here for the next ten days – well, only nine days now – so she might as well find someone with whom she was compatible, and Flora seemed to fit the bill. Alice guessed that, like herself, the woman was intelligent and quite well educated. She preferred to mix with people with whom she could hold an interesting conversation, not just idle chit-chat about the weather, or about their wonderful grandchildren. Alice had to admit, however, that that might be a question of sour grapes. She hadn't any grandchildren of her own, nor was she likely to have now.

She smiled at Flora. 'Go on then. I don't often tell folk how old I am, but I might just make an exception. You go first.'

Flora beamed. 'Well, I may not look it . . . but I'll be seventy-six next birthday! Now, what about you?'

Alice was taken aback. Good grief! She was Flora's senior by almost ten years! She was flattered, she supposed, that Flora had assumed they were the same age. And Flora was confident that she looked even younger. The idea was encouraging.

Alice had always tried to make the most of the face and figure that God had given her. She knew that she was not beautiful, not at all, but neither was she too plain. She had strong features. Possibly her nose was a little too long and her mouth too wide, but her blue eyes had kept their brightness. (She wore glasses, though, but who didn't at her age?) And her dark hair had kept its colour, with only an occasional visit to the hairdresser. Alice was above average height, but she had learnt to 'walk tall' and not feel awkward because she was taller than her friends and acquaintances, that was until the arthritis had made her stoop a little.

'Well, you may not believe it either,' she answered now, 'but I'm eighty-five. How about that then? I can give you ten years!'

Flora gasped. 'No, you're right, I would never have believed it. I thought I was doing well. But you . . . that's just incredible!'

'If you two are going to talk at the top of your voices, would you please go and sit somewhere else. You're like a couple of cackling hens. Jack and me, we're trying to watch the snooker.' The speaker was Henry, whom Alice had met at lunchtime along with his pal, Jack. She did not take offence as she might have done, were she not feeling in quite such a good mood. She had already gathered that Henry was an outspoken Yorkshireman – typical of his breed – but that his bark was worse than his bite, as the saying went. He was laughing as he spoke so she knew there was no malice in his words.

'Oh . . . sorry,' said Flora. 'We didn't realize. Come on, Alice, let's go and sit on the settee.'

'Reckon you must be going deaf,' added Henry with a sly grin. 'Ne'er mind, it comes to all of us.' He was, in fact, wearing a small hearing aid.

'That I'm not!' said Alice, rising stiffly to her feet. 'I've still got all my faculties. Sorry if we disturbed you, though . . .'

She followed Flora to a settee in the corner of the room. Some of the residents had gone to their own rooms after the midday meal, maybe for a rest on the bed, or to watch TV or read in peace. Alice was finding that this was one of the good things at Evergreen. You were left to your own devices. You could join in with the activities and with other people, only if you wished to do so. If you were a 'loner' then they were content to leave you alone.

Alice had decided before she came that she would keep herself to herself. She had brought several books to read, and a puzzle and crossword book, but, to her surprise, she was enjoying the change of company.

She looked across at her new friend. Yes, she supposed she could regard Flora as a friend. The woman was the opposite of herself as far as looks were concerned. She was what might be termed 'petite', about five foot two, but just a tiny bit plump. She had a pretty round face that was enhanced by discreet make-up and pale pink lipstick, fairish hair with golden highlights – artifice rather than nature, Alice guessed – and brown, rather inquisitive eyes.

'Yes,' said Flora, as the two of them settled themselves against the plump cushions. 'You've certainly surprised me. I hope I look as good as you do when I'm eighty-five . . . if I live that long!'

'That's something we mustn't dwell on,' replied Alice. 'We've to make the most of every year – every day – that's left to us.'

She thought, a shade guiltily, as she made the remark that she, in point of fact, had not been doing that, certainly not of late. She had allowed herself to get into a rut, never venturing far from home. When Jane was available she had taken her in the car to various places: to church on Sunday, if she felt like going; to the library; to Sainsbury's or Tesco; and occasionally into Preston to visit the market or the shops. Jane had been a willing horse, and she, Alice, had been guilty of driving her too hard.

She wasn't sure what had brought it on, but the realization of how she had been behaving was coming home to her. No wonder the girl had been tired and ready for a holiday. She decided she would have to make it up to her, somehow. Maybe the first way to make amends was to settle down here at Evergreen and try to enjoy her stay.

'So, Flora . . .' She looked enquiringly at her new friend. 'Why are you living here when you're still quite young? Young as elderly people go, I mean. I hope you don't mind me asking, I've always been forthright.'

'I don't mind,' said Flora cheerfully. 'I'm on my own, you see; no husband, no children, just one brother in Australia. I moved in here a year ago. I felt it was the right thing to do, and I've never regretted it.'

'You've had a husband, though, haven't you?' said Alice, looking at Flora's left hand. She wore a plain gold wedding ring, and her engagement ring was a large solitaire diamond, which must have cost a pretty penny!

'Yes, I've had a husband – two, in fact.' Alice grinned. 'My first husband turned out to be a gambler. I didn't know that, of course, when I married him. He was charming and plausible, and I was young and gullible. That didn't last long. Then I met Clive. I'd been on my own for quite a while. I'd had one or two boyfriends – well, men friends. I was into my thirties by then – but I didn't feel like risking it again. But Clive . . . I couldn't resist him. I went to work for him as a secretary and sort of aide. He was a successful business man, finger in all sorts of pies, something of a wheeler dealer, but an honest one. My job didn't last long because we got married and I gave up work. I must admit I lived a life of luxury. It was a magic world to me. I'd been brought up in a humble semi with parents who had been hard-working ordinary folk. They made sure I had a reasonable education. I went to a grammar school, but I left when I was sixteen to get an office job. I travelled all over the world with Clive; a cruise every year, holidays in the States, the Far East, the Caribbean . . . then he died suddenly of a heart attack, five years ago.'

'So the good life came to an end?' observed Alice, but not unkindly. Her new friend's life, though, had been vastly different from her own.

'Yes . . . I was devastated at first. I'd become so dependent on him. We had a lot of friends, but they were his friends rather than mine. When he'd gone they still kept in touch with me, but it wasn't the same. I was on my own. He'd left me very well provided for, of course: big house, more money than I'd ever need . . .' She didn't sound boastful, just regretful.

'Anyway, after I'd stopped feeling sorry for myself I decided I was too young to sit around and stagnate. I joined the local branch of the Townswomen's Guild, and a book club, and a ladies' choir.'

'And do you still keep up with all these things now that you're living here?' asked Alice.

'Of course, why not?' answered Flora. She laughed. 'We're not prisoners, you know. We come and go as we please. They run a bus to take us into Preston a couple of times a week, for those who want to go. And we have theatre trips and outings to places like Southport or Blackpool. But I take a taxi when I want to go somewhere on my own. A lot of us do that.'

Alice was beginning to realize that living in a retirement home was not like being in a sort of prison – albeit a lenient one – as she had supposed. 'But it must have been a big step for you to give up your home, wasn't it?' she asked.

'Oh, the house was far too big for me, it had been too big for the two of us to be honest. I had someone to help with the cleaning even when Clive was alive, and I'd got out of the habit of housework. I used to cook for the two of us, I quite enjoyed that, but I never got used to cooking just for myself. And then my arthritis got worse – you'll know all about that – so I decided to look around for a nice retirement home. I visited a few, but this was by far the best. It's more like a hotel really, but there's medical help there if you need it. There's a nurse on the staff, and several of the assistants have had training in first aid. I've had no regrets, Alice, about coming here, I can assure you.'

'Yes, I suppose I can understand it in your case,' said Alice, a little doubtfully, 'with you being on your own. But a lot of the people who end up in homes – nice ones like this, or others that are . . . not so nice – they have sons and daughters, don't they? It never used to be like this. I remember going to friends' houses when I was a little girl, and more often than not there was a grandma or grandad living there with the family. We had my old grandma living with us. She died when I was eight. I say old, but she wasn't nearly as old as I am now. But they seemed much older in those days, somehow.'

'Things are much different now, Alice, in all sorts of ways,' said Flora. 'Old people know how to keep themselves young, that is if they want to. There are some folk, of course, who were born old, if you know what I mean.'

'Yes, I do.' Alice smiled. 'You can be old at forty, or young at eighty. It's a state of mind, isn't it?' It was coming home to her, though, that although she looked younger than her age she had, in truth, perhaps allowed herself to become somewhat old in outlook. Maybe it was time for her to start looking at things differently . . .

'You were saying, Alice, about grandparents living with the

family,' Flora went on. 'I remember that as well, but sometimes it isn't possible nowadays. Most women go out to work as well as the men; a lot of them need to, to make ends meet. I was fortunate, but I can't imagine how some of them manage to pay the mortgage and the bills and put food on the table. And maybe it's impossible to look after an ageing parent as well. I know there are some that could do it, and don't want to, but it must be a dreadful problem for a lot of people to know what to do.'

Alice was thoughtful. She remembered the times she had remarked to Jane that old folk were put into homes because their children couldn't be bothered with them. It was dawning on her now that it was the sort of remark that a cynical embittered person might make. Was that what she was turning into? Was that how others saw her? Alice knew that she was outspoken, and she had prided herself on it, she had believed in being honest and saying what she thought. As they said in Yorkshire, she called a spade a spade. Her husband, Joe, had been born in Bradford and he was proud of it, but he had teased her by saying that his fellow Yorkshiremen had nothing on her.

Joe had been more tolerant, far less abrasive than Alice. Despite this they had lived together amicably and had had a good marriage. His tendency to live and let live had had a calming effect on her . . . most of the time at least. But since he had died the old Alice had come to the fore again, probably more than she had realized.

'Alice . . . what's up? You're miles away, aren't you?' Her new friend was looking at her curiously. 'I was just saying that it must be a hard decision for some sons and daughters to make, with regard to their parents.'

'Yes, I heard you,' replied Alice. 'It was making me think of my own situation, mine and Joe's, because we never had that problem. We were both working, and there was no way that I could have given up my job. But my parents, and Joe's, stayed in their own homes right till the end. Goodness knows what we'd have done if they hadn't been able to cope because neither of us had brothers or sisters; only children, both of us. But they all lived to a ripe old age, scarcely ailing anything.

And then both my parents, and Joe's as well, died within a few months of one another. We were fortunate, I suppose. We never needed to make any difficult decisions. Maybe that's why I've . . . well . . . perhaps I've never understood what a problem it might be.'

'It's something I never had to face with my parents, either,' said Flora. 'What did you do when you were working, Alice, if you don't mind me asking?'

'I was a teacher,' replied Alice promptly. 'We both were, Joe and I. That's how I met him, of course.'

Flora smiled. 'Now why doesn't that surprise me? I might have guessed you'd been a teacher.'

'Oh dear! Is it so obvious?' Alice grimaced. 'I don't know whether to be pleased or offended.'

'I meant it as a compliment,' said Flora. 'You have that way with you – an air of authority.'

'Bossy, you mean?'

'No . . . Not standing for any nonsense, that's what I meant. You don't suffer fools gladly, as they say. That's a daft expression, though, I've always thought.'

'No.' Alice sighed. 'I dare say I've become a bit intolerant in my old age. It's since Joe died, of course.' She smiled reminiscently, and a little sadly.

'You had a good marriage, then?' asked Flora, quietly, 'I can tell that you did.'

'Yes, so we did,' said Alice. 'It was more of a marriage of minds, though, than . . . anything else. We only had the one daughter, Jane.'

'And is she a teacher as well?'

'Good gracious, no!' said Alice. 'She'd seen enough of it with the two of us. She attended the school that we taught at because it was near our home. So she never had any aspiration to follow in our footsteps. No. Jane works for the GPO. She was a clever girl – well, she still is – and she did very well as a counter clerk. She's in charge of a sub post office now, near to our home.'

'So there are just you and Jane living together?'

'Yes, that's right. Her husband, Tom, died two years ago. He was a grand fellow . . .' And very tolerant of me, she thought to herself, but didn't say. 'His death was a terrible blow to Jane, but she seems to be getting over it now.'

'So this holiday she's on will be a nice change for her, won't it? I don't know her, but I hope she has a lovely time.'

'Yes, so do I,' answered Alice briefly. 'She missed her father just as much as I did,' she added, 'but she was married to Tom by that time, so it softened the blow somewhat. Neither Jane nor I were young when we married, I was thirty-six. I didn't think I'd get married at all. Not that I was all that bothered. I was doing the job I enjoyed. I'd always wanted to be a teacher.'

'And then you met Joe,' said Flora encouragingly.

'Yes. He came to our school in 1955 as our new headmaster. He'd only trained as a teacher when he came out of the army, but he had what it takes and he soon worked his way up the promotion ladder. They were crying out for men teachers at that time. The war had taken its toll, and the fifties were the years of the 'baby boom'; the post-war children all starting school. I was deputy head by that time, so we had to work closely together.'

'That was at a school in Preston, was it? A junior school?'

'Yes. juniors and infants, quite near to where lived with my parents. I did my training in Manchester during the first two years of the war. Most of the men teachers had been called up for war service, so there was no shortage of jobs for women. I was lucky, though, to get a post so near to my home. I didn't see it as a disadvantage, living at home with my parents. It was convenient. Girls weren't so anxious to fly the nest then and get a place of their own. So I stopped where I was, then I was promoted to deputy head.'

'And then Joe came along.' Flora prompted again.

'That's right. We got on well together right from the start. We didn't fall madly in love or anything like that, but we knew we were . . . compatible. We were right together. Then he asked me to go out with him, and we started courting – to the amusement of the rest of the staff, of course! We both knew that. No doubt we were the subject of a few ribald jokes! They were all pleased for us, though, when we got married the following year. They bought us a lovely Royal Doulton dinner service. I've still got it, at Jane's house. She was born in 1960, so I gave up teaching for a while. Then when she was five and ready to start school, there was a vacancy there, at the same place. So I went back, as an ordinary teacher, of course.

'I've only ever taught at the one school. Not like today's young teachers, seeking promotion before they've hardly got started, and wanting more money all the time. Joe retired when he was sixty, I was a few years younger, but I went at the same time. Yes, we enjoyed our retirement.'

She reflected that her retirement – in fact the whole of her married life – had been vastly different from that of Flora. She and Joe had never had any yearning to visit exotic places. They had toured around the British Isles in their family car. Jane had accompanied them until she was well into her teens, after which she had her own circle of friends. They had never been abroad, only once had they crossed the sea when they had gone on a coaching holiday touring southern Ireland. But Alice felt sure that they had been as happy, in their own way, as Flora and her Clive had been, jetting all over the world.

'You're miles away again,' remarked Flora, bringing her out of her reverie. 'Thinking about old times, eh?'

'Yes, maybe I was,' replied Alice, a little brusquely. 'But we've to think about the present and the future, haven't we? Now, if you don't mind, I'm going to my room to read for a little while. I'll see you at teatime.' Then, aware that she might have sounded rather dismissive, she turned back. 'We've had a good chat, Flora. Thank you for listening to me. I'm pleased to have met you. I'll see you later . . .'

Three

Jane was more at ease with herself when she had phoned her mother. She had felt guiltier than she needed to do when she had said goodbye to her at the home. Jane knew that Evergreen was a very satisfactory place. The staff seemed kind and helpful and, from what she had seen of the residents, they were not the bunch of decrepit old fogies that her mother had imagined. Mother was being difficult, determined to show Jane that although she had agreed to give the home a try she was there against her will.

Jane knew her mother only too well, her unwillingness to admit that she might possibly have been wrong or made a mistake. She could tell now that she was, in fact, settling down there very nicely. She had admitted that the food was good, she appeared to have made some friends, or at least, fellow residents with whom she was compatible, and she was enjoying her favourite programmes on a much larger television set than she was used to. Jane smiled to herself. She felt she could relax now and really start to enjoy her holiday.

Dave, her travelling companion, was already seated when she rejoined the coach and he stood up to allow her to occupy the window seat again.

'Have you had a good meal?' she asked him.

'Passable,' he replied. 'Fish and chips; you can't go far wrong with that. The prices though! You'd think you were paying for smoked salmon and caviar. But we're a captive audience, I suppose. I've found the motorway cafes on the continent are far more reasonable. How about you? You enjoyed your packed lunch?'

'Yes, I'm OK for now. It'll be a while before our first proper meal though, won't it?'

'Yes, at the hotel in Calais. Sometimes they ask you to dine on the ship, but it's only a short crossing to Calais. We should be there by early evening.'

Mike came down the coach, counting heads. 'All present and correct,' he said again. 'You're very good timekeepers. Now, off we go to Dover.'

'I rang my mother at the home,' said Jane, as they rejoined the motorway. Dave turned to smile at her.

'Oh, that's good. Is she settling in all right?'

'I do believe she is, but she won't admit it outright. She can be a stubborn old devil, my mother. She won't want to admit that she was wrong, or that I might have been right, of course!' She laughed. 'She's always been the same. It's because of the job she had, career, I should say. She can't bear to admit that she might have made a mistake.'

'Oh? And what did she do before she retired?' asked Dave.

'She was a teacher. Both my parents were teachers. But my father was much more easy-going even though he was a headmaster. I thought the world of my dad.'

Dave cast a surreptitious glance at his companion. She was smiling reminiscently, not sadly, though. Her words implied that she had got along with her father much better than with her mother. That did not surprise him. From what he had gathered so far the woman seemed to be a right old harridan!

'Didn't they want you to go into the same profession?' he asked her.

'No, surprisingly enough, they didn't. Fortunately for me, because teaching was the last thing I wanted to do. I'd seen enough of it at home, and to make matters worse, I attended the school where they both taught, a primary school – juniors and infants.'

'Oh dear! That sounds rather claustrophobic.'

'It was mainly because it was convenient, near to our home, you see. I know some people travel miles to their workplace nowadays, but it was more usual to have a job nearer home forty or so years ago.'

'Didn't it affect your friendships with the other children, you having both your parents teaching there?'

'No, not at all,' Jane replied. 'I had some very good friends at school and I still see a few of them. It wasn't as bad as it might have been because I was never in my mother's class, thank the Lord! My father had a rule about it, because there were one or two others whose mothers taught there. My mother was a good teacher but I know she put the fear of God into some of those children! They seemed to like her, though, despite her strictness, and they certainly respected her.'

'And your father? I should imagine he was a popular headmaster, from the way you speak about him?'

'Yes, he was very popular, both with the children and their parents. He didn't believe in corporal punishment, which was unusual in those days. It's forbidden now, of course, but there used to be a lot of heads who were handy with the cane. Dad believed in other ways of maintaining discipline; taking away privileges for miscreants – like removing them from the football team – and it seemed to work very well.

'Yes, my dad was a remarkable man in all sorts of ways. I missed him very much when he died. I must admit that I still do . . . that's not to say that I don't love my mother,' she added, almost apologetically. 'I do, but she's not all that easy to love. And since Dad died it's been just the two of us, and I suppose we tend to get on one another's nerves. My husband, Tom, was great with her. He was a sort of buffer between us, and he didn't seem to mind her nowtiness.' She smiled. 'A good old Lancashire word, that! Tom was able make her laugh, whereas all I seemed to do was to make her irritable.'

'I'm sure these ten days away from each other will do you both a world of good,' Dave commented. 'You're both badly in need of a change, aren't you? A change of scene and a change of company.'

'That's true. It's not so bad for me, of course. I go out to work each day, and I have a lot of friends, mostly married, though, and I get rather tired of their attempts at matchmaking.' Jane smiled and Dave smiled back at her. She was an attractive woman, but she obviously still missed her husband very much.

'It's different for Mother. She isn't able to get about as much now, but she seems as though she doesn't want to make the effort any longer. There's been such a change in her since Dad died. They had a good retirement together; they didn't seem to want anyone else's company, and since he died she's been so reclusive. She was such a determined, go-ahead sort of woman – well, she's still just as determined, of course! – but she's lost interest in so many things. I suppose teaching was her whole life, until she met my father. I know it was what she'd always wanted to do, and she was jolly good at it, too. She made it her hobby as well as her career. She didn't mind how much extra work she did at home, planning projects, writing Nativity plays, – she was always doing something. So now there's a big gap in her life, made worse since Dad died . . . and then Tom.'

'But you've always been there for her, Jane,' said Dave. 'She'll miss you this week, believe me. 'It will make her appreciate you all the more.'

Jane nodded thoughtfully. She was quiet for a few moments, and Dave reflected on what she had said. It seemed to him that the old lady needed a short sharp shock to bring her to her senses. Good for Jane that she had found the courage to make a break, be it only for a short time.

She was sitting with her hands folded in her lap, deep in thought after all she had said about her mother. He was finding her a restful sort of person, although he hardly knew her yet. She was easy to talk to, although he guessed that she didn't open up so readily to everyone she met. Maybe she found him compatible? He hoped so because they would be spending most of the next nine days together.

The thought did not displease him. He found her attractive, in a quiet way. Demure . . . he thought that was the word for her. She was neatly dressed in navy blue trousers and a shirt style top of pale blue and white stripes. Her short dark hair waved gently over her forehead and ears, in which she wore a pair of tiny diamond studs. Her eyes were her most outstanding feature, dark brown, glowing with warmth and what he guessed was a genuine wish to be friendly, though perhaps not with everyone she met? Her mouth was rather small and her chin was not exactly weak, but indeterminate. It prevented her from being beautiful or even pretty, but she had a quiet charm and dignity that, maybe, was not always apparent. Her remark about matchmaking suggested that she was possibly a little shy with men. Her father, then her husband, had clearly been all in all to her.

He could have done much worse with regard to a travelling companion. He considered, moreover, that he had done very well when he compared Jane with some of the folk who had sat next to him on previous holidays. There had been a garrulous middle-aged woman, then, by contrast, a very silent introspective young man who had scarcely wanted to talk at all. This was always the problem when you were travelling alone. Away from the coach you could do as you pleased, but the longish periods on the coach could become difficult if you were not at ease with your neighbour.

Dave decided that he had been lucky this time. He was not wanting anything other than a holiday friendship; neither, he guessed, was Jane. It was sufficient that they had formed a bond, in that they were both on their own, and that both their mothers were staying in retirement homes. Their circumstances, however, were very different. Dave's mother was the gentlest person you could wish to meet, so accommodating and never wanting to cause any bother. Not like Jane's mother who sounded a real old battleaxe! Dave's marital situation had been very different, too, from that of Jane. But he had loved his wife once, and had tried to think about the times when they had been happy together. It was not something he talked about to those who had not known her. The one good thing to come out of his marriage was his son, Peter, who would be managing the farm very competently in his absence.

Dave had been more than content with his work – exhausting at times but always rewarding – and the happiness he enjoyed with his son and his many friends. He had not wished for anything else, but perhaps it was now time for him to broaden his horizons, to look to the future? After all he was still young, not yet fifty.

'I'm sorry, I've talked you to death, haven't I?' said Jane after a few moments had passed. 'I'm not surprised you've gone quiet. I didn't mean to offload my problems on to you.'

'You didn't, not at all,' he answered. 'It's good to talk, as they say. I wasn't quiet because I didn't want to talk any more. To be honest I was thinking about the folk I've been forced to sit next to on other Galaxy tours. A talkative woman who hardly stopped to take breath, then there was a silent young man who hardly spoke two words. But this time, I've struck lucky, haven't I?' He smiled at Jane, and she blushed a little as she smiled back at him.

'Thank you. Yes, I hope so,' she replied. 'I'll read my magazine for a while, then you can have a bit of peace. You could read your book.' There was a paperback book in the rack in front of his seat; one of the Sharpe novels by Bernard Cornwell. 'My husband used to read those,' she commented.

'He is a good storyteller. I've read them all before, but I like a bit of escapism.' He took out the book and put on a pair of dark-framed glasses which gave him a studious air. 'I'm not tired of talking. Don't think that, Jane. But we've all week to chat and get to know one another, haven't we?'

'Yes; I'm pleased about that . . . and I think I've been lucky too,' she added shyly.

It didn't seem long before they were on the approach road to Dover. Very soon the sea came into view between the roofs of the dock buildings, and in the distance a large ship at anchor. Jane began to feel excited. Was that the ship they would travel on? She knew it was a Stena Line vessel, built to carry cars and coaches and hundreds of passengers. She found it amazing, almost terrifying, that a ship could stay afloat with such a weight inside it. But there were scarcely any accidents. There had been one several years ago due to carelessness, but she was determined to put all her fears behind her and enjoy the new experience.

When they arrived at the dock area they joined a queue of scores of other vehicles waiting to go through passport control. Then they drove up a ramp right into the bowels of the huge ship. There were several decks for the vehicles, and Mike warned them to remember that their coach was on the red deck.

'Get that fixed in your minds, ladies and gents,' he told them. 'We don't want anyone getting lost. And please remember the position of the coach on the deck. Fortunately we're near the steps, so you shouldn't have any problems. If you've travelled on one of these ships before you'll know what I mean. If you haven't, then please take care. It can all be very confusing.'

Jane cast an anxious glance at Dave.

'Don't worry,' he said. 'We'll stay together then I can make sure you don't go astray.' He grinned. 'Not that I'm suggesting you need looking after, but it can get rather fraught with people pushing and scrambling around trying to find their coach.'

'Thank you,' she replied. She hoped that he really did want to be with her and was not suggesting it because he thought she was a silly helpless woman.

'Ready now?' he asked. 'You won't need your travel bag, just your handbag. And take your jacket. It'll be warm on the ship, but it might feel cold if we go out on to the deck.'

They alighted from the coach on to the iron floor of the deck, then made their way through part of a tightly packed crowd of people, up the iron steps. There were three steep flights to negotiate before they reached the top, finding themselves in a comfortable lounge area, luxuriously carpeted, with armchairs grouped around little tables and a bar, not yet open, at one end. There were signs showing the way to the restaurants, toilets, shops and the enquiries and the foreign exchange desks. Jane already had a supply of euros tucked away safely in her shoulder bag which she was wearing slung around her body for safety.

'Be careful with your money,' her mother had warned her. 'Keep it close to you, and watch out when you're in a crowd. Especially when you get to Germany. I wouldn't trust any of them as far as I could throw them!'

'Yes, Mother,' she had replied dutifully. She felt, though, that she would sooner trust the Germans rather than the French these days. She had heard that the Germans were a very meticulous, law-abiding race of people, and that the younger generation knew very little about the last war. 'Don't mention the war!' had become a catchphrase, thanks to *Fawlty Towers*. But some of the older folk had long memories.

'Shall we go out on to the deck and say goodbye to England?' said Dave. 'The white cliffs are an impressive sight. Then we could come back and have a drink. What do you say to that?'

'Yes . . . thank you,' replied Jane. 'But I'd better pay a visit to the . . . er . . . to the ladies' room first,' she said, a trifle embarrassedly.

'Good idea. So will I,' agreed Dave. 'To the gents, I mean, of course. See you in a few minutes then.'

The ladies was busy already, as such places always seemed to be. Jane washed her hands, straightened her hair, and applied a dusting of powder and a smear of pink lipstick. She could scarcely stop herself from smiling at her reflection in the mirror. Butterflies were fluttering inside her, partly due to excitement at the start of a holiday, and partly at the thought of being in the company of a man, one that she hardly knew but already felt she liked and trusted. It was the first time since Tom died that she had looked forward to such an occasion with pleasure. She had been asked out a time or two with men who had been introduced to her by well-meaning friends, but had gone only from a sense of duty.

They made their way past the shops then another similar lounge and bar area on to the deck at the stern of the ship. There were a few people there leaning against the railings. They stood there, too, in a companionable silence, and after several moments the ship slipped away from its moorings. It was not the first time that Jane had seen the white cliffs of Dover, it was, as she remembered, a truly impressive sight. She felt a lump in her throat as she thought about the significance of this place, of the centuries that had gone by whilst the cliffs had stood there, the first sight of England to both friends and foes, to English folk and to foreigners.

On top of the cliff stood Dover castle, a bastion against the enemies who had tried in vain to conquer our tiny island. This was the shortest route across the channel, from Dover to the port of Calais; such a short distance away that the sounds of warfare in successive conflicts – the Napoleonic wars and the two more recent world wars – had been heard in the villages and farmlands of Kent. Jane reflected that the country was now at peace, or comparatively so, but it seemed that there was always news of strife and discord in various parts of the world.

She was deep in thought as the ship gathered speed and the foam-topped waves beat against the side of the vessel. She became aware of Dave looking at her.

'Are you OK, Jane?' he asked. 'You're very quiet. It's a

thrilling sight, isn't it, watching the shores of England slip away from us? I never tire of it.'

'Yes, I'm OK,' she replied. 'Just . . . thoughtful, you know? The white cliffs of Dover evoke so many stories. I was thinking that I'm proud to be British, or English, to be more specific.'

'So am I,' Dave agreed. 'I like to go abroad but it's always good to return to our own shores. Anyway, we don't need to think about that for quite a while. We can concentrate on enjoying ourselves.'

A sudden gust of wind tugged at the light scarf around Jane's neck. She gave an involuntary shiver.

'Let's go and have a drink, shall we?' said Dave. 'It's turning chilly now.'

'Yes, why not?' she answered cheerfully. She was starting to believe, now, that Dave really did want to be with her and was not keeping her company just out of politeness.

The lounge was quite crowded. They found a seat near, but not too near, to the grand piano where a man in evening dress was playing a selection of nostalgic melodies.

'Now, what would you like to drink?' asked Dave. 'Lager, shandy? Or are you more of a sherry or Martini lady?'

'I usually like a sweet sherry,' Jane replied, 'but would you think I was awfully silly if I say I would like a coffee?'

Dave agreed at once. 'Good idea,' he said. They're serving tea and coffee as well, and snacks. What about a bite to eat? It's a long time since we had our lunch, and goodness knows what time we'll get our evening meal in Calais.'

'That's just what I was thinking.' Jane realized that she was quite hungry, but with all the excitement of the journey she had scarcely noticed.

'Right. How about a ham sandwich or a buttered scone?'

'Just a scone, please. That will be enough. And a cappuccino . . . is that all right?'

'Of course it is.' Dave laughed. 'I'll have the same.'

He went across to the bar, and Jane sat contentedly humming along to the tune of 'Moon River'. She felt like pinching herself to make sure she was really there, that she would not suddenly wake up from a delightful dream. Could she be here, travelling to the Continent in the company of an attractive man who actually seemed to enjoy being with her? She looked around at her fellow passengers. A mixed crowd of people: a lot of elderly and middle-aged couples, families with children, ladies sitting quietly on their own, a group of lads laughing and making a heck of a din in the far corner. It seems that anything goes here, she thought to herself. The surroundings were elegant, but there were no restrictions, no first- or second-class lounges. Only the smokers, it seemed, were frowned upon. 'No smoking' notices were on all the tables. If you wished to indulge you had to go out into a draughty area near to the deck.

She remarked on it to Dave when he returned with a laden tray.

'Do you smoke, Dave?' she asked.

'Not any more,' he replied. There was a time when I did smoke quite a lot. When I . . . lost my wife, I found it helped to settle me down, to relieve the tension, you know? But I managed to kick the habit. Just as well in the present climate. But I must admit that I don't approve of all the paranoia about smokers. We're all lectured to far too much, in my opinion.

'Now, here's your coffee and scone. They're a bit stingy with the butter, so I pinched an extra portion or two. I don't think they noticed. And there's a little pot of jam . . .'

'Lovely,' said Jane. She reached for her bag. 'Let me settle up with you.'

'What? For a cup of coffee?' He laughed. 'Don't be silly! My treat.'

'But you mustn't. Not all the time . . .' She felt embarrassed and confused. It looked as though they might be together for a lot of the time. Or was she wrong in assuming that they might be? 'Thank you, anyway,' she added. 'It's very kind of you. But the next time . . .'

'Forget it, Jane.' He grinned at her. 'I do know what you mean, but don't worry. We'll sort it out.'

They chatted easily for a while. Dave told her about the farm, at her request. She was interested to hear about something so remote from her everyday experience. She was definitely a town girl, although she loved the beauty of the countryside when she was able to escape, occasionally, from her urban surroundings. Dave looked pleased at her absorption in what he was telling her.

Far sooner than she expected – the time had flown by – there was an announcement on the loud speaker, first in French, then in English, that they were approaching Calais. Would passengers please assemble at the various exits.

'Oh dear! Have I time to go to . . . to the ladies' room?' asked Jane in a fluster.

'Yes, of course. There's no immediate rush,' said Dave. 'It takes ages for everyone to embark. I'll pay a visit myself, then we'll make our way to our exit. Don't worry. I know exactly which stairs we're heading for . . .'

Jane was relieved to hear that. She was finding the ship very confusing, exits at every corner, people dashing hither and thither, and she did not know whether she was fore or aft. Goodness knows how she would have managed to get back to the coach on her own. It was pandemonium at the exit, crowds of folk jostling one another, anxious to get down the stairs to locate their vehicles.

'Hang on to me if you like,' Dave told her. 'I'll go first. Just be careful on the stairs, they're rather steep.'

They negotiated their way down the three flights – Jane did not cling on to Dave, but made sure she was right behind his tweed jacket all the way – and then they were back on the red deck.

'There's our coach,' said Dave. 'We're not the first back, but we certainly won't be the last.'

Mike and Bill were already there, Mike on the driving seat.

'Take your time,' said Bill. 'They're not all back yet, but it'll be about ten minutes or so, I reckon, before we're ready to drive off.'

The passengers climbed aboard, mostly couples, husbands and wives, or friends, travelling together. Bill went down the coach, counting heads. 'Two missing,' he muttered. 'Now, who are they? I don't know everyone's name yet.'

'It's the couple who sit there,' Dave said to Jane, pointing to the seat across the aisle from them. An elderly couple, possibly in their late seventies. Dave had noticed them and had thought to himself that it was an adventurous trip for them, but the lady had seemed to be very much in charge.

Mike and Bill were consulting their list. 'Mr and Mrs Johnson,' said Mike. 'Bloody hell! They're cutting it fine. That's the trouble,' he grumbled. 'You can't stop folk from travelling, even if they're getting on a bit. I bet they're turned eighty, the pair of 'em. This blasted job is getting too much for me, I can tell you, Bill.'

'Calm down, mate,' said Bill. 'Here they are, see . . .' The missing couple arrived back, just in the nick of time.

'Sorry, sorry . . .' said the woman. 'We got lost. Arthur insisted it was the other staircase. Go on, up you go.' She shoved her husband, none too gently, up the coach steps.

'Never mind, love,' said Bill. 'You're here now. No harm done. Just settle yourselves down. We'll be off in a minute or two.'

Mike breathed a sigh of relief. It wasn't the first time that this had happened, and he vowed every time that he would pack the job in. He put a smile on his face.

'Right, ladies and gents, off we go. Welcome to France,' he said as the coach drove off the gangway and Bill put on a tape which played 'La Marseillaise'.

Four

It was only a short distance across the channel from Dover to Calais, twenty-one miles – just a bit further than it was from Preston to Blackpool, Jane thought to herself – but how different it all seemed now that they were on the Continent. The styles of the houses, many of them three-storied with shutters at the windows, the names of streets and the signs on the shops – which Jane was able to read and understand having enjoyed her French lessons at school and learnt a lot from them – and, above all, the traffic driving on the right-hand side of the road.

Their hotel was situated on a side street off the main boulevard. It was an unprepossessing sort of building from the outside, opening straight on to the street. They would be allowed to park there just long enough to unload the luggage.

'Go inside and collect your keys,' Mike told them. 'Your cases will be brought up to your rooms. And dinner will be at eight o'clock this evening, so that should give you nice time to sort yourselves out. See you later, ladies and gents.'

They all trooped through the revolving door into the foyer, making an orderly queue at the reception desk. The hotel presented a more pleasing aspect inside. It was an old building, partly modernized, with a boldly striped carpet and the walls adorned with large format posters of paintings by Monet and Degas. There were two display cabinets filled with souvenirs for sale and a revolving rack with postcards of Calais on the desk. A pretty dark-haired girl handed them their keys – ones that might well belong to the outer door of a castle, suspended from a brass ball and chain – repeating their names in a quaintly accented English.

They queued at the lift, an old-fashioned one with a gate as well as a door. It would hold only four at a time, so there was a wait of several minutes before everyone was taken up to their rooms. The single rooms were on the third floor – most of the passengers had been allocated double rooms on the lower floors – and Jane found that her room was next to Dave's.

'See you in a little while,' he said, fitting his gigantic key into the lock and opening the door.

'Yes . . . see you,' she replied. She, too, opened her door, finding herself in a fair-sized room with a single bed, and a wardrobe and chest of drawers in a plain, functional design such as was found in thousands of hotels; adequate but by no means luxurious, but at least it was clean and it was only a stopping place for the night. She opened the shutters and found that the room was at the front of the hotel, overlooking the street. On the other side of the road there was a pharmacy, a *boulangerie*, and what seemed to be a shop selling ladies' wear, judging by the sign above the window which read 'Madame Yvette'. The shutters were closed on all the shops as it was now almost seven thirty. (They had been told to put their watches forward an hour on arriving in France.)

Jane flopped down on the bed feeling strangely disorientated. She was slightly dizzy and felt as though she might have a headache coming on. That was not surprising after such an unusually hectic day, but by no means an unpleasant one. She would take a couple of tablets in a minute when she had become acclimatized to her surroundings. She sat very still, gathering her thoughts together, a myriad of new scenes and experiences following one upon the other in a bewildering manner. And it was only the first day of the holiday!

She opened her bag and took out a couple of soluble headache tablets. They would need to dissolve in water. Now, hadn't she heard that one shouldn't drink the water from the tap when on the Continent? Just too bad, she decided. She had no choice and it wasn't likely that it would kill her!

She opened the door leading off the bedroom. It was not a bathroom as she had hoped it might be, just a small cubicle with a toilet, washbasin and shower. Not a handheld shower like the one she had had installed at home, but one that came straight down from the ceiling, drenching your hair as well as the rest of your person if you were not wearing a shower cap. Fortunately Jane had brought one, although there was one on the shelf above the washbasin, in a tiny plastic bag.

She dissolved her tablets in water from the cold tap – she was able to read the words '*chaud*' and '*froid*' on the taps – in the glass that was provided. Just as she had finished using the other facility there was a tap at the bedroom door. She hurried to answer it and found the hotel porter standing there with her overnight case.

'Oh . . . come in,' she said, smiling at him.

He carried her case into the room, then he stood there, his head on one side smiling pleasantly – expectantly? – at her. Oh crikey! she thought. Is he waiting for a tip? That was the trouble of travelling alone, especially without a husband; she was not sure of the protocol.

'Wait a minute . . . *un moment*,' she said, reaching for her bag on the bed. She took out her purse and found a one euro piece. She had asked for some at the travel agency as well as the notes. She handed it to him and he bowed his head, smiling more broadly.

'*Merci, madame, merci beaucoup . . .*' He backed out of the room as though he were leaving a royal bedchamber.

Breathing a sigh of relief she glanced at her little travelling clock. Only about half an hour left in which to get ready for the evening meal. Her sponge bag was at the top of her case and she took out the requisites for overnight – toothbrush and toothpaste, deodorant, soap, flannel and spray cologne. It would have to be a quick wash, there was no time for a shower even though she felt rather grubby after the long journey.

She filled the washbasin and swilled her hands and face and underneath her arms. Now, where was the 'thingy' to let the water out? The stopper was a modern design and it wouldn't budge. At last she found a little lever at the back of the taps; there was nothing to beat a plug on a chain in Jane's opinion!

She put on a silky polyester top, pale green with embroidery at the lowish neckline – recently purchased from Marks and Spencer – as it was rather more dressy than the one she had worn earlier, but she decided to wear the same trousers. A quick comb of her hair which, luckily, was easy to manage, a touch of moisturizer, pressed powder and a smear of lipstick, then she slipped on a pair of sandals with a higher heel, and she was ready.

She picked up her bag and her giant-sized key and went out into the corridor. You couldn't lock yourself out as you might do in some hotels as the door had to be locked from the outside. This she did, then she stood there unsurely. What should she do? Knock on Dave's door, or would that seem presumptuous? As she stood there pondering, but only for a moment or two, his door opened.

'Ah, there you are,' he said. 'I was going to knock and see if you were ready.' Jane was relieved to hear that. 'Let's go and see what pleasures are in store for us at the evening meal . . .'

There was no one else in the lift when it finally arrived at the third floor. Dave pressed the button for the lower ground floor where the restaurant was situated but it stopped at the first floor and two more people joined them. It was the elderly couple who had sat opposite them in the coach, the ones who had been late back on the ferry. They all smiled at one another in recognition.

'You were sitting across from us in the coach, weren't you?' said the woman. 'Do you mind if we share a table with you in the dining room? I said to Arthur that you're a nice young couple.'

'Certainly,' said Dave, looking at Jane who nodded her agreement. After all, what else could you say? You could hardly refuse and they seemed pleasant enough.

'It all depends on the seating arrangements, though, doesn't it?' Dave remarked. 'Sometimes they put a coach party all together on a long table, or two tables.'

'Aye, like a Sunday school outing,' said the older man. 'I don't care for that meself. Anyway, we'll wait and see, won't we?'

When they entered the dining room they saw that it was laid with tables for four, or for six; the ones reserved for the coach party had a notice on them saying 'Galaxy Tours'. The woman led the way to a table in the corner. They sat down, smiling at one another again.

'We'd better introduce ourselves, hadn't we?' said the woman. 'I'm Mavis, and this is my hubby, Arthur. Arthur and Mavis Johnson.'

'How do you do?' The four of them nodded and smiled but did not shake hands.

'I'm Dave, and this is Jane.' He turned to her, raising his eyebrows in an unspoken question, then he went on to say, 'We're not actually a couple, as you probably thought we might be. What I mean is . . . we only met today because we were given seats together. But we seem to be getting along very well, don't we, Jane?'

She nodded and smiled, feeling a little embarrassed. 'Yes, so we do.'

'Well, fancy that!' exclaimed Mavis. 'I thought you'd been married for ages. Of course, you can never tell these days, can you? So many folk come away with what they call partners, even a partner of the same sex. Anything goes now, doesn't it? Not that I'm bothered. Each to his own, that's what I say. Anyway, I hope you have a happy time together, the pair of you.' She beamed at them.

Jane and Dave exchanged amused glances. Jane decided to forget her embarrassment. This was bound to happen, the two of them being mistaken for a 'couple'. She would just have to go with the flow.

The room was low-ceilinged and rather stuffy. There was a faint aroma – by no means an unpleasant one – coming from the direction of the kitchen at the far end. Arthur sniffed once or twice before remarking, 'It'll be chicken tonight; it always is on t'first night. I'd've guessed that even if we couldn't smell it. It's what they always give to coach parties on t'first night.'

'I'm sure it will be very nice, Arthur,' said his wife. 'Anyway, there's your starter before that.'

'A plate of lettuce, or else watery soup, that's what it'll be,' rejoined Arthur.

His wife tutted good-humouredly, shaking her head at him in mock exasperation. No doubt she was used to all his funny little ways. He seemed like a bit of a know-all, and a grumbler, although not a cantankerous one. It was probably second nature to him to have his say about everything, rather like her own mother, thought Jane. Anyway, it was all part of the holiday, meeting different folk.

Jane guessed that Mavis and Arthur might be in their late seventies, possibly older than that, Arthur at any rate. He was a corpulent man and he seemed to have a little difficulty with his breathing. He was bald on top with a fringe of white hair at either side, and he wore dark-rimmed glasses. He was smartly dressed with a collar and tie and had his jacket on, whereas several of the men were in shirtsleeves.

His wife, Mavis, was smartly dressed as well, possibly a little overdressed in a purple satin blouse with a pattern of sequinned flowers. She obviously liked to 'dress for dinner' when on holiday. She was plumpish but by no means fat. Like her husband, she wore glasses; hers were designer ones with diamanté frames. She was grey-haired and the discreet mauve tint on her perfectly waved and styled coiffure complemented the top she was wearing. She had a lovely friendly smile which made up for her possibly too outspoken remarks. Neither of them, in fact, were afraid of saying what they thought. Jane guessed, however, that Mavis must have 'a lot to put up with' regarding her husband – as Jane's mother might say – but that they were a very contented couple.

Arthur was proved right as far as the starter was concerned, the soup was, indeed, watery, though piping hot with noodles and onion rings, served with chunks of rather dry brown bread. The chicken – another accurate guess – was a large breast portion for each of them, served with the inevitable French fries. It was very tasty and Jane realized how hungry she was. She emptied the plate, which was unusual for her, apart from a few over-crisp chips.

There had been a bit of a friendly argument when the wine waiter appeared, Jane insisting that she really must pay for her own glass of wine, and Dave saying that he wouldn't hear of it.

'Stop yer quibbling, the pair of you,' Arthur had intervened. 'We'll have a bottle of wine for the four of us. I'm paying, and that's that! White wine alright for you? That's what Mavis likes.'

They settled on a medium-sweet French wine of Arthur's choice. He seemed to consider himself something of a connoisseur. Conversation was flowing easily by the time they had almost emptied their glasses.

'We were so embarrassed when we were late back at the coach,' Mavis told them. 'I was afraid Arthur might have one of his turns with us dashing about all over the place.'

'Give over, Mavis, I've not had a funny turn for ages. It was you that was getting in a tizzy. I knew we'd get back in time. And I've admitted I was wrong, haven't I? But I was sure it was t'other staircase. Aye, I should've listened to you, I know.'

'Never mind, you got back safely and no harm done,' said Dave. 'You're not the first couple to be late back, nor will you be the last. I should imagine it's a nightmare for the drivers, especially on the Continent, waiting for people who are late.'

Conversation drifted, inevitably, to tales of the various tours they had been on before. Jane admitted it was all new to her and how much she was looking forward to the new experience. Mavis and Arthur, it turned out, were seasoned travellers on the Continent.

'We're not much for the seaside,' said Mavis, 'at least not over here. What's the point of going abroad if all you do is lie on the beach and get sunstroke? If you want to do that you might as well go to Blackpool or Scarborough.'

'Except that you're more likely to get blown off the beach than to get heat stroke,' said Dave with a laugh. 'I know what you mean though. I must admit I've never been to Spain. Sun and sand and sangria has never appealed to me, though I'd like to see the interior of Spain, cities like Madrid and Barcelona. One day, perhaps . . .' He caught Jane's eye, and she smiled and looked away.

'Arthur's not keen on flying either,' said Mavis. 'That's why we come on these coach tours. I tell him it's as safe as houses up in the air. You're far more likely to have a car crash . . . or a coach crash. God forbid!' she added hastily. 'Galaxy has an excellent record, though. We've been travelling with them for years now.'

'Aye, one trip up in an aeroplane was quite enough for me,' said Arthur. 'She managed to persuade me to go to America, about ten year ago, wasn't it, Mavis?'

'Yes, that's right,' replied his wife. 'Well, eleven years to be exact. We went to New England, in the fall, as they call it over there.' She smiled reminiscently. 'The maple trees in Vermont . . . I've never seen anything quite so lovely, before or since. You must admit it was a grand sight, Arthur.'

'Aye, it was; I'll not deny it. But you'll not get me there again. Besides, I don't know as aeroplane travel would do for me now, not with my blood pressure and what have you. I'd be happy enough to stay in Britain – or the UK as it's now called. There's some lovely places back home: Scotland and t'Cotswolds, and t'Yorkshire Dales; but Mavis likes to go further afield once a year, don't you, love?'

'Yes. Austria, Switzerland, the Loire Valley; we've even been to Czechoslovakia – the Czech Republic, that is. But it's the first time I've managed to persuade him to visit Germany, isn't it, Arthur?'

Arthur nodded. 'Aye, so it is,' he said meaningfully. 'I'd vowed I'd never set eyes on another German, not as long as I lived. I saw more than enough of 'em sixty year ago, an' I can't see as how they'll have changed all that much. Leopards don't change their spots, you know.'

'You served in the last war then, Arthur?' asked Dave.

'Aye, so I did. I joined up in 1940, when I was eighteen. I didn't wait to be called up. Of course by that time – it was after Dunkirk – most of the troops were back in England, except for the Desert Rats. So we had to bide our time. I was at a camp in the south of England. We made up for it in the end though, damned sure we did. I went over for the D-Day landings. Came through it all in one piece, thank God, at least as far as my body was concerned. But it's what it does to your mind . . . I've never talked about it, not to anyone, certainly not to Mavis, nor to my parents. I was one of them that went to Dachau, you see, to release the prisoners.' He gave a shudder. 'Enough said. It's still with me, though I try to forget what I saw. And I never go to any of their damned reunions.'

Dave did a quick calculation. He had guessed that Arthur might be eighty. By his reckoning now the man must be eighty-three, his wife possibly a few years younger.

'I've managed to persuade him that it's all a long time ago,' said Mavis, gently touching his hand as it rested on the table. 'It was a couple of years after the war ended that I met Arthur. He was a sales rep – commercial travellers, they used to call them then – and he came into the hardware shop where I worked.'

'Aye, we met over the pots and pans and kettles, didn't we, love?' Arthur looked at his wife fondly. 'It didn't take me long to realize that she was the one for me. And we've been married for fifty-five years, haven't we, Mavis?'

'That's right,' she replied, smiling. 'And never a cross word, eh, Arthur?' Her lively blue-grey eyes twinkled at him.

'I wouldn't go so far as to say that,' he replied. 'She's had summat to put up with, looking after me, I can tell you. But we've made a go of it, haven't we, love?'

Their new friends learned that Mavis would be eighty later that year. They still lived in Blackburn, where they had met, and they had two children, one of each, and six grandchildren.

After they had eaten their pudding – a slice of Neapolitan ice cream with a serving of diced fruit at the side – they went into the adjoining lounge where coffee was being served. Jane found herself sitting next to Arthur. She confided to him that her mother held exactly the same views about the Germans.

'She's the same age as you, well, a couple of years older, actually, and she still tends to think of them as the enemy. My father served in the war, like you did. He was in the D-Day landings, but I never heard him talk about it either. He didn't give the impression that he hated the Germans . . .' Jane mused that her father had been a much more placid person than Arthur appeared to be, more ready to let bygones be bygones. '. . . but of course he might not have seen the same horrors that you did.'

'No, p'raps not,' agreed Arthur. 'But my good lady says I've to put it all behind me and enjoy the trip to Germany. And that's what I've made up my mind to do, though I haven't actually told her that,' he added with a quiet chuckle. 'I've heard that the Rhine valley is worth seeing, and the Black Forest. And I believe they have some pretty good wines, don't they?'

'So I've heard,' said Jane, smiling at him. She had thought at first that Arthur might be a bit of a 'clever clogs', and one who found fault with everything, but the elderly gentleman was growing on her. On the chairs on the other side of the small table Mavis and Dave were chatting comfortably together. Arthur and Mavis were a pleasant couple with whom they would, no doubt, spend quite a lot of their holiday time. There was a coach full of people, though, some of them younger than herself and Dave, and many of them considerably older. All of them, however, judging by the lively chatter in the room, looking forward to an enjoyable holiday.

Five

Mavis Johnson awoke with a start and looked round the unfamiliar room. A faint light was filtering through the shutters against the window. She could make out the shape of a wardrobe and dressing table, and another bed a few feet away from her where Arthur was still fast asleep. For a brief moment she couldn't think where she was. Then, as a fleeting, scarcely remembered dream vanished from her mind she awoke to reality. Of course! She was not at home, she was in France, in Calais, where they had just spent the first night of their holiday, and today they would be travelling on through France and into Germany.

She reached for her glasses – she was needing them more and more these days – then glanced at her little bedside clock that she always took away with her. It was just turned six o'clock. She had set the alarm for six thirty. They had been told that breakfast was at half past seven, then they would be on their way as soon as everyone was ready, hopefully at half past eight.

Mavis heard a sound coming from the street, a sort of clanging noise. She realized now that it was the same sound that had awakened her. And now Arthur was awake as well. He made a grunt, then sat bolt upright in bed.

'What the dickens is that? What time is it, Mavis?'

'It's five past six,' she told him.

'For crying out loud! Can't a chap have any peace? We're supposed to be on holiday, aren't we? I reckon nothing to be woken up at six o'clock in the morning.'

He was always irritable when he awoke, but the mood would soon pass and Mavis had learnt to take no notice. She smiled to herself. He was a comical sight sitting up in bed, what little hair he had standing on end, his boldly striped pyjamas ruckled around his middle, and his eyes peering short-sightedly around the room. He, too, reached for his glasses.

'Can't see a damned thing without these,' he muttered. 'Six o'clock! What a time to be waking up!'

'We'd be getting up at half past anyway, Arthur,' Mavis told him, 'or we won't be ready in time. Come along now; stop being so grumpy, and I'll make us a nice cup of tea.'

A small travelling kettle and two beakers, plus tea bags, powdered milk and sugar lumps were essential items in Mavis's luggage whenever they went abroad. And the Continental plug and adaptor, of course, so that the kettle would work. Most, if not all, the hotels in the UK now provided tea-making facilities in all their bedrooms, but very few of the Continental hotels had, so far, cottoned on to the idea.

'Good idea; thanks, love.' Arthur was coming round a bit now. 'That'll be grand, there's nothing like a cup of tea first thing in a morning.'

Mavis had by now donned her dressing gown and fluffy bedroom slippers and was busy seeing to the tea-making; there was a handy plug socket over the dressing table.

'Let's get these shutters back, then we can see what we're doing,' she said, going to the window and fastening back the wooden blinds. Then, 'Oh look, Arthur,' she cried. 'Look at those young people in the street, outside the bread shop; it's called a *boulangerie*. I remember that from French lessons at school.'

As Arthur joined her at the window they saw a man in a voluminous white apron, with a baker's cap on his head, pushing up the shutter on the shop window. It made a loud clattering sound, and Mavis realized that must have been what she had heard earlier. It was a double-fronted shop. There was a small crowd, seven or eight teenage boys and girls standing by the shop all carrying long loaves. Some of them were nibbling at the end of the loaf, others tearing off chunks and devouring them as though they were starving. Then the man who had put up the shutter could be seen inside the shop, filling the window with loaves of all shapes and sizes. The youngsters were laughing and shouting and having a whale of a time.

'I expect they've had a night on the town,' said Mavis, 'and now they're having their breakfast. And look, he's got some other customers already.' A couple of middle-aged women, clad in dark coats and headscarves and carrying wicker shopping baskets were going into the shop. 'They'll be buying bread for their breakfast. I can just imagine how nice and fresh it will taste.'

'Shopping, at six o'clock in the morning!' exclaimed Arthur. 'I couldn't see you doing that, Mavis.'

'Well . . . no, I agree that I wouldn't, but it's different here, Arthur. They like to buy fresh bread each day. Those long loaves don't keep fresh like our bread does, but they taste delicious; baguettes, they're called. We might be having some ourselves for breakfast.'

'Can't see what's wrong with sliced bread meself,' replied Arthur. 'Bloomin' Froggies! They have to be different, of course.'

'We're in a different country, Arthur,' said Mavis, patiently. 'Different food, different ways of doing things. You should know that by now, we've been abroad often enough.'

It all added to the enjoyment of her holiday, how they did things in other lands. Mavis felt herself smiling at the young people, remembering a time when she, too, had been young and giddy. And she knew that Arthur didn't mean half of what he said. He always had to have his little grumble about 'damned foreigners', but she knew that, secretly, he enjoyed these holidays abroad as much as she did.

'Come on, Arthur,' she said now. 'Your tea's ready.'

'Thanks, love,' he said. 'The cup that cheers. Sorry I'm such a trial to you, Mavis love.' He grinned at her. 'I don't know how you put up with me sometimes.'

'No, neither do I.' She smiled back at him. 'But it's a bit late now to be thinking of swapping you for someone else. I reckon I'll have to make the best of it.'

'I don't know what I'd do without you, Mavis,' he said now, putting an arm around her in an unusual show of affection.

'Nor I without you, Arthur,' she answered quietly.

It was true. He drove her mad at times, but she couldn't imagine how she would manage without him . . . if anything were to happen to him. That was the expression everyone used, 'if anything happened', when what they really meant was if the loved one was to die. Something one didn't want to think about or talk about. And yet it would happen, sometime. Mavis knew that. It happened to everyone, eventually.

She worried about Arthur, more than he realized. He took tablets for his blood pressure, which was sometimes rather higher than normal, and for a rapid heartbeat that troubled him from time to time. Arthur, though, to give him credit where it was due, was not a hypochondriac. He made light of his ailments, insisting that he was fighting fit. Indeed, their doctor had given him the all-clear. Mavis had insisted that he should pay a visit to the surgery before they embarked on the holiday. It might have been different had they been flying, but neither of them really liked that form of travel.

Arthur had a little grumble again because it was a shower and not a bath. Mavis, also, preferred a bath, but was happy enough to put up with a shower for one night. There might be a proper bathroom at the main hotel, with a bit of luck. She remembered the time – twenty, thirty years ago, maybe? – when all you had was a washbasin in your room and you had to go down the corridor to the bathroom, and to the loo. Facilities had improved, both at home and abroad.

They were ready in good time for breakfast at seven thirty, leaving their suitcase outside the bedroom door, as instructed, for the porter or one of the drivers to collect. Their companions of the previous night, Dave and Jane, were already seated at the same table, so they went to join them. Mavis thought how happy Jane looked, and how attractive in a pale green shirt and neat navy trousers. There was a quiet radiance about her. Mavis guessed – and hoped – that a romance might blossom between her and that nice man Dave before the holiday was over.

There was the usual conversation about how well they had slept, or otherwise. Arthur complained that the sound of the plumbing had kept him awake half the night. Mavis bit her tongue. It would not be tactful to say that she had been kept awake by the sound of his snoring! At home they sometimes slept in separate rooms, but when they were abroad the extra cost of single rooms would have been prohibitive.

Continental breakfasts had improved as well. Mavis remembered the time when all you got was a roll with butter and jam. Now there was quite a feast laid out on a side table for you to help yourself. A choice of cereal and of fruit; brown and white bread rolls and croissants (no baguettes, but the rolls looked just as fresh and crisp); small jars of jam, honey or marmalade; there were even hard-boiled eggs, cold ham and thin slices of cheese. Coffee and tea as well, in large Thermos jugs, for the guests to help themselves. Mavis had learnt that it was as well to stick to coffee when abroad. Their Continental friends had no idea how to make tea, but the coffee, although strong and rather bitter was sure to wake you up.

After breakfast, and when the travellers had got together all their bits and pieces, and had made sure they had left nothing behind, they assembled outside the hotel whilst Mike and Bill loaded the cases on to the coach.

'A lovely day for our onward journey,' Mavis remarked to Jane. Although it was still early the sun was shining in a cloudless sky and there was no nip in the air as there often was at home in early summer.

'I've been very daring and put trousers on this morning,' Mavis whispered confidentially. 'I don't often wear them but I thought why not? I'm on holiday. You don't think they make me look fat, do you?'

'No, of course not,' replied Jane. 'You look fine.' She smiled to herself. What else could she say? She could hardly tell her new friend that she did look fat if, indeed, it were so. As it happened she was telling the truth. The older woman looked very smart in well-fitting navy trousers – very similar to the ones that Jane herself was wearing – and a crisp pink and white striped blouse. Admittedly she was a little on the plump side, but she carried herself well. Jane guessed that she always paid great attention to her appearance.

There were some women who really should not wear trousers. Jane noticed a few middle-aged ladies amongst their number whose nether regions were bulging alarmingly in crimplene trousers. But they didn't seem to be aware of how they looked, or else they didn't care. After all, as Mavis said, they were on holiday.

Jane noticed two ladies standing nearby. She had seen them

the night before in the lounge. She guessed that before the holiday was over they would all have got to know one another, at least by sight, but you were sure to know some better than others. One of the ladies caught her eye and smiled in a friendly way. Jane moved across to speak to her.

'Hello,' she said. 'Are you enjoying the trip so far?'

'Oh, very much so,' replied the woman, who looked to be the elder of the two. Jane had taken them, from a distance, to be mother and daughter. Now she could see that they were much closer in age, but this one appeared older than her friend – or sister or whoever it was – because of the way she was dressed. 'We're enjoying it, aren't we, Shirley?' She addressed the woman who was standing next to her, and she turned to join in the conversation.

'Yes we are; this is the third trip we've been on with Galaxy,' she said. 'I'm Shirley, by the way, and this is my friend, Ellen.'

They all nodded and said 'How do you do?' Jane introduced herself. 'I came on my own,' she told them. 'I was really quite nervous about it, but I've made some friends already. That's Dave, who I'm sitting with on the coach, and the older couple are Mavis and Arthur.' Those three were chatting and laughing together. 'We all sat together for dinner last night, and we got on really well. It's nice to make new friends, isn't it?'

'Oh, those are the two who were late back on the ship, aren't they?' remarked Shirley.

Her friend, Ellen, glanced at her reprovingly. 'You've no room to talk, Shirley!'

'Oh, come on, Ellen. We've never been late back,' Shirley replied with a little laugh.

'Well, we've cut it fine a time or two,' said Ellen. She turned to Jane. 'She will insist on waiting till the very last minute before we go back to the coach. "He said half past, and that's the time we're going back," she'll say. And there's me panicking and thinking they'll go without us. It's a wonder I've not had a heart attack with her goings-on!' She was smiling though, so Jane knew there was no malice in her words.

'Now you know they have to wait till everyone's back,' said Shirley. 'They're not allowed to go and leave you. Anyway, I promise to do better this time. But I like making the most of every minute, you see.'

'It's a thankless job for the drivers, isn't it?' remarked Jane. 'I bet they feel like driving away when people keep them waiting. And it's such a big responsibility, looking after a coach load of people. How do they manage to know them all? I'm sure I could never do it.'

'Maybe it gets easier with practice,' said Ellen. 'Oh . . . they're getting on now, see. Come along, Shirley. Nice talking to you, Jane. Maybe we'll chat again later.'

Jane watched them as they stood there waiting to board the coach. Chalk and cheese, one might say, but she had the impression that they were good friends. It would be interesting to find out how they knew one another. The younger one – or so she took her to be – called Shirley, was the height of fashion. She was wearing cream trousers and a smart red and white striped top with a bright blue cotton scarf tied at a jaunty angle. She was carrying a jacket that matched her trousers, and her feet – with bright red toenails – were shod in a pair of strappy red sandals.

Ellen, in complete contrast, wore a summer skirt in a floral design and a cotton blouse with a Peter Pan collar. She carried a woollen cardigan and wore sensible Clarks' sandals. She looked very neat and tidy but . . . so old-fashioned!

Jane noticed when she and Dave boarded the coach that the two women were sitting on one of the front two seats. People often booked early to get these prime positions.

'Good morning all,' said Mike, in his usual jovial manner. 'Slept well, have you? And enjoyed your first evening? Good, good . . . Now, have you all handed in your keys?'

There were one or two audible gasps, then two ladies, looking rather sheepish, handed the giant-sized keys to Mike. He laughed. 'Never mind, there's always somebody, believe me! I'll just nip back with them.'

When everyone was finally settled Mike counted heads, then, with Bill at the wheel, they set off on what would be a long journey to the Rhine valley.

Leaving Calais they headed east on the motorway that linked northern France with Belgium. It was an attractive tree-lined road, and seemed quiet compared with the M1 and M6 back home. Jane remarked on the fact to Dave.

'They have to pay tolls to use the motorways over here,' he reminded her, 'so drivers often prefer to use an alternative route. Coach drivers have to take the shortest route from A to B, unless there's something of particular interest to see.'

'Yes, of course,' said Jane. 'It's all so interesting, though. I get bored travelling on our motorways, or if I'm driving myself I get worried by all the traffic. It's so nice to be able to relax.' She gave a contended sigh, and was aware of Dave smiling at her. The place names they read as they bypassed the towns – Mons, Ypres, Armentieres – were familiar because they evoked such poignant memories. No one on board would have lived through the First World War, but they all knew of the carnage and the sorrow it had caused. There was a song that the soldiers used to sing. How did it go?

Mademoiselle from Armentieres,
Never been kissed for forty years . . .

At least that was the polite version. Jane smiled to herself. There would no doubt have been a bawdier one, but women in those days weren't supposed to know about such things. Times had certainly changed.

Now and again through the trees they caught a glimpse of war graves, row upon row of white crosses. The countryside they were passing through was where so many British soldiers – and German ones too – had died in the trenches. It was a peaceful scene now, the fields bright with golden dandelions, but here and there by the roadside were clumps of blood-red poppies, a stark reminder of what had taken place almost a hundred years ago.

Mike, who was doing a commentary on matters of interest, pointed out that some of the fields still contained tank traps – triangular concrete blocks like miniature pyramids – because they were travelling along what had once been the Siegfried Line, a German line of demarcation, but to most people, including Jane, the place where the British soldiers vowed to hang out the washing.

Now and again they passed an idyllic scene: tall poplar trees evenly spaced along a cart track and a red-tiled farmhouse in the distance, just like a painting Jane remembered having seen called 'The Avenue at Middelharnis'.

The coach sped along, eating up the miles, or kilometres as it was over here. Jane noticed that Arthur, in the seat across the aisle, had dozed off, his head nodding and his glasses slipping forward. He gave a snort, and his wife nudged him. He awoke with a start.

'Come along, Arthur,' Jane heard Mavis say to him. 'We're getting off soon, for a coffee stop.' Mike had just informed them that they would be stopping for half an hour, no more, at the next service station.

It turned out to be a pleasant place with cosy little alcoves interspersed with flowering plants and small palm trees. It seemed very attractive and welcoming compared with the hustle and bustle of the service areas on the M6; they were so huge and impersonal. Or maybe it was just because it was different and 'foreign'. Jane was still almost pinching herself at the idea of being abroad and, what was more, being in such congenial company when she had thought she might be on her own. But there was no time to linger. They scarcely had time to drink their hot fragrant coffee and pay a visit to the facilities before they were back on the coach.

Mike told them that their lunch stop, in another couple of hours, would also be in Belgium, near to the German border. It was a similar place to the former one – as in England, they seemed to follow a pattern – where Jane and Dave dined on vegetable soup with crusty bread. Jane was tempted by the apple pie and cream, but Dave reminded her that they might be having *apfelstrudel* that evening at their overnight stop on Rüdesheim; so she chose a slice of gateau instead.

She no longer felt embarrassed at being with Dave. He seemed to take it for granted that they would stay together. And he no longer insisted on paying, which was as it should be. So that was another little problem that had been solved.

Soon after the lunch stop they crossed the German border, and by early afternoon they were approaching the Rhine. Ahead of them they could see on the horizon the twin towers of the huge Gothic cathedral at Cologne, but they bypassed the city, taking the road towards Bonn.

'The birthplace of Beethoven,' Bill reminded them, putting on a tape of the composer's Fifth Symphony. The drivers had changed places now, with Mike at the wheel and Bill doing the commentary. Not that any comments were necessary to help them appreciate the lovely riverside towns and villages through which they were passing. Königswinter, Bad Godesburg, Oberwinter, with houses painted in pastel shades of cream and pink. High on the hillsides were turreted castles, and steeply sloping vineyards ran down to the river. The Rhine was the lifeline of the area, a broad silver-grey ribbon of river with parallel roads and railway tracks running alongside each bank.

They were approaching Remagen, famous for the capture of the bridgehead by the Americans at the end of the war. Jane noticed that Arthur was now wide awake and appeared to be listening intently, though with a stern expression on his face, as Bill told them the story of the bridge at Remagen. It was the only bridge that had not been destroyed by the retreating German army. The Americans had established a bridgehead there, and Hitler, consumed with rage, had ordered that all those in charge of the bridge defences must be shot. Ten days later the bridge collapsed except for two massive towers, like castles, one on each bank. One of them was now a museum of peace.

Jane knew the story. She had watched the film, *A Bridge Too Far*, on the television with her husband, Tom, although he had been far more engrossed in it than she had been. As far as she was concerned it was all a long time ago. We were all part of the European community – be it for better or worse – so what good did it do to keep looking back on it all?

They stopped at Boppard, a lively, more modern-looking town with a mile-long promenade.

'This is where you will be boarding the pleasure steamer for a sail up to Rüdesheim,' Mike told them. He glanced at his watch. 'You can go and stretch your legs for quarter of an hour, but make sure you are back here by ten minutes to three. The boat leaves at three o'clock, and you mustn't miss it; it's a lovely trip. Bill and I won't be coming with you. We're taking the coach along, and we'll meet you at the other end at Rüdesheim, that's where you leave the boat, then it's not very far to our hotel. So . . . enjoy yourselves, ladies and gents, and we'll see you later.'

Boppard was a popular tourist resort. There was a good number of holidaymakers strolling along the promenade and around the narrow streets behind the hotels and shops that faced the river.

All the passengers heeded the instructions and were back in time to board the steamer. The day had kept its earlier promise of fine weather, and the sun was shining brightly, albeit with a gentle breeze, as Jane and Dave sat on the open-air top deck enjoying the passing scenery, and the commentary, given first in German then in English, with a guttural accent.

It was reputed to be the most picturesque part of the Rhine. Pastel-coloured houses and steepled churches on both river-banks, and on every craggy hilltop another castle. Here was a village church you could enter only through the pub, as the vicar was both the publican and the priest! Here was Maus – Mouse – castle, then Katz – Cat – castle, and here was the village of St Gaur which took its name from the patron saint of innkeepers, Jane doubted that she would remember all these facts when she arrived home, but she was busy with her camera, snapping away at each interesting scene.

They rounded a bend in the river, and the guide told them that they were approaching the Lorelei rock. He stopped talking, then the boat was filled with the sound of German voices singing the song that told the story of the famous legend. Jane couldn't understand the German words, but she remembered the song that they had learned long ago at school.

> I know not what comes o'er me, or why my spirits fail;
> Strange visions arise before me, I think of an ancient tale . . .

There on a promontory running out from the cliff was the bronze statue of the Lorelei maiden. The legend told of sailors at twilight being lured to a watery grave by the maiden singing her song as she combed her golden hair. Just a story – a sad story – but there was an element of truth in that there were dangerous rocks in that part of the river, and boats had been known to come to grief there.

'Rüdesheim,' called the guide a few moments later, and the Galaxy passengers all alighted from the boat to find their coach waiting for them at the side of the road.

Mike counted heads. 'Thank goodness for that! You're all here. No one has been swept away by the Lorelei maiden. Good trip, isn't it?'

They all agreed that they had enjoyed it very much. Their hotel was no more than half a mile along the river. Bill pulled up outside a white painted hotel with a brightly coloured awning, and little tables where guests were enjoying coffee or ice cream.

'Here we are,' he called. 'Hotel Niederwald. Collect your keys at the desk, and your luggage will be taken care of. See you later, everyone . . .'

Six

Compared with its light and sunny aspect on the outside, the hotel appeared somewhat forbidding and gloomy inside, until one became accustomed to the dark wooden doors and balustrades, the deep red carpet and the subdued lighting from the wrought-iron chandeliers. First impressions, however, could be deceptive, and guests soon learnt that it was a friendly, welcoming hotel. The receptionist at the huge oaken desk, which resembled a dock in a court of law, received them all with a cheery smile and good wishes for a pleasant stay, along with – once again – a key with a giant-sized brass plate with the room number on it.

The lift, like the one in the previous hotel, was antiquated with room for only four, at a tight squeeze, as they made their way up to the second floor where the single rooms were situated. Dave and Jane were sharing the lift with Shirley and Ellen, the ladies whom Jane had met that morning. She was surprised that they were not sharing a room – it was a good deal cheaper to do so – but maybe they each liked their privacy. It could well be that having spent the day together they preferred just their own company at night.

And so it was that when they had had a wash and change of clothes – their cases arrived promptly outside the doors – the four of them found themselves sharing the lift down to the dining room on the ground floor. As was customary on coach tours, the tables were set for six or eight; there were rarely tables for two as it was supposed that the travellers would have become acquainted and would wish to dine with new friends.

Mavis and Arthur were already there, waiting for the dining-room doors to open at seven o'clock. By mutual agreement, it seemed, the six of them sat down at the same table, one with a notice saying 'Galaxy Travel'. There was another coach party staying there as well; their tables had different coloured napkins – green rather than the red for the Galaxy people – and their notices said 'Richmond Travel', suggesting that they were from Yorkshire. Or it might be the Richmond near to London. The accents soon indicated that they were Yorkshire folk. The dining room was busy, but the service was surprisingly prompt, the coach parties being served first, to be followed later by the private guests.

The watery minestrone soup with chunks of – not very fresh – bread did not bode well; but the following courses made up for it.

'There! What did I tell you?' proclaimed Arthur when the main course arrived. 'Wiener Schnitzel; they always serve that the first night.'

'How do you know, Arthur?' said his wife. 'We've not stayed in Germany before.'

'No, but that's what we got in Austria, and they speak the same language. And I reckon we'll have it tomorrow in the Black Forest.'

'Well, we'll have to wait and see, won't we?' said Mavis. 'I must say this is delicious.'

And so it was; tender fillets of veal in breadcrumbs, served with slices of lemon, fluffy mashed potatoes and green beans. The dessert was no surprise either. *Apfelstrudel*, as they had anticipated, apples and raisins, flavoured with cinnamon, encased in mouth-watering puffed pastry, with lashings of cream. Five of them, all except Ellen, shared a bottle of the Rhine wine recommended by the waiter, whilst Ellen chose to drink *Apfelsaft*.

Conversation flowed easily around the dining tables as they all talked about how much they had enjoyed the day, and became better acquainted with one another. Jane was sitting between Dave and Shirley, with Ellen, Mavis and Arthur at the other side of the table.

Many of the guests had made an effort to 'dress for dinner', especially the ladies, although it was not obligatory. Only a few of the men, the older ones, were wearing jackets and ties, the majority had opted for open-necked shirts. The ladies, though, had all tried to look their best. Jane had chosen to wear an ankle-length black skirt rather than her usual trousers, with a floral top. Shirley was dressed 'to the nines' in a long skirt and a top of heavy cream-coloured lace with a diamond (well, probably diamanté) necklace and earrings. She was carefully made up: mascara and eyeliner, delicate blue eyeshadow and shimmering pale pink lipstick. Her dark brown hair was highlighted with blonde streaks. A lady who liked to look glamorous and liked people to notice her appearance. As Jane talked with her she discovered that she was a friendly, likeable person, but possibly the teeniest bit vain?

Her friend, Ellen, was wearing a 'two-piece', a maroon dress and matching jacket made of what Jane thought was called Moygashel? Well, something like that, more the sort of suit her mother might wear. Her hair was grey and newly permed, and she wore a light dusting of powder and the tiniest smear of lipstick. It was clear, though, that she had made an effort to look nice, according to her way of thinking. She looked happy as she talked animatedly to Mavis who was sitting next to her.

'Ellen never touches alcohol,' Shirley told Jane in a quiet voice as they sipped their golden wine, but her words were not critical or derisory. 'She had very strict parents, you see – dyed-in-the-wool Methodists – and it's had quite an effect of her, poor Ellen. Although I don't know why I say "poor Ellen". She's a very contented person, she tries to find good in everything and everyone. She's a good friend to me; we've known one another for ages . . . haven't we, Ellen?' she said as her friend looked across at them and smiled.

'Yes. Would you believe we started infant school together?' said Ellen. 'We lived in the same street and our parents knew one another.'

Jane learnt that this was in the mid-fifties. She estimated their age as fifty-five or so, ten years older than herself. They had progressed to the same secondary school and had both left at sixteen, Ellen to work in a bank, and Shirley to follow her bent for fashion and design, training as a window dresser at a store in Manchester where they both lived; not in Manchester itself but in nearby Salford. Shirley had moved on to a more prestigious store in the city, where she was the chief window dresser, and Ellen still worked in the same bank.

'It's only recently, though, about four years ago,' said Ellen, 'that we started going on holiday together, although we'd always kept in touch. I was looking after my elderly parents, you see.

They died five years ago, both of them in the same year, God bless them . . .'

'And that was the time when my marriage came to grief,' said Shirley. She gave a rueful smile. 'The least said about that the better! I've decided I'm quite happy on my own. I've lots of friends, though; women friends, I mean. I wouldn't get married again. Once bitten twice shy.'

'I'm a widow, too,' said Jane quietly. She smiled. 'We were very happy. I never thought I would—' she stopped suddenly – 'what I mean to say is . . . it's the first time I've been away on my own. But I'm very glad I came.'

Shirley smiled at her in a confidential way. 'You're enjoying it then . . . more than you thought you would?'

Jane nodded. 'Yes, indeed I am,' she answered. 'I'm having a lovely time.'

Coffee was served in the adjoining lounge before they all went their separate ways.

'Shall we take a walk along the riverside?' Dave said to Jane. 'Then we could have a drink on the Drosselgasse later on. I know it will probably be heaving with tourists, but you can't come to Rüdesheim without seeing its famous street. You've heard of it, have you?'

'Yes, I have,' said Jane. 'Anyway, what are we but tourists like all the rest? I'll just change my skirt for a pair of trousers.'

They walked away from the town up to the part of the river where the cruise ships that travelled along the Rhine and Moselle were berthed for the night. They crossed the railway line that ran alongside the river to take a closer look at them. They were nowhere near the size of the QE2 and other ocean-going liners, but they were handsome-looking vessels, streamlined and gleaming white, some cabins having windows and others with portholes.

'I should imagine that's a nice leisurely way to see the sights,' observed Jane. 'Like the cruise we had this afternoon, but every day. And a different stopping place each night.'

'And not so rushed as a coach tour,' said Dave. 'Not that I'm complaining. But it's a thought for the future, maybe . . .' His words lingered on the air as they smiled at one another, crossing the railway line back to the main promenade.

'Hello there,' called a cheery voice. 'Seeing what Rüdesheim has to offer, are you?' Mike and Bill were walking towards them, smartly dressed in their regulation bright blue blazers with the Galaxy motif on the pocket and blue and red striped ties. They were both smoking as they were not on duty. This was forbidden on the coaches, of course, for passengers as well as drivers, as it had been for many years. But they often indulged in the weed when they stopped for coffee and lunch breaks, as did some of the travellers.

'Yes, it's a lovely little town,' replied Jane. 'It's the first time I've been to these parts, and it's all so new and interesting.'

'Glad you're enjoying it,' said Bill. 'See you later . . .'

'A nice couple,' he remarked to Mike, as they strolled back towards the town. 'They've only just met, at least that's how I see it. They seem to be getting on very well. What do you bet there's a romance in the air? It won't be the first one I've seen.'

'Nor me,' replied Mike. 'You're probably right. Jolly good luck to them . . . What about your love life, eh? Is it still on with the lovely Lise?'

Lise was a waitress at the hotel where they were staying that night, with whom Bill had been having a casual relationship. He visited the place every few weeks, sometimes with Mike, sometimes not, according to the schedules. Mike knew that they always had a drink together; only a half or a shandy, though, because there was a strict rule that Galaxy drivers must not drink when on duty, and they knew it was foolish not to obey. The drivers shared a room, and Mike knew that his colleague would be missing for part of the night, so he drew his own conclusions.

'No,' Bill answered curtly, in answer to Mike's question. 'I'm afraid not. It seems I've got my marching orders. She told me when we arrived that she's friendly with one of the porters now, so that's that! But I'm not bothered . . . You'll have noticed the girl – the young woman, I should say – on the front seat? She's called Christine Harper.'

'I did, and I saw you talking to her while I was driving. She's with her mother, isn't she?'

'Actually, it's her elder sister, quite a bit older I imagine.

She lost her husband last year – the older one, I mean – and reading between the lines, I think that Christine is recovering from a broken relationship. So they decided to come on holiday together, the first time they've done so.'

'So you're on first name terms. Christine, eh? You fancy your chances there, do you?' Mike was laughing, but Bill answered more seriously.

'I've between thinking it's time I settled down. I know what you think of me – a girl in every port, so to speak. I've played the field, but I'm getting older now, and it's time I looked to the future. I'm forty now, time to think about a more stable relationship; a home and marriage, kids maybe, though I might have left it a bit late for that.'

'I don't see why, if you're really serious about settling down,' said Mike. 'But our job isn't exactly conducive to a settled life, is it? My wife's been getting on to me about it. She'd like me to give up these Continental tours and do the ones in the UK. I'd see more of the family that way. They're mostly five-day tours, so you get home every weekend.'

'And how do you feel about that?' asked Bill.

Mike shrugged. 'There's for and against. I must admit I enjoy coming over here. We're not always on the same tour, and you see a bit of the world. And I try to make it interesting for the clients, you and me both, of course. I know some of the blokes just do their job, drive from A to B with hardly a word about the sights and all that. But the folk do like to know about the places they're visiting. I know they've got guide books, and maps, too, some of 'em, following the route. God knows why! They're not doing the driving.'

'Yes, I think we do our best for them,' said Bill. 'They seem a good crowd this time, a mixed age group. No problems so far, touch wood.' He tapped his forehead. 'So . . . what are you going to do? Will you ask if you can go on the UK jobs, to please Sally?'

'I can see what she means,' said Mike. 'The kids are getting to a difficult age. Tracey's fifteen now, studying for her GCSEs next year. At least she's supposed to be studying, but she's got in with a daft crowd at school. Staying out late, and Sally thinks she might be going into pubs. And she's wanting to go to late-night discos. Sally's said no to that, and it's caused friction between them. Tracey can be a right little madam.'

'So Sally wants you to be at home and lay the law down, does she?'

'I've never been much good at playing the heavy-handed father. I was a bit of a tearaway myself, till I met Sal, so I suppose I can remember what it's like. Our Gary's only twelve; he's a good kid, no problems there so far. Anyway, we'll see. I've told her I'll think about it this week.'

'I'd miss you if you were based at home,' said Bill. 'I know we're not always on the same tour. But I'm glad when we are. They're not all as easy as you are to work with.'

'Nice of you to say so.' Mike grinned at him. 'The same goes for you, of course. So . . . what about you and Christine? Have you tested the water there?'

'As a matter of fact, I've asked her to have a drink with me in the hotel bar, later tonight. I said ten o'clock. I know they'll all want to see the town first.'

'What about her sister?'

'Oh, I think I've made it clear. They were sitting with two other ladies at dinner time, and they all seemed to be getting on well. I dare say Norah – that's her sister – will take the hint.'

'Unless she's the overprotective sort?'

'Well, we'll see won't we? I tell you what, though; I must try and get some of this off if I want to make a good impression.' He patted his rather corpulent stomach. 'The trouble is I can't resist these strudels and dumplings and the Black Forest gateaux at the next place. It's too tempting, and they do feed us up, don't they, because we're doing the driving?'

Mike laughed. 'You can always say no. It's our lifestyle as well, all this sitting at the wheel every day, and lack of exercise, except for a stroll in the evening. What about your other lady friend, Olga? Isn't that a bit more serious?'

Olga was a receptionist at the hotel in the Black Forest. It was common knowledge that she and Bill were 'an item', at least whilst he was staying there. They had been friendly for a couple of years.

'I really ought to make a clean break there,' said Bill. 'We both agreed the last time we met that it was going nowhere.

I don't see how it can really. I'll see how it goes this week with Christine. She might decide she doesn't like me. But it struck me as soon as I met her that she's a nice homely sort of girl, the sort I should be looking for.'

'Pretty as well, though,' said Mike. 'I couldn't see you being interested if she wasn't. Anyway, the best of luck, mate.'

They had turned aside to look in one of the shop windows on the promenade. 'D'you think anyone buys this junk?' said Bill. 'Just look at it!'

A lot of it was junk, as Bill had said. Small statuettes of the Lorelei maiden; plates, mugs, ashtrays, tea towels, all emblazoned with pictures of Rüdesheim and the River Rhine; beer steins with pewter lids; dolls dressed in national costume; cheap jewellery, perfume bottles, souvenir pens and pencils. Amidst the dross, though, there was some merchandise for the more discerning. Hummel figurines of cute rosy-cheeked children; a boy sitting on the branch of an apple tree; a girl driving home the geese; another holding a bouquet of flowers.

There was a rack of postcards in the doorway – the shop was still open to catch the passing trade – depicting the highlights of the area. The famous Drosselgasse with its half-timbered houses and numerous Wienstuben; the Lorelei maiden on her rock; the vineyards sloping steeply down to the river; the Brömserburg Castle, the oldest one on the Rhine; and the Niederwald Monument after which the hotel was named. It could be viewed from the road, a thirty-seven-metre-high statue known as Germania, built as an expression of power following the Franco-Prussian war in the nineteenth century. A cable lift took visitors up to view the sword-brandishing Valkyrie, but there was rarely time for tourists staying for only one night to take the trip.

'Who knows what you might buy if you were on holiday?' said Mike. 'Some of it is tat, I agree, but it might well bring back happy memories. Come on, let's get back to the hotel, then you can get ready for your date with the lovely Christine. I hope it turns out well.'

Dave and Jane set off together for a stroll around the town. They ended up, as tourists did at least once, in the Drosselgasse.

As was to be expected it was crowded and noisy, but a scene not to be missed. Dusk was falling, and lights streamed out from the myriad of shop windows; many of the souvenir shops were still open along with the hamburger stalls. The sound of merry laughter and singing drifted from the many Wienstuben where tourists, and locals as well, sat at long tables drinking lager and joining in the German drinking songs, many of them familiar back home in the UK.

'Might this be too noisy for you, too raucous?' asked Dave with a grin as they stopped outside one of the wine bars.

'No, why should it be?' replied Jane. 'It's not something I would normally do, but we're on holiday, aren't we? And you can't come here without joining in the fun, just once.'

'That's all it will be,' replied Dave. 'Just once. Tomorrow night we'll be in the Black Forest, although there'll be ample opportunity for a 'knees up' there as well. Come on, let's see if we can find a seat.' He took her hand and guided her to a space on a long bench, not too far from the doorway. From there they could watch the passing crowds as well as the activity in the room.

Everyone seated at the bare wooden table was friendly and in a holiday mood.

'How do?' A man with a Yorkshire accent greeted them as they sat down opposite him. 'Enjoying yerselves?'

'Yes, very much,' answered Jane politely. 'Are you?'

'Yes, we're on a river cruise,' said the woman next to him. 'We're berthed here for the night, then we're heading off to Koblenz and the Moselle river. It's the first time we've been on one. It's champion, isn't it, Joe?'

'I'll say it is. You must try it next year, the pair of you,' said Joe.

Dave laughed. 'We'll bear it in mind,' he replied, and Jane felt herself blushing.

It wasn't long before a waitress in a dirndl skirt and peasant blouse came to take their order. Dave ordered two glasses of lager which soon arrived, full to the brim with a frothy head on them.

It was too noisy for any meaningful conversations. The voices around them were mainly English, though they could hear snatches of French, Italian and, of course, German. Jane couldn't imagine why the locals would come here, unless they were from a different part of Germany with different customs, and were on holiday, just as they were.

A little while later a group of men dressed in lederhosen; short leather breeches with coloured braces, thick woollen socks and heavy brogues and wearing green felt hats with a feather in the brim, mounted the stage at the end of the room. There followed an entertainment of dancing, consisting of stamping and thigh slapping, singing along to an accordion, and a comedy routine where they all punched and knocked each other about. It was well received by the audience, who joined in the choruses of the songs, lah-lah-ing if they didn't know the words. Jane felt her inhibitions fast disappearing as she joined in with the rest.

When the entertainment came to an end Dave put an arm round her shoulders. 'Shall we go?' he asked quietly. 'It's an early start tomorrow.'

She nodded in agreement, and he held her hand as they made their way to the door and out into the still busy street. He continued to hold her hand as they strolled back the half mile or so to the hotel, neither of them speaking very much, both deep in their own thoughts.

They collected their keys at the reception desk – they were too heavy to carry around – then they took the lift up to the second floor. When they stopped at Jane's door, Dave took hold of her shoulders; then he leaned forward and, gently and softly, kissed her lips, just once.

'Thank you for a lovely evening, Jane,' he said in a quiet voice. 'See you in the morning.'

'Thank you, too,' she replied. 'I've had a lovely time.'

As she stepped into the room she felt suffused with a quiet joy. She smiled, and almost laughed out loud. Was this really happening to her, the reserved and rather shy Jane Redfern? She couldn't remember when she had felt so happy and carefree; certainly never since . . . since Tom had died. The thought of him subdued her for a moment. She could never, ever forget him; but maybe it was time, now, to look forward and not back.

Seven

Mike had told them that it would be a nine o'clock start the following morning, which was not too early. They must leave promptly although the journey to a little village in the Black Forest, not too far from Freiburg, would not be too long or too arduous.

To some of the party, however, it seemed very early to be up and about. As they stood on the forecourt of the hotel whilst Mike and Bill loaded the cases on to the coach, much of the talk was about the sleepless night that some of them had endured.

'Those blessed trains! No sooner did I drop off to sleep than another one hurtled along the track.'

'All very well having a river view, but nobody told us, did they, that we'd be kept awake half the night by the bloody trains?'

'We were alright; our room was at the back. We were disappointed that we didn't have a nice view, weren't we, Bob? But it seems that we came off best.'

'D'you think they run all through the night?'

'Well, I suppose they must stop sometime, but they start off again too bloomin' early.'

Mike and Bill listened with half an ear to the comments of the passengers. They had heard them all before; it was the same every time. It would serve no useful purpose, though, to tell them beforehand that they might be kept awake by the passing trains. Better to let them find out for themselves. After all, it was only for one night. The rest of the holiday in the quaint little village hotel in the Black Forest would be as quiet as anyone could wish.

Maybe the residents who lived near to the river were accustomed to the traffic noise. Although the scenery along the banks of the Rhine couldn't be surpassed in its beauty and grandeur, it was, nevertheless, an important arterial route in that part of Germany with goods as well as passengers being transported by road, rail and river.

Jane and Dave listened to the remarks of their fellow travellers.

'I reckon we did OK then, having rooms at the back,' observed Dave. 'Did you sleep alright?'

'Very well,' replied Jane, 'once I'd got off. My head was full of the events of the day, especially the music and the hilarity last night. It was a great evening, wasn't it?'

'The first of many, I hope,' he answered.

The other coach party, the one from Yorkshire, was leaving round about the same time. Their drivers, also, were loading their coach; they were bound for the Austrian Tyrol.

There was an enormous stack of suitcases, but it gradually dwindled as the men humped them into the well at the side of the vehicle. They refused help from the men in the parties, although they might well have been glad of it. It was all concerned with health and safety, Bill had told them. If a client injured himself whilst helping, then the company would be liable to pay compensation.

'All aboard now,' shouted Bill when the last suitcase was stacked away. A quick count of heads, then they were off.

It was a pleasant drive along the bank of the river. Bill drove at a leisurely speed as it was not much more than a hundred miles to their destination. They made a morning coffee stop at the side of the river, then, after the lunch break near to the famous town of Heidelberg – unfortunately with no time to view the sights of the 'Student Prince' city – they turned towards the Black Forest region.

They arrived mid-afternoon at the village where they were to stay for the next six nights. The hotel – or Gasthaus – was in an idyllic setting, such as was seen on hundreds of picture postcards. It was a white painted building with green shutters at the windows, situated near a rippling stream that flowed along by the roadside. The village through which they had passed consisted of a cluster of similar guest houses, a church with a spire, and a few souvenir shops and wine bars. The 'Gasthaus Grunder' – the name was on a swinging sign by the door – was a half mile or so from the centre of the village;

there was no other guest house near to it. It would most certainly be quiet – no sound to be heard except the ripple of the stream – a vivid contrast to their hotel of the previous night.

The proprietor, Johann Grunder, came out to meet them, a portly ruddy-faced man of middle-age, clad in a voluminous white apron. He welcomed them in halting English, saying that he hoped they would enjoy their stay. When they had collected their keys there was to be a treat for them to bid them welcome. *Kaffee und Kuchen*: a piece of Black Forest gateau and coffee. And whilst they were enjoying this their luggage would be sorted out and taken to their rooms.

'How very nice!' Mavis remarked to her husband. 'What a kind thought! I must say we've been made very welcome in Germany. I've been pleasantly surprised so far. You can't say any different, Arthur.'

'I'm not trying to,' he answered. 'Aye, it's been alright so far. It's a damn good job we had a room at the back, though, in that last place.' A comment that Mavis agreed with wholeheartedly. She'd never have heard the last of it if he'd had a sleepless night.

The hotel was deceptive, as it was much larger inside than it had appeared to be from the exterior. It was a long low building, stretching back a good way, with bedrooms on the ground floor and on the one above. It was modern and simple in design and there was a pleasant smell of pinewood. Everything was light and bright and scrupulously clean. It was a family-run hotel with a small staff, consisting of the receptionist, three waitresses, and an extra chef who helped Johann Grunder – himself a trained chef – in the kitchen. Marie, his wife, made the pastries and cakes. All this information was gleaned by Mavis who was not shy at asking questions. One of the waitresses, a language student called Greta, was only too willing to chat and practise her English.

The receptionist, Olga, was a friendly and attractive young woman in her mid-thirties with her dark hair swept back in a chignon. Mavis, who missed very little, noticed that she smiled and nodded at Bill as though she was very glad to see him. He smiled back at her, but he was busy with the luggage. Mavis guessed, though, that they might be well acquainted.

Their cake and coffee was served in the dining room, along a short corridor from the reception area. The room had a cosy, homely feel with floral chintz curtains at the windows, earthenware plates with designs of fruit, flowers, and birds hanging on the walls, and a small vase with fresh flowers in the centre of every table. The tables and chairs were of pinewood, with a tapestry cushion on the seat of each chair.

The six who had shared a table the previous evening sat together now. They all agreed that the piece of Black Forest gateau was the best they had ever tasted. It would be the authentic recipe, of course, moist and rich, oozing with cherry liqueur and whole cherries, covered with chocolate frosting, and served with whipped cream.

'Much better than anything you can get in the supermarket,' said Mavis. 'Even when you have it in a restaurant it doesn't taste like this. It's all so stereotyped and stodgy, not the real thing at all.'

Arthur complained that it would play havoc with his indigestion, but he ate it all the same.

It was whilst they were chatting, having finished their little treat, that Mike came to the table to speak to Shirley. 'Mrs Carson,' he began politely. 'Could you come with me, please? There seems to be a mix-up with your luggage. I'm hoping we can sort it out.'

Shirley sprung to her feet. 'What do you mean? Are you saying that my case is missing? Well, really . . .'

'We're not sure,' Mike answered placatingly. 'Bill's checking again now. So, we'll go and see, shall we? Have you got your room key?'

'Shall I come as well,' said Ellen, sounding very concerned.

'No, best not to, Miss Walmsley.' He smiled at her. 'We're doing our best to sort it out.'

Shirley left the room with Mike; she was looking very cross and anxious.

'Oh dear!' said Ellen to the others. 'I don't like the sound of that. I do hope they find her case. I know I'd be upset if it happened to me. But for Shirley—' she shook her head despairingly – 'I think it would be a major disaster.'

Jane new what Ellen meant, at least she thought she did. She had noticed that Shirley always dressed immaculately and stylishly as well. Even during the day when they were travelling she looked chic; her hair and make-up was perfect and she paid great attention to detail, even with casual clothes. She had never looked the least bit untidy or travel weary. Her trousers looked neatly pressed and she added a touch of style to her tops with a trendy little scarf or a chunky necklace and dangling earrings. And at night she really went to town in long skirts and sequinned jumpers.

Ellen bore out Jane's impression with her next words. 'Shirley tries to look her best at all times, you see. I know we all want to look neat and tidy – at least that is what is important to me – but Shirley loves to dress up, especially when we're on holiday.'

'Yes, I've noticed she always looks elegant,' said Jane. 'I feel as though I need a good wash and tidy-up after the journey today, but Shirley looked as though she'd stepped out of a bandbox.' She laughed. 'Whatever that is; I've never been sure.'

'She's always been the same,' said Ellen. 'Even when we were at school she managed to look stylish in her uniform; she made the rest of us feel a scruffy mess sometimes. I'm not criticizing her; it's just the way she was, and still is.'

'And she'll be surrounded by lovely clothes in the department store where she works, won't she?' observed Mavis.

'Oh yes; she loves her job, and she creates the most wonderful window displays. And she's able to buy her clothes at a good discount,' she added in a confidential voice. 'That's why she has so many. Her suitcase is always bulging with all the stuff she brings. Oh dear! I do hope they manage to sort it out.'

'I expect it's just mislaid – gone to the wrong room, perhaps,' said Jane, trying to be optimistic, although she could imagine how Shirley must be feeling. 'I'm sure the drivers are very careful . . .' But I suppose mistakes happen occasionally, she thought. She had heard of luggage going astray at airports, being missing from the carousel at the end of a flight. She wondered if the Galaxy insurance would pay up if the worst came to the worst.

'It wouldn't matter so much if it was me,' said Ellen. 'I've bought a couple of new things to come away – a summer skirt and a new cardigan – but most of my clothes I've had for ages. They're still good, though; not shabby or worn. I give some to the charity shop now and again, but I've always been thrifty. It's the way I was brought up, you see. My parents weren't short of money – not wealthy but not poor by any means – but they didn't believe in wasting it or going in for luxuries. Actually, my father was a Methodist local preacher, very set in his ways . . . and it's had an effect on me,' she added, almost apologetically.

'I reckon we're all a product of our upbringing, one way or another,' said Mavis kindly. 'And we're all as the good Lord made us. I can see that you're a very good friend to Shirley.'

'As she is to me,' replied Ellen promptly. 'We get on really well, even though we're not at all alike. She's always telling me to clear out my wardrobe and have a fresh start. She says I could make more of myself,' she added in a whisper, 'but I'm quite happy the way I am.'

She probably could, thought Jane. Ellen had a roundish face and dark brown alert-looking eyes, and when she smiled, as she often did, she looked very pretty and younger than she normally seemed. Her grey hair would look better when the newness of the perm wore off. She was prematurely grey; a light brown tint would work wonders. But maybe, as she said, she was content the way she was. After all, it was what we were like inside that mattered. And Ellen was a really nice person. Jane had formed a favourable impression of Shirley, too, but she guessed she might be quite a tartar when riled, as she had seemed when she went off with Mike.

Shirley accompanied Mike up to the first floor. 'That's my suitcase!' she exclaimed when they arrived at her door. 'Oh, thank goodness! It wasn't missing after all. What a fright you gave me.'

'Er . . . no, I'm afraid not, Mrs Carson,' said Mike. 'It looks like it, almost identical, I'd say. I remember seeing yours earlier, but when we'd sorted them out, this is the one that was left. It's . . . not yours,' he finished in a halting voice. 'I'm so sorry . . .'

Shirley bent down to look at the label. 'This one says Richmond Travel.' She stood up, facing him angrily. 'That's the tour from Yorkshire, isn't it? They were staying at the hotel . . . Oh, really! This is too bad. I can't believe this is happening.'

'Bill has gone to recheck outside all the rooms. Yours may have been left at the wrong door.'

'But that doesn't explain why this one is here,' said Shirley. 'There's been a slip-up, a bad one, and you'd better admit it.'

Bill arrived back at that moment, shaking his head. 'No joy, I'm afraid, I've checked all the rooms.' The drivers looked dejectedly at one another.

Then Mike spoke. 'We're really very sorry, Mrs Carson. We can only assume that your case has gone with the luggage on the Richmond coach. You say your suitcase is just like this one?'

'Yes, I've already told you that.' Her voice was quiet rather than loud with anger. 'But how can you have made such a stupid mistake? The labels are all clearly marked, aren't they?'

Mike ran his fingers through his hair. 'We were loading up at the same time. We left just before they did. I remember seeing the two red suitcases; they were near to one another. That's all I can say. Maybe Jim, the other driver, picked the wrong one up. Or maybe I did, I don't know. All I can say is that I'm truly sorry. But don't worry; we'll get it back for you.'

'Don't worry! How can you say don't worry?' Shirley's voice was shrill with anger now. 'I'm left with only the clothes I stand up in. Oh . . . this is too bad!'

'We're really sorry, Mrs Carson,' Bill reiterated. 'We try to be so careful. This has never happened before, at least not to us.'

'But that doesn't help me, does it?' snapped Shirley. 'It's happened now. And how long will it be before I get it back . . . if ever? Where have they gone, the folk on the Richmond tour? And I suppose some other poor woman will be in the same boat as me, with the wrong case?' The label had stated that it was a Mrs and not a Mr.

'Er . . . we're not quite sure where,' answered Mike. 'We

know they've gone on to the Austrian Tyrol. I don't suppose they'll have arrived there yet; it's a longer journey. We don't know the hotel or even the resort, but the receptionist back in Rüdesheim will know.' He crossed his fingers tightly, hoping that this was so. 'We'll do all we can to get it back for you as soon as possible.'

'How?' asked Shirley.

'Well, it would mean one of us driving over there, or their driver coming here, or perhaps we could meet at a point halfway.' He was not at all sure himself, but it would need to be sorted out somehow. It was just one of the hazards of being a coach driver, although one he had not encountered before. 'I promise you we'll do our best. And for now, the least we can do is to offer you a bottle of wine tonight for you and your friends, by courtesy of Galaxy. Just a little gesture of recompense.'

'Well, that's something, I suppose,' said Shirley grudgingly. 'I'll have a look at my room now. At least I've got one or two essential items with me in my travel bag. But I won't be satisfied until my case is back.' She turned the key in the lock and entered her room.

'Phew!' said Bill. 'One angry lady, but you can't blame her. You've remembered, I suppose, that we've got excursions on the next two days? So it's going to be . . . let me see . . . Saturday before we can do anything. Unless Jim is willing to make the journey over here. Oh, what a bloody mess we're in! Let's go and drown our sorrows, mate!'

'In a drink of orange juice?' said Mike wryly, 'or a half of shandy if we really want to go mad. I know it was my fault, for what it's worth – or Jim's – I can't be sure which. But you were nowhere near those blasted red suitcases. Thanks for supporting me, though.'

'No problem, we're in this together,' said Bill, putting a comradely arm round his mate.

There was another matter on Bill's mind. He must have a word with Olga, and try to convince her that it might be better to call it a day.

Shirley entered the room and looked around. Yes, it was a very pleasant room, and in normal circumstances she would have been highly satisfied. It was a good size for one person. There was a single bed with a pinewood headboard, and a duvet with a bright floral cover which matched the window curtains. The pine theme was echoed in the wardrobe, chest of drawers and bedside cupboard. There was a reading lamp, too, and a light over the mirror on the chest of drawers, essential for fixing one's hair and make-up. The room was at the back of the building, and there was a picturesque view of the church spire in the village a little distance away, and further away the verdant rolling hills of the Black Forest region.

She flung her shoulder bag and travel bag on to the bed, then flopped down on it feeling cross and weary. The holiday had been going so well; she had been enjoying it immensely. It was good to meet different people. The two couples that she and Ellen had met – she was already thinking of Dave and Jane as a couple – were interesting to talk to and share points of view. Arthur, admittedly, was a bit of a grumbler; he reminded her of her father who had died a few years ago, both in looks and in temperament. She had not been to this part of Europe before and she had been enchanted by the scenery of the Rhine valley, and now the Black Forest. The food, too, had more than lived up to her expectations, which had not always been so in the past.

It was good to spend time with her old friend, Ellen, as well. She knew that some found it hard to understand their friendship; they were so different. But each had found in the other something that appealed to them; maybe it was because they were so dissimilar. Ellen irritated her at times, of course, with her fussiness about getting back to the coach in what she called 'plenty of time', for fear of annoying the driver. (Shirley had sometimes insisted on leaving it till the last minute, just for the sheer devilment of it!) And she knew that she aggravated Ellen sometimes by dressing up 'like a dog's dinner' as her friend might say, and keeping her waiting while she added the finishing touches to her hair and make-up, or making sure that her shoes and bag and scarf matched her current outfit. Whereas Ellen didn't care as long as she looked clean and tidy as she put it, which, of course she always did. Shirley had tried in vain to persuade her to spend some money on herself – fashionable clothes, smart shoes, even a tint on her hair, but you might as well talk to a brick wall.

Shirley sighed, a deep heartfelt sigh that reached down to the pit of her stomach. It was all spoilt now; she had no smart clothes to wear, no high-heeled sandals, floating skirts or stylish culottes – she had recently bought two pairs of those to wear as a change in the evenings. Whatever would she do? She felt like bursting into tears.

There was a knock at the door at that moment, and there was Ellen. She looked at her friend's stricken face and drew her own conclusions.

'Oh dear!' she said – one of her favourite expressions. 'You've not had any luck then? Your case hasn't turned up?'

'No, has it hell as like!' Shirley didn't often swear – she also knew that Ellen didn't like it – but this was enough to make a saint swear. She explained that her case was probably in the Austrian Tyrol by now, and goodness knows when she would get it back.

'Oh dear!' said Ellen again. 'How dreadful! Never mind, though; it could have been a lot worse. You could be ill, you could have fallen and broken your ankle or . . . it could have been raining all the time. It might not be too long before you get it back. Don't let it spoil your holiday. We're having a lovely time. And you always look nice, whatever you wear. And not everyone gets dressed up for dinner. You can wear those trousers and top tonight. You'll look as smart as anyone.'

'Tonight and tomorrow and the day after that!' Shirley retorted. It irritated her how Ellen always looked on the bright side, trying to find the good in everyone and everything – although she knew it was really an admirable character trait, one that she feared she did not possess.

'Yes, I think I can understand how you feel,' said Ellen, her eyes full of sympathy. 'It's such a shame. You wanted to wear all your nice clothes, and you've bought some new ones as well. I know you like to wear something different every night . . . But I've brought loads of clothes with me, far too many. You're about the same size as me, aren't you? You could borrow some of mine.'

'What!' Shirley couldn't believe what she was hearing. This

was adding insult to injury. She didn't stop to think what she was saying as the words burst from her. 'Really Ellen! I wouldn't be seen dead in your clothes!'

Her friend's demeanour changed in an instant. The kindly concern disappeared from her eyes, and her face started to crumple as though she was going to cry. 'Shirley, how could you!' Her voice was faint and trembling. 'What a dreadful thing to say! I know I'm not as attractive as you, but my clothes are always clean and tidy and—'

'Oh, Ellen! I'm so sorry. I didn't mean it to sound like that, of course I didn't. It's just a figure of speech, something people say, but they don't really mean it. And I'm so worked up that I scarcely know what I'm saying.' She put an arm round Ellen as she sat beside her on the bed. 'It was very kind of you to offer, but—'

'Yes, I know,' said Ellen stiffly. 'They're old-fashioned – like me – not all stylish and chic, if that's the right word. But that's the way I am. It was silly of me to even think of you . . . wearing my clothes.'

Shirley was mortified. She felt so ashamed of herself. She had upset her friend really badly and she did not know how to make amends. But she could not let this spoil their holiday any more than she could let the loss of the suitcase do so. Careless words – how quickly and thoughtlessly they were uttered, and once said they could not be taken back. She tried again.

'Ellen . . . I am truly sorry. Please, please forgive me. You know I wouldn't want to hurt you for the world. We've been such good friends, so don't let this spoil things between us. Perhaps I overreacted about the case, but I was so cross, with the drivers or whoever it was, for making such a stupid mistake. I suppose "There are worse troubles at sea", as my mother used to say . . . although I always thought that that wasn't much help to us!'

Ellen gave a weak smile. 'My mother used to say that as well. No, I don't think you've overreacted. It should never have happened. Somebody is at fault, and I know I would have been cross as well if it had happened to me. Although it wouldn't have been such a great disaster to me. Nobody really notices what I wear. I was hurt though, Shirley, it's no use pretending I wasn't, but I know you spoke in haste.' She reached out and put her hand over her friend's manicured one with the red painted nails. 'Let's forget it, eh? Don't think any more about it.'

Shirley felt like hugging and kissing her, she was so relieved, but she didn't do so. There had never been anything like that between them, and she wouldn't want anyone to get that impression. That was one of the reasons why she, Shirley, had suggested that they should have single rooms. She hadn't said that to Ellen, of course. Her friend was very naive about the ways of the world, even in today's climate, and it may not even have occurred to her.

'Thank you,' she said, simply. 'I'll try to watch my tongue in future. There is something you could lend me, though, if you don't mind.' This would be a sop to her own conscience, and no doubt Ellen would be pleased to help in some way.

'Yes, of course. What is it?' asked Ellen.

'Er . . . some underwear,' replied Shirley.

'Underwear? What sort?' Ellen looked puzzled.

'A pair of knickers,' said Shirley, more bluntly. 'I've got a spare pair in my travel bag. I always change them after a journey, but I shall need a fresh pair for tomorrow.'

'Certainly,' agreed Ellen. 'I always change my undies after a journey as well. And I've got lots of spare ones in my case. What about a nightdress? You won't have that either, will you?'

'Oh no, of course not . . .'

'Well, I've brought two with me. They're not all that glamorous, but no one's going to see you in your nightwear, are they?'

'I should be so lucky,' murmured Shirley.

'What did you say?' asked her friend.

'Er . . . no,' she said with a laugh. 'As you say, nobody's going to see me.'

'I'll pop next door and get them for you now,' said Ellen.

Shirley was pleased to see that she was back to her normal, eager-to-please self. Well . . . almost. There was still a little constraint there, but Shirley would work hard to make things right.

What would the garments be like? she wondered. But what did it matter? She was satisfied, though, when Ellen returned with a pair of ordinary white knickers. She had wondered if it might be a pair of what they used to call 'Directoire' knickers such as they sold in old-fashioned draper's shops; voluminous bloomers with elastic at the waist and knees. Her own underwear was of pretty colours. Not thongs – she couldn't imagine wearing those – but briefer ones with high-cut legs. But these of Ellen's would suffice until she could find a shop and buy some more. This was something she could not manage without. The nightdress, too, was plain and serviceable – not like her own garment with lace and ribbons – but she was very grateful to her friend.

'Thank you so much,' she said. 'These are great . . . Shall we go down and have a drink before dinner? It might cheer me up a bit.'

They agreed to meet in half an hour when they had had a wash and tidy-up; and when Ellen had changed her clothes and she, Shirley, had tried to add a fresh look to her daytime trousers and striped top. Fortunately she carried her costume jewellery with her in her hand luggage.

Eight

There was a small, but adequately stocked bar, at one end of the lounge. When Shirley and Ellen arrived there were already a few of their fellow travellers sitting around the small tables at the sides of the room. This area was carpeted, the centre of the lounge being of highly polished wood. Maybe for dancing, thought Shirley, or for evening entertainments. There was a dais at the other end of the room, a low platform where visiting artistes might perform. They had been told there would be entertainment on a couple of nights.

The receptionist, Olga, was serving behind the bar. It seemed that she helped out there when she was not occupied at the desk in the foyer.

'What would you like to drink?' asked Shirley. 'My treat tonight, so put your purse away.' They usually paid their own way on holiday – it saved a lot of arguments as to whose turn it was – but Shirley was doing all she could to make it up to her friend for her tactless remarks; and Ellen seemed to understand this.

'Thank you,' she said. 'I'll have my usual *Apfelsaft*.' It was a sparkling apple juice, popular in Germany and Austria.

'And I'll have my usual Cinzano and lemonade,' said Shirley. 'Oh . . . by the way, there's wine for us tonight, courtesy of Galaxy, for me and my friends, Mike said. It's his way of making amends, of course, for my suitcase.'

'Then make sure you choose one of the best wines,' said Ellen, rather surprisingly.

Shirley laughed. 'If I'm given the choice. They may present me with a bottle of the house white. And I'll make sure you get the tipple of your choice . . . unless I can persuade you to have a drop of wine?' she asked with a questioning smile.

'I'll see,' replied Ellen. 'You never know, I might well do that.'

Pigs might fly, thought Shirley as she made her way to the

bar. The polished floor was rather slippery and you had to watch your step. She was not wearing her high-heeled sandals as she would normally have done; they were a hundred miles or more away with the rest of her smart gear. She had to be careful, though, in the wedge heels she was wearing.

There was no one else at the bar. Olga smiled at her pleasantly, saying that she hoped she would enjoy her stay. She spoke almost perfect English. She was an attractive young woman, possibly in her late thirties, quite tall and slim with dark brown hair and eyes, a contrast to the more usual flaxen hair and blue eyes of many of the German people. She wore a plain black dress, a uniform of a sort, but it was clearly expensive and stylish, the dark shade relieved only by a silver cross and chain around her neck and small earrings.

'Cheers,' said Shirley as they settled down in the comfortable chairs, wicker work ones with bright floral cushions, complementing the pinewood and the light and airy aspect of the guest house. She raised her glass and Ellen followed suit.

'Yes, cheers,' she echoed. 'Here's to a lovely holiday. It will be, you know . . .' She looked intently at her friend. 'You look very nice tonight, as you always do.' Shirley was wearing a chunky necklace of brightly coloured beads that looked well with the plain top she had worn all day. 'Nobody really cares two hoots about what other people wear, you know.'

Shirley did not agree, but she did not say so. For her part, she always looked at other people's clothes, assessing whether the outfit suited them or not. She was just naturally interested, or maybe just plain nosy!

'Anyway,' Ellen went on, 'You could always buy one or two nice things in the shops here, couldn't you? I know it might make a hole in your spending money but . . .'

'Nice things? Here?' Shirley gave a bitter laugh, despite trying to look on the bright side as her friend had urged her to do. 'I'd end up looking like a German hausfrau!' Even as she said it she knew she was being difficult. The young woman at the bar was very smart. 'I'm not likely to run out of money,' she added. 'I've got my credit card with me.' Ellen never used one. She still used the old-fashioned way of paying by cash, or the occasional cheque, when on holiday.

'But I'm not likely to see anything I'd want to wear. Don't let's talk about it any more, Ellen. It's too depressing! Oh look . . . there's Bill. He's on his own. I wonder if they've a room each or if they have to share?'

'Does it matter?' asked Ellen, smiling at her friend. 'You're too nosy by far, that's your trouble,' she added good-humouredly.

'Yes, I admit that I like to know what's going on,' said Shirley. Ellen had voiced what she herself had just been thinking. She liked to know what made people tick.

She noticed now that Bill and Olga were deep in conversation; in fact, it looked as though they might be having an argument. She knew that Ellen would laugh, and probably tell her that it was none of her business, but she couldn't resist commenting on it to her friend.

'Oh . . . yes,' said Ellen, not laughing at all. 'It certainly looks as though they know one another quite well.'

'Maybe they've been friendly,' said Shirley. 'Well, maybe rather more than just friendly. I know that both Bill and Mike have stayed here several times before.'

'Well, it's not really any of our business, is it?' said Ellen. 'As far as I'm concerned Bill and Mike are both very nice young men, very helpful and considerate. I know you may not agree right now, but they're doing all they can to make the holiday interesting, aren't they?'

'Yes, I do agree; they're great,' said Shirley. 'But you never know what problems other people might have, do you? I wonder if they're married? Somehow, I don't imagine that Bill is . . . It's not an ideal job for a married man, is it, being away from home such a lot of the time?'

'You'll have to find out, won't you, about their marital status?' said Ellen with a mischievous grin. 'I'm sure somebody will be able to tell you.'

'You're laughing at me,' said Shirley, 'but I admit I'm curious.'

Bill and Olga were still talking, but not smiling at one another. Then two people from the coach party went to the bar to be served, and Bill walked away, out of the room.

He was quite a good-looking chap, Shirley thought to herself; a bit overweight, though. He had what was termed a good head of hair, an attractive shade of ginger and with a natural wave; such as some straight-haired women might envy, saying it was wasted on a man. He had a cheerful round face, and bright blue eyes. No doubt he would appeal to quite a lot of women . . .

The drivers dined at a small table on their own, away from the coach party, although they were served at the same time. They preferred it that way. They needed a bit of space after dealing with their clients and their problems all day. And the passengers seemed to understand that, and did not pester them at meal times.

'What's up?' asked Mike, as they sat down at their table in a far corner of the dining room. 'You look as though you've lost the proverbial pound and found a penny. Is it Christine? I thought it was all going well.'

'No, it isn't her. Like I told you, we got on famously last night, and she's agreed to have a drink with me tonight as well. I think we'll have a stroll down to the village, away from the busybodies here. No, it's Olga. I'm afraid she didn't like what I had to say, not one little bit.'

Mike looked puzzled. 'I thought you'd agreed, the last time you met, that there wasn't much future in it?'

'So we did, at least that was the impression I got. But it seems as though she's changed her mind. She says she looks forward to me coming every few weeks, and she doesn't see why we can't carry on as we are. I think, between you and me, that she's hoping I'll see a way to making it more permanent. But how can I?'

'I suppose you could if you really wanted to,' said Mike. 'Where there's a will there's a way, as the saying goes. The problem is, women get more serious about these things than men do, depending on the woman, of course. Some are just out for a good time or a casual fling, but a nice well brought up lass like Olga – as I'm sure she is – she probably wants more than just a relationship like yours, here today and gone tomorrow. You can't blame her, Bill.'

They stopped talking as the waitress brought their starter – thick pea soup in deep bowls with chunks of brown bread.

'I've got in too deep, that's the problem,' Bill continued, 'and now it's difficult to back out. I feel dreadful, really; I'm very fond of her. I suppose I've just let it drift on without thinking too much about the future. I thought she felt the same as me, you know – it was good while it lasted, sort of thing.'

'So what are you going to do? How have you left it?'

'It's stalemate at the moment. She was busy at the bar, so I just left her to her work. I'm hoping she'll realize I'm right, that it's best to call it a day. There would always be problems if we were to consider a future together. For a start, she's a Catholic, and that always causes strife in families.'

'I don't see why,' said Mike. 'It isn't as if you are much of a churchgoer, are you?'

'Christmas and Easter if I feel inclined. Olga doesn't go much either, to Mass or whatever it is. But her parents are very keen. She left home to get away from their control – they live in Stuttgart – and she's had a fair number of jobs like this one, living in hotels since she was twenty or so.'

'She must have had a few boyfriends – well, men friends, relationships, surely? She's an attractive woman.'

'Yes, I suppose she has, but I haven't enquired too closely, just as she hasn't asked too much about my past, but I think she's getting rather bored, stuck out here in the back of beyond. She's ready for a change of some sort.'

'And so are you, it seems. Olga doesn't know you've got somebody lined up, does she?'

'Good Lord, no! I've had a quiet word with Christine. I suggested we might go down to the village after dinner. She's a great girl, Mike. I really like her.'

'But you can't possibly know from meeting her just once, that she's right for you.'

'I'm not saying that. But we hit it off straight away. She's from the same neck of the woods, too, from Manchester, like me. Not the same district, but near enough; her home's in Didsbury.'

'Ooh . . . posh, eh?'

'Well, she does speak nicely, and I can an' all – I mean as well! – if I make an effort. It's an advantage, though, living in the same area, not like a friendship with someone in another country.'

'But you wouldn't be in the same town, would you? You'd be working over here. There'd only be the occasional weekends.'

'Yes, I know, but you were saying the other day that there's work in the UK. I might consider that. Some of the lads are dying to get on to the Continental tours. And we don't work during the winter, do we?'

The Galaxy drivers were laid off during the winter months, apart from doing day trips now and again, and a few Christmas tours which were a new innovation. Some of them found other part-time jobs or drew unemployment benefit. They knew that their jobs would be there for them, come the spring.

Their conversation stopped for a time whilst the main course was served. It was a typical German dish; roast pork served with dumplings and red cabbage, an introduction to local cuisine. They did not talk much as they enjoyed the succulent pork and the substantial helping of dumplings.

Bill glanced across at a nearby table where there was the sound of laughter and high spirits. 'Mrs Carson seems to have recovered from the loss of her suitcase,' he remarked. 'Unless she's just drowning her sorrows. That was a nice gesture, offering her a bottle of wine.'

'The least we could do,' said Mike. 'I'll have to get round to tracing the bloody suitcase.'

'Haven't you done anything yet?'

'All in good time, Bill. They wouldn't arrive in Austria till early evening, and then it's all go for the next couple of hours as you know. I'll ring Rüdesheim as soon as we've finished our meal and see it they've got the address in Austria. If not, then it will mean getting on to Richmond Travel in the UK. There are times when a driver's lot is not a happy one!'

At the table a little distance away the six travellers, who were by now good friends, were enjoying the bottle of Riesling wine recommended by the proprietor, Herr Grunder. It was one of the priciest on the wine list and was proving to be a great success with all of them.

'There's not really enough for all of us,' Arthur had remarked. 'I'll order another bottle of the same; no arguments – my treat.'

Dave had argued that Arthur had bought wine the first night in Calais. So after a bit of good-natured quibbling, the two men had agreed to share the cost.

'Ellen won't want any,' said Shirley, 'unless I can twist her arm . . .?'

'Do you know, I think I might!' said Ellen with a sly grin. 'Just a teeny drop, I might not like it.'

Shirley was flabbergasted. 'Well! I'll go to the foot of our stairs!' she exclaimed. The others all laughed.

'Don't ask me what it means,' said Shirley. 'It's one of those old Lancashire sayings my mother used to use. Good for you, Ellen! I bet when you've tasted it you'll want some more.'

Jane wondered if Shirley might be guilty of persuading her friend to act against her better judgement, although Ellen didn't seem the type of person to do anything against her will. 'Why don't you try a mixture of wine and lemonade, Ellen?' she suggested. 'It's called a spritzer. You can have wine with soda water, but it's nicer with lemonade.'

'Thank you; I think I'd like that,' agreed Ellen. She was quite pink-cheeked with excitement, although she hadn't drunk anything yet. And when the drink arrived she said it was refreshing and very much to her taste.

Shirley fended off all enquiries about her suitcase. 'It's a banned subject,' she declared. 'I want to enjoy my meal.'

They all agreed that the first meal at the guest house boded well for the rest of the stay. The main course was delicious, though different from anything they would eat at home. And the *Apfelkuchen* – or apple cake – that followed, served with whipped cream, left them feeling that they could not eat another mouthful.

They retired to the lounge for coffee. Arthur and Mavis, Shirley and Ellen, decided that they had had enough excitement for one day and would stay in the hotel for the rest of the evening. So it was just Dave and Jane who decided to walk down to the village.

They strolled down the leafy country road enjoying the warmth of the balmy evening. It had been another glorious summer day, and the light was just beginning to fade, the sky turning to a darker blue, tinged with golden and crimson streaks. How long could this weather last? Jane wondered. There must be rain in Germany sometimes, though maybe not so much as they had at home. They had been very fortunate so far.

After a few moments Dave took hold of her hand, and she stole a sideways glance at him. He was smiling at her.

'You enjoyed your meal, did you? I noticed you were struggling to finish your apple cake.'

'So I was; and I had to leave one of the dumplings as well. It was all very enjoyable, though a little . . . dare I say stodgy? Satisfying and filling, at any rate. Certainly more than enough for me.'

'I think it may well be the same sort of fare for the rest of the week,' said Dave. 'They don't go in for dainty meals in Germany. Their cuisine has developed from the dishes that the peasants used to eat, especially in the country districts. A meat and potato diet, such as we have at home, but more of the dumplings instead of potatoes. I'm afraid we might go home a few pounds heavier.'

'I don't put much weight on as a rule,' said Jane, 'so I'm not unduly worried. I'm not always watching my weight, like some women do. I should imagine Shirley is very conscious about that sort of thing. She's always so immaculate and concerned about how she looks. It couldn't have happened to a worse person, losing her case . . . I like her though,' she added. 'They're a nice little crowd at our table, aren't they?'

'Yes, so they are, and it makes such a difference to a holiday like this, who you sit with for meals. They very rarely have tables for two; the idea is that they want you to mix and mingle. I've found that it's better to be on a table for six rather than four. If you get stuck with a couple you don't get on with it can be deadly. But we all seem very compatible. Different, of course, but that adds to the interest . . . And I'm so glad that I met you, Jane.' He squeezed her fingers just a little as he turned to look at her.

'Yes, I'm glad too,' she replied. 'I was dreading coming away on my own, although I knew I had to do it . . . to prove that I could. And it's made such a difference, getting to know you. I'm having a lovely time.'

They had arrived at the village, which was little more than a large hamlet. The road widened a little as they approached a row of houses, a church and a few shops. A general store, a pharmacy, a butcher's shop, and what looked like a charity shop such as they had at home, with all sorts of odds and ends in the window. There was a gift and souvenir shop, too; they obviously had their share of tourists passing by.

All the shops were closed, but at the far end of the street there was a beer garden, set back from the road in its own grounds. Strings of lights flickered amongst the trees, beneath which there were wooden tables and benches. Further back there was a white painted building with more seating accommodation inside. There were a few couples sitting outside and a waiter in a long green apron taking an order at a table in the corner.

'Look at that!' said Dave, sounding surprised. 'Just the job! I was doubtful that we would find anywhere open, but this seems as though it might be a popular place.'

'How lovely!' Jane exclaimed. In her present mood everything was delightful. Here was another idyllic scene to store away in her memory along with the other sights and impressions that had followed, one upon the other, these last few days.

They sat down on a bench beneath a spreading lime tree, and Dave handed her a large menu card. They served meals, as well as lighter snacks and a wide variety of drinks. The menu was in German, with no English translation, but it would be easy enough to order as the names of the beers and wines were familiar.

'A beer for me – Helles, I think,' said Dave. 'That's what they call a blond beer, not too heavy. Some of their beers would knock you out, they're so potent. What about you, Jane? White wine?'

'The only German wine I know is Liebfraumilch,' she replied, 'apart from the Riesling we had tonight. And that was quite enough for me, for one evening. Perhaps I could have a spritzer, like I suggested Ellen should have. I rather think it was the first time she'd ever tasted alcohol.'

'It didn't seem to have any ill effect on her,' said Dave. 'A very nice lady. I hope her friend's case turns up, though, or

Ellen may well have to bear the brunt of Shirley's bad moods. She was OK at dinner time – Shirley, I mean – but she was obviously very annoyed earlier on.'

'What an awful thing to happen, though,' said Jane. 'I do feel sorry for her. I should hate it to happen to me.'

'You wouldn't let it spoil your holiday, though, would you?'

'No . . . I'd try not to. But ladies do like to have a change of clothes in the evening, I know I do. And Shirley seems to dress as though she's on a catwalk. Her clothes are jolly expensive, but she was telling me that she gets a very good discount at the store where she works.'

'She's certainly a very elegant lady,' said Dave, 'but there are other things that are far more important than the clothes we wear . . .' He stopped speaking as the waiter arrived at their table.

It was clear that he was quite used to ordering from a German menu, as the waiter seemed to understand what they wanted. Jane commented on this.

'That sounded very competent. Have you been to Germany before?'

'Er . . . yes,' he answered, a little hesitantly. 'Not with Galaxy, though . . . and it was a long time ago. My wife and I went on a couple of Continental coach tours, before our son was born, to Austria and Bavaria. The whole business of coach travel has improved no end since that time. I remember en-suite rooms were few and far between; you had a washbasin in the room, that was all – no shower or loo. And the breakfasts were very meagre: rolls and butter and jam. They have to provide more variety now to cater for tourists from all over.'

'No doubt you have happy memories, though, of your early holidays,' Jane remarked. Dave had sounded a little uneasy when he mentioned his wife. It was the first time he had spoken of her since that first day when he had told her that he, too, was on his own. She thought about the happy times that she had spent with Tom – although these had receded even further to the back of her mind over the last few days – and she guessed it might be the same for Dave. Maybe some poignant memories had returned to him as he mentioned his wife.

He was silent for a few moments before he answered. 'I'm

sorry to say that not all the memories are happy ones. I know from what you have said that you and your husband – Tom, wasn't he? – had a wonderful marriage . . .'

'Yes . . . we did,' she answered quietly.

'But it was not the same with Judith and me. We were happy at first. We were young and in love, or so we thought. I soon realized, though, that we had very little in common, not enough for a satisfactory marriage. Judith was a town girl, and she couldn't get used to the quiet of the countryside, or to being a farmer's wife.

'She had a part-time job in Shrewsbury at first – she was a shorthand typist – and she drove there and back each day. But she had to give up when Peter was born.'

'How old is your son?' asked Jane.

'He's twenty-two, and he's already engaged to a girl he went to school with. I did try to tell him, tactfully, not to rush into things. But he's a sensible young man, and I don't foresee any problems there. Kathryn's a lovely lass, and she's from a similar background. Her father's a market gardener, and she does the bookkeeping for him as well as helping out on the land. She's told him, though, that he'll have to find somebody else next year, because she intends to be a 'hands on' sort of farmer's wife.'

'Are they getting married soon?'

'Yes, next year. They'll live at the farm with me. There's plenty of room, and I shall make sure they have their own space, and plenty of it. I'm sure it will be a happy marriage, as far as one can ever predict such a thing.'

He paused, and Jane made no comment. She did not want to pry. If he chose to tell her more about his own marriage, that was OK. If not, then she would not ask. However, he went on. 'As I said, Judith was not happy as a farmer's wife, and it was worse after Peter was born. She loved him – I never doubted that – but she felt even more tied down. She still had a lot of friends in Shrewsbury, and she wanted go on meeting them the same as before. And I'm afraid that's what she did. We didn't have much of a home life, but I suppose we stayed together because of Peter. I used to worry about her being out late, especially if she was driving.'

He stopped suddenly, and Jane wondered if she had been killed in a car crash. He had not said how his wife had died, and if it had been a road accident it would still be painful to talk about it, even though their feelings for one another might have changed.

'Anyway, that's all in the past, and we have to look to the future. And it's already looking very promising.' He placed his hand over Jane's, smiling into her eyes.

'Yes,' she replied quietly. 'I knew that I had to start enjoying myself again, if it were possible.'

'And you are, aren't you – enjoying yourself?'

'Very much so. It's more than two years since Tom died. And it's longer for you, isn't it?'

'Yes, more than four years since Judith . . .' He sighed. 'But things had not been good for quite some time.' He let go of her hand and took a long drink of his beer. The waiter had put down their drinks unobtrusively whilst they had been talking. Jane sipped at her spritzer and found it very palatable.

'This is nice,' she said cheerfully, hoping to lighten the rather sombre mood that their conversation had evoked.

'Good.' He grinned at her, his good humour restored. He took hold of her hand again. 'Jane . . . I would like to think that I could go on seeing you after the holiday has ended. How do you feel about that?'

The idea had been forming in her mind as well, and she was pleased that he felt the same, but the practicality of it was another matter. So she did not say at once that she would be delighted to see him again, even though she wanted to do so.

'We haven't known one another long, have we?' she said.

'Three days,' said Dave, 'but it seems much longer. I feel as though I've known you for ages.'

Jane felt the same. They had shared so much over the last three days. They had been together constantly, except for the night times. They did get on very well together, but this was a holiday situation. How would they fare when they were back home without the excitement and glamour of new sights, new experiences? Dave lived quite a long way from her own home, and there was her mother to consider.

'Let's see how it goes, Dave,' she said, trying to be sensible and follow her head, not her heart which was urging her to throw caution to the winds. 'We do get on well, and we're having a lovely time here . . . but there would be obstacles at home. Where we live, for one thing; then there's my mother.'

Dave forbore to say that her mother was an elderly lady and would not live for ever, but that would be too unkind, and he did see the problems. 'My mother has been very accommodating,' he replied. 'You might well be surprised. And we're not a million miles apart, are we? And we both drive . . . But you're right; let's see how things go.'

They were both quiet for a little while, each deep in thought. Jane noticed a familiar figure at the other side of the garden.

'Oh, look – there's Bill,' she said. 'And isn't that the lady that sits at the front of the coach? I don't know her name.'

'So it is,' said Dave. 'It looks like another holiday friendship in the making.'

The two of them looked very friendly and happy together as they sat at a table, heads close together studying the menu. 'Good luck to them. Bill seems a decent sort of bloke – well, they both do, he and Mike. But some drivers do have a reputation for getting off with the single ladies.'

'So long as he's not married,' said Jane. 'You never know do you . . .?'

Nine

'Now, Christine, what's your poison?' asked Bill. 'I'm afraid I shall have to stick to a half of lager or Pils, or maybe a shandy. And then it'll be orange juice or *Apfelsaft*. Both Mike and I obey the rules; most drivers do.'

'And do you always obey the rules, in everything?' asked Christine with a sly grin.

'Oh, I think so,' Bill replied easily. 'I'm a pretty straightforward sort of chap. I would certainly not drink while on duty, and that goes for evenings as well. There's too much at stake with a coachload of passengers. We're responsible for their welfare.'

'Yes, I imagine there are problems from time to time, aren't there?'

'You can say that again! We've done alright this time, so far, apart from the missing suitcase. And Mike has managed to trace the hotel in Austria where the Richmond coach has gone. The main problem is when people are late back at the coach. We're not allowed to leave anyone, even though it's a blasted nuisance at times. They usually turn up in the end; they've mistaken the time, or they've got lost. If they're too long we have to go looking for them. Then sometimes people are taken ill and have to be rushed to hospital. Or they complain about the rooms or the food . . . But it's all going well up to now, touch wood.' He tapped on the table. 'What about you? You're enjoying it, are you?'

'Yes, very much, and so is Norah. She made friends with two ladies of a similar age to her. We're sitting with them for meals and we all get on well together.'

The conversation was interrupted as the waiter appeared to take their order – a small Pils for Bill and a glass of Liebfraumilch for Christine. 'I think you will find it far superior to the sort we get at home,' Bill told her.

'There's quite a big age gap between you and your sister, isn't there?' he asked when the waiter had gone.

She grinned. 'That's a polite way of asking how old I am, is it? I don't mind telling you, why should I? I'm thirty-six, and Norah is fifty-two, although she's looked older recently. Her husband was ill for a long while, and she cared for him all the time. I'm hoping this holiday will help her to look to the future again. I'm afraid she's often mistaken for my mother; she did look after me a lot when I was little. I was something of an afterthought in the family. I don't think my parents really intended to have another child! But I was loved all the same.'

'Are your parents still living?'

'Yes, both of them. We're lucky in that respect. We've all got our own homes, of course, not very far from one another.'

They stopped talking again as the waiter arrived with their drinks. Christine took a good sip of the pale golden wine.

'Delicious!' she said. 'You're right. It's far superior to the stuff I buy from Sainsbury's.'

'I think they keep the best for themselves, and export the rest,' said Bill. 'You were saying, Christine, about your home . . . You live alone, do you?'

'At the moment, yes,' she replied with a smile. 'You're asking if I'm single, aren't you?' She knew that the term 'single' no longer just meant unmarried as it used to do. Nowadays it seemed to mean anyone who didn't have a partner at that time, a partner of either sex. Whether you were widowed, divorced, or just on your own you were referred to as being single.

'It's as well to know,' replied Bill, 'so that there's no misunderstanding.'

She nodded. 'I live on my own, and I'm single. By that I mean that I've never been married. Until about six months ago I was in a relationship, but that came to an end, by mutual agreement. I'm not completely on my own, though. I live with my dog, a chocolate Labrador called Monty. He's a great companion, and just lately I've not wanted anyone else.'

'So where is he now?'

'My parents are looking after him; they love having him. My dad takes him for walks in the park, and my mum spoils him rotten. He'll be glad to see me again, though.'

'And what does he do during the day when you're at work?' asked Bill. He was yet to discover her form of employment.

'That's not a problem,' she replied. 'I have a dog parlour, you see, and I live over the premises. I'm able to keep an eye on him, and he likes to make friends with our clients.'

'Good grief! A dog parlour!' said Bill. He had imagined she might be an office worker or a librarian. 'You mean you do shampoos and sets for pampered poodles?'

'There are all kinds of dogs, not just poodles,' she answered, a trifle curtly. 'We do get a fair number of poodles because they need a good deal of care to keep them clean and tidy. But all dogs need a bath now and again, and a bit of a spruce-up. It's something they can't do for themselves, like cats do. Some owners like to bath their dogs themselves, but we're kept pretty busy.'

'So who's looking after the business this week? Or are you closed?'

'No, I have an assistant, Thelma. It's my business, but she's been with me for several years and she can manage very well if I'm not there. And we've got a young trainee girl now, Tracey. She's only sixteen, but she's shaping up very well . . . You look astounded, Bill. You didn't see me as a doggie person, eh?'

'I thought you might work in an office. I'd no idea really. But I'm sure it must be interesting work. Have you always done that sort of thing?'

'No, I had an office job when I left school. I'd always liked animals, though, and I rather fancied the idea of being a vet. But I knew the training would be very long and arduous. I did get a job eventually, working in a veterinary practice, mostly in the office. Then my grandparents died, left me some money, and with help from my parents I was able to start my own business.'

'And that's in Didsbury, is it?'

'Yes, that's right. We get a good clientele round there; some very wealthy people, and others more like my family – just ordinary folk.'

'You get some free time though, don't you? I wondered if we could carry on seeing one another – you know – now and again, when we get back home? I don't live all that far away from you – the other side of Manchester, but that's no problem. I have a car, and I expect you do as well.'

'You're not at home though, are you? You're over here working, most of the time.'

'As a matter of fact, I have a week off when we get back. It's just the way it's worked out. So . . . do you think we could meet? We could go for a meal in Manchester or . . . whatever you like?'

'But I don't really know you, Bill, do I? We've only just met.' Christine felt that she did like what she knew of Bill, so far, but she did not know very much. 'What about you?' she asked. 'Do you live on your own? You haven't told me.'

'Yes, I have a flat in Chadderton, and I live on my own; have done for ages, in between tours, you know.'

'And you are single, too?'

'Yes,' he replied, 'I'm single; and by that I mean that I've never been married. I can't say that I've never had any relationships – you wouldn't believe me if I did – but at the moment I'm as free as a bird; or else I wouldn't be trying to persuade you to give me a chance.'

Bill was metaphorically crossing his fingers that Olga would take heed of what he had said and realize that it was for the best. He had suffered from pangs of guilt from time to time about his simultaneous friendships with Lise and Olga, and neither one knowing about the other. That was why he had decided to break with both of them and have a completely fresh start.

Lise had made it easy for him by her admission that she was already seeing someone else. But it was a different matter with Olga. He didn't want to upset her. They had had some good times together, but he had never thought that she might be looking for something more permanent.

Christine broke into his reverie. 'What's the matter, Bill? That's an ominous silence.'

'Not really,' he replied. 'I'm wondering what you're going to say, that's all.'

'As I said before, I've only known you for three days. I can't say how I will feel when we get back home.'

'But friendships have to start somewhere, don't they? And we have the rest of the time here, in Germany, to get to know one another better. You said that your sister has made friends with two more ladies, so that leaves you free to spend more time with me, doesn't it?'

'You mean . . . during the day when we're on our excursions?'

'Yes, why not? We have a lot of free time at the various places we visit.'

'Don't you spend the time with Mike? What do you do, anyway, when you visit the same places time after time? Doesn't it get boring, hanging around waiting for the passengers?'

'Oh, there's always something to fill the time. If it's a bad day we might have a snooze in the coach. That's when we feel sorry for the clients, having to turn them out in the pouring rain, but there's usually somewhere they can run to – cafes or souvenir shops. But let's hope we have a rain-free week. We've done well so far.'

'But it must rain sometimes?'

'Obviously, or there wouldn't be all these forest areas. It doesn't seem to rain as much as it does at home. They have long spells of glorious weather, but when it rains you think it's never going to stop. We feel sorry for you lot then, when you've paid all that money for a summer holiday. You expect it to be fine all the time, don't you, when you're away?'

'Yes, I suppose so, but it all depends on where you choose to go. If you want endless sunshine you should go to the Costa Brava or the South of France, not to the mountains of Austria or Germany. Where are we going tomorrow? I know it's in the brochure, but just remind me.'

'Well, we start with a leisurely tour of the Black Forest; the part where we're staying, near to Freiburg is said to be the loveliest of all. Then we stop at a shop that sells cuckoo clocks, and lots of other touristy things as well, so make sure you've got plenty of euros. And you'll see what is reputed to be the largest cuckoo clock in the world. Actually, there are a few of them in the area all claiming the same! Then we drive on to Lake Titisee – a silly name, I know – for a lunch stop, and then we'll spend a few hours there before returning home. You'll enjoy it, I'm sure, and if you'll allow me I'd like to show you round the lake area. Not the gift shop – you can browse round there on your own. I've seen enough cuckoo clocks to last me a lifetime!'

'What about Mike? Won't he mind being left on his own?'

'No, why should he? He'll probably stay in the coach after lunch and read a book, or have a nap. We're good mates, Mike and me; it's just as well when we're together such a lot. But we do our own thing when we want to. What we really need for tomorrow's outing is good weather, so we'd best cross our fingers and say a little prayer.'

As Bill was looking round for the waiter, to order a second drink, he saw another couple from the coach at the other side of the garden. They nodded and waved to him, and he and Christine waved back.

'That seems like another holiday friendship that's going well,' he remarked. 'Mrs Redfern and Mr Falconer. They've only met this week, at least that's what Mike and I think. We met them taking an evening stroll together in Rüdesheim the other night.'

'It was last night,' said Christine.

'Gosh, so it was! You tend to lose track of the days when you're dashing from one place to the other.'

'I noticed those two together,' said Christine, 'but I haven't spoken to them very much as yet, only to say hello. Perhaps by the end of the holiday we'll all have got to know one another, but with – how many is it? – thirty odd passengers, it takes time to recognize everyone.'

'Thirty-six, to be exact,' said Bill. 'That's one of the hardest things for us drivers, to recognize all the people from the coach. Especially with the older couples; they all tend to look alike, although we know that they don't, not really.'

He ordered another drink for each of them. True to his promise, he had orange juice, and Christine had the same. She wasn't, in fact, bothered about a second drink, but it was very pleasant sitting there in the twilight. She was enjoying being with Bill. He was an entertaining companion and they had not run out of things to talk about. She had decided – almost – that she would like to spend time with him this week. There could be no harm in it even if, at the end of the holiday, she decided she didn't want to see him again. On the other hand, he might want to call it a day.

Bill was hoping that he would continue to play his cards right. Christine seemed to be coming round to the idea of spending time with him this week. He didn't really know what it was about her that appealed to him. She was not what you might call beautiful, but she was very attractive. Fairish hair in a simple style framed a high forehead and a roundish face; her eyes were a sort of bluey-greyish colour. But when you got to know her there was nothing 'ish' or nondescript about her. She had a lovely smile and a gentle easy-to-listen-to voice. He decided she must be a very nice person because she liked dogs. He hoped she wasn't too obsessed with them, preferring them to human beings as some people said they did. He liked dogs, too, and cats, but his job had prevented him from ever owning one. Anyway, time would tell. He must be careful not to blow it, after such a promising start.

As they strolled back to the guest house he ventured to put an arm round her, and she did not object. When they were just a few yards away he stopped and put both arms around her.

'I'll kiss you goodnight here, if I may?' he said tentatively. 'Just in case there are nosy people around. May I, Christine?'

'Yes, of course you may,' she answered. He kissed her gently on the lips, then let her go. 'Thank you for a lovely evening,' he said.

'Thank you too, Bill,' she replied. 'I shall look forward to seeing you tomorrow.'

Bill gave a gasp, an inaudible one, he hoped, as they went through the door, he with his arm around her. There at the reception desk was Olga. She wasn't usually there at this time of night; in fact, he had never known her to be there. He realized that that was because she had always spent the evenings with him when the tour was staying there. Anyway, there she was now, handing out bedroom keys to the guests. Most people left them at reception as they were too heavy to carry about.

Bill withdrew his arm from Christine as she walked up to the desk. 'Room twenty-five, please,' she said, smiling at Olga. Bill, standing to one side, saw her hand the key to Christine. Olga was smiling, but it was a sardonic smile. She raised her eyebrows as she spoke to Christine.

She pointed towards Bill. 'I see that it did not take him long to find somebody else,' she said, in her almost perfect English. 'Let me warn you: that one, he has had me on a – how do you say it? – on a piece of string since last year. He will tell you all kinds of things, but you will be foolish if you believe them.'

Christine took the key without a word. She turned towards Bill. Her face was grim and her eyes like two grey stones as she hurried past him towards the stairs that led to the bedrooms.

'Christine . . . wait,' he called, hurrying after her. 'I'm sorry. I should have told you; I can explain . . .'

'You have already said quite enough!' She almost spat at him as she dashed up the stairs.

Bill opened the door of the room he was sharing with Mike. His mate was sitting up in bed, engrossed in one of his usual thrillers. Bill flopped down on the other bed, his usually cheerful face a picture of misery.

'I've gone and blown it,' he cried. 'What a bloody fool I am! And I really liked her, Mike. I really thought I was in with a chance.'

Mike put his book down and got out of bed. He was already clad in his pyjamas. 'I'll make us a nice cup of tea,' he said. 'Then you can tell Uncle Michael all about it.'

Ten

Mavis went to the window and opened the shutters. 'Another lovely morning,' she called.

'Arthur, are you listening? It's another nice day. Aren't we doing well?'

She looked out on a pleasing vista of fields and wooded hills, a blue sky with a few fluffy clouds, and the sun already shining at seven thirty in the morning.

All she got from Arthur was a grunt as he turned over in bed. He would come round, though, after his usual early-morning grumpiness. But by the time they had washed and dressed, had their usual morning 'cuppa' and were ready to go for breakfast she realized he was not himself. He was rubbing at his stomach.

'This damned indigestion again,' he said. 'Must have been those dumplings last night, and that roast pork. It was good, though, I must say that.'

'I told you not to eat them all,' said his wife. 'Like my mam used to say, your eyes are bigger than your belly when you see something you like.' She was pleased, though, that he was enjoying the food. He was enjoying everything about the holiday so far, despite being in Germany.

They dined with their usual companions. Jane and Dave were cheerful and happy. Ellen was rather quiet, and Shirley was looking a little downcast after her hilarity of the previous night and her vow not to let the matter of the suitcase bother her. She was, of course, dressed in the same clothes as she had worn the day before.

There was a good choice of breakfast food. Cereals, fruit, different kinds of bread and copious supplies of butter and jam. It looked like home-made jam – strawberry, raspberry and apricot – in glass bowls; far preferable to those pesky little cartons with the awkward tops that they served in hotels at home. There were slices of cold meat and cheese instead of the cooked breakfast of bacon and eggs that some of them might have preferred. But it was certain that no one should go hungry.

Mavis was pleased that Arthur ate sparingly, and after he had taken a couple of Rennies he said that he felt a lot better.

Shirley seemed fidgety and preoccupied. 'I'm going to have a word with Mike,' she said. 'I want to know when I'm likely to get my case back. I'm trying to be patient, but I want to know and that's that!'

'Oh dear!' said Ellen as her friend got up and marched resolutely to the table where the drivers were sitting. 'I do hope she gets a favourable answer.'

'Yes, so do I,' said Jane who was sitting next to her. She feared that Shirley's moods had an effect on her friend. She sympathized with Shirley, too, knowing how lost she would feel if all her belongings had gone astray. 'It's another lovely day, though,' she added. 'I'm sure we'll all enjoy the trip to the lake.'

'Shirley wants to find a shop that sells – you know – underwear,' Ellen whispered confidentially. 'I've lent her a couple of pairs, but it's something you need a lot of on holiday, isn't it?'

'Of course,' agreed Jane, trying not to smile. 'A pair for each day at least.'

Shirley was having an animated talk to the drivers, and when she returned to the table it was clear that she was not too happy.

'Saturday!' she exclaimed. 'Would you believe I can't get my case back till Saturday!'

'And today's Thursday,' said Ellen. 'It could be a lot worse. It's only two days, and at least they know that it's turned up in Austria, don't they?'

'Only two days!' Shirley was not mollified by her friend's remark. 'How would you like to wear the same things all day and all evening as well?'

'No one's bothered, though, about what you're wearing,' said Jane. 'They're all very sorry about what has happened. Why can't they do anything till Saturday?' she asked.

'Because of all these excursions,' retorted Shirley. 'And they've to fit in with the driver of the coach from Yorkshire; there's only one driver, apparently, and he can't get away any earlier. We've got a long trip today, and a long one tomorrow to Baden Baden. On Saturday we go to Freiburg which isn't very far. So Bill will take us there, and Herr Grunder has offered to lend Mike his car so that he can meet the other driver at a halfway point and swap over the cases.'

'That's very kind of the hotel owner, isn't it?' said Jane.

'Yes, I suppose so,' said Shirley a trifle grudgingly.

'And the lady in Austria – at least I assume it's a lady – she'll be in the same position as you, won't she?' Jane went on. 'She no doubt feels just as fed up as you do.'

'Yes, of course she will,' Shirley agreed. She gave a weak smile. 'Sorry I'm such a misery, I'll try to make the best of it, really I will. At least the sun's shining and that makes all the difference, doesn't it?'

They set off at nine thirty for a leisurely drive through the Black Forest. Bill was at the wheel with Mike giving the commentary. It was doubtful if anyone but the people concerned noticed that Bill was somewhat subdued, or that the lady who sat at the front of the coach did not speak to him – or he to her – as she sat down next to her sister.

Mike counted heads and they set off along a route which was one of the most beautiful in the area. At every turn in the road there was another eye-catching vista of the wooded hills and peaceful valleys. They passed rippling streams and waterfalls and an occasional mill wheel – still in use for providing electricity for the industry of the valley – beside a typical Black Forest house, the roof of which reached almost to the ground.

Mike told them they were driving along part of the route that was known as the German Clock road, passing more than thirty places where clocks were made.

They stopped mid-morning at one of the most renowned clock shops which boasted that it housed the largest cuckoo clock in the world. A middle-aged man clad in the form of national dress that was still worn in the country areas – dark green jacket and hat with a feather, knickerbockers and bright red socks – boarded the coach to tell them a little of the history of Black Forest clocks. His English was good, although no doubt well rehearsed after talking to countless visitors, such as themselves.

'We have been making these clocks for hundreds of years,' he told them, in the guttural voice common to so many of his race. 'Ever since the seventeenth century . . .' The clocks were carved by the peasants of the area who were always looking for ways to supplement their meagre income. At first they were simply carved wooden clocks, then, much later, a little house in the shape of a railway station was designed for the front of the clock. No one knows who first put the cuckoo in, but these were the first of the famous clocks that were now sold all over the world. Nowadays, not only cuckoo clocks were produced in the Black Forest, but all types of modern clocks and wristwatches.

'Now, all of you will come with me, please,' he said at the end of his talk, 'I will show you the front of our cuckoo clock, the largest one in the world.'

They followed him to the side of the shop to view the enormous clock with the hands standing at almost eleven o'clock. As they stood there out popped an enormous bird from its huge wooden house, 'cuckooing' eleven times.

'He measures one metre from his beak to his tail,' their guide told them. 'Now, if you follow me, please, I will take you into the shop.'

They entered the large store and were confronted with a display of fantasy and colour that had to be seen to be believed. It was a fairyland of delights from floor to ceiling; so much merchandise that at first they could only stand and stare.

'If you wish,' said their guide, 'you may come with me to see the mechanism of the large cuckoo clock. It is worth a few minutes of your time.'

It was mainly the men, and a few of the women, who accompanied him up the stairs. Most of the ladies wanted to spend as much time as possible amongst the tempting goods that were calling out, 'Come and buy me!' They did not need the company of the menfolk, especially the ones who might say, 'Good grief! Look at the price of that!' or, 'Come on, you don't really want that, do you?' No, they just needed a purse full of euros and time to indulge themselves to their heart's content.

The pre-eminent goods for sale were, of course, the clocks. Cuckoo clocks of all sizes, some quite garishly painted in bright colours, others of dark wood, intricately carved, and most of them ticking away merrily, a constant accompaniment to the voices of the shoppers. There were other kinds of clocks as well; small mantel clocks, kitchen clocks, and larger timepieces, even a few grandmother and grandfather clocks standing against the wall.

They all walked around, up and down the aisles, examining the price tags, pondering what they could afford to buy, or what to take home for a present for a friend or relative. Some of the articles were inexpensive trifles – souvenir pens and pencils, bookmarks, simple wooden toys or cheap pottery vases and mugs – costing only a few euros. But they were in the minority. Amongst the goods for the more discerning were wood carvings of peasant folk, animals – mainly bears – and birds; brightly painted wooden nutcrackers, bottle openers, screwdrivers, salt and pepper pots in the shape of comical characters; cute Hummel figures of children; calendars for the forthcoming year with glossy pictures of the region; dolls in national costume; wooden puppets; soft toy animals, mainly teddy bears, some with the Steiff button in the ear.

'Hello,' said a voice at Jane's ear. 'Are you enjoying yourself?' It was Dave who had been viewing the workings of the cuckoo clock. Some of the men had joined their wives now, others of them had gone outside for a smoke or a chat.

'Yes, I'm quite mesmerized,' replied Jane. 'There's such a lot to look at, most of it very tempting. You could easily spend a fortune – on things you don't really need!'

'That's the idea,' said Dave with a laugh. 'To make you part with your money. You have to treat yourself, though, sometimes . . . and I must buy something for my mother and my son and his fiancée.'

'Yes, so must I, for my mother,' said Jane. 'I've been looking at the cuckoo clocks, but I can imagine her saying that the cuckoo gets on her nerves, popping out every hour! So I've almost decided on a wood carving. There's one of a deer that I think she might like; it's quite small so she should be able to find a place for it. And I shall treat myself to a little carved bear. I like bears, although I know these are really very fierce in the wild. I much prefer teddy bears! And I'll get a calendar for next year; it'll bring back happy memories.'

'Yes, my mother would like a wood carving,' said Dave, 'and I'll get a cuckoo clock for my son and his fiancée . . . but that's not really very personal, is it, seeing that we all live together? Never mind; we can all enjoy it . . . I'll get a beer stein for Peter as well, and a little Steiff bear for Kathryn.'

They went their separate ways, each of them to choose their purchases. Jane took a little longer wandering around, deliberating about this and that. There was quite a long queue at the cash desk. Most of the people from the coach – mainly the women – were carrying one of the store's baskets containing several items. The lady assistant packaged all the goods up very neatly, placing them in a distinctive carrier bag, along with a picture postcard of the cuckoo clock as a thank-you token.

Dave was waiting for her. He smiled as he handed her a bag. 'A little present for you. As you said about the calendar, it will bring back happy memories.'

'Oh, Dave . . . thank you so much!' she exclaimed. She almost said, 'You really shouldn't,' then she realized it was something he wanted to do – because he liked her? – and she must accept the gift gratefully. She peeped inside the bag, and there was a little Steiff bear with golden fur and a blue satin bow round his neck.

'Oh . . . how lovely!' She was almost crying with delight, and she wanted to put her arms round him and kiss him – they had exchanged a few kisses by this time – but of course she didn't do so.

'I'm glad you like it,' he said. 'I got one for Kathryn as well.'

Mike and Bill had come into the shop and were talking to the lady at the till.

'They'll be sorting out their commission,' whispered Dave. 'They'll get a small percentage for everything we buy. One of their perks, but you can't blame them . . .'

They all stood outside for a few moments enjoying the sunshine. Mavis had a bulging carrier bag.

'I thought she was going to buy up the whole shop!' said Arthur. 'Not that I mind what she spends if she enjoys it.' He chuckled. 'She deserves it for putting up with me!'

'How's your indigestion?' asked Jane. Arthur was not one to suffer in silence, and they had all known of his discomfort.

'Much better, thanks,' he replied. 'I'm looking forward to my lunch. I had hardly any breakfast.'

Shirley and Ellen were both holding carrier bags. Shirley looked far happier than she had been earlier. 'I've bought a couple of colourful scarves,' she said, 'They'll add a touch of glamour to my top, till I get my case back. I was looking at the sweaters, but they're not my sort of thing, far too countrified and homespun. Anyway, it's too hot for jumpers.

'And we've each treated ourselves to a little teddy bear, haven't we, Shirley?' said Ellen, as excitedly as a little girl.

'We have indeed,' replied Shirley. 'Steiff ones, no less!'

Jane smiled to herself. It seemed that all women liked teddy bears, even the sophisticated Shirley. Dave was not near them – he was talking in a group of men a little distance away – so she could not resist telling them.

'I've got one as well!' she said, a little coyly. 'Dave bought it for me.'

'Oh, isn't that nice!' said Ellen. 'You must be thrilled. You're getting on very well with him, aren't you?' she whispered.

'I think so,' said Jane, wondering already if she'd said too much. 'We'll see. It's early days yet . . .'

'All aboard,' called Mike coming out of the shop. They all climbed on the coach and stacked their carrier bags containing their purchases in the compartments above the seats.

Mike sat down behind the wheel to take his turn at driving, and Bill did a quick count of heads. 'Two missing,' he remarked. 'It's not surprising, though; it's a very tempting place to linger. They'll soon realize everyone else has gone.'

He knew who was missing. It was Christine and her sister from the front seat. They appeared after a couple of minutes. 'Sorry, everyone,' called Christine as she boarded the coach.

'No, it was my fault,' added Norma. 'I got into a muddle with my euros.'

'Never mind, it's easily done, love,' said Bill. 'We'll forgive you, won't we, Mike?'

'Sure,' said Mike. 'We'd better get moving though now, ladies and gents. We want to get to the lake in good time.'

Christine and Bill were forced to exchange glances now. He half smiled at her as her sister settled down in the seat by the window.

'I hope I'm forgiven, too?' he said, leaning down to speak to her. 'It's all over with me and Olga, really it is. If you'll let me explain . . .'

Christine nodded. 'OK,' she said briefly. 'See you later.'

What the heck! she thought. The chances were that it wouldn't come to anything with Bill, but she had enjoyed his company so far, so why not continue to do so? By the time they had arrived at their destination, the oddly named Lake Titisee, she had decided to give Bill a chance to explain if that was what he wanted to do, but not to let herself get too involved. She had been happy enough recently with just her faithful friend Monty for company, and had not even considered embarking upon another relationship. On the other hand, she did not want to turn into a 'doggie' person, a middle-aged spinster with only a canine companion. Bill had seemed amazed on finding she owned a dog parlour. She must try to rediscover her more human and feminine side.

Mike stopped the coach a little way above the village at the spot where he would pick them up again in three hours' time. So they had ample time to shop and browse, to enjoy a meal, or even to stroll all the way round the lake if they wished to do so, which would take about an hour and a half.

There was a chilly wind blowing when the passengers alighted from the coach. The lake was situated some 850 metres above sea level and the air was fresh and keen. The road which led down to the small resort of Titisee Neustadt became more crowded the nearer one got to the lakeside. There were shops and cafes aplenty, most of which catered for the tourist trade. Here were cuckoo clocks, wood carvings and souvenir items such as they had already seen in the home of the largest cuckoo clock, but many of these were of an inferior quality. It was an appealing street in spite of the touristy overtones which, for some, only added to the holiday atmosphere. The women lingered to stare into shop windows whilst the menfolk strode ahead.

There was a pleasant lakeside promenade and a landing stage from which pleasure boats left for a trip round the lake. There were a few brave souls swimming near to the edge of the lake, and further out a few waterskiers and yachts sailing in what appeared to be calm waters.

They were feeling peckish by that time. It was ages since breakfast time, but there was no shortage of eating places to choose from; posh and no doubt expensive hotels down to kiosks selling hamburgers and different kinds of wurst. (They soon recognized that the word meant sausage.)

All the lakeside cafes had their menus prominently displayed. You could dine inside away from the crowds or outside under a colourful umbrella that provided a shade from the midday sun. The problem was knowing which place to choose. There were so many serving identical dishes – bratwurst, goulash, Black Forest ham, pork with the inevitable dumplings – so how could you tell which of them had the best chef?

'You find that the busiest ones are usually the best,' Mavis remarked to Arthur. 'If there's hardly anyone there it might be a sign that the food's not up to much.'

'Well, for goodness' sake, let's sit down somewhere,' groaned Arthur. 'My belly thinks my throat's cut! I'm famished. It's ages since breakfast, and how can I keep going on a bit of bread and jam?'

'Now, you know you couldn't eat anything else. You had that bad indigestion,' Mavis reminded him.

'Well, it's gone now. Let's go in here or we'll be wandering around all day.'

'Yes, there's a table by the window, and it's nice and quiet inside.' There was a goodly number dining outside and the food looked appetizing.

The table was covered with a green and white checked cloth, and the waitress, who handed them the large menu, wore a green dirndl skirt and a white peasant-style blouse embroidered with green flowers and leaves.

'It's all in German,' said Arthur, but Mavis pointed out that the English was written in italics at the side.

'Now, nothing too heavy, Arthur,' she told him. 'You may well be hungry but there'll be a big meal tonight.'

They settled on a platter of cold meats including the Black Forest ham – which lived up to its reputation of being the best in the country – served with a simple salad of lettuce and tomatoes tossed in oil, and crisp bread rolls and butter. Arthur would have preferred his usual Heinz salad cream, but said he was comfortably full again after his meal and a half of lager.

They were not the only ones from the coach who had decided to lunch there. There was a couple whose names they didn't know who waved to them from across the other side of the room. Then Mavis noticed Bill sitting down at a table outside. But he wasn't on his own, nor was he with Mike. He was with that young lady who sat on the front seat, right next to him.

'Look, Arthur,' she said. 'There's Bill, over there, see. And he's with that nice young lady who sits at the front of the coach. It looks as though there's something going on there.'

'Don't stare at them, Mavis. It's nothing to do with us, whatever they get up to.'

'No, perhaps not, but I like to know what's going on.'

'You mean you're just nosy!'

'No, I'm not. I'm . . . interested, that's all. Jane mentioned to me at breakfast time that she and Dave had seen the two of them last night – Bill and that lady, whatever she's called. They were having a drink at a wine bar in the village.'

'Well, good luck to them then,' said Arthur. 'I dare say it'll just be a holiday fling. Coach drivers have quite a reputation for that sort of thing. Let's hope the lass has got her head screwed on the right way.'

'Oh, I think today's young women are a lot wiser about the ways of the world than we were,' replied Mavis, 'I wouldn't like her to get hurt, though. She seems a nice young woman. Bill seems a pleasant sort of fellow, too. I saw that receptionist, Olga, smiling at him when we arrived, and I thought it looked as though they might be . . . well, friendly, you know. I hope he's not playing fast and loose with the pair of them.'

'For heaven's sake, Mavis, give it a rest!' said Arthur. 'I've told you, it's nothing to do with us. Now, have you finished eating, or do you want a piece of that Black Forest cake?'

'Gateau . . . No, I don't think so, Arthur. It's very tempting, but it'll be coming out of our ears by the time we get home if we eat much more of it. Let's have a coffee to finish off with.

It's very pleasant here watching the world go by. Then we'll have a nice stroll by the lake. We're having a lovely holiday, aren't we, Arthur? Aren't you glad we came to Germany?'

'Maybe I am,' he replied, a trifle grudgingly. 'The hotel's OK, and the food, and we've seen some nice views of mountains and what have you. But I don't know about the folk, I haven't made up my mind yet. I think they have long memories; they can't forget that we won the war.'

It was Mavis's turn then to tell Arthur to shut up. She caught the waitress's eye and ordered two coffees. Arthur gave her a sheepish look. He knew by the set of her mouth that she was annoyed with him. But she would come round. She always did.

Outside on the terrace, Bill and Christine were studying the menu; at least Christine was doing so. Bill had decided that he would have Weisswurst.

'What on earth is that?' she asked. With her limited German she could work out what the word meant. 'White sausage?' she queried. 'It sounds awful. Is it really white?'

'You'll see when it arrives,' said Bill. 'What about you? Do you want to try some?'

Christine grimaced. 'No, thanks! I'll stick to the normal bratwurst, and just a few chips, or whatever they call them here.'

'*Pommes frites*, the same as in France.'

When the meals arrived, however, there were more than just a few chips. When the waitress had gone, Christine looked at the Weisswurst and shuddered.

'That looks disgusting!' she said.

Bill laughed. 'It's an acquired taste, but I've got used to it. It's a dish from Munich, really.'

The fat white sausages, made from veal had been brought to the table in a tureen of hot water. They were flecked inside with parsley, and were eaten with sweet grainy mustard. Christine watched as Bill slit the sausage along the middle, separating the edible meat from the skin.

'Don't you eat the skin?' she asked. 'We always do at home, don't we? And our sausages are pink or pale brown.'

'It's really very tasty,' he told her. 'No, you don't eat the skin. Another way to eat it is to open one end and suck out the contents. That's what the locals do, but I'll use a knife and fork.'

He laughed at her bemused expression. They had made up their differences now and were enjoying one another's company.

'I should have told you about Olga,' he had said. 'I had decided to finish it before I met you. I thought she would agree that there's no future in it. But . . . you saw how she reacted when she saw me with you.'

'And I can't say I blame her,' said Christine. 'I'll spend some time with you this week, Bill. But nothing too heavy, eh? And then we'll see.'

'Suits me,' replied Bill; but he was finding that he liked her more and more.

Everyone agreed on boarding the coach a couple of hours later that they had enjoyed the day immensely. Shirley was still feeling cross, though, as she hadn't been able to find a shop that sold underwear, let alone any decent clothing. Surely the German women had to buy knickers and bras?

'They probably do their clothes shopping in Freiburg,' said Ellen patiently. 'We're going there on Saturday, and we're going to Baden Baden tomorrow. There's sure to be a large store there that sells panties. Until then I'll lend you two more pairs,' she whispered. And with that, Shirley had to be content.

Mike put on a tape of well-known German songs as they drove back, and those who didn't doze off joined in with the singing of 'Valderee, Valderah . . .' The holiday was going well.

Eleven

The dining room was filled with the noise of excited chatter as the folk of the coach party discussed the events of the day with their table companions. It seemed as though they had known one another for ages although it was really only four days. Some, maybe, would form a friendship, exchange addresses and send a card or letter at Christmas. For others it would just be a holiday acquaintanceship, good while it lasted, but receding to the back of the mind when they were home again. Mike and Bill agreed that they were a good crowd this week; passengers that seemed to 'gel' and get along well together.

'Sounds like a bloomin' aviary in here,' Arthur commented. 'All these women chattering away like budgerigars.'

'Not only the women, Arthur,' his wife reminded him. 'The men are doing their fair share. Now, it's veal cutlets tonight for the main course, according to the menu. You'll be alright with that, so long as you go easy on the dumplings.'

'Oh, I'll be fine. Stop fussing, Mavis. That onion soup was watery. I'm ready for something more substantial.'

The veal was tender and very palatable; small cutlets in breadcrumbs served with noodles and pickled cabbage. Arthur pushed the cabbage to one side.

'Can't say I'm right keen on that. Why can't they serve it like you do? Spring cabbage with nice tasty gravy.'

'It's called sauerkraut, Arthur. Not entirely to my liking either, but you know what they say. "When in Rome . . ."'

'Aye, but we're in Germany, aren't we?' He sat back in his chair, and Mavis noticed that he winced and put his hand to his stomach.

'What's the matter?' she asked. 'Have you got that pain again?'

'Just a twinge, that's all. I've told you not to fuss. I'll just sit quietly and happen it'll go away.'

Mavis looked at him anxiously. His face was pale, almost

ashen. He sat motionless and closed his eyes as the waitress cleared away the plates.

'You'd better not have the pudding,' Mavis whispered to him. 'It's pancakes and they'll be rather indigestible. What about a little portion of ice cream?'

'No, I don't want anything,' he mumbled, as he suddenly clasped at his stomach and fell forward on to the table, knocking over a couple of glasses and making the cutlery jingle. The sound of that and of his groan of agony silenced the people on the nearby table.

Mavis sprang to her feet. 'Help him! Please help him, somebody . . .'

Dave was at his side at once, and a man from the next table. Mike and Bill were soon at the scene and together they lifted Arthur and carried him out of the dining room into the lounge area. They laid him on a settee. His face was deathly pale but he was still breathing, in strangled gasps, as he struggled to get air into his lungs.

Mike rushed to the reception desk where Olga, fortunately, was still on duty. 'An ambulance,' he told her. 'Ring the hospital, Olga. Quickly, please. A man has collapsed. It looks like a heart attack.'

Mavis sat at her husband's side, holding on to his hand. 'Arthur, I'm here with you. You're going to be alright . . .'

He could not speak to her. He looked at her pleadingly, then closed his eyes again, still gasping and struggling for breath.

'I should have known it was more than indigestion,' she whispered to Dave. 'He's having a heart attack, isn't he? Oh, dear God! Why didn't I realize what was the matter with him?'

'You couldn't have known,' said Dave. 'The symptoms are so similar. Mike's rung for an ambulance so you won't have long to wait. See . . . he looks a little easier now; he's stopped gasping for breath.'

Arthur was laid full length on the settee with cushions supporting his head. His eyes had closed and it seemed as though he had lost consciousness.

'He's not . . . he's not gone, has he?' Mavis murmured. 'Oh God, please don't let him die . . .'

Dave took hold of Arthur's wrist, feeling for a pulse. 'No,' he said. 'There's a pulse there, and it looks as though the spasm, or whatever it was, has passed. We're all here with you, Mavis, all your new friends.'

The rest of the people from the table – Jane, Shirley and Ellen – had come into the lounge. It would have been unfeeling to eat the dessert course; besides, they had all lost their appetites. The rest of the company carried on as normal with the delicious raisin pancakes in lemon sauce, but the hubbub in the room had dropped to a murmur.

It seemed a long time as they waited for the ambulance, but it was really only ten minutes before the two men hurried into the hotel with a stretcher and blankets. They talked together quietly as they examined Arthur, then they lifted him on to the stretcher, fitted an oxygen mask to his face and covered him with a red blanket.

One of the men spoke to Mavis. 'You are his wife, ya?'

'Yes, I'm Mrs Johnson,' she replied. 'You're taking him to hospital?'

'Ya . . . We will take good care of him. Frau Johnson, you come with us, please? Come with your husband. We take him to hospital, in Freiburg.'

'Oh . . . oh yes, of course. I didn't realize . . .'

'Yes, you go along with him, Mrs Johnson,' said Mike. 'He'll be in good hands there. And they'll see that you get back safely, or one of us will come and get you. Try not to worry too much.'

Jane and Dave and the two drivers went with the little party as Arthur was carried outside into the waiting ambulance. Mavis climbed into the back looking scared and bewildered, but she smiled and waved bravely to them as the vehicle drove away.

'What a shock!' said Jane as she and Dave sat down in the lounge. They had missed the pudding but there was no point in going without the coffee as well. 'How awful for this to happen on their holiday. They were enjoying it so much. Oh dear! It casts a gloom over everything, doesn't? And it was all so lovely . . .'

Dave took hold of her hand. 'Let's hope for the best,' he said. 'At least he was still breathing. My father died of a heart attack. It was very sudden, just like it was with Arthur. But Dad had gone, straight away. There was nothing anyone could do. It was a tremendous shock for us all. I don't know, of course, but I should think there's every chance that Arthur will recover.'

There was no longer the happy chatter that there had been earlier in the evening. There was a far more subdued atmosphere in the lounge. Little groups sat together talking quietly, a few playing cards, and others reading a book or magazine.

Shirley and Ellen joined Dave and Jane, all of them concerned about Arthur but trying to look on the bright side.

'I'll tell you something,' said Shirley in a thoughtful, almost penitent voice. 'I'm feeling quite ashamed of myself. Making all that fuss because I have to wear the same clothes for a few days! Whatever must you think of me?'

'We understand,' said Jane, reaching over and patting her hand. 'The women do at any rate. We all like to look our best, don't we, wearing the nice new things we've bought for our holiday? But I do know what you mean. Something like this puts our own little problems into perspective, doesn't it?'

'Yes, that's what I meant,' said Shirley. 'Poor Arthur! And Mavis, too. She thinks the world of him, doesn't she? You can tell she does.'

'And he of her,' added Ellen. 'Such a nice old couple; though I'm sure they don't think of themselves as old.'

'No, and it's a lesson for all of us,' said Dave, 'to make the most of the time we've been given. Seize the moment. You never know what's round the next corner.'

Jane was aware of Dave looking at her, and they exchanged a brief and rather sad smile. Shirley and Ellen left them before long, both deciding they would go to their rooms and read. It wasn't long before the other two decided that they would do the same.

'I'll go and read my adventure story,' said Dave. 'It might help to take my mind off things.'

'And I'm in the middle of a Maeve Binchy,' said Jane. 'A nice comforting read.'

He kissed her fondly as they said goodnight at her bedroom door, and she clung to him for a moment.

'Try not to worry,' he told her. 'There's nothing we can do . . . except to say a little prayer. And I'm sure we'll have a lovely day again tomorrow. Goodnight, Jane . . . my dear.'

It was after eleven thirty when Mavis arrived back from the hospital. The staff there had been very kind to her and had sent her back in one of their smaller vehicles as there was a temporary lull at that time.

The hotel was in darkness apart from one light shining in the reception area. Fortunately she had her key with her, and she crept along the corridor towards her room at the far end. Then she stopped in her tracks. She didn't feel like going into an empty room, not just yet. Surprisingly she was wide awake, not tired by the events of the day, and relieved, of course, that there was now slightly more encouraging news of Arthur. It would be good to have a chat with someone, and perhaps a cup of tea before turning in for the night.

Jane! She would go upstairs and see if Jane was not yet in bed. She had told Mavis that she sat up late reading before going to sleep. Jane's room was on the first floor. There was, in fact, only one floor above the ground level. The light was on a time switch, allowing only just enough time to climb the stairs before you were plunged into darkness again. Jane's room, too, was at the end of the corridor, and Mavis hurried along before the light went out again. Everything was dead quiet and a little eerie with no one around. There was a fanlight above each door, so you could tell whether the occupant was still up or had gone to bed.

Good. There was still a light shining in room thirty-two; Mavis had noticed the number on Jane's gigantic key. She lifted her hand to knock, then she hesitated. Supposing Jane was not alone? Supposing . . . Dave was with her? She knew that the couple were getting very friendly, and she had seen the way they looked at one another. Unless she was very much mistaken the two of them were falling in love. They had known one another for only four days, but feelings could be heightened in the free and easy holiday atmosphere. And who could blame them if . . .

Mavis prided herself on being broad-minded. She had a

daughter a few years older than Jane, happily married, fortunately, and a son two years older who had been married, divorced, then married again. So she had been with them in their various joys and sorrows. She guessed though, that Jane was a very circumspect sort of woman and would not commit herself until she was very sure.

The corridor light went out, and she decided to take a chance. She knocked at the door. A moment or two passed before she heard the sound of quiet footsteps. Then the door opened just a fraction and a nervous voice whispered, 'Who is it?'

'It's me . . . Mavis,' she answered. 'Sorry if I'm disturbing you, but your light was on and I felt as though I needed to talk to someone before—'

'Oh . . . Mavis, of course!' Jane interrupted as she opened the door fully. She was wearing a pretty pink housecoat and matching slippers. 'Come on in. I was startled for a moment, wondering who it was. Anyway, how is Arthur? That's the important thing.'

'He's recovering quite well, at least that's what I'm trying to tell myself,' said Mavis as she entered the room. Then she suddenly burst into tears. Jane put an arm round her and guided her across to the bed, where they sat down.

'Oh, Jane, I'm so sorry,' she began. 'It's been such a worry and I've been trying to be brave. I thought he was dying, really I did.'

'But he's getting better?' Jane asked encouragingly. 'He's come round now, has he?'

'Yes, he regained consciousness when we got to the hospital. He recognized me, but he didn't speak. It was a heart attack, like I thought. Well, I thought it was just bad indigestion at first. We'd no idea that Arthur had a bad heart. He's had palpitations in the past, and his blood pressure is high at times; he takes tablets for that. But we never expected this.'

'He's in the best place now,' said Jane. 'And they've let you come home . . . well, come back here. It's not home – no doubt you wish you were there – but you've got friends around you here. They must be satisfied with his progress.'

'Yes, he's in intensive care at the moment, or whatever they call it here, and he'll have to stay in hospital for a few more days. We'll have to take a day at a time with regard to the holiday and everything. I shall go back there and stay with him tomorrow; they said it didn't matter about sticking to visiting hours. I can be there with him till we see how things go. I'm afraid we've rather spoilt the holiday for everyone, haven't we?'

'We're all very concerned,' said Jane. 'And they'll all be pleased that Arthur's recovering. Now, Mavis; how about a cup of tea?'

'That would be lovely,' she replied, 'if you're sure it's not too late for you?'

'I was on the last chapter of my Maeve Binchy,' said Jane. 'That's why I was up late. I'll finish reading it tomorrow. I'm ready for another cuppa now.'

Mavis stayed a little while with Jane, until they both realized that they were trying to suppress their yawns. It had been a long and eventful day, especially for Mavis. She kissed Jane on the cheek as she said goodnight, as though she was an old friend.

'May I ask, do you go to church?' she enquired. Jane replied that she did, not all the time, but that she did believe in God.

'Would you say a little prayer, then, for Arthur?' asked Mavis. 'I believe that it might help.' Jane assured her that she would do so, straightaway, before she got into bed.

Mavis switched on the corridor light and made her way along the passage and down the stairs to her own room. Whatever had happened – or was still to happen – on this holiday, she felt that she had made a few good friends, ones that she hoped would stand the test of time.

Twelve

Mavis was touched and overwhelmed at breakfast time the following morning by the enquiries about Arthur. Almost everyone from the coach came to ask about him and send their good wishes. And at the end of the meal Mike gave her a 'Get Well' card signed by them all, to take to him. She guessed that this sort of thing had happened before, a passenger being taken ill and rushed into hospital. It was a very thoughtful gesture that she appreciated and she knew that Arthur would, as well.

She hoped that what she was telling them all – that he had come round and was recovering nicely – was true, and that he hadn't had a relapse during the night. She would know soon enough; she would be returning to the hospital in a little while, while the rest of the company prepared for the day's excursion to the spa town of Baden Baden.

Mavis was pleasantly surprised when Herr Grunder, the proprietor, offered to run her to the hospital. She had intended taking a taxi, but he insisted on taking her. It was above and beyond the call of duty, and very kind of him. Everyone was being so kind and thoughtful. She hoped that Arthur might be changing his mind about this country and its inhabitants.

The trip to Baden Baden would be the longest excursion of the week, and so the coach party set off at the rather earlier time of nine o'clock. It was some seventy miles away – or 110 kilometres, if you had got used to the metric calculation – and it was hoped that they would arrive in time for lunch, after a morning coffee stop en route.

Bill was at the wheel, and the now seasoned travellers settled back comfortably in their seats. Mike gave the commentary as they drove along. Most of them listened, especially if they wished to learn and – hopefully – remember as much as they could about their holiday. Others dozed off after a little while, but not really because they were tired. The motion of the coach had a soporific effect.

They were travelling northwards along the route which led, eventually, to France and Switzerland. The spa town was situated in the most northerly foothills of the Black Forest.

'Baden Baden is so good they named it twice, like New York!' said Mike.

He told them that it had originally been know just as Baden, but had been given its double name later partly because it was the town of Baden in the state of Baden Wurtenburg but also to distinguish it from other towns with the same name: Baden near Vienna and Baden in Switzerland.

It had long been a celebrated resort visited by the rich and famous, partly for health reasons – its hot springs had been known about since Roman times – but also because it was the popular place to be, the premier European capital of pleasure in the nineteenth and early twentieth centuries. Queen Victoria had stayed there. So had her son Edward the Seventh, lured there by his love of horse racing and gambling at its famous casino, and by his pursuit of lovely ladies!

Kaiser Wilhelm, and the Emperor Napoleon, had stayed there too; the composers Berlioz and Brahms; and several of the Russian writers. Tolstoy's novel, *Anna Karenina*, had been set partly in Baden Baden, although it had been given a different name in the story.

Jane, listening to the commentary, thought to herself that that was one of the books that she had always intended to read, but had never got round to it. It was not so much the length of it that had put her off, but the unfamiliarity of the Russian names. She found her mind wandering a little until Mike started to tell them of the attractions of the town and the places of interest.

'You ladies will think you're in Wonderland today,' he said. 'I hope you haven't spent all your euros, although credit cards are very acceptable, of course, provided you don't get carried away. I'm rather glad my wife isn't here! You'll find shops there to rival those in London or Paris; boutiques and jewellers and antique shops, whatever takes your fancy.' He laughed. 'Bill and I will be heading for one of the taverns. Not to drink, I assure you – you know our strict rule about that – but to have a jolly good meal. You'll find plenty of eating places to suit every pocket. I know you're all going to have a great day. Now, I'll shut up for a while and let you enjoy the scenery.'

He put on a tape of 'easy listening' music, some of the lighter pieces by Beethoven, Brahms and Mozart.

Shirley, also, started to listen intently when Mike told them about the shops in Baden Baden. She nudged her friend.

'Did you hear that, Ellen? It sounds as though it might be my lucky day, that is if what he says is true. We've seen nothing so far that I'd look at twice.'

'Yes, I heard what Mike said,' replied Ellen resignedly. Thank goodness for that, she thought to herself, for something to put a smile back on Shirley's face. They had both been pleased to hear the news about Arthur, but Ellen knew that it still niggled at Shirley and hurt her pride that she was unable to look her best each day in her smart holiday clothes.

'We'll have a good browse round the shops, Shirley,' she assured her. 'I might even treat myself if I can find something that I like.'

'To wear, you mean?'

'Yes, why not? I rather like the nice trousers and tops that some of the ladies wear. I've never really liked to wear trousers. My father used to say that they weren't for women; that trousers were only for men.' She chuckled. 'What he really meant, of course, was that he had to be the only one in the house to wear the trousers!'

'Very true,' agreed Shirley. 'Your father ruled the roost, didn't he? And you and your mother had to toe the line, if I remember rightly. You were a good obedient daughter, Ellen. I know jolly well that I'd have rebelled; but it's time for you to please yourself now. We can't live in the past, none of us.'

'Yes, I'm realizing that,' said Ellen. 'We're having a good time, aren't we? We were all upset about Arthur, and it's hard to go on enjoying yourself when someone else is in trouble. There's not much we can do, but I said a little prayer for him . . .'

Shirley smiled at her fondly. 'You're a saint, Ellen.'

'No, I'm not!' her friend retorted. 'Far from it. I had some very un-Christian thoughts about my father sometimes, and my mother, too, for kowtowing to him like she did. But I knew that I mustn't upset them . . . I know I'll never get married, not now,' she added in a whisper. 'That was something I really wanted at one time, but my father disapproved of the young man I liked. But I've got used to being single now, and I'm quite happy with it.'

'Why shouldn't you be?' Shirley laughed. 'Who needs men, anyway?'

It seemed a long way to their destination. They had a brief stop after a couple of hours, what Mike called a coffee and comfort stop, then arrived at Baden Baden at twelve o'clock.

'Now, we have a nice long stay here,' he told them. 'Be back at the coach for half past four, and please try to be on time. I've arranged for us to have our dinner a little later tonight, so that we can make the most of our day here.'

He showed them the way to the town through the Kurhaus gardens, a place where they could linger on the way back. They were all anxious, though, at the moment, to get to the town to have a meal and to savour the delights of the shops, particularly so for the ladies.

'You won't want to spend all day with me,' Jane said, tactfully, to Dave. 'I remember how my husband used to get bored with the shops after so long. I'll stay with Shirley and Ellen, if that's OK with you?'

'That's fine with me,' Dave assured her. 'I shall find some antique shops to browse around, or book shops. I may not understand the language, but they usually sell all sorts of other things as well. You go and have a good time with the ladies.'

Christine also had a word with Bill. 'You spend today with Mike,' she told him, 'and I'll go with my sister and our new friends. I'm sure boutiques and jewellers are not much in your line. I'll see you later tonight . . . that is, if you still want to?'

'Of course,' replied Bill. 'Off you go and spend your money. We'll have a drink together after dinner.' They had been getting along well together since they had sorted out the problem with Olga. The receptionist seemed to have got the message now, and Bill had to accept that she was ignoring him. He would have preferred them to part more amicably, but he knew that he had only himself to blame. He might, unwittingly, have given her false hopes. He decided that he must not make the same mistake with Christine. It must be one girl at a time from now on for Bill. He had a feeling that this one might well be the right one for him.

Jane had decided at the outset that she must not be too 'clingy' with regard to Dave. Besides, she would welcome a day with 'the girls'. She suggested to Shirley and Ellen that she might spend the day with them, if they didn't mind, and they seemed delighted at the idea.

Dave walked on ahead, catching up with Mike and Bill. There didn't appear to be any other men on the coach tour who were on their own; but Jane was sure that Dave was the sort of man who would not be bored with his own company.

The extensive gardens of the Kurhaus housed the famous casino and conference centre which attracted people from all over the world. They walked through tree-lined avenues and flower beds ablaze with colour at the start of the summer season. Those that were able walked at a fast pace to reach the town and find a place to eat.

Baden Baden did not disappoint them. It was a mixture of the old and the new. There were wide streets with all kinds of modern shops, whilst the old town was a maze of picturesque cobbled streets and narrow lanes. There were exclusive boutiques, and small quaint shops selling all manner of things – jewellery, antiques and other 'collectibles', second-hand books, handmade chocolates, perfumes and body lotions – as well as bistros and taverns, and cafes with seating both inside and out.

Shirley had to be discouraged from stopping and staring in every shop window.

'Lunch first,' the other two told her. 'We'll come back afterwards,' said Jane. 'If we start shopping we'll have no time to eat.'

Shirley was reluctantly steered away from a very tempting boutique. 'I only hope we can find it again later,' she said, as they walked up one little lane and down another. 'We must try and remember where it is.'

'I feel it might be rather expensive anyway,' remarked Ellen, 'and there are plenty of other shops in the modern part of the town.'

'It depends on what you want to buy,' said Shirley, with a longing glance at an emerald green trouser suit at the front of a shop window. There was no price ticket on it, though, which was sure to mean that she couldn't afford it.

She sighed. 'OK then, girls. Lunch first, as you say. Look, there's a place over there that looks promising. Let's go and see, or we'll be wandering around all day.'

The bistro looked clean – which was an important consideration – and inviting, with gaily patterned tablecloths and attractive menu cards with the items written in English and French as well as German. There were several people dining there which, again, was a good sign, but there was still plenty of room.

They opted to go inside rather than dine out on the street as the pavement was not very wide and the streets were crowded. They chose a table by the window, then pored over the menu. There was an extensive range, as there seemed to be in all these places, but their choice was simple. Pizzas for each of them, though with different toppings, sprinkled liberally with Parmesan cheese, accompanied with a drink of fresh orange juice.

They decided against a sweet, as the pizzas were enormous, and they would, no doubt stop for refreshment again later in the afternoon. They did, however, have coffee to end the meal, strong and fragrant, such as they rarely had at home, but to which they were becoming familiar. It was a pick-me-up that was favoured on the Continent more so than in the UK. When they had sorted out the bill and worked out how much the tip should be, they set off for their afternoon shopping spree.

Closer scrutiny of the garments in the boutique windows proved that the prices were way out of their range, so they decided – reluctantly on Shirley's part – not to venture inside the little shops. They bought some handmade chocolates, though, for themselves, and some as a little treat for Mavis, from the three of them. It was such a shame that she was missing today's trip and would, possibly, have to forgo the other excursions as well.

They fared better – as Ellen, in her practical way had suggested they might – in the larger shops in the more modern part of the town. There were numerous shops there selling ladies clothing, and Shirley was forced to admit that she had been wrong. The clothes were not of a fuddy-duddy style, suitable for German hausfraus. They were, in the main, very stylish and modern.

Besides being able to replenish her stock of necessary underwear, Shirley, as was only to be expected, had a whale of a time.

'Go steady, you'll get your suitcase back tomorrow, won't you?' Ellen reminded her. But she took little notice. She was like a child in a sweet shop.

When their shopping spree was finished she had bought a pair of flared trousers in royal blue, and two snazzy tops, one striped and one with polka dots that would go well with the trousers. Also, a floaty chiffon skirt in pastel shades, a pair of high-heeled blue sandals, and a blue and white shoulder bag that was suitable for day or evening wear.

'Now, come along, Ellen,' she kept urging her friend. 'You said you wanted some trousers. I'll help you to choose them.'

Ellen could not be persuaded to buy flared ones. She preferred the straight style, and the others admitted that they suited her better. She felt she was being extravagant as she was coaxed, though not unwillingly, into buying two pairs, one in navy blue and the other in fawn. She bought two pretty tops as well, not as bold as the ones her friend had chosen, but in colours that she liked, lemon and coral pink.

'And for heaven's sake, ditch those old-fashioned cardigans of yours,' Shirley told her, 'and buy a nice smart jacket.'

She did as she was bid, choosing an edge-to-edge terylene jacket which, she told herself, was a serviceable colour and would go with most things. Never had she spent so much money all in one day. Never had she used her credit card so much. Her parents had paid for everything in cash, with the occasional cheque, and she had always done the same. She was surprised that she did not feel guilty, but she knew she had money in the bank to cover the expense. She knew she must watch herself, though, and be careful not to turn into a spendthrift.

Jane, not to be outdone, treated herself as well. She enjoyed watching her new friends choosing their clothes. She didn't very often have the chance to go shopping for clothing, and when she did she invariably went to her favourite store, Marks and Spencer, or to Debenhams.

With Shirley's help she chose a floral dress in a silky fabric, in shades of green and blue, ankle-length with elbow-length sleeves – she did not like to show too much bare arm – and a neckline that was not too low. 'For those special occasions,' as Shirley told her.

There had not been too many of those recently, but Jane was hopeful that there might be in the future. She also bought some green summer sandals and a bag to match. Then she decided that that was enough; but she couldn't remember when she had enjoyed a shopping expedition so much.

Mike and Bill invited Dave to join them for lunch in a little place they knew of near to the main square of the town. It was a tavern, rather than a restaurant, with subdued lighting and wood panelled walls, giving it a more masculine feel. They assured him that the food, and the drink, too, was excellent, although the two drivers restricted themselves to a small glass of lager each, then went on to apple juice. Dave indulged himself with a pint – or the equivalent – of Dunkles, a strong dark German beer. At their recommendation he dined, as they did, on goulash, so full of vegetables that you could stand a spoon in it, with crusty bread rolls (*brutchen*) and butter.

Dave found the two men very affable and easy to get along with. In their forties, he guessed, as he was, but possibly a few years younger. He learned that Mike was married, as he had thought, and that Bill was single and had not yet taken the plunge into marriage, as he put it.

'But he's hopeful, aren't you, Bill?' said Mike. 'He's met the girl of his dreams this week.'

Bill laughed. 'I wouldn't go so far as to say that. It's early days, and I nearly messed it up at the start. I'd been seeing Olga, the receptionist, you see, and Christine wasn't too pleased when she found out – neither was Olga! But enough said about that. Yes, she's a really nice girl; well, young woman, I should say.'

'You've been let off the leash today, haven't you, Bill?' teased Mike.

'Well, I spent yesterday with her at the lake, and we'll have a drink together tonight. But, like I said, it's too soon to . . . well, you know. She wanted to go shopping today with her sister and their new friends, so I thought that was a good idea.'

'Yes, so did Jane,' replied Dave. 'I've . . . er . . . got friendly with the lady who sits next to me. It was totally unexpected. I wasn't looking for anything, neither was she, but we just seemed to hit it off.'

'Yes, we'd noticed, hadn't we, Bill?' said Mike. 'Not that we're being nosy, but we are aware of what goes on with the passengers, to a certain extent. None of our business, of course, any of it, but we have to try to get to know them all, one way or another. Not always easy, is it, Bill?'

'Good grief, no!' replied Bill. 'It's the elderly ladies, all with grey hair and glasses. I do get them confused, but that's usually on the tours at home. Over here the clientele is rather different, younger on the whole. We do get elderly couples, though, like Mr and Mrs Johnson. And it's not the first time we've had to deal with someone being rushed into hospital. All in a day's work, isn't it, Mike?'

'Yes, that's true. We have to be prepared for anything and everything.'

'You mean . . . like somebody dying?' enquired Dave.

'Yes, it does happen, occasionally. It's only happened to me once, thank the Lord! Bill wasn't with me. I was on my own, doing a tour at home – in Torquay, actually – so it wasn't quite so complicated as being abroad. Traumatic, though; it puts a downer on the holiday. We're just hoping the old chap will be OK, aren't we, Bill?'

'I'll say we are! For his sake, and his wife's, of course. Anyway, let's look on the bright side, eh? This lady you've met – Mrs Redfern, isn't it? – she seems a very pleasant person. Are you hoping to go on seeing her when we get back? Not that it's anything to do with me . . .'

'I certainly hope so,' replied Dave. 'I intend to say something before the holiday comes to an end. It's complicated, though. Family issues, you know . . .'

'You're single, though?' enquired Bill.

'Oh yes. I've been married, but I'm not now. But we live

miles from each other. Not Land's End to John O' Groats, but far enough. Jane's in Lancashire and I'm in Shropshire.'

'Not far on the motorway . . .'

'No, but Jane has an elderly mother; rather a harridan from what I gather! And there are other things on my side that I haven't mentioned yet.'

Dave didn't explain any further, and Mike and Bill knew better than to ask.

'I hope it works out well for you, Dave,' said Mike. 'And for Bill here, of course. But that's a different problem. It could put an end to gadding about on the Continent . . . That reminds me, I must ring Sally tonight and see how things are at home. She's not too happy about me being over here so much.'

They talked for a little while about the pros and cons of working abroad, then when they had settled the bill they went their separate ways.

Dave mooched around the old part of the town, enjoying himself in his own quiet way. He had never been bored with his own company; sometimes he liked to be entirely on his own for a while. It would be good to meet up with Jane again, though. And Mike's remark had reminded him that he must ring up his son that evening and see if everything was going well at home.

They were all walking back through the Kurhaus gardens at roughly the same time, making sure they did not arrive back late at the coach. Dave caught sight of Jane with the other two ladies and hurried to catch up with them. They were all laden with carrier bags and were chatting and laughing together.

'Oh, hello Dave,' said Shirley. 'We've had a great time. Mind you, we'll have to live on bread and corned beef when we get back!'

'So I see,' said Dave, laughing, knowing full well that all of them had good jobs and could afford to indulge themselves occasionally. He guessed that for Jane it would have been a real treat. 'You'll be dressed in your new finery tonight, will you?' he asked Shirley.

'You bet I will!' she replied, 'But we've all had quite a spree.'

He and Jane smiled at one another, glad to be together again even though it had been only a few hours. He offered to carry her bags, and she agreed to let him take the heavier one.

'Have you bought anything?' she enquired.

'A book with photos of the region in the last century,' he told her, 'and two CDs – Mozart concertos for woodwind, and German overtures.'

The four of them stopped at a cafe near to the casino to refresh themselves with lemon tea and a slice of gateau. Then they had to step on it so as not to be late back for the coach.

Mike, also, stepped on the gas for the return journey, taking a more direct route. The passengers chatted for a while, then some of them dozed and some looked out of the window at the now familiar scenery. Dave took hold of Jane's hand and held it for the whole of the journey. She smiled contentedly to herself.

Thirteen

Shirley caused quite a sensation in the dining room that evening in her royal blue flared trousers and her eye-catching white top with blue polka dots. Everyone had sympathized with her over the missing suitcase and were pleased to see her looking so smart again – although she always did, whatever she was wearing.

Ellen wore her new beige trousers and the coral pink top, feeling a little self-conscious about 'the new you', as Shirley had called her. Ellen was aware that she looked different – quite modern, and younger, too – but she didn't want anyone to comment too much about her changed appearance.

The four of them at the table were delighted when Mavis joined them for the meal. She had spent all day with Arthur, and the news was encouraging. He was now in the normal ward for heart patients, in a little side room on his own. He would need to stay in hospital for at least another day, but all being well he would be able to travel home with the rest of the party. A relief to everyone, not least to the drivers. His heart attack had not been as severe as it had at first appeared to be, but it was a warning that he had to take extra care of himself.

'So you will go and stay with him tomorrow, will you?' asked Jane, full of concern for the woman she now regarded as a friend. 'It's a shame you're missing the excursions, and Arthur is as well.'

'His health is far more important, my dear,' replied Mavis. 'Freiburg tomorrow . . . I'd like to have seen the shops there, but we have a free day on Monday. Perhaps by then . . . But Arthur says I must definitely go on Sunday to Lake Constance and that island where there are all those gardens. Anyway, we'll see. Now, tell me all about your day. Did you enjoy it?'

It was clear from the happy chatter in the room that they had all had a most enjoyable day. Dinner was later that evening because of the long excursion, and they did not finish until after nine o'clock. The five of them sat together in the lounge. Most of the passengers were all too tired to venture out to the village or even to take a little stroll, but it was pleasant to just sit and relax. Both Jane and Dave said that they had to make phone calls to relations. Mavis had been in two minds as to whether to ring her son and daughter to tell them about their father, but she had decided against it. He was recovering, thank God, so there was no point in alarming them.

The hotel phones were busy that evening. Many of the group had mobile phones but it wasn't easy to get a satisfactory signal in the mountainous region. 'And about time too!' was Alice Rigby's opening remark when she went to the phone to receive her daughter's call. 'I was wondering when you'd remember to ring and see how I'm getting on.'

Jane sighed quietly to herself. But had she really expected anything any different?

'Sorry, Mother,' she said. It came naturally to her to apologize even if she hadn't done anything wrong. 'I didn't think it had been all that long, and I didn't promise to ring every day. Anyway, how are you going on? You've settled in OK, have you?'

'Yes, I suppose so. I've been here five days now, and there's another five to go. I'll be glad to get home, I can tell you. There's nothing like your own bed or your own armchair.'

'But it's a comfortable place, isn't it? I thought the lounge looked very nice and homely, and there's that big television set . . .'

'Yes, I suppose it's alright – could be worse.'

'And what about the other people there? Are you getting to know them?'

'Some of 'em aren't so bad. I've got friendly – well, sort of friendly – with a woman called Flora. She's a bit younger than me, but we get on alright. She's had the life of Riley, though; more money than she knows what to do with. She's OK, though.'

'And are there some men there as well?'

'Of course there are. More women, though. It seems as though women live longer. But there's Henry and Jack – they're not so bad. A bit argumentative, like, but I give as good as I get.'

'Yes, I'm sure you do, Mother.' Jane smiled to herself.

'What's that supposed to mean?'

'Nothing at all . . . I'm glad there are some people you can talk to. They're not all zombies, then, like you thought they might be?'

'No . . . no, I have to admit that they're not losing their marbles. Funny ideas, though, some of 'em. I don't always agree, and I'm not afraid to say so. There's Henry, for instance. His son comes to see him, with his latest lady friend. He's been married twice already, so Henry says, and this one – well, he might marry her or he might not. Living in sin, they are – that's what they used to call it in my young days – but it doesn't seem to matter any more. Henry doesn't think it's important.'

'I suppose we have to move with the times, Mother.'

'Well, some of us don't want to move. I'm old-fashioned about marriage, and I don't care who knows it.'

'But it's really none of our business, is it? I don't know why we're even talking about it.' Jane was getting cross. There was her mother, wittering on about the views of some old chap, and this phone call was costing her an arm and a leg. 'Aren't you going to ask me about my holiday?'

'Oh . . . yes, of course I am. I haven't forgotten you're gadding about in Germany. Enjoying it then, are you?'

'Yes, very much, thank you, Mother. I'm having a lovely time. Germany's a beautiful country, and the people are nice and friendly, too. We've been on some interesting trips, and this hotel is very good, especially the food, and that's one of the main things of course. Some of it is rather like we would have at home . . .' Jane stopped, realizing she was beginning to sound like a travel brochure. 'Yes, it's all very nice.'

'I'm glad you're having a good time. Make the most of it while you can.' Was her mother inferring that it might be her one and only such trip? 'What about the folk on the coach? Are you getting on alright with them?'

'Oh yes, they're a very friendly crowd. You don't get to know everyone, of course, but I've got friendly with two ladies and . . . some others as well.' Now was not the time to tell her mother about the very attractive man she had met, or about the elderly man who had had a heart attack. 'Yes, it's all turning out very well, Mother. I think that's all we can say now, isn't it? You're OK, and so am I. So I'd better say cheerio. It's costing quite a lot to ring from here, but I'll call you again, perhaps after the weekend.'

'Are you on that mobile thing?'

'No, it's the hotel phone. The signal's not good here, for mobiles. So . . . 'bye for now, Mother. Take care of yourself, and I'll see you soon.'

'Yes. You take care of yourself as well. I'm glad you're having a nice time. You deserve it.' Her mother's last words were uttered quietly, and Jane wondered if she had misheard them. Then, 'Goodbye, Jane . . . love,' she said. 'See you soon.'

She heard the phone go down, and she, too, hung up. That hadn't gone too badly. It was hard to tell with Mother, but, reading between the lines, it seemed as though she might well be enjoying herself at the Evergreen home, more than she was letting on.

'Hi there, Dad,' said Peter. 'Great to hear from you. Are you having a good time?'

'Wonderful, thanks,' said Dave. 'Yes, I'm really enjoying it all. But tell me about you and Kathryn, and the farm. All going well, is it? No problems?'

'No, none at all. Everything's going well. Kathryn's been helping me with the cooking, not my strong point, you know. And she's coming to stay for the weekend. Her dad said she could have a couple of days off, so she'll be here till Monday. Everything will be nice and shipshape when you return.'

'Very good,' said Dave. He had a relaxed attitude regarding his son and his fiancée. Kathryn sometimes stayed the night with Peter, and he knew it would be considered stuffy to make an issue of it nowadays. They were sensible young people and well, it seemed to be the norm these days. 'I know you won't let things go to pot on the farm. It's your livelihood as much as mine, isn't it?'

'Yes, and it means a lot to Kathryn as well. Anyway, like I

said, it's all OK here. What about you? You're having a great time, then? You certainly sound on top of the world.'

Yes, everything's just fine. The scenery, and the hotels, and the food. Germany's a lovely country. A good crowd on the coach, too. Nice, friendly people. And . . . I've met someone, Peter. Somebody I like very much.'

'Well, well! I take it you mean a lady?'

'Of course I mean a lady!'

'Come on then, Dad. Tell me more.'

'There's not a great deal to tell at the moment. She has the seat next to me on the coach. She got on at Preston – that's where she lives – so we met when I joined the coach at the next stop in the Midlands. She's called Jane; a few years younger than me, and she's very nice. We just seemed to click, if you know what I mean.' Dave laughed. 'That's an old-fashioned word, "click." It's what they used to say ages ago when you got off with a girl.'

'So, you and this Jane have clicked, have you?'

'I'm hoping so, Peter.'

'Well, good for you, Dad. I've been telling you for ages that it's what you should do – find someone to share your life. There's no point in dwelling on the past, especially as it wasn't very happy. So, do you think it will go any further with Jane? Have you said anything to her?'

'I think she knows I'm getting fond of her, and she of me, at least I hope so. Yes, I'm sure she is.'

'And does she know about the circumstances? About . . . Mum?'

'Er . . . no. I must confess I've not told her everything, not yet. She thinks I'm a widower, although I didn't actually say so. She probably assumes I am because she's a widow. Her husband died two years ago. They were very happy together, from what I gather. So, it's rather different for her, you see.'

'But you deserve some happiness now, Dad. Why don't you tell her how things stand? It's not your fault that my mother's being so damned difficult.'

'I like to think I might have a future with Jane, although it's early days yet. We've known each other for less than a week, although it seems much longer. But she's the sort of girl – woman, I should say – who would want something permanent, if it ever got that far.'

'But you don't really know until you ask her, do you?'

'No, but another problem is that she has an elderly mother, an awkward so and so, from all accounts! They live together, but the old lady's staying in a home this week, very unwillingly.'

'You never know, she might decide she wants to stay there. Gran did.'

'I rather think Jane's mother is a very different kettle of fish from your gran. Anyway, we'll see. It's my problem, but I don't want it to be too much of a problem right this minute because we're having such a good time together, Jane and me. She's a lovely person. I know you'd like her.'

'Yes, I'm sure I would. But listen, Dad – nothing ventured, nothing won. Put your cards on the table and see what she says. You might be able to sort it out.'

'I'll wait for the right moment. I don't want to spoil things. Perhaps towards the end of the holiday. I'll be more certain then about how we feel about each other.'

'Yes, you do that, Dad. We'd better say cheerio, hadn't we? You're running up quite a bill. Anyway, all the best . . . to both of you. Take care, and I'll see you soon.'

'Yes, you take care as well. Good to talk to you. Love to Kathryn, see you next week. 'Bye for now.'

'Hello there, Sally. Sorry I've been so long ringing you, but you know how it is. I've been so busy, what with one thing and another.'

'What do you mean, I know how it is? How should I know what you're getting up to over there, Mike? You promised to ring, and it's five days now. And here I am, over here, tearing, my hair out.'

'Hey, steady on, Sal. What's the matter? This isn't like you.' His wife sounded really uptight and Mike was concerned. She was normally quite a placid person, took things in her stride, although she had been getting on to him lately about being on her own with the children, and the problems she had with them, at least with Tracey.

'What's up, Sal?' he asked again. He was even more worried when he heard Sally, at the other end of the phone, give a sort of choking sob.

'It's our Tracey, isn't it?' she managed to gasp. 'She's only got herself excluded from school.'

'What! She's been expelled?'

'No, not expelled, excluded, I said. Just for a few days, her and two friends of hers. But it's bad enough. I'm so ashamed, and she seems to think it's all highly amusing. At least she did until I grounded her. She's not allowed out, and I've confiscated her telly and phone until she goes back to school on Monday. Oh, Mike! I don't know what I'm going to do. I've told you, it's getting too much for me to cope with on my own.'

'Yes . . . yes, I can see that, love.' Sally sounded really distraught. 'So what's she been doing to get excluded? I'm sure it can't be anything too dreadful. Not our Tracey.'

'She's only been stealing from the Tuck Shop near to the school, hasn't she? Her and that Nicky and Kim. I never did like those two girls! They were caught red-handed by the chap that owns the shop, and he marched them right back into school. And of course Miss Fielding sent them home right away, when she'd written all the parents a severe note – that we had to reply to to prove we'd received it – saying how they'd let the school down and all that. Honestly, Mike, I've never been so ashamed in my life.'

'Yes . . . yes, I can see that it's quite serious, it really is,' said Mike. He was remembering, though, the time when he and his mate, Colin, had pinched some sweets from Woolies. They'd not got caught, and they'd had a real good laugh about it. But Mike, secretly, had felt ashamed. He had been brought up to be honest and trustworthy. His dad would have belted him if he'd found out, though he had never done so, only threatened it. He appreciated, though, that it was regarded as a serious offence by the school and by Sally as well. 'What has she to say for herself?' he asked.

'She says they only did it for a dare. Some other girls egged them on. She's really getting out of hand, but maybe this will teach her a lesson.'

'What did they pinch?'

'Oh, a packet of crisps and two Mars bars. What the heck does it matter what it was! It's the humiliation of it. I'll never be able to lift up my head again, everyone knowing she's a thief.'

'Now come along, Sally love. It's not as bad as all that. Get it into perspective. It's just a silly prank, very childish really, for girls of fifteen. Now if she'd been bullying other girls I'd have been more worried. They had an incident of that not long ago at the school, didn't they?'

'Yes, they did. And Tracey wasn't involved, thank God. No, she would never do anything like that. She's always been a kind-hearted girl. She's just got rather out of hand recently.'

'Well, try not to worry too much, love. I'll be home on Wednesday, then I've got a day or two off until the next tour; that's to Scotland, for a week. But I'll see what I can do about staying in the UK permanently. Bill and I have been discussing it.'

'So how's the tour going?' Sally sounded a little calmer now. 'No problems?'

'Well, just a few. We mislaid somebody's suitcase. It went off to Austria on another tour, so I've to go and collect it tomorrow at a halfway point. And an old chap had a heart attack and was rushed to hospital, but they think he's going to be OK.'

'Good grief! It sounds as though you're earning your money this week. There might not be so many problems if you stayed in the UK.'

'I wouldn't say that. There's always something to cope with. But I'd be home more often, that's for sure. Bill's thinking of packing in the Continental tours as well. He's met a lady on the coach this week. He seems really taken with her.'

'So he's decided it's time to settle down, has he? Goodness knows what you coach drivers get up to! Somebody said that to me, but I told her I can trust my husband.'

'And so you can, love . . .'

'I just want to see more of you, Mike. And so do the kids. I'm sure Tracey would be better if you were over here.'

'I'll see what I can do, I promise. Now, are you feeling a bit calmer? It's not the end of the world, you know. It'll be a nine day's wonder at the school, and I'm sure Tracey will have learnt her lesson.'

'Yes, I'm feeling a bit easier now I've told you about it. It was all getting on top of me.'

'Yes, I know. Try not to worry any more. I'll see you soon. Love to Tracey and Gary. Don't tell Tracey her father's cross with her, or anything like that! You know I've never been hard on them, but I will try and be there with you more of the time. Anyway, I don't think we can say any more at the moment. 'Bye for now. I love you, Sal . . .'

'Love you too, Mike. Take care, won't you? See you soon . . .'

Fourteen

The coach party would be setting off later on the Saturday morning as the excursion was a half-day one to Freiburg, just a short distance away. They would leave at ten o'clock, have lunch in Freiburg, then set off back at half past two, leaving them free for the rest of the afternoon to do as they pleased.

Mike had already set off in Herr Grunder's car to meet the driver of the Yorkshire coach at a halfway point and retrieve Shirley's suitcase. Bill was left in sole charge of the group.

'Now, don't forget it's our al fresco meal tonight,' he told them. 'We will be having a barbecue meal outside, weather permitting, and it hasn't let us down so far. Then we're being entertained by a group of local lads and lasses with dancing and singing and all manner of jollity. We'll have a rare old time, I promise you. So, ten o'clock at the coach this morning, please, ladies and gents.'

Bill suggested to Mavis that she should travel to Freiburg with the rest of the group and spend some time in the town before going to the hospital to see Arthur. 'I'm sure he won't mind you spending an hour or two with your friends, will he?' he said, 'especially as he's feeing so much better.'

'I'd love to,' agreed Mavis, 'and of course he won't mind, but he might be expecting me to come earlier.'

Bill offered to phone the hospital and say that she would be there at around two o'clock. She would get a taxi to take her the short distance and spend the afternoon with him.

Arthur was, indeed, feeling much better. It had been a heart attack, sure enough, but milder than they had thought at first. He was vexed, though, that he was still stuck there in hospital – albeit in a little room to himself – instead of enjoying the holiday with the rest of the group. And Mavis was missing the trips as well, although she didn't seem to mind about that, bless her. She was full of concern for him, spending hours each day with him and trying to keep him cheerful.

'Could you imagine I'd be stuck here at the mercy of a load of Germans,' he had complained to her, though half jokingly. 'Who'd have thought it would come to this, eh?'

He had to admit, though, that he was being treated with kindness and consideration and the German doctors and nurses seemed to know what they were doing. They spoke good English, too.

'And that's more than you can say for us,' Mavis told him. 'Us speaking German, I mean. We haven't a clue.'

'They learnt it at school,' said Arthur, a trifle dismissively. 'They had to when we won the war; they were a conquered nation and our troops were over here. Still, I can't complain about the treatment I'm getting.' He was finding that there was very little to grouse about.

He was greeted on Saturday morning at about ten o'clock by a young nurse whom he hadn't seen before.

'Good morning, Mr Johnson,' she said, which was unusual for a start. They usually used the title of 'Herr', rather than the English version. 'I have a message for you from your wife. She will be coming to see you, but it will be later, at two o'clock. She is spending some time in Freiburg with her friends . . . I think the message is correct. You understand it, yes?'

'Yes, that makes sense,' he replied. The nurse was a pretty young woman, neat and trim in her blue uniform which matched the colour of her eyes. Her dark hair waved attractively under the brim of her little cap. She reminded him rather of Mavis when she was young; Arthur could still appreciate a pretty face and figure. From her name tag he read that she was called Ingrid Hoffman.

He smiled at her. 'I haven't seen you before.'

'No, I have just returned after a few days' leave. I will be looking after you now. You are recovering well, I am told?'

'Yes, I'm doing nicely, thanks,' he replied. 'I must say that you speak good English. The others do, but yours is very good indeed.'

She laughed. 'Yes, thank you. That is because I am part English. Just . . . a quarter English. Oma, my grandmother, was from England – from Yorkshire. She married my grandfather after the war. He was there, in England, you see.'

'You mean they met during the war?' Arthur was beginning to understand what she meant, but it was difficult to put it tactfully.

'Ya . . . yes. He was prisoner of war.' Whilst she tidied his bed, checked his temperature and his pulse, and made him comfortable she told him more.

'My grandfather – Opa, I call him – he was in the Luftwaffe, air force, you say, and his plane was shot down. He was not hurt, that was lucky. He was in a camp, then he worked on a farm. And there he met my Oma. She worked on the farm, too. So they were friendly, you see?'

'She was in the Land Army, was she?'

'Yes, she said she was a land girl. My grandfather, he stayed in Yorkshire after the war. They were married, two years later, I think, and they lived there for a little while. But he wished to come home. The hills in Yorkshire were very lovely, but they were not the hills of home. That is what he said to Oma. So she came with him to Freiburg, to his home, and they had their family. My father, then my aunt . . . then I was born. So, you see, I know a little about England. My grandmother, she tells me, and she speaks to me in English, sometimes. She is a lovely lady.'

'So your grandmother is still living?'

'Yes, and my grandfather. They will be same age as you, I think.'

'Yes, they would be, I suppose.' Arthur nodded thoughtfully. 'You talk about the war . . . I was in the war, in the army though, not the air force. I spent some time here afterwards. But it is all a long time ago now.'

'Yes, and we are all friends now, are we not?' said Ingrid. 'We have the European Union. And your Tony Blair, he likes to – how do you say it? – keep us on our toes.'

'You can say that again!' answered Arthur, but he did not want to be drawn into politics.

'He is good ambassador for your country, I think . . .'

'We could do worse,' said Arthur, thinking again that his new nurse had an excellent command of English.

'I am very pleased to meet you, Mr Johnson,' she said. 'Now I leave you in peace. I bring you your lunch in a little while.'

A very pleasant young woman, he mused, when she left him. And that was very interesting, her grandfather bring a prisoner of war in Yorkshire. He had heard that they were very well treated, and many of them had met and married English girls. He felt that he would not have liked it if his sister, for instance, had decided to marry a German. She hadn't, of course, but if she had he would not have approved.

All the same, it seemed to have worked out well for this family. This Ingrid was a lovely young woman. What age would she be? he wondered. Probably in her mid-twenties; the same age as one of his granddaughters.

She returned with his lunch at twelve o'clock; a sort of hamburger with a small amount of mashed potato and cabbage.

'I have an idea,' she told him. 'You go on eating while I tell you. Do not let your lunch go cold. My Opa – I tell you he was in camp in Yorkshire – I think he would like to meet you. He lives here, in Freiburg, with my Oma. I finish here at six o'clock and I will phone and tell him about you. It is coincidence, I think, very good coincidence. I ask him to come and see you, yes?'

Arthur was nonplussed, but how could he refuse? She was such a nice friendly girl and she was doing her best to please him. 'Why not?' he answered, smiling at her. 'It will be good to have a visitor, but don't pressure him. Do you know what I mean? Make sure he really wants to come.'

'Yes, I understand, but I know he will be very pleased to meet you. Now, you eat your lunch. I bring you cup of coffee soon, then your wife, she will be coming to see you. Yes?'

'Yes, so she will. Thank you . . . Ingrid. May I call you Ingrid?'

'Yes, of course you may. It will please me very much.'

Mavis spent an enjoyable morning in Freiburg with Shirley and Ellen who had insisted that she should accompany them. Most of the people on the coach continued to enquire about Arthur, and she felt that she was amongst friends. Now that he was improving she decided that she must try to relax and make the most of the day. It was a pity he couldn't be with her, but she would see him again soon.

They found that Freiburg was a delightful medieval city with a modern shopping area as well. They wandered through the narrow streets of the old town, alongside fast flowing rivulets at the sides of the road. They had once been sluices carrying away the sewage, but were now perfectly clean and added to the charm of the place. They admired the Rathausplatz with its early Renaissance town hall, and the Zum Roten Baren – the Red Bear Inn – which claimed to be the oldest inn in Germany.

When they were tired of wandering they ended up in the Munsterplatz, the main square of the city. They looked in admiration at the Munster, reputed to be one of the most splendid medieval minster churches in Germany. Its 380-foot tower loomed over the square. In its shadow was the picturesque town market, buzzing with activity, especially on a Saturday morning. The tourists mingled with the housewives doing their weekly shopping, stopping now and again to listen to the street musicians and hearing the ranting of an itinerant preacher near to the church.

The stalls were a wondrous sight, a medley of rich colours and appetizing smells against the background of chatter and laughter and the cries of the stall vendors. There were fruit and vegetable stalls galore, with all manner of produce. Piles of oranges, and apples in russet, green and red; luscious strawberries, raspberries and gooseberries, figs and fresh dates; enormous cabbages and cauliflowers; strings of onions, lettuces, tomatoes, huge bunches of radishes. The tourists, in the main, did not want to shop there, but they gazed in wonder at the tempting displays which seemed, somehow, to be more attractive than they were at home.

Farmers' wives were selling the produce of their farms – eggs, cheese, butter, jars of jam and marmalade, pickles and chutneys. There were flower stalls, too, the fragrance of the lilies and roses, and the more pungent dahlias and chrysanthemums scenting the summer air. Pot plants as well – begonias, fuchsias and geraniums, sturdy and healthy looking blooms – but the ladies decided they would be impractical to transport all the way back to England.

Across from the fruit and vegetable stalls were stalls of possibly more interest to the tourists. Here were all sorts of gifts and handicrafts, many of them produced locally. Pottery mugs and plates; wooden toys; floppy dolls, clowns and furry animals; embroidered tablecloths, napkins and mats – probably machine made but still most attractive – and dried flowers fashioned into posies and garlands to hang in a kitchen.

The three ladies meandered amongst these stalls for a while, trying to decide what they would like to buy. There were so many things to tempt them. They met others from their coach tour, notably the women, wandering around like children in a toy shop. The menfolk, on the whole, had decided it was not much in their line and had drifted away to have a smoke or to partake of a beer in one of the many cafes and bars around the square. Not surprisingly they bumped into Jane, on her own for once.

'Where's Dave?' asked Shirley. 'Not far away, I guess?'

'No, he's having a mooch round on his own. There are some old Dinky cars and some old German toys on a stall over there, and ancient postcards and books. More to his liking than this sort of thing. Some of it's a load of tat, isn't it?' she remarked, lowering her voice. 'But I must admit I like those tablecloths, and the floral arrangements are very attractive.'

'Yes, so they are,' agreed Shirley. 'But you have to be discriminating or you'll end up buying a lot of junk! You arrive home and ask yourself why on earth you bought it.'

After another ten minutes or so of lingering and pondering they all decided to buy a dried flower arrangement, of varying designs, and embroidered tablecloths for that special occasion, such as Christmas or a birthday. Jane chose some dressing table mats for her mother, maybe a little old-fashioned she thought. They were not used so much now, but Mother liked that sort of thing and they had a rose design and a pretty crocheted edging.

Jane was meeting Dave for lunch at a cafe they had already picked out, overlooking the market square. The other three went with her, and found him already sitting there enjoying an ice-cold lager. Jane joined him under the shade of the large green umbrella, and the others sat at a vacant table nearby.

They were glad to escape from the heat of the sun and to rest their aching feet.

After they had enjoyed the lunch of their choice – as usual the menu was vast and varied – it was time for Mavis to leave the others and find her way to the hospital. Shirley and Ellen went with her to locate a taxi at a rank not far away, leaving Jane and Dave to enjoy a refreshing lemon sorbet, then a cup of strong coffee to fortify them for the rest of their time in Freiburg. The city streets, quaint and charming as they were, felt claustrophobic in the midday heat.

'I've enjoyed it, but a half day here is long enough,' said Jane. 'We're not used to this heat, are we? It will be nice to get back to the hotel and rest for a while.'

Dave agreed. 'Yes, and it's party time tonight. I wonder what they've got in store for us?'

'Whatever it is, I'm sure I'll enjoy it,' said Jane contentedly.

Dave knew what he intended to do. Tonight he would ask Jane if she might consider planning a future with him.

Mavis found Arthur much improved. His colour was better; the pale grey pallor had gone and he was in good spirits. She told him about the pleasant morning she had spent in Freiburg.

'It's a lovely old town, Arthur. I'm so sorry you missed it. It was tiring, though, walking round in the sunshine. We kept trying to find patches of shade, so it might have proved a bit too much for you. Anyway, I'm pleased to see you looking so much better. Is there any news about when you can come home? Come out of here, I mean. We'll be able to travel back on the coach on Tuesday, won't we? Or would the journey be too much for you?'

'For goodness' sake, Mavis! We've got to get back somehow, haven't we?' A touch of the old irritable Arthur showed for a moment, then he grinned again. 'The alternative would be to fly, and you know I won't do that. They wouldn't let me anyway, not after I've had a heart attack, The doctor's coming to see me this afternoon while you're here, so he'll tell us when they're going to let me out.' He chuckled. 'Sounds as though I'm in jail, doesn't it? But I can't complain. They're treating me very well.'

And that, coming from Arthur, was praise indeed! Not even a remark like, 'Considering that they're Germans!'

Mavis had another surprise when a pretty young nurse came into the room and greeted Arthur as though she had known him for ages.

'Hello again, Mr Johnson.' She beamed at him. 'And this is your wife, yes?'

'Yes, this is Mavis, my good lady wife. Mavis, this is Ingrid. She's looking after me now.'

The two of them shook hands. 'I am very pleased to know you, Mrs Johnson,' said Ingrid. 'Your husband, he tell me about you. And I understand because, as I tell Arthur, my grandmother – my Oma, I call her – she is English. And so we have – what is it you say? – some things in common?'

'That's good,' replied Mavis. She was certainly a pretty girl. No wonder there was a gleam in Arthur's eye! 'Thank you for looking after him.'

'It is no problem. And tonight he will have a visitor. I already ring my Opa, Mr Johnson, and he say yes, he will be pleased to come and see you.'

Mavis was mystified. 'What's all this about?' she asked.

Arthur explained, a little apologetically, she thought. 'Ingrid's grandfather – her Opa, she calls him – he was in the war, like me. He was . . . er . . . his plane came down, in Yorkshire, so he was a prisoner, you see. He worked on a farm, and he met an English girl. Then he married her after the war; she's Ingrid's grandmother. And Ingrid thought . . . she wondered if I would like to meet him. So I said yes, I would.'

'Good for you, Arthur!' said Mavis. My goodness! she thought to herself. That was a turn up for the book. Arthur agreeing to meet a former enemy! She couldn't make any comment, though, with that nice young nurse being there.

'I hope you have an interesting time together,' she said, 'reminiscing about . . . everything. I'm sure you'll have a lot to talk about.'

'Yes, I'm sure will,' said Arthur, with a touch of irony, or had she only imagined that?

'So I won't come and see you this evening, then you can have a good chat with your visitor, just man to man.'

'Aye, I suppose so.' He nodded thoughtfully. She could tell he was none too sure about it.

'Anyway, there's a party on at the hotel tonight,' she told him. 'I was feeling guilty about being there without you, but now I won't feel so bad.'

'Yes, you go and enjoy it, love,' said Arthur. 'What sort of a party? I don't suppose it will be a wild abandoned affair, will it?'

'I doubt it.' She smiled. 'It's what they call an al fresco meal. You know, a barbecue sort of thing, eaten out of doors. Then there's an entertainment by a local group, singing and dancing and that sort of thing. It'll be a nice change.'

Ingrid didn't stay long. She took Arthur's pulse and temperature again before saying goodbye to Mavis.

'It is a pleasure to meet you, Mrs Johnson. Now, you look after Arthur when you get back to England. I am hoping he will be well, for a long long time.'

'I hope so, too,' said Mavis. 'Goodbye, my dear. Lovely to meet you.'

'I couldn't very well refuse, could I?' said Arthur, 'when she asked me if I'd like to meet this chap. What have I let myself in for, I wonder?'

'It will be fine, Arthur,' she told him. 'He married that English girl, didn't he? So he must have got to know quite a bit about life in our country. You'll be polite and friendly towards him, won't you, Arthur?'

'Of course I will! What d'you think I'm going to do? Start an argument as soon as we meet? I'll be as nice as pie, I promise you.' He chuckled. 'Who'd have thought it, though, eh? Me having a tête-à-tête with a German!'

The doctor who was in charge of Arthur came to talk to them soon after Ingrid had left. He was far more impersonal than the nurse; friendly to a point, but with an abrupt way of speaking.

'We are satisfied with your progress, Herr Johnson,' he said. His English bore scarcely a trace of an accent. 'Your condition is not so bad as we at first thought it to be. The heart attack was quite a mild one, made worse, I believe, because of your fear of being ill in a strange place. It is a warning, though. You must take care. You must not try to run before you walk.' He managed a brief smile.

'Thank you, doctor,' said Mavis. 'So. we'll be able to travel home with the others, will we?'

'Yes, of course. You may leave here in the morning, Herr Johnson. We will make arrangements for you to travel back to your hotel. Then you enjoy the rest of your stay here, in our lovely Black Forest. You behave quietly, though. You must not get too excited.'

He shook hands with Arthur, then with Mavis, giving a curt bow and a nod of his head. 'Goodbye, Frau Johnson. You look after your husband, yes?'

'Yes, of course I will, Doctor. Thank you very much for all you've done for him.'

She stayed for a little while longer, then took a taxi back to the hotel, feeling, for the first time since it happened that all would be well. It had been only two days since Arthur had been taken ill, but it had been the longest two days of her life. She knew they would not live for ever, but she would thank God every day now for the time they had left together.

Fifteen

Arthur was feeling a little apprehensive as he waited for his visitor that evening. He had combed what little hair he had and straightened his crumpled pyjamas. Fancy greeting a visitor in these old pyjamas! But at least they were his own, not the awful regulation nightwear from the hospital. Mavis had brought them in for him, with his shaving tackle and the book he was reading; a war story, but not about the last lot, but the exploits of Sharpe in the Napoleonic wars.

There was a knock at the door at just after six thirty, then a nurse entered – not Ingrid, she had gone off duty – accompanied by a tall distinguished-looking man.

'Here is your visitor, Herr Johnson,' she said. 'This is Herr Hoffman. I hope you have good time together.'

The man approached the bed, smiling and holding out his hand. 'Herr Johnson,' he began. 'I am delighted to meet you. Ingrid told me about you, and of course I said yes, I would be pleased to see you. So, how are you, my friend?'

'Not so bad, thanks,' replied Arthur. 'Much better actually. I've had a scare and it put the wind up me, I can tell you. But they say I'll be alright.' He smiled. 'I'll be here for another few years, please God! I'm pleased to meet you too, Herr . . . er . . . Herr Hoffman. Ingrid's told me about you. Sit yourself down then. There's a chair over there.'

Arthur was feeling more conscious than ever about his appearance now, compared with the spruce-looking gentleman who had come to see him. He was a tall upstanding man, with not the trace of a stoop. He had a good head of silver grey hair, and blue eyes that did not look the least bit faded behind rimless spectacles. A handsome chap with classic Germanic features. He was wearing a smart grey suit with a blue shirt and a striped tie, the picture of elegance.

Especially so compared with me! thought Arthur, clad in boldly striped 'old man's' pyjamas, and wearing glasses with heavy frames. He was used to them because he had had them for years, and he refused to change them for a more modern design. But the man seemed pleasant, and the first hurdle was over with.

His visitor pulled the chair closer to the bed and sat down. 'Now, you will allow me to use your first name, yes?' he said. 'I cannot go on calling you Herr Johnson. I believe my granddaughter said you are called Arthur?'

'Yes, that's right. And your name is . . .?'

'I am called Wolfgang,' he replied, with what sounded like a touch of pride.

'Same as the composer,' said Arthur. 'Yes, I like that name. I like Mozart as well.'

'Just as I do,' said his visitor. 'So, we already have something in common. Now, tell me, Arthur, where do you live, in England?'

'My wife and I live in Blackburn,' said Arthur. 'It's in Lancashire. That's just over the Pennine hills, the next county to Yorkshire. It's an ordinary little town, not what you'd call a beauty spot, but we live on the outskirts, and there's a nice view of the hills from the back windows. Ingrid said that you were . . . that you lived in Yorkshire. It's a lovely county, one of the best in England, I reckon, though happen I shouldn't say that, being a Lancashire lad, born and bred.'

'Yes, I agree. It is a most beautiful part of your country, although I haven't seen all of it. My wife and I, we have visited London, and many years ago we travelled to Scotland. And, of course, we visit Yorkshire again, several times.'

His English was perfect, but then it would be with his wife being from England. They had no doubt done their courting in her language, thought Arthur. She wouldn't have known any German until the two of them had met.

'Where were you when . . . where was the farm you worked at?' asked Arthur, trying to choose his words carefully. 'I believe you were at a farm in Yorkshire during the . . . er . . . the war?'

'Yes, so I was.' Wolfgang smiled. 'Do not be afraid to mention the war, Arthur. I tell you, I was glad when I knew it was all over for me, when I became a prisoner. I did not know how

I could carry on much longer with all the dreadful bombing raids. But the way I see it, the good Lord, he rescued me. I could not admit that to my fellow Germans, but I believe that many of them felt the same about the war. It was frightful, horrific.'

Arthur nodded. 'Yes . . . yes, so it was.' His visitor was shaking his head, gazing into space unseeingly. But he soon recovered.

'Yes, the farm. It was near a town called Settle. A very beautiful place, but lonely as well. Those hills, so wild and bare, they seem to close in on you. As I say, I was glad of an escape from the war. No more worry about the next time we go up in the air, what we had to do. But then I feel sad and depressed as well, missing my family at home here in Freiburg. They would not know, perhaps, what had happened to me. Then it all changed . . .' He smiled. 'Because I met Elsie.'

'Your wife? The girl you married?'

'Yes, of course. My dear Elsie. She came to work as land girl at the farm. She lived there, she and her friend, Paula, with the farmer and his wife, Mr and Mrs Strickland. They were very kind people. They treat us well, my friend Johann and I. But Paula, I think she did not like me very much. She did not approve, you understand, of Elsie and me being friendly.'

'Yes, I see. I suppose there might have been some bad feeling.' said Arthur. 'The war would be at its worst perhaps, then?'

'Yes, it was 1942. I joined the Luftwaffe, as so many young men did, at the start of the war. We felt we must, you understand? I expect it was the same for you. There was unrest in Germany. The older people felt it was not good after the first war, the treaty and everything. Then the new regime, it seemed at first as though it could be the answer to the problems. We were carried along with it all for a time. By . . . Herr Hitler.' He spoke the name scathingly. 'We did not know until afterwards, when it was too late. Such dreadful things; we did not believe they could happen. So many of us, we felt the same after the war when we heard about it. We felt guilty, ashamed that they were our people, that they were Germans who had done all that. And I think we had bad reputation for a long time.'

'Yes, there was bad feeling for a time,' said Arthur. 'And some of us, we saw too much. I was at Dachau, when it was all over . . . but I never talked about it, not to anyone.'

Arthur knew, though, that it had influenced his feelings about Germany and the German race as a whole. He had always known, deep down, although he would not admit it, that there were many decent peace-loving Germans who had not wanted to be a part of it all. Like this gentleman, Wolfgang. He was, indeed, a perfect gentleman. Arthur felt that he would be pleased to have him as a friend, if that were possible. He knew now that it was time to set aside his prejudices. He knew, also, that he had exaggerated them at times for effect, sometimes just to be awkward.

'I must admit I didn't want to come to Germany,' he said now. 'I still had bad memories, and I wouldn't let myself forget the past. But my wife persuaded me to come, and I'm very glad I did.' He looked into the eyes of his new acquaintance and smiled at him. 'And I'm very pleased to have met you, Wolfgang.'

'You are glad you came. In spite of being ill?'

'Yes, maybe the heart attack was a wake-up call. It's made me see things differently. Anyway, it might have happened at home. Who can tell? These things happen at our age, quite unexpectedly. We've got to make the most of our years now, haven't we? I'm damned sure I'm going to enjoy mine, what's left of 'em.'

'You must not do too much, though, Arthur. You must be careful for a while. My Ingrid says that is what you must do.'

'Yes, I know that. She's a grand lass, isn't she, your Ingrid?'

'Yes, and she is the image of my wife, Elsie, when she was young, of course. I sometimes feel I am seeing my young Elsie again. But my wife is still a very lovely lady. She is eighty now, but still beautiful, I believe.'

'And . . . what did her family think,' asked Arthur, 'about their daughter and you? Was there any opposition, any trouble about it?'

'I did not meet Elsie's family until the war ended,' said Wolfgang. 'Her home was in York, a good distance from the farm where we worked, and she did not go home very often. But she told them about me, when we fell in love. We did so, soon after we met. We both knew how we felt, but it was difficult at first to admit that it had happened. I was afraid to do anything, to say anything to upset Elsie. But in the end I took hold of my courage and I told her. I said that I loved her. And it was the same for her. She had been waiting for me to tell her.'

'So you were married in England, were you, after the war ended?'

'Yes, that is so. When I left the camp it was a little while after the end of the war. I went to live at the farm with Mr and Mrs Strickland. Elsie and Paula had gone home, and I had a small room in the attic. The farmer had asked me to stay and work for him, as a paid worker this time.' He smiled. 'I was happy there, I enjoyed working on the land. It was very new to me. Here, in Freiburg, my work was in an office, very boring job. But I knew now that this was what I wanted, to work outside.'

'So you changed your job, did you, when you came back here to Germany?' Arthur felt that he was asking a lot of questions, but it was an interesting story and it seemed as though Wolfgang wanted to tell it.

'Yes, that is correct. Elsie and I were married in York the year after the war. When her parents met me they decided I was not so bad.' He laughed. 'We lived in Settle. We had two rooms rented to us by a family. I was working at the farm, and Elsie, she had a little job in a shop.

'But then, it was in 1947, I knew I wanted to come back home. I was missing my family and they missed me, too; and they wanted to meet my new wife. And Elsie, she wished to please me, and so we came back here. I found work with a man who had a small farm, just crops and vegetables and a few chickens. Then, later, I had a small place of my own. And so we stayed and were very happy. We have two children, Karl and Eva, and four grandchildren – you have met Ingrid – and now there is another little one on the way, our first great-grandchild.' He smiled contentedly.

'But I talk too much, all about myself. Now, you tell me about you, Arthur. You were in the air force, too?'

'No, not me,' said Arthur. 'I was a soldier – in the army. Joined up when I was eighteen, didn't wait for them to call me up. Like you said, we felt we had to do it. I didn't see much action for a long time. It was after Dunkirk, you see, and all the troops were back in England, just waiting. So I went out with the D-Day lot, and managed to get through it all without any injuries, thank God! Then, well, I told you about Dachau . . . then eventually I was demobbed. My war was quite uneventful, I suppose, compared with a lot of chaps. You, for instance. It must have been hair-raising being part of a bomber crew. Did you pilot the plane?'

'Oh no, not at all!' Wolfgang shook his head. 'I was not an officer, you understand? I was just an ordinary flyer. But we had lost so many men – just as you did – and the rest of us, we took their place. I was a navigator . . . not a very good one, I fear.' He gave a wry smile. 'Our plane got lost, crossing the hills, and we were shot down. There were no casualties among the crew, but we were all taken as prisoners. A happy escape for me, as I told you. Now, that is enough about the war. You tell me, Arthur, about your work in England and your family.'

The nurse who had brought Wolfgang to the ward came back with cups of coffee and biscuits. They chatted together like old chums for another half hour or so. It was not an official visiting time, but an allowance had been made as a favour to Ingrid. Arthur found, when talking to his new friend, that his tendency to grumble and to look on the gloomy side was not apparent. In fact he found himself looking at things from a more positive point of view. It became clear that Wolfgang was an optimistic sort of man, one to whom the glass was always half full, rather than half empty, as it often was with Arthur. He made up his mind to watch himself in future, starting with a determination to enjoy what was left of his holiday in Germany.

At the end of the visit the two men exchanged addresses and promised to keep in touch. Arthur was not much of a letter writer – he left all that sort of thing to Mavis – but at least they would be able to send a Christmas card, if nothing else. And who could tell? He might even get round to penning a few lines himself.

The al fresco meal at the guest house was most enjoyable. They all sat around at small tables, helping themselves when they felt inclined to a variety of food, both hot and cold. There were sausages – bratwurst – and chicken legs; chunks of beef, pork and veal cooked on the barbecue; large platters of cold meats, and dishes of sauerkraut, potato salad and lettuce and tomatoes tossed in oil; and crusty brown bread and butter. And it you were still hungry following that, there was a choice of the inevitable Black Forest gateau, *apfelstrudel*, or ice-cream.

Despite it being an informal meal the ladies had dressed up to look their best. Particularly so for at least three of the ladies, who had purchased new clothes in Baden Baden. Shirley and Ellen wore their new trousers and tops, and Jane wore her floaty dress in shades of green and blue, and her green high-heeled sandals.

She knew that Dave kept glancing at her admiringly during the meal, and when their eyes met he smiled tenderly and knowingly at her. She felt that tonight would be a turning point in their friendship. She was sure now that she was falling in love with him.

Following the meal there was an entertainment by a local group of men and women all dressed in national costume. This took place in the lounge, where the tables and chairs had been pushed to the sides leaving a large empty space in the centre. There the troupe danced and sang and played musical instruments, putting on a show very similar to the one that some of them had seen in Rüdeshiem, on their first night in Germany. A lady played a huge piano accordion that was almost as big as herself and a man blew down an alpenhorn more than six feet in length. There were fiddlers, too, and harmonicas to accompany the thigh slapping knockabout dance by the men, then the gentler landler, danced by the men and the ladies.

There was enthusiastic applause as they finished their act, then departed with smiles and waves to the audience. After a short interval a local disc jockey played recorded music for the company to sing along and dance to, or just listen. It was not the ear-shattering sound such as was heard in the clubs and discos frequented by young people, but more gentle nostalgic tunes considered suitable for the clientele from the coach tour. Familiar songs, mainly from a bygone era, though not so very far distant. Hits by the Beatles, the Pet Shop Boys, Boyzone, Simon and Garfunkel, the Beach Boys . . . And the haunting songs of Nat King Cole, Matt Monro, and Andy Williams.

'Do you dance?' Dave asked Jane. They had been sitting quietly, hand in hand, contented in one another's company.

She laughed. 'Are you asking me?'

'I'm just wondering if you do . . . if you did? It's something we haven't talked about.'

'Well, if you're asking me, then I do,' she replied. 'At least I used to dance; I'm afraid I'm rather out of practice.'

'Well, that makes two of us,' he said. They took to the floor to the strains of 'Unforgettable', sung by the truly unforgettable Nat King Cole.

Dave held her close to him, her head resting on his shoulder. She was just a few inches shorter than he was. The foxtrot had never been her forte, but they glided rather than danced, their steps in time with one another. Jane was sure that their minds, also, were attuned to one another and that Dave felt just the same as she did.

There were several couples dancing, but not all of the company had taken to the floor. Mavis was sitting with Norah and the two new friends she had met that week, and Norah's younger sister, Christine, was dancing with Bill, the driver. Norah confided to Mavis that the two of them were getting very friendly.

'I worry about her, you know,' she said. 'My little sister, she's quite a lot younger than me, and I feel responsible for her. I thought it would just be a holiday fling, but they seem to be quite taken with one another. Anyway, time will tell. He seems a decent sort of fellow, though, from what I've seen of him.'

They certainly seemed very 'lovey-dovey' together, thought Mavis as she watched them dancing. How lovely it was to be young, she mused, although there were always problems to be encountered along the way. She hoped that all went well for them, and for Dave and Jane. The two of them were oblivious to everything but one another as they swayed in rhythm to the sentimental melody.

Shirley and Ellen were dancing, too. Not with one another but with two men from the coach tour. They were brothers, both widowed and in their sixties, holidaying together. They had been seen in company with the two ladies, not that there would be any romantic notions there, thought Mavis. But it was good to see Ellen's face light up at the unaccustomed attention.

The evening's festivities ended at eleven thirty. Dave and Jane danced again as Engelbert Humperdinck sang of the last waltz with you, the song that told of two lonely people together. Jane thought how lovely it would be, never to be lonely again. But was that just an impossible dream?

Dave's next words surprised her. 'Let's go to my room,' he said. 'I've got a bottle of wine, and we can have a nice quiet drink together to finish off the evening.'

Jane burst out laughing. She couldn't help it. 'Well, that's a good chat-up line if ever I heard one!'

Dave laughed too. 'Yes, I suppose it sounds like it, but I didn't mean it like that . . . I don't intend to seduce you,' he added in a whisper. 'Everyone's going now, and we can't very well stay down here. Besides, I want to talk to you, Jane.'

They went up the stairs to their rooms. 'Oh dear! There's only one glass,' he said. 'You'd better bring your own.'

Jane felt bemused as she went along the corridor to Dave's room with the glass provided by the hotel. She had already had quite enough to drink, but she knew that what Dave had said would be true. She knew he was not the sort of man to take liberties with her.

It was the first time she had been in anyone else's room. They were almost identical with regard to decor. Not elaborate, just homely and functional with pine furniture and folkweave curtains and cushions. Dave had already drawn the cork from the bottle of Riesling and he poured out a glass for each of them.

'It's been a good evening, hasn't it?' he began, as they perched together on the edge of the bed. There was nowhere else to sit apart from one semi-easy chair at the other side of the room, and she felt it might look rather stand-offish if she sat there.

'Cheers.' He raised his glass and she did the same. 'Here's to the rest of our wonderful holiday. It's been a very happy one, unexpectedly happy, thanks to you, Jane.'

He put his glass down on the bedside table and put an arm around her. She put her glass down as well, welcoming his embrace and his tender kiss. But he did not continue kissing her. He took hold of both her hands, looking earnestly into her eyes.

'Jane,' he began, 'I've only known you for a few days, but I feel that I already know you so well; that we both know each other really well . . . and I believe that I love you. No . . . I'm sure that I love you. And . . . dare I hope that you feel the same?'

'Yes . . . yes, I do,' she answered. 'But it's less than a week since we met. I've been trying to tell myself that it's just a holiday thing; that we've been thrown together and that it was inevitable that we should get friendly.'

'But if we'd disliked one another on sight we wouldn't have even tried to be friendly, would we?' said Dave. 'There are spare seats on the coach; one of us could have moved. But we didn't, because the attraction was there, right from the start.'

'Yes, so it was,' said Jane. 'And I do believe I'm falling in love with you.'

He kissed her again. 'It sounds corny to say that I've never felt like this before, but it's true, I haven't . . . well, not for ages. And I've been very cautious about showing my feelings to anyone. But now, I would like to think that we might have a future together, don't you, Jane?'

'Yes, I do,' she replied. 'I know that we're both single, as they say nowadays. I'm a widow, which is what they used to say, and so are you . . . a widower. But it isn't quite so simple, is it? There are other commitments.' She shook her head. 'What on earth would I do about Mother? She depends on me so much. And you have your farm to run, and we live so far apart.'

'Not so very far, love,' he said. 'A hundred miles or so. What's that? Yes, I know there are difficulties, but I'm sure we could carry on seeing one another. We both drive, it shouldn't be too impossible.'

He did not kiss her again, not just then. He picked up his glass of wine and she did the same. He knew that he was not being entirely truthful with her, in fact he was allowing her to believe something that was a lie. What was more, he had had the chance to tell her the truth, and he felt he couldn't do it, not after they had spent such a lovely evening together. Jane believed that his wife had died. He had said that he had lost his wife, and Jane had presumed that she was dead. But Judith was very much alive. She was in a relationship with another man, as she had been ever since she had left Dave, but she refused to consider a divorce because of her Catholic upbringing.

'Is something the matter?' asked Jane. 'You've gone very quiet.'

'No, not really,' he replied. 'I was just thinking about what you said, mainly about your mother. There must be some way round it all. She wouldn't be so heartless as to deny you a chance of happiness, would she?'

'I don't know. If she met you I feel sure she would like you. Let's just wait and see, shall we, Dave, and enjoy the rest of our holiday? We have to return to reality in a few days' time. This is an unreal situation in a way, isn't it? A carefree holiday, no worries, no decisions to make. Let's see how things go when we get back home. Of course I want to carry on seeing you. I shall do all that I can to make sure I do, so long as we both feel the same?'

'I will, my darling. I assure you, I will.' It was the first time he had used the endearment. He kissed her again and again. Their embraces became more passionate until they both realized it was time to call a halt.

Jane stood up rather abruptly. 'I must go, Dave.' She kissed him lightly on the cheek. 'Don't let's worry about it, not just yet. Goodnight, sleep well.'

'Goodnight, my dear, See you in the morning.'

He would tell her tomorrow, Dave decided. Tomorrow night when they had returned from the excursion. He didn't want to spoil what promised to be one of the best days of the tour. Maybe she would understand and not think it too much of an issue. There was a much more relaxed attitude now about couples living together out of wedlock. It was something Dave had thought he would never do; he was a trifle old-fashioned in that respect. He knew now, though, that his life had not been complete. He had been contented enough on his own, with his work and his family . . . and then he had met Jane. He did not want to miss out on the chance of being happy and fulfilled again.

Sixteen

There was a resounding cheer on Sunday from the company of the Galaxy tour, when Mike entered the dining room carrying Shirley's missing suitcase. They had all sympathized with her, understanding how they might feel if parted from their possessions. As it turned out she had managed quite well. She had come to realize that there were others with far worse problems and, on the lighter side, she had enjoyed a good spending spree and had persuaded Ellen to do the same.

The Sunday excursion was to Lake Constance, a large lake, almost an inland sea, which bordered on three countries, Germany, Austria and Switzerland. The distance from Freiburg was around a hundred miles, so they would need to make an early start.

Arthur was due to come out of hospital that morning and, to Mavis's delight, the doctor had said that he might be allowed to go on the excursion with the rest of the group, provided he took very great care. He would be facing a long journey home in a few days' time, so this would get him used to the coach travelling again.

Both the hospital staff and the coach drivers did all they could to help. He was taken back to the guest house in an ambulance, and Mike delayed the start of the journey for fifteen minutes to make sure he was comfortably settled in his seat.

'By heck! This is grand,' he said to his wife as the coach sped along the road. They were using mainly the Autobahn route as the journey was quite a long one. 'I'd never have believed that I'd be out and about again so soon. They've worked wonders at that hospital. I tell you, Mavis, I was scared to death when I came round and realized where I was. I thought I'd had it, really I did.'

'Well, thank the good Lord you're still here with us.' Mavis took hold of his hand and squeezed it gently. 'I was worried, too, that night when I left you in hospital. You seemed to be recovering, but I was scared that you might have a relapse. But it wasn't as bad as we feared, after all.'

'No, and I'm still here to tell the tale.' Arthur laughed quietly. 'It was quite an experience meeting that German fellow last night. He's a grand chap, Mavis, and he did me a world of good. I'm sorry you couldn't meet him an' all.'

'Yes, I'm sorry, too. You were able to swap stories then, about the war?'

'Aye, but we didn't dwell on it too much. He felt the same as I did, that it was horrific, just . . . dreadful.' He shook his head sorrowfully. 'He said he was relieved when he was taken prisoner, so that he could escape from what he was being forced to do. All that bombing and destruction . . . He didn't want to be a part of it at all, especially when he realized what was going on. They didn't know, Mavis, a lot of 'em, not till afterwards. They weren't to be blamed. It was just that Hitler and his cronies.'

'So you're changing your mind about the Germans, are you?' Mavis smiled at him understandingly.

'Aye, I suppose I am. I've had to, haven't I? The ones I've seen so far, they're great folk. A bit humourless, maybe; a bit prim and proper. Not Ingrid, though, she was a real lively young lass. She reminded me of our Melissa, she was so bright and cheerful. She made me feel tons better, same as Melissa always does. Well, like all our grandchildren do. We've a lot to be thankful for, haven't we, Mavis?'

'We certainly have,' she replied. Arthur sounded like a different person since his traumatic experience. She couldn't help but wonder if the old Arthur might surface again when they got back home. What did it matter, though? She still cared deeply for him, warts and all.

'Just relax now, Arthur,' she told him. 'Look at the scenery, or have a little doze. It'll be a long day, so just take it easy now.'

They had a coffee and comfort stop mid-morning, and arrived at their destination, the lakeside town of Constance – the same name as the lake – in time for lunch. It was a pleasant town with a new pedestrianized zone as well as the old town with narrow cobbled streets and alleyways, similar to other German towns they had already visited. From the harbour there was a magnificent view across the lake to the Swiss and Austrian mountains.

They stayed only a short time in the town, to have a stroll around or a quick bite to eat if they so wished. The main part of the tour was to the flower island of Mainau, situated in the German part of the lake and reached by a causeway from the town. They were to be there for three hours to see all the sights that the island had to offer. A short enough time, and they all agreed afterwards that they could have spent a whole day there and still not seen it all.

When they arrived at the island Mavis discovered to her relief – she had been rather worried – that wheelchairs were available and, what was more, there was no shortage of men who were willing to push Arthur around. It was finally decided that Trevor and Malcolm, the two brothers who had formed a casual friendship with Shirley and Ellen, were to take turns with the wheelchair. And so the six of them set off together to view the delights of the island.

They had already been told by Mike, in his commentary, that the island had been created by Frederick the First, the Grand Duke of Baden in 1853. He had been responsible for the planting of the arboretum and for the building of the Baroque summer palace.

Throughout their stay there the people from the coach tour kept encountering one another at the various places of interest: the gardens, hothouses and numerous cafes. The island was an enormous flower-filled park with enchanting vistas at every turn.

The little group of six stopped to take a rest in the Italian rose garden, a fairyland of pergolas, sculptures and fountains, containing, it was reputed, more than five hundred varieties of rose. Their fragrance scented the air, and the varied hues of the flowers, from purest white to lemon, gold, delicate pink, scarlet and deep purplish red, were a wondrous sight to see.

They strolled through the Mediterranean terraces, a haven for palm trees, colourful pot plants, and purple bougainvillea cascading from gigantic urns. At every turn there were rhododendron and azalea bushes, coming to the end of their flowering period. The hothouses were filled with exotic blooms too delicate to exist out of doors, and in one of the conservatories there was a myriad of butterflies flittering amongst the flowers.

At the end of the afternoon when they arrived back at the coach they could not stop enthusing about all that they had seen.

'We've had some wonderful tours this week,' said Dave, speaking for them all, 'but I think this one beats the lot. Thanks very much, Mike and Bill, for bringing us to this lovely place.'

Mike laughed. 'Don't thank us, thank Galaxy Travel. They arranged it all. We're glad you enjoyed it. By the way, it's the last trip you'll take with Bill and me, apart from the journey home, of course. Tomorrow we have to take a rest day – the company is very strict about that – so that we're in good shape to travel back to the UK. So it's a free day for you folks tomorrow to do as you wish. You could take a bus into Freiburg again, or have a saunter round the countryside. We'll tell you later on about the starting off time on Tuesday. Now, relax and enjoy the journey back. It's full speed ahead now, back to our hotel.'

Several of them felt dejected thinking about going back home in two days' time. Jane was one of them. It was all coming to an end. It had been so exciting, such a happy time, just like a dream, and all so unexpected. She thought about what Dave had said last night. Could she dare to hope that they might have a future together? She hadn't rung her mother for a few days. She was loath to burst the bubble of happiness that enclosed her, She decided it would be time enough to break the news to Mother – if she could ever find the courage to do so – when she saw her again.

Dave, also, was deep in thought. He knew that he would have to talk to Jane again, later that evening, and this time he would have to be absolutely truthful with her. He was in a quandary. He could not ask her outright to be his 'mistress', an outdated expression that he would not use, but it amounted to the same thing. But he had to make it clear to her that he wanted her to be more than a friend, although he was unable to promise her the security of marriage. Did it matter, though, nowadays? He was coming to the conclusion that living together – not straight away, of course, but sometime in the future – was the only solution. He was sure that he and Jane could be happy together. But how would she feel about it?

Dinner was a little later that evening to give everyone a chance to freshen up after the tiring day. After the meal Dave asked Jane if she felt like taking a stroll down to the village, if she was not too tired.

'We could have a drink at the beer garden, like we did the first evening,' he suggested. 'That is if you feel up to it?'

'Of course I do,' she replied. That had been a memorable evening, with the feeling of a developing romance. Dave had kissed her a few times on the way back to the hotel, and she had known that she was growing very fond of him. She was sure now that she would like to think – to hope – that they could have a future together. But was that all that it amounted to, just a forlorn hope?

They walked hand in hand down the country road that led to the village, and to the beer garden they had discovered the first evening. There were a few others from the coach party sitting in the garden area, including Bill and Christine. Jane and Dave said hello to them then found a secluded table at the other side. Not that they wanted to be unfriendly but they both knew that there were personal things that they wanted to talk about, and their time together was growing shorter, only two more days and they would be on their way home. It was clear, as well, that Bill and Christine were very contented on their own.

'White wine for you?' asked Dave when the waiter appeared.

'Yes, please . . . Well, a spritzer, I think,' she replied. It would last longer, and more than a couple of glasses of wine – which she had already drunk at dinner time – made her feel woozy. Dave ordered the drinks – lager for himself – then they sat quietly until they arrived.

When he had taken a good gulp of his lager Dave looked intently at Jane and took hold of her hand. 'Jane,' he began, 'I have to tell you something.'

She guessed by the serious tone of his voice that it was something of importance. She wondered for a brief moment if he was beginning to regret what he had said about them sharing a future together. Maybe she had not seemed enthusiastic enough about the prospect, putting obstacles in the way, chiefly the problem of her mother. She looked at him in silence, waiting for what would come next.

'I haven't been entirely honest with you,' he went on. 'You are under the impression that I am a widower, and I know that it is my fault. I have let you go on believing so, when I should have told you. The truth is . . . I'm so sorry, Jane . . . I still have a wife. Judith is very much alive.' She gave an involuntary gasp, and Dave leaned closer to her.

'I feel dreadful about this, my love, please believe me. It wouldn't be so bad if I could say we are divorced, but we're not.'

Jane shook her head in bewilderment. 'But . . . I don't understand. What are you saying, Dave? You are separated . . . living apart, aren't you?'

'Yes, of course we are. Judith left me four years ago to go and live with someone else, someone more exciting than I am who can give her the sort of life she wants to live – glitter and glamour, parties and exotic holidays. She's still with him – I've never met him – but according to my son, Peter, they're very happy together.'

'Then why are you not divorced? That's what you said, isn't it? Surely there are grounds for divorce?' Jane was stunned. This had come right out of the blue. She could scarcely take it in. She was so sure that he had said his wife had died. Now she remembered that what he had actually said was that he had lost his wife. So what else was she to think? That was what the words implied; that the woman was dead. And he had let her go on thinking so.

Dave sighed. He let go of her hand and took another good drink of his lager. 'Yes, there are grounds for divorce, ample grounds; anyway, divorce is so much easier now than it used to be. It is what I want and she knows it. The problem is . . . Judith is a Catholic. Not even a practising one any more. That's what makes me so mad. She hasn't attended Mass, or whatever, for years. But she insists that it's her conscience, what she was brought up to believe. They still don't accept divorce, and she's going along with their teaching. Her parents are still living, and I guess that has a lot to do with it. They are more Catholic than the Pope, as the saying goes. They never approved of her marrying me. We had to be married in a register office because there was no other way round it. I refused to be married in her church, nor she in mine. I admit I don't go to church all the time, but I'm a believer, Jane, and I would always say with pride that I am Church of England. So, I suppose our marriage got off to a shaky start with regard to that. And it was never really a satisfactory marriage, I soon realized that.'

'But if you were only married in a register office . . . Sorry, perhaps I shouldn't have said 'only'. It's still a marriage, isn't it? What I mean is, do Catholics – people like her parents – regard it as a proper marriage? Why haven't they objected to her living with this other man who she's not married to, if they are so strict about everything?'

Dave shook his head. 'I honestly don't know, Jane, my dear. I know it doesn't make sense, but she's sticking to it like grim death. I know that the top and bottom of it is that she's being damned awkward. She refuses to think about a divorce, and that's that. She's very happy living with this chap Roger – that's what he's called. Maybe he still has a wife, I don't know because I haven't asked.'

He was silent for several moments and so was Jane, trying to take in all that he had said. Eventually, after what seemed ages, she said quietly, 'I wish you had told me at first, Dave. Right at the start . . . you should have told me then.'

'I know – I know I should,' he almost shouted. 'But it doesn't alter how I feel about you. I love you, Jane. I know I do. As I said before, I would like to think we might have a future together. Not right away, of course, but sometime, maybe in the not too distant future.' He took hold of her hand again. 'Does it really make so much difference, my dear, that I'm not free to get married again?'

'I don't know, Dave,' she said, quietly. She was remembering something her mother had said when she spoke to her on the phone a few days ago. Something about a man in the home whose son was 'living in sin'. Those were Mother's exact words, and that was how she regarded it and always would as far as Jane could see. This fellow had been married twice, and was now living with another woman, and they might or might not get married. Some such tale, the subject of gossip in the home. Jane hadn't taken much notice, but it all came back to her now. Mother was so set in her ways. She would never understand.

'Maybe . . . maybe we might be able to go on seeing one another when we get back home,' she began. 'But as far as anything else is concerned, I just don't know. You say that we don't live all that far apart, and I suppose that is true. With the motorway and everything a hundred miles isn't the obstacle it used to be. But you must admit there would still be problems. Your farm for a start. You can't keep taking time off, can you, no matter how well your son can cope in your absence? And, of course, there is . . . my mother.'

Yes, your mother! thought Dave, but he did not give voice to his somewhat uncharitable thoughts. From what he could see, Jane's mother was always going to be the stumbling block if Jane continued to go on regarding her as such.

'Bring her over to meet me,' he said impulsively. 'You could easily get to Shropshire and back in a day, if you set off early. And she would enjoy a day out, wouldn't she? My daughter-in-law – well, she isn't yet, but she soon will be – Kathryn, she would cook a nice meal for us all. You don't need to say any more than that I am a friend you met on holiday, for a start, that is. Then we would just have to see how things worked out.'

Jane looked pensive and a little sad. Dave knew he had dropped a bombshell that had been a tremendous shock to her. He felt truly sorry that he had disappointed her, as he knew that he had.

'I'm really sorry, Jane,' he said again. 'I can't tell you how much I regret it now, not telling you about my wife. My ex-wife – that's all she is. But even if I had been widowed, as you assumed, there would still have been problems, wouldn't there? Exactly the same problems regarding where we live, and the question of your mother.'

'Let's not think about it any more now, Dave,' said Jane. 'Going over and over it only makes it seem more complicated. Let's forget it, shall we? Well, put it to one side, at any rate.'

He nodded. 'Very well then. As you say, we're not getting anywhere, just mulling it over. But we won't let it spoil the rest of our holiday, will we?'

'No, I hope not,' Jane replied.

'We still have tomorrow, a free day for us, before we set off for home on Tuesday. Let's try and make the most of it and not think about the problems. I know I've upset you, but you'll forgive me enough to spend the day with me, won't you?'

Jane smiled, a little ruefully. 'Of course I will. After all, we've only known one another for a week, haven't we? That's all it is. Tomorrow it will be exactly a week since we met.'

'And what a fantastic week it has been,' said Dave. 'Whatever happens, I know I shall look back on it as one of the happiest weeks of my life. And that is thanks to you, Jane. We've had a wonderful time together. And I do hope it is something we can build on, not just look back on as a memorable week.'

'Yes, I hope so, too,' she replied. But she knew, and Dave knew, too, that her words lacked conviction.

They did not talk very much on the way back to the hotel. They walked hand in hand, but they did not stop to kiss from time to time as they had done before. When they reached Jane's bedroom door he kissed her gently on the lips.

'Goodnight, Jane, my dear,' he said tenderly. 'See you in the morning.'

'Yes, see you, Dave,' she replied. She hurried inside quickly and closed the door.

She did not burst into tears. Her mother had always been a stiff upper lip sort of person, and a lot of it had rubbed off on Jane. She felt sad, though, unutterably sad that her dream – or maybe it had always been an impossible dream? – might be coming to an end.

Seventeen

'Checkmate!' cried Henry with obvious delight as he moved his last piece into the strategic place.

'You've done it again!' said Alice, sounding vexed, but smiling at the same time. 'I shall beat you one of these days, Henry Collins, just you see if I don't!'

'Well, you'll have to hurry up about it, won't you?' replied Henry. 'You've only a few days left, haven't you? When is your daughter coming to pick you up?'

'Oh, I think it will be Thursday morning. She gets back on Wednesday, but I expect it'll be late by the time she arrives home. Yes, Thursday. That gives me three days to get even with you.'

'You're doing very well,' said Henry, just a trifle patronizingly. 'You wouldn't want me to let you win now, would you?'

'Let me win? I should think not! I shall beat you fair and square or not at all. Now, how about a cup of tea before we call it a day?'

'Good idea. Let's go and join Jack and Flora.'

Henry led the way across the lounge to where his mate, Jack, was talking to Flora the woman with whom Alice had become friendly since coming to stay at Evergreen. The four of them were often to be seen together, chatting or watching TV, or playing a board game that required more than two people.

Alice, during the week she had been there, had been relearning how to play chess.

She and her husband, Joe, had used to play. It was Joe who had taught her to play and she had become proficient, though never as good as he had been. Since he died there had been no one for her to play with. Jane, for some reason – although she was very intelligent – had never taken to the game, although her father had tried to teach her. Anyway, Alice realized that the lass was tired when she had done a day's work, as well as the shopping and cooking. It was little wonder that Jane wanted to relax, watching the TV or reading a book, or, on rare occasions, going out with a friend.

Whilst she had been staying in the home Alice had been thinking about how much her daughter did to make her life so much easier. She found, to her surprise, that she was missing Jane very much and was looking forward to seeing her again. She appreciated now, more than ever, that the two of them, mother and daughter, had needed a break from one another. They had spent far too much time together, apart from the time when Jane was out at work, and Alice knew that that had been her own fault. Her daughter had tried to encourage her, many times, to join this or that.

She remembered Jane saying, 'There's a branch of the Townwomens' Guild not far from here, Mother. Why don't you go and join? It would be just up your street. Intelligent ladies that you could chat to, and I believe they do all sorts of interesting things.'

Or, 'There's an Over Sixties group at church, Mother. They meet every Tuesday for a social afternoon – a talk by a visiting speaker, and a cup of tea and a chat. Mrs Evans down the road goes there. I could ask her to come and pick you up in her car. I'm sure she wouldn't mind.'

But Alice had always had an excuse for why she wouldn't do this or that. How would she get there, with Jane working all the time? And she wasn't going to be beholden to people giving her a lift. Yes, she knew there were taxis, but she wasn't going to spend her money on taxi fares, they were far too expensive. Anyway, she didn't know any of the people, and she'd heard that they could be very 'cliquish' in these organizations. Yes, she knew some of the women at church, but they weren't really her cup of tea. From what she had seen of them they spent all their time gossiping about one another.

The truth was – and Alice could see it only too well now – that she just couldn't be bothered. She had got into a rut and hadn't wanted to make the effort to join anything or to make new friends. And so after a time Jane had stopped trying to persuade her to do anything. She remembered how she had taken a great deal of cajoling to even consider coming to stay at Evergreen.

But how glad she was, now, that she had agreed to Jane's suggestion. She had been determined, after she had finally given in and said yes, that she was not going to like it, but her resistance had been broken down, even on the first day. She sat at ease now, on the Sunday evening, enjoying a cup of tea with Flora, Henry and Jack, the three people she had come to know best whilst she had been staying there.

'Well now, did you manage to beat him this time, Alice?' asked Jack.

'Did I heck as like!' she replied. 'No, I'm beginning to realize that Henry is streets ahead of me. If I had more time I'd catch up with him, you mark my words. But I'll be going home in a few days' time.'

'We'll miss you, Alice,' said Flora.

'Aye, we will that!' echoed Jack.

'There's nothing to stop you coming back for a visit, is there?' said Henry. 'We could have a game of chess, you and me. You could swot up on your moves at home. I'd look forward to another session.'

'I've no one to play with at home,' said Alice, sounding regretful. 'Our Jane's never learnt to play. Besides, she's too busy. I'm glad I've got into it again, though. It's jolly good exercise for the brain cells, isn't it? I think mine were beginning to stagnate with lack of use.'

'You certainly seem a lot brighter than you were when you came here,' said Flora. 'I could tell you were here under sufferance, but we soon jollied you up a bit, didn't we? We made you realize it wasn't all that bad living here.'

'Yes, so you did,' replied Alice thoughtfully. 'I must admit I've changed my mind about old folks' homes, and I never thought I'd say that. But you can't really compare this one with the majority of homes, can you? My daughter told me it was more like a residential hotel, but I didn't believe her. I was determined not to like it, but she was right.'

'Aye; you don't like to admit you're wrong, do you, Alice?' said Henry with a chuckle.

'Less of your cheek, Henry Collins!' she retorted. 'I thought just the same about you when I first met you. He's a bloomin' awkward so and so, I thought. Then I realized that you're a lot like me, aren't you?'

'Well, it takes one to know one,' he replied.

'Yes—' Flora looked at Henry and then at Alice – 'you two make a good pair, you're two of a kind. Hard on the outside, but quite soft underneath, like those hard chocolates with a creamy centre.'

'Aye, maybe we are, but I'm not right keen on those soft centres meself. I like a nice chewy caramel, at least I did until my teeth started sticking to 'em. I know this about Alice and me; we haven't much time for folks who won't make an effort to help themselves.'

Rather like I was before I came to stay here, Alice thought, with a sharp twinge of guilty conscience. But Henry had not seen that side of her, and she was determined that she would never go back to the way she had been before.

'. . . and who won't have a go at summat new,' Henry went on. 'You're never too old to learn. Look at Alice now, how she's got the hang of chess again. She's nearly as good as me, and all it needs is a bit of perseverance.'

'Oh, shut up Henry, for goodness' sake!' said Jack. 'You and your flippin' chess! Just because Flora and me don't want to be bothered to learn. It doesn't mean that we're stupid.' He winked at Flora to show that he wasn't really as cross as he sounded.

'I never said you were. Don't be so damned touchy, Jack Perkins! But there's a few of 'em here who are content to sit around and let life pass them by. I'm going to make the most of it till I draw my last breath, and I reckon you will an' all, won't you, Jack?'

'Yes, I hope so. But I've never got the hang of that chess game. Draughts is exacting enough for me, and dominoes. Flora and me, we'll stick to our draughts, and leave the chess to you and Alice.'

They all retired to their rooms soon afterwards. Alice's room was on the ground floor, something she was pleased about. It was getting more and more difficult to climb the stairs, and she hated having to use a stick, even for walking. Jane had suggested that they should have a stair lift installed at home – which was very thoughtful of the lass, she supposed – but she had refused to even consider it.

'Do you want me to lose the use of my legs altogether?' she recalled saying, rather snappily. 'That's what it would come to if I got one of those contraptions. No, I'll get upstairs even if I have to crawl on all fours.' Which was what she had to do sometimes . . . And, there again, Jane had stopped making the suggestion.

Alice had also refused, so far, to have an operation on her knee. 'It would make a world of difference to you,' several people had told her. All about Mrs Whatsit who had had a knee replacement and she was a changed woman. You wouldn't believe the difference it has made to her. And so on and so on . . .

Her doctor had told her that her heart was strong, and that was the main issue, even though she was turned eighty. That had been a few years ago, but still she remained obdurate. So long as she could hobble about what was the point of putting herself through the trauma of an operation? And the more people tried to persuade her the more she dug her heels in. She was not going to be told what she must or must not do.

The truth was that Alice had an irrational aversion to hospitals. She had had the good fortune never to have been ill enough to stay in one. When she had given birth to her daughter she had insisted on staying at home. At that time there had been a lot of home births. Her husband had died, quite suddenly, at home. But she had seen both her parents go into hospital and die there. Her father had died when Alice was ten with a lung complaint, the legacy of a gas attack he had suffered in the trenches in the Great War. Her mother had died from cancer many years later.

She knew that conditions had improved drastically since those days, with the availability of new drugs and up-to-date procedures with anaesthetics. And hospitals were much more patient-friendly than they had used to be, or so she was told. But she remembered the stark clinical feel of the wards, and the rows of iron beds. The hospital staff, too: the stiff and starchy matron, the sisters and nurses, all immaculately dressed without a hair or a button out of place. Like prison warders, she had thought, remembering one particularly brusque sister with whom she had had words regarding her mother's condition.

She knew they were much more relaxed nowadays with regard to dress and their relations with patients and visitors, much more friendly and approachable. Possibly too familiar, though. She did object to being called Alice by some chit of a girl young enough to be her granddaughter . . . if she had one. That was how doctors' receptionists addressed you now, instead of affording you the courtesy of your proper title.

'So what exactly do you want, Mother?' Jane had asked her, not long ago, when she had been telling her about the casual attitude of the dental nurse, her use of Christian names and the way she was dressed, in what looked like a pink romper suit. And the dentist as well, Alice had complained about. He was dressed in a pale blue tunic and trousers, as though he was about to break into a song and dance act.

'You object to being called Alice,' Jane had said, 'but she's only being friendly and it's what they do today. It doesn't bother me, it makes me feel younger. But you say that the old-time nurses were unfriendly. There's no pleasing you sometimes, is there, Mother?'

But Jane had been laughing, so Alice had been forced to admit that she was perhaps being a mite unreasonable. 'Yes, I'm a contrary devil, aren't I?' she had agreed. 'Nothing's ever right, but things have changed so much, Jane, and not often for the best.'

'Hospital treatment has changed,' Jane had told her. 'That's why I think you should have that operation while you can. You can't afford to wait much longer, timewise, I mean. Or you could even afford to have it done privately.' But Alice had refused to budge. Now, as she looked around her room at Evergreen she realized she had been stubborn and pig-headed about a lot of things. This was a pleasant room and it was beginning to feel almost like home. The owners had certainly done all they could to give an individual feel to each room. She had been in Flora's room, and hers was similar in many ways, but with a different style and colour scheme.

Alice's room looked out on to a pleasant garden at the back of the house. The curtains at the double-glazed windows were a Laura Ashley design, patterned with spring flowers in shades of green and yellow, and there was a matching duvet cover on the bed. It was a fair-sized room with a green carpet, a wardrobe and dressing table in light wood, and a small television set on a corner cupboard. There was a comfortable chair with plump yellow cushions and an upright chair as well, and two framed prints on the wall of paintings by Monet, floral scenes to match the decor.

Opening off the room was a cubicle containing the toilet, washbasin and a low bath with grab handles and a handheld shower. Alice was glad about the bath. She could still get in and out of a bath, provided it was low enough, and she much preferred that to a shower.

Flora's room had more of an autumnal feel, although it was equally attractive with curtains of a William Morris design in brown and orange, a rust-coloured carpet and prints of paintings by Constable.

Alice decided to make herself a mug of hot chocolate to drink in bed. Another bonus was the provision of a kettle and a beaker, also tea bags, sachets of coffee and drinking chocolate and packets of biscuits, just the same as you would get in a hotel. Alice had been very surprised to find this facility here, in what she had originally thought of as a home for old people. She had found out, however, that a kettle was only provided for those guests who were capable of using it without any chance of an accident. There were several who were incapable, but, by and large, Evergreen's guests were still quite active and mobile.

Alice undressed and had a wash, then settled herself in bed with the mug of chocolate on her bedside table. There was a reading lamp provided, too, also an alarm bell to ring if assistance was needed during the night. She was contented, much more so than she had imagined she could ever be, away from her home in a place full of strangers. But that was one of the best things about her stay there, the people were not strangers any more. She could even class some of them as friends.

She opened her book, intending to have a good read before

she went to sleep, as she did every night at home. It was the latest Ruth Rendell book, one of her murder mysteries involving Inspector Wexford. She loved watching them on TV as well; George Baker personified him so brilliantly. She had also brought a Barbara Vine book – Ruth Rendell's alter-ego – usually more creepy and psychological, and another mystery by P.D. James.

She had thought that she would spend a good deal of her time reading, as she did at home. She did little else at home, reading avidly, or watching the television. Her TV viewing habits had changed since she had been living with Jane. At one time she would have scorned the 'soaps', but now she was a great fan of *Coronation Street* and *Emmerdale*. She enjoyed *Midsomer Murders* too, and *Foyle's War*. That was possibly her favourite of all; a contradiction, really, as she had often said she had seen enough of the war to last her a lifetime. But this was more about the Home Front, not the war that had been raging in Europe, and the characters were so convincing.

She had become engrossed in this make-believe world but, when all was said and done, it was not real life and, however well it was portrayed, it was just a form of escapism. The TV programmes and the books she enjoyed had become a substitute for her lack of friends and human companionship. She hardly ever conversed with anyone, apart from Jane. She spoke briefly to people at church and to shop assistants, to her doctor – on rare occasions, to the milkman, maybe, or the postman. Her life had become sterile and empty, but she hadn't realized it until she had spent a few days at Evergreen.

She read a page or two of her book – she was only halfway through it although she had been here for a week – but she found that her mind was wandering . . . That had been a jolly good game of chess tonight, with Henry. She knew, though, that however much she said it, she was unlikely to beat him. Henry was a 'whizz' at the game. That seemed to be the term they used nowadays.

He was very good company, too, and she enjoyed talking to him. She had made up her mind at first, in her usual forthright way, that this was a man she was going to dislike. He was so argumentative, always so sure that he was right. Then she had come to see that he was very much like herself. And the twinkle in his eyes when he was arguing that black was white, showed that he didn't mean the half of it.

To her surprise she found that he kept coming to talk to her, actually seeking her out as though he enjoyed her company, and they didn't always argue. Then he had asked her if she played chess – there was no one in the home who could give him a decent game – and this had become a shared interest for them.

She found herself smiling as she thought about Henry. Never since she lost Joe had she found anyone – let alone a man – with whom she was so compatible. But then she hadn't wanted to meet anyone; she had missed Joe so much and knew there would never be anyone else to compare with him. Pull yourself together, Alice! she told herself sternly now. Having silly thoughts about a man, at your age! She wasn't falling for him. Of course not, the very idea was ridiculous! All the same it was very encouraging to feel that someone, especially a man, should want to be with her.

She had learned, during their many conversations that week, that Henry Collins had been a joiner by trade. He had retired, of course, many years ago.

'I left school when I was fifteen,' he told her, 'I had to because my parents needed me to go out to work and earn some money. There were four of us; me and my brother and two sisters, and I was the eldest. It was just after the war started, 1940, and my dad had been injured. He'd lost a leg early on in the war, so he was never able to work again. Anyway, I was lucky enough to get apprenticed to a good trade, and I've done all right; had my own business in the end, and my eldest son took it over when I retired.'

Alice knew that although he had left school at an early age he had a keen brain and had done what he could to further his education.

'I didn't have the chances like you had, Alice,' he had said. 'No sixth form and college and all that for me, but I was determined to do what I could to make up for it.'

He had attended night school to obtain the qualifications for his carpentry and, years later, he had studied French and learnt to speak the language quite fluently as he and his wife had used to travel abroad each year.

Henry was five years younger than Alice. He had just celebrated his eightieth birthday, but didn't look anything like his age. His hair was grey, of course, a silvery grey and he had not lost any of it. He was tall and upstanding, with no sign of a stoop, and he walked without the aid of a stick, something that Alice found very galling when compared with herself. This, above everything else, made her feel her age.

'You've no sign of arthritis then, Henry?' she had asked him. 'You're lucky if you haven't.'

'At my age, you mean? No, that's something I seem to have escaped, thank goodness. I can walk nearly as well now as I could when I was thirty. Not that I was ever a great walker, fell walking and all that. But I used to cycle, and I played a fair game of cricket, and bowls as well. I still have a game of bowls now and again. Jack goes with me sometimes to the green down the road, and there are one or two fellows there who play with us.'

Alice had been surprised at the number of residents at the home who still got out and about to follow their various interests. Flora had told her about her own activities, and there were others of them who were just as active. There were some, though, who preferred to stay put and do very little. They were the ones who were more difficult to get to know.

'The least you do, the least you want to do,' Flora had remarked. It was true that the least active folk among them tended to become insular and preoccupied with themselves and their problems and ailments.

'Thank God there's nowt very much wrong with me,' Henry had said. 'A bit of chest trouble; I get bronchitis in the winter and I have to keep an eye on my blood pressure. Apart from that I'm as fit as a fiddle.'

'Then may I ask, what are you doing here?' Alice had enquired in her usual outspoken way, 'Why did you decide to come and live with a lot of old folk?'

'Age is an attitude of mind, Alice,' he replied. 'You are just as old as you want to be. You can be young at heart even at our age if you take an interest in what's going on around you.

I know I'm a bit crotchety and I like to argue, but I've always been like that. I don't know how my wife put up with me. She was a very patient lady, one in a million, my Esther.'

Not very much like me then! thought Alice to herself. And it had struck home to her what Henry had said about age being an attitude of mind. She was realizing that she had allowed herself to become old in her mind – set in her ways – even though she still prided herself on looking younger than she was.

'She looked after me too well,' Henry went on, and I missed her so much when I lost her. Not because of what she did for me, being a good housewife an' all that, but the house seemed so empty without Esther. I didn't know how I would ever stand being there on my own. I stuck it for about eighteen months, then I found this place and thought I'd give it a try, and I've never looked back.'

'Wasn't it a big wrench, though, leaving your home – all your possessions and everything?' Alice asked.

'In a way I suppose it was. It felt strange at first, but I reckon that sort of thing might be worse for a woman than a man. It was Esther who made the house into a home; she was the one who was interested in furniture and colour schemes and what-have-you. She was a real homemaker, and it was never the same after she'd gone. And apart from all that I was never much good in the kitchen.' He laughed. 'I could make a cup of tea and boil an egg – although they're damned tricky things to get right – and put bread into the toaster. Apart from that I was pretty useless.'

'So what did you do when you were left on your own?' she asked.

'Oh, I managed the best way I could. Meals for one from Marks and Spencer or Sainsbury's that I could put in the microwave, or I went to the local chippy. My son asked me round for a meal now and again, him and his wife . . . I told you he's been married twice, didn't I? The last one was a rotten cook, though; happen that was part of the problem, I don't know.

'But I could never have gone to live with Barry – he's too much like me – not that he's ever suggested it. It doesn't always work out, does it, living with a son or daughter?'

Alice had learnt that Henry's daughter lived in the south of England, and he had another son who had emigrated to New Zealand, so he was pretty much on his own.

'No, perhaps not,' Alice had replied. 'It isn't ideal living with Jane, but I knew it was the best thing to do at the time. And I must admit she's made me feel that it's my home just as much as hers. I took a lot of my own belongings with me. I suppose she might miss me if I wasn't there . . . I don't mean if I died – if I was to leave.'

'Why?' asked Henry. 'Are you thinking of coming and living here permanently?'

'No,' she answered decidedly. 'No, of course I'm not . . .'

Eighteen

The guests at Gasthaus Grunder awoke on the Monday morning – their last day in Germany – to grey skies and lowering clouds. There was no sign of the sun that had blessed them all week, and it was already starting to rain.

Jane opened the shutters, then felt her heart plummet as she looked at the dismal scene. She was already feeling downcast following the revelations from Dave the previous evening. They had not fallen out about his disclosures, but she felt very let down and disappointed in Dave, whom she had thought of as such an honest and straightforward man. But they had agreed that they would spend their last day – that was the last day apart from the journey home – together, and try not to think too much about what the future might hold for them.

She made a cup of tea, which always brought her round and made her feel more able to face the day ahead. She was like her mother in that respect. Alice said she only felt half alive before she had drunk her first cup of tea.

Jane found herself thinking almost fondly about her mother now. It would be good to see her again, although it had been great to have these ten days away from her. She would ring her later today and see how she was faring at Evergreen, and assure her that she would pick her up on Thursday to take her home. She could imagine her mother saying, 'About time too!' or some such remark, although Jane had a sneaking feeling that she might have enjoyed her stay at the home rather more than she had let on.

The two of them would then have to settle down again to their life together. Perhaps it had been just an impossible dream to imagine that it could be otherwise. How could she go off and live her own life when her mother was so dependent on her? Dave still seemed convinced that there was a way round it, but Jane was trying to become reconciled to the fact that this last week had been a lovely idyll, a memory

– lots of memories – to look back on with pleasure and nostalgia when she was back in her normal routine.

She washed and dressed, putting on a cardigan because the day felt chilly, something she had not needed to do since the start of the holiday. Dave was already seated at the breakfast table, and he greeted her cheerily, ready to carry on as though everything was hunky-dory.

'It's a miserable sort of day,' she commented, but Dave was determined to be cheerful. 'It'll probably clear up later,' he said. 'We can't let it spoil our last day here. We've done very well so far, and a drop of rain won't hurt us. It isn't as if we're not used to it back home.'

They helped themselves to cereal and fruit at the breakfast bar. Then Mavis and Arthur arrived, both of them looking happy to be together again. In reply to Jane's question he said that he was feeling fine, and was glad to know that his condition was not as bad as he had feared. He was looking forward to being home again, when they had got through the long journey back.

Shirley and Ellen were the last to arrive at the table. 'Our last breakfast together,' said Ellen. 'It's rather sad, isn't it?'

'It isn't our last breakfast,' Shirley told her. 'We'll be here tomorrow morning, then we'll have a breakfast in Calais on Wednesday before we cross the Channel.'

'Yes, I know that,' said Ellen, 'but I mean it's the last real day of our holiday. We'll be travelling for the next two days, and we'll be having our breakfast at some unearthly time tomorrow morning. What time did Mike say we were setting off?'

'Eight o'clock,' said Shirley. 'Cases packed and ready to load by seven. Yes, I agree it's damned early, but there's a heck of a distance to cover from here to Calais.'

They were doing the return trip to France in one day instead of the two more leisurely days they had taken on the outward journey.

'So, what are we all going to do on our last day?' Shirley asked the others. 'Have you anything planned?'

Jane and Dave looked at one another uncertainly. It was Dave who answered.

'Take a bus into Freiburg, I should think; that's the nearest place. I know we've already been there, but there's a lot to see.'

'And shops to go into if it keeps raining,' said Jane.

'Oh, it'll stop, you'll see,' answered Dave, a shade impatiently. 'We've got to look on the bright side of life, like it says in that song.'

'My mother used to say, "Rain before seven, fine before eleven,"' said Arthur. He turned to look out of the window. 'It's still pouring down, but I think it might be getting a bit lighter.'

Mavis turned to look out as well. 'Is there a little patch of blue?' she said. 'No . . . I can't see one, but it might clear up. My mother used to say that if there's enough blue in the sky to make a sailor a pair of trousers it will be a fine day.'

Arthur laughed out loud. 'It looks as though your sailor will be without his pants at the moment, love. But never mind, eh? I don't mind if we have to spend the day here. We can get some lunch here at the hotel.'

'Yes, I think Arthur and I will have a quiet day here,' agreed Mavis. 'We're just relieved that everything has turned out so well for Arthur. What about you two?' She was speaking to Ellen and Shirley. 'How are you going to spend your last day here?'

Shirley grinned mischievously. 'Well now, Ellen and I have got a date, haven't we, Ellen?' she said, rather to her friend's discomfiture.

Ellen blushed and looked warily at Shirley. 'I wouldn't say that we could call it a date. We're not exactly teenagers, are we?'

'It doesn't matter how young or how old we are,' Shirley replied. 'Don't be such a spoilsport, Ellen. What would you call it then, if it's not a date?' She laughed as she turned to explain to the others. 'We sat with Trevor and Malcolm in the bar last night – you know, those two brothers. Yes, of course you know, how silly of me. They helped to push Arthur along in the wheelchair, didn't they? Well, they've asked Ellen and me to have lunch with them today. We'll probably go into Freiburg. I expect most of us will end up there. It's no big deal, but Ellen's getting all of a fluster about it.'

'Well, isn't that lovely?' said Jane. 'I hope you enjoy it. They seem to be very nice friendly sort of men, from what I've seen of them.'

Shirley started talking to Mavis who was sitting next to her, so Jane spoke in a quiet voice to Ellen. 'You look very attractive in your new top and trousers,' she said, 'and it's great for you to have a change of company. You don't need to get all worked up about it. I'm sure you'll have a lovely time.'

'It's ages since I went out with a man,' Ellen whispered. 'Well it's not really 'going out' is it, because there are four of us? Not a proper date, like Shirley was saying, but I know she was just teasing me. I've not had a lot to do with men, you see, except for those I work with, and they're married, of course, just colleagues. I had a boyfriend once,' she added in a confidential tone, 'when I was about twenty. My parents were very strict, you see, so I hadn't been out with many young men. But I really liked this one and we were getting quite fond of one another, but my parents disapproved of him because he liked to go for a drink, and they were afraid he would encourage me to do the same. So, it just fizzled out. There was never anyone else after that. And then, of course, I looked after my parents when they became ill.

'I'm not complaining, though.' Ellen smiled so brightly that Jane felt sure she meant it. 'I've enjoyed my job at the bank, and I have some good friends, as well as Shirley. And this week – it's been just wonderful. I do hope we'll all be able to keep in touch, Jane.'

'I'm sure we will,' replied Jane. 'We'll exchange addresses before we say goodbye.'

She was sure that these words had been said many times before by people who met on holidays such as this one. Maybe some kept up the friendships – though possibly by email or phone these days, rather than the conventional letter – whilst others lapsed apart from the odd Christmas card. For her part, Jane felt that she would like to keep in touch with Ellen. She experienced a kinship with her, knowing that Ellen, like Jane herself, was somewhat diffident when it came to friendships with the opposite sex. Ellen had been discouraged, even prevented, it seemed, from forming any meaningful relationships, until now she assumed it was too late.

Jane could not complain about her parents in that respect. She had never had the close bond with her mother that she could have wished for, but neither of them had ever objected to her having boyfriends. There had been one or two, but no one of any importance until she had met Tom. She understood how Ellen must feel now, nervous and unsure about getting friendly with a man, as she had felt after Tom died. Jane did not know, in fact, whether the four of them had formed themselves into two couples. Probably not, at least not so far. But it might work out that way, she thought to herself; foursomes usually did. Maybe it would just be a holiday companionship, not leading to anything afterwards. But however it turned out, Jane hoped that Ellen would forget her fears and have a really enjoyable time.

As for herself, she had soon overcome her shyness on meeting Dave. It had seemed that their friendship might be going somewhere, but now the future looked more unsure than ever.

The two drivers had breakfast together rather later than usual. As a rule they liked to dine before the guests appeared. They were glad of a complete day of rest, which was what the management insisted on before they embarked on the long journey home. They were not allowed to drive at all on this rest day. On the UK holidays the drivers were permitted to do an extra tour, usually a half day, and this was regarded as a bonus for the driver; he was allowed to keep the fare money for himself, less the amount used for the fuel. This little tour on the last day rounded off the holiday nicely, but on the Continental tours the clients were left to their own devices.

'So, what do you have planned for today?' Mike asked his co-driver. 'Are you seeing the lovely Christine?'

'As a matter of fact, I am,' said Bill. 'You don't mind, do you?'

They had sometimes spent the last day together, mooching around doing not very much at all, glad of the time to be on their own without the responsibility of a coachload of passengers.

'Why should I mind?' said Mike. 'I'm pleased it's going well for you, old chum. No further trouble from Olga?'

'No, thank goodness! I suppose I was rather a heel, dumping her like that, but I thought it was a mutual decision. Anyway, she seems to have got over it and we're speaking to one another again. It would be better, though, if I didn't have to do this tour any more. I would miss it, but I've almost made up my mind to ask about being transferred to the UK tours.'

'You and me both, then,' said Mike. 'I shall ring Sally today and see how things are going with Tracey. She was in a real tizzy the last time I spoke to her, and I know it's time I thought about being nearer home. Like you, I would miss my trips over here, but there'll be plenty of lads waiting to step into our shoes, you can be sure. Are you serious, Bill, about giving this up? Are you and Christine . . . well, is it going to carry on after you get home?'

'I'm hoping so,' said Bill. 'Fingers crossed and all that. It's not gone very far yet, if you know what I mean. Anyway, she's not the sort of girl to rush into anything like that. That's what I like about her. I don't think she trusted me at first, especially when she found out about Olga. But we've been getting on fine these last few days. I'll have to be careful not to blow it, though. I've planned something special for today.'

'Have you, indeed! What have you got in mind? The weather's not too good at the moment.'

'No, but I'm hoping it will clear up because I thought we'd have a run out to Schneider's Vineyard. We can do the wine-tasting bit and have lunch there. It's much nicer to dine outside, but it's comfortable inside if it's still raining.'

'How are you going to get there? Will you borrow Herr Grunder's car?'

'No, it would be a cheek to ask and he's been very good to us. Anyway, we're not supposed to drive at all, are we? I thought we'd take a taxi; it's not all that far.'

'My goodness, you're going mad, aren't you? You must think she's worth it.'

'It's only once in a while. Anyway, I've saved up a fair bit this year, and the crowd this week should be good for a few extra quid, don't you think?'

'I try not to be so mercenary,' said Mike with a grin. But he knew what Bill meant. The drivers were not highly paid, but the tips they received at the end of the holidays – and most of the clients were pretty generous – made quite a difference to their wages.

'We may not do so well back in the UK,' Mike added, 'but there may be advantages. It's swings and roundabouts, I suppose . . . I hope you have a good day. What time are you going?'

'I said I'd meet Christine in the foyer at half past ten. So I'll see you later, Mike.' Bill stood up, ready to make a move. 'Wish me luck, won't you?'

'Oh, I do, as much luck as you deserve!'

'And how much is that? Not a lot, eh?'

'All the luck in the world,' said Mike. 'Yes, I mean it. I hope all goes well for you.'

The name 'Black Forest' brought to mind a region of mountains and dense forests. There were, however, gentler hills where small farms and vineyards were to be found in the valleys. They were mainly family concerns, the vineyards producing comparatively small quantities of wine, red and white, from sweet to dry, which was sold mainly in their own region. Such a vineyard was the one owned by Rudolph Schneider and his wife, Eva, a few miles outside Freiburg.

'We used to visit it on our tour,' Bill told Christine on their way there in the taxi, 'then the itinerary was changed. There isn't enough time in a week to see all the places of interest, but it may well be included again sometime in the future. It's a shame to miss it, though, and I know Herr Schneider will be pleased to see us. I haven't told anyone else about it,' he added with a wink. 'It's just a secret for you and me. We're not likely to meet anyone from the coach there, and that suits me just fine.'

'They're a good crowd, though, aren't they?' asked Christine. 'No one causing any trouble. I'm sure you must have lots of problems sometimes.'

'No, we can't grumble this time. It's all gone smoothly, apart from Mr Johnson's heart attack and the missing suitcase. They're a good crowd as you say, but the best thing is that I've met you.' He turned to smile at her and took hold of her hand.

It took only twenty minutes or so to drive to the vineyard. A rather faded sign at the entrance held the name of the proprietor and the opening times, surrounded by a border of grapes and leaves; then a short drive led up to a long low white building which Bill said was the restaurant.

'I believe they do very well in the evenings,' said Bill. 'The locals dine there, and Eva is a splendid cook, with a very good team of assistants, of course. But if it's fine it's nicer to dine outside, in the daytime, I'm still hoping we might be able to do that.'

The taxi driver drove round to the back and pulled up in the courtyard. Christine noticed a coach parked there, and the sign on it indicated that it was from Lille in France. Bill paid the fare and explained in halting German interspersed with English – that the man seemed to understand – that he would phone him when they were ready to go back.

The proprietor must have been expecting them because he appeared at that moment, a tall thin man with greying hair and a goatee beard, and dark piercing eyes that lit up with an expression of delight at seeing them. He greeted Bill like a long-lost friend.

'Ah, Bill, it is so good or see you again. It has been too long. And your friend . . .?'

'Yes, this is Christine. She's on the tour and I wanted her to see your place.'

'That is very good. We have a party here just now. They are tasting the wines, if you would like to join them?'

Christine looked around curiously. At the rear of the restaurant there was a paved terrace with wooden tables and benches, with flowering plants and small bushes in terracotta pots; a rustic setting where it would be nice to dine if the rain stopped. It was still drizzling, and she was wearing her anorak, the first time she had needed it during the holiday. A veranda stretched over the area though, so it might be possible to sit there later.

Despite the weather it was an idyllic setting. Beyond the huddle of buildings, which included the red-roofed bungalow where she guessed the family lived, a gentle slope rose upwards where the rows of vines were growing, and in the distance a backdrop of wooded hills. The scene was far different from the steep slopes they had seen along the Rhine valley, mile upon mile of vineyards reaching down to the river.

That was the chief wine producing area of the country where vast quantities of somewhat less expensive wines were produced, such as those sold in supermarkets all over the UK. Connoisseurs were inclined to disregard these products as being inferior, only produced to suit the tastes of a largely undiscerning market.

In the Black Forest region the wine was produced on a much smaller scale catering mainly for the local population and not sold abroad in large quantities. It did, however, find its way across the channel in the bags and boxes of tourists who had been on a wine-tasting trip.

'Come along with me, if you please.' Herr Schneider led them into a building where a group of people were sitting at tables with a row of tiny glasses in front of them. Christine assumed that these were the French visitors from the town of Lille. The proprietor spoke to them in French, and they smiled and nodded at the newcomers, inviting them to sit down and join them.

The young man assisting with the distribution of the wine was a younger edition of Herr Schneider. Christine guessed, correctly, that it was his son, Sebastian. The French contingent had already sampled a few of the wines, but Bill's and Christine's glasses were soon filled so that they could catch up.

'It's a good job you're not driving,' she whispered, after drinking the contents of three glasses, albeit minute ones. 'This stuff's pretty potent. Not like your common or garden Liebfrau, is it?'

'I shall be careful, don't you worry,' said Bill. 'I'll have an odd drink at lunchtime, then keep off the booze tonight so that I'll be fit and ready for the journey in the morning.'

Sebastian walked around the tables filling each of the glasses in turn, whilst his father told the visitors, first in French and then in English, about the wine that they were tasting. There were various kinds of whites and reds, ranging from dry to very sweet, with names that Christine had never heard of before. There was a particularly sweet red wine, which seemed to be a contradiction because reds were usually dry, but this was a wine that was favoured by the local populace and not widely sold abroad. There were bottles of this, however, and of all the other wines, for sale in the shop.

As was only to be expected, at the end of the session they were led into the adjoining shop where they were left to browse among the row of laden shelves. There were wines in abundance, of course; they were by no means cheap, but, according to Rudolph Schneider, you were paying for the quality, that extra something that was not to be found in the mass-produced wines.

There was a vast array of eatables and souvenirs as well as the wine. Chutneys and jams; honey and marmalade; packets of biscuits, fudges and chocolates; carved wooden animals, teddy bears, dolls and trinkets, such as they had seen in the shop with the large cuckoo clock, but on a smaller scale.

Christine had already shopped that week at every place they had visited, so there was nothing else she wanted to buy here apart from the wine. She felt obliged to buy a couple of bottles – it seemed that most of the visitors felt the same judging by the items in their baskets – but she wanted to do so, as well, as a souvenir of her holiday. She chose a medium white, similar to a Liebfrau but rather more mellow and fruity, although she was by no means a connoisseur, and a bottle of the rich red which had almost the consistency of a liqueur.

Bill didn't purchase anything, but then she didn't expect him to. He must have been there many times before. Christine waited in a queue to pay for her purchases and when they left the shop the rain had stopped. A break in the clouds gave promise of a sunny afternoon.

'That's good,' said Bill. 'We'll be able to have our meal outside. And it looks as though we might have the place to ourselves.'

It seemed that the French people were paying only a short visit to the vineyard then moving on to somewhere else. Christine and Bill sat down at one of the rough wooden tables on the terrace.

'It's much posher inside the restaurant,' Bill told her, 'but the food is just the same. Is this OK for you?'

'It's fine by me,' she answered. 'It's a lovely place. I'm glad you brought me here.'

There was a superb view beyond the slope of the vineyard to a wooded mountain range in the distance. The clouds were quickly dispersing as the sun shone through the morning mist and rain. As Christine feasted her eyes on the beauty of the landscape a rainbow appeared over the faraway hills. She was reminded, as she always was at the sight of a rainbow, of the story she had heard long ago in Sunday School, of Noah's Ark and God's promise, following the flood, that He would always be there in the midst of trouble. She did not go to church now – well, hardly ever – but the moment seemed to be filled with a special meaning. She was happy that she was there, happy that she had met Bill, and hopeful that there might be something for the two of them in the future.

Bill nudged her. 'You're miles away,' he said with a laugh. 'Are you thinking of the pot of gold at the end of the rainbow?'

'Something like that,' she replied. 'It's a stunning view, isn't it?'

'I must admit that it is,' he said, 'although I'm not one to wax lyrical. I know I'm ready for something to eat.' He handed her the large menu that was held between the paws of an upstanding wooden bear. 'What do you fancy?'

Her eyes scanned the extensive list, then she realized that several of the items were only available in the evening. But there was still a goodly number of hearty snacks for lunchtime.

'I'm spoilt for choice,' she said, scanning the list of pizzas, pastas and salads. 'You choose for me, Bill. I'll have the same as you.'

'We'll have Flammkuchen, then,' he replied. 'It's a sort of flambé tart. It's truly delicious, home-made by Eva Schneider. I know you'll enjoy it.'

He gave their order, plus two glasses of Riesling, to the waitress who was dressed in a dirndl skirt and peasant blouse. There were a few more customers now, seated at the tables, who looked like locals. It was always a good sign when the local people dined there.

'We may have to wait a little while,' said Bill. 'Everything is cooked specially as you order it, but I can assure you it will be worth the wait. So Christine . . . are you looking forward to going home?'

She didn't answer for a moment, then, 'Yes, I suppose I am really,' she replied. 'It's always good to get home again after a holiday. There's no place like home, as they say. But it's been a fabulous trip, far better that imagined. I've really enjoyed it.'

'Good . . . and could there be any special reason for that?' He raised a questioning eyebrow as he smiled at her.

'You're fishing for compliments, aren't you? I've enjoyed your company, Bill. You've made it all very interesting, showing me places and telling me all sorts of things about the area.'

'And have you thought any more about what I said? About us seeing one another when we get back home?'

'I've thought about it,' she replied. 'But it all depends on Monty. I'll have to see what he thinks about it.' She gave a roguish grin.

'Ah yes, of course, Monty, your chocolate Labrador. Do you think he might take a dislike to me? I like dogs, you know. I've never been able to have one of my own, but I know they're very loyal companions. He'll be missing you, won't he?'

'I'm sure he will, but he'll be OK with Mum and Dad . . . No, I don't think he'll take a dislike to you, Bill. I was only teasing. I've never known him to take a dislike to anyone. He's a very friendly dog. Labradors are, you know. That's why they make such good pets; they're so gentle with children. I'm not sure about being a guard dog, though. He hardly ever barks and I don't know how he'd react to a burglar.'

'You still haven't answered my question. Shall we give it a try, Christine? I'm absolutely sure that I want to . . . if you do?'

'Yes . . . yes, I do, Bill,' she answered. 'We've got along well together this week and yes, I'd like to go on seeing you.'

They were interrupted at that stage by the arrival of their lunch. 'That looks good,' said Christine. 'It's enormous, though.'

The tart filled the large round platter. It was a sort of thin pizza, covered with crème fraiche, crisp bacon pieces and golden fried onions. And it turned out to be just as delicious as it looked. The dry white wine was the perfect accompaniment.

'I'm really chuffed that we can go on seeing one another,' said Bill. She knew that he was not one for flowery phrases, and she felt, now, that she was able to trust him. He had assured her that it was definitely all over with Olga. She guessed that there might have been others, plenty of them, but she was ready to give him a chance.

'I shall ring up the boss as soon as we get back to the hotel,' he told her. 'I'll tell him that I'd like to work in the UK for a while, maybe permanently. I know there are several lads who will jump at the chance of working on the Continent. So now . . . well, it all depends on Monty, doesn't it?'

Nineteen

The phone lines from the Gasthaus Grunder to places in England were busy on that Monday afternoon. Bill, as he had promised, rang his boss in Preston as soon as he and Christine arrived back at the hotel.

'What? You as well!' said Charlie Baldwin, the manager of Galaxy Travel when he heard Bill's voice and had listened to his request. 'I've already had Mike on the phone saying the same thing. What's up with the pair of you? I thought you were both OK, and you get on well together, don't you?'

'Yes, like a house on fire,' said Bill. 'We're good mates, but we both have our reasons. I didn't know Mike had spoken to you, I've not seen him since breakfast time.'

Charlie admitted that he did know why Mike wanted to work in the UK. 'Family problems, I gather,' he said, 'and I can understand that. Wives get fed up when their hubbies are working away, and Mike's been doing the Continental tours for about three years now. He's ready for a break. But what's the problem with you, Bill? You're a single bloke, and I thought you liked it over there.'

'So I do,' replied Bill, 'but I'm the same as Mike; I feel that I'm away from home too much.' He didn't want to say that he had a new girlfriend, one that he had met on this tour and that he was hoping to make a go of it. 'I don't have family commitments in the way that Mike has, but I do have a family – parents and a brother and sister, and grandparents who are getting on a bit. And there are things I like to do like go to football matches, and I'm in a darts team – at least I used to be – and, well . . . I just feel so out of things while I'm over here. I know it has its compensations, and I've enjoyed it, but the shorter tours at home would suit me better.' He decided he'd said enough and maybe he was overbuttering the bread, or whatever the saying was.

'Yes, I see . . .' said Charlie. 'You have a free week after you get back, don't you? And then I think we've got you down for one of the French tours, in the Loire Valley . . .' One of the problems with Galaxy was that you never knew where you might be asked to go from one week to the next.

'I'll think about it,' Charlie told him. 'That's the best I can say at the moment. I've more or less told Mike that it'll be OK for him – he did ask first after all – and there's young Steve dying to have a chance to work on the Continent. He's ready for it now, but he'll have to have someone with him the first time to show him the ropes. I'll see what I can do, Bill, but it's a pity, you were starting to get more experienced over there. It's not a job that anyone can do. Leave it with me, and I'll try to rearrange the schedules.'

'Thanks very much Charlie. I'm grateful to you. It's hard to explain but—'

'Say no more, Bill. We always try to oblige if we can. It makes for a happier workforce. See you on Wednesday then? It's been a successful trip, has it? Apart from the couple of problems I've heard about—' that was the suitcase incident and Mr Johnson's heart attack; they had to report back to HQ about everything that happened '—but you and Mike seem to have coped very well. Anyway, bye for now, Bill.'

At the other end of the line Charlie Baldwin reflected that, knowing what he did about Bill, there was probably a lady involved. But they had a fair number of drivers and there were always men waiting to join the firm; women, too, in these days of equal opportunities.

Bill found Mike in their bedroom, lounging on his bed reading a spy thriller.

'So you beat me to it.' said Bill. 'I've just rung Charlie and he said you'd been on the phone. I get the impression that you're home and dry – you did ask first – but he's going to think about my request. So it's fingers crossed.'

'I hope you get what you want then, if you're sure about it. You had a good day with Christine then, did you?'

'Terrific, thanks! We've agreed to give it a try, and I've a week off when we get back, so . . .' Bill winked and made a thumbs up sign.

'All power to your elbow, then,' said Mike. 'Don't go mucking things up if you think you're in with a chance.'

'I'll try not to. How did you go on with Sally? I take it she's still anxious for you to work at home?'

'Absolutely, but she was a lot calmer, not in such a tizzy as she was the last time I rang.'

He had phoned her around lunchtime, just before she started her afternoon shift at the supermarket.

'Hi there, Sal, it's me,' he began. 'How are things with you?'

'Hello, Mike. I guessed it might be you.' At least she sounded much calmer, and he breathed a sigh of relief at not having to hold the phone away from his ear. 'Things are better here, I'm pleased to say. Our Tracey went back to school this morning with her tail between her legs, as you might say. I've never seen her so subdued. She was cocky about it at first – at least she pretended to be – as though it was just a laugh. But she had a real good telling off from me, and she was grounded all weekend, and for this week as well, unless I relent.'

'Good for you, Sal! She's not a bad kid, though, really, is she? We've done our best to bring her up in the right way, although I must admit it's been largely up to you in the last few years. I'm going to have a word with Charlie about working nearer to home. I shall talk to him today instead of waiting till I get back.'

'That's good,' said Sally. 'Thank you, Mike . . . We do miss you, you know. I know you'd probably be away all week, but at least we would have all the weekends together.'

'We'll have to cross our fingers that Charlie agrees, then. I'll put in an earnest plea.'

'Tracey misses you a lot. I hadn't realized how much, but last night she said to me, "I really miss Dad, you know. It's awful that he's away so much." And she even said, "I'm sorry I've been such a nuisance, Mum." That's all she said, but you could have knocked me down with a feather.'

'It's nice to know I'm missed so much.' Mike felt very touched at what Sally had said, and he was more determined than ever not to be such an absentee father. 'Listen, love, I'll have to go now. Goodness knows how much this is costing.

Bye for now, Sal. love you, and love to the kids. Take care now . . .'

'Will do. See you soon, Mike. Love you too . . .'

Jane phoned her mother when she returned to the hotel in the mid-afternoon.

She had spent the day with Dave in Freiburg. The low cloud and grey skies during the early part of the day had not helped her downcast spirits. But towards midday the sun had appeared, and by this time she had managed to cast off most of her gloom.

It seemed that Dave intended to act as though there was nothing wrong. She realized he was a pretty sanguine sort of fellow, determined to look on the bright side and not allow himself to be downhearted. Did that mean that he was unable to feel things as deeply as she did? She had not really known him long enough to have found out everything about him. She knew, though, that men and women often had a different outlook on problems.

They had had a pleasant enough day, although there was that constant niggle at the back of her mind all the while that this might be the last time they would be alone together. In a couple of days she feared they would have to say goodbye, and that would be the end of their all too fleeting romance.

They had dined at lunchtime under the veranda of a cafe in the market square. It was not so busy as it had been on Saturday, but there was still a good number of tourists around and they kept meeting other people from the coach. They had seen Bill and Christine setting off somewhere in a taxi earlier that morning, looking very happy together. Whilst they were having their lunch Shirley and Ellen walked past with the two brothers, Trevor and Malcolm. Jane was not quite sure which was which, but Shirley was walking with one of the men, and Ellen with the other, not arm in arm or hand in hand, but they seemed very relaxed in one another's company. Ellen gave a shy smile and a little wave to Jane as they passed.

'Ellen's a lovely person, isn't she?' Dave remarked. 'She seems to be getting on well with Trevor – at least I think that one is Trevor. I get the impression that she's dominated by Shirley a lot of the time, so this should do her a world of good.'

'Yes, I hope so, even if it's only a holiday friendship . . .' Jane's voice petered out. She said no more, but she felt that Dave knew what was in her mind. He nodded but made no comment.

They had a last wander around the square when they had finished their lunch, then took a bus back to the village, which was the nearest stop to the hotel.

'I must finish my packing now,' said Jane, halting at her bedroom door. 'I'm taking back far more than I came with.'

'Me too,' said Dave. 'I'll see you at dinner time then? If we go down early we could have a drink at the bar?'

'Yes, maybe . . .' She smiled brightly as she entered her room. 'See you later, Dave.'

A few moments later, after trying to get herself into the right frame of mind, she went down to the foyer to phone her mother.

'Hello, Mother. It's me.' She hoped she was sounding happier than she felt. The carefree attitude she had tried to assume all day was fast disappearing.

'Yes, I guessed it might be you,' said Alice. 'You'll be setting off back tomorrow, won't you?'

'Yes, eight o'clock in the morning. I'm just going to finish my packing.'

'You've had a good time, have you? You feel the holiday has done you good?'

'Yes . . . yes, I'm sure it has. It's all been lovely. Good weather, and lots of interesting places to see, and nice people on the coach.'

'You've made some new friends then?'

'Yes . . . yes, I have. One or two people I shall keep in touch with.' She had a chance then to mention a particular one, but she did not do so. She might have done, had not Dave told her his true circumstances. But Mother would never get her head round that. 'What about you, Mother? I expect you've made some friends at Evergreen, haven't you?'

'Yes, I suppose so. Like you, there's one or two I might keep in touch with. I said I might pop back and see them sometime. I told you about Flora, didn't I? We get on quite well, and there are one or two others. It's been better than I expected, but I'll be glad to get home. There's nothing like your own bed and your own things around you.'

'I'm glad you've enjoyed it. I said you'd be OK there, didn't I?'

'Yes, maybe you did. I said I'd give it a try, and that's what I've done. Now, when are you coming to collect me? You won't be back till late on Wednesday, will you?'

'No, it'll be too late. I'll come on Thursday morning, so make sure you're ready. It'll be nice to get home,' she said, realizing that, in spite of everything, she had missed her mother. 'It's been a great holiday . . . but all good things come to an end.' She felt her voice breaking, and her mother picked on it at once.

'Jane? What is it? There's nothing wrong, is there?'

'No, nothing at all. It's just . . . it's nothing, Mother. I'll see you soon . . .'

She put the phone down quickly, trying to stem the tears that were welling up in her eyes. She hurried back to her room where she made a cup of tea and tried to compose herself.

She dragged her suitcase from the top of the wardrobe, ready to start packing. It was easier packing to go home as one didn't need to be so careful about folding the clothes. She had a large plastic bag in which she put the items that were ready for washing, but some things would only need a quick iron to be ready to wear again.

There was so much more to take home than she had brought with her. As a result of her shopping sprees in Baden Baden and elsewhere her case was bulging and the adaptable straps stretched to their furthest limit. Then there were all the bits and pieces she had bought as souvenirs or for presents. She had been given a sturdy carrier at one the gift shops and that would hold her purchases and fit into the overhead compartment above her seat. One bonus with coach travel was that the luggage was taken care of – although, occasionally, maybe not as well as it might have been! – and the passengers did not need to carry their heavy cases around.

By the time her case was packed, with the clothes she had decided to wear for the last day's travel in the UK at the top, she was feeling more composed. She washed, then dressed with care for the final evening in Germany. That morning in Freiburg, egged on by Dave – he had been determined to carry on as though everything was OK – she had bought a pair of flared trousers in a deep coral shade, and a top with pink and blue flowers on a white background. She knew that they suited her – made her look younger – and she decided as she applied her make-up and combed and rearranged her hair, that she must do her utmost to be cheerful and carefree that evening, and put to one side the jumbled thoughts that were whizzing round and round in her head.

She sat and read her book, getting engrossed in other people's joys and sorrows which was a distraction that helped her to focus her mind on something else, if only for a short time. Dave knocked at her door at six thirty, and she greeted his cheerful, 'Ready, Jane?' with a bright smile.

They sat in the bar area enjoying a pre-dinner aperitif along with several other Galaxy travellers. In fact, by the time they were ready to go for their final dinner almost all of the party had congregated in the lounge. They all knew one another by this time, some better than others, of course. There was plenty to talk about and conversation flowed easily. Jane chatted to one, then another, relieved that she did not have to talk exclusively to Dave.

Just before seven o'clock, which was the set time for the evening meal, Herr Grunder appeared in the lounge. 'We have a little extra treat for you this evening, ladies and gentlemen,' he announced. 'After your meal we will have a get-together – that is how you say it, I think? – here in the lounge. You may not know – my wife, Marianne, and I have only just found out – that this may be the last time that our good friends Mike and Bill will be staying here.' There were surprised exclamations from a few people as he went on to say that the two drivers had decided to give up their Continental tours to work in the UK.

'We have known them for quite some time,' he said, 'Mike rather longer than Bill. They have become good friends to us and we will miss them. And so, ladies and gentlemen, there will be a farewell drink for you all after the meal, "on the house" as you say, then a little entertainment. We will dance and sing and have a good time together, yes? You have been excellent guests, all of you very happy, I think, and no complaints. Marianne and I, we thank you very much. And now . . . your last evening meal awaits you. Please enjoy it.'

There was a round of applause before they all trooped into the dining room. There was a festive air to the room with candles burning – safely in glass holders – on each table, and vases holding fresh flowers: roses, Sweet Williams and sweet peas, their fragrance scenting the air.

The meals at Gasthaus Grunder had all been good, some more palatable than others to English taste, but on the whole their plates had been cleaned each time, apart from one or two dumplings that had proved to be rather too filling. The guests all agreed that the meal on the final evening was one of the best that Herr Grunder and his assistants had prepared that week. Onion soup with noodles was followed by the main dish of succulent roast pork served with asparagus tips, broccoli and potato slices in a cheese sauce. The dessert was Sachertorte, as was served in Viennese cafes, a rich chocolate cake with a layer of cherry jam, served with whipped cream.

The party of six – Mavis and Arthur, Dave and Jane, Shirley and Ellen – had got to know one another quite well over the six days they had spent at the guest house, and they talked to first one then another, with ease. Jane, as usual was seated between Dave and Ellen. Ellen looked very attractive that evening. Her grey hair, which at first had had that tight permed look, was now arranged in a softer style. The coral top she was wearing matched the pink lipstick she had applied sparingly and brought a radiance to her rather pale face. Jane commented that her hair looked nice, and Ellen said that Shirley had washed and set it for her. Most of the ladies had done an impromptu styling of their hair as ten days was too long to go without their usual shampoo and set or blow dry.

'And how did you enjoy your day in Freiburg?' asked Jane. She guessed that the glow that was emanating from Ellen was not entirely due to her discreet make-up and her hairstyle.

'You and Trevor looked very contented together. The man you were with – he is Trevor, isn't he?'

'Yes, that's Trevor.' Ellen smiled, a gentle, secretive sort of smile. 'He's two years older than his brother. Malcolm's just turned sixty, and Trevor's sixty-two. They've both retired recently – they worked in local government – but they decided that they'd worked long enough and want to enjoy their retirement. Trevor is seven years older than me,' she added in a whisper, 'but that's not very much, is it?' She looked questioningly at Jane.

'No, not at all,' Jane replied. 'It doesn't matter how old you are, or who is older than who, so long as you get on well together.' She felt that Ellen was dying to confide in her. 'Are you saying that you and Trevor are getting . . . friendly? That you like one another . . . quite a lot?'

Ellen gave a quiet contented sigh. 'Yes, I think so. He wants us to meet when we get back home. He lives not very far away from me, in Stockport. It's only a short journey away from Manchester on the train, although we both drive a car.'

'Do you really?' said Jane. For some reason it surprised her that Ellen could drive.

'Yes, I decided, when I was in my forties, that it was something I must learn to do. It was handy for driving my parents about. My father had never learnt to drive, but he became very much a back-seat driver! They were glad of the convenience of it, though. I don't drive as much now, it can be murder driving in Manchester. I'm near enough to my work to walk there, but I've kept up with my driving licence. It's handy sometimes.'

Still waters run deep, thought Jane. 'And . . . what about Shirley and Malcolm?' she asked. Shirley was not listening. She was talking animatedly to Dave.

'Oh, I think they're getting on OK together,' replied Ellen, 'but for Shirley it's just someone to be friendly with on holiday, and I think Malcolm feels the same about it. Trevor's the quiet one of the brothers – more like me – but Malcolm's much more lively, more like Shirley. I haven't said very much to her. You know what she's like, she'd tease me unmercifully. No, I think that's the last she'll see of Malcolm, after this holiday.

She's had a few men friends, you know, since her divorce, but she doesn't want to get married again.' Then she looked at Jane in some consternation.

'I'm not saying that Trevor and I . . . nothing like that, but I really think he means it when he says he'd like to see me again.'

'I'm sure he does,' said Jane, 'and I'm really happy for you. We must keep in touch, then you can let me know how you're getting on.'

'And you and Dave, as well,' said Ellen. 'You two are very happy together, aren't you?'

'Yes . . .' replied Jane, a little uncertainly. 'I thought so, but things aren't always as simple as they seem. I've got a mother who's getting on in years, and Dave . . . well, there are one or two problems.' She decided not to say exactly what they were. 'He's a farmer, you know, and he has a lot of responsibility. We'll just have to wait and see how things work out.'

When the meal ended they all adjourned to the lounge for coffee and, after a short interval, the festivities of the evening began. An 'on the house' drink of white wine, lager or fruit juice was brought round to all the guests by the waitresses and Marianne, all dressed in what must he their best National dress they wore for special occasions: dirndl skirts in forest green with a fancy red border at the hemline, richly embroidered peasant blouses, white stockings and highly polished black patent leather shoes with silver buckles.

Then Herr Grunder appeared, dressed likewise in National costume – dark green jacket, knickerbockers and bright red socks. Everyone stopped talking as he stood on the dais at the end of the room.

'Ladies and gentlemen,' he began. 'I would like you please, in a moment or two, to raise your glasses and we will drink a toast to our two very good friends, Mike and Bill.' The two drivers were sitting together near the dais and, as Johann Grunder motioned towards them, they stood, each giving a somewhat embarrassed nod to the assembled audience. Then they sat down again as the proprietor went on with his speech.

'Marianne and I have known these two worthy gentlemen for quite some time, Mike for a little longer than Bill. They have come here several times each year bringing you lovely people from the United Kingdom, and we have had some happy times together. Now they have decided that it is time for a change. I know it cannot be easy spending so much time away from their families and friends at home. And so, as I think you may know, they have decided to carry on with their work as drivers in your own country. I confess that Marianne and I have never visited the place you call the UK, but perhaps when we retire – or maybe before – we will pay a visit to your country, to see London and the other places I have heard you talk about: your Lake District, your Yorkshire Dales, and your Scottish Highlands. And your seaside towns, all around the coast of your little island. That is something we do not have in our own Black Forest.

'So, ladies and gentlemen, we thank you for being such pleasant and friendly guests this week and we hope we may see you again, although it will not be with Mike and Bill. So—' he raised his glass of lager – 'good luck, good health, and a happy life to our friends, Mike and Bill.'

'Mike and Bill . . .' they all echoed as they stood and drank the toast to the men who had become more like friends than drivers over the week that they had known them. Then there came the applause and cries of 'Speech, speech . . .'

But Mike and Bill, unusually, could not be persuaded to say very much. It was Mike who answered. 'Thanks, ladies and gents, for your good wishes, and Johann for his kind words. You have been a grand crowd this week, and I hope we may see some of you again on our holidays in the UK. That's all I've got to say except . . . enjoy the rest of your evening.'

There was time then for general chatter amongst the thirty-six members of the coach party who all knew one another well enough now to find something to talk about. They were all present there that evening, the older ones as well as the younger ones, eager to make the most of their last evening in Germany.

Johann and Marianne Grunder proved that they had other talents as well as those involved in being host and hostess to a guest house full of visitors. Johann took to the stage carrying a huge piano accordion which he played competently to accompany Marianne as she sang some traditional German songs in her melodious mezzo-soprano voice. The words were not familiar – nor did any of them know sufficient German to understand the lyrics – but some of the melodies were well known. Soon everyone was humming or lah-lahing, clapping or tapping their feet to the rhythm of the catchy tunes.

After they had finished their recital, to prolonged applause, it was time for the audience to let their hair down, or to sit back and watch and listen, if they preferred. It was obvious that Herr Grunder, over the years, had collected tapes and CDs of music and songs that would appeal to the visitors from the UK. *Songs from the British Isles* included 'Lassie from Lancashire', 'Blaydon Races', 'Maybe it's because I'm a Londoner', 'We'll keep a Welcome', 'Loch Lomond', and 'When Irish Eyes are Smiling.' Everyone joined in all the songs with gusto, although they were all from the north of England or the Midland Counties.

The more energetic amongst them danced along to 'YMCA', the 'Birdie Song' and the 'Hokey Cokey'; then there were tapes dating back to the time of the Twist, when it became the norm to 'do your own thing' and dance with or without a partner. There were tapes or CDs of Dolly Parton, Bob Dylan, the Beatles, the Rolling Stones, Cilla Black, Matt Monro and Andy Williams.

Jane, as usual, sat with Dave. They talked from time to time, they joined in some of the communal dances, they danced together to a waltz or quickstep rhythm. The problems that they had discussed previously were not mentioned, although Jane guessed that they must be present at the back of Dave's mind as they were in hers. She watched with interest the people with whom she had become most friendly over the last week.

Mavis and Arthur, of course, did not take part in the dancing, although she felt sure they would have done so at one time. They sat close together, holding hands from time to time and smiling at one another, clearly so happy that Arthur's illness had been short-lived.

Shirley and Ellen sat with the two brothers, Malcolm and Trevor. A very different Ellen now as she talked and laughed in a way she had not done at the start of the holiday. Not as unreservedly, though, as her friend, Shirley, who was having the time of her life and whose laughter could be heard above the general hubbub of voices. She and Malcolm – possibly two of a kind – seemed to be having a riotous time, whilst Ellen and Trevor sat quietly together. Jane saw him take hold of her hand as he spoke quietly to her. He was still a good-looking man in an unobtrusive sort of way, with greying hair and kindly grey eyes behind rimless spectacles. She looked away, aware that she was being nosy. But she had become fond of Ellen and felt that she deserved some real happiness in her life, just for herself, as she had spent so much time caring for others.

Bill and Christine, the lady he had met this week appeared very happy and relaxed together. Jane guessed that it might be because of Christine that he, as well as Mike, had decided to work in the UK.

But what about herself and Dave? It had all started so unexpectedly, the attraction they had felt for one another, then had gone on so well, until he had dropped the bombshell that had made her think it had all been a hopeless fantasy.

'Penny for them,' said Dave, taking hold of her hand. 'Come along, let's have a dance. It's a waltz, something I can do quite well.' She smiled at him, and they took to the floor to the tune of the once popular song, 'Around the World'.

'For I have found my world in you . . .' she hummed to herself. She had believed it might be so, only to have the wonder and magic of it all snatched away again.

Twenty

By Tuesday morning, two days before she was due to go home Alice had reached a decision. She usually had every confidence in the decisions she made and, in her self-assured way, would ask for advice from nobody. This time, though, she felt that she wanted to talk it over with someone. And who else but the person she had come to know best during the last week, Flora, the woman she was now regarding as a friend. Alice knew that she had made few – if any – new friends lately, and the ones she had had in the past she seldom saw any more.

Breakfast was a meal that Alice had enjoyed very much at Evergreen. There was a choice of menu – not a big fry-up, bacon and sausage being available only at weekends – but there were eggs cooked in various ways, cereals, porridge, toast and fruit, and muesli for those who liked it. Alice had always thought it tasted of sawdust. This morning she had enjoyed tinned grapefruit slices and a poached egg on toast. At home it was usually cornflakes and toast. When Jane was dashing out to work she had little time to prepare anything more, though she sometimes made bacon sandwiches as a treat on a Sunday. Alice was beginning to appreciate more and more all that her daughter had done for her, and, she admitted to herself, for very little thanks.

When breakfast was over they adjourned to the lounge, and Alice drew Flora away to a corner away from the rest of the guests. 'There's something I want to talk over with you,' she said. 'Let's go over there away from the telly and all the chatter.'

They settled themselves on the settee at the far end of the room. Flora smiled at her. 'Fire away,' she said. 'I'm all ears.'

'I'm thinking . . . well, I've already thought,' Alice began, 'and I've decided – well, almost – that I'd like to stay here permanently.'

'Wow!' exclaimed Flora. 'That's a turn-up for the book, isn't it? When I think how set against it you were when you first came here, determined not to like it . . .'

'I know, I know,' said Alice, just a little tetchily. 'You don't need to remind me what I was like, but I've changed my mind. I know I'll have to eat humble pie. I said to Henry the other day that I most definitely would not come and live here.'

Flora laughed. 'I think that Henry, for one, will be very pleased if you decide to stay here. That couldn't be the reason, could it? Henry and you, you're getting on very well, aren't you?' she said with a twinkle in her eye.

'Don't be ridiculous!' scoffed Alice. 'Yes, I get on well enough with him, and I'm determined I'll beat him at chess one of these days. I hope he'll be pleased if I decide to stay.'

'We'll all be pleased,' said Flora. 'Those of us who have got to know you, at any rate. I would really miss you now, Alice. I was feeling quite dejected at the thought of you leaving us on Thursday. We've found that we have quite a lot in common, haven't we?'

'Yes, so we have,' Alice agreed. Apart from our previous lifestyles, she thought to herself, but didn't say, and the fact that Flora was loaded whilst she, Alice, would have to consider the financial aspect very carefully because Evergreen was far from cheap. One of the most expensive homes in the area, she guessed, but then you got what you paid for, as with everything in life.

'So, how has all this come about?' asked Flora. 'Why the sudden change of heart. I thought you were looking forward to going home and seeing your daughter again. After she rang you the other day you said she sounded a bit low.'

'So she did,' said Alice. 'And that's one of the things I have to think about carefully. I just wonder how she would feel if I decided to stay here. I really like it here now. I've settled down far better than I ever imagined I would.' She gave a wry smile. 'I've realized what an awkward so-and-so I'd turned into, finding fault with everything and everybody. I was well on the way to becoming a crotchety old woman. It's no wonder people didn't like me, because I didn't try to like them.'

'Oh, come on now,' said Flora. 'Don't be too hard on yourself. 'I think you're a great person, and so do a lot more of us. Yes, you're dogmatic, and you're not afraid of speaking your mind, but that's because you're such a strong character. There's nothing wrong with that. We're all as the good Lord made us.'

'Yes . . . I know,' said Alice. 'But we can all recognize our own faults if we look for them, can't we? And try to change them.' She hesitated for a moment, pondering the issue that was uppermost in her mind.

Flora prompted her. 'You mentioned your daughter. You think she might not be happy about you coming to live here permanently?' She could not help thinking to herself that the young woman might well have been relieved at her mother's decision if Alice was always so difficult and hard to please as she had seemed on first acquaintance.

'I really can't say,' replied Alice. 'I'm sure she must have wished sometimes that I was somewhere else. We did tend to get on one another's nerves living together – just the two of us – for so long. But as I've just said, I know now that I've not been the easiest person to live with.'

'Are any of us?' said Flora, diplomatically. 'We all have to try to get on with the people we live with, but it isn't always easy. It's a question of give and take, isn't it? In marriage and in other relationships as well.'

'Give and take, yes,' repeated Alice thoughtfully. 'Jane has shared her home with me – Jane and Tom at first, of course. And they both assured me it was my home as much as theirs. But I like to think I've pulled my weight, especially since Tom died and Jane was left on her own. I've helped quite a lot financially, and I'm concerned about how she would manage if I wasn't there to help. I know she has a reasonably well-paid job and her widow's pension, but there's still a mortgage on the property, then there are all the bills and the maintenance of the house and the cost of running her car. I don't want to swan off and leave her to manage on her own.'

'People do manage,' said Flora. 'I know it's easy for me to say because money has never been a problem for me, not for many years, at any rate. But, as you say, she has her job and her pension, and – who knows? – she might get married again.'

'She hasn't shown any signs of wanting to so far. She and Tom were so happy together – just right for one another – and I've heard her say that there could never be anyone else. It would be nice for her if she did find someone, but she's a very reserved sort of girl – more so since Tom died – and she keeps herself to herself a lot of the time. She has a few close friends, and she seems content to leave it at that. I was really surprised when she decided to go on that holiday on her own. It must have taken some courage.'

'And she seemed to be enjoying it, didn't she?'

'Yes, everything seemed to be going well. Good weather and good hotels, so she said, and she'd met some nice friendly people. But the other night, like I said, she sounded a bit down. Perhaps because it was coming to an end or . . . well, I just don't know, do I? But I can't very well tell her, as soon as I see her, that I've decided to come and live here . . . can I?'

'You don't need to blurt it out as soon as she arrives, no, of course not. Just play it by ear, as they say. Anyway, have you made enquiries? Do you know if there's a room for you? They keep pretty busy, you know. Sometimes there aren't any vacancies. You might have to wait a little while.'

'That's what I intend to find out today. Then I'll talk it over with Jane. It would be a big step for me, of course. When I went to live with Jane and Tom I had to get rid of a lot of my furniture and bits and pieces. They talk a lot about 'down-sizing' on those house-hunting programmes, don't they? It seems to be one of the 'in' phrases at the moment. Well, I've downsized once, but this time it would be even worse, wouldn't it? There's not a great deal of room here for your own bits and bobs, is there?'

'We manage,' said Flora. 'A few of your own possessions around you, photos and ornaments and books, and it soon comes to feel like home. In fact you're quite at home here already, aren't you?'

Alice nodded. 'And then there's the financial side of it. It costs a pretty penny to live here, doesn't it? I'd have dismissed it out of hand at one time. Good grief! It costs as much as a three-star hotel.'

Flora laughed. 'You can't take it with you, Alice. I don't know how you're fixed with regard to money, but you have your teacher's pension, haven't you? And your widow's and state pensions as well? Those could cover the cost of staying here.'

'They may well do so,' said Alice. 'And I've a bit put by from the sale of my house. I hoped I'd be able to leave it intact for Jane to inherit, but no doubt I'll have to break into it.'

'From what I've heard about your Jane I'm sure she would want what was the best for you.' Flora smiled at her. 'I'm really pleased and honoured that you decided to talk it over with me, Alice, and I hope I've been able to help you. I'd love you to stay, but you must do whatever you and Jane think is best.'

'Yes of course,' said Alice. 'I'll see what Jane is like when she comes to pick me up on Thursday. If I feel she might be quite agreeable to the idea of me staying here, then I'll tell her what I'm considering. But if I think she might not be too happy about it, then I might have to put it on hold for a while. I don't want to upset the lass. Like I was saying, I got the impression that there was something on her mind. I know we've not always got on together as well as we might, but I know her inside-out by now. I should do, she's my only daughter . . .' And one who is very dear to me, she added, silently to herself. 'I'll just have to wait and see. Thank you for listening to me, Flora. You've helped me a lot, but I know it has to be my decision in the end.'

The journey home, across Germany, Belgium and France, all in one day, was quite a marathon for the passengers as well as for the drivers, and there was not the same excited chatter as there had been on the outward journey.

They had set off from the guest house at seven thirty in the morning, following a breakfast during which none of them felt as bright and bushy-tailed as they had on previous mornings. It was early for the staff to be up and about, and the guests had served themselves coffee, left on the table in large flasks, and a more limited choice of breakfast foods.

Johann and Marianne Grunder were both at the coach, however, to wish them goodbye and a safe journey home. They all agreed that they had been a marvellous host and hostess. Mike and Bill were particularly sad at the thought that they would not meet up with them again, although it had been their own decision to finish with the Continental tours.

As the miles – or kilometres – sped by, the passengers dozed, catching up with lost sleep, or tried to read, or just watched the scenery, firstly the hills and woods to which they had become accustomed, then the flatter fields and the nondescript towns of Belgium, viewed in the distance from the motorway as they flashed past the window.

There were stops every few hours, as was obligatory, at service stations, and from time to time, Mike or Bill put on a tape of 'easy listening' music, or one of an Irish comedian – a tape very popular with the coach drivers – whose jokes and witticisms had many of them quietly chuckling. Anything to relieve the inevitable boredom of the long and rather tedious journey.

Mavis was concerned about Arthur. He dozed for much of the time and appeared to be coping very well with everything, considering his recent heart attack. She was watching him continually, though surreptitiously – Arthur hated anyone fussing over him – but she knew she would utter a prayer of thanks when they had finally crossed the Channel and had set foot once again on English soil. It would probably be the last time they would travel abroad, but she hoped they would have several more years together, and there were lots of interesting places to visit nearer to home.

Shirley and Ellen chatted together, although it was Shirley, as usual, doing most of the talking. They had known one another for many years but they were never short of things to say or discuss. Ellen was filled with a quiet happiness that she was keeping very much to herself. She had had a lovely evening with Trevor and, at a time when Shirley and Malcolm were dancing together and the two of them were on their own, they had exchanged addresses and telephone numbers. Trevor had seemed eager that they should arrange to meet when they got back home, and Ellen believed that he was sincere in what he said. She was hugging the secret to herself. She would tell Shirley, of course, in her own good time, but at the moment she did not want her private affairs shouting from the roof tops. The four of them, Shirley and Ellen and the two brothers sat together at the coffee and comfort stops, chatting as a foursome. Trevor seemed to understand how Ellen felt – which boded well for the future – and was careful not to draw attention to their blossoming friendship.

Conversation between Jane and Dave did not flow as easily as it had done on the outward journey when they were getting to know one another and had found lots of things to talk about. Now, of course, although they knew much more about one another, a certain constraint had built up between them. Dave, far more sanguine than Jane, tried to chat unconcernedly, but Jane, although she tried to act as though things were quite normal, was finding it difficult to respond. They did not refer, during the long journey back across the Continent, to the problems that had arisen in their relationship, but Jane knew – and she was sure that Dave knew as well – that something would need to be said before they parted company back in England the following day.

They both read their books, or tried to do so, although Jane found that her mind was wandering. She could not concentrate even on the latest Ruth Rendell offering. She had finished her Maeve Binchy, a nice comfortable read, and maybe she was not in the mood for murder and intrigue, although she kept her eyes glued to the page, making a good pretence at being engrossed in the story.

The motorway cafe in Belgium where they had their lunch stop was very busy and they waited in a long queue to be served with soup and a bread roll, and a slice of apple tart. A situation that might have seemed unique and interesting on the outward journey – the chatter of foreign voices, the pleasant aroma of the various foods being cooked, and the exciting feeling of being abroad – now seemed to have lost its appeal. Jane was only aware of the crowded eating place and of the way they had to hurry with their meal. Because of the length of the journey Mike could allow only forty-five minutes for the lunch break, although it seemed certain that not everyone would be back in time.

As it happened they all managed to return to the coach only a few minutes later than requested. Arthur and Mavis were the last, but nobody minded about that. Arthur had been determined not to 'gobble my dinner and have an attack of indigestion'. Or worse, thought Mavis, who was in total agreement. This journey was proving to be very tedious. How relieved she would be when they arrived at the hotel in Calais and she was able to get her feet up and rest her swollen ankles, a hazard of coach travel that she had found to be worse than ever during this holiday.

It was six o'clock in the evening when they arrived at the Calais hotel, where they had stayed on the outward journey. It was, therefore, familiar to them, and knowing their way around did help somewhat when they were feeling tired and maybe a little irritable. However, a wash and brush up and, in many cases, a drink at the bar did revive everyone's spirits and put them in a better frame of mind for the evening meal.

This time the tables were set for eight. Jane remembered that on the first visit she and Dave had sat with and become friendly with Mavis and Arthur. The four of them sat together now, with two other couples whom they had met up with now and again during the holiday. They all knew one another now, to a certain extent, and conversation was largely about the sights they had seen, what they had enjoyed the most and, inevitably, polite enquiries about Arthur's present state of health. How had he coped with the wearisome journey? He answered their questions with as much patience as he could muster, telling them he was as fit as a fiddle, but he would be glad to sleep in his own bed again, a feeling that they all endorsed.

The meal was pretty much the mixture as before – onion soup, roast chicken and *pommes frites*, followed by fruit and ice cream. Everyone was hungry after a makeshift lunch and there was very little left on any of the plates.

Coffee was served afterwards in the lounge, but by that time it was turned ten o'clock. Mavis and Arthur declined the coffee saying that they would go straight to bed. Jane and Dave sat with a couple they had dined with, for the sake of politeness more than anything. Then they, too, decided it was time to call it a day.

The two of them took the lift to the third floor. As before, their rooms were adjacent. They paused at the doors ready to enter the rooms with their giant keys. Dave leaned towards Jane, taking hold of her shoulders in a gentle grasp.

'Don't worry, my dear,' he said. 'It will all sort out, I feel sure it will.' He kissed her gently on the lips. 'Goodnight now, and God bless. See you in the morning.'

'Yes . . . see you, Dave,' she replied, smiling bravely at him.

Tears were threatening as she entered the room and closed the door behind her. She blinked them away, determined not to give in to the negative thoughts that were invading her mind. Could there be a glimmer of light at the end of the tunnel? Dave seemed to think so.

'Don't worry,' he had just said. 'It will all sort out . . .'

Did he really believe that, or was he just trying to cheer her up? Maybe she had been living in a fool's paradise ever since she met him just over a week ago. He did not know her mother like she did; in fact, he did not know Alice at all. If he did then he might have a better idea of what she was up against. She and her mother lived together. Jane had offered to share her home with her, willingly – well, as willingly as she was able, she confessed to herself – and that was that. How could she, now, cast her aside, 'like an old worn-out coat.' She could almost hear her mother saying the words, or something similar.

And that was not the only problem, even if the living arrangements for Alice could be sorted out. Her mother would go ballistic at the idea of Jane consorting with a man who was still married, even if it was only in name.

Stop it! Stop it! Jane scolded herself. Going over and over the problem only made it worse. Resolutely she undressed and washed and got into bed, setting her little clock for six o'clock. Their cases had to be outside their rooms by seven, and after an early breakfast they would depart at eight for the short journey to the docks.

Fortunately her tortuous thoughts stilled when her head touched the pillow. It had been a tiring day. Sitting still for hours on end on a coach could be just as wearying as a ten-mile hike. Despite her worries she slept until the alarm clock woke her the following morning.

Twenty-One

The sky was grey and overcast and there was a chilly wind blowing when they boarded the coach on the Wednesday morning, following a somewhat hurried breakfast. A very different outlook from the sunshine that had greeted them on their arrival in France and had blessed them for almost the whole of the holiday.

The cross-channel ferry was not so crowded as it had been on the outward journey. They were all used to the procedure by now; they knew the whereabouts of the cafes, bars, shops and toilets, and it no longer seemed quite so strange. Once again the coach was parked near to a staircase, so should be easy to locate when the journey of ninety minutes or so was completed.

Jane and Dave were still together. There seemed to be no way they could separate without appearing impolite or difficult. After all, they had not fallen out, but just come face to face with a load of problems.

Jane, however, did go off to the shops on her own when they had enjoyed a cup of strong coffee and a scone. The breakfast had been rather a hit and miss affair with no one feeling particularly hungry.

'Yes, off you go and treat yourself,' said Dave. He grinned at her. 'You don't want me hanging around.' Shopping, especially in gift shops and the like was something that men only did under protest. She recalled that Tom, an ideal husband in many ways, had preferred to leave Jane to shop on her own, and no doubt Dave was of the same inclination.

Jane felt her spirits rise when she entered the shop. There was a fragrant aroma of perfume, and the shelves were full of all manner of tempting goods, many of them less expensive than in the high street shops . . . but still by no means cheap! Radley handbags and purses, silk scarves, watches and exquisite costume jewellery. Jane looked but did not linger. To indulge in a new scarf or earrings, for instance, would be an extravagance.

But she did ponder at length over the various perfumes: Chanel, Dior, Estée Lauder, Givenchy, Lance, Rochas. There were tester bottles available, and she sprayed each wrist and the back of her hands trying to decide which one she preferred. In the end she was quite bewildered as all the scents merged into one.

An attractive girl with an oriental look came to assist her. 'May I help you, madam?' she asked politely.

'Yes, please,' said Jane. 'Something light and flowery, not too musky . . .'

After sampling one or two more she finally decided on 'Dolce Vita' by Dior. Expensive! But cheaper than in it would be in Debenhams, and what did it matter? She had several euros left and it would save the trouble of changing it back into sterling currency.

The adjoining shop sold cigarettes, wines and spirits, none of which was of interest to Jane, but there was a tempting display of confectionery and chocolates. She bought two boxes of marzipan chocolates, one flavoured with strawberry and the other with apricot brandy, for herself and her mother; then a huge bar of Toblerone, which she had loved ever since she was a little girl. Her purchases had taken care of most of her remaining euros. She felt much more light-hearted now. It was amazing what a spot of retail therapy could do, although it was something in which she rarely indulged.

'I thought you'd got lost overboard!' said Dave when she reappeared in the lounge. 'All spent up?'

'Almost,' she said with a smile.

He stood up. 'Just time to pay a visit,' he remarked, 'then it'll be almost time for us to find our way back.'

All the passengers arrived back at the coach with time to spare.

'We were nearly the first,' boasted Mavis. 'Weren't we, Arthur? We didn't keep you waiting this time.'

'Aye, so we were,' said Arthur. 'I was damn glad to get off that boat, rocking and rolling like a switchback.' He looked rather tired and pale, and Jane was sure it would be a great relief to him, and to Mavis as well, when they were safely back home. The sail had, indeed, been slightly choppy, but not unduly so. Ships were far more stable now than they had been years ago. She remembered her first trip abroad on a school visit to France. No one had actually been sick, although they had felt decidedly queasy.

Anyway, here they were, back on English soil, and as the coach pulled away from the dock area it was raining. Not pouring down, but a steady drizzle from a grey sky that showed no sign of a break in the cloud; a day that was typical of many in an English summer.

'Put your watches back an hour, ladies and gents,' Mike told them. So it was only ten minutes past nine, although they all felt that they had been up and about for ages.

The coach sped along the motorways, heading northwards. Not the most interesting of journeys, but the quickest route back to the north of England. There was friendly chatter and laughter along the way as new friends called to one another, exchanging addresses and promising to keep in touch.

Jane saw that Mavis and Arthur in the seat across the aisle were holding hands for much of the time. A real Darby and Joan couple, she reflected. Whatever might happen between herself and Dave she must not lose touch with these two elderly friends. Their home town of Blackburn was not very far from Preston. It would be easy to pay them a visit, and her mother might enjoy meeting them, too, if she could be persuaded to go.

They stopped mid-morning at one of the huge impersonal motorway services. Jane left Dave chatting to another couple and sought out Mavis and Arthur.

'Here's my address and telephone number,' she said to Mavis, handing her a postcard with a picture of the market square in Freiburg, 'and could you give me yours, please? You can write it here at the back of my diary.'

'Of course, my dear,' said Mavis, getting out her biro. 'We would love to see you again sometime – and quite soon, I hope – wouldn't we, Arthur?'

'I'll say we would,' he agreed, beaming at Jane, and she could tell that he meant it. 'It's been lovely meeting you this week, and your nice gentleman friend as well!'

'How is it going, my dear?' asked Mavis in a confidential tone. 'Forgive me if I'm being nosy, but I know the two of you have become . . . quite friendly.'

Jane had not told anyone of the problems that had arisen, only hinted to Ellen that they had encountered one or two snags. Her face dropped a little as she replied.

'We're not too sure. There's my mother to consider, and Dave's farm. It's not all that easy.'

Mavis patted her hand. 'Life is seldom easy,' she said, 'but he's worth fighting for, believe me. One only has to see the pair of you together . . .'

Jane nodded and tried to smile, but she felt incipient tears pricking at her eyes as she remembered that very soon she and Dave would be parting company. And he was still putting on a front of cheerfulness and normality. Or was it just a show of bravado?

'Must go now,' she said. 'It's nearly time to go back to the coach, and I need to visit the ladies' room.'

The lunch stop was at a similar venue further north. All these stopping places were much of a muchness, and at midday were usually crowded with long queues for sandwiches, soup, salads, hot meals, Costa coffee, soft drinks, or 'do it yourself' tea and coffee. Then there was the ubiquitous WH Smith shop where you could while away the remaining minutes before it was time to continue with the journey.

No one had a packed lunch this time, and so were obliged to pay the exorbitant prices charged to a captive audience. Jane opted for a triangular pack of cheese and chutney sandwiches whilst Dave queued for fish and chips. She was not very hungry, and she had learnt from experience that your meal was apt to go cold while you were waiting in a queue to pay for it. Dave, however, seemed quite phlegmatic about the experience, tucking into his battered fish and greasy-looking chips with enjoyment.

Jane left him finishing his meal and went to speak to Ellen and Shirley who were sitting at a nearby table with Trevor and Malcolm. She gave her address, written on souvenir postcards, to the two ladies, as she had done with Mavis, and they, in turn, wrote their addresses in her diary. Ellen was the one with whom she most wanted to keep in touch, and she felt sure that Ellen was of the same mind. She included Shirley for the sake of politeness, knowing that they were not likely to do more than send a token Christmas card, possibly for only the first year.

'It's been a grand holiday, hasn't it?' remarked Trevor. 'Good weather, lovely scenery, good hotels . . . nice company. What more could you want?'

'What indeed?' replied Jane. 'Yes, it has come up to all expectations.' She left them with a surreptitious wink and smile at Ellen, who smiled back coyly.

They boarded the coach once again. For some of the party it would be the last time. The next stop would be in the Midlands at the Galaxy depot where roughly half of the passengers would be leaving the tour. This was where Dave would leave, and Jane knew that something would need to be said before the two of them said goodbye. After they had sat in silence for about half an hour Dave turned to her, lightly taking hold of her hand.

'Don't be despondent, Jane,' he began. 'I've a feeling that things will work out just fine for us. It may take time, but I'm sure we'll be able to sort something out. That is . . . if you still feel the same way about us, about you and me?'

Jane nodded numbly. 'Yes, I do . . . I'm trying to, but I can't see any way ahead at the moment. Mother . . . I can't just abandon her – anyway, she's so set in her ways. She would never approve.'

'Surely she would if she met me,' said Dave, squeezing her hand and giving a quiet chuckle. 'Who could resist my dynamic personality, to say nothing of my handsome looks! I'll have her eating out of my hand, you'll see . . .'

Jane knew he was trying to make light of the situation, even though he might well be as unsure of the outcome as she was. 'Of course,' she said. 'Who could resist you! No, seriously, Dave—'

'Say no more,' he interrupted her. 'There's no point in going over and over it. We'll wait and see what happens. Here are my telephone numbers, my landline and my mobile numbers. We can't lose touch with one another, Jane, when we've had such a lovely time together.' He was speaking gently and earnestly now. 'I've told you how I feel about you, and I'm sure that you feel the same. You know there was an almost instant attraction between us, don't you?'

She nodded again. 'Yes, I believed so . . . but we were

thrown together, weren't we? Sitting next to one another. A holiday friendship; we're both away from home with our problems left behind us for a little while. But we have to return to the real world, and the problems are still there. They won't disappear overnight. I let myself believe, for a short time, that it might be possible for us to continue our friendship. But I know I was kidding myself.'

What was it her mother had said the last time she phoned her? She'd be glad to get home; there was nothing like your own bed and home comforts. She had admitted that Evergreen had not been too bad, but that didn't mean that Jane could go gadding off any time she felt like it. Those were her exact words, 'gadding off'. So how would she feel about her daughter gadding off to meet a man in Shropshire, a man who still had a wife? And it was during the previous telephone conversation that she had been going on about some man or other at the home whose son was carrying on with a woman to whom he was not married. 'Living in sin', Alice had said.

Jane was silent for a few moments as these thoughts ran through her mind.

'Come along, love, never say die,' said Dave, a trifle impatiently. 'We can't give up before we've even tried.' He pressed the paper with the telephone numbers into her hand and she pushed it into the pocket of her trousers. 'I shall be waiting to hear from you. I refuse to believe that we won't see one another again. Now, give me your phone number, please. Just your mobile number if you don't want your mother intercepting calls from a strange man.'

But Jane shook her head. 'No, let's just leave it as it is, Dave. It will only upset me if you keep ringing up and I have to tell you that it's no use. Mother isn't going to disappear. God forbid! I don't want anything to happen to her.'

'No, of course you don't. But who knows what might have happened while you've been away? Your mother might have a gentleman admirer at this place where she's been staying. I've heard of it happening. There was an elderly couple where my mother lives, both well into their eighties, and they became friendly and got married!'

Jane gave a wry laugh. 'Now you're talking nonsense! You

haven't met my mother. No, I'm trying to be sensible, Dave. I promise I will ring you if I can see any light at the end of the tunnel, any hope of us meeting again. That's all I can say. Let's just leave it at that, eh?'

'Very well, if you say so . . .' Dave sighed. He could see there was no point in saying any more. Jane was feeling despondent. Maybe she was given to highs and lows of mood? He didn't know her well enough to have found out everything about her. But it wouldn't matter to him if she was. He had seen a glimpse of a happy, fun-loving Jane, and he felt, against all odds, that he would be with her again, sooner rather than later, he hoped.

The coach sped on along the M6, eating up the miles until, just north of Birmingham, they reached the Galaxy depot in the Midlands. A good number of people would be leaving there, including Bill, the driver. His home was further north, in the Manchester area, but he was based in the Midlands and would be dealing with the directing of passengers to the various minibuses that were waiting to take them home.

Many of the people who were leaving expressed their thanks to the drivers, in the usual way, as they left the coach. Others, including Jane, had thanked them the previous night. Monetary tips were much appreciated to supplement a reasonable, but not over-generous, wage.

Bill gave a cheery wave to the remainder of the group as he departed. 'So long, folks. You've been a grand crowd and I've enjoyed your company. Hope I'll see some of you again if you decide to holiday at home for a change.'

He said a quiet unobtrusive goodbye to Christine on the front seat. Her home, too, was in Manchester, so she was remaining on the coach. No doubt they had already said their goodbyes in private. Jane hoped that things worked out well for them.

It was time now for her to say goodbye to Dave. He took hold of her hand and kissed her gently on the cheek, '*au revoir*, Jane, my dear,' he said quietly. 'It's not goodbye.'

She smiled bravely. 'Yes . . . *Au revoir*, Dave,' she repeated. 'I hope so, anyway.' She knew that '*au revoir*' meant 'until we meet again'.

She watched him alight from the coach and then wait whilst

Mike and Bill sorted out the suitcases. Then he lifted his hand to wave at her, though not all that cheerily, as he walked towards the waiting minibus.

Jane leaned back on her seat and closed her eyes as the coach set off again. She was determined not to give way to tears. She knew that she must put on a brave face when she said goodbye to her other friends who, like herself, were travelling northwards to the depot near Preston. She took the paper that Dave had given her out of her pocket. She glanced at it briefly, then, scarcely aware of what she was doing, she tore it in half, then into quarters, screwed them up, then shoved them into her shoulder bag.

They had an obligatory 'comfort' stop an hour or so later, but there was little time to chat to anyone, and no one really felt like drinking yet another cup of tea or coffee. She had managed to compose herself by mid-afternoon when they arrived back at Preston.

Mike, at the wheel, said his goodbyes on behalf of himself and Galaxy Travel. 'You have been a wonderful crowd,' he told them. Jane wondered if he said the same thing every time. But to give him the benefit of the doubt, she was sure he meant it. 'Thanks to you all for your enjoyable company, and I hope I shall see some of you again. So it's goodbye for now, and God bless.'

The remainder of the passengers, those who lived near and others from a little further afield, alighted at the Preston depot. Jane's home was not far away, and there would be two couples travelling with her in the same minibus. Mavis and Arthur, bound for Blackburn, would be in the bus for mid-Lancashire. There was a third one which would take Shirley and Ellen, Trevor and Malcolm, and the two sisters, Christine and Norah, to the Manchester area. The added bonus with Galaxy Travel was that you were transported, as they advertised, 'from door to door'.

They all milled around as Mike unloaded the cases. Jane said a fond goodbye to Mavis and Arthur, and to Shirley and Ellen. They were all a little emotional, as they had bonded so well over the past ten days, and it felt as though they were bidding farewell to old friends, not ones whom they had, in reality, known for only a short time.

Mavis hugged Jane, holding her close for a moment. 'Thank you for being a good friend to Arthur and me,' she said. 'You've been such a comfort to me, Jane . . . and I hope that all goes well for you and Dave.'

Jane had not told her about the complications that had arisen, but Mavis had obviously become aware that there were problems. 'Don't worry about me,' said Jane, bravely. 'You take care of Arthur, and of yourself; I'll pop over to Blackburn to see you before long, I promise.'

After a speedy goodbye to Shirley and Ellen – the cases were loaded and the drivers were anxious to be on their way – Jane stepped aboard. She had the seat next to the driver, so she could not converse with the others who were sitting at the back.

Her home was the nearest one to the depot, so it was not long before she was getting off again. She waved to the couples in the back as she accompanied the driver, who was carrying her case, up the garden path to her door.

'Cheerio, love. Take care now,' he said, as she put her key in the lock and opened the door.

The house felt strange and empty; everything looked a little unfamiliar as though she had partly forgotten her surroundings. To be alone again, after the constant hubbub and excitement of the last ten days – apart from the night times, of course – was a shock to the system.

A cup of tea first. That was always the priority. Then she would make herself a meal. She had bought a loaf at the last service station, so beans on toast would suffice. It felt odd without her mother there to greet her. How often in the past, she had longed for a bit of peace and quiet, but to have someone to talk to now would take her mind off her problems. She realized she was looking forward to seeing her mother the following day, and maybe, she thought, surprisingly, to having her home again.

Twenty-Two

Jane thought when she arrived at Evergreen the following morning that her mother would be waiting with her bags packed, ready and raring to go. But that was not the case. Jane was shown into the lounge by Mrs Meadows, the supervisor, to find her mother sitting comfortably in an easy chair, with another woman, rather younger than herself, in the opposite seat.

'Here's your daughter, Alice,' said Mrs Meadows. 'I'll go and make some coffee for you, and then you can have a chat.'

Jane was nonplussed. She stooped to kiss her mother's cheek and to give her a quick hug. 'Hello, Mother,' she said. 'You're looking well. I thought you'd be ready to go, but—'

'Oh, there's no hurry,' Alice broke in. 'Sit yourself down and relax for a few minutes. You've had a good holiday, have you? You've caught the sun, but you're looking a bit tired and strained. Is everything alright?'

'Yes, I'm fine, Mother,' she replied. 'It's been a busy ten days, though . . .' She looked enquiringly at the other woman, and smiled at her. 'Aren't you going to introduce me to your friend, Mother?'

'Give me a chance,' snapped Alice. 'Yes, this is Flora. I wanted you to meet her. She helped me to settle down when I was left here, feeling like a fish out of water.' She was never able to resist a sly dig.

Flora, however, winked at Jane as she shook hands with her. 'Hello, Jane,' she said. 'I've heard a lot about you and I'm very pleased to meet you. Take no notice of what your mother says. She's had a whale of a time here, haven't you, Alice?'

'I'm pleased to meet you as well,' said Jane. 'Thank you for looking after Mother. I had guessed that things weren't as bad as she was making out.'

'Well, I must admit it's been alright, all things considered,' replied Alice. 'I reckon it must be one of the best of these old folks' homes.'

'Now, come on, Alice,' said her new friend. 'You've said yourself that it's not like an old folks' home, it's more like a three-star hotel.'

'Did I say that? Oh well, maybe I did.' Alice actually gave a chuckle, and Jane looked at her in amazement.

'Well, I'm glad you've enjoyed yourself, Mother,' she said. 'I told you it would be OK when you got used to it.'

She glanced round the room. They were in a quiet corner, but there were several other men and women sitting near to the large television set, one or two others reading, and another lady happily knitting in a quiet corner.

Mrs Meadows arrived with the coffee in a silver pot, with china cups and saucers on the tray. We're being treated like royalty, thought Jane, still mystified as to why her mother was not anxious to be on her way home. Flora set out the cups and saucers – four of them – on a small table.

'I'll go and ask Henry to join us,' said Alice. She stood up, and with the aid of her stick, hobbled across to the television area. She returned with an elderly man, tall and upright and, to Jane's eyes, still quite handsome.

'This is Henry,' said Alice, a trifle abruptly. 'He's another friend who's helped to make it not so bad for me. This is my daughter, Jane.'

His handshake was firm, and there was a twinkle in his eye. 'Hello, Jane,' he said. 'Good to meet you. Your mother is quite a character, isn't she? Not so bad, though, when you get to know her and take her remarks with a pinch of salt. And I must say she plays a fair game of chess. She might even manage to beat me, one of these days.'

'Oh, that's good,' said Jane, surprised at the revelation. 'Yes, she used to play chess with my dad, but I never managed to learn . . . You didn't tell me, Mother.'

'There hasn't been any chance, has there?' said Alice rather sharply. 'We had to do something to pass the time. You can't sit watching telly all the while, like zombies.'

They drank their coffee and chatted for a while. It was mainly Flora and Henry who enquired about Jane's holiday, appearing genuinely interested. It seemed that Flora had been something of a globetrotter in the past. She must be the one who, according to Alice, had more money than she knew what to do with, thought Jane. Flora remarked that the memories were still very precious. Henry, too, had enjoyed several holidays abroad. Mother hadn't mentioned him during her phone calls, at least not to say that he was a friend. He might, however, be the one whose son was 'living in sin'.

After a little while Henry and Flora left the mother and daughter on their own. 'We'll leave you to have a little talk together,' said Flora. 'Nice meeting you, Jane.'

Jane wondered when her mother would decide it was time to go home. She did not seem at all anxious to make a move.

'You've made some nice friends here, Mother,' she said. 'You'll be sorry to say goodbye to them. But I could bring you back to see them, sometime, if you feel like it. And fancy you taking up chess again! Now that would be a good interest for you if you started playing again. I remember how good you were. You managed to beat Dad sometimes, didn't you?'

'Yes, so I did, but I've got a bit rusty with not playing for so long. I've told Henry that I'll pop back – sometime – and we'll have another game. And Flora . . . she's a nice sort of woman. Had an easy life, though, since she married her second husband; never done a day's work for goodness knows how long . . .'

'She's the one with more money than she knows what to do with, I take it?'

'Yes, she is. But I must admit that she doesn't boast about it, and she's certainly not a snob. She was brought up quite ordinary, like the rest of us, until she married into money.'

'And what about Henry? He seems a very pleasant sort of man. He's certainly no fool. You couldn't pull the wool over his eyes.' And he's got you weighed up, Mother, she thought, but didn't say. She could imagine sparks flying between the two of them.

'Yes, Henry's OK,' said Alice, briefly. 'A bit argumentative, like, and always thinks he's right. But he's not so bad.'

'Is he the one whose son has been married twice, and has a lady friend. You told me about him when I phoned you.'

'Yes . . . yes he is. Actually, I met his son – Barry, he's called – on Sunday afternoon, and his . . . friend. And I must admit she seems a nice sort of woman; homely and friendly and they're obviously very happy together. I'd imagined some tarty, flashy sort of lass, but she's not like that at all.'

Jane smiled to herself. 'You shouldn't jump to conclusions, Mother. Things aren't always just as they seem.'

'No, perhaps not. But I've always had my standards, Jane, you know that. I still think there's too much chopping and changing of partners, these days. In my day marriage was for life, till death do us part. That was what we promised.'

'Circumstances alter cases, sometimes,' said Jane, cautiously. Could it be that there might be a slight glimmer of light at the end of the tunnel? Mother seemed to be a shade more tolerant after her stay here. 'Anyway, we'll get off now, shall we, if you're ready? You've got your case packed, have you?'

'Yes . . . I have. But there's something I want to talk about before we go. And Mrs Meadows said she'd come and have a chat with you. You see, Jane, I've been doing a lot of serious thinking this last week. And – you may not believe this – but I've realized that I might be quite happy if I came to stay here, permanently, I mean.'

Jane could scarcely believe what she was hearing. Her mouth dropped open in shock and bewilderment as she stared at her mother. 'But . . . after all you've said. It's hard to believe . . .'

'Yes, I know what I've said,' retorted Alice sharply. 'And I still haven't changed my mind about old folks' homes, or about sons and daughters who want to get rid of their parents. But this place is different, or else I wouldn't consider it.'

Jane still continued to stare at her mother, too stunned to smile or to begin to think that this could be an answer to her prayers – because she had dared to ask for a little help from above.

'I know there's a lot to consider,' Alice went on, 'and if you don't want me to, then of course I won't do it. I can see you're not too happy about it, and I can understand that. You might not want to live on your own, and I know that the upkeep of a house is getting more expensive every year. But I won't live for ever, and I've got quite a bit put by . . .'

'Stop, Mother, stop!' cried Jane. 'I wouldn't mind at all, of course I wouldn't. I think it's a splendid idea, but—' She suddenly burst into tears, whether of happiness or sadness she didn't know. They were more like tears of frustration; the pent up anxiety that she had felt for the past few days had to have a release.

'Jane, whatever's the matter? I didn't mean to upset you.' Her mother leaned forward and took hold of her hand in a very uncharacteristic gesture. 'Come on now, love. Don't take on so, we'll be able to sort something out.'

Jane blinked back her tears and tried to compose herself. 'You've not upset me. It's just that . . . you see . . . while I was on holiday I met a man. A lovely man called Dave, and we got friendly. I know we've only known one another a short while, but we would like to carry on seeing one another, but I told him it was no use.'

'Now, why ever did you do that?' Her mother was showing an understanding that Jane had hardly ever seen before. 'I like you to have friends, even men friends, but you've never seemed bothered since Tom . . .'

'I know, Mother. I've never been interested. But Dave is . . . different. We got on so well, but there were problems.'

'What sort of problems? Where does he live? Has he been widowed, like you?'

'He lives in Shropshire. He has a small farm that he runs with his son.'

'A farmer, eh? Well, well!'

'And . . . he has been married, of course. I thought he was a widower, then he told me that his wife is still living, but she won't grant him a divorce. She's a Catholic and she thinks it's wrong; but in spite of this she's living with another man. Living in sin, as you might say, Mother.'

'Now, Jane, don't throw my words back in my face. What did you say before? Circumstances alter cases. Well, perhaps they do. I won't stand in your way if you want to go on seeing this man. You know where he lives, don't you? And he knows where you are?'

Jane shook her head. 'I've been a stupid fool,' she said. 'I wouldn't give him my address or phone number. He gave me his, and I said I would ring if I could see any way round the problem.'

'Well then, you can do so now, can't you? Not this minute,

but when we get home. Yes, I am coming home for the time being. The room I had will be in use for the next fortnight – a short-term resident like I've been – but then I can move in permanently. Mrs Meadows will come and talk to you before we go.'

Jane sighed. 'I've done something very very stupid, and I don't know why I did it. I tore up his phone numbers – I was feeling so miserable and confused – and they're all in pieces at the bottom of my bag.'

Alice shook her head. 'Honestly, Jane! Sometimes I despair of you. But there must be a way round it. You know the name of the farm, don't you? And you know where it is? Directory enquiries will help you. Come on now, what's it called?'

Jane wracked her brains. 'It's near Welshpool. He's called David Falconer. Hillside . . .? Woodside . . .? No, I think it's Cragside . . . Yes, I'm sure it is; Cragside Farm, near Welshpool.

'There you are, you see,' said Alice. 'Problem solved. Jane could tell that she wanted it solving for her own sake as well, but it was great, all the same, that she seemed so pleased about the situation.

'And here's Mrs Meadows. She'll tell you anything you want to know, although I think you found out quite a lot when you came to look round, didn't you?'

'Yes, I knew it was a place with a very high standard,' said Jane, 'and now you know that for yourself, don't you, Mother?'

'Alright; don't rub it in!' retorted Alice, in a quiet voice, as Mrs Meadows sat down beside them.

She was a woman in her fifties, the owner of the home and in overall charge. She and her husband lived in a bungalow nearby, and the residents saw little of him. He worked as a joiner in his own business and was very handy for doing odd jobs from time to time. Jane could tell that she was friendly and had a pleasant way of dealing with the residents, never patronizing them or talking down to them, but she would stand no nonsense.

Jane told her how her mother had said that she would like to come and live there permanently and that she, Jane, was very happy, though surprised at her decision.

'Yes, I think she was a little unsure about us at first, weren't you, Alice?' Mrs Meadows smiled at her knowingly.

'Yes . . . happen I was,' agreed Alice, 'but it didn't take me long to change my mind.'

They talked about the necessary details; the weekly terms, the methods of paying, etc. It was agreed that Alice should return for good in two weeks' time. Jane was amazed at the way her mother waved a cheerful goodbye to the folk in the lounge.

'Cheerio for now, but I'll be back before long. Take care now, and behave yourselves!'

Most of them smiled and waved, apart from one or two who were too engrossed in the chat show on the television.

'Come on now, ring this fellow of yours,' said Alice when they arrived home. 'Are you sure you can't read the telephone number?'

But Jane could not decipher the writing on the screwed up bit of paper. It was surprising how quickly the woman at directory enquiries came up with the number she required.

'Go on, what are you waiting for?' said her mother. 'I'll go upstairs and sort out my things.'

Thankfully she left Jane on her own. Her hands trembled a little as she picked up the receiver and dialled the number.

'It was a woman's voice that answered. 'Hello, Cragside Farm. How can I help you?'

'Could I speak to Mr Falconer, please?' asked Jane.

'Yes, of course. Do you want Mr David Falconer, or his son? They're both outside, but they're not far away.'

'Oh, David, please . . .'

'And who shall I say is calling?'

'Just tell him that it's . . . Jane.'

'Oh . . . oh yes, right away.'

Jane waited, her heart beating rapidly and her stomach churning with butterflies. Then she heard a familiar voice. 'Jane . . . Is it really you?'

'Yes . . . yes, it's me, Dave.'

'And . . .?' That was all he said, but it was a loaded question.

'And . . . it's going to be alright, Dave. I can't believe it, and neither will you. My mother's decided she wants to go and live in the home, for good! So we'll be able to meet. Isn't that wonderful?'

'It's incredible! I could hardly believe it when Kathryn said it was Jane on the phone. That was my daughter-in-law . . . to be. You'll be able to meet her soon, and Peter. I've told them about you, and they know I've been waiting and hoping . . . How soon can you come? Tomorrow?'

Jane laughed. 'No . . . I'm afraid not. We'll have to wait a couple of weeks until Mother goes back to the home.'

'Oh dear! So long?'

'Yes, I know you said, once, that I could bring Mother to meet you – and I know she'll be looking forward to that – but it will be better if I come on my own at first, don't you think so?'

'Whatever you say. I'm just so delighted, Jane, my dear. It didn't take you long to change your mind!'

'I never had any doubts about you and me. It was Mother who needed to change her mind, about all sorts of things. And I really believe she has.'

'That's wonderful . . . I shall be counting the days, the hours. It's almost too good to be true . . .'

'It's true, Dave. It really is. I must go now, but I'll see you soon.'

'Yes, not soon enough for me . . . but I understand. Goodbye for now, or as I said before, *au revoir*. And . . . I love you, Jane . . .'

'Yes, *au revoir*, Dave,' she replied. And then, a trifle shyly, 'I love you too . . .'

BAKEMONOGATARI
Monster Tale
Part 02

NISIOISIN

Art by VOFAN

Translated by Ko Ransom

VERTICAL.

BAKEMONOGATARI, PART 02

First published in Japan in 2006 by Kodansha Ltd., Tokyo.
Publication rights for this English edition arranged through Kodansha Ltd., Tokyo.

Published by Vertical, Inc., New York, 2017

ISBN 978-1-942993-89-6

Manufactured in the United States of America

First Edition

Vertical, Inc.
451 Park Avenue South, 7th Floor
New York, NY 10016

www.vertical-inc.com

CHAPTER THREE SURUGA MONKEY

CHAPTER FOUR NADEKO SNAKE

CHAPTER THREE
SURUGA MONKEY

SURUGA KANBARU

001

The name Suruga Kanbaru belongs to a celebrity known the entire school over, which of course means that I too heard it my fair share of times. My classmates Tsubasa Hanekawa and Hitagi Senjogahara may be no less celebrated, but that's strictly among third-years. Yes, despite being a year below me, Tsubasa Hanekawa, and Hitagi Senjogahara and thus a second-year, Suruga Kanbaru's renown is so extraordinary that it reaches the ears of a senior like me who's fairly estranged from those kinds of rumors. That's not normally supposed to happen. You can act like a grandee and chortle that she's sure impressive for someone so young, but in her case, the statement would be uncomfortably close to the truth.

Maybe you'd get a better sense of who Suruga Kanbaru is if I said "star" rather than "celebrity." While Tsubasa Hanekawa and Hitagi Senjogahara are seen (despite the latter's true nature) as so-called model students, diligent pupils with good grades and excellent conduct, that's not the image here at all—though, being a "star," it's not as if she's known as a rough-and-tumble ringleader of a gang of bad girls. In contrast to Tsubasa Hanekawa and Hitagi Senjogahara and their primarily academic dominance, her mastery is in the realm of sports. Suruga Kanbaru is our school's ace basketball player. After she joined the club in her first year, she was on the main roster in no time at all, but if that were it, you could reason that an unknown, perennial first-round knockout of a girls' basketball team was a joke anyway. But it would be strange to treat her as anything but a star when she ended up building a monstrous legend by leading the unknown, perennial first-round knockout of a girls' basketball team, which was a joke anyway, to the national tournament. There's no better way to put it than "ended up building" because you almost wanted to ask what she thought she was doing and scold her, the legend was so abrupt. Our girls' basketball team blew up and was elevated into an honest-to-goodness crack squad that boys' teams from neighboring high schools requested, for real and not in a haw-haw way, to play against, for practice—all thanks to one girl.

She isn't unusually tall or anything.

She's built like the average high school girl, too.

If anything, she's a little on the small and slender side.

The term "dainty" would suit her well.

But Suruga Kanbaru—can jump.

Just once, a year ago, for some reason or other, I had a chance to take a peek at a game Suruga Kanbaru was playing in—and she was so quick and agile that she didn't just pass by the other team's defenders but threaded them, and like in the sports manga that once swept Japan, scored with a clean dunk—one dunk after dunk, dozens of them, as if it were the most pleasant activity, with comfort, with ease, with the refreshing smile of an athletic girl never leaving her face. When girls' basketball teams make most of their shots using both hands, how many high schoolers can expect to witness a dunk of all things? From my position in the crowd, more than being overwhelmed by her, I felt awful for the players on the opposing team as they visibly lost their will to play, overwhelmed by her, and couldn't watch anymore, it was so painful, and had to leave. I remember it like it was yesterday.

In any case, while my high school is an academically oriented prep school, it's still a high school, full of sensitive mid-teen youths, so flashy sports heroes getting showered with more attention than evident model students who merely excel at their studies is a natural outcome—and Suruga Kanbaru doing this or that in response to whatever, every detail of her behavior that hardly seems to matter and hardly does, turns into gossip and courses through the school. I'd have enough for a book if I collected all of it. Even if I'm not interested and actively try to avoid it, information about Suruga Kanbaru reaches me anyway. If you go to our school, regardless of your year, whether she is ahead or behind you, anyone who cares to can find out, on a given day, what she ordered at the cafeteria. It's easy, you just ask someone nearby.

But rumors are rumors.

Half-serious.

They aren't necessarily true.

In fact, a lot of the rumors that make it all the way to me lack credibility and are difficult to take at face value—or rather, it's not rare for two perfectly opposed rumors to be making their rounds at the same time. She's irritable, no, she's gentle; she cares about her friends, no, she's cold; she's modest, no, she's arrogant; she goes from one wild romance to the next, no, she's never dated a boy before—anyone who actually satisfied those conditions would be a broken person. Someone like me who has seen her but never spoken to her, who probably has never come within fifteen feet of her, has to leave it to the imagination on those points. But as a practical matter, there's altogether no need for me to exercise my imagination, altogether none—we're in different years, after all, and there's no way a sports star and ace basketball player (since club activities are only for first- and second-years at my school, I feel I can at least go ahead and trust the rumor that she's been made captain) is going to have anything to do with a washout third-year like me.

We don't have the first thing to do with each other.

Naturally, she must have no idea who I am.

There ought to be no reason for her to know.

That's how I saw it.

That was my assumption.

I learned that I was mistaken as May was drawing to a close, when we'd be changing to our summer uniforms come June. By then, my hair had grown out to where it nearly hid the two small holes gouged at the bottom of my neck, and I felt relieved that wearing a band-aid for a couple of weeks should do it... Ten or so days had passed since Hitagi Senjogahara and I started seeing each other, as they say, following a

002

"Ah…Mister Ah-ah-ah-gi."

"It's Araragi."

"I'm sorry. A slip of the tongue."

As I biked down a slope getting home from school on a Friday, ahead of me I saw a little girl with pigtails carrying a backpack, namely Mayoi Hachikuji, so I hit my brakes, came to a stop to her left, and called out to her, at which she blinked and acted surprised and mispronounced my name like always.

While a small part of me was touched that my name could still be mangled in a new way, I, ever conscientious, corrected her.

"Don't be turning me into some sidekick who takes his name from his cluelessness."

"I think it sounded quite cute."

"I sounded like a total loser."

"Hmm. Well, I think that might be surprisingly fitting." The fifth grader could let some mean words slip out of her mouth. "In any case, I'm glad to see that you're doing well, Mister Araragi. I'm delighted that we're able to meet like this again. How have you been? Has anything in particular happened since then?"

"Huh? Oh, no, not really. That kind of thing isn't common. I've been living in peace. Peace, or maybe quiet. Oh, but I do have my skills test coming up soon, and there hasn't been much peace or quiet in my life when it comes to that."

About two weeks earlier—May fourteenth, Mother's Day.

I met her, Mayoi Hachikuji, in a park that day, and found myself getting wrapped up in a bit of a case as a result… Well, what happened wasn't concrete enough to be called a case, nor general enough to highlight or spotlight, but at any rate, I was involved in *an experience that wasn't quite normal.*

When I say it wasn't normal, I mean it wasn't normal.

But we were able to solve it in the end thanks to the help of an unpleasant dude, namely Oshino, and Senjogahara—and everything was fine, but if what happened on May fourteenth was fate and not a fluke, then spending every day of the following two weeks in peace and quiet must have also been fate and not a fluke.

As far as I could tell, Hachikuji was doing okay too—which seemed to mean that the Mother's Day incident had come to an amicable end. This was rare since the experience wasn't a normal one. In that regard, for me—and Hanekawa—and Senjogahara—what came after our not-quite-normal experiences, their aftermath, was actually tougher to deal with—or much crueler. More miserable, even.

Mayoi Hachikuji.

In that regard, I envied her.

"Oh, is something the matter? How indecent of you, Mister Araragi, to stare at me with such passionate eyes."

"…What passionate eyes?" And indecent? This was some low passion.

"Stare at me with such eyes a second more and you'll make me go *hic.*"

"What's wrong with your diaphragm?"

Eek, maybe.

Well, considering her circumstances, it wouldn't be right simply to feel envious of her…because in a way it's Hachikuji who has it the toughest and cruelest, neither me nor Hanekawa nor Senjogahara. I'm sure many people would be inclined to take that view.

As I mused, two high school students passed to the left of my bike. Both of them were girls. They were wearing uniforms from a different school than mine. The pair looked at Hachikuji and me with clear suspicion, and unsubtly hushing their voices, whispered as they passed by, in an extremely grating display… I suppose high school senior Koyomi Araragi engaging in earnest conversation with fifth grader Mayoi Hachikuji appeared very dodgy to ordinary sensibilities.

Fine.

The cold gaze of society didn't bother me.

I hadn't accosted Hachikuji without the necessary resolve. Why, all that really mattered was that she and I understood the truth. Shallow prejudice was powerless against the friendship that she and I had forged.

"Oh dear, Mister Araragi, it seems those two figured out that you're a pedophile. My deepest condolences."

"Don't you be saying that!"

"There's no need to be embarrassed. Being fond of little girls isn't, in and of itself, against the law. Your preferences and predilections are your own. It's just that you mustn't practice your abnormal philosophy."

"You know, even if I did like little girls, I'd hate you!"

We hadn't forged any friendship.

I seemed to be surrounded by people like her.

I glanced behind me.

We were alone now.

For the time being.

"…You're a scarily promising kid, you know that? But Hachikuji, what're you doing here wandering around at this hour? Did you get lost on your way somewhere again?"

"Isn't that quite the rude way to put it, Mister Araragi. I've never been lost since the day I was born."

"That's an impressive memory you got there."

"You're making me blush with your compliments."

"No, it really is impressive. Being able to forget all the stupid, inconvenient stuff."

"Oh, not at all. By the way, who are you again?"

"I've been forgotten!"

It was a pretty neat riposte.

She had good taste.

"…Really, though, even if it's a joke, it's depressing to be forgotten by someone, Hachikuji."

"I forget all the stupid, inconvenient people."

"Hey, I'm not so stupid that you can call me that! And I said stuff, not people!"

"I forget all the stupid, inconvenient...stuff."

"Good, good, that's…not right! It's not right at all! You shouldn't go around calling people 'stuff'!"

"But you said to, yourself."

"Be quiet. No playing gotcha."

"You're very self-centered, aren't you, Mister Araragi? Very well, then. I'll be considerate and put it another way."

"Let's hear it…"

"Stupid, convenient people."

"………"

It was a fun conversation.

To be honest, I did have some reservations about myself, this high schooler named Koyomi Araragi who chatted with a fifth grader like we were peers, but it did feel pretty similar to talking to my sisters, who were in middle school, so… Plus, maybe it was the difference between elementary and middle school girls, but Hachikuji wasn't strangely touchy or oddly cynical, and our conversation had a better flow to it than when I talked to my little sisters.

"Haa…"

With a sigh, I got off my bicycle.

Pushing its handlebars, I began walking forward.

Talking with Hachikuji was fun, but standing around and running on for too long could have an adverse effect on my later plans. Not that I was particularly pressed for time, but I still decided to push along my bike as we spoke. Better to walk and talk than stand and talk. Hachikuji must have been wandering around without a specific destination because she strolled alongside my bike without a word or gesture from me. I bet she just had nothing to do.

There was another reason that I chose to get going—I glanced behind again, but it looked like I didn't need to worry on that account for the time being.

"Where are you headed, Mister Araragi?"

"Mm. Home, for now."

"For now? So will you be going out after that?"

"Yeah, I guess—remember what I just told you about the skills test being soon?"

"Your skills, which is to say your very worth, will be facing a moment of truth?"

"It's nothing that big... The moment of truth is simply whether or not I'll graduate."

"Is that so. The moment of truth of whether you'll not graduate."

"........."

It meant the same thing, but the nuance was so different.

Such a tricky affair, this language thing.

"Mister Araragi, you are, after all, a convenient person mentally."

"I'd honestly be happier if you just said I was stupid."

"No, I'd never. There are some things that are better off taken for granted."

"But not better off left unsaid, I see!"

"Oh, um, don't worry. I don't have the best grades either, so we're in the same boat, the same boat, okay?"

"......"

I was being comforted by an elementary schooler.

In the same boat as an elementary schooler.

Not only that, when it came to herself, she wasn't stupid but merely didn't have "the best grades." Mayoi Hachikuji was slyly deceptive.

"Well, it actually hits close to home for me," I said. "I'm seriously going to be in a bad spot if I bungle this skills test."

"Will you be expelled?"

"No matter how preppy of a prep school it is, I'm not going to be expelled over a low test score. I mean, any prep school where I would sounds like a setup to a joke. So the worst that can happen is that I'll have to repeat a grade, but... But I do want to avoid that."

If I could.

No, not if I could. I had to.

"Hm. In that case, Mister Araragi, are you really in a position to be going out again today? You should hurry and lock yourself in at home and study for your test."

"Surprisingly solid advice, Hachikuji."

"'Solid advice'? That's two words too many, sir!"

"But 'surprisingly' was fine?!"

What a born entertainer.

"Well, there's no need for you to worry, Hachikuji, if anything you've hit the nail on the head. I don't need to be told. You see, I may be going out, but it's not to play or to shop. I'm going out to study."

"Hrm?" Hachikuji tilted her head like a grownup. "So you're saying you're going to study at the library or something? Hmm. I personally think that the best environment for studying is a familiar one where you can relax, like your own room… Oh, or will you be going to a cram school or something?"

"If I had to say, cram school would be closer to the mark," I answered. "You remember Senjogahara, don't you? Well, she gets some of the top grades in our whole year, and she promised to coach me at her place today."

"Miss Senjogahara…"

Hachikuji folded her arms and faced down.

Wait, had she forgotten? Not because it was inconvenient, but possibly out of fear?

"Her full name is Hitagi Senjogahara," I tried to remind her. "You know, the lady with the ponytail who was with me the other day, who helped—"

"Oh, that *tsundere*?"

"………"

She did remember.

It appeared as though Senjogahara was being granted the "t——e" title all around town… Was she okay with that? I needed to ask her how that made her feel, just so I'd know how to react, on my part.

"She was an endlessly tolerant women, I recall. She carried me on her back the entire time as she showed me the way."

"Those are some really embellished memories, you know?!"

Senjogahara was functioning like a trauma for Hachikuji. Considering their respective circumstances, that almost made sense…

"Hmm," murmured Hachikuji, her arms still crossed. "Oh, but… if I'm not mistaken, you and Miss Senjogahara are—well, um, how to put it."

Hachikuji seemed to be choosing her words with care. I had a good idea what her question was, but I got the impression that she was reluctant to phrase it in a bald way and was searching for a different expression. While I wouldn't call it curiosity, I was somewhat interested in the selection process her fifth-grade vocabulary would undergo, so I stood there and watched, offering her no lifeline.

Finally, she said, "You've entered into a lovers' contract, correct?"

"You couldn't have done worse!"

To no one's surprise, I found myself yelling at her.

Another textbook interaction between us.

"Excuse me? Did I say something odd, Mister Araragi?"

"On the surface, you didn't use any funny words, but few people would fail to smell something rotten from their nuance…"

"If the word 'contract' is the problem…then what about 'transaction'? A lovers' transaction."

"You did manage to make it worse! Just speak like a normal person, I don't care!"

"Hmph. All right, as you wish. I'll speak like a normal person. Normal comes easy to me when I feel like it. Here I go, are you ready? If I'm not mistaken, you are Miss Senjogahara's gentleman caller."

"…Um, I guess."

Now she was coming at me with an awfully musty locution.

That was her idea of normal?

"So this claim that she'll be coaching you is surely no more than a pretext, and you'll end up trading caresses?"

"………"

Another musty expression.

Something was definitely off about her vocabulary.

"Mister Araragi, if I may, visiting your lover's home right before a skills test that will ascertain if you can repeat a grade is nothing short of suicidal."

"It'll ascertain if I can graduate." She seemed to think that I was a pretty big idiot. You poor thing, I pitied myself. "And don't be calling it 'suicidal,' either."

"All right, then. It seems like nothing short of suicide."

I was being bullied by an elementary school kid. You poor thing, I pitied myself. "Watch it," I warned her, "or I'll bust you up, sooner or later…"

"Bust me up? Are you talking about my chest? What exactly are you seeking from my elementary-school body?"

"Shut up. Don't play gotcha when you haven't even gotten me."

I bonked Hachikuji on the head.

In return, Hachikuji kicked my shin.

Draw declared, out of mutual respect.

"Well anyway, Hachikuji, no need to worry on that point… Senjogahara is ridiculously strict about these things."

"She's strict about studying? How Spartan. Ah, now that you say so, she didn't seem the type to suffer fools gladly."

"Yep. She said as much herself."

That's why she found children insufferable.

Including Hachikuji.

Maybe she found me insufferable, too.

Though, of course, I wasn't only talking about studying when I described Senjogahara as "strict"… Well, let's just agree that she's a model student.

"So she's like Gunnery Sergeant Heartful," Hachikuji said.

"Whoever that is sounds like the friendliest NCO ever."

"Um, I believe Miss Senjogahara's home is near that park—"

"No, I think I already told you, but she moved away a while ago—I've already been there once, a little before I met you, and it's pretty far. If I go home, switch bikes, and head over… Ugh, now that I'm looking at the time, I kind of need to hurry."

"If you're in a rush, I won't be so boorish as to keep you."

"No, I don't have my back against the wall or anything yet."

I may have been heading to Senjogahara's, but it was still to study, and the honest truth was that I couldn't quite get in the mood…though who knew what acid-tongued abuse Senjogahara would unleash if I told her that.

Oh boy.

Hitagi Senjogahara.

It was true of Hachikuji, too, but Senjogahara was certainly—

"Hey, Hachikuji…are you—"

Just then.

Mid-sentence, I heard a sound from behind me.

A sound.

The sound of footsteps.

A sharp and lively rhythm, less a series of strides than leaps, outright jumps, *tup, tup, tup, tup, tup, tup*—such footsteps.

There was no need to glance behind me to confirm.

Yeah, I guessed not…

In terms of not being able to enjoy some peace and quiet, I was burdened with another dire threat on top of the skills test…

Just when I thought I'd shaken it.

Tup, tup, tup, tup, tup, tup.

The footsteps got closer and closer.

There was no need to confirm, but still—

I couldn't help it.

Tupp!

Just as I completed my reluctant, recalcitrant turn—she leapt.

She, Suruga Kanbaru, was leaping through the air.

Across more than just several feet, as though performing a long jump, airborne with an ideal form and trajectory that seemed to ignore the law of universal gravitation—and passing me to my right still air-borne, almost at eye level—

She landed.

Her fluttering hair settled when she did.

A school uniform.

This time, needless to say, it was my school's.

Her scarf was colored second-year yellow.

By the way, leaping in her uniform meant that her skirt, modified to be shorter as they are these days, had flown up as well, but since she wore bike shorts that reached to her knees—the pleasure wasn't mine.

Her skirt, too, fell back into place just a moment later.

Suddenly, I noticed a smell like burning rubber.

The source seemed to be intense friction between the asphalt and the soles of her unmistakably expensive sneakers… How exceptionally athletic was she, anyway?

Then our basketball ace, Suruga Kanbaru—turned around.

Though not thoroughly adult, her expression was cool and commanding in a way most third-years couldn't pull off, and her handsome eyes—looked straight at me.

She placed her hand on her chest as if she were about to make a pledge.

Then she flashed a little grin.

"Hello there, my senior Araragi. What a coincidence."

"I've never heard of such a contrived coincidence!"

She'd obviously sprinted in my direction.

When I looked around, Hachikuji was clean gone. Despite being blunt and brusque toward me, Mayoi Hachikuji was a surprisingly bashful kid, and she'd exercised a snap judgment and fleet-footedness to go with it. Of course, just about anyone would flee if a strange woman came dashing at such an unholy speed (it must have looked like Kanbaru was heading straight for her from where she stood).

Still, she really wasn't much of a friend, was she…

Fine, fine.

When I looked back at Kanbaru, she was nodding over and over again like she was utterly enchanted and profoundly moved for some reason.

"…What's the matter?"

"No, I was just pondering your words, to engrave them deep in my heart. 'I've never heard of such a contrived coincidence'… The perfect line for the occasion, the kind that everyone hopes to come up with but fails to. That's what I call a razor wit."

"………"

"Yes, you're right," Kanbaru said. "I did come chasing after you."

"...Um, yeah. I know."

"Ah, so you did know. Anything a fledgling like me tries to pull is transparent to someone of your caliber, I take it. This is awkward, and I could not feel more embarrassed, but I am duly impressed."

"........."

What are you supposed to say to that?

God knows what kind of expression was stuck on my face at that moment, but Suruga Kanbaru paid no mind and brandished her vivid smile at me.

Three days earlier.

As I walked down the hallway, the very same Suruga Kanbaru approached me with resonant footsteps and began talking to me like it was nothing. So much so that I ended up replying normally, but this was the star second-year, a celebrity known the school over, someone whom even I, a third-year estranged from such gossip, knew of—but never dreamed of having anything to do with in any conceivable way—so I was quite surprised.

But what really surprised me was her personality. Well, I don't know what to call it, but I do know it's bizarre... Suruga Kanbaru possessed a disposition, a character I'd never encountered in my whole life.

And.

Ever since, meaning from three days ago to this exact day and moment—I'd been followed around by her like this. No matter when, no matter where, no matter who might be watching, *tup, tup, tup, tup, tup, tup*, Kanbaru was dashing towards me.

"Putting break periods aside," I asked her, "didn't you have practice after school? Should you even be here?"

"A-ha. So astute, as I've come to expect. You're like the hero of a detective story who never misses the slightest discrepancy. You'd give Philip Marlowe a run for his money, a barefoot run."

"A national-tier basketball player shouldn't be here at this hour, it's just odd, so enough with the flattery."

If that was all it took to send the hero of a detective story running to his mommy, then I didn't want to read that series.

Kanbaru was beaming. "Such modest words of self-admonition,

you never fail to value humility as an asset that's second only to your life... I'm prone to overestimating myself and ought to learn from you, starting right now. Ha ha, they say that one bad apple spoils the whole barrel, but I can feel myself growing as a person just from being with you. Now I know what 'emulating' is all about."

There was no malice in her smile.

...In my life so far, I'd taken "a good person" to mean someone like Hanekawa, but I wondered if the ultimate specimens were actually more like Kanbaru.

In other words, they were even worse than Hanekawa.

Even more of a pain than our class president.

"But see, my hand is like this right now," Kanbaru said, sticking out her left arm.

Her left arm, wrapped tight in a white bandage. Over every inch, from all five of her fingertips to her wrist. The long sleeves of her school uniform hid the rest of her arm, but the bandage probably extended up to around her elbow. I'd heard that a little while ago, she'd suffered a mishap during a solo workout and given herself a nasty sprain, or something—well, I'd heard that as a rumor, right before Kanbaru talked to me.

Rumors are rumors.

Suruga Kanbaru with her athletic prowess and flexibility spraining herself, solo workout or not, was hard to take even with a grain of salt—but since her arm was bandaged, I supposed it was the truth. Everyone makes mistakes, to err is human, even monkeys fall from trees.

"Since I can't play, I'd only get in the team's way at the gym. That's why I'm refraining from going to practices now."

"Still, aren't you the captain? Even as it is, the team's morale is sure to drop without you."

"I'm disappointed to know that you think I'm carrying the whole team on my back. My team isn't so feckless that their morale would drop just because I'm not around," Kanbaru said in a tougher tone. "Basketball is a harsh sport. You can't count on any single person to win the game. Sure, the position and role I play means that I stand out, but it's only thanks to everyone else. The praise that gets showered on me ought to be shared by the whole team."

"...Uh, I guess you're right."

What was the word for someone like her?

Decent? Virtuous?

What was it.

It seemed that, not just now but in general, Kanbaru was incredibly sensitive to people insulting her teammates (not that I was trying to). When she was a first-year, she flipped a table when the school newspaper was interviewing her because they said something rude about one of her elder comrades—or so one rumor went (if you're curious, the rumor ended up being false, but something similar did happen).

Heheh, a laugh escaped Kanbaru's lips. "I know. You were putting my aptitude as a captain to the test, weren't you?"

"........."

What was this second-year saying to me now with such a smug and triumphant look?

Turn that gaze away from me.

"My senior, in recording your words for future generations, the writer better bold and underline them so their impression is imparted to the readers. The weight you invest in each word is overwhelming. 'It's not what you say, but who says it'—they often mean that in a negative sense, but you're the one person who gives it a positive spin. Please, relax. I don't intend to abandon my responsibilities as captain; I'm not so self-absorbed as to be that negligent. I'm aware that I have to live up to being our ace and made sure to issue workout routines. If anything, they're focusing on practice with greater ease thanks to my absence. When the devil's away, the mice will play."

"The devil, huh? Well, I'm relieved to hear it anyway."

"Sport or not, it's just a club activity for students. Moreover, ours is a prep school. At the end of the day, an extracurricular is a way for us teens to have some memories, so fun, free, and friendly does it. Even so, most of my betters wouldn't bother to have anything to do with me, but not only are you looking out for my relationships, you're even thinking of my teammates. I feel bad for making you so concerned. Such depth of character expands my own horizons—to think that you'd even play the villain for the basketball team's sake. Only someone who truly cares about his juniors could go that far. I've never met a person like you before, sir."

"I've never met a person like you before, either…"

She was breaking new ground…

A natural-born killer with kindness…

"Is that so," she said. "There's no greater honor than to hear that from you. Heheh, what is this feeling, inspiration? It's as though getting praised by someone as gracious as you has opened up a whole new well of courage in me. I feel like I can do anything now. From this day on, whenever I feel down, I'm going to come to you. A few words from my mentor will make me pick myself back up again, I know it."

Kanbaru's smile refused to leave her face even for a moment.

Her expression almost looked unguarded—but it wasn't, due to an undeniable strength that resided at its core. Only someone with absolute confidence in herself could wear such a smile.

We belonged to completely different worlds.

We belonged to completely different categories.

Well, that went without saying—not even counting our personalities, the athletic girl Kanbaru, the school star, and Koyomi Araragi belonging to different worlds, different categories, was self-evident, so the question was why someone like Suruga Kanbaru had chosen to talk to me.

Not just chosen. Why she continued to.

Why she dashed toward me—and continued to do so.

It couldn't be that she was, in her own words, coming to me because she felt down and needed to cheer herself back up. I didn't have that kind of supernatural power. If I did, I'd be using it liberally on myself.

I'd lost count of how many times I'd asked the question over the last three days, but I asked again. "So, Kanbaru. What do you want from me?"

"Ah, yes…" She'd been making quick, eloquent replies thus far, but now for the first time seemed to be searching for the right words. But it only took a second before her cheeks were lit by a smile and she opened her mouth. "You must have read the international section of today's paper, yes? I wanted to hear your thoughts on the unfolding political situation in Russia."

"Current events?!"

What a topic to ask about, too. I barely knew anything about Japanese politics, but we were crossing the sea and talking about Russia?

"Oh, would India be more to your taste?" she offered. "But as you can guess, sadly I'm something of a jock, an outdoors type, who's weak on IT-related topics. I have a better feel for the problems facing Russia."

"I didn't read the paper this morning," I gave an excuse so blatant I couldn't possibly play it down myself. Actually, I do read it, but can't make enough of anything to partake in a discussion…

Yet Kanbaru merely said "Oh," and her eyes took on a tender cast. "Well, you are a busy man. I can see how you might not have the time to read the paper in the morning. I apologize, I should have thought of it before blabbering so inconsiderately. We can put the topic off until tomorrow in that case, if that's all right with you."

"Sure…"

"How generous of you. I didn't expect to be forgiven so easily. There is simply no way someone with your gravitas didn't find my remark superficial, but you let it go without so much as hinting at your displeasure. Now that's what it means to be a diplomat. I never thought that I could come to like you even more."

"Well, thanks…"

"No need for gratitude. I'm only telling you how I feel."

"……"

Regardless, she seemed pretty smart.

Being both smart and athletic wasn't playing by the rules at all… It wasn't like Hanekawa and Senjogahara were bad at sports, but they couldn't begin to compare to this second-year. Sure, Senjogahara may have been the star of the track team in middle school, but the gap in her résumé after starting high school wasn't negligible—more so if you added in her special circumstances.

Well, of course, I didn't really think that Kanbaru wanted to debate me on the political situation in Russia—that was clearly a pretext. No matter how many times I asked her what she wanted from me, she was this way and wouldn't give a straight reply.

She had to have some objective, but I didn't have the first clue.

Why in the world was she following me around, and so suddenly? She, the star of the entire school, and I, a third-year washout, hadn't a single thing in common.

I ought to be a total stranger to her.

"By the way, did anything odd happen to you today?" she asked.

"Hunh? Not really… Everything's normal." Aside from her. Well, I was starting to get used to her, too. "I have a headache thanks to the skills test we have coming up, I guess?"

"Oh, the skills test. Hm, yes. It's been giving me a headache as well. It's quite a pain, as someone involved in an extracurricular. Our school prohibits any practices for a week before the test, so your only choice is to train solo."

"Huh."

So that's how it worked. I had trouble understanding her logic that if the school banned it, she had to work out on her own, instead of just taking a break. But hers was a different world.

"But Kanbaru, isn't that a good thing, at least from your perspective? Your sprained left hand should heal by then."

"Hm? Oh…true." She looked down at her hand. "Impressive, you simply see things in a different way. Always trying to figure out how to make everyone around you happy. You're a real master of positive thinking."

"Hey, I could think positively for a hundred years and never get to your level…"

What kind of upbringing turned out people like her?

It baffled me.

"I know it's a cliché," she conceded, "but it is a student's job to study. As annoying as they are, skills tests are skills tests, and I'm not going to take mine lightly."

"Good thing it wasn't your right hand."

"Well, I'm actually a southpaw," Kanbaru said. "Being left-handed means you have to deal with a lot of day-to-day inconveniences, but the one place it can be an advantage is the world of competitive sports. I treasure my birthright."

"Huh, really?"

"Mm. That's common knowledge for anyone in competitive sports. In Japan, parents still tend to correct their children's left-handedness, so only one out of ten athletes, at most, is a southpaw. What do you think that ratio means in the sport of basketball? It's a five-on-five game, so on average there's only one on the court. And that would be me. It's one of the reasons I was able to become our ace."

"Huh…" I felt convinced, but of what I wasn't sure.

"Still, when something like this happens, be it the result of my own carelessness, all I'm left with is a bunch of inconveniences."

"A southpaw, eh… I don't really understand any of that because I don't play sports, but being left-handed just seems cool."

That was my honest take.

Well, it was more of a preconception, even a prejudice, but somehow every little thing lefties did seemed more stylish to me.

"You say that, but aren't you left-handed too? Heheh, I noticed immediately because you have your watch on your right wrist. Lefties are quick to pick up on fellow lefties."

"……"

I wore my watch on my right wrist just because I felt like it, but now I didn't dare tell her… Was I going to have to write and use chopsticks with my left hand in her presence going forward? Lefties seemed stylish to me, but not to the point where I'd reverse-correct myself…

"So," I said, "taking the test will be quite a challenge for you. With your good hand in that shape, the Japanese exam will suck bad."

"True, but since this is a skills test, we won't have to write essays in any subject, and a few oddly shaped characters here and there shouldn't be an issue. I'm sure the teachers will take my situation into account, too. Pardon me, it sounds like I've caused you undue concern. I do have to say, though, you really do look out for your juniors. To be able to worry about someone like me because you feel so relaxed. That's no simple feat."

"…Uh, I don't know about relaxed." Far from it. Putting aside whether I'd worry about my juniors if I were relaxed, I was anything but at the moment. "In fact, I'm about to go to a study session today."

"A study session?" Kanbaru's confusion was apparent. It wasn't ringing any bells for her.

"Um, I guess a simple way to put it would be that my grades until now haven't been the best…plus I had a pretty bad attendance record during my first and second years of high school, so…"

Why was I having to explain to her?

Star or not, she was a year below me, my junior.

"In short, this skills test is my big chance to make a comeback," I found myself putting a good face on it. I felt small.

"Hmm. I see." Kanbaru nodded. "I don't really understand because I'm not the type to hustle when it comes to exam prep, but now that you mention it, my classmates do gather at someone's house before a test…I think?"

"Yeah, that's pretty much what I'm doing."

"Okay. So you're about to head to a friend's house. But," Kanbaru said a little uncertainly, "unlike with sports, I don't see how working together can help…"

"Don't worry. I said it was a study session, but it's a one-on-one where someone's going to be teaching me, that's all. It's like I'm going to be tutored. There's someone in my class with ridiculously good grades who's going to be helping me out."

"Huh… Ohh." As if she'd just remembered, Kanbaru added, "You're talking about my senior Senjogahara."

"…What? You know her?"

"Who else could it be if it's someone with good grades in your class? I've heard rumors about her."

"Huh… Well, yeah."

Senjogahara was famous, after all. Maybe it wasn't surprising that a second-year knew about her.

Hm?

But wait. As far as being famous for good grades went, the first person to come to mind should have been the even more famous Hanekawa, who'd never once ceded her spot at the top of our year. At the very least, it didn't make sense to be saying it couldn't be anyone else. Also, if someone mentioned a study session, wouldn't you normally assume that it was a same-sex affair and bring up a boy's name, not a girl's?

Why was she bringing up Senjogahara out of nowhere?

"I shouldn't get in your way, then," Kanbaru said. "I think I'll get going for today."

"Okay."

It was very Suruga Kanbaru to stick in the "for today" even as she made a show of not overstaying her welcome.

She squatted and stretched her legs.

Warm-ups.

She took her time stretching her Achilles tendon, and then—

"May fortune smile on you."

No sooner than she said so, she dashed back the way she came, her footsteps ringing *tup, tup, tup, tup, tup, tup*. She had strong legs—not only was she fast, she was abnormally quick to hit her top speed. While I doubt her hundred or two hundred meter times are that outstanding, she must be a good match even for members of the track team at ultra-short distances like thirty or fifty feet. That's where Suruga Kanbaru, an athlete specializing in basketball, a sport where you run in every direction within a limited play field, shines…and then, before I knew it, she was out of sight. Her short skirt flew up from her vigorous motions, but that surely didn't bother Kanbaru, who wore bike shorts long enough to extend below her skirt.

…Still, I thought, she ought to wear a tracksuit when she runs. That way she'd spare onlookers like me from getting our vile hopes up.

Sheesh, though.

It felt like a weight had been lifted from my shoulders.

This encounter had been relatively brief, but…if she didn't hurry up and reveal why she was following me around, I couldn't rest easy, since this situation might drag on. Sure, it wasn't causing me any actual damage or harm, so leaving her be was technically an option, but that personality of Kanbaru's did more than a little to tire out people like me. No, was there anyone out there who wouldn't get tired talking to her? If there was—

Yeah. Maybe Senjogahara was the only person on that list.

"Mister Rararagi."

"...You're asymptotically closer to the right pronunciation compared to the last thing you called me, but Hachikuji, don't sing my name like you're a cartoon dog. My name is Araragi."

"I'm sorry. A slip of the tongue."

"No, you're doing it on purpose..."

"It was a srip."

"Or maybe not?!"

"It was a trip."

"What were you seeing?!"

Hachikuji was suddenly back by my side.

She must have returned after realizing that Kanbaru had left. I couldn't be sure, as this was Hachikuji I was dealing with, but given how promptly she'd come back, maybe she felt her fair share of guilt for running off and leaving me on my own. Perhaps this time, she really had mistaken my name on purpose, to hide her embarrassment.

"What was with that person?" she asked.

"You couldn't tell by watching us?"

"Hmm. Since she referred to you as her senior, if I may don my thinking hat, is she your junior at school?"

"...That's some impressive thinking hat."

If I were Kanbaru, this was where I'd whip out Marlowe or some other classic detective to praise Hachikuji to high heaven, but no—for a moment I thought I might try to borrow a page, but my heart was refusing to let me...

"Even so, Mister Araragi. I was all ears, but it was very hard to understand what that person was getting at. To the very end I couldn't figure out the gist of your conversation. Had she chased after you to chat about nothing in particular?"

"Um... Well, Hachikuji, don't ask me because I don't know, either."

"You don't? I can't help but be receptacle."

"So you turned into a trashcan while you were gone?"

Skeptical, I assumed.

I decided to tell Hachikuji exactly what was going on. "That girl's been stalking me."

"Stalking? Like what women wear over their lower bodies?"

"That's a stocking."

"Are you sure?"

"Do you really not know the word? She's been following me no matter how much I try to skirt around her."

"Skirt? Like what women wear over their lower bodies?"

"How did Mister Araragi become so obsessed with what ladies wear below their waists in your mind?"

I thought for a bit to see if I could come up with a word Hachikuji might confuse with bike shorts. Unfortunately, my vocabulary wasn't up to the task, so I gave up and kept the conversation moving.

"I don't understand why, but for about three days now, she's been shadowing me blatantly and then popping up and starting a conversation. One-sidedly, so like you said, I can't figure out what she's trying to get at… I don't know if you'd call it chatting, and I honestly have no idea what her goal is."

Her goal—well, she had to have one.

But I didn't have the first clue what it was.

She was deflecting my attempts to find out, for sure.

The athletic grounds are about the only place third- and second-year students see each other, which means we almost never meet by coincidence—in other words, Kanbaru was making the most of short breaks during the day to seek me out… I'd figured that out, but not much else.

"Hmm. You know, Mister Araragi, isn't there an easy answer sitting right there? Doesn't she just like you?"

"Wha?"

"I believe she said something to that effect."

"…Oh, I guess? Nah, give me a break. It was just a manner of speaking. I'm not a dating sim protagonist, it's not like I'm going to wake up one day and suddenly have girls all over me."

"You're right. Because if you were a dating sim protagonist, I'd be one of your flagged targets, and that's absolutely not happening."

"……"

Did elementary school kids know about dating sims?

Not like I had ever played one, either.

"But if you were," Hachikuji continued, "I'm sure I'd have a high difficulty rating."

"No, I get the feeling you'd be a pushover..."

If not for her shyness attribute, it'd all happen very quickly... In a game with six heroines, she'd be around the fourth to go down.

Of course, if you took the age issue into account, she'd be a high-difficulty character indeed.

"Kanbaru isn't," I objected, "that kind of... Ah, now that you mention it, I guess there are rumors that she goes from one wild romance to the next. Still, she and I had literally nothing to do with each other until now, okay? Unlike them...unlike Kanbaru and others, I'm not a school celebrity or anything."

But upon further thought, I realized she had at least known my name and what class I was in when she first spoke to me.

Why?

Could she have...asked someone?

"Maybe she saw you picking an abandoned cat off the street," Hachikuji said.

"I've never done that."

In fact, I'd never once stumbled upon a so-called abandoned cat. In the first place, would a cat plunked in a cardboard box labeled "please adopt me" just sit in place?

That would be one well-trained cat.

"Then perhaps she saw you picking garbage off the street?"

"Hold on, did you just put cats on the same level as garbage?"

"It was only a manner of speaking, as you put it, so stop scrounging for reasons to criticize me. That's a very vulgar hobby you have, Mister Araragi, finding sport in castigating weak little girls for things they never said."

"Apologize to catkind. Cats can be scary, you know."

"In any case, love at first sight does exist. They even say that relationships between people in general are based on first impressions. At least, looking at it that way explains why you're being followed around, doesn't it?" Hachikuji was yelping gleefully. She was an elementary schoolgirl in that way. “I'm certain of it, the woman in me is telling me that I'm right. So what will you do, Mister Araragi? She's only nibbling now, but she might confess her feelings for you soon enough. What will you do, what will you do, what will you do?”

“Listen. I don't like how people try to see everything in romantic terms. The ‘power of love’ they go on about in old foreign films? Imagine how peaceful the world would be if that did solve everything. No way, no how. Some simple, small-time, realistic goal makes much better sense.

“And anyway,” I said. “I've already cleared the highest difficulty character of all.”

003

"I feel like someone said something unpleasant about me," Hitagi Senjogahara suddenly mumbled.

The comment was so abrupt and unprovoked that, out of shock, the pencil in my hand froze in place on my notebook.

Yet it seemed she was mumbling entirely to herself because she switched topics.

"Still, teaching is so difficult."

After that, I'd walked back home with Hachikuji talking about all sorts of things, including about Kanbaru, and parted ways when I arrived. The little girl wandered around in one place or another all the time, so I was sure I'd meet her again somewhere. Then, after taking off my backpack, changing my clothes, and stuffing my textbooks, notes, and study-aids into a Boston bag, I switched from the granny bike I rode to school to my mountain bike and headed to Senjogahara's. My little sisters had already returned and almost got around to interrogating me, but luckily I managed to escape.

As I'd mentioned to Hachikuji, Senjogahara's place was fairly far from mine, a distance I normally wouldn't travel by bicycle. But taking the bus actually meant having to walk more, so going by bike felt quicker to me—which was subjective, and since this was only my second time visiting Senjogahara's, and the first time straight from my place, I couldn't say for sure.

The Tamikura Apartments—a two-story wooden building.

Room 201.

A hundred-or-so square feet, a small sink.

It was so cramped that two high school students of average build facing each other across a low table with their study materials spread out around them filled up the space. It was what you'd call a single-father household, and Senjogahara what you'd call an only child, and her father what you'd call stuck at work until late at night, so we were, of course, alone.

Koyomi Araragi and Hitagi Senjogahara.

Two healthy teenagers by themselves in a cramped room.

A man and a woman.

Who were officially going out, too.

Boyfriend and girlfriend.

And yet.

"...Why am I studying right now," I said.

"Hm? Because you're stupid?"

"What a mean way to put it!"

She was absolutely right. But.

It couldn't hurt if there was a little more going on.

We started dating on the same day we got ourselves mixed up with Mayoi Hachikuji, on Mother's Day, May fourteenth. About two weeks had passed since then, but it would be no exaggeration to say that absolutely nothing sexual had taken place between us in that time.

....

Hold on, we hadn't even gone on a date yet.

Come to think of it.

We met in the morning at school, talked during break...ate lunch together...then walked home together partway...and said see you tomorrow. That was about it. That was the kind of thing that the cooler kids did regardless of gender if they were friends...

I wouldn't say that I particularly craved a sexual turn of events, but some development you'd expect between lovers would have been nice.

"In my life so far, Araragi, I've never struggled at anything involving the word 'study,' so I don't have the slightest idea what's giving you so much trouble and what you're stuck on… I don't understand what you don't understand."

"Is that so…"

She really knew what to say to get me down.

How wide was the gap between her academic abilities and mine, anyway? Was it a canyon so vast you couldn't see the other side?

"Are you acting like you don't get it," Senjogahara asked, "just to make me laugh?"

"Like I'd go that far… But it's not like you were born smart, right, Senjogahara? Isn't it thanks to blood and tears that you maintain your place near the top of the class?"

"Do you think that's the kind of thing people who work hard worry about?"

"…Okay."

"Oh, but don't get me wrong. There are people whose hard work never pays off, who don't even know how to begin working hard, like you, and I do pity them."

"Please don't pity us!"

"I despair for you."

"G-Gah! Is the rule that whenever I make a quip about it, you get even harsher?! Even begging for mercy is a risky move!"

Bizarre game we were playing.

"No weed actually goes by that name," she said, "but 'small fry' is an actual species of fish…"

"There's no such fish, either!"

"No weed actually goes by that name, but there are people who do…"

"Only if other people call them that!"

"Anyway, I'm feeling motivated because helping you pass this skills test will let me take another step forward as a person."

"Don't be treating my grades like they're your rite of passage… And there are other things you ought to attend to first if you want to grow as a person."

"Oh, be quiet. I've strangled you to death."

"In the present perfect tense?! Am I already dead?!"

Getting her to teach me may have been a mistake… Hmm, should I have just asked Hanekawa?

However.

Despite my protestations to Hachikuji, I had to admit to a motive so cute it would be embarrassing even to call it ulterior, that just maybe something might happen if I was alone with Senjogahara in her home…

I looked up from my notes to glance at her.

She looked unconcerned as always.

Her expression never really changed.

She wasn't going to reveal a special face that she'd never show anyone else just because we were going out… In that sense, she wasn't a tsundere at all.

Her attitude didn't change one bit, either.

Hmm.

Or was I expecting too much, as I tended to do? I'd vaguely imagined that conversations grew more special once you started going out, but maybe what you discussed with another person didn't change all that much whatever your relationship? Were my thoughts of sweet talk between lovers nothing more than an idiotic fantasy?

"………"

In all likelihood.

Considering Senjogahara's experiences, the events that made Hitagi Senjogahara into Hitagi Senjogahara—she certainly had her notions regarding chastity and all, but apart from that, in all likelihood she was satisfied with the current state of our relationship.

She'd told me she didn't like silent partnerships.

Since she said so, she probably didn't.

…No.

Even then…

It was hard to imagine that Senjogahara didn't feel a thing in this situation. In fact, it had developed in a much more sexual way the last time I'd visited the Tamikura Apartments… It wasn't like she was too unworldly not to have a clue about what it meant to invite her ostensible boyfriend to her home with no guardian around… And when I looked at it that way, Senjogahara did seem to have put a little bit of work into the outfit she was wearing across the low table from me, but the awfully long skirt sat on my mind. Her stockingless legs were bare, but I could hardly see them thanks to that long skirt of hers. It felt like it was caution she had put into her outfit, not thought.

Phew.

Or maybe it was my role as the man to show some initiative? Of course, I'd never gone out with a girl before, so I hardly even knew what initiative looked like.

"What's the matter, Araragi? Your hands have stopped."

"Nothing... I was just thinking about the high challenge rating."

"But this one isn't so hard. What am I going to do with you?"

Showing no interest in making out my mood, Senjogahara just gave me an utterly appalled look. Her eyes seemed accustomed to dispensing condescension.

Then she mumbled, melancholically, "I guess that's it."

"Huh? Hold on, Senjogahara, you're putting your mechanical pencil aside like you're fed up and giving off this tired air, but is quitting on me actually an option for you?"

"I won't say that it isn't," she declared. "60-40...no, 70-30, maybe?"

"Whichever is the seventy, that's an awfully realistic ratio..."

It would have been easier on me if she'd said 90-10.

Really, which was the seventy?

"I'm conflicted, you see. Trying and failing would hurt my pride more than not trying and failing."

"Please don't quit on me..."

If she did, I'd have to ask Hanekawa after all.

At the end of the day, that wasn't something I wanted to do.

Being tutored by our class president, who bought wholesale the commonsensical notion that you did well in school if you just tried, was out of the question...

"Well, if you're going to go that far, then I won't quit on you."

"You'd really be helping me out."

"Not at all. I accept all comers and won't let any go."

"What a frightening philosophy!"

"Don't worry. If I'm doing this, I might as well die doing it."

"You don't have to die! Maybe just tire yourself out! What the hell do you have in mind for me?!"

"...Then again, Araragi. I want to say you're good at math, at least?"

"Huh? Oh, yeah."

How did she know?

Before I could throw the question at her, Senjogahara said, "Hanekawa told me."

That made sense. Hanekawa knew my grades better than anyone.

"Huh," I grunted. "I never saw Hanekawa as the type to go around discussing other people's grades, though."

"Oh, maybe I didn't word it right. I was secretly listening in when you and Hanekawa were talking the other day."

"...You certainly didn't word it right."

Hearsay was bad enough, but now we were at eavesdropping.

"You think?" deadpanned Senjogahara.

She was such a handful.

"I do all right in math because it isn't all about memorization," I explained. "Aren't formulas and equations almost like special moves? An Ultra Beam or a Kamehameha or something. If only other subjects had them, too..."

"If things were so convenient, no one would have a hard time of it. But putting aside actually learning about the subjects, there are tried-and-true techniques, if not special moves, when it comes to studying for tests." Senjogahara picked her mechanical pencil back up. "One of them is trying to guess what'll be on the test, which you don't want to make a habit of because it's like gambling. While I generally don't recommend it, stopgap measures might be our only choice at this point. If we get down to it, you just need to avoid getting F's. If we say the cutoff line is half of the average score..."

She scribbled numbers in her notebook.

The expected average score, and a number that was half of it.

I had to say, when she put them out there like that, it did seem attainable—as my perfect score, that is.

"In memorization-heavy subjects, teachers have 'questions that they have to ask,' so we need to set our sights on those. In other words, we're taking a laser-focused approach instead of making wild guesses. You don't want to get bogged down by questions you can't answer and miss the chance to score on ones you can. Do you understand what I'm saying so far, Araragi?"

"...Sure, I get it."

Still, smart kids really did see tests in a completely different way... The teacher's mindset in preparing them was something I'd never given any thought to. Actually, no, maybe I did back in middle school, when I still got decent grades... But that felt like a forgotten fable.

Back in middle school.

I didn't miss those days at all.

"So," Senjogahara said, "let's start with an easy subject. World history."

"World history is an easy subject?"

"It is. All you have to do is memorize all the important terms."

"......"

"But like I said, I'm not going to expect you to do even that much. Still, Araragi. You'll probably pass this skills test if you start studying right now with my help, but what in the world are you planning on doing after that?"

"After that?"

"After you graduate," replied Senjogahara, pointing the tip of her mechanical pencil at me.

"After I graduate... This is kind of sudden."

"You're at the end of your second month of your last year of high school. You must have given it at least a little bit of thought. I know you said something along the lines of only caring about making it to graduation, but does that mean you're going to find a job right away? Do you have some sort of concrete plan? A connection or an in at some company?"

"Umm..."

"Are you going to be a temp at first? Or maybe you'll just be a NEET? I don't really like any of that terminology because they oversimplify a real issue, but of course, your own views and wishes take precedence. Oh, but I suppose you could always learn a trade at a vocational school to start off?"

"What are you, my mother?"

She was getting very detailed about this.

Peppering me with all these questions wasn't going to drag an answer out of me... Couldn't Senjogahara tell that I was already overwhelmed by the skills test staring me down?

"Your mother? What are you talking about. I'm your girlfriend."

"......"

The straightforward reply.

Her special move.

In a way, it was even deadlier than her acid tongue.

For me, at least.

"After I graduate... Hmm. You're right, I do need to decide soon. Well, how about you, Senjogahara?"

"College. Probably on a recommendation and scholarship."

"...I see."

"Was saying 'probably' too modest of me?"

"By your standards."

"Anyway, college."

"College, huh."

She said it like it was only natural.

Maybe it was, for her.

As with what she'd earlier, it was probably going to be a mystery to me for the rest of my life if I didn't get it now, but I wondered how it felt like for a smart person to be a smart person.

She added, "The tuition issue certainly narrows down my path. Saying 'fortunately' might be too self-deprecating, but it's not like there's anything in particular I want to do, so I guess I'm letting that path guide me."

"Well, no matter where you go, you'll be you, I'm sure."

"Right. But," Senjogahara said, "I'd like to walk the same path as you if I can."

"Er...that's a little..."

I was honestly happy to hear that, but the laws of physics practically ruled it out...

Right, Senjogahara nodded. "Ignorance is a crime, but stupidity isn't. Since it's not a crime, it's the punishment. If you'd only been more virtuous in your past life like me, poor Araragi, then this wouldn't have happened. Now I know exactly how the ant felt as it watched the grasshopper freeze to death. Getting me to identify with a bug is no mean feat, mind you."

"……"

Bear it…

A retort would only cause the knife to dig in deeper…

"Why not just let it go and drop dead?" Senjogahara continued. "Even a grasshopper becomes useful as a carcass when the ant deigns to feed on its nutrients."

"Next time we meet, it'll be in court!"

I couldn't bear it.

I lacked the necessary mental fortitude.

"You say so, Senjogahara, but doing different things after graduation doesn't have to mean not walking down the same path, yeah?"

"True. You're absolutely right. But if I have a sudden change of heart in college because I'm going to co-ed mixers all the time, what will I do?"

"Ready to make the most of campus life, are you?!"

"In that case, should we live together after graduation?" she suggested all too casually. "That way, even if we're doing different things, we might spend even more time together than we do now."

"Well…that's not a bad idea."

"Not a bad idea? I don't like your tone."

"…Yes, I'd like to. Please, let's do that."

"You think?"

With that, she cast her eyes back down on her textbook in the most unassuming manner. She was acting nonchalant, and the timing of her remark had made it sound almost frivolous, but even someone as unobservant as me saw by now that she wasn't the type to jest at such a moment.

This was Hitagi Senjogahara I was dealing with.

…Anyway, she seemed to be thinking two steps ahead.

Or instead of taking it that way—maybe I should receive it as a sign of Senjogahara's earnest interest in our relationship. Not many high school couples took going out as seriously as she did.

Going out, though. What did that mean?

It was a verbal promise not backed up by anything.

Sigh.

It was no good. I'd never gone out with a girl before, so I didn't just not know how to take the initiative, I had no idea how to react in my situation.

Not even the first clue.

May I ought to have played some dating sims.

They'd have served as reference, at least.

Then again, beating a game was one thing, while you could never "clear" reality.

"You're sighing a lot, Araragi. Did you know that a small happiness slips away every time you sigh?"

"If that's true, I'd have to measure my loss in K's…"

"How many you've let away doesn't concern me at all, but I wish you wouldn't sigh around me. It makes me sick."

"You're horrible."

"What I meant is lovesick."

"…Er, as the straight man, I don't even know how to respond to that one."

I was even feeling a little happy.

A clever trap for the straight man.

"By the way, Araragi," Senjogahara said, "I've never broken up with a boy before."

"………"

No, this was an example of why wordings mattered.

She made it sound like she was a smooth gal with many suitors, but wasn't she simply announcing that she had no prior experience whatsoever with men?

"So," she continued at any rate, "I don't intend to break up with you, either."

Her expression remained placid. It didn't shift even a little, not an eyebrow moving. It made me wonder if she had any emotions at all. But—she still had to be thinking about it.

Two years.

Since the time between middle school and high school, when she'd been neither a middle schooler nor a high schooler nor even on break, Hitagi Senjogahara had shunned all contact with other people. If she had forgotten how to interact with human beings, if she'd grown extraordinarily passive or unnecessarily timid—you couldn't blame her for it. It was like dealing with a cautious stray cat—though Hanekawa fit the bill better as far as cats go.

Maybe neither of us knew how to take the initiative.

"...Hey, Senjogahara?"

"What is it."

"Are you still carrying staplers and stuff?"

"Now that you mention it...not lately."

"Ah."

"I must have gotten careless."

"Careless, huh?"

Well—you could still call that progress.

It wasn't big enough of a change to make her a tsundere, but if that was her personality—

...Hm, by the way. Speaking of Senjogahara two years ago—

"Hey, weren't you the star of the track team when you were in middle school?" I asked.

"Correct."

"You don't do that anymore?"

"Correct. Because there's no reason to," she answered pretty much instantly. "I have no desire to go back to that time in my life."

"Hmph..."

Apparently, Senjogahara had been a nice, sociable person, kind to everyone, a hard worker, not at all stuck-up, the respected star of the track team in middle school—cheerful and full of energy. It was no more than a rumor, but I found it pretty credible.

That all changed right before high school.

Then, two years later.

What had changed about her was back to normal.

Back—but not everything, of course.

Certainly not if she lacked the desire.

"I don't see the need or necessity, and above all, the good it would do me at this point, Araragi—there's a lot more I have to carry with me now. I'm already a third-year, anyway. But why do you ask?"

"Oh, I was just interested in what you were like back when you played sports… And yeah, given the hiatus, I see why you might not bother."

Just as cats meant Tsubasa Hanekawa, sports were now synonymous with Suruga Kanbaru for me, and I'd asked with her in the back of my mind, but…that's what you called a brusque response.

You could say Senjogahara was facing forward—but.

Was refusing to look back the same as facing forward?

Senjogahara, I began to think, was still…

"Don't worry," she said. "I don't need to play sports to maintain my figure."

"…Hey, that's not why I was asking."

"You were drawn to these supple, carefree limbs that have never known a breakup, weren't you?"

"Stop assuming that I'm after your body!"

And that phrase "carefree limbs"…

It was a bit much.

"Oh. So it wasn't my body?" she inquired innocently. "I guess that means you can wait for a while."

That's what she wanted to say?

If so, it was so roundabout—and awfully devious, quite unlike her trademark straightforward approach.

Chastity, eh?

But it had to be about more than that.

"Araragi, I know you aren't a shameless, stingy bastard who pays for an all-you-can-eat buffet only to wonder if you've 'eaten your money's worth' and rushes to 'try a little more so it won't be a waste' when it's going to be the same price anyway."

"……"

I wasn't quite sure what her analogy was trying to imply, but it had to be some sort of pickoff move…

She was timid with people.

Prudent in her relationship with me.

Well, I was willing to go along with that.

I still didn't get what going "out" with her was about, but if that's what I was doing, then I was going along with all of her.

"…Oh, right," I remembered—and decided that I needed to tell Senjogahara about Suruga Kanbaru. I'd kept mum not so much because Senjogahara might get worried over nothing, but rather simply to avoid annoying her, but interpreting Suruga Kanbaru's motives in light of Hachikuji's eminently grade-school take and the remote possibility that she was right, it didn't feel all that fair, given my position, to withhold the fact from my (ostensible) girlfriend.

And I did have Kanbaru in the back of my mind just a moment ago.

There was something I was curious about, too.

"Hey, Senjogahara."

"What is it."

"Do you know Suruga Kanbaru?"

"………"

She replied with silence.

Or I should say, made no reply.

In terms of what was and wasn't fair, my question itself probably wasn't fair at all—I mean, who didn't know about the school star, Suruga Kanbaru? The fact that she was stalking me would circulate as a rumor by the beginning of next week at the latest, if it wasn't out already. I could rest assured that it would be treated as a false one—but that was precisely why my question took on an odd significance. I was suffering the silence I'd brought about and restraining myself from following up, when—

"Yes," Senjogahara said, "Suruga Kanbaru. That name takes me back."

"…Oh."

So—they were acquainted after all.

I'd thought they might be.

When I mentioned my study session, Kanbaru had immediately named Senjogahara and not Hanekawa, who has the best grades in our year—and that wasn't all. I'd picked up the same suggestion from various remarks that she'd made. The possibility that Hachikuji raised had eluded me thanks to my vague, no, clear sense that Kanbaru wasn't after me, but some other goal—

"Is that why you asked me about middle school just now?" added Senjogahara. "Yes, she used to be my junior, in middle school."

"Well, she still is. You go to the same school, don't you? Or wait, do you mean that girl was on the track team in middle school?"

"No, she was on the basketball team from the time she was in middle school. 'That girl'... You sound awfully close with her."

In an instant, the look in Senjogahara's eyes turned hostile. Normally free of any emotions at all, they now gleamed with danger. Not waiting even a second to see if I'd offer some sort of explanation, she took the mechanical pencil in her right hand and thrust it forward, the tip homing in on my left eye at an alarming velocity. My first instinct was to get out of its way, but even as she moved her right hand, she climbed over the low table on her knees, indifferent to all the notes she sent flying in the process, and used her left hand to cradle the back of my head, preventing me.

The tip of the mechanical pencil—was so close to my eyeball it seems absurd to say she stopped short of anything. It was so close I couldn't blink, freezing me in place. In fact, I had to wonder if the left hand cradling my head was a considerate gesture meant to hinder extraneous movements on my part that might spoil her precision, that's how perfectly orchestrated it was.

...H-Hitagi Senjogahara.

You might not be carrying a stapler now, but you haven't changed one bit!

"What about that girl, Araragi?"

"......!"

Hold on!

Was she this jealous?!

It was almost laughable how committed she felt... And how did that even sound like we were close? I'd referred to a junior as "that girl," no more. This was my punishment for merely knowing another girl without Senjogahara's knowledge? What in heaven's name was she going to do to me if I actually cheated on her?

While I did find myself in a ghastly situation, I was also relieved that I'd decided to tell her early.

Thank goodness—I'd learned about this side of Senjogahara through a case where I had plenty of excuses to give!

"You heal from injuries incredibly fast, right? So a single eyeball can't be that bad, can it?"

"Stop, no! No, an eyeball would still be bad! There's nothing here I ought to feel guilty about, I don't see us as close at all, you're the only girl for me, Senjogahara!"

"Oh, am I? I like how those words make me feel."

And then—she pulled back the mechanical pencil. She spun it around a couple of times in her palm, placed it on top of the low table, and rearranged the scattered notes and textbooks. I tried to calm my still-pounding heart as I watched her.

"I might have gotten a little excited there. Did I surprise you, Araragi?"

"...You know you're going to kill someone one of these days."

"And when I do, I'll make sure it's you. You're going to be my first guy. I wouldn't choose anyone else. I promise."

"Don't spout scary stuff like they're sweet lines! Listen, I love you, but not enough to be killed by you!"

"To be loved to death, to be killed by the one you love. Could there be any better way to die?"

"I'd rather take a pass on that kind of twisted love!"

"Really? That's too bad. And I can't believe you'd say that. If it was by your hands, Araragi—"

"You wouldn't mind being killed?"

"...Hm? Oh, uh, well, I guess."

"What a vague answer!"

"Well, um, I suppose I would?"

"Followed by a vague refusal!"

"What's the big problem? Just accept it for what it is. If I were to kill you, Araragi, I would be the one by your side during your final moments. Isn't that romantic?"

"No. If I'm going to get killed, you're my last choice for the killer. No matter who kills me in what way, for me, it's better than getting killed by you."

"What? I won't have that. If someone else ever kills you, Araragi, I'm going to kill whoever did it. Aren't promises made to be broken?"

"……"

Her love was already pretty twisted.

I did feel loved, nevertheless…

"In any case, we were talking about Kanbaru," Senjogahara tossed aside our frightening line of discussion and put the conversation back on track with her usual aplomb. "While we played different sports, I was the star of the track team while she was the star of the basketball team. Even though we weren't in the same year, we did associate—and also."

"And also?"

"Well, it's not really worth mentioning now, but in our private lives away from sports, you could say that I caused her a bit of trouble, or maybe that I troubled myself over her… Wait, Araragi." Senjogahara turned the subject to me. "What we should be talking about right now is why you brought up that kid. If you're not guilty of anything, you shouldn't mind explaining."

"S-Sure."

"Of course, if you were guilty, I'd have you explain anyway."

"………"

Senjogahara might actually kill me if I tried keeping secrets from her, so I told her that Suruga Kanbaru had been stalking me for the past three days. A second-year who dashed up to me with a quick and rhythmical *tup, tup, tup, tup, tup, tup*, who rambled for a while, and who left without hinting at any objective at all—Suruga Kanbaru. She had to have one, but I didn't know what it was.

As I explained this, I began to think.

Kanbaru was probably choosing moments when Senjogahara wasn't around and coming up to me then. With the exception of today, when she dashed over my way even though I was with Hachikuji, she was basically lying in wait for me to be alone. In other words, it wasn't by chance that Senjogahara hadn't known about the stalking until now.

And there was something else I started to think about.

Wasn't Senjogahara the one referring to Kanbaru in a familiar way? Calling her "that kid" even if she'd been a year behind in middle school sounded more than a little—no, maybe it was just a manner of speaking, too.

Just as Senjogahara's emotions didn't show on her face, they didn't seep into her voice. No matter what she said, it was almost all in the same flat tone. You shuddered to fathom the strength of will she was exerting to control herself.

But—*that kid.*

"I see," Senjogahara finally nodded after hearing most of the story. And yes, she still had the same expression and flat tone. "Um, Araragi?"

"What is it."

"What's flooded on top and in blazes on the bottom?"

"…"

Why a riddle all of a sudden?

Wondering when she'd turned into the kind of character who asked riddles, I decided to humor her for the time being. I knew the answer to this one, fortunately.

"A cauldron, right?"

"Bzzt. The correct answer is," Senjogahara enlightened me in the same monotone, "Suruga Kanbaru's house."

"What are you planning on doing to the home of our school's basketball star?!"

Now I was really scared!

Her eyes were so still, too!

"Jokes aside," she said.

"Your jokes are no joke, okay? Not when you might follow up on them."

"Really? But since you insist, Araragi, I'll keep my jokes non-practical."

"That's only normal…"

"Kanbaru found out about my secret a year before you," Senjogahara told me like it was nothing special—in her usual tone, only a tad irritated. "I'd just become a second-year, so it was right after Kanbaru started at Naoetsu High. Considering its location, I'd already foreseen that a junior who knew me would be coming to our school, so I'd thought about what to do—but with Kanbaru, I guess I let my guard down a little."

"Huh."

Hitagi Senjogahara.

The secret she'd borne—

I'd learned it by catching her after she'd tripped on the stairs—by chance, so to speak. But on the flip side, you could say her secret was so precarious that mere chance was sufficient to expose it. In fact, Senjogahara had told me I wasn't the first to find out—so Kanbaru...

Knowing Kanbaru's personality.

"I bet that gir...Kanbaru probably tried to save you or something, didn't she?"

"Yes, indeed. Though I refused," Senjogahara replied calmly, as if coupling those phrases were a standard construction, a grammatical staple. "I dealt with her the way I did with you. You tried to get involved anyway, Araragi. Kanbaru never came back after that. That was all our relationship amounted to."

"...She never came back."

So that was a year ago.

The refusal—must have been thorough. It must have been immeasurably more intense than in my case since Kanbaru knew about Senjogahara's past as a middle school track star quite well. Otherwise—Kanbaru, given her nature, wouldn't have given up without a fight. I recalled that according to Senjogahara, at the May eighth stage, when I learned her secret—the only person who knew about *it* at that moment apart from me was Harukami, the health teacher.

At that moment.

In other words, Suruga Kanbaru had noticed her secret in the past, but Senjogahara had forced her to forget. One of the poor victims...no, casualties—but had Kanbaru, of all people, really been able to forget about Senjogahara?

"...You were friends, weren't you?"

"Yes, in middle school," Senjogahara admitted. "It's different now. We're complete strangers."

"But your...situation has changed compared to a year ago. I mean, we cleared up that secret of yours, so—"

"Didn't I just tell you, Araragi?" she cut me off. "I don't intend to go back to any of that."

"......"

"That's how I've decided to live my life."

"Oh..."

Well.

If that was her decision about her own life, it didn't seem like my place to butt in—at least that's how the logic usually went. And Senjogahara wasn't so glib as to offer to bury the hatchet with someone she'd rejected so harshly just because her condition had become a thing of the past.

"Still..." I said. "I get your relationship with Kanbaru, but that doesn't explain why she's following me around, does it."

"She must have found out that we're going out. We started dating two weeks ago, and the stalking started three days ago, so the timing seems to work out fine."

"What? You mean she's curious what kind of guy Hitagi Senjogahara's boyfriend is...and she's checking me out?"

"I think it's something like that. Sorry for the trouble, Araragi. I won't mouth any excuses. This is on me for not being able to liquidate my relationships."

"Liquidate..."

What a word to use.

Knowing her, it didn't even sound figurative.

"Not to worry," she assured. "I'll take responsibility for—"

"Don't! Don't take responsibility! God knows what you mean by that! This is nothing, it's my problem so I'll take care of it!"

"Why so shy? Don't be so standoffish."

"I'm just afraid you'll turn it into a different kind of standoff..."

Hrrm.

In any case, or even so, it didn't make sense to me.

"You shooed Kanbaru away in no mild fashion a year ago, right? And it's been that way since? Would she still care if you got a boyfriend?"

"If it were an everyday case of an estranged senior finding a boyfriend, then sure—but this is different, isn't it? Araragi. You did something she couldn't, so actually I'm not surprised. The way she sees it, you succeeded where she failed."

"Ah…I get it."

She learned Hitagi Senjogahara's secret…but was turned away, rejected, harshly and mercilessly. A little reasoning was all it took to arrive at the assumption that I, as the boyfriend, couldn't possibly not know the secret, and seeing me by Senjogahara's side *even as I knew* surely must have given Kanbaru some food for thought.

At the same time.

Kanbaru probably didn't realize that the secret itself had been resolved. Because if her reasoning were that good, she'd have reached out to Senjogahara instead of me, or so I assumed.

"Hitagi Senjogahara was someone Kanbaru looked up to, if I do say so myself," Senjogahara divulged, averting her gaze from me. "I knew I was in that position, and I did try to act the part. What could I do? I think there was nothing else I could do. So in rejecting her, I was extra careful to make a clean break—yes. But I guess the kid hasn't forgotten about me after all."

"…You shouldn't say that like she's annoying. She's not doing it out of malice, right? And anyway, people forgetting you is a pretty depress—"

"She's annoying," Senjogahara declared without a shred of hesitation. "The presence or absence of malice isn't the issue."

"Come on, don't be like that… If she looked up to you, and she's still concerned about you…well, it might be weird to call it 'making up,' but don't you have some room in your heart for her?"

"I don't. It's already been a year, it was in middle school that we were friends, and yes, it would be weird to call it 'making up.' I told you I'm not going back to any of that. Or are you saying I should walk up to her after all this time and apologize for making her wait so long? That would be the height of idiocy."

Then, as if to close the door on that conversation, and also as if she'd just come up with something, Senjogahara changed the topic. She was, as always, slick.

"Oh, right. By the way, Araragi, do you have plans to meet Mister Oshino anytime soon?"

"Oshino? Well, I guess you could say I do..."

Maybe not Oshino—but I needed to let Shinobu drink my blood, and it was about time for me to go by that abandoned cram school. It was Friday, so I'd make some time tomorrow, or maybe the day after tomorrow...

"Okay. In that case."

Senjogahara silently stood up, grabbed an envelope from atop her dresser, came back to me, and held it out. The envelope had a post office mark printed on it.

"Could you give this to Mister Oshino for me?"

"What is this... Ohhh."

I realized as soon as I'd asked.

Mèmè Oshino—

That frivolous Hawaiian-shirted bastard's payment for services rendered.

What he required to remove Senjogahara's secret, the calamity that had befallen her—his remuneration, or simply put, his payment.

A hundred thousand yen, if I remembered correctly.

I checked inside to make sure, and indeed, ten ten-thousand-yen bills were inside. Exactly ten bills, crisp and probably fresh from the bank.

"Wow...you got that together faster than I thought you would. You made it sound like it would take you a while. Weren't you going to take a part-time job or something?"

"I did," Senjogahara said nonchalantly. "I got my father to let me help him out with his work. Well, I guess it'd be more accurate to say I forced him, but that's how I earned the money."

"Huh."

Senjogahara's father worked at some foreign company—and maybe that was the right choice for her? Regular part-time jobs didn't seem suited to her personality, and our school forbade us from taking them in the first place.

"I was reluctant because getting help from my father somehow felt like cheating, but as someone who grew up in a family mired in debt, attending to money matters is a must. There was a little bit left over, so I'll buy you lunch some time at the cafeteria. The food at our school is pretty good but reasonably priced, so you know, order anything you want."

"...Thanks."

Still, it was the cafeteria.

A weekday lunch break.

Did she not intend to go on a date with me, ever?

"But in that case," I asked, "why not just go and give it to him yourself?"

"Nope. Because I hate Mister Oshino."

"Understood..."

She was so direct about her savior.

What was mature about Senjogahara, though, was that she still felt grateful towards him.

Of course, it wasn't like I loved Oshino, either.

"If I had my way," she said, "I'd never meet him again, and I don't want to have anything to do with him in the future. Not with someone who acts like he sees through people."

"Yeah, I think you're right that you and Oshino are incompatible. He has that frivolous and mocking attitude, and it clashes with your personality," I said, placing the envelope next to my floor cushion. I slapped the envelope and nodded at Senjogahara. "Okay, I get it. If that's how it is, I won't say another word. I'll take good care of this, and I'll be sure to give it to Oshino the next time I meet him."

"I appreciate it."

"Yup."

Then I thought—

Compatibility.

Attitude.

Personality.

Wasn't that second-year Suruga Kanbaru's out-of-left-field character—the exact flip side of Senjogahara's? In terms of compatibility, attitude, personality, and everything else.

Senjogahara had been the star of the track team in middle school.

Moreover, she'd been admired. The worshipping gazes that she'd drawn—couldn't have been Kanbaru's alone. In that position, Senjogahara had played a certain character—she must have played a character that was the polar opposite of her current verbally abusive, acid-tongued self.

Abuse and flattery.

Acid tongue, soothing tongue.

Polar opposites.

Flip side.

Which meant.

"So, Araragi." Senjogahara's eyes were devoid of emotion. "Let's get back to studying. Are you familiar with Thomas Edison's famous observation? He said that genius is one percent inspiration and ninety-nine percent perspiration. A great quote, worthy of a genius. But I bet he thought the one percent was more important. Don't they say that's about all that separates a human's genes from a monkey's?"

004

It was two years for Senjogahara—and two weeks for me.

The start of Golden Week to its finish for Hanekawa.

For Hachikuji, who knows. I can't say exactly how long.

I'm talking about the periods we were in contact with aberrations—the amounts of time our *abnormal experiences* lasted. It was over those periods, those spans that our improbable, dreadful experiences, which were anything but normal, lasted.

Take Koyomi Araragi.

My case.

In this day and age, amidst our twenty-first-century civilization, it's so embarrassing that it makes me want to find a hole and jump in it, but I fell victim to a venerable old vampire—a bloodcurdlingly scary terror, a traditional and legendary vampire, sucked every last drop of blood from my body.

She sucked me dry.

And I became a vampire.

I was afraid of the sun, hated crosses, avoided garlic, and kept my distance from holy water, and in return, gained physical abilities that were tens, hundreds, thousands of times greater than a human's, but once again in return, I felt an absolute hunger for human blood—like one of those nightwalkers so popular now in manga, anime, and movies. Really, it felt unfair to have become such a true-to-form vampire. These days they were fine walking around in daylight, wore crosses as accessories, ate garlic bread and washed them down with holy water, but still had absurd physical abilities—wasn't that just mainstream now?

And yet.

A vampire having to suck human blood seems to be the one constant.

They're bloodsucking demons, after all.

In the end, it was a dude passing by, not a vampire hunter, not a Christian spec ops team, not a vampire who hunted his own kind, but a regular dude passing by, a frivolous Hawaiian-shirted bastard named Mèmè Oshino who saved me from that hell—but that did nothing to erase the fact that I'd lived through those two weeks.

A demon.

A cat.

A crab.

A snail.

Still, I couldn't allow myself to forget that there was a decisive difference between me and the other three. An especially large one, in particular, between Hitagi Senjogahara's case and Koyomi Araragi's.

I don't mean the length of time, but the depth of our loss.

She didn't intend to go back to that—she said.

But despite her talk about there being no need or necessity, didn't she mean that she couldn't go back to that time in her life even if she wanted to?

I say that because...for two years, she'd refused anything and everything you could call social contact. Hitagi Senjogahara had spent two years associating with no one in her class—and now that those two years were over, nothing had changed.

Aside from me, nothing had changed.

Koyomi Araragi was merely a unique exception for Senjogahara, and she hadn't changed at all aside from that.

There was no difference between her before and her after.

She just stopped going to the nurse's office.

She just started participating in P.E. class.

She sat in the corner of the classroom—and read silently. As if reading a book, in our classroom, was a way to build sturdy walls against her classmates—

She talked to me now, but that really was it.

She ate lunch with me now, and that was it.

A quiet model student prone to illness—that was still the position she occupied in our class. All that our classmates thought was that her condition must have improved somewhat, to whatever degree.

Hanekawa, our class president, innocently welcomed it, however, as a major change—but I couldn't share her simple optimism at the new picture.

Maybe Senjogahara hadn't lost anything.

Maybe she'd thrown it away.

But you ended up with the same result.

I absolutely don't want to sound like I know it all, and I probably won't learn the truth no matter how I relate to her going forward—and I bet I shouldn't be second-guessing her.

Interfering, meddling, all that doesn't seem right.

But I can't help but wonder.

What if.

If Senjogahara not carrying a stapler around anymore is progress… if that is a change, then might not there be a *furthermore*?

Not just in relation to me.

About the other stuff, too, if—

"Hello?"

"Yes, thank you for waiting. This is Hanekawa speaking."

"……"

Sure, that was a very proper way to answer a call, but wasn't it a bit odd on a cell phone?

Tsubasa Hanekawa.

The class president—a high-end model student.

A woman who seemed like a born class president.

A class president among class presidents elected by the gods themselves—I'd meant it as a joke at first, but after spending two months working alongside her as class vice president, I came to see how seriously fitting the description was. All knowledge ought to be cherished by human beings, but I wish I'd been spared this particular tidbit.

"What's the matter? It's not every day that you call me, Araragi."

"Nothing, really—it's just, I had a question I wanted to ask you."

"A question? Sure, that's fine with me. Oh, is this about what our class will be doing for the culture festival? I think it'd be better if you didn't give it much thought until after the skills test—you're in a pretty tight spot, right? I can take care of all the busywork, of course. Or did you want to rethink what we're doing? That'd be tough since we took a survey. Oh, or is there some problem and do we have no choice? We need to deal with it right away in that case."

"...You didn't even give me a chance to nod along."

Hanekawa really advanced the conversation all on her own.

Not only was she quick to make assumptions, she was an even quicker talker.

It was hard work to find your opening with her.

Eight at night.

I was on my way back from the Tamikura Apartments, Senjogahara's home, and was pushing my bike down the asphalt road instead of striding the saddle. It wasn't because Hachikuji was by my side, nor because Kanbaru had spotted me and dashed up to me, that I was pushing my bike rather than pedaling. I just needed to think a little.

I ended up cramming until eight at night.

Despite naive hopes that maybe I'd get the chance to eat Senjogahara's cooking for dinner, she didn't even hint at it. When I casually brought up feeling hungry, unable to bear it any longer, she sent me on my way with nothing more than, "I see. Then let's call it a day. I'm sure you remember, but there aren't many streetlights in this area so do be careful on your way home. See you later, alligator." Hitagi Senjogahara essentially lived alone because her father often worked late into the night, so she had to know how to cook, but...

She had such a high difficulty rating.

Of course, I didn't get very hungry anymore, so my complaint was mostly a lie.

In any case.

I needed to think, but this was me we were talking about, someone whose tutor, Senjogahara, didn't trust to earn an average score, so it wasn't going to be particularly productive. It was mostly for my own satisfaction. Now, self-satisfaction did for some matters in the world, but not others, and this was the latter.

So.

Pushing my bike with my right hand and walking, I'd called Hanekawa on her cell. It was eight-thirty at night—whether that's an appropriate hour to call a girl you aren't that close to is a question I couldn't answer, but Hanekawa's reaction suggested that it fell within the boundaries of acceptable behavior. The incarnation of seriousness, a moral paragon, she'd tell me if I were acting out of line.

"Um, Hanekawa. This might go a little long, do you have a minute?"

"Hm? That's fine. I was only doing some light studying."

"......"

Saying that without a hint of sarcasm was what made her a class president among class president elected by the gods themselves.

Light...what sort of studying could she mean?

"Well, okay," I said, "I'll try to keep it as brief as possible... You went to the same middle school as Senjogahara, right? What was it called again—oh, Kiyokaze Public Middle School?"

"Yup, that's it."

"So you must know a girl a year younger than you called Suruga Kanbaru."

"Well yeah, of course? I mean, is there anyone who doesn't? Even you know who she is, don't you? She's the captain of the basketball team, a school-wide star. I've gone with my friends to cheer from the stands at some of her matches."

"No, listen. I'm not talking about now—I wanted to ask about the middle-school Kanbaru."

"Hmm? You do? Why?"

"Why not?"

"Huh... Well, it was more or less the same in middle school. She was the star of the basketball team and everyone knew her. It sounds like she was team captain there, too, starting around the second half of her second year. Why do you ask?"

"Oh, um—"

I couldn't tell her.

I couldn't say the words.

I couldn't possibly convince her.

That of all things, that star was, to put it unkindly, stalking me, of all people.

As it was, how much of this I should be babbling about was an issue, but then again we were talking about Hanekawa, so maybe it was okay to share a bit of my predicament. I'd of course fudge certain aspects as needed.

"I heard that she and Senjogahara were friends in middle school—were they?"

"Hmm? No, I think I told you, but it wasn't like Senjogahara and I had any physical contact to speak of just because we went to the same middle school. She was a celebrity, so frumpy old yours truly just knew about her unilaterally—"

"I'm as moved as ever by your modesty, but if we could put our usual exchanges aside for today—"

"The Valhalla Duo."

"Wha?"

"You just reminded me. That's what they were called, the Valhalla Duo. Senjogahara from the track team and Kanbaru from the basketball team."

"The Valhalla Duo? What does that word mean again, I feel like I've heard it somewhere. And why'd they be called that…"

"Kanbaru's 'baru' and Senjogahara's 'hara' gives you 'Baruhara.' And Valhalla, from Norse mythology, is the heavenly hall where Odin, the supreme deity, resides and welcomes the spirits of heroes who died in battle. It's like holy ground for the war god, so—"

"…Ah, Kanbaru's name starts with the character for 'god' and Senjogahara's with the ones for 'battlefield.'"

"Thus the Valhalla Duo."

"Phew…"

You couldn't hope for a more snug fit.

How some people exercised their wits to come up with a mere nickname... If I were to nitpick, it sounded too pretty, so you could only sigh and actually found yourself in a hard spot, but that's just the career straight man in me griping.

"Since they were called a duo," Hanekawa noted, "I assume their relationship at least hadn't been bad or hostile. Senjogahara was on the track team until right before graduation, so they must have hung out as fellow athletes at the minimum."

"You really do know everything."

"I don't know everything. I just know what I know."

The same exchange as always.

In any case...I had confirmed their background.

And now that I had—what next?

How would I approach the foreground?

"I know I've already asked you this before," I said, "but when Senjogahara was in middle school...she was nothing like she is now, right?"

"True, she wasn't. Senjogahara seems to be changing a little bit lately, but she's still not who she used to be."

"Oh..."

She was changing.

But only when it came to me.

So—she wasn't who she used to be.

"I guess she must have been popular with her juniors?"

"Yes, both the boys and the girls. And not just her juniors, you know. Her seniors loved her when she still had seniors, and she was well-regarded by students in her year—"

"Loved by everyone—young or old, male or female."

"Middle school only lasts for three years, so 'young or old' would be an overstatement. But if I had to choose one specific group, then she might have been most popular with girls who were her junior. That's what you were trying to ask, yes?"

"...I'm glad you're so observant."

She was a little too observant, though.

She wasn't Oshino, but it felt like she saw through me.

"But, Araragi, you like Senjogahara as she is now, regardless of who she was in the past, right?"

"........."

I hoped she knew she was acting just like a fifth grader.

By the way, while we hadn't particularly stated the fact to anyone at all, everyone knew that Senjogahara and I were going out. We weren't openly mocked or excessively teased about it. Senjogahara was considered a mild-mannered model student by our class, so of course she wasn't, and for my part I was simply not the type of classmate who attracted that kind of behavior. But even so, the entire situation was common knowledge, a tacit understanding.

Rumors were scary things.

It must have taken the rumor a little bit of time, at least, to hop the wall between third-year and second-year students and reach Kanbaru... Well, when you considered that Senjogahara was a celebrity together with the fact that she weighed on Kanbaru's mind, it had taken quite a while, but that's how it is between different years.

"Araragi, I know I've told you this over and over, but keep your relationship proper and platonic. Watch out so there won't be any indecent rumors. Senjogahara seems like a serious girl, though, and I doubt your relationship will turn crass."

"Serious, huh..."

Come to think of it, Hanekawa still didn't know the real Senjogahara... Our other classmates were one thing, but deceiving the Amazing Class President Hanekawa, who knew we'd be going out before we actually did—Senjogahara, too, was a formidable player. In that respect, you could say she was showing me a side of herself she showed no one else... Hmm, but that didn't make me particularly happy. That's not what being a unique exception is supposed to mean.

But really, that was more or less the state of our relationship. She wouldn't even cook for me, so how could our relationship ever become sleazy?

......

Oh.

If she was rebuffed—then regardless of how it had been in middle school, Kanbaru knew Senjogahara's true nature quite well. If she was coming up to talk to me anyway, then she—

"Senjogahara is a tough one, okay?" Hanekawa said suddenly.

When she did—I recalled that she'd said something similar to me in the past, too. This was Hanekawa talking, of course, so it couldn't be about Hitagi Senjogahara's challenge rating.

"Not that I'm some kind of expert," Hanekawa continued, "but she's created an impregnable force field around herself like in a game."

"........."

"And you're someone else with one, Araragi. Everyone has one around them, putting aside how strong it is—call it a sense of privacy—but you and Senjogahara have built fortresses where you've holed up. People like that find human interaction annoying in general. Rings a bell, doesn't it?"

"Are you talking about me? Or about Senjogahara?"

"Both of you."

"Well, yeah."

Of course.

But in that case.

"Still, Araragi, not liking to deal with people and not liking people are two different things."

"What? Aren't they the same?"

"'Annoyances come / In forms none greater than that / Of the visitor'..." recited Hanekawa in a calm and quiet voice, "'But then of course I speak not / Of yourself, my esteem'd friend'... I don't care how bad you are at literature, Araragi, you must get what that poem is saying, right? And what I'm trying to say?"

"...I get it."

I couldn't reply any other way.

I did resent being treated like a child, though.

Even so—all I could do was thank her.

"Thanks. Sorry for wasting your time with this nonsense."

"It isn't nonsense. It's normal for you to want to learn more about your special someone."

Hanekawa actually said that.

She didn't think twice about saying something so embarrassing.

A class president among class presidents, indeed.

"But," she added, "I think it's better not to go digging around your lover's past too much. Don't let it turn into fun and games. Stay within limits."

Having put one last fat point on it, she appended a "Bye, then," and fell silent.

I was puzzled as to why she said bye but didn't hang up, until I remembered how she'd taught me over spring break that the etiquette was for the caller to do so.

Oh, what a frighteningly correct girl…

Thinking such thoughts, I told her, "Bye, see you tomorrow at school," and pressed the button to end the call. I folded my cell phone and put it in my back pocket.

So, now what.

As someone who once stood in the same position and underwent the same kind of experience as Senjogahara, I of course understood her words and deeds to some degree—but I found my sympathies lying with Kanbaru.

If possible—I thought.

If only.

It would be a needless intervention, an overstepping of bounds, an unsolicited favor—Senjogahara had revealed her eccentric philosophy to me whereby generosity was an act of aggression, and this didn't even smack of generosity.

After all, part of it was my own underhanded calculation. A motive so conceited that I balked at the thought, let alone expressing it.

But I couldn't help but think—

I wanted Senjogahara to get back what she'd lost.

I wanted Senjogahara to pick up what she'd thrown away.

Why?

Because those were things I could never do—

"Asking Oshino about this wouldn't do any good… That jolly idiot probably doesn't give a damn about aftercare and following up. Not that I'm one to talk… Wait, hold on."

Important but forgotten details often come back in a flash for no reason whatsoever, and that was exactly what had happened. I opened the zipper of the Boston bag hanging off my shoulder and checked inside. I didn't need to in order to find out, but I was hoping against hope. Sure enough—the envelope I received from Senjogahara wasn't inside.

The envelope containing Oshino's fee for services rendered.

"I left it on that cushion next to me… Ugh, what now?"

This was about money, so it was best taken care of at the earliest convenience, but there was no need to feel that rushed, and I could get it from Senjogahara when I saw her at school the next day, but…what to do? Though I doubted it, I couldn't rule out the possibility that I'd put it in one of my pockets and that it had fallen out without me noticing as I walked talking on the phone with Hanekawa, so maybe I should call Senjogahara and make sure, just in case… No.

I was pushing my bike alongside me as I walked, so I couldn't have covered that much distance. If I biked my way back to the Tamikura Apartments, I would be there in no time. In that case, the right course of action was to go back immediately to get it. There was the risk that I'd end up having to meet Senjogahara's father considering how late it was, but the probability seemed negligible given what I'd heard about how hard he worked.

Sure, a phone call would get the job done just the same, but I wanted to see Senjogahara as often as I could.

Not that I knew how to take the initiative.

I could be forgiven for acting at least a little like her boyfriend.

"Okay, then."

I straddled my bike seat, turned around—

And wondered if it had started to rain.

Not because a drop of water hit my cheek or anything, but because of what I saw right in front of me after turning my bike around—a human figure, right in front of me as if it had been tailing me the whole time, entered my vision.

A human figure.

Dressed in a raincoat from head to toe.

It wore its hood deep.

Black rubber boots…and a pair of rubber gloves.

If it were raining, the outfit would provide perfect protection from the weather…but though I opened my palm, I didn't feel a single drop after all.

The stars were in the sky.

We were in a rural town some ways from a provincial city—so other than a few shreds of clouds, nothing in the night sky was so boorish as to challenge the starlight.

"…Um."

Oh…

I knew… I knew what was going on here… I knew it well, very well. It was what had played out during spring break, what I had experienced more than enough of…

Yet I couldn't wipe the smirk, a completely inappropriate expression for the occasion, off of my face. The sensation was so familiar that I nearly felt a pang of nostalgia, oddly enough. I recalled my experience with Hanekawa during Golden Week as well.

If there was an issue here…it was that unlike during spring break, my body was no longer immortal and that I wasn't a vampire.

It was no time for me to be keeping my cool…but cool was exactly what I needed to be to discern it and its nature. You could say that over the past few months, I had become a little accustomed, inured—

To dealing with aberrations.

…I hoped it was a physically harmless aberration like the one on Mother's Day, Hachikuji's snail…but my instincts told me that I had to flee. No, not my instincts, but the vestigial instincts of a legendary vampire that surely nested somewhere inside my body—

I tried to turn my bicycle back around—but in the heat of the moment, decided to dive off it and tumble to the ground.

It was the correct decision—in exchange, however, I lost my oh-so-precious mountain bike for good. Raincoat leaped in my direction too fast for my eyes to follow and punched, with its left fist, the center of my mountain bike's handlebars just as I jumped out of the way—crushing and denting my bike and sending it flying like a weightless scrap of paper caught in a raging tornado. By the time it slammed into a telephone pole and fell to the ground, the object formerly known as a mountain bike had lost any traces of its original form.

If I hadn't dodged—it would have been me.

I bet?

The wind pressure generated by the fist was enough to tear my clothes. My Boston bag's straps snapped, too, and it fell from my shoulder to thud at my feet.

"...I-It's on a different level."

Even my smirk—vanished from my face.

I'd only been on the periphery of its attack, and I couldn't believe its intimidating presence... It may not have rivaled a legendary vampire but was impressive enough to bear comparison...an aberration that brought bodily terror in its wake.

Forget about Mother's Day.

This was, without question, spring break.

I'd lost my bike.

Could I still run away, on foot?

At least from what I'd seen of Raincoat's moves... Well, I didn't actually see them, but judging by its invisibly quick moves, getting away on foot was impossible.

Plus.

Even if it was to run away, I didn't want to turn my back on this aberration—nothing felt scarier than turning my back on Raincoat, taking my eyes off of it. My fear was irrevocable, primordial.

So I take back what I just said.

You never become accustomed to such a sensation.

You don't get inured no matter how many times you undergo such an experience.

You don't even want to remember.

Raincoat twirled around towards me. Its hooded face made it difficult to read its expression—in fact, rather than an expression, what was there was akin to a deep pit. It was dark—so dark that I couldn't see a thing.

Like it had been chipped out from this world.

Like it had been left out of this world.

Then, Raincoat stepped towards me.

Its left fist.

It came too fast for my reflexes alone to dodge—but it described a perfectly straight line like the blow that had destroyed my mountain bike, so I was prepared to react at the first sign of motion and was able to evade it again, by an inch—and the left fist that I'd evaded penetrated the concrete-block wall behind me like it was nothing. It was almost like a catapult launch.

While stunned by its hilarious destructive potential, I thought I'd be able to use the time lag to regain my stance as Raincoat pulled its left hand out of the wall, since it was like a monkey with its closed hand stuck inside a jar, but no, of course not, things weren't going to be that convenient, and Raincoat wasn't giving me a few seconds. As if a dam were collapsing around a leak, a dozen feet of the concrete-block wall crumbled and fell with a tremendous clatter.

That took me back.

So, no time lag.

Raincoat seemed to twist its entire body around as its left fist came right at me—this time there was no sign, no initial motion, only a determined attempt to punch me from its current position.

A catapult.

Forget about evading it, I couldn't even defend against it.

I didn't even know where it hit me.

A moment later, my world began to spin, then again, three times, four, and as if my thought processes were being scrambled, intense G's assaulted me every which way, up and down, left and right, and the world began to warp and bend before I was slammed prone against the asphalt.

I learned what it might feel like for my entire body to be grated.

I felt like a block of cheese getting turned to curly shreds.

Yet—it hurt.

And if it hurt, I was still alive.

My body hurt from head to toe, but my abdomen most of all—I must have been punched in the gut. I tried to stand up in a panic, but my legs trembled and shook so much it was all I could do to go from prone to supine.

Raincoat was awfully far away. It looked that way. I thought it was some optical illusion—but no, it really was far away. That one blow seemed to have sent me flying an incredible distance. It truly was a catapult.

My innards—felt yucky.

The pain I was feeling…I'd felt before.

It wasn't my bones.

A number of my organs had ruptured.

While they may have been destroyed, the *shape* of my body was, you could say, fine. Right, bicycles and humans were made different, so even if they took the same punch, one of them didn't turn into a crumpled piece of paper. Nice one, joints. Viva muscles.

Having said that…

I couldn't move thanks to the damage I'd taken.

And Raincoat was approaching me—this time at a relaxed pace, slow enough for me to see it clearly and for its figure to be burned into my brain. Perhaps one more shot, and if not, two or three more and it would all be over—in other words, there was no need for it to feel hurried or impatient now.

That did make sense. It was a reasonable decision.

But…what was going on?

This aberration was practically a thrill killer… It was clear by now that, no matter how humanoid in shape, it wasn't "human" given its power to crush a bicycle and smash through a concrete-block wall—but why was this aberration attacking me?

For every aberration, there was a reason.

They weren't just cryptic.

They were rational—grounded in reason.

That was the most valuable thing I'd learned from Oshino, and from my time with the gorgeous vampiress—thus, the logical conclusion was that there was a reason for this aberration, too, yet I couldn't think of anything—

What was the cause?

I thought back to the day's events.

I thought back to whom I'd seen.
Mayoi Hachikuji.
Hitagi Senjogahara.
Tsubasa Hanekawa—
My two little sisters, my homeroom teacher, my classmates whose faces were fuzzy, and…
As I was coming up with names in no particular order—
I remembered Suruga Kanbaru's at the tail end.
"………!"
Just then—Raincoat turned around.
Its humanoid body turned a perfect 180 degrees.
No sooner than it did, it took off in a dash—
And vanished.
It was so sudden that I found myself at a loss for words.
"Wh…Whaa?"
Why would it do that all of a sudden?
I looked up at the sky as the pain that reigned over my body turned from dull to sharp—and the starlight was still beautiful. It was such a discordant sight given the faint smell of blood wafting in the air from all over my body.
My mouth was filled with the thick taste of blood.
Yes, my organs were definitely wounded. My guts had been vigorously churned. But it shouldn't be enough to kill me… And I wouldn't even need to go to the hospital. Though my body may no longer be immortal, I still retain a modicum of regen capabilities. A night's rest would have me back up and running. So I'd managed to escape with my life barely intact…
But…
Suddenly, and for no particular reason, I recalled the moment before I was hit. Raincoat's left fist was aimed in my direction—I had a flashback focused on that fist, and that fist alone. Maybe it was when it punched my bike, or maybe when its fist went through the wall, but the friction of the blow must have destroyed the rubber glove, opening up a line of four holes at the base of its fingers—and just like the inside of Raincoat's hood, they seemed somehow chipped out, left out, hollow,

but.

The contents of that gloved fist.

It belonged to some kind of beast—

"Araragi," I heard a voice call from above me.

A flat voice, so cold it was below freezing.

When I looked toward it, I met an equally cold, emotionless gaze—it was Hitagi Senjogahara.

"...Hey, long time no see," I said.

"Yes, it's been a while."

It had been less than an hour.

"I'm here to give you something you forgot." With those words, she shoved the envelope in her right hand in front of my eyes. She didn't have to bring it so close, I could see that it was the envelope containing the hundred thousand yen fee she was paying Oshino. "Brazenly forgetting something I handed to you is a capital crime, Araragi," she scolded me.

"Yeah...sorry."

"Apologize all you want, I'm not forgiving you. I came here so that I could bully you to my heart's content, but it looks like you've already punished yourself. Quite an admirable show of loyalty, Araragi."

"Listen, I'm not one of those guys into punishing myself..."

"You don't have to hide it. In light of your loyalty, I'll half-forgive you."

"......"

She was lessening my sentence but not absolving me.

The Senjogahara Court seemed to be tough on crime.

"Joking aside," she said, "what happened, did you get hit by a car? I see that precious thing you called your bicycle over there, and it looks like it's been heavily damaged. Or rather, it's sticking out from a telephone pole. A convoy would have had to run over you for it to end up like that."

"Umm..."

"You remember its license-plate number, I hope? I'll go and avenge you. I'll start by turning the car into scrap metal, and then I'll put the driver through so much pain he'll be begging for me to finish him by running him over and over with a bicycle."

Hitagi Senjogahara never hesitated to say the most alarming things.

I was relieved that she was the same as always. I had to admit, though, it felt both weird and amusing that Senjogahara's acid tongue was making me feel alive…

"…No, I just tripped and fell. I need to watch where I'm going… I was pedaling my bike while I was on the phone…and slammed into a telephone pole…"

"Did you, now. Okay then, would you like me to destroy that pole at the very least?"

She just wanted to vent her anger.

It wasn't even a misbegotten grudge.

"Please don't. I'm sure the neighbors around here would be annoyed if you did…"

"Okay, then… But you know, Araragi, you have a very flexible body if you were able to slam into that concrete-block wall hard enough to break it and only come away with a few cuts and scrapes. I'm impressed. Maybe someday you'll actually be able to make good use of that flexibility. Oh, I could call an ambulance, but…I guess you don't need one?"

"Nah…"

Had Senjogahara gone through the trouble of bringing that envelope because, like me, she wanted us to meet as often as possible? Maybe she'd meant to take the bus to bring the letter to my house. If so, it still wasn't enough to make her a real tsundere, but I could almost feel elated…

Also, she'd saved me.

However unexpectedly.

Because Raincoat must have noticed Senjogahara—and vanished as a result.

"If I just rest a little longer," I said, "I'll be able to move."

"Oh. Okay, I'll reward you with a very special something."

Stride—

Senjogahara stepped one foot over and across my face-up head.

I'd like to reiterate, her outfit that day featured a long skirt. She had stockingless, smooth, slender, bare legs—and now, from where I was lying, the length of her skirt didn't matter so much.

"Enjoy it until you can move again."

"……"

To be honest, I could have gotten up already—but I decided to take the opportunity to think some things through. Not that thinking was a productive activity for me…but for the time being.

For the time being, I thought about Senjogahara.

And about tomorrow.

005

Suruga Kanbaru's home was about thirty minutes away by bike from the front gates of our school. It was also about thirty minutes away on foot if you dashed the whole way. At first I tried telling Kanbaru to get on the back of my bike so we could ride together, but she demurred. It's dangerous for two people to ride on one bicycle, and it's against the law to begin with, she said. Well, I couldn't argue with that, and perhaps she was reluctant because getting on the back meant holding on to me the whole way. In that case, I thought, I could push my bike and walk alongside her or leave it at school, but Kanbaru told me not to worry about her and to ride. Then what's she gonna do, I wondered, until she told me, like it was the most natural thing, "Okay, let me show you the way," and dashed off on her two feet. This was just as true now as when she stalked me, but for Suruga Kanbaru, "dashing" seemed to be a mode of transportation just like "by foot, bike, car, or train." This seemed unusual to me, even for jocks. *Tup, tup, tup, tup, tup, tup*, Kanbaru's sharp and lively rhythm went as she guided my bike—with the white bandage on her left hand. When we arrived at our destination, her breathing completely unperturbed, she had somehow only worked up a small sweat.

It was an impressive Japanese home.

I could practically feel the history coming from it.

I knew that it must have been her home from the nameplate reading

"Kanbaru" on the gate, but the premises had an air of solemnity about them that gave me pause nevertheless.

Still, I was going to go inside.

I intruded on the premises with the same indescribable feeling that overcame me when I visited a shrine or a temple on a school field trip, and after we walked down a hallway that faced a traditional courtyard, bamboo-pipe fountain and all, I was shown into Kanbaru's room beyond a sliding paper-screen door.

...As I looked around, I wondered how she could have allowed in a senior whom she didn't even know that well.

Her futon hadn't been folded up; her clothes were strewn across the floor (including her underwear); many books, be it textbooks, novels, or manga, lay open face-down on the floor; a mountain of cardboard boxes that belonged in a warehouse stood in one corner; and worst of all, her trash didn't sit inside a waste basket but was left carelessly all over the tatami mats, packed into plastic bags from her neighborhood supermarket or just as-is. In fact, the room seemed to lack any container burdened with the quaint notion of holding trash.

It should have felt spacious, at over two hundred square feet.

But there was nowhere to take even a first step.

"I apologize for the mess."

Suruga Kanbaru said this briskly with an innocent smile on her face, her right hand on her chest. Maybe the words were fitting for the occasion, but I'd always thought of them as a modest disclaimer you uttered upon inviting someone into a room that was at least somewhat tidy.

What's flooded on top and in blazes on the bottom?

Well said, actually.

Oh god...

There were even some hygiene products...

I reflexively looked down at my feet.

If I didn't, I might find plenty of things that would be even worse to see. Self-confidence is a good thing, but being shameless is something else, Suruga Kanbaru...

Oh.

That applied to Senjogahara too, didn't it…

True, there wasn't a speck of dust to be found in Senjogahara's room… Still, she'd had a major influence on Kanbaru back in middle school not limited to her personality, and it just seemed to have ruined Kanbaru's character, if anything.

"There's no need to be modest," my hostess urged. "You're hesitating to enter the room of a girl you don't know well, which speaks to your delicacy, which I find rather charming, but I don't think this is the time for that."

"…Kanbaru."

"Yes?"

"I'm very aware of the fact that this isn't the time for it, but…please, I have a request for you."

"Sure thing. Whatever you want. I'm in no place to turn down any from you."

"I just want an hour, no, thirty minutes… Just give me some time to clean this room up. Also, give me a big garbage bag."

I didn't see myself as a clean freak…and it wasn't like my room was particularly tidy, either, but this was just awful…cruel, even. Kanbaru seemed confused, as if she didn't have a clue as to what I was talking about, but that must have also meant that she had no real reason to refuse. With an "Okay, then," she went to get me a garbage bag.

Fast forward.

Well, actually.

The disaster that was Kanbaru's room wasn't, of course, something that could be rectified in thirty short minutes, not to mention that at the end of the day, this was the room of a girl I didn't know that well, which meant that while I could grab some things, there were others that I couldn't touch for ethical and moral reasons. So pretty much all I did was gather up the scattered trash and tidy up her books and magazines (or so I say, but with no bookshelves in Kanbaru's room, I simply stacked them up according to size). It was a halfhearted attempt, like sweeping a circle in her square room, but even so, once I folded up her futon and stored it in her closet and folded up her clothes and put them in a corner (she didn't have hangers, let alone a dresser), the sight became bearable, or at least, there was enough space for Kanbaru and I to sit facing each other and talk.

"Incredible, my senior Araragi. So that's the color of my floor mats. I wonder how many years it's been since I last glimpsed them."

"You're counting in years..."

"I'm grateful."

"...Once this is settled, let's take a full day...no, I'll even stay over to spend multiple days cleaning up this room. Next time I'll bring a full set of serious cleaning supplies, like liquid cleaner and spot remover, okay?"

"Sorry for making you fuss over me. Basketball is about the only thing I'm good at, and cleaning up or tidying up or finishing up or whatever it's called isn't my forte."

"......"

She was wearing such a broad, self-assured smile that I didn't know what to say... During those thirty minutes, she'd stood idle and absent-minded in the hallway and shown no signs of helping out. I didn't think she was lazy or slovenly, only really that inept at tidying up her room, but still, though it was none of my business, the sight had been one to hide, at all costs, to be withheld, absolutely, from the eyes of students at our school who considered her a star. She hadn't invited any of her classmates here, had she? Friends were one thing, but if she invited one of her club juniors, she ran the risk of traumatizing them. Among the many things I'd stuffed into the garbage bag were crushed soda cans, candy wrappers, and empty instant noodle cups... What was an athlete on the national level doing eating and drinking that stuff?

I knew that a quirk or two could actually cause a celebrity to be more likable, but this was going too far no matter how you looked at it. Try as you might, you wouldn't find such a character adorable...

"Okay, then—"

It was tomorrow.

The day after Friday, in other words.

Saturday.

While most of society has long taken the two-day weekend for granted, Naoetsu High, the private prep school of note that we attend, regularly holds classes even on Saturdays. Even after tomorrow turned to today, not having arrived at any kind of conclusion, I used the break between first and second periods to head to the building for second-years. I was going to be talking to a famous star, so there was no need for me to look up her class. Class 2-2. While the other kids were abuzz that a third-year had visited them (a familiar yet fresh feeling for someone like me who no longer had senior schoolmates), Kanbaru—being Suruga Kanbaru—walked up to me with a majestic gait as I waited in the hallway.

"Hello there, my senior Araragi."

"Hey, Kanbaru. There's something I need to talk to you about."

"I see. In that case," Kanbaru replied, no questions asked, as if everything had been worked out in advance, "please come with me to my home after school."

And—

There I was at her home, the Japanese mansion.

There was no need to go all the way there if all we were going to do was talk. We could have done so in an empty classroom, on the roof, on the athletic grounds, or even at a nearby fast food restaurant if we had to do it off campus, and I'd told her as much, but Kanbaru seemed to want to do it at her home for a reason.

If she had a reason, I'd oblige.

I wasn't going to ask.

"So," she said, "where should we begin? Of course, as you can tell, I'm not much of a conversationalist so I'm not sure how this is supposed to go, but first things first." Kanbaru re-crossed her legs and bowed her head. "I'd like to apologize for what happened last night."

"Yeah..." I'd recovered in a day's time—though I might have felt some lingering pain in my stomach, which I rubbed for a moment before nodding. "So that was you, after all."

The raincoat.

Rubber gloves, rubber boots.

They had been—among the clothes that I'd just finished putting away.

Needless to say.

"'After all,' huh," Kanbaru echoed me. "I don't know how to feel sometimes when I hear you speak. You're so humble. You saw straight through it, didn't you? You wouldn't have come to me otherwise."

"Not really…I was just guessing. Based on your build, your outline, your silhouette, that kind of thing. I added filters, like people who were aware that I was paying Senjogahara a visit for a study session, and ran a search, so to speak… And if I went to you and I was wrong, I'd just be wrong. It's not like there would be an issue."

"Hmm, I see. How astute of you." Kanbaru sounded genuinely impressed. "I've heard that some boys can identify a girl by the shape of her hips. Was that it?"

"Not even close!" How could I when she was wearing a raincoat?!

"I apologize. I hadn't meant to do that."

Kanbaru bowed her head again.

To me—she seemed sincere.

But if she hadn't meant to…then what had she been up to? It was clearly an attempt on my… Or was that not the case, either?

"Well," I said, "apologies are great, but what I wanted to hear was your reason. Actually—we can put aside the reason."

Her reason.

It wasn't that I had no clue.

I wasn't going out of my way to say it now, but it was the very bit, the hint that pointed to Raincoat being none other than Kanbaru.

But—

"In any case, that power, that abnormal power—"

Abnormal power.

Aberration.

It crumpled my bike like paper.

It demolished a concrete-block wall with a single strike.

It took a human and—

"That's what I want to ask about," I continued. "What, exactly, did you…"

"Hrmm. I was wondering where to begin, but that would be where, I suppose. Fine… But first, I'd like to ask if you're the type of person who can accept the absurd."

"The absurd?"

That must have meant—oh, right. Of course.

Kanbaru didn't know about my body. About my once-immortal body—while she had dealt me significant damage the night before, I didn't heal so quickly you could see it taking place, so of course she didn't know. Thus her preface—but wait, no.

Even if Kanbaru didn't know about me, she knew about Senjogahara, having learned her absurd secret before me. And—as her boyfriend, I had to know the absurd secret, in Kanbaru's mind—in other words, maybe she was sounding me out at that very moment.

"Did that not make sense?" she asked me. "My question is whether or not you're able to believe what you see with your own eyes."

"I only believe what I see with my own eyes. Which is why I've believed everything I've seen. Naturally, that goes for Senjogahara, too."

"...Oh, so you even figured that out." Without a hint of guilt or shame at my remark, however, Kanbaru continued, "But. I don't want you to get the wrong idea. It's not like I've been following you around recently because I want to learn more about her."

"Huh? You weren't?"

I'd been—completely convinced of that.

She was trying to confirm the rumor that Koyomi Araragi and Hitagi Senjogahara were going out—wasn't she? And then, when she heard that I was going to Senjogahara's home for a one-on-one study session, she felt certain—didn't she?

Well, I was probably right about that.

My read wasn't mistaken, but—was there a separate reason for the stalking?

"You and Senjogahara were called the Valhalla Duo as the basketball star and the track star, I've come to understand."

"Yes, exactly. I'm impressed you know that much, I underestimated you. I thought I'd praised you as much as I could, but it looks like I still fell short. I could never measure your greatness with my own piddling values. The more I get to know you, the further away you feel."

"...Someone told me, that's all."

Despite all her flowery praise, she wasn't coming across as a sycophant or brownnoser to me, which in a way made her a work of art.

"How it was derived, too," I added. "It's a really well thought-out moniker."

"Isn't it? I came up with it myself."

Kanbaru puffed her chest out with pride.

...She'd thought of it herself.

I hadn't felt so heartsick in a while...

"I thought about it for the longest time before coming up with that one. By the way, I also came up with a personal nickname for myself, 'Li'l Suruga Can-do,' but that one didn't stick, unfortunately."

"I'm feeling very disappointed, too."

"Oh, so you sympathize?"

Yes. On account of your poor sensibility.

"You're such a compassionate senior. Of course, now that I say it out loud, it was a little long to use as a nickname. I can see why it never caught on."

"If we're gonna postgame it, that was the least of your errors."

Kanbaru seemed to have been surrounded by wonderful people in middle school.

Including Senjogahara back in those days...

"Anyway, yes," she said. "Putting aside the Valhalla Duo, perhaps I'll only annoy you by spelling things out considering how perceptive you are, but in middle school Senjogahara and I were—no, before I go into that, there's something I want to show you. That's why I asked you to spare some of your valuable time to trek all the way here."

"You want to show me something? Oh, I get it. That something was at home, and that's why we couldn't talk at school or just anywhere."

"No, that's not it. It'd stand out at school, or maybe you could say I was afraid of people seeing it... I'd prefer it if no one else did."

Saying so—Kanbaru began to unwind the white bandage on her left hand. She undid the clasp holding it wrapped around her arm, and methodically, starting with her fingers—

It came back to me.

The night before.

It had destroyed my bike, smashed through the concrete-block wall, and ruptured my organs—

It had been the doing of a left hand balled into a fist.

"To be honest, I don't really want people seeing this. After all, I'm a girl."

She unwound the entire bandage—and rolled up the sleeve of her uniform. What I saw there was Kanbaru's girlish, slender, soft-looking upper arm, and connected to it from the elbow down—a bony left hand covered in thick, black hair you'd expect to see on *a wild beast*.

It had peeked through the holes worn through the rubber glove.

The scent—of a beast.

"Well, this is how it is."

"........."

Could it have been an odd-looking glove or hand puppet—no, clearly not. It was far too long and thin—and anyway, apart from how it looked, I had witnessed something *similar* though *not quite the same* for certain over Golden Week—so I knew.

That it was nothing but an aberration.

An aberration.

I called it a wild beast—but I'd be hard-pressed to say what kind. It felt like it could be any animal, but also like no animal in existence. While it looked like everything, it seemed to belong to nothing. But if I had to say, given the five reasonably long fingers and the shape of the nails extending past them, only if I had to say—

Although I don't think it's a very appropriate way to describe a girl's body part.

"A monkey's paw."

Those were my words.

"It looks like—a monkey's paw."

An ape—as in the general term to describe any non-human primate.

"Huh."

For some reason—Kanbaru was looking at me with admiration.

Then, she smacked her knee and said, "I knew it. It is impossible, after all, to measure just how discerning those eyes of yours are. I'm stunned, it's like they work in a completely different way. You were able to figure out what this is at a single glance. I'm simply amazed. There's no comparing the knowledge you possess to the resources of a plebeian mind like mine—that must mean there's no need for me to explain anything else."

"H-Hey, don't feel convinced all on your own!"

No way I could let her stop explaining now.

She might as well have hung me out to dry.

I told her, "I just said the first thing that came to mind. I haven't discerned a thing."

"Really? That's the title of a short story by William Wymark Jacobs—'The Monkey's Paw.' The theme of the monkey's paw has been used so many times in all kinds of media that it's been spun off into different patterns—"

"Never heard of it," I confessed.

Oh, Kanbaru said. "That you would utter the truth without knowing makes me wonder if you enjoy some celestial being's blessing. Intuiting the essence, no logic required!"

"...Well, my intuition does enjoy a little bit of a reputation."

"I knew it. And now I'm proud of myself. I'm nowhere on your level, of course, but to the extent that I laid store in you, my intuition was spot-on."

"Oh, really..."

If you asked me, her sights were misaligned.

Um, I said, looking at Kanbaru's left hand again. A beast's hand—a monkey's paw. "C-Can I touch it?"

"Yup. It's fine *for now.*"

"O-Oh..."

With her permission, I brought my hand close to her wrist—and touched it gently.

Timidly, fearfully.

The texture, the flesh...the heat, the pulse.

It was alive.

So this aberration—*was a living aberration* after all.

...So even Suruga Kanbaru, who had no issue with me seeing her room in that state, did mind showing people this left arm of hers...

What she'd said about spraining it while doing solo workouts was nothing more than talk. The bandage wasn't to protect her injury but a way to hide her arm... And yes, I'd found it a little strange that she didn't disfavor the left side of her body despite the sprain...but I guess it's not very convincing of me to say that after the fact.

Then again.

It made sense she wasn't able to play basketball with that left hand.

Without thinking.

Squeeze—I tightened my hand around her wrist.

"Mm, ahh, no," she moaned.

"Stop with that weird voice!"

Without thinking, I let go.

"But you were touching me in a weird way," she objected.

"I wasn't touching you in any weird way."

"I'm ticklish."

"Okay, but that's no reason for you to moan in a way that contradicts your character so far..."

When I thought about it, Senjogahara had pulled the same trick a few times. It had to be in a diametrically opposite way from her current self, but if Kanbaru had it down too, then Senjogahara's repertoire included it since middle school...

"Kanbaru, just in case you've forgotten, this is your home and your room, okay? What do you think is going to happen to me if your parents heard you moaning like that?"

"Oh, that's okay," she replied jovially. "You don't need to worry about them, at all."

"...Fine, then."

Huh?

Why was she saying that like she didn't want me to bring up the topic, like she was openly refusing to pursue it any further? While her tone was as upbeat as ever, it really did seem out of character.

So anyway, Kanbaru rushed to get us back on track, opening and closing her left hand. "As you can see, it moves like I want it to right now—but there are also times when it won't. No, I guess you might say there are times it moves like I don't want it to—"

"Like you don't want it to?"

"Want, or hope—hmm, what's the right word. It's hard to say. I guess it would be when I'm trying to explain something that I don't understand very well myself… However. It was me who attacked you last night, it was definitely me—yet I barely remember a thing. It was like a waking dream, or maybe a reverie—it's not like I don't remember anything at all, but it felt like I was watching something on television, like I couldn't step in—"

"A trance," I interrupted her explanation. "You were in a trance—that's what it's called. I know all about it… Aberrations that possess humans come in and have their way with your mind and body."

That wasn't the case with me—but it was in Hanekawa's, the occurrence with Tsubasa Hanekawa's cat. That's why she remembered practically nothing about what happened over Golden Week, when she came into contact with an aberration. As a case, this one seemed close—there'd been a similar type of phenomenon where Hanekawa's body transformed, too—

"You know a lot," Kanbaru admired. "So that's what this is called, an aberration—"

"I'm not particularly well-informed, though. It's just that I've had a lot of experiences with them lately for whatever reason, and there's someone who is well-informed about them—"

Oshino.

This—was right up his alley.

It was Oshino's domain.

"—that I met."

"Okay. Well, I'm fortunate you're so broadminded. We wouldn't be able to talk if you ran away the moment I showed you this arm. And I would feel hurt. More than a little."

"Luckily, you see, I've gotten used to dealing with the absurd, so don't worry. The absurd…meaning Senjogahara, too—of course."

At this rate, I should tell her later about how I got involved with an aberration myself and temporarily turned into a vampire… From an accountability standpoint, maybe I needed to tell her now, but there were still too many unknowns about the aberration that was Kanbaru's left hand for that.

"Still, I was a little surprised," I shared. "You made me hiccup, as my fifth-grade friend would say. But since you've started with the most surprising part, I'm confident that nothing else you tell me will shock me."

"Ah. Of course, that's why I had you look at my arm first. We've cleared the biggest hurdle from the get-go. All right, to business, then."

With a smile Kanbaru went on.

"I'm a lesbian."

"……"

I fell over in shock.

Like in a Fujiko Fujio comic.

"Oh, I see," Kanbaru mumbled at my reaction. "Maybe I was a little too blunt, given that you're a man. Umm…" She cocked her head. "Allow me to correct myself. I'm a sapphist."

"It's the same thing!"

I had yelled, in an attempt to keep myself grounded.

Huh? What? So, what did that mean?

Is that why she and Senjogahara were the Valhalla Duo back in middle school? A year apart, were they? Senjogahara calling her "that kid"? Hunh? Is that what she meant the day before when she said she'd never broken up with a boy?

"Oh, it's not like that. I only had a crush on her, there was nothing the other way around. To me, she was purely perfect, a senior I could look up to. I was content just to bask in her presence."

"Content just to bask in her presence…"

That sounded nice.

That really did sound nice. But.

An unrequited crush, she'd gone ahead and told me…

Hachikuji, I thought, the woman in you led you in a completely wrong direction… No, I needed to calm down. I couldn't reject stuff out of prejudice… Right… Maybe this is how girls were these days. Maybe my worldview was dated. Maybe I needed to be less serious and more liberal.

"I see, a sapphist… All right, then."

"Yes, a sapphist."

Kanbaru looked happy for whatever reason.

Be that as it may…

Whether it was vampires, cats, crabs, or snails, class presidents, always-ill girls, or grade schoolers, cat ears or tsunderes or lost children, or even sapphists, the world was, how should I put it, full of new challenges, or maybe insatiable.

It was a free-for-all.

Did Senjogahara know that about her? Probably not, given the way Kanbaru had said it. But whether she did or not, I doubted it concerned a middle-school Senjogahara very much.

The star of the track team and the star of the basketball team.

The Valhalla Duo.

"She was popular with everyone," Kanbaru related, "but I'm pretty sure my feelings for her went beyond that. I'm certain of it, in fact. I was even ready to die for her sake. Yes, you could say I wanted her, dead or in love."

"……"

Uh…what?

I wasn't sure if that was clever or not.

"Mm," she hummed. "That came off better than I expected. Pretty inspired of me to play on 'alive' and 'in love,' if I do say so myself. Wouldn't you agree?"

"Uh huh. I wasn't sure at first, but now that you've explained it to me, I've made up my mind."

It was a bad pun.

Anyway.

I told Kanbaru to go on.

"Go on? I don't know, it's not like we're discussing the past. To speak of continuing, it's of a piece with the present. I chose Naoetsu High in the first place to chase after her."

"Yeah… That's what I assumed after hearing your story. If anything, it all makes better sense."

I ran the risk of insulting Kanbaru's teammates all over again depending on how she took it so I kept the words to myself, but a basketball star in middle school should have been able to play in a better environment via an athletic recommendation or something. Yet, for whatever reason, Kanbaru had decided on Naoetsu High, a school that put as good as zero focus on extracurriculars, basketball included. Why? What could have been her motivation?

Her devotion.

Well, even then, it was all too straightforward.

"I was so taken with her that I would've licked a candy that came out of her mouth."

"......"

Was that an image she ought to be putting into words in front of other people?

"My third year," she lamented, "the whole year after she graduated, was colored gray."

"Gray, you say."

"Yes. A gray Sapphic existence."

"......"

She really liked that term.

Sure, if that's what she wanted.

"My gray matter's gray Sapphic existence," she said.

"That's not even remotely clever."

She was trying too hard to insert jokes into our conversation.

This could stay a tad more serious.

"How strict of you," she complained. "You're setting too high a bar for me with your tough standards. It's strange, though. Knowing that you're doing it for my own good eases me into accepting them."

"Uhh... What happened to your gray Sapphic existence next?"

"Yes. That year drove home just how important she'd been for me. That year we were apart may have weighed more on me than the two years we were together. That's why my plan was to tell her how I felt if I got into Naoetsu High and could meet her again. With that goal, I spent all of my time studying for entrance exams."

So said Kanbaru.

She was as full of confidence as ever, but it seemed like her cheeks were flushed. She must have been embarrassed, plain and simple. Uh oh…it was kind of cute. I was busy being confused and bewildered when she was stalking me, but now for the first time I was starting to feel fond of Suruga Kanbaru, my junior. Gosh, a whole new Sapphic-*moé* territory was opening up inside of me…

I found myself barely caring about Kanbaru's beastly left hand…but no, I knew that was where the meat of this story lay…

"Forget about candy. Gum," she averred. "I was so taken with her that I would have chewed a piece of gum that came from her mouth."

"Your standards are a mystery to me…"

There had to be a nicer image.

"But," Kanbaru said, her tone sagging exaggeratedly, "she had changed from the senior I knew."

"Ah…"

"She had changed completely."

A crab.

Hitagi Senjogahara had encountered—a crab. She'd lost much, thrown away much, and rid herself of much—and she rejected everything. It must have seemed like Hitagi Senjogahara had transformed into a different person altogether for those who'd known her in middle school, like Hanekawa. And for Kanbaru, who had worshiped Senjogahara—the transformation must have been too thorough to take.

So thorough it made her doubt what she saw with her own eyes.

"I had heard that she became seriously ill after entering high school—and that she had quit running because of how protracted it was. I knew that much coming in. But I never imagined she could have changed—that much. I thought it was all a bunch of nasty rumors."

Seriously ill, eh…

Well, she wasn't wrong to look at it that way… Ultimately, Senjogahara had a chronic condition that still dogged her.

"But—I was wrong. Those rumors were so off the mark that they didn't even scratch the surface. Something far worse had happened to her body. I noticed—and I thought I had to do something. I had to save my senior. How could I not? She was really good to me when I was in middle school, and I've never forgotten it. We may have been in different years and on different teams, but she was extremely generous."

"That generosity..."

That generosity—what had it meant to Senjogahara? But this wasn't the time to speak or inquire about it, was it?

"And that's why I tried to save her—I wanted to. But I couldn't even begin to approach her. She refused."

"Ah..."

It seemed like too much to expect her to tell me exactly how. She was probably covering for Senjogahara... Kanbaru would never speak a single bad word about her, no matter what.

Yes, it wasn't hard to guess that she'd had something just as bad, if not worse, done to her... Frankly speaking, I didn't care to know.

For my sake, and for Kanbaru's.

For Senjogahara's sake, too.

Stapler.

"I thought I could do something." Despite an air of chagrin, of regretting it from the bottom of her heart—Kanbaru was forcing herself to sound calm and collected. "I thought I could do something about whatever she was burdened with. Even if I couldn't get rid of the cause, even if I couldn't relieve her symptoms, I could be by her side—and heal her heart."

"......"

"What a joke that was. I was such a foolish girl. Looking back on it, it's nothing short of comical."

Because Senjogahara didn't want anything like that at all—

So said Kanbaru, with downcast eyes.

"She told me, 'I don't think of you as a friend or even as my junior—not now, nor did I ever.' To my face."

"Well..."

That did seem like something she would say back then. If there was any weapon she carried deadlier than her stationery, then it was her acid tongue and bitter abuse.

"At first I thought that meant she thought of me as her lover, but it wasn't the case."

"That was quite positive of you."

"Yes. So she was even more blunt the next time. Being friends with a talented junior like me would boost her own reputation, and that was the only reason she was nice to me, the only reason she acted like a caring senior—she said that."

"...That's awful."

Senjogahara's goal was to hurt her—

Her goal was to make her go away, so—

Yet, only yesterday, Senjogahara had called Kanbaru "that kid" and her junior in middle school, and confirmed that while it was no longer true, they were friends back then. Perhaps I was interpreting her words to hear only what I wanted to hear—but still.

"I was happy that she called me a talented junior, though."

That was positive of her.

Through and through.

"But—that's when I learned how powerless I was. I was so conceited to think that I could heal her with my presence. If anything—she didn't want anyone at all near her."

There are some people in the world—who aren't lonely when they're alone.

It wasn't hard to pin Senjogahara down as one of them—at the very least, she probably hadn't ever appreciated herding for its own sake. Even as her middle-school sociable self, she must have thought so quietly—but.

Not being lonely when you're alone.

That's different from wanting to be alone.

Just as not liking to deal with people and not liking people aren't the same.

"That's why I never accosted Senjogahara after that day. It was the only thing she wanted from me, after all. Of course, I could never forget her—but if stepping away and not doing a thing, if not being by her side could save her—I could agree to that."

"...Kanbaru."

I didn't know what to say. It wasn't simply her gallant attitude that moved me, but her choice of words: the decision wasn't helpless or inevitable, but one she could agree to. According to Senjogahara, Kanbaru never came back—but that wasn't it. Kanbaru had stepped away of her own will.

She was so—serious.

About Senjogahara.

From middle school until a year ago, Kanbaru's feelings for her only grew stronger—and.

Even now.

"I was careful not to run into her. I made sure that my field of activity wouldn't overlap with hers, whether that meant meeting her by accident in a hallway, catching a glimpse of her at morning assemblies, or crossing paths with her at the cafeteria. I made arrangements, not just so that I wouldn't have to worry, but so that she wouldn't have to worry about me, either. Of course, I couldn't help people talking about me when I did well in basketball games, so I manipulated the rumors myself to make sure they were a mix of fact and fiction."

"...Which is why the gossip about you is so all over the place, you seem to have a personality disorder."

I got it now.

But to go so far... Might I say, not stalking but...reverse-stalking?

"I managed to do that for one year. It wasn't a gray Sapphic existence, it was a black one. Hard to say whether all of that getting directed into even more enthusiasm for basketball was a good thing or a bad thing... But then, after a year—I learned about you."

"......"

Considering how much she cared about Senjogahara, you'd think she'd have found out sooner, but maybe it wasn't simply because we were in different years—wasn't it because Kanbaru went out of her way to avoid hearing about Senjogahara?

And yet.

She ended up learning about Koyomi Araragi.

"I couldn't hold back any longer—for the first time in a year, I consciously...visited her. Or tried to. Of course, there'd been a few careless mistakes in the span of a year, but this was my first time intentionally seeing her. And she—was in a classroom that morning, chatting and cooing away with you. There was a happy smile on her face, too, of the kind she never showed me even back in middle school."

"……"

Which particular pile of abuse was Senjogahara heaping on me then? That's about the only time a smile comes across her otherwise expressionless face.

"Do you understand?" Kanbaru looked at me straight. "Something I wanted so very much, that I wanted so very much but had to give up on, you did like it was the most natural thing in the world."

"Kanbaru… No, that—"

"At first, I was jealous," Kanbaru said, punctuating every word. "I tried not to be," she went on, her voice holding back a torrent of emotions. "To the end, I was jealous," she concluded.

"……"

"I wondered why it couldn't have been me. I was jealous of you, and I was disappointed in her. I wondered if she would have accepted me if I were a man. I wondered if the problem was that I was a woman. She didn't need friends or juniors but didn't mind having a lover? In that case…"

In that case—Kanbaru glared at me with an accusatory gaze for the first time.

"In that case, why couldn't it be me?"

I knew she was my junior, a girl who was younger than me, and that she wasn't the type to begin putting her hands on me in a frenzy—but her eyes were so irate I was scared she might.

"I was jealous of you and disappointed in her. And—I was appalled at myself. I was going to heal her heart? I was going to step away? It was a lie, all of it. It was all my ego. It meant I didn't care as long as I was happy. Was I hoping she'd praise me, or what? Ridiculous. You couldn't be any more hypocritical. But even then—I wanted things to be like before. I wanted her to be kind to me. Even if it was selfish, I wanted to be by her side—which is why."

Then.

With her right hand—she touched her left.

Touched the beastly left hand.

"Which is why I wished upon this hand."

006

I'm sure there's no need to give a synopsis of "The Monkey's Paw" by William Wymark Jacobs—but not having known about the story before, I thought why, yes, what a well-made ghost or horror story. A textbook tale of dread, tried and true—indeed, once I heard it, I felt as if I'd heard it somewhere before.

It was a classic, in other words.

According to Kanbaru, the monkey's paw was a pretty well-known item, though it didn't compare to vampires, and was reused in lots of different media in lots of different ways. Spun off into a bunch of different patterns, splitting from one new version to the next like an evolutionary tree, but with one shared, underlying factor common to them all, the biggest factor that makes the monkey's paw the Monkey's Paw—

The Monkey's Paw grants its owner's wishes, the story goes.

But not in the way its owner intends, the story goes—

Those two elements.

It was the kind of item you described by appending "the story goes."

Say that you wished for riches. You might wake up the next day to find that your family has died and that you'll be receiving their life insurance. Say that you wished for a promotion at work. You might wake up the next day to find that the company has taken a turn for the worse, that the upper management has been fired, and that you're being promoted at a failing company.

That kind of thing.

It seems the Monkey's Paw was an item created in India by an old mystic to teach people that they should live according to their fate and that terrible disasters await those who defy it. A reputation that it can grant three wishes for three people, for instance, accompanies its entry into the story.

The first thing I think of when I hear about three wishes being granted is the magic lamp in the *Arabian Nights*, but how did that story go and end? Similar tales can be found all over the world. Considering how subject humans are to endless, insatiable desires, narratives where some sort of being capable of granting any wish presents itself to people might be a fundamental form of storytelling. The best known of its kind among ghost stories seems to be "The Monkey's Paw"—

"So—what's his name again, Mèmè Oshino? Did I hear that right?"

"Yes, but he's not cute like his name makes him out to be. I already told you this, but he's some older dude who likes wearing Hawaiian shirts. I don't want you getting your hopes up or anything. He doesn't *look the part* to say the least, so I want you to be prepared for that."

"No…that's not what I meant. His name is just so striking, or maybe symbolic… It doesn't matter, though. Still, 'Mèmè' would be hard to turn into a nickname…"

"Huh, yeah… I wonder what people called him when he was a kid. I have to admit, I'm curious… Actually, I can't even begin to imagine what he was like as a kid."

Oshino dwelled in an abandoned four-story cram school a little ways away from any residential areas—to put it simply, these were ruins. Ones that children wouldn't dare each other to enter, that people living in the vicinity might not even register as a building—these ruins existed as scenery. They were so aged that a large earthquake would probably raze the whole thing—well, I say aged, but the cram school went out of business only a few years ago when one of the large chains opened up a branch right in front of the station. The site was like a cadaver meant to teach us what a horrible state buildings ended up in after only a few years of disuse. So while I say Oshino dwelled there, it wasn't official in any way, and you could call it a grand case of squatting. He'd been living there for the two months since spring break, surrounded by signs that read "Private Property, No Trespassing." The desks left behind serving as his bed, he roamed around town all day.

Roamed.

Yes, that's right. It wasn't as if he stayed put.

So I could come to see him, as I was doing then—but actually finding him there was a matter of chance. He didn't have a cell phone, or even a PHS, and to be honest, there was a lot of luck involved in meeting him.

It took a little more than an hour to get there on bicycle from Kanbaru's Japanese estate.

It also took a little more than an hour to dash over, if you were Kanbaru, of course.

The two of us looked up at the abandoned cram school.

"By the way," she asked me, "you said you were attacked by a vampire, but—was that your first time with an aberration…or whatever you call them?"

"Yeah, probably."

Maybe I just hadn't noticed earlier instances.

It was the first case that I was aware of.

"Spring break for you, and then her, and now me… It seems suggestive of something, doesn't it? Nothing before, and now three in quick succession."

"Yep." It was actually five if you counted Hanekawa and Hachikuji, but I decided to be somewhat vague and hide that fact out of respect for their personal privacy. "Once you experience it, you're more likely to experience it again—apparently. So maybe it's always going to be like this for me now."

"That sounds tough."

"Not really… It's not all tough. Experiencing an aberration means having an experience that's out of the norm, and you probably come away from it having noticed and gained new things."

Although I said that, it sounded like I was papering over it or covering my tracks to avoid telling her how I felt. Just thinking back to my spring break experience told me that I was beating around the bush by saying that it wasn't all tough. Partly because I felt awkward, my eyes wandered over to Kanbaru's left hand—and the rewound white bandage. I couldn't see what it concealed, but once you knew, you could tell nonetheless that there was something slightly off about the length and shape. Even if she did her best to make it hard to notice by wrapping some areas multiple times…

"My senior Araragi, she and you have been in the same class for three years in a row even though our school shuffles homerooms every year. I assumed that you two were at least a little close from before—but from what I've heard, you only spoke to her for the first time three weeks ago."

"I don't know if I could say it was the absolute first time, but…I wouldn't have noticed her secret if she hadn't gone and slipped, and we probably wouldn't have started dating. And—if I hadn't known Oshino, I doubt I could have helped her out… So in that sense, it was luck. I guess it was convenient…or that I was inconvenienced? You knew about the Monkey's Paw, Kanbaru, and I knew a vampire. That's all."

Upon learning Senjogahara's secret a year ago—Kanbaru was able to believe it so readily, I presumed, thanks to knowing the monkey, just as I'd experienced the demon and the cat by that point. Which meant the only difference between us was that I knew Oshino, a way to fight back.

That's why I couldn't help but think.

What if Kanbaru had known Oshino—no, not necessarily him, but some sort of spiritual technocrat who could aid Senjogahara—and solved her secret a year ago? Wouldn't Kanbaru be in my position then—rather than me? Putting aside differences in age and gender for the time being—

Sheer luck.

You could call it a fated meeting—but it was chance.

"I appreciate how considerate you're being," Kanbaru thanked me, "but I wish you wouldn't say that. She isn't that kind of person. She wouldn't confuse gratitude for love. That was just what got the ball rolling." Kanbaru's words were tinted with a pale desolation. "And that's exactly why it's so frustrating. When she rebuffed me, I stepped away.

Meanwhile, you chased after her. If anything made a difference, it wasn't vampires versus monkeys, nor knowing this Oshino, it was that."

"......"

I'm sure of it, she muttered.

Talking to her like this made me realize how surprisingly introspective she was...the complete opposite of what you'd expect from her image of an athletic girl full of vim and vigor. But if she was remorseful, I felt like I was, too.

What was it?

This emotion akin to remorse as I chatted with Kanbaru, as if there were pins being pricked into my heart—I knew there was no need but found myself constantly trying to paper over things.

And that made me feel even more remorseful.

"Yes...but," Kanbaru said, "I am honestly glad that her problem was already gone. It might be strange for me to be thanking you, but that's what I'd like to do, from the bottom of my heart."

"Well, like I told you, it wasn't me, the credit should go to Oshino—actually, no, it wasn't him either. Senjoghara got saved thanks to Senjogahara. She simply went and saved herself all on our own."

That's how it was.

Oshino and I had barely done a thing.

There were no two ways about it, that was it—

"Ah...maybe you're right. But can I ask you one more thing?"

"What is it?"

"I get why she fell for you. It puts my jealousy and disappointment to shame... Yes, I think I get it. But what is it about her that made you fall for her? You said she was just another classmate for over two years, a classmate you'd never even spoken to."

"Well..."

It was hard to answer when she put it so bluntly. Part of me was embarrassed, but the bigger issue was being asked for a specific reason... It was just that in that park on that day, on Mother's Day—

Oh, of course.

It made sense.

That was the source of my remorse.

"...Why do you ask, Kanbaru?"

"Well. What I'm trying to say is that if it's just her body you're after, I think I could take her place."

"........."

An incredible proposal.

With her right hand and her bandaged left, Kanbaru grabbed her own breasts and squished them together and up. She was still wearing her school uniform, and enhanced by the immodest mismatch, her enticing pose exuded an almost unnatural allure.

"I think I'm pretty cute."

If she did say so herself.

"I think I'd look a little more feminine if I grew my hair out, and I'm not indifferent to skin care. Plus, thanks to having always played sports, my body is nice and toned, with just the right kind of waistline. I've been told I have the kind of figure that men savor."

"Bring over whoever told you that, so I can kill him."

"It was the basketball team advisor."

"This world is done for!"

"You can't kill him. We'd get suspended from matches."

So what do you think, Kanbaru asked for a second time.

She didn't seem to be joking or half-joking or jocular, but absolutely serious, and she bore down on me to give her one of two answers: yes or no.

"I'm ready to do this, you know. All you have to do is ask, any time and any place, and I'll be the bottom for your top."

"Bottom?! Top?! Why would I ask for that?!"

"Hm? Oh, I see. You don't have any grounding in BL. That's surprising."

"I don't want to talk about BL with a younger girl!"

"Hm? BL just stands for 'Boys' Love.'"

"I know that! It's not like I got that wrong!"

Yes, I'd noticed.

When I cleaned her room, there'd been so many books scattered around with those kinds of covers!

I'd gone out of my way to avoid the subject!

I'd pretended I hadn't seen anything!

"Oh, so you weren't confused. I was sure you were, judging by your reaction. Then what exactly are you so mad about? I didn't mean to offend you with anything I said. Could it mean you're a bottom?"

"Not another word about this!"

"I'm more of a sub, so I don't think I can top."

"Wha… Um, you lost me."

A sub-what?

Were we entering forbidden territory here?

I felt like our conversation was treading on thin ice.

"And anyway, Kanbaru, why would a boy and a girl have to do BL anything? There's zero need for that."

"But you see, I want to preserve my maidenhood for her—"

"I don't need to hear it!"

The thin ice had cracked. This conversation was underwater!

Hitagi Senjogahara and Suruga Kanbaru, are the two of you conspiring to smash into dust every illusion I have about women?! I'm sure of it now, the crisis management part of my brain is telling me outright, it's unmistakable, you're old acquaintances, the Valhalla Duo!

Tiptoeing and sneaking off, or running away on fleet feet, my chances at happiness were abandoning me in droves. I could feel it with my whole body and heaved a sigh.

Ahh… They were grinding away at my sanity with all this risqué talk about "going after her body" and "supple, carefree limbs, the kind of figure that men savor"… Though precocious in her own way, talking with Hachikuji the day before was fun because she never sounded weirdly jaded—or so I thought back fondly to my conversation with a grade school kid.

I was a terminal case.

"I'm sorry, but if you'll allow me to be intrusive," warned Kanbaru, "I don't think you'll be able to make it very far in the adult world if you can't talk smut with girls younger than you. Be smart and jettison your precious notions about femininity as soon as you can."

"If there's anything I don't want to be scolded about by a girl younger than me, that would be it."

And her choice of words, "talk smut"…

Not that putting it another way would have made it fine.

"Still," she insisted, "I don't want to belabor the point, but expecting me to be chaste thanks to these flimsy illusions of yours presents actual problems that start with saying hello. Don't blame me, girls are interested in dirty talk, too."

"Uh huh…"

This whole episode was liable to foment its own set of illusions about women, though… Was I wrong to think that with Senjogahara or her, the context was different?

"All right," Kanbaru said, "then let's get back to if you're a briefs guy or a boxers guy."

"I don't think that's what we were talking about?!"

"Huh? Was it whether or not I wear panties under my bike shorts?"

"Excuse me, but you don't, Miss Kanbaru?!" I was so shaken I found myself speaking politely. "Th-Then those bike shorts peeking out under your skirt are…!"

"Even if that's the case, why be shocked? Bike shorts were originally designed as a form of underwear."

"All the more so then! You mean you're walking around with your underwear out for the world to see!"

Moreover…that skirt of hers got blown in every direction but down when she ran and jumped!

"Hmph. Yes, I suppose you could say that, but just think of it as the chic dispensation of a sporty girl."

"No! It's the perverted behavior of an exhibitionist!"

"Oh, now I remember, that's not what we were talking about, either. It was whether I could serve as a replacement for—"

"Hold on, don't rewind the conversation and leave such a question hanging! Tell me right now if you're wearing anything underneath!"

"Can we gloss over such vulgar matters, please? It's a triviality."

"It isn't a triviality, it's a watershed moment—is my junior a sporty girl or an exhibitionist?!"

Smuttiness aside, we were going on and on about nothing in particular.

"Okay, then," conceded Kanbaru, "why don't you look at it this way. I'm both a sporty girl and an exhibitionist. For those who see me as a sporty girl, I am that; for those who see me as an exhibitionist, I am that too."

"Stop with these word games! That kind of line stops being cool once you get out of middle school! What are you, my little sister?!"

Our conversation about nothing in particular reached a peak.

It could only be about something now.

"...But listen, Kanbaru. Seriously, no matter how hard you try, you're not going to take Senjogahara's place."

"......"

She wasn't going to take her place.

I was talking about more than what she'd said.

"You're not Senjogahara, after all. No one can take someone else's place, and no one can become someone else, either. Senjogahara is Hitagi Senjogahara, and you are Suruga Kanbaru. No matter how much you love her, no matter how much you idolize her, no matter how much more you do."

"...You're right." Kanbaru nodded after a brief pause. "You're exactly right."

"Yeah. So let's stop wasting time chatting, and get going. And also, can you knock it off with that pose already? You've turned me into someone who has an extended conversation with a high school girl who's groping her own breasts. That's too surreal a picture for me."

"Guh. I didn't notice."

"Notice." It went for other stuff, too. "The sun will go down if we don't hurry—it's bad news if it gets dark, right? For your left hand."

"Yes. It also means everything's fine as long as it's bright out. I'm completely okay for another few hours at least."

"Oh... Being active only at night somehow can't help but remind me of vampires..."

Kanbaru and I walked alongside the chain-link fence that surrounded the building until we found a large hole. Three weeks earlier, Senjogahara had gone through it with me—this time I was with her junior, Kanbaru.

I'd never thought I'd have anything to do with her.

The webs we weave.

Ties that bind.

"Watch your feet."

"Yes. Thank you kindly."

I pushed forward through the wall of unkempt grass, trying to make a path for Kanbaru as she followed behind me. Wondering how it was going to be in summertime if it was this way now, I entered the crumbling, or you might say already-crumbled, cram school.

It was still a mess.

The concrete fragments, empty cans, signs, shards of glass, and who knew what else were still a mess, a royal mess. The building was already dim in the late afternoon as it had no power, making it seem even more decayed than otherwise. I thought Oshino could at least tidy up the building if he had so much free time on his hands. Didn't living in such a place depress him?

I guess it was a little better than Kanbaru's room…

Senjogahara had scowled at the building's wretched state and Oshino's insouciance, but I wouldn't have to worry with Kanbaru…

"It's filthy," she said. "I can't believe it. If this Oshino person lives here, he ought to clean up."

"……"

I guess she was tough on others about certain things?

Or maybe it was that she wasn't self-conscious… I thought her brazen attitude came from her confidence, but perhaps there was another side to it.

That was one way she and Senjogahara were different.

Senjogahara was abnormally self-conscious.

Oshino primarily roosted on the fourth floor.

I walked—in the dim light.

The farther we got from the entrance, the deeper the darkness grew—what an oversight on my part. I'd been to the building so many times, I could have at least brought a flashlight. I'd brought the envelope containing a hundred thousand yen that Senjogahara had entrusted to me—in other words, I'd planned on coming here regardless of how my conversation with Kanbaru panned out. I could have spared the idea some thought.

But, well.

It depended on the time and the place, but for the most part, I was fine with darkness...which is why I found myself forgetting such obvious things.

Mementos from my time as a vampire.

"......"

I turned around when we reached the stairs to notice that Kanbaru's steps were incredibly timid and wobbly. She must not like the dark, I thought. When you considered that she was normally a fearless sportswoman, her gait appeared all the more precarious and uncertain. In her state, walking up stairs would be an ordeal. Whatever was up with her left arm, it'd be a big problem if she hurt her legs, too... I remembered how I'd led Senjogahara by the hand when we came here together...

That was the first time I had held her hand.

Hmm...what to do? Kanbaru must have declined to ride behind me out of such considerations, and come to think of it, I'd learned only yesterday just how strict Senjogahara could be about cheating...

"Hey, my junior Kanbaru."

"What is it, my senior Araragi?"

"Hold out your right hand."

"Like this?"

"All right. It's docking time."

I pulled her hand toward me by the tip and had her grip the belt that I wore on my school-issued slacks.

"We're about to climb up some stairs, so don't trip. I'll be sure to walk up slowly, so be careful."

"......"

No matter how strict Senjogahara's guidelines were, this degree of physical contact couldn't possibly count as cheating. It was a brilliant idea. It seemed like sophistry, I admit, but I would at least have a proper excuse prepared for Senjogahara.

"Aren't you kind," Kanbaru said, tugging on my belt as though she were testing its strength. "You must get told that often. That you're a good, kind person."

"Who wants to get told, and often, the kind of thing you tell someone who doesn't have a personality?"

"Even when it comes to guiding me through the dark, you're minding both her and me, and I'm grateful from the bottom of my heart. I'm pained by your consideration. I'm envious of your discretion."

"...Was my thinking that transparent?"

She was a sharp one.

You usually wouldn't catch on to that.

But since she did, why go and spell it out? I felt so awkward. The jokey way I'd gone about it made it so much worse.

"My senior, there's something I want to ask you."

"What is it? Ask whatever you want, as long as it's not about tops and bottoms."

"Oh, then I'll put that bit off until later."

"It's on your list of questions?!"

"As are panties and exhibitionism."

"We already played it out!"

"To be frank, only dirty talk interests me."

"I won't have such a character! Just hurry up with your question!"

"Judging by everything you've said...it seems like you haven't talked to her about me at all."

"Hunh? No, I have. That's how I learned you two were the Valhalla Duo."

To be exact, I'd heard that from Hanekawa, but I hadn't understood their relationship until I checked with Senjogahara. I might have guessed, but guesses were all they were going to be. I wouldn't have thought to ask Hanekawa.

"That's not what I meant," Kanbaru said. "About my left hand. About my left hand attacking you..."

"Oh, that. Yeah, I haven't had the opportunity... I was in no state to last night, and I didn't know the truth of the matter anyway, or that your left hand was like that. I wasn't even close to sure you were behind the attack in the first place. It was just speculation. As far as she knows, I ran into a telephone pole on my bicycle."

"Will that do, with all the collateral damage?"

"Well, I can't get the police or a hospital involved thanks to my formerly vampiric body. If things go public, it'll be just as annoying for me. I don't plan on keeping what happened with you a secret from Senjogahara forever, of course, but...I just thought it was something you should tell her, not me."

"I should?"

"See, I'm not a kind person or a good person. It's just that I have my motives—"

My underhanded calculations.

My scheming persistence.

Something I, myself, could never do—

"...Hm? Whoa there."

Shinobu was there on the landing between the third and fourth floors.

Shinobu Oshino.

A blond girl who looked to be about eight years old, her skin so white it seemed translucent, wearing a helmet and a pair of goggles—she was there on the landing sitting directly on the floor, legs folded, arms around her knees. You might have mistaken her for the spirit of a dead child from Japanese folklore if not for her golden hair.

I yelled in surprise despite myself.

Shinobu glared intensely at me and Kanbaru as we came climbing up the stairs. It was a loaded gaze full of hate and gravity, of unspoken words and unfulfilled desires.

"......"

I ignored her.

I ignored her, averting my eyes, and walked around her, refusing to pay her notice, to proceed to the fourth floor... But why was she sitting on the landing, of all places? Could she have gotten in a fight with Oshino?

"H-Hey, what was with that girl?" asked Kanbaru in a mildly agitated, flighty voice once we were on the fourth floor. Then again, it would have been weirder for her to pay no mind to a girl like Shinobu mysteriously sitting on the floor of some ruins... Well, part of Kanbaru's body had turned into an aberration. Could she have sensed something from Shinobu?

"She was super freaking cute!"

"You said that with the biggest smile you've shown all day!"

"I want to hold her in my arms… No, I want her to hold me in her arms!"

"You fall for anyone, don't you?!" I'd thought there was only one girl for her. Plus, this was a child she was talking about. "Just keep that stuff to yourself…"

"I don't want to keep any secrets from you, though."

"You still don't need to put out the naked truth."

"Naked?"

"Don't react to just that word! Do I have to watch every single phrase I use now? I've never met someone who's harder to talk to!"

She was a real horn dog, or rather, she wasn't Sapphic only for Senjogahara… Every one of my illusions, and not just ones about women, was being blown to pieces like it was a carpet bombing. Swearing to myself that I'd never allow her to meet Hachikuji, I gloomily conveyed a warning.

"…Well, you should stay away from—that."

A vampire.

—husk of.

A vampire.

—dregs of.

That was what Shinobu Oshino, the blond girl, was.

When the devil is away—the mice.

"Hm. I see… Too bad," Kanbaru lamented.

"And now that you've said so with the saddest face you've shown all day, here we are. Time to find out whether Oshino's in or not… We can't just put this off until tomorrow if he isn't, though. My life's in real danger."

"…Sorry."

"I'm not trying to be mean or anything. Don't feel bad about it."

"Well, I don't feel good about it, either. I think I need to make it up to you somehow. Ah, right, what's your favorite color?"

"Huh? My favorite color? Are you giving me a present? I don't know if I have one, but if I had to say, I guess aqua blue?"

"Okay, got it." Kanbaru nodded. "Then I promise from now on, whenever I meet you, I'll do my best to be wearing aqua blue underwear."

"Don't drag me in to your dirty talk or make it seem like I'm the reason! It's all on you and your sexual frustration!"

There were three classrooms on the fourth floor. The doors to all of them were broken. If Oshino was in the building, he would be in one of the three, but—

The first room was a miss.

We checked in the second room—and there he was.

"You're late, Araragi. I've been waiting so long that I nearly fell asleep."

Mèmè Oshino—lay there on a linoleum floor so cracked and ripped you wouldn't just trip but get deep cuts if you walked across it with bare feet, a piece of cardboard box so discolored it must have been rotting as his only bedding. And without getting up, he greeted us off the bat with those words in his usual all-knowing tone, despite not knowing the first detail about our situation.

His crumpled, psychedelic Hawaiian shirt, his shaggy hair, and his generally filthy appearance. Words like "clean" or "refreshing" existed on a separate plane from the man. You could say it was an appropriate look for the ruins he lived in, but what he could have ever looked like before coming to them was by now beyond my imagination.

Oshino scratched his head like even that was a bother.

Then, and only then—did he notice Kanbaru, who, out of anxiety or alarmed by the very questionable Oshino, was trying to hide behind me and holding tight to my belt with her right hand though we were already here.

"Oh. So you're brought yet another girl with you today, Araragi. You're with a new one every time we meet—why, I'm quite glad for you."

"Shut up. Don't keep spouting the same lines."

"You say that, but what am I supposed to do when it's the same situation? My repertoire is limited. Hm? And another girl with straight bangs, at that. Judging by her uniform, are you two classmates? Does your high school regulate hairstyles? Interesting, that's a very antiquated system they've kept around."

"No, we don't have such rules."

It was just coincidence.

Or rather, though Kanbaru wore hers short, it was probably because she was imitating Senjogahara that they had similar hairstyles. I wasn't aware of any reason behind Senjogahara's, but as for Hanekawa, well, as a symbol of seriousness? That had to be it more or less.

"So it's what you're into, after all," asserted Oshino. "Hmph. In that case, I'll cut little Shinobu's hair, too, for your next visit. She just lets it grow out, and it's about time she had a haircut. In exchange, do you think you could bring a girl with a one-length haircut next time? I might be wasting my breath, but I'm putting the request out there."

"...I saw Shinobu on our way up. What's she doing there?"

"Oh, she's sulking because I ate one more than I should of her snack-time Mister Donuts. She's been like that since yesterday."

"......"

What kind of a vampire was she?

And what kind of a dude was he?

"I tearfully handed over the Pon de Ring, so she's one narrow-minded little girl. I think I need to teach her the phrase, 'quality over quantity.'"

"I don't care... I couldn't care any less. Also, Oshino, one correction. She's not my classmate. Take a close look, her scarf isn't the same color as Senjogahara's or Hanekawa's, right? She's a year younger than me, and her name is Suruga Kanbaru. Kanbaru as in 'god' and 'plains.' And Suruga as in...umm."

Oops.

I knew how to write it, but it was hard to explain...

The barely literate Koyomi Araragi was showing his colors.

"Suruga as in 'Suruga-toi,'" Kanbaru chimed in helpfully.

Thank goodness...but wait, what exactly was that?

I'd never heard the term before. Was it *toi* in the sense of "question"?

Like some famous quiz? A riddle like with the Sphinx?

"Ah, 'Suruga-toi.' Of course, of course." Oshino nodded in clear comprehension.

Ugh, if he hadn't known, I would've gotten an explanation without having to speak up… I clicked my tongue, but I hated having to wonder, so I asked Kanbaru, "What's 'Suruga-toi'?"

"It's a famous method of torture from the Edo period. They'd hogtie your hands and legs behind you, hang you from the ceiling, put a heavy rock on your back, and spin you around."

"Don't use a torture method to explain your name!"

"It's something that I'd love to undergo sometime in my life."

"………!"

So she was a sapphist, a BL fan, a sub, a bottom, a pedo, and a masochist?!

How could all of that apply to any one person…

The star of our school didn't need to spread conflicting rumors about herself. She already had a personality disorder.

I was at a loss for words.

"Anyway, I'm Suruga Kanbaru."

The exchange seemed to have relaxed her, and finally letting go of my belt, Suruga came out of half-hiding—and in her usual proud, confident, and unhesitating way, stated her name, her right hand in front of her chest.

"I'm Araragi's junior. Nice to meet you."

"Nice to meet you, missy. I'm Mèmè Oshino."

While Suruga was smiling—

Oshino was smirking.

Written out, "smile" and "smirk" look similar, a difference of only two letters, but seeing their expressions up close, I received very dissimilar impressions that were pretty much diametrically opposed. It proved to a painful degree that looking happy wasn't enough. Yes, Oshino's was lighthearted too, but so much so that it felt unpleasant. The man was just sculpted to seem fake.

"…Hmph. If you're his junior, that makes you missy tsundere's junior as well."

As he said this, Oshino's eyes were unfocused and distant as if he were looking at Kanbaru's back—and me and Senjogahara both being third-years and Kanbaru therefore being Senjogahara's junior as well didn't seem to be his entire point.

But maybe I was reading too much into it.

"Oshino—anyway, I should start by giving this to you. It's from the very same missy tsundere, Senjogahara."

"Hm? An envelope? Oh, money. Money, money. Perfect, I was just starting to feel squeezed. This should last me until the rainy season. Once it starts, I won't die of thirst, but I thought I'd be keeping a stiff upper lip in the meantime."

"What a thing to say to sensitive adolescents."

It was amid such dire straits that they'd fought over their Mister Donuts... No wonder Shinobu was sulking. Vampire or not, she did come from a noble bloodline. Cohabitating in these ruins with a filthy older guy was like plunging to the lowest depths... Since I was partly to blame, I didn't know what to think...

Oshino checked the contents of the envelope.

"Yep, exactly a hundred thousand yen. This clears out any balance between me and missy tsundere. You know, she's made a good impression on me, giving this to you instead of coming to hand it to me herself. She seems versed in the way of the world."

"Huh? Shouldn't it be the other way around? It feels like giving it to you in person would be a show of good faith, or good grace—"

"It's all the same whether you make gestures like that or not. But I don't intend on having that argument with you, Araragi, it'd be a pointless one at best. So—what's up with this missy?" Oshino asked casually, jabbing his chin in Kanbaru's direction as he crammed the envelope (those fresh bills, all for naught) into the pocket of his Hawaiian shirt. "I'm sure you didn't bring her here just so you could introduce a cute junior to me. Or did you actually do it just to show her off? If that's the case, I underestimated the kind of man you are, Araragi... Ha hah, but that couldn't possibly be it. Which means—hm, could it be that bandage? Ah..."

"Mister Oshino. I'm—" Kanbaru began to say something.

He slowly waved his hand as if to cut her off. "Let's start from the beginning. It doesn't seem like a very happy story. Stories about arms never are, in my experience. Especially if it's your left hand."

007

Mixed among the crushed soda cans, candy wrappers, and empty instant noodle cups I found while cleaning up Suruga Kanbaru's room was a single item that gave me pause, a long and thin paulownia box. I could feel its age from the color of the thing, and though it was covered in scratches, probably due to how carelessly Kanbaru treated it, the box seemed thick and sturdy. I assumed that it held some sort of curio—maybe a vase. Its presence, or that it might contain some such object, didn't seem odd given how impressive the Japanese home I stood in was.

But.

The box was empty.

That of course wasn't enough for me to classify it as trash, so I placed it on top of some cardboard boxes for the time being, but around when we got down to business, Kanbaru made a show of reaching out, grabbing the box, and placing it between the two of us. Then she asked me what I thought had been inside the box. A vase or something, I replied candidly.

"So even you can be wrong sometimes… This might be rude of me, but I'm relieved. Saved. I feel like you've given me a glimpse of your humanity."

"…And what was inside it?"

"A mummy," she replied straightaway. "*A mummified left hand*—was in it."

"………"

A mummified left hand, inside a paulownia box.

According to Kanbaru, she used it for the first time—in elementary school. Her mother had given it to her eight years ago when Kanbaru was still in third grade.

It was apparently the last time she ever saw her mother.

A few days after Kanbaru was given the box, both of her parents died in a traffic accident—the timing was so perfect it was as if her mother had known what was going to happen. Kanbaru said it happened while she was in math class at her elementary school. They'd died instantly in a multiple car pile-up on some far-off highway. Their car caught fire, and the remains were left in an awful state.

Kanbaru was taken in by her grandparents on her father's side.

Taken in—to the Japanese home where we sat.

She said she'd lived with her parents in an apartment until then, just the three of them—because her mother and father had eloped. Their wedding had brought them no blessings or congratulations. Her father came from a traditional and storied family, while her mother's world was far removed from any of that…or so Kanbaru told me. I had to wonder if those kinds of things still happened in this day and age, but she said they do all the time.

"My mom suffered because of that. My dad—rebelled against such customs, but it was no use. His family pretty much cut ties with him. In fact, I hadn't met my grandparents until the day of my parents' funeral. I didn't even know their names—and they didn't know mine, either. That was the first thing they asked me, what my name was."

"Huh…"

Flooded on top and in blazes on the bottom.

You don't need to worry about them, at all.

Those kinds of things—happened.

But despite whatever strife had intervened with her mother, Kanbaru was their son's only daughter—their grandchild. Taking her in was the natural thing to do, and so Kanbaru left the town where she'd lived her entire life, of course transferring schools in the process.

She wasn't able to fit in.

"The way I spoke was different. I might talk like this now, but when I was still with my parents, we were all the way out on the tip of Kyushu, probably to get as far away as possible from this home. They talk in a thick accent there, and well...I wouldn't call it bullying, but I was made fun of, and I didn't have any friends."

"Um...so it wasn't the same elementary school as Senjogahara's?"

"Right. I met her in middle school."

"Okay."

It made sense, address-wise.

She probably wasn't with Hanekawa back then, either.

"When I think back to it, I was throwing everything off balance in my new environment, and I wasn't completely blameless. It's obvious to me now, but my parents' death had hit me hard, and I'd closed off my heart. You can't expect people to treat you kindly when you've closed off your heart. But, and I can only say this because so much time has passed—back then, I was still deeply mired in my parents' death. Not that I was able to sit back and reminisce about them. I couldn't even drown myself in my memories of them. That was because my grandfather and grandmother threw away every last one of my father and mother's possessions. It was like they wanted to raise me as someone who had nothing to do with my parents."

But just so you know, Kanbaru said.

"My grandmother and grandfather are both people of character—I do respect them, and I'm truly grateful that they've looked after me all this time. It's just that their relationship with my parents is beyond me."

It made sense.

Too much time had elapsed for it to be mere past strife.

And that was why the only mementos she had left of her parents were whatever memories she retained, along with, yes, that paulownia box her mother had given her.

It may have been sealed tight.

But she hadn't been told not to open it.

So she did.

The mummified left hand.

But back in those days—the mummified hand *only went down to its wrist.* There was also a letter from her mother inside the box. Well, it wasn't so much a letter, given what was written on it—but a simple user's manual for the left hand.

It stated that it was a tool for making wishes come true.

It would make any wish come true.

It would make three and only three wishes come true.

It was such an item.

She'd gone up a school year to become a fourth grader and was either nine or ten years old—whichever she was, whether you believed that kind of fantastic story was a tossup at that age. Just barely yes, or just barely no, one or the other. It's probably an age group where the split between kids who believe in Santa Claus or not is about fifty-fifty. Or maybe that's just an illusion that people of my generation and above hold... At least, I don't think I believed in Santa Claus when I was in fourth grade, but maybe some of the special gadgets in cartoons were credible to me.

Kanbaru—was straddling that line.

In other words, she half-believed and half-doubted it would work, and just as she might try a charm printed in a girls' magazine, with a casual attitude really, she made a wish upon the mummified hand.

It didn't matter what the first one was.

It was like one of those charms.

She was just trying it out.

"Though I did know what my second wish would be if the first one worked," Kanbaru said.

Of course she did.

I knew already—it had to be a wish about her parents, right?

Something about their being alive.

I want to be able to run faster.

Such was the wish the fourth grader Suruga Kanbaru made—to the mummified thing. She was apparently a notoriously slow runner back then...and that, just as much as her accent, contributed to her being teased. From a high schooler's perspective, it seemed as ridiculous of a reason to make fun of someone as an accent, but being a slow runner is, in any case, a serious cause of distress for a grade school kid. It just so happened that field day was coming up soon at her school—and she'd made the wish thinking that everyone would look at her in a new way if she could just win the foot race.

"I was fatally unathletic at the time. I'm not talking about having slow reflexes or slow anything, but actually tripping over myself just walking around."

"Huh… But now."

Our basketball ace.

A star.

"…Wait, so does that mean—"

"If only it did," Kanbaru said. But instead. "I had a dream that night. A dream of children being attacked—by a *monster wearing a raincoat.* A nightmare—where they were tucked into bed and the monster's *left hand* attacked them mercilessly."

"……"

"I'm sure someone with your intuition has already figured out how this story ends. When I woke up the next day and went to school—four students were absent. And all four of them were supposed to run in the same race as me at field day."

The Monkey's Paw.

The Monkey's Paw grants its owner's wishes, the story goes.

But not in the way its owner intends, the story goes—

"I was terrified. I went to the library in a panic to find out what the mummified thing really was—and I came across Jacobs' 'The Monkey's Paw' in no time. My shoulders trembled with fear… If I'd made my second wish first, what would have happened, I wondered. As it was, those classmates of mine could easily have died… Fortunately, it wasn't that serious, but it could have turned out that way."

Kanbaru returned the thing to its box, sealed it even tighter than before, and stuffed it in the depths of her closet. There would be no second or third wish, of course not—she wanted to pretend none of it ever happened. She wanted to forget it all.

But.

She couldn't.

No matter how much she tried to forget about it, she found that she couldn't. Because there was still time until field day—and during practice the next day, they decided to place Kanbaru in another group.

There were five others this time.

She would be racing against—five other people.

"What do you think I did?"

"……"

"What do you think I should have done?"

Whatever I thought, if she sat and did nothing—well, the consequences were as clear as day. The same thing would happen…and repeat itself over and over again. Normally, the only way out of the situation would be to make another wish upon the paw—to ask it to cancel the first wish. But Kanbaru was afraid to. Now that she'd learned about the paw, she was afraid. It granted wishes, but not in the way its owner intended—and she had no idea how the revocation might come true.

Which is why Kanbaru ran.

She ran, and ran, and ran.

She was slow—

So she worked to become fast.

"My only option was to fulfill my wish on my own. Because if I did, there'd be no reason for the paw to attack my classmates. And fortunately, I started getting the hang of it as soon as I started—there wasn't any physical issue that made me slow, like being heavy or having a bad leg, so while I didn't become athletic overnight, I improved when it came to running. I managed to come in first at field day… Thanks to that, I started to make friends with my classmates. It of course took a good bit of time, though."

Having made her own wish come true—she never stopped working, even after field day. To say that she must have been talented to begin with would perhaps be unkind. Her continued efforts only continued to flower, to the point that she began hearing from middle school track teams not long after entering sixth grade.

Tup, tup, tup, tup, tup, tup.

But Kanbaru couldn't join a track team. She couldn't put herself in *a place where people might be faster than her*—because she didn't know the reach of her first wish. Maybe it expired the moment she took first place at field day—maybe it would last forever. There was no way to find out. Since there wasn't, the latter possibility was a source of fear.

For Kanbaru.

She already knew she wasn't made to be a distance runner—mini-marathons in grade school were one thing, but she couldn't keep going in middle school and high school. If anyone were even a little bit faster than her, all her efforts would be for naught, end of story.

That was probably why she decided to join the basketball team in middle school—if her field only extended as far as those courts did, no one could catch up to her.

"Forgoing clubs and sports might have been an option, but not only did I need to stay in good shape, just in case, but also athletics were a more or less compulsive refuge for me by then. If I didn't do something—I felt like I'd be crushed. People call me sporty, but I'm not sure if I'm the real deal. I was just motivated by fear."

But.

Playing basketball ended up being fun.

She ended up liking it.

Her speed, which had been a compulsive refuge—she could now put to positive use. She'd thought of her legs merely as a means to run away from the paw, but she could apply them constructively—towards an actual goal.

Plus.

Becoming the star of the team—

She ended up getting to know Hitagi Senjogahara.

"She was the star of the track team...and she came to watch me since I had a reputation for being fast. She might have forgotten by now...and even if she does remember, she might not think anything of it, but she was the one who came to me first."

"Huh..."

That was a bit of a surprise.

Even if it was the middle-school and not the current-day Senjogahara, it was still a surprise.

"She asked me to run a hundred-meter race with her, saying that it didn't have to be official or anything. It killed me to have to turn her down. This was a charming person who was a year above me. It might not have been love at first sight, but I'd fallen for her by the third day of talking to her. I started wanting to be near her. Being with her was therapeutic."

Therapeutic.

The word was as far removed from Senjogahara today as Pluto is from the Sun—but it really seemed that meeting her allowed Kanbaru to put out of her mind the mummy she'd received from her mother, the paulownia box stuffed in the closet.

It let her forget.

It let her forget—what she wanted to forget.

But.

"It was still there in the back of my mind, sitting in my subconscious, and more than once after that day, I was seized by a sudden impulse to use the paw. I'd be seized by an urge to rely on it. Like when we faced a really strong team in basketball. Like when I got in an awful fight with a friend. Like when I wanted to get into Naoetsu High where my senior Senjogahara was… Like when she rejected me."

Each time—she held out.

Each time, she managed to make it happen on her own.

Or, each time, she gave up on it.

By then, she understood why her mother had given her the box—it was as a sort of wish that Kanbaru would become someone who handled any problem she came across by herself. Unlike the one in "The Monkey's Paw," which taught you to accept fate, her mother's lesson must have been to alter your destiny with your own hands. It had been passed down again and again—her mother had gotten it from her mother, and her mother's mother had gotten it from her mother, and her mother's mother's mother, and so on. The lesson passed down for generations had to be that you fulfilled your own wishes. So it was all thanks to herself that Kanbaru was fast and also smart.

She hadn't been—born with it.

It was the result of work, of blood, sweat, and tears.

She always remained aware of that.

Hence.

She might have been able to solve Senjogahara's secret, her problem, by wishing upon the paw, but didn't even then.

Quietly.

She stepped away.

She gave up—on being by Senjogahara's side.

She gave up—balling her fists, biting her lip.

She didn't mind dying for Senjogahara's sake.

Suruga Kanbaru had told me that—in no uncertain terms.

Kanbaru smothered her own feelings for Senjogahara's sake.

Stood by and watched her own heart die.

What she didn't want to forget.

What she couldn't forget—she did forget.

"But a year later…I found out about you. I ended up finding out about you and her. I ended up seeing her by your side."

She couldn't hold out anymore.

She couldn't do it.

She couldn't give up.

She had no recollection of when she'd opened the closet, when she'd taken the paulownia box out of it, when she'd undone the seal, or when she'd wished upon the paw—she hadn't paused *even when the paw that had only gone down to its wrist was extended to the elbow*—and when she noticed.

Her left hand—had turned into an aberration.

Her arm had turned into a beast's paw.

Kanbaru—

Felt truly terrified for the first time in seven years.

"…And so you started stalking me after that. Come to think of it, every time we met, you asked me if anything odd had happened to me."

So—that's what she meant.

She wasn't making small talk.

She wasn't trying to spy on Senjogahara, either… Unable to play the sport she loved with her arm in that state, Kanbaru must not have wanted to go out in public at all, but she went as far as to bandage it up and hide it—because she was concerned about my safety?

But then, four days after she started stalking me.
The night of the fourth day.
That's when—it happened.
Kanbaru said she had a dream—
A dream where a monster in a raincoat attacked me.
And that was why she seemed so calm from the moment I stepped into Class 2-2.
She already realized everything—
Knew what had happened.
This backstory was quite different from my analysis.
I'd surmised that an aberration was involved, but Kanbaru actually didn't intend the phenomenon… It was all the paw's doing.
The Monkey's Paw grants its owner's wishes, the story goes.
But not in the way its owner intends, the story goes—
The simplest way to be by Senjogahara's side was to eliminate her current boyfriend, Koyomi Araragi—thought the paw.
Probably.
And afraid of that, Kanbaru was stalking me—
But her premonition was on the mark.
In truth, if I wasn't who I was…if Koyomi Araragi wasn't Koyomi Araragi, the formerly immortal human with an experience of being a vampire, I would have certainly died at that point. I wouldn't have been able to dodge the first two strikes, and even if I had, the third blow would have been lethal. That was its absurd potential and capacity for destruction. My guess was that those four elementary school kids had been spared thanks to Kanbaru's body still being a fourth grader's and also still being unathletic—but now she was on another level. Ironically, the body she'd forged to escape her first wish was making her second wish inflict that much more damage. Only her left arm had attacked me, but the incredible speed that my eyes couldn't even track—that physical capacity belonged to Suruga Kanbaru. It was an upgraded version of the same.
Capacity—destructive capacity.
A capacity for violence.
And.

It was far from over—nowhere near over, since I had survived. Once the sun set and night came, the monster in the raincoat would attack me, again and again—Kanbaru would keep on having dreams about that fiend assaulting me.

Over and over, until I died.

Until her dream came true.

Until her wish was granted.

Until Kanbaru's second wish was granted.

She wanted to be by Hitagi Senjogahara's side.

That was all she had wished for—

"'Annoyances come / In forms none greater than that / Of the visitor / But then of course I speak not / Of yourself, my esteem'd friend'—"

"Huh?" Kanbaru opened her eyes dubiously when I recited the poem. "What was that?"

"Nothing… I was just wondering if the person we're visiting will welcome us—"

And then.

Without changing our clothes or eating lunch, we went straight to the remote, abandoned cram school where Mèmè Oshino and Shinobu Oshino lived, me riding my bike and Kanbaru dashing on her own two legs.

And that—finally brings us to now.

The present moment.

Kanbaru and I were facing Oshino on the fourth floor. Despite giving him the rundown, he showed nothing resembling a reaction, simply looking up at the fluorescent lights hanging (just hanging, of course, since there was no power) from the not-so-high ceiling. He wiggled the unlit cigarette he'd stuck in his mouth midway during the explanation—but didn't speak. I'd said everything there was to say, including about Senjogahara, and didn't have any more cards to play.

A vague awkwardness drifted in the air.

Normally Mèmè Oshino gabbed more than he should as if he were born full-formed from a tongue, but he sometimes sank into these deep silences, which made him really hard to deal with… He was cheerful and happy-go-lucky on the surface, but at times like these, I wondered if he might not be an awfully gloomy guy at heart.

"The bandage," Oshino said—at last. "Could you undo that bandage for me, missy?"

"Oh, okay—"

Kanbaru glanced at me beseechingly. To put her at ease, I told her, *It's all right*. At that, she started to unravel her bandage using her right hand. *Whip whip*.

Then—the beastly hand appeared.

Without being prompted, she rolled her sleeve up—all the way to her upper arm. She bent her elbow, as if to indicate where the monster's arm and her human arm connected.

Taking a step forward she asked Oshino, "Like this?"

"...Yes, that's good. I see. That's what I thought."

"What you thought?" I cut in. "And what's as you thought, Oshino? Damn you, acting as inscrutable as ever—you constantly leave people hanging on your words. Pretending to be omniscient can't be that fun, now."

"Don't prod me like that. You're feeling spirited, Araragi. Something good happen to you?" Spitting out the cigarette in his mouth without ever having lit it—well, actually, I've never seen Oshino smoking one—he directed his trademark flippant and frivolous smirk at me. "Araragi, and you too, missy. To start off with a correction—that isn't a Monkey's Paw."

"Wha?"

Oshino had overturned the premise out of the blue—and I was shocked. Kanbaru looked like she'd been caught off-guard, too.

"There've been so many versions since Jacobs that it's hard to know what's true without seeing one for yourself—but from what little I know, I've never heard of the Monkey's Paw combining with the owner's arm. A crab for missy tsundere and a monkey for missy here would be like the old Japanese folktale and downright neat, but the world isn't so accommodating. You researched it yourself, missy, didn't you? And found nothing? No story where the Monkey's Paw merges with the owner. If there is one, that means uneducated old me has a big hole in his knowledge."

"…I did some research, but I was still in grade school."

"That's what I thought. So how did you get it into your head that it's a Monkey's Paw? Your mother *absolutely* must not have said such a thing to you… But I guess the conditions did match by and large."

"The conditions?" I asked. "What do you mean?"

"There are a pair of them in how *the story goes*, Araragi. The Monkey's Paw is an item with a story attached to it. It grants its owner's wishes, the story goes. But not in the way its owner intends, the story goes—was that it?"

Heh, Oshino snorted with an unpleasant smile.

It was the smile of someone with an awful personality.

Or may I say, rotten to the core.

"I suppose it was a convenient interpretation for you, missy—or maybe a comforting one? It doesn't really matter. What's for sure, though, is that it's not a Monkey's Paw—originally it was mummified, right? And it gained life by melding with you. Then—my guess is that it's a Rainy Devil."

"Rei...?" I blurted out when he spoke the name, but without allowing me a question, or even a moment, Oshino pushed on.

"So, Araragi. Have you read *Faust*?"

"Huh?"

"Thank you for the reaction, I see that you haven't. In fact, it seems like you haven't even heard of it. But I'm not the least bit surprised, not anymore. I've decided to get accustomed to these reactions of yours. What about you, missy? Have you read *Faust*?"

"Ah, umm." Kanbaru sounded surprised to be put on the spot but replied, as if it were a spinal reflex, "No, I'm not very well read, so I haven't. Of course, I'm familiar with the plot and rough outline of the tale."

"I see. No, that's par for the course. Yup, yup. Usually, a high schooler would at least know that much. Uh oh, how embarrassing, Araragi."

"Don't make fun of him! He just happened not to know, that's all! To begin with, he's not someone you can fit into existing frameworks like 'reading'!"

Suddenly incensed by Oshino's words, Kanbaru had raised her voice to scold him. Puzzled by her unlikely reaction, he turned his eyes toward me for an explanation.

I couldn't bring myself to meet them.

...Kanbaru.

I appreciated that she was getting mad on my behalf... I never imagined someone getting mad on your behalf would be so heartening, but yelling at Oshino there came too close to agreeing that I'm stupid...

"Kanbaru," I said. "Could you please drop that routine for now? It's amusing, yeah, but if you pull that every time Oshino makes fun of me, we're never going to get anywhere ..."

"Hm. I see. Profound words, befitting someone like you who faces any person with an open heart. Honestly, I struggle to accept your wisdom, as lacking in virtue and as quick to spite as I am, but if you say so, I'll restrain myself and persevere." Kanbaru nodded and bobbed her head in a bow to Oshino. "I'm sorry."

She was a girl who could say sorry.

Good girl.

"...No, I don't mind," Oshino excused her. "And it was amusing. But considering that one of your arms has turned out that way, you're a spirited missy. Something good happen to you? Well, in any case—*Faust*. Johann Wolfgang von Goethe was the leading author of the Storm and Stress, or *Sturm und Drang* epoch, and his career-crowning achievement was the drama *Faust*. It's about—do you think you could tell him, missy? Whatever you know is fine."

"Um, sure."

Kanbaru looked at me hesitantly.

She seemed almost apologetic.

Like when she gave me the outline of Jacobs' "The Monkey's Paw," Suruga Kanbaru's personality was such that she couldn't instruct her elders about anything without feeling presumptuous.

"As Mister Oshino said, it's Goethe's masterpiece, and...well, to mention a simple characteristic, it's a story split into two parts. *Urfaust* and *Faust, a Fragment* led to *Faust, Part One* and *Faust, Part Two*. It's a massive accomplishment that took him over sixty years to complete.

I can only bow to it. Goethe is also famous for *The Sorrows of Young Werther* and *Elective Affinities*, but if we were to pick a single work he put his whole body and soul into, the unanimous answer would be *Faust*. The protagonist, Doctor Faust, sells his soul to a devil, Mephistopheles, in order to gain all knowledge—and that ought to do for an introduction. I won't go into details because I don't want to spoil it, but *Part One* is about his romance with the commoner Gretchen, while *Part Two* depicts the establishment of an ideal nation. It's generally read as a sort of philosophy or, I should say, a narrative about the pursuit of knowledge. I'm sure you're aware, but it even gave rise to the expression 'Faustian impulse,' which describes the drive, the intellectual desire to know and experience everything."

"……"

Why in the world did this jock junior of mine think that her senior who hadn't heard of *Faust* knew of any "Faustian impulse"?

Oshino took it from there. "The heart of the story is that he sells his soul to the devil—Doctor Faust tries to fulfill his namesake impulse by having his wish granted that way… Of course, if you want to learn what happens in the end, Araragi, I recommend that you head to your nearest bookstore. But yeah, that's what it is. Missy's explanation is what you'd consider common knowledge, so if you know that much, it makes my job easier. I'm impressed that she was able to give such an eloquent speech about it despite not having read the book. If there's anything I should add, it's a bit that surprisingly few people know about—you'd find it in any commentary about Goethe, of course, but people these days don't read the classics. I'm not talking about you, missy, but people think there's no reason to go through and actually read a famous story when they feel like they already have. So yes, you can't blame people for not knowing, but the *Faust* story is based on a real person."

"What? Really?" Kanbaru sounded surprised.

As her *Faust*-ignorant senior, I didn't even know why that should be surprising.

"Johann Faust. It's said he lived during the Renaissance period… While I say he was real, there are different theories about that, but stories about him ended up turning into folklore. A wandering physician or magician who, yes, sells his soul to the devil Mephistopheles, and in exchange for all kinds of knowledge and experience, promises to act as an enemy of Christians, for twenty-four years he lives according to those 'Faustian impulses'—and the moment the contract expires, he meets a sad end. Look it up yourself, you can find the details in *Doctor Faustus*."

"Huh…I didn't know."

Kanbaru sounded impressed by Oshino's trivia. Putting aside *Faust*, the story did have to do with folklore, his field of expertise, so this level of erudition was nothing new, but at this rate was she going to start flattering him, too? In fact, I didn't understand Kanbaru's standards for that. It wasn't like she indiscriminately bombarded everyone she met with praise…

"I was convinced Goethe had come up with the whole thing himself," she said. "But he'd based the thing on local legends."

"Well, he arranged a lot of the story in his own way, so at the end of the day, it's the Goethe edition of *Doctor Faust*. It's similar to Dazai's 'Run, Melos!' or Akutagawa's 'Rashomon.' The medieval folktale and Akutagawa's version feel pretty different, don't they? Same deal. The Faust legend has been turned into stories by lots of other people, too. A famous instance would be the English author Marlowe. Do you know Marlowe? Not Raymond Chandler's Phillip Marlowe. Christopher Marlowe. He's often spoken of as a forerunner of Shakespeare, but he did write *Doctor Faustus*."

"It's kind of interesting that it was Faust who was the doctor," Kanbaru noted, a bit of bashfulness sneaking into her voice.

Huh, Oshino tilted his head in puzzlement, and I could tell that the reason for her bashfulness was lost on him.

"But…Oshino," I attempted to wade into their exchange, afraid that we were getting off track, though I still didn't know much about *Faust*. "So what? I don't mind that you're as frustratingly longwinded as ever, but I don't see how it has anything to do with Kanbaru's current predicament. I think we've gotten derailed and are skidding sideways. Yeah, the part where the devil grants wishes in exchange for your soul resembles the Monkey's Paw, but it's not like Kanbaru's arm is the arm of this Mephistopheles from *Faust*, right? As if it's not a Monkey's Paw but the hand of the devil—"

"Well, that's exactly it, Araragi. You're on point today."

Oshino—

Pointed his finger at me pretentiously.

"The hand of the devil on missy here, whose name starts with the character for 'god,' seems to line up a little too perfectly, but it's not as bad as a crab-monkey spat or what happened with that lost girl the other day. It's just a plain old hint this time around. Mephistopheles isn't particularly terrifying, as far as devils go—he's more of a vulgar one. Low-ranking, or maybe not part of the rankings at all, just a familiar. That would normally make it extremely difficult to identify its exact category, but a raincoat-wearing devil with a monkey arm narrows it down, of course—and if it merges with its owner, then it's a Rainy Devil."

A Rainy Devil.

"It's not a Monkey's Paw, it's a Devil's Hand. Ha hah, isn't this much simpler if you think of it that way? I mean, why would an ape grant human wishes without asking for anything in return? It's said the Monkey's Paw grants them because an old Indian ascetic imbued it with mystical power, but you don't need any explanation or reputation if it's a devil. Of course it'll grant wishes, it gets a soul in return."

"A soul—"

"What kind of devil wouldn't grant three wishes in exchange for a soul?" Oshino puffed a laugh through his nose. He was in full mockery mode. "Anyway, the Monkey's Paw is a right hand, not a left hand."

"...Really?"

"It's an item you hold with your right hand to use, so I assume that it's a right hand itself. But a Devil's Hand. It might not be a devil, taxonomically speaking, but I'm still surprised. You might not be shocked by much these days, Araragi, since you already encountered a vampire...but it's incredible to come across such a devil in Japan. It's a notable find. Though, of course, there's no shortage of Japanese *yokai* that would grant wishes in that manner. I don't know, what with li'l missy class president, li'l missy tsundere, and our li'l lost girl...this is one strange town. Seriously. How's it all going to end, with someone summoning the ruler of all hell to this place? …Missy, you said your mother gave you that left hand, yes? Kanbaru must be your father's surname. Do you know your mother's maiden name?"

"In fact—um, it's a bit of an unusual name." Kanbaru spoke slowly as if she were trying to remember. "I think it was 'Gaen.' *Ga* as in the phrase 'hell or high water' and *en* as in 'smoke screen.' Toé Gaen was her full maiden name."

"…Huh. Oh, all right. And Toé must be written with the characters for 'far' and the one for 'river' used in *Yangtze*. The same way you'd write Totomi, the name of the old Japanese province. So that's where your name comes from. Ha hah, nicely done."

"Of course, after she got married, she was Toé Kanbaru. Why does that matter, though, Mister Oshino?"

"Why does it matter? Did you just ask me that? Oh, no, it doesn't matter at all. I was trying to fill some time, it doesn't have anything to do with your situation. And who cares about that background stuff in this case. So, Araragi, and you too, missy. Now you know everything. Whether that hand is a Monkey's Paw or a Devil's Hand might not make a difference to you, but having come here to visit me, what's your plan going forward?"

"What do you mean—"

"You see, Araragi, I am what you might call an expert in this field. As a semi-passable excuse for an authority, in situations like these, I'm not opposed to helping out."

"You—" Kanbaru leaned forward. "You'd save me?"

"I'll do no such thing. I'll only help out. You're going to get saved all on your own, missy. You've come to the wrong place if you're seeking salvation, and it wouldn't be my scene. But considering the situation—Araragi, what should I do?" Oshino asked in a mean-spirited tone—but then fell silent, as if he hadn't meant it rhetorically and were really waiting on my answer. Why was that? What should he do… Wasn't it obvious?

"Hey, Oshino…"

"I'm wondering how exactly I should help, Araragi. Should I help missy's second wish come true? Or should I help annul it? Should I help turn her left arm back to normal? All of the above? That might be a little too greedy—but what I can say is that none of the above is going to be simple."

"Well...um."

If I said all of the above—would that come to pass?

But.

"There are two easy ways to solve this phenomenon for the time being," Oshino said. "The first is for you to be killed one night by the monster in the raincoat—the Rainy Devil. That will turn missy's arm back to normal and probably grant her wish. The other is to take that beastly left arm that's turned into an aberration and to lop it off."

"L-Lop it off?" I started fretting at Oshino's alarming proposal. "...Can you cut off just the part that belongs to this monkey—or devil? Will her old arm grow back?"

"It's not a lizard's tail, so it's not going to be that convenient. Still, an arm is a small price to pay to solve this whole situation," he said casually—but it was no joke.

You got what you paid for, with a vengeance...

Plus, it would be bad enough for anyone, but even worse for Kanbaru. If we did that, she'd never be able to play basketball again. Given how the sport had saved her, and how it continued to sustain her, the proposal really didn't bear voicing even if it came to mind.

"A-Ah," Kanbaru spoke up. "That, I don't think I could—"

"You tried to kill another human being, all right? It would only be fair," Oshino tossed the harsh words at her when she immediately balked at the idea—he was merciless at such moments. He'd acted the same way with Hanekawa and Senjogahara—

"Then again," he said, "Araragi getting killed is nice and simple as far as solutions go."

"H-Hey, Oshino, I take your point, but hold on. She tried to kill another human being... That's me you're talking about, right? But that's not what she wished for. She only wanted to be by Senjogahara's side—"

"Only to be by her side? What a riot," Oshino continued to me in his harsh tone. "You're so kind, Araragi. You're a good, kind person—what a good and kind person. Makes me sick, really. How many more people do you have to hurt with that kindness until you're satisfied? It was the same with little Shinobu. Only to be by her side? Did you believe those saccharine words just the way they came out of missy's mouth?"

"...You're saying that wasn't it?" I asked Oshino and glanced at Kanbaru. She was silent. "Hey, Kanbaru—"

"For example, Araragi. You don't find it odd? That story of her first wish when she was in grade school. Why do you think the left hand didn't just make her faster and roughed people up instead?"

"Well—that's because the Monkey's Paw grants its owner's wishes in an unintended way—"

"But it's not a Monkey's Paw," Oshino declared. "This was in exchange for a soul. The wish ought to be granted exactly as it's made. The Rainy Devil may be a low-level demon, and it may have a nasty habit of rushing to violence, but a contract is a contract. A deal is a deal. If your wish is to be faster, that's normally what should happen. How does roughing up her classmates make her any faster? Doesn't that causality seem off? It's obvious that beating them up would only get her placed in another group."

"......" I couldn't argue with him if he put it that way. "Then why? Why did the monster in the raincoat go to her classmates and—"

"Because she wanted to beat the shit out of them, of course. Unable to fit in at her new school, missy was constantly being teased. She says it wasn't what you'd call bullying, but that's what bullied kids say. If you've just had your parents die on you and you're persecuted at school on top of that, wanting revenge isn't weird at all. If anything, it'd be weird if she didn't want any."

"I..." Kanbaru said—then fell silent.

How had she wanted to explain herself?

Why did she decide not to after all?

What did she realize?

Oshino went on. "I'm sure it wasn't a conscious decision. I do think it was in the realm of the unconscious, okay? If it had been intentional, she'd know. I'm sure the way she saw it, she made a wish to become faster. On the face of it, yes, but not on the flip side. Behind her wish was a dark desire to get back at her classmates—to beat them up. That's what missy wished for, even if it was unconscious. The devil saw through to that desire. It read what was on the flip side. But deep down, missy must have known that, all right? It might have been unconscious, but those were her honest feelings all the same. But not wanting to accept that, she sought a different interpretation for the phenomenon…and arrived at the Monkey's Paw. Not the stuff about *granting a wish*, but *defying the owner's will*—that was the axial part, wasn't it? A psychological excuse that it wasn't her intention at all to attack her classmates. Well, that kind of thing is important."

A psychological excuse.

A question of interpretation.

"It's not just true for the Monkey's Paw, most cases involving aberrations that grant wishes end horribly for the protagonist—and in that sense, when missy looked them up in grade school, she could easily have found a different one. She just happened to come across Jacobs' 'The Monkey's Paw.' But what would you say? Have things turned out horribly for missy? Is she miserable because her wish came true? Araragi, would you say missy is truly miserable because those classmates who teased her were made to suffer? Isn't the normal response to that a quick and tidy 'serves them right'?"

"The normal response… But Oshino—"

"Ha hah, Araragi, are you wondering what evidence I have to be so sure? Well, it's obvious if you actually listen to her story. Clear as day. That arm of hers…how was it in grade school, again?"

"………"

Now that he mentioned it.

The mummified hand that only went down to its wrist at the time—how was it then?

"I heard nothing about bandages—" pointed out Oshino, "and until she went to class the next day and found out those four were absent, she didn't notice that it had happened, right? If her left hand turned out like that, she surely would have. What does that mean? You see, when her classmates got beaten up that night, her wish came true. The aberration merged with missy's left hand overnight without her realizing it, and likewise unattached overnight. It unattached *with a bit of her soul equivalent to the wish*—and grew from the left wrist into a forearm, I bet."

"...Wait, Oshino, that would mean—"

It made sense.

But his argument suggested...

"Your initial thinking was on the mark, Araragi. You'd actually arrived at the right answer for once. Didn't I tell you? You're on point today. There was no need to get tied up into knots, you just had to use your common sense to think it through. You're such a chump to believe your assailant's excuses. You'll never make it onto a jury, Araragi. You stole away her idol for yourself. It's hardly bizarre if she felt murderously jealous. There's no way missy's own intention had no part in this, all of it was exactly her intention. Left hands don't have any."

So said Oshino.

008

The Rainy Devil is apparently a very violent devil—there's nothing it loves more than human malice and hostility, vengeance and chagrin, jealousy and envy, negative emotions in general. It sees into the darkest side of a person, provokes it, draws it out, then makes it real. It listens to people's wishes out of spite and grants them out of spite. The contract itself—is in the form of three granted wishes in exchange for a human soul. It's said that once the three wishes are granted—it takes that person's life and body. In other words, he or she becomes the devil by the end. That was its nature. So if Kanbaru had made a wish to resolve Senjogahara's secret upon learning about it a year ago, it probably wouldn't have been granted. The Rainy Devil can only grant violent, negative wishes.

The devil reads the flip side of a wish.

There's always something—on the back.

She wanted to become faster because she hated her classmates.

She wanted to be by Senjogahara's side—because she hated Koyomi Araragi.

Yes, it reads the backside.

Yes, it looks at the backside.

It sees into our unconscious desires.

The devil—sees through us.

She may not have regretted stepping away—but resented anyone stepping into that position. If someone could, why not her?

Why couldn't it be me.

The Rainy Devil.

A devil told of in Europe since long ago.

It's often depicted as a monkey wearing a raincoat.

In that sense, it might be correct to call that left hand a monkey's paw—but either way, both the first and the second wishes had been Kanbaru's own unconscious ones, clear but hidden.

Against the classmates who teased her.

And me.

Her classmates in grade school had gotten off with injuries, while I was nearly killed… Was that due to a difference in how strongly she felt, the volume of her negative emotions? What I'd posited about Kanbaru's maturation as an athlete must have had something to do with it too, but there was also a greater psychological factor.

Well, anyway, Oshino was right.

Maybe I hadn't given it enough thought.

If Kanbaru had really wished to the Rainy Devil to be by Senjogahara's side, it didn't make sense for her to feel concerned about my safety—given the grade school episode, her violent left hand would try to eliminate Koyomi Araragi, but how could Kanbaru, from her standpoint, know that for sure? Precisely how her left hand would grant the wish, in what unintended manner it would go about it, should have been opaque to her.

But she unconsciously knew what she unconsciously wished for.

She knew that I was in danger.

If the monster in the raincoat didn't appear before me as soon as the aberration melded with her left hand, that was because Kanbaru was trying to control the impulse, according to Oshino. She was right on the edge, in conflict with it, struggling against it.

"Working hard to become faster is like the ultimate in self-regarding excuses. The paw wasn't doing anything because she made her own wish come true—what a patently ridiculous idea. Missy herself might've believed it, might've wanted to believe it, and that was by no means wrong, but the wish the Rainy Devil violently granted was the backside rather than the front. Still, her stance of always having managed on her own had a good effect this time around...and while the aberration merged with her arm, she was able to suppress it. When you look at it that way, aberrations like these are really like items. The owner's mindset is a factor...but to be realistic about it, in this case it's just an arm, so the Rainy Devil must be unable to exercise too much of its power, a devil though it may be. It couldn't draw out of her an unconscious to surpass her consciousness. In other words, her left hand didn't activate while she was concerned about your wellbeing. All of her stalking since four days ago had exactly the effect she wanted, though it might not have been missy's intention, since all of this occurred in the unconscious. But—yesterday, was it? She learned that you and li'l missy tsundere would be meeting all alone for a so-called study session. Until then, your dating was only a rumor, it might have been untrue, but that's when, alas, missy became certain. And—she couldn't hold back anymore. It's exactly as you surmised, Araragi."

The devil found an opening and wormed its way into her heart.

Oshino didn't put it that way, of course.

He thoroughly despised that sort of spoiled weakness.

But—

It was jealousy, from beginning to end—and Kanbaru had been saying as much.

She'd been saying it.

"Mm, that ought to do," I told Shinobu.

I'd had her suck my blood right up to the limit, locked in an embrace, and now I tapped her tiny back twice. Shinobu gently removed her fangs from the two holes in my neck—and licked clean the few drops of blood that dribbled in the process. Maybe I needed to start wondering if our embrace fell under Senjogahara's definition of cheating, but since this was the only way the task could be accomplished, I'd have to beg her to let it go. Unlike during spring break, Shinobu's figure was now so minute and helpless, and hugging her as I did felt like hugging fog or mist, there was so little in my hands.

"...Oops."

I stood up from my crouched position—and felt a little dizzy. It was natural, of course, but I did feel almost anemic right after having my blood sucked—and this time, especially, I'd given her a lot.

Nearly five times more than the default amount.

I hopped up and down a bit.

Then again, my senses and bodily sensation didn't feel much different from usual… All of my stats got raised across the board, so it wasn't easy to discern exactly how I compared to my normal state.

Shinobu was already back to sitting on the floor.

Sitting there…with both of her arms wrapped around her legs as if to confirm her own presence.

She didn't even look in my direction.

"……"

A good and kind person, huh?

I could insist that I wasn't either of those things all day long, but when it came down to it, the prime victim was still this blond vampire… I supposed I couldn't blame Oshino for his cutting remark.

Forget me. For Shinobu…

I grabbed her goggled helmet and gave it a good shake right and left. For a while, she ignored it and didn't react, but it must have gotten legitimately annoying because she swatted my hand away.

Yeah.

Satisfied for the time being, I did as Oshino advocated and left without parting words, turning my back on her and climbing the stairs down to the third floor from the landing. I'd bring her a present next time, maybe donut holes or something, I thought as I bypassed the third floor and headed to the second.

Across from me, in front of a door on the opposite side of the hallway—awaited Mèmè Oshino, his arms crossed, leaning back against a wall, casually dangling one foot in the air.

"Hey. I've been waiting, Araragi. Looks like you took longer than expected."

"Yup. I had a little trouble figuring out the limit. I might have shorted her…but it's better than letting her go overboard. For me and for Shinobu."

"Hmm. I guess that's true, but you don't need to be so sensitive about little Shinobu. Because her existence is bound by my name, nothing extreme is going to happen. Naming is taming. If anything, I'm more worried about her starving. You're going to be grappling and fighting it out with a devil in a moment, Araragi, so you can't afford such concerns, I don't think? You don't want to end up being the comic relief. Hitting the ceiling still wouldn't give you good odds for this match, okay? Even if your opponent is no more than a left arm."

...Our measure against the Rainy Devil.

An authentic exorcism is a major affair that takes lots of time and effort, and despite the Rainy Devil's low ranking, it would be no cakewalk even for Oshino. This was coming from him, so I took it with a grain of salt—but I was convinced, at least, that he didn't intend to partake this time.

Unlike with Senjogahara's case.

You could call Senjogahara's crab another kind of aberration that granted a wish—but that was a god, and this was a devil. Even an amateur like myself could tell it wasn't going to be simple.

Kanbaru, with "god" in her name, and a devil.

It was not so much a hint as plain irony.

But—we didn't have the time or the effort to spare.

If we didn't hurry, my life might come to an end that very night. Me getting killed, or Kanbaru's left arm getting cut off—unfortunately, I wasn't so unattached to living as to accept the former manner of resolving the story. But cutting off Kanbaru's left arm was flat out of the question.

Which left us with option three.

"The contract, huh?" I said. "Well, I hope that's all it takes for the devil to go back to its demonic or spiritual or whatever world."

"The demonic and the spiritual aren't different worlds, they refer to 'here'—but the complicated stuff will start to feel like an argument we've already had, so maybe next time. It's going to work, I'll guarantee you that much, Araragi. *If the contract can't be fulfilled*—it becomes void. I won't call it a 'cooling off' period, but missy's wish will be properly invalidated too. The poor incompetent devil who didn't cut it will slink off without a word."

The devil will slink off.

If it can't fulfill the contract.

"In other words—*if the devil can't kill me.*"

"Hyup." Oshino chuckled. "Having given little Shinobu as much blood as possible only means so much, though… If you went about it like you had a mere tenth of the power you manifested over spring break, when you were actually a vampire, you'd still be overestimating your capabilities."

"…That's a pretty bleak fraction."

"But you're facing *just the left hand* of that Rainy Devil—you'd have no chance against the whole thing, but with the 'dead weight' of a human being on top of it, I'd say you have a ten or twelve or fourteen to one chance of winning," Oshino assured most ambiguously.

The Rainy Devil is a completely different type of aberration from the Monkey's Paw—the only trait the two have in common is that they grant wishes, and the devil, as you can tell from its association with a raincoat, has a full set of body parts (how you define 'body' is relevant here, but let's leave that aside). Yet I was facing just the left hand—and it had been mummified, too, probably thanks to a reliable seal, according to Oshino.

"Missy's mother's lineage seems to have been the issue—could it also have been why they ended up eloping? Well, I don't mean to expose or nose around a stranger's family situation with an offhanded guess. A mummified devil is actually quite a feat, though I've heard of mummified mermaids and the like. Hm, personally, if it only went down to the wrist when missy got it, what happened to *the remaining parts* does make me curious."

Mother…

Hitagi Senjogahara, Mayoi Hachikuji.

Both of their aberrations—involved their mothers.

Suruga Kanbaru was continuing that trend, then.

Apparently, just like her father, her mother had been disowned by her parents after eloping and Kanbaru was completely estranged from that side of her family, so there didn't seem to be any hope of finding out more…

"By the way," I asked, "what if this Rainy Devil had all of its body parts? Could it even beat Shinobu at her peak?"

"Not a chance. It's a low-level fiend at the end of the day, toothless against a real vampire. We aren't even talking about Mephistopheles here, so it'd take her no more than a couple of seconds. She'd pulverize every one of its assembled limbs, slurp up every fluid in its body, and that would be it. Have you forgotten that our little Shinobu used to be a fearsome, legendary vampire? Of course it'd be no match for her. Given the Rainy Devil's ranking, I'd say that even li'l missy class president's lust-besotted cat was easily stronger than it. Oh, but don't try to have Shinobu help out, okay? That may let us defeat the thing, but we'd have to cut off missy's arm for real. You, yourself, defeating it—that's the whole point."

"The Rainy Devil takes over a person's body by granting wishes, right? Every time it grants one, you get closer to the devil… The mummified hand must have grown from the wrist to the elbow because it granted Kanbaru's first wish, but then what, Oshino? If her second wish, her murderous hatred for me, and some third wish were granted, what would happen to her? At that rate, wouldn't taking over her just mean growing up to her shoulder or so?"

"I can only reply to that question like a bureaucrat: there's no precedent I can refer to. But considering the ratio, it seems reasonable to presume as you just did that it'll only go up to the shoulder even if it takes over her. Still, Araragi, that doesn't change anything. Being usurped up to your shoulder is the same as being usurped whole. It's like a publicly traded company having thirty percent of its stock acquired."

"…I guess."

"Her soul would get extracted either way, and she'd be an empty husk. Oh, I'll hold on to your bag and any valuables, Araragi. It'll be hard for you to maneuver carrying all that."

"Oh, yeah… Thanks. Could you take these, then?"

I pulled my cell phone and house keys out of my back and jacket pockets, tossed them into my backpack, and handed it to Oshino. *Okay,* he said, slinging it over his shoulder.

"But Araragi—can I ask you just one question?"

"What is it?"

"Why help even someone who tried to kill you? It might have been unconscious, *the flip side of her wish*—but missy hated you. She saw you as a hated rival in love." His usual mean jabbing—didn't seem to be what this was. "To begin with, why did you decide to hear missy out when you learned that it was her in the raincoat? Normally, at that point, there'd be no more need for questions or answers—you ought to have skipped her right then and come straight to me."

"...Everyone's going to have someone they hate. That's part of being alive. I don't have any interest in being killed, but if Kanbaru was doing this because she pined for Senjogahara—"

For every aberration, there was a reason.

If that was her reason—

"—I can forgive her."

If I was right from the start as Oshino said, then nothing had changed. I'd just gone back to the beginning, and Monkey's Paws and Rainy Devils didn't have anything to do with it. True, I hadn't imagined that she saw me as her rival in love, but even then.

Underhanded calculations.

Scheming persistence.

Maybe I was a good and kind person, but I wasn't exactly pure and virtuous like Hanekawa.

Tsubasa Hanekawa.

The girl with a pair of mismatched wings.

...If I was jealous of anyone, it was her.

I really was—envious, even.

"Oh. Well, if that's what you've decided, Araragi, then sure. It's fine by me and none of my business. In that case, get in there and help missy out. I should caution you, once you enter, you won't be able to leave until it's over. The door absolutely won't open from inside. Brace yourself because escape is not an option. Think very well back to spring break about situations from which there's no turning back, and be prepared, understand? ...And of course, whatever happens, little Shinobu or I won't come save you. Don't forget that I'm an inordinate pacifist and an ill-timed humanitarian. I'm going up to the fourth floor to get some sleep once I see you enter this classroom, so the rest is up to you. No need to say bye to me when you leave, neither you nor missy. Little Shinobu will be asleep by then, too, so just leave on your own."

"...Sorry for the hassle."

"Don't mention it."

Oshino moved from his spot on the wall to open the door.

I slipped in without hesitation.

As soon as I did, Oshino shut the door.

I couldn't leave now.

A classroom located in the back of the second floor—it was laid out the exact same way as the fourth-floor classroom but was the only one in the entire ruins whose windows were sealed. That isn't to say that there weren't shards of glass all over the floor here too. Rather, numerous planks of thick wood were nailed over the empty window frames just like people used to do when hurricanes came along. So single-mindedly many boards that it made you wonder why. Once the door shut, not a ray of light shone in—it was already the middle of the night, but not even starlight.

It was pitch black.

But—I could see.

Just having given plenty of blood to Shinobu, I could see through the darkness. In fact, in my current state, I could see better in the dark—and I slowly took in my surroundings.

I found it in no time.

It was there, standing in the not-so-large classroom—

Raincoat.

"...Hey," I called out to it, but there was no response.

It seemed she was already—in a trance.

The body was Suruga Kanbaru's—but its left arm, and for now, its soul was the Rainy Devil's... If you're wondering about the raincoat, Kanbaru ran off to grab one from the nearest general store while I was having Shinobu drink my blood. You could say the raincoat wasn't necessary, or at least it was an optional, non-essential item, but it served as per usual a ceremonial purpose to set the mood and scene.

The desks and chairs in the classroom were in the way and had been removed—so now only Kanbaru and I stood there. The Rainy Devil's *left arm* and a mock-vampire *nonhuman*.

Two beings that were not quite. It seemed like an even fight.

No—actually, I couldn't let it be an even fight.

I had to overwhelm the devil.

Just like the night before, beneath the raincoat's hood lurked a deep pit, and I couldn't make out what was in there, let alone any expression—

"........."

The most standard measure against an aberration that grants wishes, like Rainy Devils and Monkey's Paws, is to wish for something it cannot grant.

A wish that's too grand.

Or a contradictory wish.

A wish that is completely impossible.

A wish that would put it in a double bind, between a rock and a hard place.

Like a bucket with no bottom, as Oshino put it. That lets you drive off the aberration, see beyond the aberration—or so he said.

But Kanbaru had already made her wish in this case—she wanted to be by Senjogahara's side. And for that—Koyomi Araragi was in the way. She hated Koyomi Araragi, and she wanted to kill Koyomi Araragi, she ended up wishing unconsciously. The Rainy Devil was trying to answer to that wish as stated.

A wish can't be canceled.

Since she did think it, even for a moment, it was too late.

In which case, the logic needed to be turned on its head.

The very same wish should be made impossible.

Koyomi Araragi should be an entity that no mere Rainy Devil could kill—

"I guess this is a case of being able to argue your way out of anything—a little on the sophistic side if you ask me, like we're monkeying around with the rules, but hey, if it works... Oops!"

I don't know what triggered it—but Raincoat suddenly leapt toward me. Suruga Kanbaru's jumping chops—amplified by the intensity of her hatred. Normally, the speed would have defied my eyes like the night before—but things were different now.

I could see just fine.

And also react—

"Wait, wh-whoa!"

With a centrifugal twist of my torso, I dodged Raincoat's left fist—a very close call. Completing the spin, I moved away—it was lame, but I needed to regain my footing.

What was going on?

I wanted to say it was even faster than the night before—no, my eyes were still adjusting, that was all. Anyway, if I evaded Raincoat's left hand's attacks and waited for my opening, then targeted the "dead weight" that was Kanbaru's body, caught it, and pinned it down—

"........kk!"

It was already—on me.

Ridiculous, I didn't expect to overwhelm Raincoat when it came to speed, but mine ought to have been enhanced far beyond last night thanks to Shinobu, and yet, as easily as this—Raincoat brandished its left fist at me. I couldn't dodge to the left, I needed to get on its right somehow, outside—

The bared, dark and hairy arm grazed my cheek and missed. I felt like the gusts in its wake were ripping my body apart—but kicked at Raincoat's exposed flank.

...I'm sorry, Kanbaru!

I apologized to her in my heart.

As expected, apart from its left hand Raincoat was fairly normal—its body flew straight in the direction of my kick, lost its balance, and fell on all fours to the linoleum floor.

Indeed, controlling just the left arm posed a disadvantage for Raincoat. It was horribly imbalanced and obvious that the rest of the package couldn't keep up.

But then, what was up with its speed? Had Raincoat not been serious the night before? Did it get faster in response to my enhanced abilities? But what need was there for an aberration to hold back?

I didn't get it.

I still didn't—as Raincoat got up.

Hmm… Even ignoring the fact that the body was Kanbaru's, I couldn't bring myself to kick an opponent who was down…

I knew I had to, but I was reluctant, even though I couldn't afford to be in this case.

A good and kind person.

Ugh, I hated that label.

How nice that your lack of personality was getting smoothed over.

In a beeline, Raincoat's left fist smashed into my right shoulder this time—that catapult of a fist. It must have aimed for my median line, but I was able to avoid that…not completely, though. I couldn't fully acquire it—it was too fast. I hurtled back about ten feet… With my sense of equilibrium, I flipped midair and landed on my feet. Raincoat's left hand had turned my bicycle into a crumpled piece of paper and demolished a concrete wall, but unlike yesterday, my body neither flew an absurd distance nor got wrecked. I suffered some damage, of course, but not to the extent that I couldn't move. My shoulder was dislocated and probably also fractured, but it was nothing that my vampiric regeneration couldn't heal right away. The sharp pain went away in an instant, too. If anything felt nostalgic, this was it. Oh, I couldn't wait for sunrise… Just how badly was I gonna get burnt?

But I didn't have time to be thinking about that. Because Raincoat followed up where I landed—and follow up, it did. Raincoat knew no doubt. Its left fist now went for my head. The punch caught me right in my face with its eyes that had yet to adjust. I was treated to the sound of my nose snapping. That was in my current state, which meant a normal human head would have been blown to smithereens; the destructive force was that terrifying even to imagine. I pathetically crawled away to get some distance from Raincoat, and as I did, my broken nose healed. I loathed the feeling. It was as if I'd become an amoeba or something. And this was at a tenth—my spring break had been hell.

I was able to dodge the next punch.

But the one after that nicked me.

"……Dammit!"

Why?

Why couldn't I dodge them altogether?

Though the strikes themselves described efficient straight lines, Raincoat's overall attacking motion, merely thrusting out its left fist with such brute force I half-expected it to go flying off its shoulder like an anime robot's rocket-propelled punch, was crude—it didn't telegraph its movements, but that was all, and I should have been able to track it, so why couldn't I? Why couldn't I get out of its way? It was clearly several notches faster than the day before. Not so much its power…I could take one or two, no, a few dozen clean shots and still be in the fight with my current build, so why was just its speed so out of sight?

Something wasn't like yesterday…

Raincoat…

The bared left arm, the beastly hand.

…Its right arm was bare too, but like whatever lurked under the hood, it had the air of some deep pit that you could and could not see—wait, no. That was what had changed. Raincoat had been wearing rubber gloves the day before—neither of its arms had been exposed. But what of it? Wearing rubber gloves shouldn't have slowed it down.

And then I realized.

I realized my mistake.

Not the rubber gloves—the rubber boots!

Kanbaru had only bought a raincoat at the general store… She hadn't gotten rubber gloves or rubber boots—not because we decided that setting the mood didn't require the whole getup, but simply because we didn't think of it. I didn't know how the original Rainy Devil was depicted, but the raincoat had been enough of a hint to tip off Oshino. If just a raincoat did a good enough job of expressing the aberration and its character, then Kanbaru and I weren't exactly amiss.

But—if Raincoat wasn't wearing rubber boots, then that meant it was wearing sneakers. One glance was all I needed to confirm the fact. Its feet weren't bare just because its hands were. Raincoat was still wearing the shoes that Kanbaru had on.

The unmistakably expensive sneakers.

Compared to rubber boots—they let you move at a different definition of speed.

Especially if you were an athlete of Suruga Kanbaru's caliber.

"…Yikes."

Openly shackling or binding Kanbaru's feet or attaching any kind of weight to her body would have been out given our strategy, or objective—but a simple pair of rubber boots was certainly a feasible handicap… Why had we gone and created conditions where Raincoat could make full and unfettered use of its powers? Suruga Kanbaru's body was supposed to serve as dead weight, to drag not her feet but her left hand down, but instead she was acting as a nimble attachment to that arm!

Urk…

I couldn't believe how bad I was at closing the deal…

Just evading was no longer an option. Since my body wasn't going to accumulate any damage, I wouldn't be chipped to death like in a fighting game as long as I barely managed to avoid half of its attacks, but that wouldn't complete my assignment of pulling off *an overwhelming victory*. It didn't seem like an issue of my eyes adjusting. I needed to face Raincoat's attacks head-on even if both of us might go down as a result. I lowered my hips and held my hands out like a goalie preparing for a penalty kick—or was a man-to-man basketball defense the more appropriate analogy?

However, another catapult strike, a clear violation of the rules of basketball (what would that violation be called?), shot toward the base of my neck, and I tried to stop it with both of my hands, my right hand meeting Raincoat's fist, my left hand grabbing its wrist, and the rest of my body wrapping around its left arm—but didn't make it in time. No, in fact, my right and left hands did make it in time, but I couldn't stop the catapult. I felt a number of my finger bones breaking, then the left fist striking my collarbone immediately after. My body lurched backwards, but I somehow stood firm on my back foot—I hadn't stopped the blow but at least reduced its force before it reached my torso.

Before Raincoat could pull back its fist, I used both of my hands, their fingers already healed, to grab its left arm—finally accomplishing my initial goal of halting its movements. At last, I had gotten ahold of Raincoat. All right, and now—

"I'm sorry, Kanbaru!"

Apologizing out loud this time, and pinning the left arm with both of my hands as Raincoat struggled to shake free, I attacked its legs, stomach, and chest with three successive sidekicks. It was an impossible attack for a normal human body to perform given the way we're built. Unlike Raincoat, who could only attack with its left fist, I could use all four of my limbs and had to make full use of my advantage.

Raincoat's left arm flailed like mad.

It was vulnerable.

Oshino was right. I probably didn't stand a chance against a fully formed Rainy Devil as I was, but I could overwhelm it if I denied it its left arm—the fist's damage, I could heal instantly as long as I didn't take multiple hits in a row, which meant the bigger threat was Kanbaru's boosted leg strength, and the bit about her sneakers was indeed unexpected, but having trapped it like this—all I had to do was kick the Rainy Devil into submission. If it wouldn't cry uncle, then until it was no more. It was nearly like torture, the right equivalent of *Suruga-toi*, so it didn't feel great, but we weren't going to tear off Kanbaru's left arm, and we certainly weren't going to end her life, so my only choice was to continue attacking and inflicting pain until the devil left her—

Raincoat's legs buckled.

My constant low kicks were finally paying off—or so I thought, but it wasn't the case. The leg that I—no, that it threw off balance came arcing at my jaw along the shortest and quickest possible route. Not its left arm, but its left leg—Kanbaru's long leg threaded its way past the rest of my body to land a high roundhouse kick right on my temple. The force of the blow was of course nothing compared to the left arm's, but this was still Kanbaru's dash burst converted into attack power, plus I had been caught completely off guard.

My brain was rattled and my vision blurred for a moment. Damaging the sensory organs of a (mock) vampire was definitely effective—an important lesson I had learned over spring break.

I had to let go of Raincoat's left arm.

To defend against the kick that followed.

I held my arms out like a cross and took it, and while inferior to the left-arm catapult—the impact scrambled my thoughts due to its sheer inexplicability.

It could use more than its left arm?

But hadn't Oshino said "dead weight"?

"…Does this mean *what I think it does*?"

I could only come up with one possible answer.

If the Rainy Devil's source of energy was human negativity, then it was feeding off of Suruga Kanbaru's jealousy toward me—if the left fist was a catapult, then Kanbaru's body was the aircraft carrier itself. Her heated passions, her inflamed emotions created the high-pressure steam channeled into her muscles. That's why her body wasn't dragging the left arm down as dead weight—well, perhaps it did under normal circumstances but wasn't loath to mount a defense when the Rainy Devil was in a pinch?

No, that was sophistry.

If I was going to say that I forgave Kanbaru, I mustn't resort to arguments that circumvented the truth—it wasn't fair to describe it as some spinal reflex, like an electrical current jolting a frog's leg.

In other words.

Kanbaru's legs moved of her own will.

Suruga Kanbaru's will had a part in this.

Unconsciously, Kanbaru was—refusing.

To lose her Rainy Devil left arm.

To let her second wish go unfulfilled.

To let me live.

She wasn't giving up—Senjogahara.

"…Scheming persistence."

I understand how you feel.

So much that it hurts.

So much that I hurt.

Because—I lost, threw something away, too.

Because I'll never get it back.

For some reason, Raincoat stood still. Having sent its left fist after me so tenaciously in simple straight lines, like a simple magnet being drawn toward an object, now it stood unmoving—almost as if it were puzzling over something.

Or maybe.

As if it were doubtful.

Raincoat's unhesitant movements—had stopped.

...Suruga Kanbaru.

Hitagi Senjogahara's junior.

The basketball star.

Please, just cut it off—she'd said.

Right after Oshino had revealed the truth, that her left arm wasn't a Monkey's Paw but a Devil's Hand, that her wishes had been granted as she'd made them, after the awful truth that didn't need to be exposed had been...she'd cast her eyes down for a few seconds, faced up bravely, and looked at Oshino and me in turn to say so.

"I don't need this left hand."

For once, without that smile of hers.

In a flat, plain, unemotional tone—oddly enough, the current-day personality of the senior she admired so.

"Please, just cut it off. I want you to sever it. I beg you. I know it's a hassle, but I beg you. I can't cut off my own arm..."

"S-Stop it."

I hastened to push her outstretched arm back toward her. The hair felt disgusting as it brushed against my hand. It was creepy.

It was scary.

"Stop being ridiculous—I couldn't ever. What about basketball?" I asked.

"It's like Mister Oshino just said. I tried to kill another human being. I think it's only fair."

"N-No—really, Kanbaru, I don't mind at all—"

Laughable. Clownish.

How far from the point could I get?

It wasn't about whether I minded or not.

What's more, whether I forgave her or not had nothing to do with it, either—the question was whether Suruga Kanbaru could forgive Suruga Kanbaru.

The girl who didn't want to injure her classmates and so kept running.

Who suppressed and overwhelmed all negative emotions.

She who had sealed them away.

That strength of will—also bound her.

Castigated her.

"A-Anyway," I said, "there's no way we're going to cut it off. Don't be ridiculous. What are you thinking? You're an idiot, a real idiot. Way to be simplistic about things. How can you take such an idea seriously?"

"Ah. You're right, cutting off my arm isn't something to impose on people. It's not a favor you can carry out just because someone asked, is it? Okay, I'll think of a way on my own. I'm sure it can be done with the help of a car or a train."

"That's—"

A car or a train?

That amounted to suicide.

It wasn't suicidal—but plain suicide.

"If she wants to cut it off, there's a good way, isn't there," Oshino interrupted with a reminder. "Why aren't you telling her, Araragi? How inconsiderate of you when someone's clearly in distress. You just have to get little Shinobu to cooperate. A heart under her blade—with that prized sword of hers, we'd be able to sever that left arm with no time for missy to feel any pain. Little Shinobu's blade might not have the edge it once boasted, but cutting off a slender arm would be as easy as pie, or slicing tofu—"

"Shut up, Oshino! Hey, Kanbaru! Stop tormenting yourself about this! You shouldn't be feeling responsible, not one bit—isn't that obvious?! This is all because of the Monkey's Paw…I mean, some aberration called the Rainy Devil—"

"The aberration only granted her wish, didn't it?"

Oshino wasn't shutting up.

Eloquently, loquaciously, he weaved his words.

"It only gave her what she wanted, yes? Wasn't it the same with li'l missy tsundere? It's not like what happened to you over spring break, Araragi. It's nothing like little Shinobu's case—Araragi, *you didn't wish upon an aberration*."

"……"

"Which is why—you don't understand how she feels. Not her remorse, and not her regrets. Not in the slightest," he told me. "By the way, in the original 'The Monkey's Paw,' after having a first and a second wish granted, the third wish of the first person to use the paw was to die. I don't think I need to explain the full significance of that?"

"Oshino—"

What he said was right.

But, Oshino, you're mistaken.

Facing off against Raincoat—immobile like we were in a standoff, I took my time recollecting.

Because I actually do understand.

So much that it hurts, that my wounded heart hurts.

Hitagi Senjogahara's feelings.

And Suruga Kanbaru's, too, okay?

No, maybe I don't, after all.

Maybe it's nothing more than a conceited and misguided notion.

But—

We bear the same kind of pain.

We share it.

Who's to say you won't use a wish-granting item that presents itself to you? Like with my spring break, though it might not have been wished for. Even the pure and virtuous Hanekawa was bewitched by a cat due to the slightest discord and torsion—

At its base, my relationship with Shinobu was no different from Senjogahara's relationship with the crab, or Kanbaru's with the devil.

"I don't mind, Araragi," she said.

"Well, I do—how could I not? What are you saying? And what about Senjogahara? I wanted you and her to—"

"I'm done. About her too. I'm done now." Her words must have literally pained her. "It's fine. I'll give up."

No way.

Giving up isn't fine at all.

Make your own wishes come true—that's why your mother gave you that mummified devil. It couldn't have been to teach you to give up on your dreams—

So don't make that face.

Stop looking like a deep pit where your face should be.

You can't ever give up on anything on the verge of crying like that.

A rainy devil—and a weepy devil.

Its origin is said to be a child who ran away from home after getting in a fight with his parents over nothing one drizzling day. He got lost in the mountains and was killed and eaten by a pack of wild monkeys. Mysteriously, no one from his family or settlement could recall the child's name—

"...Bastard!"

Unable to take our standoff, mentally—unable to bear the shadow play of thoughts that beleaguered me, I charged Raincoat. Including the night before, it was the very first time I went on the offensive instead of just reacting. You could say that the pressure of maintaining an interceptive posture was getting to be too much.

Staying on our feet wouldn't do. Even if I trapped its left arm again, a kick would follow without delay. I needed to go at Raincoat with a mind to pin it down like this was judo or wrestling—

I spread my arms out as though to clamp down on Raincoat, but I couldn't catch it—had it moved left or right, I might have been able to respond, but that's not what it did. Yet it didn't back away, either—in that case I would have only needed to take another few steps.

Raincoat had jumped.

It jumped—and with both of its feet stuck to the classroom's ceiling—stayed up there and dashed. *Tup, tup, tup, tup, tup, tup,* it defied gravity—and dashed across the ceiling, ignoring the universal law.

Then it came down—and landed on the floor.

And jumped sideways next.

And landed on the rickety blackboard—and jumped again—and landed on the thick planks sealing a window shut—and jumped again—and was back on the ceiling.

Every which way, plus a few more.

With bewildering speed—Raincoat jumped.

Like a pinwheel firework, it went from wall to wall, from wall to ceiling, from ceiling to floor, from floor to wall—jumping on its two legs. Raincoat was jumping around on Suruga Kanbaru's practiced legs.

Or like a super ball fired at high speed.

A raucous dance of reflected angles.

Bounding, then bounding again.

My eyes couldn't keep up.

It was moving faster than my eyeballs.

It was accelerating like a body in free fall and going faster and faster, gradually, boldly picking up speed with every jump—the difference between rubber boots and sneakers a quaint detail, it gradually and boldly and unmistakably toyed with my vision.

Simply going from two to three dimensions had such a huge effect—the classroom had been turned into a sealed boundary by Oshino to limit the damage and to ensure a decisive outcome…and also out of a straightforward calculation that a narrow field offered advantages over a wide one in fighting the quick and agile Raincoat—but it was the complete opposite. That was totally backfiring.

Backfiring.

How could we not have foreseen it?

The reason Kanbaru had joined the basketball and not the track team—was that her legs shone most brightly as a weapon that made her faster than anyone else on the narrow field that is a basketball court! Despite her height and build Suruga Kanbaru had the jumping chops to dunk the ball with ease, and what did that mean in a constrained space with a low ceiling?!

It was backfiring, everything was.

I couldn't have miscalculated more flagrantly. What was I, stupid?

I never gave up a good chance to be wrong.

As Raincoat jumped around making a fool of me, my heels seemed nailed to the ground and I couldn't take a single step. In particular, the vertical movements from the floor to the ceiling, and from the ceiling to the floor, confounded me—it was a design issue in that the human eye was physically capable of handling lateral movement but wasn't as prepared to shoot up and down. My vision couldn't keep up with Raincoat's movements.

Rapidly getting around behind me where I stood—

Raincoat jumped from the ceiling toward me at last. Spinning its body midair, heels over head like in a Sepak Takraw roll spike, it drove the tip of its foot into the crown of my head with the momentum it gained—I felt my skull collapse. As I lurched forward from the force of it, Raincoat, having already landed, met my jaw with a Muay Thai knee. The consecutive blows, the Sepak Takraw-Muay Thai combo, were nearly simultaneous timing-wise, and the impact of being sandwiched by a virtual pincer strike, something that exceeded pain, assaulted me. My brain felt dented along with my head, and I lost consciousness for a brief moment—suddenly comatose.

But I didn't die.

My wounds healed immediately.

Man, it was hell.

Sañjīva, the Buddhist hell of revival.

Crushed into dust, then mended and restored by a gust of wind, crushed again, mended again, crushed, repeatedly, into dust, crushed for eternity, one of the eight great hells—it was exactly like my spring break.

"Tsk..."

I extended my arm—and Raincoat evaded me. Then it cocked its fist, and I reacted—no, I didn't, my reflexes did. I'd focused on that left arm for so long that I was overly sensitive to its motion. What I ought to have taken more deeply to heart was Raincoat's earlier attack, consecutive kicks delivered *by choice* despite its left arm being free. Or what the abrupt onset of its bewildering high-speed three-dimensional disruptive acceleratory movement, that terrifying footwork, meant. The significance of using not just the Rainy Devil left arm but all four of its limbs to maneuver.

Play with the devil and become the devil.

Forget whatever coming true, selling your soul, bodily possession, and all that—

Wish upon the devil and become the devil.

The left fist was a feint.

Only having mounted linear attacks at first—now Raincoat was finally employing footwork, combos, feints, that is to say, combat techniques.

No, not a feint.

A fake, was more like it. Because the tactic wouldn't have been accessible to Raincoat without Suruga Kanbaru's cooperation—

Bracing myself for the left fist fatally exposed my opposite flank, and the tip of Raincoat's toes connected, thrice this time, and in the same precise location—and as my body folded in a sideways V thanks to an attack that contradicted the theory of relativity and struck the same coordinates simultaneously three times in a row, the sole of Raincoat's other foot shot through my chest.

Like a catapult.

Overpowered, I fell over backward, but placing my hands on the floor as if to perform a back roll, I spun myself upright and put distance between myself and it—Raincoat immediately closed in.

The kick had struck one of my lungs.

It had probably collapsed.

It hurt to breathe.

Dammit, it wasn't healing right away—did it mean that Raincoat's kicks now had more power, more destructive potential than its left fist?

Did Kanbaru's thoughts surpass the devil?

Jealousy.

Hatred.

All her negative emotions.

Why not me, then.

"*...Because you just*," I said—with my still collapsed lung, "*because you just won't do, Suruga Kanbaru—*!"

No one can ever replace someone else, and no one can ever be someone else. Senjogahara is Hitagi Senjogahara, and Kanbaru is Suruga Kanbaru.

And Koyomi Araragi is Koyomi Araragi.

The difference between me and Kanbaru.

Whether or not we knew Oshino.

Whether or not we stepped away.

Whether it was a demon or a monkey.

Random encounters, chance.

It did give rise to feelings of remorse.

I was remorseful, towards both Kanbaru and Senjogahara. But when it came to trading places if I could, I didn't feel that way—I had no desire to cede my position.

Right.

If I'm your hated rival in love—then you were mine, and I'd have done better to hate you, Kanbaru.

Maybe my remorse sprang from there too.

I hadn't considered Kanbaru my equal.

I'd condescended.

Made light of her.

Deigning to mediate between Kanbaru and Senjogahara to bring about their reconciliation, while I rested on an absolutely secure perch with consummate ease—how thoroughly repulsive a deed was that? Such a good, kind person. Such a bad, callous person.

If a wish.

If a wish is something you fulfill on your own, then—

Giving up on your own ought to be fine.

Giving up, provided you don't forget—ought to be fine.

"…! …! …!"

Relentless attack after attack splashed across my body, each impact so intense it actually remolded me—I wasn't able to dodge even one in four anymore. My body repaired and regenerated itself, destroyed part after destroyed part, but Raincoat's assault now outpaced the process.

Before I knew, I was trapped in a corner of the classroom. As if invisible strings were binding me, I couldn't move back or to either side. Raincoat no longer bothered with any footwork—if this were boxing, you'd say it was fighting on the inside, legs planted, and unopposed at that. No matter how nice the sneakers, the friction from the sustained, impractical acceleration would wear out the rubber soles, I'd vaguely hoped based on nothing, but even my optimistic projection was now bankrupt. Every permutation of fists, elbows, shins, toes, and heels tormented my body all over in quick succession. I wasn't even allowed a moment to scream out in pain, it was the ultimate combo chain.

It no longer fell under the rubric of strikes.

Pure pressure.

It wasn't just my bones breaking; the spots where I got hit were tearing, my skin and muscles were ripping and sundering. Raincoat's stance was that much more rooted and weighted forward than before and seemed to add to its left fist's destructive power by the moment.

Still—

Not to the extent of Suruga Kanbaru's legs...

"Uni...form."

My body may have been immortal, but my clothes weren't.

They'd been torn to shreds by that point.

Ugh. I'd ruined yet another one.

My high-collared jacket, when we were only a few days away from changing into our summer uniforms...

What excuse was I going to offer my sisters this time?

"Guh...kk."

At this distance...

At least, at this distance, if Raincoat offered me the slightest opportunity, I could render it immobile by hugging Kanbaru's body... and force it down to the ground with all I was worth and turn around the fight.

I still had a path to victory.

Even now, while I was trapped in a corner in positional terms, I wasn't actually cornered—attack me as Raincoat might, I had nothing to fear as long as my regenerative healing abilities were kicking in.

It was only painful.

Like Kanbaru's heart, it was only painful—

Being in pain meant I was alive.

"I hate you."

I heard a voice.

"I hate you I hate you I hate you I hate you I hate you I hate you."

It was the voice—of Suruga Kanbaru.

From the deep pit under the raincoat's hood, as though appealing directly to my psyche, it resonated—and I heard:

"I hate you I hate you I hate you I hate you I hate you I hate you I hate you I hate you I hate you I hate you I hate you I hate you."

"........."

Hatred—more hatred than any one person could bear.

Malice, hostility.

The negative emotions of a positive junior.

It seemed to swirl—to be brimming in Raincoat.

Its surface tension stretched to the limit.

"How dare you how dare you how dare you how dare you."

Along with the strikes, the voice continued.

The voice of hatred continued.

"I can't stand you I can't stand you I can't stand you I can't stand you I can't stand you I can't stand you I can't stand you I can't stand you—"

"...Kanbaru, sorry."

Out loud again.

I apologized to Kanbaru.

"Me, I haven't the least bit trouble standing you."

Rivals in love though we may be.

You and I might not match up at all—but, you know?

Can't we be friends at all?

"...■■■■■■!"

Some sort of piercing shriek came from the deep pit—and Raincoat's kick penetrated my abdomen. Penetrated. It wasn't just that my organs ruptured, but rather, perfectly ignoring my joints and muscles, crushing my ribs and spine, it literally and non-figuratively penetrated clean through my belly so that the heel reached the wall behind me. I was skewered.

The damage—far outpaced my healing abilities.

It...

Zlrp, the leg pulled out.

It felt like my entire digestive tract was being tugged out.

The whole mess.

Dragged out—and my body was the deep pit now.

There was nothing inside the pit.

"Kanbaru—"

Uh oh.

With a large hole gouged in my abdomen—I couldn't stand straight, and twisting my body even a little threatened to jerk apart my upper and lower halves. Which meant that I couldn't make any more careless movements. I was still conscious, but one more blow in my state—would end it. It was me who'd gotten overwhelmed. How pathetic. At this rate, Kanbaru's second wish was going to come true. That was the one thing I had to avoid at all costs…

Or maybe it was an option?

It was only her second wish.

If Kanbaru could…hold out and not make a third wish—wasn't it fine? Her arm would go back to normal, and since a wish was a wish, she'd be by Senjogahara's side—because putting aside the manner, the wishes came true.

I wasn't ready to cede.

I wasn't ready to cede.

But I was ready to forgive.

I was supposed to have died during spring break, in the first place… so as Oshino said, it was nice and simple as far as solutions go.

Yes, I did feel attached to life.

But it wasn't like I was in trepidation over the thought of dying.

"Aa—ah, uh," I moaned.

For no reason I simply moaned.

They were like death throes.

I wouldn't be ruining my uniform again.

"Suruga, Kanbaru—"

That's when.

Raincoat's combos, which had gone on without a break for dozens of minutes already, ceased.

Abruptly they ceased.

It was—the opening I'd been waiting for.

But I couldn't carry out my plan to pin down Raincoat. There was of course the fact that the damage from the large hole opened in my abdomen seemed inestimably far from healing, and also the fact that my consciousness, which I needed to execute the move, was already fading, but more than that—I, too, had frozen in place.

Probably for the same reason as Raincoat.

I found myself frozen.

"...You seem to be enjoying yourselves."

The door to the classroom opened.

The door that never would from the inside opened, from the outside.

Allowing someone to enter.

Hitagi Senjogahara, in her street clothes.

"Looks like you're having fun without me, Araragi. How unpleasant."

Her emotionless expression—her flat voice.

Confronted with this awful spectacle, she merely narrowed her eyes somewhat.

She always—appeared without warning.

Wearing a pair of jeans with no belt, a tank top in the same color, and a comfy largish hoodie, her hair tied loosely behind her, as if she'd stepped out of her room without changing, Hitagi Senjogahara stood there in her street clothes.

"S-Senjogahara..."

I couldn't speak well with the wind hole that had been opened in my abdomen—I had been left without a voice, and it was hard even to call out to her.

Why are you here?

I wanted to ask her.

But I already knew the answer without having to ask. Oshino had called her here, of course—what other answer could there be? But how? He had no possible way to contact her—as if Hitagi Senjogahara would give her cell phone number to Mèmè Oshino, whom she disliked. There shouldn't have been any opportunity to do so, either.

A cell phone?

Oh, of course.

That asshole—not caring one bit about the sanctity of people's personal info, he'd gone and messed around with my phone in complete violation of my privacy. Yes, that cell phone in the backpack I'd given Oshino to hold on to before entering this classroom... It wasn't like I used a password to lock the thing, and no matter how bad Oshino was with gadgetry, given enough time he could surely find the contacts list or call history. Plus, Senjogahara would have given him a crash course on how to use a cell phone that time they met on Mother's Day—

But why?

For what purpose did Oshino summon Senjogahara here of all places, to this situation of all situations—

In a flash.

Raincoat leapt backwards, and via a few stops each on the ceiling and walls, moved from one corner of the classroom to the other, diagonally across and far away from me.

Why would it do that?

One more blow and the fight would have been over.

The wish granted.

Was her consciousness as Suruga Kanbaru temporarily suppressing the unconscious she'd provided to Raincoat? Was it thanks to Senjogahara's entry, and if so, had that been Oshino's aim? But how would that serve as anything more than a temporary measure? The Rainy Devil fed off of a person's negative emotions, and until we got rid of them, nothing would change. This wasn't some old foreign movie, and the power of love wasn't going to solve everything. Why summon Senjogahara when you could come in yourself, Mèmè Oshino?!

As if she couldn't care less about Raincoat's antics, however, Senjogahara glared at me with cold eyes as I hovered near death's door. They were the eyes of a bird of prey zeroing in on a kill.

"So you lied to me, Araragi."

"...What?"

"You duped me saying you ran into a telephone pole and also kept this stuff about Kanbaru secret. Didn't we promise when we started dating? We said we wouldn't do that. About aberrations at least, we wouldn't keep any secrets from each other."

"Ah, well..."

That—was true.

I hadn't forgotten or anything.

"You deserve to die a thousand times over." A chilling smile spread across Senjogahara's face.

An enormous mass of fear like I'd never felt even while Raincoat was beating me senseless shot through my body like a bolt of lightning. Scary… Damn, she was scary. What was she, Medusa? How did she muster such a gaze…against her boyfriend, no less? And wait, really? She was telling me this now, in this situation, with me in the state I was in? Way to read the room, Senjogahara!

"…But, Araragi, I guess you already did die a thousand times." With the door still flung open—Senjogahara sprang off her back foot toward the corner where I huddled. "I might let you off the hook this one time..."

Well.

A thousand times was probably an exaggeration.

Raincoat immediately reacted to Senjogahara's advance—and likewise began dashing toward me. Out of nowhere, Hitagi Senjogahara and Suruga Kanbaru were having a foot race in lieu of the one they never did in middle school. In a straight line, Raincoat was about twice as far from me as Senjogahara, mathematically speaking, but the former track team star had a two-plus-year gap in her resume, while Raincoat was now drawing on Kanbaru's leg strength—no, was the devil itself. The first one to get to my immobile form was, of course, Kanbaru.

Raincoat took the opportunity to wind up its left fist, ready to deliver me a final blow—but Senjogahara belatedly arrived to stand between it and me.

Watch out.

But I wasn't even allowed the interval to think that.

A moment before impact—Raincoat was knocked away. Knocked away? Who could possibly do that, the way Raincoat was now? Not me, and Senjogahara even less. Then the sensible view was that, rather than being knocked away, Raincoat had leapt back of its own accord. Even if it did clumsily end up supine in the process.

I was dumbfounded.

That move—what was up with the unnatural move, as if Raincoat feared getting Senjogahara mixed into this, as if it eschewed hurting her above all?

Suruga Kanbaru's conscious mind must have—no.

That would be far too convenient.

Aberrations are consistent.

They are rational to the bitter end.

It's just that the rationality doesn't always make sense to humans.

But in this case—

"Araragi. Knowing you, I bet you thought like an idiot that your death would solve everything," Senjogahara continued to speak to me—her back still turned to me, her eyes not on me, but also paying Raincoat no mind. My wretched condition, covered in blood and wounds—wasn't why she wouldn't look at me, of that I was certain. "Don't kid yourself. Your feeble self-sacrifice is totally uncalled for. If you died, how would I not do anything in my capacity to kill Kanbaru? I told you that once, didn't I? Are you trying to turn me into a murderer?"

...She'd seen through me.

Oh boy, what a devoted woman.

I couldn't even go and die cheerfully.

A wholehearted—twisted love.

"What infuriates me most of all is that you'd have thrown yourself into this even if your body weren't that way. If you were being so stupid just because you could ride your immortal body through it, then I might as well tell you to do as you please, but you went with the flow like there was no choice and end up looking like this—I don't know what to say."

"......"

"But coming from you, I guess I don't mind unsolicited favors and needless interventions and counterproductive meddling—"

Without gracing me with another glance to the very end, Senjogahara took a steady step toward Raincoat's collapsed figure. Still on the floor, Raincoat began to crawl backwards as if it were terrified of her.

As if terrified...

As if terrified...why?

Come to think of it—faced with it now, it had been the same way last night. Raincoat had blasted me away then suddenly disappeared. That was because Senjogahara had shown up with the envelope I'd forgotten… But why should her entry usher Raincoat's retreat? It seemed so unnatural when you thought about it. A *human* street slasher or thrill killer might—but an *aberration* wouldn't care about witnesses. And anyway, Senjogahara couldn't have presented an obstacle for Raincoat given its mighty left arm.

So then why did it run?

Because the person who came on scene was Senjogahara?

What did that mean?

Was it really the power of love?

Did Suruga Kanbaru's feelings for Senjogahara outclass the devil, conveniently enough? Could earnest thought brush aside aberrations, the world itself, and open up a circuit to the heavens? No.

No.

That wasn't it… Right. The thought.

Even after Kanbaru had made her second wish to the Rainy Devil left hand, turning hers into a beast's—it still took four days for it to activate. That was because she just barely managed to suppress her hateful thoughts toward me. Her stance that you fulfilled wishes on your own suppressed the devil's violence. The stance that had grown firm roots in her over the seven years since her first wish—Oshino had laughed and called it patently ridiculous, but not in the conventional sense.

She was by no means wrong—he'd said that, too.

Her thought.

Thoughts—Suruga Kanbaru's wish.

The Rainy Devil sees through us to find our darkest emotions—it sees and reads what's on the back. It sees the flip side of our wishes. You want to run faster because you hate your classmates. You desire to be by Senjogahara's side—because you hate Koyomi Araragi.

But that was just the flip side.

Just as the front has a back.

The back—has a front.

If the Rainy Devil hurt Hitagi Senjogahara—then whether or not it could kill the target of hatred, Koyomi Araragi, Kanbaru's *obverse wish* could no longer be granted… Right, it wasn't anything moving or sensitive like the power of love but a more sober and primitive matter.

A contract.

A deal.

The Rainy Devil could only grant the flip side of wishes, but that didn't mean it could neglect the top side. In fact, even when Kanbaru was in grade school—it granted her flipside wish of getting revenge on her classmates, but in the end, her topside wish of wanting to become faster came true as well. It properly came true apart from that whole causality. What was patently ridiculous was that this was exactly what the Rainy Devil intended—it simply interpreted the front as the back, but didn't pull the latter out of thin air. The reverse couldn't exist without the obverse. No, going again by what Oshino said, left hands didn't have intentions. It was all Suruga Kanbaru's unconscious mind—it established the causality between an obverse and a reverse side that never intersected, as a contradiction.

A contract with the devil.

In exchange for your soul.

A cooling-off period.

Wishing an impossibility.

A double bind—between a rock and a hard place.

Between the obverse and reverse.

That was why—precisely why the Rainy Devil couldn't raise its hand against Senjogahara. That was the contract, that was the deal. As long as Senjogahara shielded me—it couldn't raise a hand even against me, the hated, hated me.

It couldn't raise that left hand against us.

If one method was for me to overwhelm the devil and make it impossible for the flipside wish to be fulfilled—then there was also another, which was to make it impossible for the topside wish to be fulfilled.

And now, Senjogahara even pledged in front of the devil that she'd kill Kanbaru if I died. Claiming ignorance was not an option. The Rainy Devil's situation was already locked down.

Always acting like he saw through everything…

Like he saw through everything more than any devil.

Oshino, you… Your badness and callousness make me pale in

comparison—!

"It's been a while, Kanbaru. I'm glad you seem to be doing well," Senjogahara said.

Then, she went over to Raincoat, who tried to slide away on its back—no, to her old acquaintance Suruga Kanbaru—and slowly covered her body with her own, pinning her down.

Even after getting in a wretched state—

I hadn't been able to.

But finally she did what I could never do.

Taking that beastly left arm.

And the human right arm, and holding them, soothingly.

Senjogahara's stapler—

Was no longer on her.

"...My senior Senjogahara."

A mutter from beneath the hood.

The voice resonating, pleading.

What lurked under the hood was no deep pit. What lurked there was no face on the verge of crying. Not on the verge—it was crying. Reflected clearly in my eyes was the teary-eyed, crying, and cry-laughing face of a girl.

I—wracked with sobs, she voiced her thought.

"I love you."

She voiced her wish.

"Oh. Me, not so much." Direct, unfiltered, in the same tone as ever. Senjogahara said flatly, "Will you stay by my side anyway?"

Sorry I made you wait so long, she said, most flatly.

...What a fool.

The height of folly!

Jeez—I'd be lucky to call myself a tomato can here.

A master class on how to play the comic relief, if I do say so myself, and I'm pretty used to it. My uselessness was almost exemplary.

A good girl who can say sorry.

I thought I knew very well how greedy a woman Hitagi Senjogahara was. I thought I knew very well how bad at giving up she was.

If it really mattered to her.

Senjogahara would never give it up.

Unsolicited favors, needless interventions.

Counterproductive meddling.

Even so…I don't know, all of these people around me are really warped—

They have two sides to them.

And the obverse and reverse are one and the same, like in a Möbius strip.

Well, I guess the power of love is one interpretation, then.

It's pretty depressing to be forgotten by someone, after all.

Thinking such thoughts, waiting for the large hole in my stomach to close up, I just decided to watch, without wisecracking, the Sapphic spectacle unfolding before my eyes. If I were Oshino, I would have put on nihilistic airs as though they suited me, perhaps stuck an unlit cigarette in my mouth, and asked the two of them if something good had happened to them, but unfortunately, I was a minor.

009

The epilogue, or maybe, the punch line of this story.

The next day, I was roused awake as usual by my little sisters Karen and Tsukihi, and rubbing my drowsy eyes, I prepared to head to Senjogahara's house for an all-day Sunday study session as I'd promised, in high spirits, holding out hope that perhaps this was the day I finally got to eat her home cooking, but just as I straddled my commuter bicycle, the only one left in my possession, and opened the gate and left my home, I encountered a bored-looking girl who was stretching in front of a telephone pole for whatever reason. She was in casual clothes, but the combination of the short pleated skirt and the bike shorts peeking out past them made her look mostly the same as she did in her school uniform—it was the star of Naoetsu High, my junior Suruga Kanbaru.

"Good morning, my senior Araragi."

"...Good morning, Miss Kanbaru."

"Hm? Oh, I don't deserve such a formal greeting. Starting with everyday good manners, you're pure quality. Have your injuries healed?"

"Yeah... If anything, the sun is the tough part for me now, but it's not as bad as I thought. That and my healing damage are about even. So, Kanbaru, how do you know where I live?"

"Aw, acting like you have no idea. Are you setting up the scene for me? I used to stalk you. Of course I'd have ferreted out your home address."

"……"

Her cheerful laughter did nothing to dispel my bewilderment.

"And is there something you need?" I asked her.

"Yes. I received a call from her this morning, and she told me to come get you. Oh, let me carry your bag." Almost as soon as Kanbaru said this, she plucked my backpack out from my bicycle's front basket and held it in her left hand. She looked at me with a beaming, innocent smile. "I oiled up your bike chain, too. And if there's anything else you need, don't hesitate to ask."

She'd gone past being friends with Senjogahara and was her gofer.

While I had no interest in having the star of the school at my beck and call, if the pathologically jealous Senjogahara had assigned such a task to Kanbaru, then was their relationship mended, and was the Valhalla Duo back together again, or was I reading too much into it? I probably was reading too much into it.

"How about a massage before we leave? You say you're fine, but you must be tired. I'm pretty good, I'd have you know."

"…But what about your team? You have practice on Sundays, too, don't you? With the exam break looming, you need to hustle."

"No, I can't play basketball anymore."

"Huh?"

"It might seem premature, but I'm retiring."

Still holding my backpack, Kanbaru showed me her left hand. That left arm of hers—was wrapped tight in a long white bandage up to her elbow. You could tell nonetheless that there was something slightly off about its length and shape.

"It was all so half-baked. The devil left, but in the end my arm didn't go back to normal. There's no way I could keep playing basketball. Still, it's powerful, in its own way, and actually feels quite handy."

"…Give me my bag back. Now."

What could I say.

If only by half, her wish had been granted.

Then that much was only fair, it seemed.

CHAPTER FOUR
NADEKO SNAKE

NADEKO SENGOKU

001

Nadeko Sengoku was my sister's classmate. I have two little sisters, and Nadeko Sengoku was friends with the younger one. Unlike the current pathetic state of my personal relationships, I was a fairly normal kid in elementary school as far as how many friends I had, but even back then I suppose you could say that while I enjoyed playing with everyone, I never enjoyed playing with specific someones. So I might have had fun with my classmates during recess, but I rarely did anything with them after school. What an unpleasant kid. Unpleasant to talk about, unpleasant to think about. In fact, I would prefer to not do either. Still, you can't teach an old dog new tricks, or maybe the other way around, but either way I'm trying to say that I've always been like that. Which is why I'd always go home right after school, even though I didn't take any lessons, and I'd sometimes find Nadeko Sengoku at play when I got there. My two sisters are now attached to each other, side by side no matter when, where, what, or why to the point that I am more creeped out than worried, but back in elementary school they tended to act on their own. The older one was the total outdoorsy type, while the younger mostly stayed indoors, and about once every three days she would bring a friend from school over to our home. Nadeko Sengoku wasn't particularly good friends with my youngest sister, but more like one of her many friends, I imagined. I qualify that statement with a somewhat uncertain "I imagined" at the end because I don't remember that time in my life very well to be honest, but when I try, of the friends my little sister used to bring home, I at least do remember Nadeko Sengoku. That's because, coming home without having played with my friends, I ended up having to play with my little sister (My two sisters and I shared a room back then. My parents only assigned me my own room once I started middle school), mostly to liven things up by filling an open spot in a board game or the like, but I'd be called over with ridiculous frequency if Nadeko Sengoku was the one my little sister was playing with. In other words, my little sister had lots of friends (This can still be said about both of my little sisters, but they're both incredibly talented when it comes to standing in the center of attention. I couldn't be any more jealous, as their older brother), but out of all the classmates she brought home, Nadeko Sengoku was the rare girl who liked to do things on her own. To be frank, all of my little sister's friends seemed the same to me, but I would of course remember the name of the girl who was always on her own, at least.

Her name was about it, though.

Yeah, I didn't remember much, after all.

And so I'm going to have to apologize for appending yet another uncertain qualification, but Nadeko Sengoku was a reserved girl of few words who constantly looked down at the floor—I thought. That's what I thought, but, well, I don't know. Maybe I'm describing another one of my little sister's friends, or maybe one of my own friends at the time. When I was in grade school, actually, I always found it annoying and irritating when my little sister had friends over. Add to that the fact I was forced to play with them, and of course I'd be left with a poor impression. When I look back at it, it must have been more annoying for those girls to have to play with their friend's older brother, but in any case, that was in the past, so please understand a grade schooler's sensibility. Once I started middle school, my youngest sister invited friends over less often, and even when she did, stopped inviting me to play with them. There was the fact that our rooms were now separated, but there must have been some other, bigger reason. That's how things are. Most of her personal relationships must have been wiped clean when she graduated because both of my little sisters ended up going to a private middle school. Nadeko Sengoku was my sister's classmate in grade school, but not now, because they went to different schools. So—it's more than two years ago that I last saw her according to the most favorable estimate, and in truth it's probably more than six.

Six years.

More than enough time for a person to change.

At least, I thought of myself as having utterly changed. Even when I say I was always like that, back then and now just aren't the same. Taking a look at my elementary graduation photo album or the like now is just too painful. I know I just said something about a "grade schooler's sensibility," but comparing my high school self to myself in those days, I wouldn't dare argue that I am now better or superior. We tend to look at the past through rose-colored glasses, yes, but what's cringe-worthy here perhaps isn't my grade school self, but the person I am now as seen by the grade school me. No, embarrassingly enough, even if he and I ran into each other in the street, we wouldn't recognize the person standing in front of us as ourselves.

I don't know if that's a bad thing or not.

Not being able to boast of my current self to my past self.

But sometimes it's like that.

Maybe we're all like that.

Which is why when I met Nadeko Sengoku again, I didn't realize it was her at first—it took some time for me to remember. If only I'd noticed immediately, or even a little faster—if I'd noticed that she was entwined with a snake, perhaps this story wouldn't have ended the way it did. A poignant thought, but it's not as if my regrets mean anything either to her or to the aberration. To start this story off with its conclusion, it seems as though Nadeko Sengoku, a friend of my little sister's whom I barely remembered, ended up a unique someone that I could never forget.

002

"I'm sorry I made you wait, my senior Araragi."

June eleventh, a Sunday.

I'm not sure if "jockish" is the best way to put it, but at 10:55 a.m., exactly five minutes before we'd agreed to meet in front of the main gate of our school, Naoetsu High, Suruga Kanbaru, the former star of the basketball team and one year my junior, came dashing, and unable to stop, jumped, sailed easily past my head, landed, turned, and spoke those words with a fresh smile on her face and her right hand in front of her chest… I realized that I wasn't particularly tall for a high school student, but I'd never considered my height a non-issue that a girl shorter than me could clear with a scissors jump. It seemed like I had some reconsidering to do.

"No, I just got here myself. I haven't been waiting."

"Wow… Being so transparently considerate just to avoid causing me undue mental stress testifies to your good nature. You're just born magnanimous. The likes of me can only take three steps back and look up to take in all that you are. I'm truly stunned that you'd move me with your largeness within a mere few seconds of seeing you. Seems like I have no choice but to spend all the respect I can muster in my lifetime on you alone. Good heavens, I think I nearly resent you for that."

"………"

She was the same as ever.

And hey, don't go around calling people transparent.

The best response to casual kindness is to feign ignorance, okay?

"No, I really did just get here," I assured her. "And in any case, you came early, too. There's no reason for you to apologize."

"I won't have any of that. No matter what you say, the fact that I wasn't here before my senior is cause enough for an apology. I think it's an unforgivable sin to waste the time of someone above you."

"I'm not above you."

"You're a year ahead of me so you are."

"True, but..."

That was just a matter of age.

Or how tall we were, I guess (physically speaking, I was above her).

Not that she couldn't easily leap over me, though.

Suruga Kanbaru—a second-year at Naoetsu High.

She was our ace basketball player until just a month earlier, and her name was known across the whole school as its biggest celebrity and star. Whether she wanted to admit it or not, it was her who had led our private prep school's weak little sports organization to the national tournament the same year she joined it. She was a frightening junior, and a half-assed washout third-year like me would normally be unable to so much as speak to her, or even step in her shadow for that matter. Just the other day, she gave her position of team captain to one of her juniors because of an injury to her left arm, then quit the basketball team early—and it was still fresh in my mind the way the whole school was shaken by the impact of the news. I doubted the memory would ever go stale.

Kanbaru's left arm.

It was still wrapped tight in a long white bandage.

"Yes," Kanbaru began to say in a quiet voice, "as you can see, I've retired. The only thing I was ever good at was basketball, and now I have nothing to offer the school. So you ought to deal with me accordingly."

"What do you mean, 'deal with' you? For all the confidence you seem to have, your self-esteem can be weirdly low. What you've done for the basketball team won't go away just because you're retiring early."

Guilt over her early retirement—wasn't exactly it, but then again, it seemed unreasonable to expect her to stay the exact same after *all that happened* to her. Personally, though, I did wish that Kanbaru wouldn't be so self-deprecating.

"Thanks," she told me. "I couldn't appreciate your concern more. I'll gladly take those feelings into consideration."

"Take the words into consideration, too. Okay, why don't we get going."

"Yup," she said before scurrying over to my side and taking my open left hand into her right in what could only be described as a natural motion. She didn't "hold my hand" as much as wrap her fingers around mine. From there, she pushed her body into my arm, sticking to me like she was about to embrace me. Her chest was right around my elbow because of our height difference, and the delicate, nerve-dense area of my body was beset by a sensation like mashed potatoes.

"No," corrected Kanbaru, "I think the usual comparison is to marshmallows."

"Wait, what?! Did I voice that stupid monologue out loud just now?!"

"Ah, no, you didn't, you didn't. Don't worry, I only heard it telepathically."

"That'd make it an even bigger problem! Everyone around here must have heard it, then!"

"Heheheh. Well, we'll just have to show them, in that case. It's not like I'm someone who worries about appearing scandalous anymore."

"Stop smiling and saying what a girlfriend might say when you're just my junior! You know it's not you I'm dating, it's your senior who you respect very much!"

Hitagi Senjogahara.

My classmate.

And girlfriend.

And—the senior that Suruga Kanbaru admired.

She, Senjogahara, was what had connected the school's biggest celebrity and star to the ever-nondescript average student that I am. Kanbaru and Senjogahara had been junior and senior since middle school, and while this, that, and the other happened between then and now, the two were still friends as the Valhalla Duo. For a time, Suruga Kanbaru stalked me because I was the person who was dating her admired senior.

I told her, "It's not like you ever worried about scandals to begin with. Now get off of me."

"No. I read that you're supposed to hold hands when you're on a date."

"A date?! When did I ever call this a date?"

"Hrm?" Kanbaru tilted her head as if that were the last thing she expected to hear. "Now that you mention it, maybe you never did. I was so excited when you asked me to go somewhere with you that I didn't really listen to what you were saying."

"Oh…I guess you were mumbling your replies the whole time…"

"Still, I don't know about that. I'm on the open side when it comes to sex, and I do want to follow your wishes wherever possible, but you'd proceed to the deed without even going on a date first? I worry about your future."

"We're not proceeding to any deed so stop worrying about me! And a high school second-year shouldn't be talking about how open she is about sex!!"

"Then again, we've already come this far. This pleasure cruise has already set sail."

"So you are enjoying it after all!"

I caught a look of how Kanbaru was dressed.

Jeans and a T-shirt, with a long-sleeved shirt on top. Expensive-looking sneakers. On her head was a baseball cap, probably in part because the sun was getting stronger. It suited a sporty girl like her perfectly, but we'll put that aside for now.

"You're technically wearing long sleeves and long pants like I told you…"

But.

Her jeans were stylishly ripped here and there, while her T-shirt was short enough to show off plenty of her curved waist. It almost seemed a little much… Of course, people were free to dress as they wanted on Sundays, but still…

"...You really weren't listening to a word I said, were you?"
"What do you mean?"
"We're about to go up into the mountains."
"The mountains? So we're performing the deed in the mountains?"
"There'll be no deed."
"Hm, pretty wild. I think I like it. That's quite manly of you. I'm into being treated rough now and then."
"I said no deed! Listen to me!"
I was certain I'd told her to wear long sleeves and long pants to protect herself from bugs, snakes, and the like in the mountains, yet she'd showed up in clothes with plenty of openings... It didn't seem like they'd do her much good...
"Fine," she said. "Wherever you go, I'm willing to come along with you. Even if you try to tell me not to. Neither rain nor snow nor heat nor overcast skies will stop me."
"Overcast skies don't sound like much of a deterrent..."
In fact, I could have used some clouds with all the sun we were getting.
But even the day before, when I called Kanbaru's home, she wouldn't listen to a word I was saying and made the same kind of distracted replies ("You don't even need to tell me where we're going. The needle of my compass is always pointing in whatever direction you're headed," and so on)... It was actually impressive in a way how prone to making assumptions she was. She went about it in a different way than Hanekawa, like she had tunnel vision and could only see straight ahead.
"In any case, this isn't a date," I clarified.
"Oh, so it's not... I was so sure that it was. I'd gotten myself fired up for it."
"Fired up?"
"Yup. I mean, this is my first-ever heterosexual date."
I decided not to comment on the "heterosexual" part.
I wasn't confident I could make a good quip about it.
"I was so fired up," she continued, "that I broke my solemn vow to myself and bought a cell phone just for today, the first one I've ever owned in my seventeen years alive."

"……"

…Please let's keep this light!

"It'd be awful if I somehow got separated from you and couldn't get in contact," she explained. "We live in an age where pay phones have all but disappeared, so a cell phone is an essential dating tool."

"W-Well…you're right. Heh, heheh. But there still are a good number of pay phones left out here in the countryside…"

"That's not all. I woke up at four to make us lunches. One for me and one for you. Since we were going to meet at eleven, I assumed I'd get to eat lunch with you."

As she said this, Kanbaru presented me with a bundle her bandaged left arm held… Yes, I'd noticed from the beginning, but judging by its tall rectangular shape, it was one of those multiple-box affairs…

Could we keep this light, please?

I mean, literally now…

I certainly knew we'd be together for lunch, so my plan had been to take her out to a fast food place once we were done, like a good senior. But it seemed that this junior of mine operated on a more deadly plane.

So that was her move. Homemade lunches…

It was a surprise attack.

"I was so happy and excited about getting to go on a date with my revered senior that I could barely get any sleep and also woke up early, so it was a nice diversion."

"A diversion, huh? Is all of that for lunch, though? It's a lot of food… I should let you know up front that I can't eat that much."

"I made it for us to split half and half, but I can just eat whatever you don't finish. I hate wasting food, so I did take that into account."

"Okay…"

I took a look at Kanbaru's fully exposed navel.

Maybe around ten percent body fat, at the most?

She basically had an hourglass figure.

Fit Sugaru's hourglass figure.

It almost seemed like a palindrome…

It wasn't, though.

"Hold on, Kanbaru. Are you one of those people who don't get fat no matter how much you eat?"

"Uhm, it's more like I'm one of those people who lose tons of weight unless they eat like crazy."

"People like that exist?!" That would make girls envious of her... In fact, even as a boy I was envious of her! "How exactly do you get your body to do that?"

"Simple. First, start off with two sets of ten-mile sprints every morning."

"Okay, never mind."

So that was it.

What she considered a normal amount of exercise was on a different level.

It seemed that Suruga Kanbaru was still making sure to work out every day, even after her retirement from the basketball team. Impressive. It made perfect sense, though. She might have claimed she quit because of an injury to her left arm, but the truth lay elsewhere.

"Ah..." she let out an exaggerated sigh. "But it looks like it was all a waste... So it wasn't a date after all. I was really looking forward to it, too. I feel like an idiot, the way I went off and got myself excited for nothing. I'm red with embarrassment. My dreams were too big for reality. It seems so obvious that a noble senior such as yourself would never bother dating a fool like me. I couldn't have been any more conceited... I'm sorry to have troubled you with my wild assumptions. Well, this cell phone and these lunch boxes are pointless now. They're just going to weigh us down, so I'll toss them somewhere. Wait here just a minute, I'll change into a tracksuit real fast."

"Actually, this is a date!"

I lost.

Such a weak man...

"Today was a date after all, Kanbaru! Yeah, I just remembered I was, um, really looking forward to today, too! Hooray, I finally get to go on a date with Miss Kanbaru! Okay? So hold onto your phone and those lunches! You don't need to change your clothes, either!"

"Really?" Kanbaru's expression started to glow.

Uh oh. She looked super cute.

"I'm glad. You're very kind," she said.

"Yeah…though I have the feeling my kindness is going to be my downfall one of these days…"

………

I was going on a date with Kanbaru, Senjogahara's junior, before I ever went on a date with Senjogahara herself, my girlfriend. I doubted she'd count this as cheating, given how unusually lenient that tsundere girl was with Kanbaru, but it was still undeniable proof of how weak-willed I was…

Also, we were still holding hands the entire time we were having this conversation, our fingers still entwined. I made a sly effort to disentangle them, but we were locked tight as if our hands were in a rugby scrum. It felt like my hand was a piece in a wire puzzle or the victim of a submission hold.

Like a snake had wrapped itself around it.

"Still, Kanbaru. Button up that shirt you're wearing on top. You have to agree that baring your navel is a bad idea when we're going into the mountains. As far as those distressed jeans—well, I guess you'll be fine with those as long as you're careful."

"Hmm. Okay, as you wish."

Kanbaru followed my instructions and buttoned up her long-sleeved shirt, hiding her curved waist from sight. I had to admit that a small part of me regretted it, but I knew I shouldn't be having such wicked thoughts about my girlfriend's junior.

"Now let's get going," I said.

"Oh, now that you mention it. Are you going to be walking today?"

"Yeah. We're heading to a mountain. I don't know where I'd be able to park a bike, plus I can't afford to have my only bike stolen." The mountain bike I'd used for trips had been smashed to smithereens, after all, thanks to a certain someone's left arm. Not that I'd say that to her since it could only come out sarcastic. "It's not like this is much of a trip. Look, you can even see where we're going from here. That mountain over there…"

As I said this, I suddenly remembered something. When I'd first started to speak to Kanbaru a month ago, she was so averse to touching the body of the boy dating her idol Senjogahara that she declined to ride on the back of my bicycle, opting against all common sense to run alongside me as I pedaled… And now that same girl was holding my hand, wrapping her fingers around mine, and shoving her chest into my body…

"Heheheh." Kanbaru wore an innocent and bashful grin and nearly skipped down the street. "My senior, Araragi, my senior, Araragi, my senior, Araragi, my senior, Araragi~~~"

"………"

Well, hasn't she grown attached!

She's even humming to herself!

"By the way, Kanbaru… I've always meant to tell you this, but could you stop calling me your senior?"

"Huh?" She seemed puzzled, like she hadn't expected to hear that. "Why? I call you my senior because you are my senior. I couldn't imagine calling my senior anything but my senior."

"Well, there's a lot of other things you could call me."

"Like 'my senior, Kesennuma'?"

"Don't change my name."

No, the other part.

Plus "Kesennuma" was a place name.

"I'm talking about the 'my senior' part. It's so stiff and formal."

"Please don't say that. Stiff and formal is exactly what I want to be."

"O…kay. Well, sure, I suppose I am your senior, but it just sounds too serious. And 'my senior, Araragi' is a mouthful like my full name."

My full name is Koyomi Araragi.

Seven syllables.

The same as "my senior, Araragi."

"Hmm. Should I call you 'Mister Araragi' in that case?"

"I guess that's one solution? But I'm only a year older, so I don't think there's any need for you to be so proper and uptight with me. And I feel kind of weird about being called 'Mister' in the first place. There's a grade school kid I know who always calls me that, but in her case, she speaks in this weirdly polite manner."

Her personality couldn't be any worse, though.

That reminded me. I hadn't seen Hachikuji lately.

……

That made me feel kind of lonely.

"Kanbaru, I know a lot happened between us over Senjogahara, but I'd like us to treat each other more like equals."

"I see. I'm glad to hear that."

"Then again, I'm not sure I'm on even ground with our school's biggest star."

"Oh, don't be ridiculous. Nothing could ever make me happier than being with you like this. Getting to know you makes me nearly as happy as reconciling with my other esteemed senior Senjogahara. If there's anything about you that I'm dissatisfied about, it's that I didn't meet you sooner in life."

"…Uh huh."

She really did have low self-esteem.

I could understand why, though, considering what I'd learned a month ago.

She had a lot going on, too.

"So," she confirmed with me, "I'm getting the sense that it would be okay for me to refer to you in a more intimate way than 'my senior'?"

"Yeah. You can call me whatever you want."

"All right, Koyomi."

"………"

……

Only my family calls me that!

"And Koyomi, you can call me Suruga."

"You're going on again like we're an item! And why do these milestone events keep on happening between me and my girlfriend's junior?! Even Senjogahara still calls me 'Araragi'! Do you have any idea how much of a leap you just made?!"

"Please don't get so worked up. You know that was supposed to be a joke, Koyomi."

"Why are you still calling me that then, Suruga?!"

"The 'Dashing Knight of Lightning' Koyomi."

"And now you're sticking some weird slogan on my name? My

grandfather gave me my name, stop messing around with it! There's nothing dashing or lightning-like about me, and I'm not a knight, either! And that's like, twice as long as my full name, anyway! You're losing sight of our initial goal here!"

"The 'Last Hero of Our Century' Koyomi."

"The last one this century?! Isn't that a little premature?!"

"Well, in any case, I can't bring myself to address my senior casually. So 'Koyomi' is out. I don't feel comfortable not using a title. But if a slogan is too much, can we try a nickname?"

"A nickname..." Her sensibility could be a little off the mark... or more like off target. I couldn't imagine her giving me a proper nickname, but then again, you never know. "Fine, then try coming up with something," I told her.

"Yup." Kanbaru closed her eyes for a bit as if she were deliberating. A few seconds later, her head popped up. "I thought of one," she said.

"Wow, that was fast. Hit me with it."

"Ragi."

"That's a lot cooler than I thought it'd be! Too cool, in fact!"

Like she was purposely using a nickname that was too cool for me just to make fun of me... It sounded too edgy to be the nickname of a Japanese high school kid...

"I took the bottom half of 'Araragi' to come up with it."

"So I gathered... But shouldn't nicknames be a little softer and more charming?"

"You have a point. In that case, we can take a bit from 'Araragi' and a bit from 'Koyomi' to get..."

"To get?"

"Ragiko."

"Now you're obviously making fun of me!"

"Don't be shy, li'l Ragiko."

"Go home! I don't need you after all!"

"Ragiko is being mean to me... But I actually don't mind, heheheh..."

"Agh! I forgot, yelling doesn't work on a masochist! Are you the strongest opponent I've faced yet?!"

I was having fun talking to her.

Maybe a little too much fun.

I was nearly losing sight of what we were setting out to do.

"I know it's probably inappropriate to say this, but...Kanbaru. Not to seize on what you said earlier, but if I'd met you before I started going out with Senjogahara, I wonder if we'd be going out instead..."

"Yes. I was actually thinking the same thing. What if I'd met you before becoming drawn to her. It's so rare for me to feel this way about someone of the opposite sex."

I sighed.

Of course, I wouldn't have come to know Kanbaru if it wasn't for Senjogahara, and the same went for Kanbaru, making this hypothetical no more than that.

"What do you say," she offered, "to the two of us killing and burying that nuisance of a woman?"

"You're scaring me!"

We've talked enough, but I still can't pin down your character! I can't fathom your depths! Just how much is there to you, Suruga Kanbaru?!

"I know that you respect Senjogahara as your senior, but...you're surprisingly wicked."

"Don't shower me with praise. You'll make me blush."

"That wasn't praise."

"I'm happy to be called anything by you."

"I can't believe you, you little masochist..."

"Ooh, little masochist. I like that. Keep going."

"......"

While I'd harbored fears that Kanbaru might find herself lost after coming into contact with the true nature of her middle school idol Senjogahara, it seemed that thanks to such a proclivity I didn't need to worry.

In any case, about Suruga Kanbaru.

She was actually a sapphist.

As you could probably tell from our conversation up to this point, she not only worshiped Hitagi Senjogahara as a senior but also loved her from the bottom of her heart. You could even say that yes, Kanbaru and I were rivals in love—and yet we were walking arm in arm. It was hard to say what was going on. Then again, it was probably that she felt indebted to me for what happened at the end of last month, or maybe that she felt grateful, or something along those lines…

It didn't feel bad having one of my juniors get attached to me, but it didn't feel great that the attraction was due to a misunderstanding.

To borrow a phrase from Oshino—just like with Senjogahara.

Kanbaru simply had gone and saved herself all on her own—

"………"

But yes, I couldn't deny it.

Indebtedness or misunderstanding or whatever, it seemed like I needed to do at least something to adjust Kanbaru's overblown image of me. Or maybe to destroy my image… If her impression of me stayed too positive, she'd be that much more disappointed when everything went south.

Which is why I hatched Operation Ruin Koyomi Araragi's Image.

Part One.

A man who was loose with money.

"Kanbaru, I forgot my wallet. Think you could lend me some cash? I promise to give it back right away."

"Okay, sure. Is thirty thousand yen enough?"

She was rich!

Hmm…someone who was loose with other people's time… wouldn't be very convincing after I'd arrived before her at our meeting spot today…

Operation Ruin Koyomi Araragi's Image, Part Two.

A hopeless lecher.

"Kanbaru, you know what I'm interested in right now? Girls' underwear."

"Oh, what a coincidence. Me too. I consider women's underwear works of fine art. I never thought we'd agree on this point."

She agreed!

Right, I could never hope to match Kanbaru when it came to smuttiness… Wait, no! Regular lechery might be out, but maybe I stood a chance if I went in some strange direction…

"I'm particularly interested," I proclaimed, "in elementary schoolgirls' underwear!"

"I couldn't agree more! Wow, I always knew you weren't the type to be constrained by what society thinks. You know how to live!"

"My stock rose?!"

Why?

Hmm. Okay, then it was time for Operation Ruin Koyomi Araragi's Image, Part Three (I was having too much fun with this and already losing sight of my original goal).

A megalomaniac who goes on and on about his dreams.

"Kanbaru, you're talking to a man who's gonna be big one day!"

"You don't need to be telling me that. In fact, I think you're already huge. I don't know if there'll be any space left by your side if you get any bigger."

"Nkk…!"

No, this much was to be expected!

I needed to keep going!

"I'm gonna become a musician!"

"Oh? Then I think I'll become your instrument."

"I don't even know what that means, but what a cool line!"

Her stock had gone up in my ledger.

Man, why?

"What's all this about?" Kanbaru asked me. "You don't need to tell me these things because I couldn't possibly love and respect you more than I already do."

"Yeah, it's useless…" Just as she was happy whatever I told her, she was going to worship me no matter what kind of person I was. "I don't get it, though. Why do you overrate me that much?"

"Listen to you." Kanbaru laughed. "Until just now, I'd always thought that there was no such thing as a stupid question, but I stand corrected."

"………"

It sounded like a cool line to me for a brief moment, but then I thought about it and realized that someone here was just an idiot.

"I vowed to devote this life of mine to you," she added. "Not because you helped mediate between me and her, but because I think you're worthy of that kind of vow."

"A vow, you say..."

"Yes. I thought I'd make my vow to the sun, which never stops shining upon us and bestowing its gifts, but the thought came to me at night, so I chose the closest street lamp instead."

"That's the most arbitrary thing I've ever heard of!"

"But street lamps shine upon us and bestow their gifts, too, don't they? Life would be pretty tough without them."

"True, but..."

Vow to the moon, at least.

Maybe it had been cloudy.

"But perhaps," Kanbaru conceded, "I, myself, am not worthy of vowing to spend my life preying upon your good graces."

"I don't know where to begin with you, but that spelling mistake..."

Urkk.

Operation Ruin Koyomi Araragi's Image was at an impasse!

"...Hmph."

Koyomi Araragi.

Suruga Kanbaru.

Come to think of it, there's one thing other than Senjogahara that we have in common.

Neither of us is *human*.

Well, actually, both of us are mostly human. Only—

Koyomi Araragi's *blood*.

Suruga Kanbaru's *left arm*.

Each is something other than human.

No small part of my blood is a *demon's*—and Kanbaru's left arm is altogether that of a *monkey*. Just as I grew out my hair to hide the fang marks left on my neck by a vampire, Kanbaru hid her monkey's left arm by wrapping it in a long bandage. That's the real reason the once bright and shining star was forced to retire from the team early. What else could she do? There's no playing basketball with a monkey's arm.

Both Kanbaru and I had gotten ourselves involved with aberrations.

...And speaking of aberrations, Hitagi Senjogahara, my girlfriend and Kanbaru's senior, had also encountered one.

For me, a demon.

For Kanbaru, a monkey.

For Senjogahara, it was a crab.

But Kanbaru and I were different from her in a decisive way—Senjogahara faced her aberration every day for over two years but finally exorcised it and *became human again*. Kanbaru and I got rid of our aberrations—but parts of our bodies were *still not human*. You could say that we were like aberrations ourselves—we'd gotten involved with them and become them.

It was—

A sad thing to have in common.

"Hm? What's the matter?" she asked me.

"Oh... Er, nothing."

"You're going to spoil this date with that gloomy expression of yours."

"Date... Fine, whatever."

"By the way, I meant to ask you earlier, but what are we going to do once we get to this mountain? Is there anything to do up there, other than our deed?"

"If you're being serious right now, please stay far away from any Wandervogel clubs... But I take it you haven't been to the mountains very much?"

"My team did do some runs through the mountains as part of our training back in middle school, kind of like mock cross-country races. We ended up having to cancel them after some students started getting sprains, though."

"Hunh."

So to her, even the mountains were just a spot to work out.

Then again, it wasn't her technique per se that had made her our basketball ace, but rather that overwhelming leg strength of hers that easily hopped over my height.

"Does that mean you're at home in the mountains?" she asked me.

"No, not particularly..."

"But don't boys scrounge around for rhinoceros and stag beetles when they're little?"

"Stag beetles..."

"Yes. So precious they're like black mold."

"That doesn't sound too valuable..."

But why would I look in the mountains for them?

That was called illegal dumping.

"I suppose it's not exactly the kind of place to go on a date—especially considering the season," I admitted. "I'm pretty sure I gave you a full explanation yesterday, but you know, it's a job from Oshino."

"Oshino? Oh, Mister Oshino."

Kanbaru's expression turned ambivalent as soon as she heard the name. The reaction was an uncommon one from her, but it did make sense.

Mèmè Oshino.

Me, Kanbaru, Senjogahara—the man had saved all of us. No, he would never agree to that word choice. We'd gotten saved on our own, that was the only way to put it.

An expert on aberrations, and a rolling stone and vagrant.

A frivolous man who wore a tacky Hawaiian shirt.

He was by no means a respectable adult, but it was the immutable truth that we were obliged to him.

"Yeah," I said. "There's apparently a small shrine up in the mountains that isn't being used anymore, and he said to stick this talisman on its main hall—that was the job he gave us."

"...What's with that?" Kanbaru sounded mystified. "The talisman part doesn't make any sense, but to begin with, can't Mister Oshino just do it himself? He has all the time in the world, doesn't he?"

"I agree, but that's our job. I went into a ridiculous amount of debt when he helped me out... Doesn't the same go for you, Kanbaru?"

"Huh?"

"I know it's a little fuzzier in your case, but he's a professional, despite everything else about him. He's not so kind that he'd lend you a hand pro bono. You're indebted to him, and you need to work to pay it off."

"Ohh, so that's why..." Kanbaru nodded, seemingly convinced.

"Yup," I picked up where she left off, "that's why I asked you to come out here. Oshino asked us to do this yesterday when I went to have Shinobu drink my blood. He said to make sure to bring you along."

"Now that you mention it, Mister Oshino did insist that he was lending me a hand… Huh. I see, it meant that I'd be in his debt."

"There you go."

"All right. No point in arguing if that's the case."

Kanbaru squeezed and latched on to my arm even tighter. There seemed to be a complicated meaning behind the act that I couldn't hope to understand, but at any rate, it looked like she'd made up her mind. She certainly came across as the upstanding type who honored her end of the bargain.

"Still," she said, "I've been near that mountain a few times but never knew there was a shrine."

"Me, neither… Even if it's fallen out of use, you'd at least expect to have heard about it. Why does Oshino know about spots that locals like us aren't aware of? I guess the same goes for that abandoned cram school he's living in now."

Maybe he was actually more knowledgeable about ruins than he was about aberrations. At the same time, like our pay phones, it really is the mark of a rural town that a forgotten shrine and cram school aren't getting overrun by weirdoes… Then again, that could be exactly how you described that cram school since Oshino and Shinobu lived there…

"But—if you're going to put it that way," questioned Kanbaru, "why hasn't my other dear senior come along with us? Both of you owe Mister Oshino a—"

"Senjogahara is astute about that kind of thing, so she already paid back her debt. Remember I gave Oshino a hundred thousand yen when you were there? That was it."

"Ah, now that you mention it, you did discuss some such matter. I see, so that's what you meant… Hm, now there's my senior."

"In her case, it's not so much about being upstanding, it's more like she hates being indebted to people. She's the kind of person who'd endure life all alone."

"Did she say anything about today?"

"Hmm? No, not really. Not even a 'be careful.'"

She really hadn't.

Since I was technically bringing "her" junior along with me, I did make sure to bring it up with her before calling on Kanbaru, but Senjogahara's reaction had been bland, as if I shouldn't have troubled her with such a trivial matter. I found myself wanting to complain that it was thanks to her attitude that I'd ended up going on a date with her junior before I went on one with her, conveniently turning a blind eye to my own weak will.

"Did she say anything to you, Kanbaru?"

"Mm. She said to have you pamper me."

"........."

She really did indulge Kanbaru.

Jeez, a tsundere was supposed to show her sweet side to her boyfriend, not her junior.

"She told me something else. 'If Araragi tries to lay a finger on you, don't hide it from me but report it right away. He can choose between being buried in the mountains and becoming fish food, whichever he hates more.'"

"Whichever I hate more?!"

She was merciless.

But—well.

It did seem like Hitagi Senjogahara was heading in the right direction. She'd encountered an aberration before entering high school, and apparently she'd thrown everything away, given up on everything—so this meant she was getting back to where she used to be. For someone who'd endure life all alone—learning how to interact with others couldn't be a bad thing.

I was actually glad to see it.

Since she was human—that was good.

"Oh, right, Kanbaru. Talking about Senjogahara reminds me. It's her birthday soon, isn't it?"

"Yes. July seventh."

"…Sounds like you don't need to check your calendar for that one."

"We're talking about someone I love."

"Well, I have a request about it."

"Anything you want. This body belongs to you, to begin with. There's no need to check with me over every little thing, use me as you see fit."

"No, it's nothing that big, just that it's a special day that I thought we could celebrate. The only thing is that I've been fairly detached from those kinds of events for a while now, and I don't know how they go. That's where I was hoping you could help me out, Kanbaru."

"I see. You need me to strip?"

"Even I know that birthdays aren't that kind of event! What kind of occasion are you trying to turn my girlfriend's special day into?!"

"Ah. I jumped the gun."

"There isn't going to be a time when that gun ever goes off. Go back and sit on the bench. For the rest of your life. Well, actually, I'd appreciate it if you could help out with the setup and planning. I know there was a gap in your relationship, but you probably know more about Senjogahara than I do. That's all."

"Hmm. I don't know, this is her first birthday since you started going out, so don't you think you should set the mood and spend the day alone together? I feel like me trying to help out would only get in the way."

"Get in the way?"

"Yes. An unwanted kindness can be a pain in the butt, just a nuisance."

"Ahh. I did consider that, but I thought a livelier celebration might be good for our first birthday together. I was thinking of inviting Oshino and Shinobu, and maybe this one grade schooler that I know, and holding a nice little birthday party."

The idea did have issues in that Senjogahara disliked Oshino, Shinobu, and Hachikuji, but that was something I needed to power through. I had to do my best to create a situation where she couldn't say so outright.

"Well—if you're okay with it, so am I," Kanbaru consented.

"Really? That sounds evasive."

"Well, if you don't mind me saying so, while I do have the utmost respect for your intentions, she might want to spend the time alone with you."

"You think she's that sanctimonious about our relationship?"

She hadn't even gone on a date with me.

I'd been asking her out pretty clearly, too.

Of course, it hadn't been the right time, what with Kanbaru and the skills test right afterwards.

Her defenses were just so tight.

"At any rate," I noted, "you seem to care about me and Senjogahara in a pretty normal way when you and I are supposed to be rivals fighting over her."

"Well, true… But right now, it's like I'm in love with her even as she's going out with you… And I love you, her boyfriend, almost as much as I love her."

"……"

Did she just confess to me?

Uh oh, my pulse was rising.

She might even feel my heartbeat through our arms.

What a simpleton I was.

"…You know, you're letting Senjogahara influence you a little too much," I scolded her. "The sun or a street lamp or whatever you made this vow to, you don't have to see me in such a positive light just because I'm Senjogahara's boyfriend. You don't need to like someone just because she does—"

"No. That's not what it is," Kanbaru said awfully bluntly.

I felt a little cowed by her forceful gaze.

If something needed to be said, she said it, juniors and seniors be damned.

"Then," I asked her, "could you still be carrying around baggage from last month? I don't mind at all, really… You know what they say, hate the sin, what's for dinner—"

"It's not that—either," Kanbaru stated, seemingly overlooking my gaffe. "I'm fortunate that you're able to forget and forget, but that isn't what it is."

"Forget and forget..."

She made me sound so feebleminded.

I had a feeling she wasn't wrong, though.

And it certainly was simpler that way.

"Please, listen to me," she said. "I was stalking you, okay?"

"......"

What a thing to say so unabashedly to my face.

Like I was the one who needed a talking-to.

"So—" she continued, "I think I have a very good idea about the kind of person you are. I really believe that you deserve no less. Even if you weren't her boyfriend, even if last month never happened, no matter how we'd met—I would have seen you as someone worthy of my respect. I swear, upon my legs."

"...Oh."

Well, in that case.

It was foolish even to contemplate other scenarios where Kanbaru and I could have met...

However.

"If it's upon your legs—what can I say."

"Right... I respect you so much that even if you're bringing me to some lonely mountain on the pretext that Mister Oshino has a job for us, only to force upon me every single lustful desire that your heart cradles, I can forgive you with a smile."

"I don't want that kind of respect!"

And "pretext"?

She didn't trust me at all!

"Huh? Hold on," she said. "Are we really not proceeding to it?"

"Don't act so genuinely surprised!"

"Wait, are you having the girl make the first move? A-ha... Your plan is to insist to your lover that it wasn't cheating because you'd been tempted."

"Now I get it, Kanbaru, that's what you're trying to do! You're plotting to wreck my relationship with Senjogahara through this! You're using your body, no less!"

"Oops..."

"Don't stick your tongue out at me! You look so damn adorable, moron!"

So scheming.

Well, I knew it had to be a joke, of course.

...It was a joke, right?

"But speaking of birthdays," she said, "it seemed a little suggestive to me when I heard that a crab had possessed her."

"I don't know if 'possessed' is the right word, but...pardon me? Suggestive? What's suggestive about a crab? And what does it have to do with her birthday?"

"Well, she's a Cancer, isn't she?"

"Huh?" July seventh, right? "What are you talking about? July seventh would be Gemini."

"Huh? No...um, I don't think that's correct."

"Really? Am I the one who has it wrong? When I heard she was born on July seventh, I assumed that she was a Gemini..." I remembered it well because I'd thought then that Senjogahara having an identical twin with the same personality would suck to high heaven. "Well, it's not like I know the exact dates of the zodiac or anything... No, but wait. I want to say Cancer starts on July twenty-third?"

"Oh." Kanbaru seemed to have realized something. "...A quick pop quiz."

"Why?"

"What sign is someone who's born on December first?"

"Huh?" Come on, that didn't even count as a quiz. "I know the answer to that one, at least. Ophiuchus, right?"

"Pfft!" Suruga Kanbaru burst out laughing. "Ha...haha, ahaha!"

It seemed to hit her so hard that her knees shook and she couldn't stay standing, and she was even clinging to my arm. She went from pushing her chest against my elbow to trapping my upper arm in her cleavage, but her irritating laughter made it extremely hard for me to register my good fortune.

"Wh-What's so funny... Did I make that bad of a mistake?"

"O-Ophiuchus... Pff, pffahaha! Ophiuchus... Ahaha, in this day and age, y-you're using the thirteen-sign zodiac..."

"........."

Oh.

So that's what it was.

Right, I understood now. July seventh was Cancer in the twelve-sign zodiac...

"Ah, that was a good laugh. Five years' worth."

Kanbaru finally raised her head. There were tears in her eyes. I understood why she might have found it so funny, but she'd laughed at me way too much.

"Okay, let's go, li'l Ragiko."

"You're openly treating me worse! All of that respect you had for me as your senior, gone! This actually hurts pretty bad!"

"O-Oh. My mistake, dear senior Araragi."

"Cover for me as thanks for making you laugh that much."

"Cover? How, when you sounded so sure? To begin with, why are you even using the thirteen-sign zodiac?"

"I mean, what can I say? Didn't we switch from a twelve- to a thirteen-sign zodiac a while ago?"

"We tried, but it didn't spread and people gave up on it. How could my esteemed senior Araragi not know that?"

"Hmm...maybe that was right around the time I stopped caring about astrology..."

Okay...

So it never caught on...

"I guess aberrations are the same," I mused. "You could have the most terrifying ghoul or ghost imaginable, but it never existed if it didn't catch on."

"No, I don't think it's anything so deep..."

"I wonder what Ophiuchus is, anyway."

"It's a summer constellation with the alpha star Ras Alhague. It's well known for containing Bernard's Star, which has the largest proper motion of any fixed star."

"No, I'm not talking about the stars themselves... I'm wondering why it has that name. Does it have to do with snakes or something?"

"I want to say that it represents the master physician Asclepius from Greek mythology. He's grasping a snake in the constellation, which is why it's known as Ophiuchus, or the 'serpent-bearer.'"

"Huh." I nodded. I'd had no idea. "Kanbaru, I'm surprised you know all that, both about the stars themselves and the constellation. Do you actually know a lot about stars or something?"

"Does it seem unlike me?"

"To be honest."

"Hm. Well, I wouldn't go so far as to say I know a lot about them, but I do like looking up at the night sky. It's a simple one, but I also own a telescope. Twice a year, I go to a stargazing event they hold at an observatory in another prefecture."

"Huh. So not just a planetarium. Experience over knowledge, huh?"

"I like planetariums too, but those places don't have shooting stars, do they? Fixed stars and constellations are nice, but I prefer fleeting shooting stars."

"I see. How romantic."

"Yes. I hope that someday soon, Earth becomes a shooting star, too."

"Is humanity going to be all right?!"

I couldn't believe her.

Where was the romance in that?

That was a disaster movie.

"...And it looks like we've arrived after all of that talk," I told her. "There should be stairs around here, according to Oshino—oh, there they are...Well, more like a game trail..."

A roadside mountain.

I didn't know its name.

Oshino didn't, either.

I should say the road had been paved to bypass the mountain, but branching off from the sidewalk, toward the peak, were steps—or at least their traces. Well, actually, you could still call them steps. I'd heard that our athletic teams came jogging all the way here, as Kanbaru mentioned too, but I doubted any of them took these stairs up the mountain. It was overgrown with foliage, and if I hadn't known in advance, I probably wouldn't have noticed or recognized them as such.

A game trail.

Mm, no—I saw signs of trampled grass when I looked closer. Footsteps. So the stairs weren't totally unused, but then, whose tracks could they be? If I remembered correctly, Oshino hadn't even approached the shrine, so they couldn't be his. He also said the shrine was already out of use, so it couldn't be anyone who worked there…

Was it overrun with weirdoes?

Unlikely.

"……"

I looked at the girl attached to my left arm.

Her guard was always so low, just like now, but she was such a cute girl… Would she be okay? If there were weirdoes who were textbook cases of weirdoes up there…I could protect her only so well alone. Some vampire blood still coursed through me, but that merely improved my metabolism and healing, anyway.

"Balkan, my junior."

"What is it, Ragiko?"

"Your left arm—how's it feeling?"

"Huh? What do you mean?"

"Well, I was just wondering if anything was new or unusual about it."

"Not in particular."

Not in particular—she said.

True, she'd been holding that heavy-looking bundle in her left hand without switching the whole time, like it was nothing…

Maybe there was no need to worry…if having the power of that monkey left arm on top of her base stamina was the new normal for Kanbaru…

"Yup," she assured, "it's still strong enough that I can shove you down onto a bed with my left arm alone."

"I'm not really seeing why it has to be onto a bed."

"Then, strong enough that I could bridal-carry you with my left arm alone."

"It's not a bridal-carry if you do it with one arm, it's more like a bandit making off with a village lass… But I guess I'm fine with that one."

"Heheheh," Kanbaru let out a vaguely obscene laugh in reply. She seemed to be enjoying herself. "You really are kind…worrying yourself over me, of all people. Ahh, I could feel safe entrusting my body and soul to you…"

"Why are you blushing and saying that like you're deeply moved? What are you, a mind reader? Stop digging up every little thing that I'm thinking or I'll have to get out my tinfoil hat."

"I may not look it now, but I was once our basketball ace. I can figure out most of what people are thinking by looking into their eyes. And we're talking about the thoughts of a senior I respect very much! As your faithful subordinate, I practically have you wrapped around my little finger."

"Don't have me wrapped around your little finger, then. What are you, a femme fatale? Hmph… All it takes is a look into my eyes? Yikes. I mean, that really does sound like telepathy… Okay, Kanbaru, what am I thinking right now?"

"Probably something like, 'Would this woman take off her bra if I asked her to?'"

"Is that how you see me, Kanbaru?!"

"Want me to take it off?"

"Um, nkk… No, of course not!"

I'd hesitated for a moment despite myself.

Kanbaru only gave me a brisk nod along with an "Oh, then," and continued to cling to my arm… Her complete non-reaction to my hesitation seemed to be intended as a show of tolerance, almost maternally broad in scope, for the ulterior motives of men, and it honestly got under my skin…

She was the one who'd gone in that direction.

Where did she get off acting like I was her younger husband?

"Let's go," I urged. "We haven't even climbed up this mountain and I'm already tired…"

"Mm."

"Do be careful where you step, though. Aside from bug bites, it sounds like there's a ton of snakes around here."

"Did you say 'snake'?"

Pfft, laughed Kanbaru.

I must have reminded her of our earlier conversation about Ophiuchus.

I continued, unperturbed, "Well, apparently they aren't poisonous. Snakes have long fangs, though, and you wouldn't want to get a bite wound out here."

"...Yours is on your neck, right?"

"Yeah. It's from a demon, though, not a snake."

We spoke as we climbed the mountain's stairs. Our coordinates hadn't changed much, but the humidity seemed to shoot up the moment we entered the mountain, and it was sweltering. The stairs led to this shrine according to Oshino, but I hadn't asked how high up it was. I didn't imagine it was actually on the summit, but...that would be okay. It wasn't that tall of a mountain.

"My left arm," Kanbaru said. "Mister Oshino told me it should heal by the time I'm twenty."

"What? Really?"

"Yes. Well, only if I *don't do it again.*"

"That's good to hear. So it means you can play basketball again after you're twenty."

"Right. Of course, that hope will be crushed if I slack off, so I need to keep working out on my own." After saying that, she asked me, "What about you?"

"Huh? Me?"

"Are you going to be—a vampire for the rest of your life?"

"...I."

The rest of my life.

A vampire—for the rest of my life.

A mock human.

Something other than human.

"I'm fine with it. In any case—unlike your left arm, it's not that much of an issue. The sun, crosses, garlic, and all that stuff doesn't bother me at all. Ha ha—and I heal right away if I get hurt, so I got a good deal, you know?"

"I don't want to hear you acting tough. What Mister Oshino told me—is that you resigned yourself to being a vampire to save that girl Shinobu."

Shinobu.

That was what the vampire who'd attacked me was called now.

That blonde vampire.

She was now—living in the ruins of that cram school together with Oshino.

"......"

That bastard really was loose-lipped.

I hoped he hadn't told Senjogahara. I assumed it was on account of the left arm that he provided Kanbaru with an example she could reference, so I probably didn't need to worry...

"That's not true," I maintained. "They're just *residual effects*. As far as Shinobu—well, she's my responsibility. I wouldn't go so far as to call it saving her. We have an understanding, and I'm sticking to it. It's fine... I'm no basketball star so I can't tell just by looking into your eyes, but you're worried about me, aren't you, Kanbaru?"

"...Well."

"I'm fine. Your worries are misplaced—just like with the deed you kept bringing up."

I cut the topic short with a little joke at the end. Kanbaru seemed to want to say more, but probably realizing it was better left unsaid, fell silent. If something needed to be said, she said it—but if she only wanted to say it, she could hold her tongue. She was too good of a woman to be wrapped around my left arm, honestly.

"Ah."

"Oh."

Just as our conversation ended, someone came down the stairs. Perfect timing. The person was jogging down the treacherous steps a bit precariously.

A girl, probably in middle school.

She was fully protected in her long sleeves and long pants.

There was a bag around her waist.

A hat, pulled far down on her head.

I was very unsure if she could see in front of her, and even if she could, she was running down the stairs looking only at her feet, so a couple of false moves and she might have collided with us head-on. It was a good thing that Kanbaru and I had just hit a pause in our conversation; we noticed her quicker than we normally would have and shifted to one side of the stairs to dodge her.

The moment she passed by.

She looked at the two of us—and seeming to notice us for the first time, made a startled expression, and just as soon, began descending the stairs at an even faster pace. Her figure was out of sight before we knew it. She'd sped up so much that I expected her to trip and fall at least twice before she reached the street.

".........?"

Hmm?

There was something about the girl...

It was like I'd seen her somewhere before, or maybe not.

"What's the matter?" asked Kanbaru.

"Oh, nothing..."

"Well, I didn't expect to run into someone on this mountain trail. I didn't want to say it in front of you, but I was convinced we were on a road to death. She was pretty cute, too. You said the shrine isn't being used anymore, but maybe some people still visit it, after all?"

"A girl like that, though?"

"Faith knows no age."

"Sure, but still."

"Just as love knows no age."

"You didn't need to add that, did you?"

Even as I spoke, I tried to remember where I'd seen the girl before, but I couldn't in the end. Then again, I thought, maybe I didn't know her in the first place. I came to the conclusion that it might have been a simple case of déjà vu.

"Well, let's keep climbing," I told Kanbaru. "If someone came from up there, that means there has to be something above us. I was wondering the whole time if Oshino might be playing a prank on me, but this rules it out."

"Yep. As it almost does the possibility that you're tricking me."

"It not only actually existed but hasn't been ruled out yet?"

"I'll forgive you with a smile on my face."

"Not a word more about how sexually frustrated you are, okay?"

"You can call it a mistake, I won't mind. I don't intend on pestering you afterwards."

"You're already pestering me."

"Oh. In that case, how about this? You just go ahead and relieve my frustration, and I'll probably stop harassing you. It's the easiest and fastest way to calm a bitch in heat."

"Well, that's a first, a woman referring to herself that way…"

"It's only embarrassing in the beginning. Let's hurry and get this out of the way so there's less trouble down the line."

"I'm going on ahead."

"Abandonment play, I see."

"And you can go home!"

"So cold to my advances… Do you not like women who take the lead? I guess I need to act like I don't really want this, then."

"Whatever, I don't care."

"Just imagine. We're holding hands against my will now… You left me with no choice, threatened me with violence, and ordered me to. And I hesitantly ask you, 'L-Like this?'"

"Uh…if you thought that'd get me excited, actually—it doesn't, dammit!"

Nope.

Absolutely not.

"Hmph. A prude. More indifferent than cold. Being treated like air is making me lose confidence in my feminine charms. Do you not care about me at all?"

"No, that isn't true. But I have a girlfriend, and her name is Senjogahara. If I didn't behave indifferently, that would be a problem, no?"

"But you two seem to have a platonic relationship. I'm sure you need some space where you can unleash your pent-up sexual desires."

"No, I don't! And don't volunteer to be part of that space!"

"She can take care of your emotional needs while I support your physical ones. Behold, a golden triangle."

"No, you behold, that's a muck of a love triangle! Why would I ever want to get dragged into that kind of Three's Misery situation?!"

"While he said so, Araragi seemed unable to take his eyes off my breasts. At the end of the day, he could not resist his male instincts."

"Why are you voicing a monologue?!"

"This one is a side story, so I get to be the narrator."

"What are you even talking about?!"

And anyway.

Side story or no, she could never become the narrator.

We'd need to shrink-wrap it before it went on the shelves.

"Hmph. This isn't going as well as I thought," Kanbaru lamented. "With a body like mine, I expected the likes of you to become my plaything in no time."

"Is that what you really thought about me?!"

A platonic relationship…

That was one way to describe a cool girlfriend who wouldn't even go on a date. Either way, it looked like others could tell. I always made fun of manga where couples who're supposed to be going out drift apart and make up over and over again and cajoled them in my mind to just get on with it, but now that I had a girlfriend, I knew that's really how it is.

Uh-uh.

You didn't just get on with it so smoothly.

"If you're going to call me a prude, then what about her?" I said. "She's totally chaste."

"And why not? It makes sense when you consider her past, and it only makes her that much more moé as long as you think of her as a bashful, innocent girlfriend."

"Bashful… I don't know, I feel like once you start identifying a trait as moé, it starts to feel less moé and more like a selling point."

"Well, if she is selling, I don't see how it's wrong to take her up on the offer."

"You're right about that."

We climbed the stairs.

The grass trampled underfoot that I noticed down below must have been that girl's, I thought, and arrived at the shrine about five minutes later… Like the stairs, it was in such a state of disrepair that I wouldn't have recognized it as such if I hadn't been told beforehand. My concerns about weirdoes hanging around were proved utterly meaningless. Countryside or not, weirdo or not, no person would choose to be there for a single second. I could just barely tell it was once a shrine from the *torii* gate, but it wasn't clear which of the structures was the main hall. I'd have to figure it out based on the layout.

Could the girl from earlier have been here too?

For what, though?

There clearly weren't any gods in this shrine.

Even a god would have fled.

To put it like Oshino might, the gods are everywhere—but even so, it didn't feel like they'd be here. Whatever… I'd get my job out of the way. All I had to do was place the talisman, which ranked it among one of the easier jobs that Oshino had tasked me with so far. I took the talisman I'd received from him out from my pocket.

But then.

"Ungh."

Kanbaru—hopped off of my arm.

That pleasant sensation that had been with me for so long disappeared from my elbow.

"What's wrong, Kanbaru?"

"…I guess I'm feeling tired?"

"Tired?"

From what?

Climbing those stairs?

Yes, it was a decent number of steps, but it didn't seem like enough to wind a jock like Kanbaru. Even I was only breathing a little heavier than usual.

But Kanbaru really did seem tired, and her face looked pale, somehow. It was the first time I'd ever seen her in such a state.

"Hunh… Wanna take a break somewhere around there?" I offered.

"Um…I guess the only place you could sit would be…on top of a rock… But I feel like sitting down on the wrong rock in a shrine could get you cursed…"

Putting aside whether there were any gods around at the shrine to curse us—something still felt wrong about it. I knew from experience that when my guts warned me like that, it was best to stop.

What to do in that case, though?

As I worried over the question, Kanbaru proposed, "How about we just have lunch?"

"Lunch?"

"Yes. It might be an impolite request and a breach of etiquette for a junior to suggest that we eat, but when I don't feel well, it usually goes away if I fill my tummy up with food."

"………"

She was like a manga character.

What a funny junior, even when she didn't feel well.

"He did say not to eat until we placed the talisman, though… Something about keeping our bodies pure. Okay, then why don't you go and find a place where you can spread out all those lunch boxes? I'm not the biggest fan of lunching at a deserted shrine, but I guess it has a charm of its own. I'll run over and slap on this talisman while you do."

"Mm. Yes, let's do that. Sorry, but I'm going to leave the job in your hands."

"Later."

Turning my back on Kanbaru, I pushed through the grass toward the structures. Oshino had said to place the talisman on the main hall, but I wasn't sure where exactly it needed to go… Inside, or could I just put it on the door? I would say that Oshino's lack of directions was at fault for my ignorance, but then, his directions were always lacking. Maybe he was trying to tell me to think for myself.

Anyway, I decided to take a look at the edifices, and as I did, I thought again about the girl we'd passed earlier. I didn't know why, but she bothered me… No, it wasn't that.

It was like I'd seen her.

Like I'd met her.

But more immediately—I *felt* something about her.

Not that I knew what that something was.

"I do feel like I've met her before, though… Where was it? It's not like I get to know middle schoolers often…"

My little sisters were one thing, but…

My little sisters?

"Hm…I wonder."

I ended up placing the talisman on the door of a building that I took to be the main one. Actually, I felt like it might collapse in on itself if I opened the door, so you could say I had no other choice.

I gently walked away and returned to the gate. Kanbaru hadn't returned yet. I thought about pulling out my phone…but realized that she'd never told me her number. And now that I thought about it, I hadn't given her mine, either.

That cell phone of hers was useless after all.

"Heyyy, Kanbaru—!"

And so I ended up yelling out loud.

But there was no reply.

"Kanbaru!"

I tried yelling in an even louder voice—but the result was the same.

I suddenly felt anxious.

She couldn't not have heard my voice if she were around. While Senjogahara might, Kanbaru of all people would never leave me and head back home without a word. Losing sight of someone in a place like this could only mean—

"Kanbaru!"

I started to run, confused.

She said she wasn't feeling well. Maybe she collapsed while looking for a place to eat… Was that what it was? Worst-case scenarios crossed my mind. How would I deal with the situation then—what would be the right course of action? If something happened to her, I'd never be able to look Senjogahara in the eyes again.

But fortunately, no worst-case scenario came to pass in any form. Running around the shrine grounds, I was finally able to find her, facing away from me.

The lunchboxes were on the ground by her side.

She looked befuddled—and stood completely still.

"Kanbaru!" I said to her, placing my hand on her shoulder.

"Hyeek!" A jolt shook her, and she turned around. "O-Oh… It's just you."

"What a warm greeting."

"Ah…I'm sorry. What an unthinkable thing to say to someone I'm greatly indebted to. I was just so surprised… You suddenly grabbed my flesh, after all."

"'Flesh'? Come on."

Her shoulder.

"Allow me to make up for my faux pas with my body," she said. "I might pretend to resist a little, but it's all a performance to make the scene more exciting, okay?"

"Good, you seem to be in a normal state of mind if you're able to prattle on like that. I'm relieved. Yeah, I'm fully aware that you're saying that to be ridiculous. So enough of that. You really do shriek in a cute way, you know."

Her face—was still pale.

In fact, she looked even worse.

It didn't seem like the right time to be poking fun at her unexpected shriek.

"What's up, are you okay? If you're feeling that bad—yeah, if I cleaned it up a bit, you could probably lie down on the porch of the main shrine back there. Let's do that, I can carry you there on my back. If you're worried about how sanitary it might be, I could lay down my jacket—"

"No…that's not it." Kanbaru pointed—directly ahead. "Look at that…"

"Huh?"

I did as she said and looked in the direction she pointed.

At the forest a bit past the shrine grounds.

She pointed at a single thick tree.

At the base of that tree—was a snake chopped into pieces.

A snake, slain, cut into five—its long, winding, squirming body, chopped.

Into five.

Slain.

But its head looked alive.

Its tongue flicking and its mouth open wide.

It was moaning in agony.

Or so—it looked.

"………!"

I was struck silent by the sight—

And I suddenly remembered the kid's name.

The girl we'd passed.

Right.

The girl's name was—Nadeko Sengoku.

003

"This one—and then this one, I guess. Oh, that book might not be very useful. My apologies to whoever wrote it, but all it really does is tell you to memorize things. This book should be better if you're aiming for efficiency," Tsubasa Hanekawa said—pulling one book after another off the shelves and handing them to me.

One, two, three, four, and five.

The location—a big-box bookseller not far from Naoetsu High.

Monday, June twelfth.

After school.

Hanekawa, class president, and I, class vice president, headed to a bookstore together on the way home from meeting and preparing for the culture festival, which loomed later in the week on Friday and Saturday. Well, it was more like I'd asked Hanekawa and she agreed to come with me.

Braids, glasses.

A class president among class presidents.

Tsubasa Hanekawa, the ultimate model student.

"Sorry, Hanekawa...but I'm about to go over my budget."

"Huh? What's your budget?"

"Ten thousand yen. I have a little more back at home, but that's all I have in my wallet."

"Oh. Yeah, study-aids are fairly expensive. You can't complain when you consider what's in them, of course. Okay, then I'll take cost-effectiveness into consideration on top of the positives and negatives. So let's return this book for…this one instead."

Tsubasa Hanekawa—

Another person who had become involved with an aberration. But perhaps she needed to be placed in a different category from me, Kanbaru, and even Senjogahara—the reason being that she had no recollection of her involvement. She'd forgotten every last bit of that nightmare of a Golden Week that rivaled even my personal hell of a spring break.

But I remembered.

For me, a demon.

For Kanbaru, a monkey.

For Senjogahara, a crab.

And for Hanekawa—a cat.

"But," Hanekawa said abruptly, "it makes me kind of happy."

"…What does?"

"Being asked by you to help pick out study-aids. It's like maybe all my efforts didn't go to waste if you're going to take school seriously."

"………"

No.

Her efforts didn't have much to do with it.

She did force me to become class vice president in a rehabilitation attempt, having mistaken me for a delinquent…

She could be off, or more like a runaway train.

"Er, I'm not sure if I'm taking school seriously," I disabused her. "It's just that I should start thinking about what to do after graduation."

"After graduation?"

"Maybe I should say college? Senjogahara and I were talking about it the other day. And I heard what school she was trying to get into…"

"Ah. Senjogahara wanted to get into the local national university, right? She'll be admitted on a recommendation."

"…You know everything, don't you."

"Not everything. I just know what I know."

It was the same back-and-forth as always.

Actually, Hanekawa had taken an interest in Senjogahara before

I ever did, so maybe, as the class president, it was natural for her to know that much. Come to think of it, Senjogahara didn't seem to hate Hanekawa too badly for her excessive fussing. Inviting Hanekawa to the birthday party I was currently planning for Senjogahara probably wouldn't earn her full wrath.

But, having a girlfriend who might get angry that I planned a birthday party for her…

"So, Araragi. Are you actually trying to get into the same university as her?"

"Don't tell her yet, okay? I don't want to get her hopes up in some weird way." I hid my embarrassment—or not exactly, but still flipped through a random study-aid within my reach. "Actually, I feel like she'd say something standoffish to me."

"Brutal… Aren't you two boyfriend and girlfriend?"

"Well yes, but. It's like she believes that good fences make good strangers…"

"Huh? Oh, I get it. A gag based on 'good fences make good neighbors'? Ahaha, you're funny, Araragi."

"Don't go around explaining people's jokes!"

And don't call it a gag.

And don't call me funny.

"Ahaha, Araragi! You must have been thinking that one up from the moment you said, 'I feel like she'd say something standoffish to me'! It would've been easy to tell that I'd reply, 'Aren't you two boyfriend and girlfriend?' Oh, you can be so elaborate!"

"Please, stop stripping down how I talk!"

I felt buck naked.

I put us back on track.

"It's not like I have a specific goal, but I did better on the skills test the other day than I expected. I was just trying to avoid a failing grade… It of course pales in comparison to you or Senjogahara, but I did all right thanks to studying seriously for the first time in a while."

"I forget, did you study one-on-one with her?"

"Yeah."

In case you were wondering, Senjogahara effortlessly got the seventh highest overall score while watching over this washout as he studied. It was impressive, or maybe brilliant. She was at the level where my only possible reaction was admiration.

One more fact, in case you were wondering. Tsubasa Hanekawa got the top overall score.

It went without saying.

She took first place in every subject.

Close to a perfect score, apparently.

Putting that aside, while my scores weren't worthy of being posted and ranked in any subject aside from math, they had still dramatically improved compared to all the skills tests I had taken up to that point.

They'd improved to the point that I was starting to have a little dream.

It was now June.

So if I hunkered down and studied for the next half-year—

It was enough to make me think along those lines.

"With Senjogahara tutoring me, I felt like I understood how to study for the first time in a while… It reminded me of how it used to feel in middle school. I'd given up on that kind of thing at some point during my first year here."

"Huh… I think that's a good thing. I do think that wanting to go to the same university as your girlfriend is a bit impure as far as motives go, but the doors to scholarship are always open. Yes, in that case, I think I'll do everything I can to help you, too."

"………"

Being educated by Senjogahara was scary, but education-by-Hanekawa was a pretty frightening thought, too…

Not that I told her that.

In fact, no matter how I looked at it, I needed Tsubasa Hanekawa's help if I wanted to get into college.

"So," I asked her, "if I can get a good idea of where I stand, I might start going to a test-prep school starting summer break. Do you know of any good ones?"

"Hmm. I can't say that I do. I've never gone to a cram school or anything."

"I see…"

Damned genius.

"But I'll ask my friends."

"You really know how to look out for people, you know that? I appreciate it. Of course, while I may not be able to get in this year, if I plan my studies with the understanding that I'll take a year off after high school, I think I can do it."

"Why are you setting your sights so low before you've even started? If you're going to do this, try getting in on your first attempt… And when are you thinking of telling Senjogahara?"

"Again, once I have a good idea of where I stand…I guess? I know I'll need her help, too. It sounds like the national university Senjogahara is trying to get into offers various exam types, so I could choose a set that focuses as much as possible on math…"

"Makes sense." Hanekawa handed another study-aid to me. "Okay. That's ten thousand yen on the dot."

"…What? No way. You found a combination that costs exactly that much? You can really pull off a trick like that?"

"It's just addition, you know."

"………"

It was just addition, sure… But these were mostly four-digit numbers, in her head, while having a conversation… I'd thought math was my strong suit… It seemed I couldn't hope to compare to Hanekawa even when it came to arithmetic.

The thought sapped my motivation a little, or put a dent in me…

I was feeling discouraged from the very start.

In other words, I'd have to spend half a year busting my ass and in the throes of an immeasurable inferiority complex toward Hitagi Senjogahara and Tsubasa Hanekawa…

Well.

I just had to bust my ass.

"Incidentally, Araragi."

"Why so formal all of a sudden?"

"Tell me more about what you said earlier. You found the corpse of a snake cut into five at the overgrown ruins of a shrine—what happened then?"

"Huh? Oh, that."

I'd told her about it after school while we were getting ready for the culture festival. I'd only meant to update her on Oshino, but it had happened only yesterday. I couldn't stop myself from talking about it given how fresh it was in my mind. I didn't go into any detail because hearing about the cruel deaths of small animals could only be unpleasant, but it seemed to have grabbed Hanekawa's attention.

"Nothing, really. Kanbaru and I did at least dig a hole for the snake and bury it…but when we wandered around the area after that, there were dead snakes all over the place."

"Dead—all over the place?"

"Yeah. Chopped-up snakes all over the place."

Several of them.

And then I stopped counting.

I gave up—on burying them, too.

Kanbaru had looked legitimately sick.

"So we ended up going straight down the mountain… And then we ate the lunch that Kanbaru made at a nearby park. I was surprised at just how good it was, but when I asked, she told me that her grandma helped her make them. Actually, the other way around. It was more like she helped her grandma make them. When I asked her what exactly she did, it was 'I got the knives ready' and 'I boiled some water' and 'I watched to make sure the pot didn't boil over, but it did.' Wanting to be a good cook when she's already so athletic is a bit greedy, huh?"

"That might be true. But it's too bad about Kanbaru. She'd be right in the middle of a tournament right now if not for her arm injury."

"……"

Oh, right.

I was keeping that part a secret.

I'd nearly slipped up and run my mouth.

The only people at Naoetsu High who knew the truth behind Suruga Kanbaru's retirement were me and Senjogahara. No one would be added to that list, and that seemed perfectly fine.

The funny thing was that once we ate lunch, Kanbaru really did feel better again. In typical born-athlete form, her body seemed to be unusually efficient at absorbing energy.

"Well, Araragi… That must have been a handful."

"Yeah. Killing snakes that way seemed like a ritual or something and made me think. Kind of gave me the chills, it's a very uncool thing to do. Plus the place is an abandoned shrine, you know? Oh, by the way, did you know there was a shrine there?"

"Yup." Hanekawa nodded briskly, as if to say, of course she did. "Kita-Shirahebi Shrine, right?"

"Kita-Shirahebi?" North Whitesnake Shrine—

"Yes, I guess they must have worshiped a snake god there. I'm not that familiar with it, though. I just happen to know as a local."

"I feel like it's precisely the kind of place you don't know as a local… Plus, you already seem plenty familiar with it, but huh… Killing snakes in a spot where they were once worshiped… It really does seem like a kind of ritual to me. Maybe I should…report it to Oshino?"

An aberration.

I hoped I was making too much of it.

But—there was the bit about Sengoku, too.

Nadeko Sengoku.

"………"

…I didn't want the conversation going in this direction.

Hanekawa had forgotten her involvement with an aberration. She remembers being helped by Oshino, at least, but the part where she was charmed by a cat and *everything else that followed*—she has no memory of it. That isn't the only reason, but I don't want Hanekawa to have much to do with aberrations. She doesn't need to know about what happened with Senjogahara, or Kanbaru, or Hachikuji—not now, not later.

That's how I see it.

Because she's a cool person.

My concerns turned out to be extraneous here, though.

"But you know, Araragi, that's not what I wanted to talk about. I meant that dealing with Kanbaru must have been a handful."

"……"

If anything.

It seemed like I needed to be worrying about myself.

"Dealing. With. Kanbaru," she punctuated her words. "Must have been a handful, I'm asking."

She was grinning.

Her smiling face was actually scarier than anything...

"O-Oh... Yeah, she did suddenly start feeling unwell. I wondered what it could be, but...it was nothing, fortunately."

"That's not what I'm talking about," Hanekawa said in a serious tone. Well, she said just about everything in a serious tone, but especially this time. "Don't you think it's a problem being a little too friendly with your girlfriend's junior? I think it's fine for you to be somewhat friendly with her since you were the one who helped them make up, but you shouldn't be linking arms, should you?"

"What was I supposed to do? She's a friendly girl."

"Do you think that passes as an excuse?"

"Well..."

It didn't, did it.

No matter how you looked at it.

"Part of me can understand," she said. "I suppose this must be the first time you have a junior who looks up to you. You didn't have any extracurriculars in middle school either and went straight home then, too, right? It's nice to have a cute little junior. Or could it have simply been that you enjoyed how Kanbaru's breast felt? You perv."

"Ngkk..."

I found it vaguely difficult to argue.

She was wrong, but even if I told her that, there was no way to keep it from sounding like a lie.

Hanekawa continued, "I'm sure Kanbaru is feeling insecure to some degree because of her retirement, but isn't that where you should jump in and set the record straight?"

"Uhhm..."

"Wouldn't it be a shame if the Valhalla Duo split up over you when you helped bring them back together?"

"Yeah, that's true."

Weak-willed.

Feeble me.

"But in that sense," observed Hanekawa, "I guess Kanbaru doesn't have much experience with men, either. This is an odd way to put it, but maybe being treated like a star for so long deprived her of those kinds of opportunities."

"Probably."

Plus, she was a sapphist.

Plus, she was in love with Senjogahara.

Those were secrets, too.

"And you don't seem too good at communicating about this stuff, either," the class president went on. "While that's sometimes a valid excuse, it isn't always."

"I dunno. Senjogahara keeps telling me to take good care of Kanbaru. 'I won't overlook any rudeness toward my junior,' and that kind of thing. It makes me wonder who really has the power here. Like, if this is a love triangle, it's one hell of an isosceles. It even sounds like Kanbaru was told by Senjogahara to have me pamper her."

Right.

What didn't make sense here was Senjogahara's psychology.

What on earth was she thinking?

"Well, okay. Couldn't it be like this?" Hanekawa gently reached for my head with both of her hands. They sandwiched it and stayed there. My own hands were full carrying a pile of study-aids so I couldn't swat hers away.

"Huh? Wait, what?"

"Okay, go ahead."

Hanekawa used her hands to adjust the angle of my head and pointed it directly toward her own upturned face. Our eyes met. Or so I thought, but Hanekawa's were shut. Behind her glasses were two closed eyes, and her eyelashes seemed to be trembling. Her lips, sealed too, naturally appeared to convey a message—

"Huh? Huh? Huh?"

Wh-What was going on here?

Or rather, where was this going?

Hanekawa was the class president and someone I was indebted to, just as much as, no, even more than I was to Oshino—

B-But did I need to do something here?

She did tell me to go ahead…

Those glasses would get in the way a little, but…wait.

Wasn't the right move here to not do anything?!

"…Like that, I guess?"

Her eyes blinked open.

Hanekawa let go.

A mischievous grin spread across her face.

"Araragi, were you about a second away?"

"N-No… What're you saying?"

I admit, my voice was obviously cracking.

What was *I* saying?

"See. Weak-willed, feeble you."

"………"

Coming from someone else, those words really struck me.

Not only that, I couldn't deny it.

I wouldn't say a second away, but it was the undeniable truth that I'd wavered.

"You're kind to everyone, right, Araragi? I think that when Senjogahara sees that side of you, it makes her pretty insecure. You're the only one for her—but to take it to an extreme, it's like you'd be fine with anyone."

"…Insecure?"

Was she that sentimental of a person?

Then again, it was to help get rid of that part of her that I'd acted as a mediator between her and Kanbaru. So was Senjogahara, in turn, trying to help get rid of that part of me? No, it didn't make sense. I didn't see how that could possibly follow.

"You're quick to go with the flow, and you don't want to hurt people. Being kind is usually a good thing, of course, but it doesn't always serve the people around you. Senjogahara might not want you to become too friendly with Kanbaru, you know? But she could never tell you not to befriend her and might even end up saying the opposite—am I wrong? Like she's fine if you're friends, she wants you to be friends, in fact, but wants you to draw a clear line… Maybe Senjogahara wants you to choose her after you've compared her to Kanbaru."

"What the hell? You're not making any sense."

"Don't you think Senjogahara is in a dilemma of her own? You're very important to her as her boyfriend, and Kanbaru is very important to her as her junior."

"Uhh."

In addition, Kanbaru was a sapphist.

And Senjogahara already knew that.

Our relationships were pretty complicated when you took that into account.

"And Senjogahara is a tsundere," Hanekawa said as if to wrap up our conversation. "I don't think you should ever try to understand her actions in a simplistic way. You need to always be looking for the reasons behind them. If Senjogahara is important to you, I don't think you should let your heart waver over a tiny little temptation. It really is a little irresponsible to be kind to everyone."

"Yeah… Don't worry, that part has hit home."

Her live-fire exercise had worked.

I felt like I now knew for sure how flimsy I was.

…Though I did wonder about concluding our conversation with "And she's a tsundere"… Wait, so Hanekawa knew what that word meant…

She really did know everything.

Maybe she was even starting to see through Senjogahara's feline subterfuge.

Cats were Hanekawa's specialty, after all.

"Speaking of which," I asked her, "where were you planning on going to university? Tokyo, I guess? Or do students who get nationwide top scores on practice tests like you end up going overseas?"

"Huh? I'm not going to college, okay?"

"………Wha?"

Where did that bombshell come from.

She'd honestly caught me by surprise.

"You're not…going to college?"

"Nope."
"Is it a money problem? But this is you we're talking about, I'm sure you can get a scholarship…"
Schools would be scrambling to grab her as their first draft pick.
I could even see her getting paid to go to school.
"It's not like that. There isn't really anything I'd want to study in college, anyway… Yeah, I guess I could tell you, Araragi. I'm going to go on a little journey after I graduate."
"A-A journey?"
"I want to spend two years or so seeing the world. There are a lot of World Heritage sights you need to visit now, or they might disappear. There are times when I find myself relying on nothing but knowledge, so I think I should go out and experience more things. And if I do want to go to college, I can afterwards, and it won't be too late."
"……"
It was the kind of idea that floats into your head when you're daydreaming.
But that wasn't what it seemed to be…
Hanekawa didn't have the grades of a student who needed an escape from the harsh realities of the struggle to get into a good school. You could tell her that entrance exams were tomorrow and it wouldn't matter, she had the chops to handle it unassumingly. You could spring the exams on her at that very moment and she'd probably waltz her way into any school you cared to name. That's who I was dealing with, which meant these travel plans of hers must have been fairly worked out, to the point that they weren't going to change…
"Keep it a secret for now from our teachers and others, okay? I think they might be surprised if they heard."
"Yeah…I'll bet."
"My plan is to watch and wait for the right time to bring it up."
"I see… Well, I have a feeling that no matter when you bring it up, there's going to be a little more than a surprised commotion…"
It would be total pandemonium, I was sure.
If the top student at a prep school made that kind of decision, leaving behind a precedent, it could even affect the institution's legacy. This

was Hanekawa, someone they held greater than great expectations of. She had to know all of this full well…

"Please don't tell," she requested. "In exchange, this time around, I'll keep everything about Kanbaru a secret from Senjogahara."

"Hey, I don't feel like I've done anything particularly questionable…"

"And neither have I. But, you know?"

"Yeah. I get it."

Hmph.

Could Oshino—have influenced her?

Hanekawa treated that rolling stone with the utmost respect. You couldn't discount his influence, at the very least. If that were the case, it felt like Oshino had a lot of blood on his hands… What a meddlesome bastard.

So…that's how it was. I was convinced that Hanekawa would continue to be some kind of class president even after she graduated from high school, that the gods had decided her destiny was to be a class president, but she wouldn't be a class president or anything if she went off on a journey by herself.

I kind of felt like sighing.

Things never went smoothly.

I, a washout, was deciding this late in the game to try to go to college.

Tsubasa Hanekawa, a model student, aspired to become an outsider.

Suruga Kanbaru had retired from the basketball team early.

Mayoi Hachikuji couldn't go back to the way things were, either.

The only one who could go back was—

Hitagi Senjogahara.

"…Ow!"

Then.

Hanekawa suddenly placed her right hand against her head.

As if to support it.

"Hm? What's the matter?" I asked.

"No, it's just—I've got a headache."

"A headache?"

I recalled how Kanbaru had suddenly started to feel unwell the day before at the shrine, and I instantly began to fret. But Hanekawa soon raised her head.

"Oh, I'm fine, I'm fine. They come now and then, I started getting them a little while back. My head starts to hurt out of nowhere."

"Whoa, hold on… That doesn't sound fine at all."

"Hmm. But it gets better right away. I don't know what causes it, though… Maybe it's because I've been so busy preparing for the culture festival lately that I've slacked on my studies."

"You get headaches when you skip out on studying?"

How exactly did her body work?

Was she wearing some ring on her head like Monkey in *Journey to the West*?

She deserved to be in the diligence hall of fame.

Down to her marrow.

"Do you want me to walk you home?" I offered.

"No, it's fine. My home—"

"Oh…right."

A blunder.

I shouldn't have said that.

"Sorry, I'm going to head back," she announced. "You stay here a little longer and pick out study-aids. The ones I gave you are my suggestions, but personal preference ends up playing a big role in that kind of thing."

"Okay. See you…"

"Yup."

With that, Hanekawa left the bookstore like she was fleeing.

Maybe I should have walked her back until she was in the general area of her home anyway—but she was pretty headstrong, or rather, she didn't like the idea of showing weakness to others. Since she said she was fine, I shouldn't be a busybody.

But.

A headache…

It made me wonder a little.

For Hanekawa, a headache meant…

"........"

Hanekawa knew nothing about Senjogahara's crab, Hachikuji's snail, or Kanbaru's monkey, nor anything about her own cat, at this point—

But she did know about my demon.

Not that it meant anything.

But nothing could change the fact that I owed a debt of gratitude to Hanekawa. It wasn't simply over my aberration—I couldn't begin to tell you just how often her words had saved me.

Like today.

That was why I always wanted to help her out in some way...

Sigh.

I'd have loved to be a busybody.

"...Might as well check out some of the other sections."

Though I heeded Hanekawa's advice and continued to flip through study-aids, I just wasn't used to it, and they all looked the same to me. I decided to go ahead and buy the ones she'd picked out (It ended up being six books in total. I did take the time to add up the prices, which did come out to ten thousand yen on the dot. Wow) and left the study-aids section. I was at my budget exactly so I couldn't buy anything else, but the great thing about books is that it doesn't cost a thing to peruse them. I'd look stupid checking out the latest manga with my hands full of study-aids, but on the other hand, I felt smarter just carrying them around, so maybe spending some time there wasn't such a bad idea... Actually, I was already thinking stupid...

"...Hm?"

While I didn't have a destination yet, I decided to start moving—and that's when I froze. Having seen something impossible, I couldn't help it. I nearly dropped all the study-aids I was carrying.

No.

It wasn't exactly impossible.

The chances of two people living in the same town encountering each other at the largest bookstore in town couldn't be particularly low—at least, it was far more likely than passing by each other on a path that you could easily miss, on stairs that led to a deserted shrine.

And even the probability of that wasn't zero.

So—if they occurred on consecutive days.

It wasn't a mystery.

"...Sengoku."

There in front of the sorcery and occult shelves, located just next to the study-aid section, and reading a thick book, was Nadeko Sengoku—my little sister's old friend, Nadeko Sengoku.

She was wholly focused on reading the book—so she hadn't noticed me. It's not as if I could pass directly in front of her, so I could only see her in profile, but...I could tell it was her. Sengoku, who'd come to my home to play when she was in grade school...or who'd been brought to my home to play. It was an unusual name, Nadeko Sengoku, so I'd remembered it in full. Especially the name "Nadeko." Anyone else whose name was written with those characters would be named "Nadeshiko," and even as a grade school kid, I'd wondered where that one syllable had gone...

She was the same age as my youngest sister.

That meant—she was now in the second year of middle school.

I couldn't tell because she wasn't wearing her uniform, but she probably went to the public middle school that I'd graduated from. Few kids all the way out where I lived chose to go to private school like my little sisters did.

"........."

I remembered Sengoku.

But did she remember me?

She looked surprised when we passed each other the day before—but that could just have been the sight of people other than her climbing up that mountain. Your friend's older brother isn't normally the kind of person you remember...which would make saying something to her odd.

But.

Snakes.

Yes, snakes—

As I was thinking, Sengoku returned the book she was reading to its shelf and began to walk. I promptly hid myself so as not to be spotted.

There wasn't any particular reason for me to hide and I'd only done so reflexively, but I missed any chance I might have had to call out to her. I took a detour, using the bookshelves as walls, made sure she was gone, and stepped over to where she'd been standing until moments earlier.

I wanted to know what book she'd been reading.

I looked at its title.

"Hold on… This is—"

The book—was a hardcover priced at twelve thousand yen.

Not a book a middle schooler could buy. Even a high school kid like me couldn't purchase it with the cash I had on hand. I wouldn't be able to buy any of the study-aids.

That must have been why she contented herself with reading it in the aisles.

But—more than that.

The issue was the book's title.

I left the section in the back of the store to look around for Sengoku, but she was already nowhere to be found. Maybe she was hiding somewhere in another section, but it seemed more likely that she had exited the store. And those clothes she was wearing…

Long sleeves, long pants.

A hat pulled far down on her head, and a bag around her waist.

If my intuition was right…then yes.

"Damn… Give me a break."

I decided to go to the cash register and pay for the time being. There was a long line of shoppers waiting, but I toughed it out. Nothing good could come from getting flustered and rushing. I needed to start by calming myself down. Still unsure what to do, I placed a ten-thousand-yen bill on the cashier's tray. The clerk seemed surprised that my total came out to ten thousand yen on the dot, but what did I care. The honor didn't belong to me.

Hmm.

She was an old acquaintance…but me alone might not do.

There's only so much you can do on your own.

I had to seek someone's assistance…and the circumstances led me to just one person. Someone who might be particularly suited to this case… Hanekawa had just warned me, but I couldn't help it.

With a bag filled with study-aids in my left hand, I took out my cell phone as soon as I left the store and called the number I'd learned after we were done the day before. I was reminded again of how nervous I felt about calling a new number for the first time, just like two days ago when I'd called her house.

The phone rang about five times.

"This is Suruga Kanbaru."

No sooner than it connected, she answered with her full name. The oddly uncommon act surprised me a little.

"Suruga Kanbaru. My special move is double jumping."

"Liar. No human can do that."

"Hm? Judging by that voice and the quipping, I'd say it's my dear senior Araragi."

"You're right, but…"

That voice and the quipping? That's how she figured it out?

I'd given her my number the day before, too. Hadn't she put it into her contacts list? Now, that was sad… Well, never mind, she just hadn't mastered using a cell phone. She didn't seem too good with tech.

"If you have some time, Kanbaru, there was something I wanted you to help me with… What are you doing right now?"

"Heheh," Kanbaru laughed daringly for some reason. "Whether I have time or not, I'll go anywhere you ask me to, no matter how far. I don't even need a reason, just give me your location and I'll be there right away."

"No, putting all that aside… If you're not free, you don't need to force yourself. I dragged you along with me just yesterday, so I'm already feeling bad. Where are you right now, and what were you doing?"

"Umm…if you must know, well…"

"That's a pretty half-hearted reply. So you're busy? In that case—"

"No, uh…yes," Kanbaru said as if she'd made up her mind. "I can't keep any secrets from you. I'm in my room at my home right now reading dirty books and indulging in dirty fantasies."

"………"

I shouldn't have been so insistent.

Now I felt like a sexual harasser.

"Oh, but don't get me wrong," she cautioned. "They might be dirty books, but it's all boys' love."

"Please, why couldn't you at least let me get that part wrong!"

"New releases came out today, you see, and including ones I couldn't buy since we were in the middle of tests, I got around twenty."

"Huh… Not one for paring down your selections?"

"Tsk tsk tsk. You ought to know that I love every pairing under the sun."

"Oh, shut up!"

So Kanbaru had been at this same bookstore after school… It was probably the only one in the neighborhood big enough to have a dedicated boys' love corner. But that meant our town really was tiny… If my life were a dating simulator, new flags would be popping up all the time.

"In other words, you're not busy."

"I guess I couldn't argue if you put it that way. Thinking about how you and Mister Oshino would work together doesn't exactly make me busy."

"That's what you meant by 'dirty fantasies'?!"

"So where do you need me to go?"

"Don't change the topic, no, wait, don't put us back on topic! You'd better tell me, Kanbaru, who's on top and who's on bottom?! I'll never forgive you if you say I'm on bottom!"

It was a stupid conversation.

Talking to her was always like this.

"Good grief, Kanbaru. It'd be nice to have an intelligent conversation with you someday… You're supposed to be pretty smart, right?"

"Yeah. My grades are definately good."

"From the way you spelled that, though…"

Anyway, I said.

Even as we entertained our idiotic conversation, Sengoku was getting farther and farther away from the store… Well, she could go as far away as she wanted—I knew where she would end up.

She was in street clothes.

Her sense of fashion wasn't refined, but that wasn't the point.

The point—was her long sleeves and long pants.

As if she was about to head to the mountains.

"The shrine we went to yesterday," I said. "We'll meet on the sidewalk by the stairs that lead up there. Um, location-wise—you must be closer, but I should get there first since I'm on a bike. I'll wait for you there."

"Really? Do you think I'm going to make you wait on me two days in a row? Your faith in me must be at rock bottom. I have my pride, and I'm not going to let a comment like that go unanswered. I'll use this opportunity to clear my name and restore my honor. I absolutely will get there first."

"I don't even know how to respond to your weird sense of pride… but either way, get there as soon as you can. Oh, and don't forget. Long sleeves and long pants."

I was on the way back from school, so I was still in my uniform. We had just changed to our summer attire, which meant I was wearing a short-sleeved button-down, but there was nothing I could do about that now. I was wearing slacks for pants, so good enough. An insect or snake bite wouldn't be a big deal for me anyway—those vampiric "residual effects," once again.

"Okay. Your wish is my command."

"All right, see you," I said and hung up, circling behind the bookstore to the bike parking and unlocking my bicycle. More than ten minutes had passed since Sengoku left the store… I didn't know how she was getting there, but the day before, I hadn't seen any bicycle that might be hers near where those stairs began. She most likely walked… Well, either way, if she was heading to that shrine, I wouldn't catch up with her.

Now that I thought about it, Kanbaru really didn't ask me why I was summoning her…

How frighteningly loyal.

Senjogahara was obviously my superior in Kanbaru's chain of command, but being served so assiduously by someone as high-status as Suruga Kanbaru made me feel, to be honest, more scared than happy…

There didn't seem to be any way of ruining her image of me, though, which actually made me want to start acting like the ideal senior around her and not betray her overblown expectations.

Well—it didn't seem like a bad thing.

"I wonder what Senjogahara was like."

In middle school—during the Valhalla Duo's honeymoon phase, what had it been like between them?

As I was thinking that, I reached my destination.

The entrance to the shrine on the nameless mountain.

I got there fast. That's a bike for you.

Or so I thought, but Kanbaru was already there.

"........."

Were there wheels on her feet or something?

There was a limit to being fleet-footed... She might have no trouble passing the average scooter and leaving it in the dust. I doubted that the automobile would have ever been invented if all of mankind could run as fast as her. If she'd gotten ready to go right after I hung up... Well, no, she'd changed into long sleeves and long pants like I'd told her (plus, having learned from the day before, she wore unripped pants and wasn't showing her navel)...

"Uh-uh," she said, "it didn't take much time at all for me to put these clothes on. In the summer, I'm always in my underwear at home."

"Kanbaru... I'm saying this purely out of concern for you, but you know I can't make any guarantees about your chastity if you keep fanning the flames of my earthly desires."

"I'm prepared for that."

"Well, I'm not, okay?!"

"I trust your sense of reason."

"I don't trust it myself!"

"Really? I'm surprised to hear that. Do you find girls only wearing underwear when they're at home so moé?"

"Not even if you were dressed in cat ears and a maid outfit would I find you moé!"

"I see. So if we turn that around, as long as it's not me, cat ears and a maid outfit work for you?"

"Ack, it was a trick question!"

I decided to go ahead and park my bike at least.

While I did feel somewhat guilty about parking it illegally, it wouldn't be for long. I'd beg the law's forgiveness. If it did get confiscated, I'd just resign myself to my fate. Beggars couldn't be choosers.

"Even taking that into account," I remarked, "you really are fast… You could probably make it into the Olympics or something if you really tried."

"You don't get to go to the Olympics just because you're fast… And I'm not cut out for track competitions, anyway."

"Oh, I guess not."

Senjogahara was on the track team in middle school, and they'd first met when Senjogahara heard that the basketball ace was quick and went to see Kanbaru—or something along those lines.

"From my point of view," I said, "your speed doesn't even seem human."

"Hm. If it isn't human, would that make me…amphibian?"

"Try naming an amphibian that's a fast runner!"

"You got me there."

"I mean, what do you stand to gain by comparing yourself to an amphibian?"

"It's not about gain. If you would call me that, I'd present myself as such with great joy."

"Uh oh, 'great joy'?"

"Hurry and please call me your 'lowly, filthy pet'!"

"There are actually two equally important things I have to say to that, and while I'd normally ignore them because it'd be hard to without tripping over my words along the way, I like you so much, Kanbaru, that I'm going ahead and pointing them out anyway! First of all, I wouldn't keep an amphibian as a pet, and second of all, your great joy has nothing particular to do with amphibians anymore!"

If you're curious, I'd thought of a cheetah.

Of course, they aren't animals you'd keep as pets, either.

Agh, and I even admitted to her that I liked her a lot.

Yippee, the feeling was mutual.

"Please, don't be so cold and just say it," Kanbaru pleaded. "'Lowly, filthy pet!' You have to try it out just once. I'm sure you'll understand if you do."

"Why are you acting so desperate?!"

"Urk… Why won't anyone understand? She told me no, too…"

"Even Senjogahara didn't want to?!"

Well, actually.

Of course she wouldn't want to.

Saying it was one thing, but Kanbaru feeling great joy?

"So, what do I need to do?" she asked me.

"Oh, right. This was no time to be amusing ourselves with small talk."

"Do you need me to strip?"

"Why so eager to take off your clothes?!"

"If you have to take them off for me instead, I wouldn't mind."

"We're not talking about who should perform the action! What are you, the embodiment of my middle school fantasies?!"

"I'm someone who tries to pursue a cheerful sexy."

"I don't care about your creed…"

"Okay, then let me put it this way. I'm a fairy who tries to pursue a cheerful eroticism."

"Oh my god! All you did was change 'sexy' to 'eroticism' and 'someone' to 'fairy' and you've turned what you were saying into something sublime…in no way whatsoever!"

What would it take to teach this woman that men could be sexually harassed, too? It seemed like an issue I needed to address.

"Then what do you want me to do?" she complained. "Just say it, don't hold back. I'm not a refined person, so subtlety doesn't work on me. Whenever people are roundabout, I just get esaxpera… Esapxer… Esapxer…"

"Do you have any idea how exasperating you're being right now?!"

"I'm sorry. I'm starting to get all beduffled."

"Yeah, and you're befuddling me, too!"

"So, what is it?"

"Oh—well, I'm pretty sure that up there," I pointed at the stairs, "is someone I used to know."

"Hm?"

"Do you remember that girl who passed by us as we were climbing these yesterday?"

"Yes. She was petite and cute."

"I don't know about remembering her that way..."

"To word it like you might, she was a girl with 'pretty' hips."

"I wouldn't say that!"

Well, whatever.

She was a sapphist, after all.

It made for a smoother conversation than if she didn't remember her at all.

"I'd thought I'd seen her somewhere before...but I only remembered later. While I wasn't a hundred percent certain yesterday, after I saw her again today at the bookstore, I knew for sure. She's an old friend of my youngest sister's."

"Really, now?" Kanbaru seemed taken aback. "What a coincidence... I'm shocked."

"Mm-hm. I was surprised, too."

"Mm-hm. I haven't been this surprised since I woke up this morning and saw that my alarm clock had stopped."

"That's awfully recent! And that's not much of a surprise at all! It's way too commonplace!"

"Hmm. Okay, then allow me to correct myself. Uh, I haven't been this surprised since the Cambrian explosion."

"Now you've gone too far back, and this isn't that amazing! Don't bring up the greatest event in Earth's history for a coincidence like running into an old acquaintance in a small town! I'm even beginning to feel like it wasn't such a big surprise after all now that I really think about it!"

"You can be so demanding. So—you're saying that girl is here again today?"

"Right. Probably."

Judging by her reaction, even Kanbaru's quick feet hadn't managed to get her to the stairs before Sengoku. Of course—while I could be somewhat certain that Sengoku had come straight to where we were after leaving the bookstore, it was ultimately just my guess. If she wasn't here, she wasn't here, and that'd be the best outcome of all.

But—the book that Sengoku was reading at the bookstore.

That was the problem.

"The book she was reading?" asked Kanbaru.

"Yeah. Well, I can tell you more about it later. Anyway, about what I wanted to ask you—I may have known this girl in the past, but it's still awkward for me to speak to her. Actually, I don't even know if she remembers me, and it might look like I'm using some weird pick-up move on her—the defensive instincts of a freshly pubescent girl can be a scary thing."

"You say that like you speak from experience."

"Well, I won't deny that."

All sorts of people have told me that I'm kind to everyone, but there was a price: I'd gone through some bad experiences because of it. Not that I felt like my efforts were a waste, but it didn't feel great when I ended up not being able to help someone I might have otherwise.

"On that note, Kanbaru. You must be good with girls younger than you. You're the biggest star at our school, after all."

"That's not true anymore, and I don't feel like it ever was, but I see what you're getting at. You're an excellent judge of people. I really am good with younger girls."

"I thought as much. I knew you were the right person to call."

While not on Hanekawa's level, Kanbaru did seem to look after others.

She'd been captain of her team in both middle school and high school.

In that sense, she was the complete opposite of the way Senjogahara was now… Or maybe I should say that Kanbaru succeeded the middle-school Senjogahara.

"To be specific, count on me," Kanbaru boasted, "to seduce any girl younger than me in ten seconds, tops."

"Bringing you here was the biggest mistake of my life!"

I didn't need that kind of goodness!

I wasn't here to ruin a girl's life!

"Don't tell me that you saw the basketball team as nothing more than a personal harem..."

"I wouldn't go that far."

"How far would you go?!"

"I'd take out the 'nothing more than.'"

"That barely changes anything!"

"Hm? So she's your youngest sister's friend... Which means that you have a little sister... In fact, two or more..."

".........!"

Oh no!

The sapphist now knew about my little sisters!

"Heheheh... I see, your little sisters... Heh heh heh, heh heh heh. Are they anything like you, I wonder—"

"Don't get any funny thoughts...and jeez, what is with that awful grin I doubt I've ever seen before?! Is that a smile you ought to be pointing at me, the object of that selfless devotion you pride yourself on?!"

If you're curious.

They do look like me. Both of them.

"Oh, please," scoffed Kanbaru. "I would never lay a finger on your little sisters. Yes, seducing a younger girl or two might come easier than breathing to me, but there's no reason for me to ever do such a thing—as long as you and I stay close."

"Damn you, that's a veiled threat..."

"A threat? Oh my, what a grating accusation. Such shocking words from a revered senior might cause a nervous person like me to panic and, well, who knows what I might do? Don't you think there's, oh, something else you ought to be saying to me right now?"

"G-Gah..."

It was happening...

She was absolutely being influenced by the present-day Senjogahara!

The very definition of a bad influence.

"Ah, I think my chest is feeling a little stiff from running here. I wonder if I could find someone to give me a massage."

"How do I not come out ahead in that deal?!"

"Joking aside," Kanbaru said, switching to a serious tone. "Of course I wouldn't hesitate to help since you're asking me—but you're taking into account *what happened yesterday*, aren't you?"

"Well—yes."

"*So—that's what this is.*"

"...Yeah."

"Sheesh." Kanbaru shrugged, as if she had no other choice. She raised her bandaged left arm to scratch her head—before stopping and doing so with her right hand instead. "You're kind to everyone—that's what she told me, and it seems like it's true. Sure, I learned that well enough while I was stalking you—but I get a different impression now that I see it in person."

"Kanbaru..."

"It feels so pointless to be indebted to you—that's how she put it."

"......"

"It's fine. I'm talking to myself. No, I'm talking out of turn. Okay, let's go. If we don't hurry, this girl might finish her business."

Her business.

Her business at a deserted shrine.

"Yeah...you're right."

Side by side, the two of us took the first step up the same stairs we had climbed the day before.

Today—Kanbaru wasn't holding my hand.

"Hey, Kanbaru."

"What is it?"

"Any plans post-graduation?"

"Post-graduation... Before my arm turned out like this, I thought college on a sports scholarship, but that's not going to happen now. My plan is to take entrance exams and get into a school fair and square."

"I see."

While her left arm would heal, it wouldn't until she turned twenty. Now seventeen, those three years had to seem long and gloomy to Kanbaru.

"I haven't decided on a specific school," she said, "but I'd like to go to one with a strong basketball program—so I guess a Phys Ed school."

"You're not thinking of going to the same university as Senjogahara?"

"What, is that what you're planning?"

"Actually, yeah."

But keep it a secret from Senjogahara, I said.

Yes, Kanbaru nodded.

When it came to heeding my wishes, she was my cute junior. I hated to admit it, but Hanekawa was right about this… Just having a cute junior made me happy.

"With your grades," I asked, "couldn't you try to chase after Senjogahara?"

"I don't know about that. I'm a striver, which also means my current scores are already the best I can do."

"Ah, right. But—"

"Also," added Kanbaru, "what would come of spending all my time tracing her footsteps?"

"……"

That seemed—like a real change in her mindset.

It wasn't like Kanbaru to say that…or maybe I had misjudged and underestimated her on this point. Still, wasn't the woman I met a month ago dedicated to tracing Senjogahara's footsteps?

Did something change?

Thanks to the aberration?

Aberrations—weren't all bad.

Good or bad wasn't the question to begin with.

"Well, I say that," Kanbaru continued, "but no matter what path I choose, I'd like to stay involved with both you and her even after we graduate. It'd be nice if the three of us could get together and take a commemorative photo for the final episode."

"Final episode…"

"Or maybe I gaze up at the twilight sky to see the two of you reflected there in the final episode…"

"Did you just kill off me and Senjogahara?!"

What a crappy ending.

To what sounded like a crappy story.

"So there's this girl named Hanekawa in my class."

"Hm."

"Do you know her?"

"No—I'm not aware of her."

"I guess you are in different years... But she's famous among us. She has the best grades of our whole year, after all. She hasn't given up her seat at the top a single time since she started at our school and is the very picture of a model student. Sounds like a joke character or something, doesn't she? I heard the other day that she didn't do the best just here but nationwide on a practice test once. I'm pretty sure she went to the same middle school as you and Senjogahara."

"Is that so. There are some incredible people out there..."

"But that incredible person says she's not going to college."

"...Is that so."

"She wants to go on a journey because there are a lot of things she wants to see. I don't even know what to make of that, but it did make me think, you know? Oh, and I guess this also needs to stay secret. It'd be a huge deal if the school found out."

"I understand... But yes, it does make you think. You could say that Naoetsu High, being what it is, doesn't even offer any paths apart from college—so setting out on an uncharted road without qualms is something."

"Without qualms—or with them, I don't know. But it sounded like she'd made up her mind."

It was probably because we already knew the way, having taken it once, but Kanbaru and I climbed up the stairs and reached the shrine sooner than we had the day before.

It goes without saying, but the shrine was just as desolate as yesterday.

Out in the distance—I could see the talisman I'd placed on the shrine's main hall. My eyesight was enhanced after letting Shinobu drink my blood on Saturday, and I could see everything down to the individual characters written with a red-ink brush.

It was the only difference from yesterday.

"........"

I glanced over—and Kanbaru was pale. She wasn't just moments ago, we'd been carrying on a regular conversation, but now she was visibly tired.

That was also the same as yesterday.

No—she looked worse.

It—wasn't from climbing the stairs.

She wasn't feeling ill.

It happened *the moment we entered the grounds—the moment we passed through the gate.*

"...Hey, Kanbaru."

"I'm fine. Let's—just hurry."

Despite her state, Kanbaru replied firmly, encouraging me to move forward and not stand idle. She was obviously forcing herself to keep going. I started to say something but ended up doing as she said. Right now, our top priority was to attend to what we were here for.

This shrine.

It had something.

A *something* that messed with Kanbaru's body.

It was originally—a job from Oshino.

And Oshino—would never give us a simple job.

"...Sengoku!"

As soon as I spotted a girl—long sleeves, long pants, hat pulled far down, bag around her waist—crouching in front of a large rock across the grounds, my reaction was to shout her name. So much for bringing Kanbaru all the way here.

But I couldn't stop myself from shouting.

In Sengoku's left hand, fingers pinched around the neck, was a snake.

In Sengoku's right hand, a chisel.

Pressed against the rock—

The snake was still alive.

However—it was about to get killed any moment now.

"Stop it, Sengoku!"

"Ah..."

Sengoku—looked at me.

Using the chisel to push the brim of her cap, worn low over her eyes, back up.

Nadeko Sengoku—slowly looked at me.

"Big Brother Koyomi..."

You.

You'd still call me that—

The thought ran through my head as if I were some dark hero who once walked the line until a lapse in judgment derailed him, who, after battling through trials and hardships that you do not relate or sit through without tears, now sat among the top echelons of a shadowy organization and committed an endless chain of unspeakable, unwatchable atrocities, in the midst of which a comrade from bygone days while he was still on the side of justice appears and calls him, by his old name.

004

"A *Jagirinawa*."

After pondering for a while, so began Oshino—in a frightfully weighty voice, almost as if he detested the name. He tended to speak in a flippant, or even snide way, and this wasn't a tone you often heard him take.

"The only thing it could be is a Jagirinawa. That's all it could be, and I can state that for a fact. Though it's sometimes called a *jakiri*, a *janawa*, a *hebikiri-nawa*—snake cutting, snake rope, snake-cutting rope—or even just *kuchi-nawa*."

"A 'mouth rope'? So just one way to say 'snake'?"

"Right. Snake," Oshino repeated.

Snake.

The general term for reptiles in Class Reptilia, Order Squamata, Suborder Serpentes.

Noted for their long, thin, cylindrical bodies covered in scales.

They have hundreds of vertebrae and are able to squirm about freely.

So it went demon, cat, crab, snail, monkey—and now snake.

Putting aside the demon as a special case—snakes felt like they had the worst reputation of the bunch. They felt like such an ominous symbol. Cats, crabs, snails, and monkeys had nothing on them when it came to spookiness.

Ha hah, Oshino laughed as always in his falsely carefree way, forcing himself to ditch the gloomy tone.

"Well—you're not wrong to have that impression, Araragi. Since long ago, snakes have been seen as *that sort of thing*. There are a ton of snake-related aberrations, after all. They're carnivores, I guess, and we do have sayings like 'a snake in the grass.' Plus, some of them have lethal poisons…so I suppose you can't blame people for feeling that way. In the way of venomous snakes, here in Japan we have pit vipers, tiger keelbacks, habus. But then on the other hand, some see snakes as holy, or at least there's a tradition of worshiping serpent gods—it's common to nearly every region in the world. A symbol both holy and wicked—that's the snake."

"And that shrine—it was for worshiping a snake god too, wasn't it?"

"Huh? Wait, why do you know that? I kept it a secret from you. Oh, I see. Missy class president told you."

"…How'd you figure that out?"

"Well, she's the only one around you who'd know—ha hah, maybe I should have given the talisman job to her? You manage to reel in trouble no matter where you go. Missy class president seems like she has a better head on her shoulders."

"She—already finished repaying you, remember?"

"Did she now," Oshino played dumb. It was the kind of reaction I'd come to expect from him.

"Still," I said, "snakes just feel evil to me. I don't really get people worshiping some serpent god. The only snake I can think of that doesn't seem evil is maybe the *tsuchinoko*."

"Ah, yes. Now that takes me back. I once did everything I could to find one of those damned things hoping to collect a reward. Never caught any, though."

"I don't know about an expert going for that. Plus, you couldn't even find any… Oh, how about that thing, isn't it an aberration? The *ouroboros* or whatever? The circular one that's eating its own tail…"

"Oh, that. If you're going to bring that up, it's not quite a snake eating its own tail, but some snakes eat other snakes. The king cobra, I think? It's quite a sight to see photos of a snake swallowing its own kind."

"Huh… Well, personally, I find snakes scary, not on some rational but instinctual level. Just looking at one stops me in my tracks."

"Land-based creatures shaped like that are rare, I suppose. It's like watching a fish swim on land. That certainly qualifies as unique, so I guess it's only natural for people to see them as bizarre. Like, don't you respect the first person who ever ate a sea cucumber? Ha hah. And on top of that, snakes have extraordinary vitality. You can try and try, but it takes a lot to kill one—you know? You hear about 'half-dead' snakes, but what that really tells you is just how many hit points those things have. For something of that size, it's off the charts, huh? It's important to know that snakes aren't considered pests to humans, though. You must've heard of snake wine, right?"

"I've never had any, of course."

"Then what about eating one? I've had sea snake paired with snake wine in Okinawa. They say eating snake is good for longevity."

"I don't really see myself ever eating snake… But I suppose it doesn't seem as bad as a sea cucumber."

"You're so narrow-minded. Or rather, you're so gutless, balking at a mere snake. Over on the mainland, there are regions where they eat woofy-woofs, okay?"

"I don't have any intention of repudiating anyone's food culture, but could you at least not say 'woofy-woof' when you're talking about eating them?"

Another one of these conversations with Oshino.

It was that, yes.

However—his expression was still vaguely dark—or so it seemed. Maybe it was just my imagination.

The abandoned ruins of a defunct cram school.

The fourth floor.

There I stood facing an eccentric man with an unlit cigarette in his mouth, a frivolous Hawaiian-shirted bastard to whom I owed my gratitude—Mèmè Oshino.

I was alone.

I'd asked Suruga Kanbaru and Nadeko Sengoku to stand by and wait. If you're wondering where—they were in the Araragi family home, sitting in my room. Putting aside my parents, my two little sisters were definitely inclined to enter my room without asking, but with the door locked, it was most likely fine for a few hours… I had to admit that some part of me did feel it was dangerous to leave Suruga Kanbaru, with her personality, not to mention her Sapphic bent, under the same roof as Sengoku and my little sisters without any supervision, but well, I just had to trust my junior.

And.

Above all—I had a reason to avoid bringing Kanbaru and Sengoku here. A reason I didn't want to bring them along to meet Oshino—

Afterwards.

Kanbaru and I brought Sengoku along with us—and headed to my home. I had Sengoku sit on the back seat of my bike. Kanbaru ran alongside us without breaking a sweat. As I'd half-expected, Kanbaru's condition returned to normal as soon as we climbed down the mountain. That bit the day before about her feeling better after eating lunch seemed to be a misunderstanding on my part.

Luckily, no one was home.

Both of my little sisters looked to be out (there were signs that they had come home once). Since deceiving their eyes would have been the trickiest part of slipping into my home, for which I hadn't devised any concrete plan coming back, my reaction was one of honest relief. My youngest sister, in particular… If she didn't remember her friend from grade school offhand, seeing her in person would do it. My sister would certainly wonder what was going on if her brother came home with an old pal of hers.

We went straight to my room.

"Big Brother Koyomi…" muttered Sengoku in a vanishing voice. Her face was cast down, and I barely heard her. "You…changed rooms."

"Yeah. I'm in my own room now. Both of my little sisters are still in that room, though… I think they'll come back after a while. Do you want to see them?"

No, Sengoku shook her head listlessly.

Her voice was muted—and so were her reactions.

It made her body seem somehow smaller.

She should have had six years of growth and development—yet she seemed far smaller than when we'd played before, relatively speaking, of course. Maybe it was only because I'd also seen six years of growth—

For some reason, I fell silent.

Then—

"Huh. So this is my senior's room," Kanbaru said in her plucky voice, smashing through the mood before it could grow awkward. She took a look around. "It's a lot tidier than I expected."

"Sure, compared to your room…"

"Heheheh. This is my first time in a boy's room."

"Oh…"

I realized as soon as she said it.

Come to think of it, this was also my first time having a girl who wasn't family in my room. Even Senjogahara had yet to visit my house. Gauchely inviting a girl into your room was a standard rite of passage for a teenager, but I'd let in my girlfriend's junior prior to my girlfriend… Was this okay? First a date, and now this… But fine, my little sister's old friend was with us too—and it was an emergency.

Sengoku had told us at the shrine.

In her tiny little voice.

I'll tell you why—so take me somewhere indoors where people won't see us.

Why.

Why what?

Why—she killed those snakes.

Why she sliced them up.

The first place that came to mind was Kanbaru's home, but I shot the idea down internally before she could suggest it. Because Kanbaru's room was so messy I'd call it lawless terrain, as hinted above—no, I'd go so far as to call it a warzone. I couldn't show that kind of room to an innocent middle schooler. That left my home as the only option. And anyway, Sengoku would probably feel anxious if we took her somewhere completely new. My home was a place where she'd played more than a few times in the past.

"Okay then, why don't we look around for some dirty books?"

"That's what guys do when they go to their male friends' rooms! Just sit over there!"

"I'd find it worthwhile to know your tastes."

"Not only do I not find it worthwhile, I find it actively harmful!"

"Ah, so you admit owning books that are harmful to minors..."

"Says the living harmful book! Take your pick, Kanbaru, sit down or jump out of that window!"

"I'm just kidding, of course. I looked into your tastes long ago, when I was still stalking you. I know every dirty book you've bought lately."

"What?! No way! I was certain no one else was in the store! I made sure!"

"Your tastes are quite out there, aren't they."

"You're down to one option, jump out that window!"

"I'm sure most girls would, faced with that kind of fetish. Heh, but that's like child's play for me, I could withstand it."

"She's proud of it!"

When I looked.

Sengoku was snickering but trying to hide it.

She seemed tickled by our exchange.

Guh. I was embarrassed.

I'd been wondering the whole time on the way back: how friendly should I be acting with this old acquaintance of mine?

Not to mention—Sengoku was quiet, if anything.

She seldom spoke, and only ever did so shyly.

Since Shinobu, Oshino, Hanekawa, Senjogahara, Hachikuji, and Kanbaru were all voluble and garrulous despite their various inclinations (Shinobu: rampant arrogance, Oshino: frivolous sarcasm, Hanekawa: moralizing instruction, Senjogahara: bitter abuse, Hachikuji: two-faced politeness, Kanbaru: fawning flattery), dealing with this new silent character was refreshing. Of course, Shinobu had grown taciturn after becoming a child...

Was Sengoku quiet now just as she had been as a child? Yes, it did feel like she always had her head down—but honestly, I couldn't recall the details vividly.

I couldn't remember.

She was introverted, spoke little, and always faced down—

But.

She seemed to have remembered me.

Big Brother Koyomi.

Yes, Nadeko Sengoku—once referred to me in that manner. As for what I'd called her—well, I'd forgotten. Maybe Nadeko, maybe Nadeshiko. Either way, I couldn't call her that anymore.

Sengoku—was Sengoku.

"Big Brother…and Miss Kanbaru," Sengoku said at last, quietly of course. "Could you…please turn away for a moment?"

"……"

We silently did as she said.

We turned our backs on Sengoku and faced the wall.

While I may have told Kanbaru to jump out of the window, I felt relieved that she was with me after all. In fact, after I called out to Sengoku at the shrine, I was at a loss as she stood there stiffly, and it was Kanbaru who singlehandedly pulled off the feat of getting her to open up. Seducing any younger girl within ten seconds had been no idle boast. I was willing to admit that Big Brother Koyomi alone would have been useless. I'd have fretted miserably and that would have been it. Looking back on it, Sengoku hadn't just frozen in place—her shoulders slumping as if the world were coming to an end, she'd gone completely blank. *Drawing her back out* would have been nigh impossible with my meager skills.

"My dear senior," Kanbaru whispered as we looked at the same wall. She seemed to be hushing her voice so that Sengoku wouldn't hear, and I replied likewise.

"What is it?"

"You might not welcome it, but my plan is to start livening things up."

"Huh? What's that supposed to mean?"

"I think you may have already noticed—but that girl, Sengoku, seems to be quite emotionally unstable. I've seen a lot of girls like her, both older and younger than me. She's a serious case. The slightest shock could drive her to self-harm."

"Self-harm..."

Those chisels.

I'd forgotten—to take them from her.

They were inside the bag around her waist.

Everything from a triangular blade to a cutting blade, a full set of five.

It didn't sound exaggerated.

In fact.

If Kanbaru hadn't intervened exactly when she did after I yelled Sengoku's name—that totally *could have been.*

Even I could tell.

"You're a kind person," Kanbaru murmured, "so it might be hard for you to act merry when someone's feeling down, but synching with her depressed state would only make things worse here. I wouldn't say it's like Maxwell's demon, but I need to lift Sengoku's spirit right now."

"...Huh."

So was that the reason for the earlier talk about dirty books? You know, it seemed I had underestimated Kanbaru. I'd wondered if she was just obtuse when she'd said that, but my judgment had been too superficial. Suruga Kanbaru gave more thought to her actions than I knew.

"Okay, then," I said. "If that's how it is, go wild. I'll follow along."

"Yes. I might get carried away and assault you, but I'd like your generosity to extend to that possibility, too."

"I can't be 'generous' about that! How exactly were you planning to liven things up?" I managed to pull off the impressive feat of yelling in a whisper. "Ack, now I'm starting to feel bummed out, too... The slightest shock could drive me to self-harm."

"There's no need for despair. You know what they say. Though it may be winter, the ice age isn't far behind, and night is always followed by a century of darkness."

"No one says that! What would those sayings even mean?!"

"No matter how bad things may seem now, it's as easy as it's ever going to be."

"What a seemingly positive but horribly pessimistic message!"
"There is no rain that doesn't turn to a flood."
"Yes, there is! It rains without turning into a flood all the time!"
"Heheheh. See? Now you sound positive again."
"Agh! You tricked me!"
I suddenly heard a stifled laugh from behind me.
Like someone was struggling to keep quiet.
It was Sengoku.
It seemed she just barely heard us.
If that was Kanbaru's plan all along—
She really was something.
"It's okay now. Please turn back around," Sengoku said.
When I did, I saw Nadeko Sengoku fully in the nude—standing straight on the bed as she looked down in embarrassment.
No—she wasn't completely nude.
She had taken her hat off, naturally, and even her socks, but was still wearing volleyball shorts. Other than that—there wasn't a thread left on her body. Though she did use the palms of her hands to hide her modest breasts.
"...Wait, volleyball shorts?"
Huh?
Just as I'd guessed, Sengoku attended the same middle school that I graduated from, but hadn't they retired volleyball shorts and introduced baggier athletic shorts by the time I started there?
"Ah well," Kanbaru said, "I just 'happened' to be carrying those around and lent them to her."
"I see. You just 'happened' to be carrying around volleyball shorts."
"They're a simple and tasteful part of a young lady's life."
"No, that'd be a sick and twisted plot on a young lady's life."
"I had them ready in case something like this came to pass."
"What did you think was coming to pass? What exactly did you think I wanted when I summoned you today? You're making me doubt my own credibility. And where did you even get a pair of those things, anyway? If this were an old-timey manga, that's the kind of item that would prompt lines like, 'Impossible! That tribe was supposed to have

been wiped out long ago!'"

"Yup. While I may not look like it, I have excellent foresight. I saw that the culture would some day be wiped out and decided to conserve a hundred and fifty pairs of them beforehand."

"Isn't that over-hunting, rather than conserving?"

Hadn't she made them go extinct, to be honest?

"........."

A high school boy and a high school girl having a lively and jovial discussion about volleyball shorts while a nearly naked middle school girl stood there on a bed. An outside viewer might see it as a fairly serious case of bullying.

Sengoku's bangs, hidden earlier by her hat, were longer than I expected, covering her eyes. Or maybe she was doing it on purpose out of embarrassment. The cuticles of her lustrous black hair shone. It seemed she'd hidden her clothes under my comforter after taking them off. The fact that she was wearing those shorts as per Kanbaru's ministrations and that she'd taken even her bra off suggested that displaying her underwear was more embarrassing than baring her skin for this old female acquaintance of mine. She undoubtedly looked more provocative than she intended, there in nothing but volleyball shorts, but I didn't understand middle school girls' sensibilities...

But.

Unfortunately—I guess you might say?

Sex appeal had nothing to do with this situation.

"What is...that?"

It had taken me a while, but the surprised words found their way out of my mouth—when I saw Nadeko Sengoku's skin.

Her skin—was covered in traces of scales.

From the toes of her two feet up to her collarbones.

Clear traces of scales—on every inch of her body.

For a moment I wondered if scales had grown directly on her body, but I looked closer to realize that wasn't the case. The scales were imprinted onto her body, like with a woodblock print—pressed onto her skin as it were.

"Reminds me of rope bondage marks," Kanbaru said.

Indeed, there did seem to be signs of internal bleeding here and there on her body, and the painful-looking markings made it look like she had been tied up—asking Kanbaru why she had such intimate knowledge of rope bondage marks would only complicate things, so I decided to let it slide for the time being.

No—maybe not rope bondage marks as much as…

Something going from her toes up through her legs all the way to her torso—

It was as if something was gripped around her.

Something we couldn't see.

Traces of scales, on every inch of her body.

Gripped around her.

Gripping—possessing her.

The only parts of her body without those marks were her arms, as well as her head from the neck up. There was no need to go the extra step of having her show us her hips and lower abdomen, now hidden by those volleyball shorts.

Scales.

So if they were scales—fish?

No, these weren't fish scales, but a reptile's—

A snake.

Snake…*serpent.*

"Big Brother?" Sengoku said.

Her voice still vanishingly small.

Her voice shaking.

"You're a grownup already…so you aren't having any dirty thoughts seeing me naked, are you?"

"Huh? O-Oh. No way. Right, Kanbaru?"

"Yes? Umm…I…guess?"

"Hey, play along! Where'd all that loyalty of yours go?!"

"Sengoku, it might do you good going forward to know that some people think dirty thoughts when they see little girls nude precisely because they're adults."

"You've betrayed me! And we'd gotten along so well until now!"

"I don't know, though. I think in this case, it only makes you more suspect as a man if you show no interest whatsoever in seeing her naked, or maybe, it's just rude to her?"

Kanbaru seemed fairly solemn as she said this to me.

Thinking about it, I had to admit she was right.

While the situation was anything but sexual, and while there were snake scales imprinted along her entire body, it still felt impolite to see a girl naked and not feel a thing. I seemed to recall Senjogahara saying that providing some feedback was just good manners.

I turned to face Sengoku.

I spoke to her in the most serious voice I could manage.

"Let me correct myself. I do have a few little dirty thoughts seeing you nude, Sengoku."

"……urr." Sengoku's shoulders began to shake, as though she were trying to stifle her anguish. "Uh, urrr…uurk."

Tears began to stream from her eyes—and she began to cry.

"Hey, Kanbaru! I've made a middle school girl cry because I took your advice! A middle school girl! Do you understand? It's all over for me! How are you going to make this right?!"

"No one could have guessed that you'd put it so directly…"

Kanbaru was looking at me, appalled.

It didn't seem like she'd been trying to trick me.

"I," Sengoku said, crouching down on my bed—her head bowed, mumbling so quietly it was barely audible—

And yet.

The words were certain.

"I—hate having this body."

"…Sengoku."

"I hate it… Save me, Big Brother Koyomi," she said—in a tearful voice.

005

And then—

An hour later.

I was visiting a derelict building inhabited by Oshino and Shinobu that once housed a cram school with only a day separating me from my last visit on Saturday.

"You're late. I've been waiting," Oshino greeted me in his arrogant, all-knowing tone.

Mèmè Oshino.

An expert on the subject of aberrations.

A specialist, an authority.

The man who lifted me from the veil of darkness I found myself under during spring break after being attacked by a vampire and getting turned into one myself in this day and age—my savior.

A Hawaiian-shirted dude, age unknown.

An awful role model with no fixed address who went from journey to journey.

Tsubasa Hanekawa, when she was charmed by a cat.

Hitagi Senjogahara, when she encountered a crab.

Mayoi Hachikuji, when she got lost with a snail.

Suruga Kanbaru, when she wished to a monkey.

All of them—received help from Oshino.

I don't know if I'll ever fully repay the favor—but to be frank, if he weren't my savior, I wouldn't want to get to know his type very well. By no means.

He had an awful personality. He was no font of good will. He was like an avatar of caprice. While I'd known him for some time since spring break, I still couldn't understand large swaths of his personality.

He sat cross-legged on top of a makeshift bed he had fashioned by tying together, with plastic rope, a number of desks that kids must have once used to study away. After I'd explained all of the above, Oshino said in a tormented voice almost as if he detested the name—

"A *Jagirinawa*."

"A Jagirinawa, huh… Never heard of that one."

"It's pretty famous. I think it's a form of serpent shamanism."

"Serpent shaman? Not serpent-bearer?"

"Serpent-bearers are from Greek mythology. Serpent shamanism is domestic. You know, like serpent-god mediums… I guess there isn't much point in talking to you about that. Still, a Jagirinawa… Hmm. So would that make this girl…your junior?"

"It doesn't really feel like it because of how much younger she is. So—she's my little sister's friend."

"A-ha. So she's like a little sister to you."

"Don't go around assigning my acquaintances to whatever position."

"She does call you her big brother."

"………"

I'd told him too much.

What an honest chump.

It was like I couldn't tell a lie…

No, I was just bad at hiding things.

"And that 'big brother' of days gone by," Oshino added, "is now 'li'l Ragiko'… Time really does fly like an arrow."

"I don't get called that! That was just a joke Kanbaru made!"

"I think it suits you well, though."

"Forget about it!"

"You know, I've been calling those girls 'li'l missy' tsundere and 'li'l missy' class president all this time, while you are simply Araragi, and I was beginning to feel prejudiced. From now on, I'll be more impartial and call you li'l Ragiko."

"Please, don't! I'm begging you!"

"It does feel like it could stick."

After we went back and forth like that for a bit, Oshino got back on track.

"At any rate. You managed to finish your job on time regardless. Good work, Araragi."

"Oh… Yeah, I guess." I'd never expected to be thanked by Oshino. I was so taken aback that my reaction must have seemed a little odd.

"I have to say, I couldn't ever have done it myself. Give my thanks to that missy, too. Er, uh—"

Oshino started to think.

He must have meant Kanbaru, but… Ah, he wasn't sure what to call her. That made me realize he hadn't settled on a tag for her yet. Hanekawa was li'l missy class president, Senjogahara was li'l missy tsundere, and Hachikuji was li'l lost girl… So Kanbaru would be, say, li'l miss sporty?

"That li'l miss pervy."

"……"

It seemed that Oshino saw Kanbaru more as a pervy character than as an athlete.

Not that I didn't see where he was coming from.

I thought he'd hit the mark, myself.

"Couldn't you at least draw the line at something like 'li'l miss sapphy'? She is, despite it all, a girl…"

"Huh? You think so? Okay, I'd be fine with that. Anyway—both you and her are now even with me. Let her know that."

"Even? So—we don't owe you anything?"

"Right."

"There's something I wanted to ask you just to be sure, Oshino—may I?"

"What is it?"

"It seemed like the moment we entered those shrine grounds, Kanbaru suddenly started feeling sick… Is that relevant?"

I'd had Kanbaru wait at home because I wanted to ask Oshino the question when she wasn't around.

Hmm, Oshino said with a sidelong glance.

"Araragi—what about you?"

"Huh?"

"How did you feel? Did you get sick or anything?"

"No—I was fine."

"I see. Well, you'd given little Shinobu your blood the day before—so I guess it makes sense. It means you were lucky."

"Lucky?"

"Remember what I just told you? It isn't something I could have ever done. That shrine used to be the center of this town."

"The center? Really? If anything, I'd say it's placed—"

"Not in terms of location. Well, it stopped being used long ago. There shouldn't be anything to the place nowadays, seeing how everyone has forgotten about it, but—Shinobu."

"Shinobu? What about her?"

"You know how she wandered into this town—she's a legendary vampire from a noble bloodline. A vampire, the king of aberrations. I guess you could say her influence activated the spot. *Bad things—were starting to gather there.*"

"There? You mean—at that shrine?"

That shrine—even the gods seemed not to visit.

Bad things.

"Yep. You could say it had become like an air pocket, or maybe a kind of hangout—places like that exist, centers. Part of why I stayed here even after Shinobu's case ended was to find that hangout—though my main goal, of course, was to collect aberrations. Ha hah. I got to meet missy class president and missy tsundere thanks to it, so I will say I had my fun."

"When you say *bad things*—what exactly do you mean?"

"*Various things.* It's not something I can put concisely…or rather, these *things* don't have names yet. You couldn't even call them aberrations at this point."

A haunt frequented by the bizarre.

That—is what it had become.

What gathered there—weren't humans.

The literally bizarre had.

"And Kanbaru started feeling sick—because of that?" I asked.

"That's right. Li'l miss sapphy's left arm is still a monkey's—so it's easier for her to be affected by *bad things*. It's the same for you, but as aberrations, there's an overwhelming difference in rank between her monkey and Shinobu. It means that while she's lost her resistance against those kinds of phenomena, you've actually built up a decent resistance to *bad things*."

"...Did you know all along, Oshino? That Kanbaru would feel *that way*?"

"Don't glare at me. You're always so spirited, Araragi, something good happen to you? It's not like li'l miss sapphy suffered anything in particular. And—she owed me. She wouldn't be paying me back unless she went through a few struggles. Her, especially. Don't you agree?"

"......"

He—may have been right.

It was just that I couldn't see it in such a strict light. Maybe that suffering was something Kanbaru needed to experience. At least, I couldn't see her complaining to Oshino even if she found out. That was the kind of person she was.

"Well, the rest is up to her now," Oshino said. "The fate of that left arm is her problem. If she can make it to twenty without incident—she'll be freed from her aberration."

"That'd be nice."

"Hm. You're a good person, Araragi. As usual..."

"What's that supposed to mean? It sounds like you're trying to imply something."

"Not really. I was just wondering if you weren't a little jealous. Of her going back from fellow non-human to human again."

"...Not really. I've already made peace with myself when it comes to my body. It's all sorted and settled, so—stop trying to stir up trouble by saying those kinds of things. Don't say anything unnecessary to Kanbaru, either. I don't want her to feel like she owes me anything."

"You're right, I'm sorry. You stuck the talisman on the door of the main hall, right? That's a little bit of a lazy job, but it's fine. It should scatter those *bad things* to some degree."

"To some degree?"

"A talisman placed by an amateur isn't going to change things that dramatically. In fact, it'd be an issue if they did. We only need to nudge the natural flow of things—or else who knows what could happen elsewhere. In that sense, the choice to do a half-assed job by placing it on the door might not have been a bad choice at all."

"...Why couldn't you do it? Whether it's aberrations or whatever *bad things* that precede them—that's your field of expertise, isn't it? Or is this a case of you forcing yourself to come up with a job so that Kanbaru could pay off her debt to you?"

"I won't say that wasn't a factor, but it really would've been hard for me. Just look at me, I'm as thin and wimpy as I seem. I don't have the stamina to climb up a mountain."

"That's not the line of a wanderer going from journey to journey."

"Ha hah. Was I being transparent? Well, yes, that was a joke. Physical stamina isn't the issue—it's more of a mental thing. Just like what happened to you and li'l miss sapphy *because you're aberrations*—I stimulate those *bad things* needlessly *because I'm an expert*. I'd have no choice but to do something if they decided to attack me, and in that case, I'd end up turning that hangout into a perfect vacuum. There's no telling what might stream into it next—worst case, we'd have another Shinobu."

"I don't really get it...but is it like how humans shouldn't affect the balance of the natural world just to make things more convenient for us? Sending someone like me or Kanbaru instead of the too-powerful Oshino going there helped to keep them calm?"

"Yeah, something like that," he brushed me off.

The truth must have been a bit more complicated—or maybe it was something else entirely—but there didn't seem to be any point in delving into the matter.

Kanbaru and Oshino were even now.

Just as long as that much was clear.

"Not just her, you know," Oshino said breezily. "Your debts with me are all settled now, too."

"...Huh?" I couldn't hide my surprise. Those didn't seem like words he would ever speak. "I owed you...five million yen."

"In cash terms, yes. That was how much your job this time was worth, though. You essentially managed to prevent the Great Yokai War from taking place."

"I-It was that big of a deal?"

I wished he would've told me earlier.

But when I thought about it, the job was big enough to instantly cancel out Kanbaru's bill despite her headache of a case—so I should have expected him to deduct a suitably sizable chunk of my debts, too. Not taking yourself into account sounded beautiful, but in reality it just made you feel like an idiot...

"We're all settled," Oshino assured, "but I almost feel like I owe you a little bit of change. Whatever. Let's talk about that girl—the missy who's like your little sister. You're making this sound like a pretty urgent matter, after all."

"Am I?"

"It's only her arms and neck and head that's unaffected, right? Ouch. Once the Jagirinawa comes up to her face, that's it. Araragi. The Jagirinawa is *an aberration that kills people.* I need you to understand that. This case—is a rather serious one."

"........"

I'd thought—that might be so. Those scale marks had a sinister air. But it felt so much more grave coming from an expert's mouth.

It wasn't a deathly aberration.

It was a—killing aberration.

"Snake venom can kill humans—they say. Neurotoxins, hemotoxins, cardiotoxins, the whole gamut. If you don't go at it with a serum, you can get pulled into it. Snakes—are tricky, you see."

Though, surprisingly enough, the poisonous ones tend to taste better—Oshino added.

"Oshino... Exactly what kind of aberration is the Jagirinawa?"

"Before I let you know, tell me the title of the book missy was reading in the bookstore aisle. You said to miss sapphy that you'd tell her later, but you never did, did you? What book was it? Looking at it made you feel certain that there was *something about that girl.*"

"Oh… Well, it's exactly what you'd expect. A twelve-thousand-yen hardcover called *A Complete Collection of Snake Curses.*"

"…The title makes it sound like a recent book. Not from before the war or the Edo period."

"Yeah. The cover looked brand-new, too."

But that title—was more than enough to make me think of the dead snakes, chopped into five, that I'd seen the day before. Of course, as soon as I witnessed the carcasses on Sunday, I vaguely suspected Sengoku, whom we'd just passed on the stairs…but it was when I saw the book's title that my suspicion turned into certainty.

Long sleeves, long pants.

But her long pants—may not have been for entering the mountains, and more a way to hide the scale marks imprinted on her legs.

In fact, that had to be it.

This body.

I hate having this body—she'd said.

Kanbaru must have understood the way Sengoku felt. The bandage wrapped around her left arm was there to hide her monkey's arm. When I thought about it, that was on a different level from me growing out my hair in the back to hide my bite marks. And come to think of it, when Kanbaru wanted to show me what lay under the bandages, she'd invited me to her house—not wanting anyone else to see.

In that sense, those two faced similar circumstances.

Those two.

What could they be—talking about right now?

……

Miss sapphy, you better not be seducing her.

I'm trusting you… I'm trusting you, all right?

"My limited knowledge doesn't cover what kind of book that is," Oshino admitted, "but it must include information on the Jagirinawa. Serpent shamanism is basically synonymous with snake curses, after all…"

"So are serpent shamans like witch doctors or something?"

"Well, yes. These aren't naturally occurring aberrations—they're commanded by someone's clear, or explicit, malice... Well, it doesn't necessarily have to be malice, but siccing the Jagirinawa on someone sounds like nothing else."

"Oh...I heard that, too."

"Hm? You did?"

"Well, yeah."

Sengoku didn't give me a name.

It was partly my fault because I didn't feel like grilling an introvert like her—but Sengoku stubbornly refused to give up a name.

The culprit's name.

But—she did tell me it was someone in her class.

A friend—from her class.

What with a curse placed on her, I thought "former friend" was more like it.

I told Oshino, "It's a middle schooler's idea of a charm—some sort of fad, apparently. These charms go a little deep into the occult... Most are complete whiffs, of course, but I guess you could say Sengoku is the unlucky exception."

"Unlucky, huh?" Oshino echoed suggestively. "Charms and curses. I suppose the two are similar. But Araragi, from what you're saying, the perpetrator is a rank amateur, a middle schooler... The Jagirinawa isn't supposed to be the kind of aberration that a beginner can handle."

"Like a broken clock getting the time right, couldn't it have been a fluke?"

"Could it? Hmm. Why did this classmate want to curse missy to begin with?"

"According to the bits and pieces I gathered from her, it was actually over love. Someone being head over heels. This friend had a boy she liked, and that boy told Sengoku he loved her, but not knowing any of that, Sengoku turned him down—earning her resentment."

"Hm. How typical."

"Well, this is a middle-school romance we're talking about." Not that the views of someone who'd never dated a girl until his last year of high school counted for much.

"If she started dating him without knowing, that's one thing," commented Oshino, "but you'd think turning him down wouldn't have mattered."

"It's about feelings, I guess. Maybe when Sengoku turned him down, the other girl resented something precious to her getting dissed?" I made it sound like my interpretation, but it was Kanbaru's take. How could I hope to understand the mentality of a middle school girl? If Kanbaru thought so, I could only suppose that she was right.

"Huh. Well, who cares about the reason. People don't need reasons to hate each other. So things soured—and ended with a curse. Ah, how fleeting friendship is. That's why I don't make friends."

"…Is that so." I wanted to retort to that, but if I tried to quip at everything Oshino said, our conversation would last through the night, and then some… I needed to control myself. I couldn't leave those two waiting forever. "Sengoku said she was reading *A Complete Collection of Snake Curses* because she wanted to figure out how to get rid of hers. Today wasn't the first time she read that book, either. She'd been going back to it over and over for a while now, almost every day, reading, then reading some more, and consulting it—to try every curse removal, ritual purification, exorcism, and the like by herself."

That's what those were.

The sliced snakes.

It wasn't like a ritual—a ritual was precisely what it was. Using a chisel struck me as grotesque at first, but it seemed that those were the only bladed objects Sengoku owned. Maybe the most readily accessible edged tools for a middle school girl was in fact her chisel set.

"Removing a snake curse by killing snakes—the idea smells fishy to me," I continued. "And actually, she said her condition started to get worse when she started killing snakes like that—"

"No, Araragi. Repelling a Jagirinawa by cutting up snakes isn't wrong. Actually, it's the right and proper thing to do. The method was probably listed in the Jagirinawa section of the so-called *Complete Collection*… But she's quite the brave young lady, isn't she? Catching snakes on her own and killing them. It's wonderful. You keep describing her as docile and quiet, but I find that hard to believe."

"Well, this is the countryside at the end of the day. You can't let yourself be surprised by a girl who picks up snakes with her bare hands."

"That's hard for me to accept, as a city boy."

"What about you makes you a city boy, exactly?"

Well.

You could say Sengoku had been pushed to that point by the curse—by the Jagirinawa.

She'd cried.

There was nothing brave about her.

If anything, she was delicate. Too delicate.

"It's not that killing snakes will remove a snake curse, Araragi—what's important here is the *cutting up* of snakes. Here, the snakes are a metaphor for rope. Jagirinawa—*nawa*, rope. No matter how tightly you're bound, cut the rope and you'll be free."

"Bound..."

Rope bondage marks.

She was being bound—by a snake.

A rope, huh?

Oshino went on. "There's a saying that once you're bitten by a snake, you'll jump at the sight of a rope, and in this case, snake equals rope. What makes a rope a rope is that it can be cut."

"...That doesn't seem to make sense, though. Sengoku said she's already killed more than ten snakes at that shrine. But far from going away..."

The curse was—only getting worse.

The more snakes she killed, the faster the scales *climbed up rolling* from her toes—that's what she told me. It was proof that the curse was progressing.

"Well, like I always say," reminded Oshino, "when it comes to these things—the process matters. This missy who's like your little sister is a complete, rank amateur—right? In general, it's harder to remove a curse than to place one, so of course her condition is going to get worse if she goes by her half-knowledge. If you kill snakes while a snake is possessing you, of course you're going to make it mad. You're right in that regard, Araragi."

"……"

"But this conversation is helping me see why a curse placed by another complete amateur of a middle school girl has been so successful. My initial assumption was that hell has no fury like a woman scorned, but I guess I missed the mark. It's bad luck."

"What do you mean?"

"Missy probably learned that a curse had been placed on her before it ever began to work. Judging by the fact that she knows exactly who it was, she must have heard it straight from the girl. 'Damn you, I placed a curse on you!' or something. Missy panicked, went to the bookstore to find out how to get rid of it, and climbed up a mountain that's known for having a lot of snakes—so she could cut 'em up. I guess she found the shrine by accident? Well, maybe she knew about it in advance. Then, she got busy killing those snakes."

"What about that is 'bad luck'?"

"The spot. Remember what I said? *An air pocket, a hangout—*"

"Oh."

A place where bad things—gathered.

Those *bad things* that Shinobu's presence had activated.

"And that—strengthened the curse?" I asked.

"Not strengthened, most likely it wouldn't have triggered at all if not for that spot. Unlike you and miss sapphy, her body must be a regular human one—so while she probably didn't feel unwell, the *bad things* affected her in the form of the Jagirinawa."

She had no way to fight back—no resistance.

A rank amateur.

"So it's like she deepened her own wounds," I said.

"It's like she wounded herself. Although it's a cruel way to put it, nothing would have happened if only she'd done nothing. Actually, the description in this *Complete Collection of Snake Curses* might be half-assed to begin with. I try to refrain from speaking ill of books I haven't read, but it's a strong possibility. On top of it all, you have an amateur edition curse-removal ritual in a spot like that. Those *bad things* must have worked in a *bad direction.*"

"What a quagmire."

"A quagmire, indeed."

Your bad luck—could get that bad?

"I suppose the silver lining for her was being reunited with you right as matters were coming to a head—you do plan on doing something for the girl, right?"

"...Am I wrong to?"

"No, not necessarily. Neither seek nor shun the fight, after all. But it is a little tough for me to understand. I get taking pity on her, but why go so far? Because she's your little sister's old friend? Or because her last name reminds you of your girlfriend's?"

"Huh? Oh, because Sengoku is a 'thousand *koku*' as in how they used to value territories, and Senjogahara means 'battlefield'? Actually, I'd never considered that one. I only realized for the first time now. Well, no—I mean, she's in such distress. Isn't it normal to—want to do something?"

"What a good person," Oshino said.

He gave it such an unpleasant ring.

"There's a book called the *Compilation of Snake Curses* that was put together in mid-Edo—it's an odd tome containing nothing but snake-related aberrations. That's where the Jagirinawa first appears in print. With an illustration, to boot."

"An illustration? What does it look like?"

"*It depicts a man who's being constricted by a giant snake. The tail's design resembles a straw rope, while the snake's head is—in the man's mouth.* His jaw is open as far as it can go, almost as if he's a snake—that's the picture. Snakes can swallow animals as big as chickens whole, after all."

"Constricted—"

"Gripped. Possessed."

"......"

"In other words, Araragi. Missy's body is—*in the grips of such a giant snake as we speak.* A snake is gripping and possessing and constricting her. Tightly—and mercilessly."

"But...she said it doesn't hurt."

"That's a lie, of course it does. She's trying to endure the pain. Don't I keep on telling you that trust is key? You're dealing with a quiet kid, you need to try to read what's in her heart—looking into her eyes."

"Looking—into her eyes."

That reminded me, when Sengoku said it didn't hurt, Kanbaru seemed to want to say something… So that's what it was? She said things that needed to be said—but kept her mouth shut if she only wanted to say it. That certainly would have been very Kanbaru.

"Wrapping around a prey's body and pulverizing its bones to make it easier to eat before swallowing it is typical snake behavior. It's not easy to get a snake to release you once it has you in its grip."

"I see… Right, it's an aberration, so it can ignore her clothes."

Those marks were only on her skin, and she seemed to be able to take off and put on clothes freely, volleyball shorts aside. That had kept me from thinking that an aberration might have Sengoku's body in its grip, but what did I know—*I just couldn't see it.*

"A rope—right?" I asked Oshino. "And bound? So those scale marks across her body aren't traces—at this very moment, an invisible snake is *manifestly gnawing into her.*"

This giant snake, the Jagirinawa, was invisible to my eyes, to Kanbaru's, and of course to Sengoku's, so we *only saw through to the effect* that the aberration was having on Sengoku's skin.

"Even then," Oshino explained, "I think it's only because you and miss sapphy are essentially half-human, half-creature that you can see those marks at all. The same goes for missy, who's in its grip. I'd imagine that anyone other than you three—missy tsundere or missy class president, for example—wouldn't even see the marks. They might be able to see the internal bleeding, though."

There was no need for her to hide the marks with long pants.

No reason to be ashamed of her body.

That's what Oshino said.

But that didn't seem like the problem to me. Yes, that might be the case, logically speaking—and maybe it was another instance of Sengoku's bad luck that Kanbaru and I happened to be the ones to see her body—but didn't it more than qualify as an issue *if she saw herself that way?*

"Maybe," Oshino admitted. "Yes, you might be right."

"That was an awfully quick admission."

"Even I can be honest and upfront at times. I don't have anything better to do right now."

"You can't be honest and upfront if you aren't just chilling?"

"Come to think of it, I get that she dresses in long sleeves and long pants when she goes out, but what's she been doing at school so far? Do the girls at your old middle school not wear skirts as part of their uniforms?"

"Not really, they're more like dresses. Kind of an all-in-one? Have you seen them on your research forays?"

"Ah, yes. So that's your alma mater. Those are cute—but wouldn't they still leave her legs exposed?"

"That's why Sengoku's been taking school off since those marks became visible, though she managed while she could still hide them with socks—well, okay, Oshino, what about this? Is there some way to make the body of this Jagirinawa visible? Would you be able to see it?"

"No way, I'm just a human."

Mr. Expert didn't seem to mind at all that he couldn't.

He was practically shirking his duties with that line.

"And not just me," he said. "In this kind of case, it's basically hard for others to see what the possessed can't see themselves. No matter how much of a former vampire you may be. As a side note, it isn't the person in the Jagirinawa's grip but the one who cast the snake who can see it—and this is an accidental case, so I doubt even she could. This friend probably hasn't even realized that the curse took. Otherwise, it'd be a huge deal in their class… Well, no, maybe that friend is just keeping quiet about it. That really would be full-blown malice…but I don't think that's what it is. Missy would be long dead if it were. But there's no point in going over all these possibilities. Talk about guesswork. Oh, but one thing—while you may not be able to see it, Araragi, you just might be able to touch it."

"Hm…like you did once?"

"Uhhh, what're you talking about?" Pretty pointlessly in my view, Oshino was playing dumb. "If you can touch it, you should be able to peel it off…but you might not want to. Snakes are savage animals. Do that and I'm sure the Jagirinawa will attack you. And even if you somehow escape it, it'll seek out the classmate who cast the curse next."

"The curse turning on the caster."

"You know what they say—when one is cursed, two holes are dug. This girl must not have meant to kill missy and probably doesn't believe in curses to begin with. I think she honestly intended to just go, 'Damn you, I placed a curse on you!' out of spite. Hmm. I don't like that she decided to get the occult involved over something so petty, though... How's an outsider like me supposed to make a living? This business is bad for me."

"I can't tell if you misspoke there or not."

"Ha hah. Well, I guess it's fine."

With those words, Oshino got off his makeshift bed. He then plodded away and tried to exit the room, so I hastily called out to his back.

"Hey, where are you going?"

"Eh. Wait here a second."

That was all he said before leaving the classroom for real.

He was a fickle person. Actually, he was just being selfish.

Now what... If I had time, I wanted to check up on Shinobu, but if I missed Oshino in the process, that'd be stupid... Which classroom was Shinobu in, anyway? It was rare for her and Oshino to be in different ones. Had she gotten into another fight with Oshino over some Mister Donuts?

Fine, I would just file a status report.

I pulled out my cell phone and tried calling Kanbaru—Sengoku, by the way, still didn't have one, in typical fashion for a rural middle schooler. Then again, even if my parents found them, this was Kanbaru so she'd do just fine ... As long as they didn't discover that she was a pretty serious pervert and a real-deal sapphist, Kanbaru was an exemplary young woman who excelled at academics as well as athletics.

But the moment I tried to open my contacts list—

"Thanks for waiting."

Oshino returned.

That was quick.

So quick that I wondered if he knew what I was about to do.

He really acted like he saw through everything.

"Hm? What's that modern convenience you have there? Were you about to call someone?"

"Well...I was just thinking of contacting Kanbaru and Sengoku in advance. It seems like this will take more time than I thought."

"No need to call in that case. I'm already done talking here. Take this."

From his position at the entryway, Oshino tossed straight at me whatever he was holding in his right hand. The sudden projectile threw me off balance, but I was somehow able to catch the item without dropping it.

It was a traditional amulet.

It was shaped like a standard amulet—but the pouch said nothing.

There were no words indicating if it was for, say, traffic safety or fertility.

A blank design.

"What's—this?"

"You can purify it with that. The Jagirinawa."

"......"

"There's a talisman inside of it. What you might call a protective charm. It's different from the one I had you place...and the pouch it's in is nothing, just a sheath. The talisman is a bit of a powerful one, so safety measures are required. Safety measures, or maybe a limiter. Don't get it wrong, though, it's not as if all you're going to have to do is place that talisman on her forehead like she's a *jiangshi* or something. In fact, don't ever take that talisman out of its pouch. Like I said, it's a safety measure, a limiter. There's no telling what might happen. I'm going to tell you the correct method for this, so do your best to remember for later. I could go out there myself, but it's probably better if I don't—as far as building a relationship of trust with the young lady, you and li'l miss sapphy are already set. That claim of being able to seduce younger girls within ten seconds doesn't sound like false advertising, either. I'm so impressed. I'm so jealous. Ha hah, and while you seem to have forgotten, it seems missy's memories of you are rather nice ones, no? She wouldn't be able to strip on a moment's notice in a man's room otherwise, Big Brother Koyomi."

"……"

I didn't know about that, to be honest.

When it came to people who never stopped talking like Senjogahara, Kanbaru, Hanekawa, or Hachikuji, I could make some sort of guess about how they felt—whether those words were frank ones or not—but it was hard to deal with someone who spoke so little. Someone with a shy personality. Who buckled under pressure and cast her eyes downward at the smallest provocation—

When I thought about the situation, it was surprising that this very same girl had flatly turned down a boy. Someone with her personality seemed like the type who couldn't say no and got dragged into being someone's girlfriend… But, once again, I had no right whatsoever to be talking about these affairs of the heart.

"I think it's like how you wouldn't be embarrassed to strip naked in front of a doctor," Oshino said. "That's what a relationship of trust is. Oh, wasn't Asclepius from the constellation Ophiuchus a patron saint of medicine? Another hint, perhaps."

"But, Oshino…is it really okay?"

"Is what okay?"

"For you to be so…quick and simple with a way to purify her. You normally act more pompous, you know? You go into these tiny little details, or you're never really cooperative. I feel like you went easy on your usual mountain of trivia too. Don't tell me you're not being serious about this now that I don't owe you anything."

"Oh, Araragi. You just love nagging me, don't you? You and I know full well that you'll complain if I do pile on the trivia. I'm starting to think that the real tsundere here is you, not li'l missy tsundere. How so spirited, something good happen to you? I didn't use to say all that to be mean or anything. It was the same for missy class president, missy tsundere, li'l lost girl, miss sapphy, and especially you, Araragi. *Each of you stuck your own neck into an aberration, didn't you?*"

"Well, that's…"

That's.

"If I may," Oshino continued, "all of you were *perpetrators*. Whether or not you meant to be, you were *complicit* with your aberrations. For people who've gotten their hands dirty to wash their feet, a certain process becomes necessary. But it's different in this case, isn't it? *Nadeko Sengoku is clearly nothing more than a poor victim.* She's done nothing wrong. Even the reason the Jagirinawa was set upon her is weak. *For every aberration, there is a reason*—but none of that reason here is missy's doing. Ten snakes, was it? She may have killed them, but even that was her trying to defend herself. She was unlucky, it wasn't her day—that's it. I'm not so unreasonable to hold accountable the victim of someone's malice. What people like that need is to be saved."

"........."

So that's what it was.

Sorry, Oshino, I thought you were acting that way to be mean...

It made sense now... That was why his tone sounded so grave from the moment he first named the Jagirinawa. It didn't have anything to do with the Jagirinawa itself. That was purely Oshino thinking about the victim, Nadeko Sengoku.

"Crimes need to be atoned for, but you can't allow someone to be judged for a crime they never committed. People in trouble need to be saved—right? Yes, I may not be the nicest guy, but even I have that much kindness for others left in my heart. Though that isn't to say I'm doing this entirely as volunteer work—this is my job."

"Yeah, I figured as much."

"But it's fine. This can be the change left over from the work you and miss sapphy did for me. The missy who's like your little sister doesn't need to do a thing in return."

"...I see."

Yes, there may have been that issue of perpetrator versus victim.

But even then, it felt like he was playing favorites.

Maybe he liked middle schoolers.

"But, Araragi. Let me give you just one warning—when one is cursed, two holes are dug. I know I'm saying it again, but I want you to keep the words close in mind, and I want you to think closely about them."

"Oh... Well, that won't be hard, it's not unheard-of advice. You don't need to do anything special to learn that. I've had plenty of chances to find out what it means that have nothing to do with aberrations."

"I'm sure that's true—but, Araragi. I don't know how you see this, but it's not as if I'm going to be living here forever," Oshino said, his tone staying frivolous. "Eventually I'll be done collecting and researching. After all, you and miss sapphy have solved one of my main concerns, or rather, achieved one of my main goals. I will leave this town some day. And when I do, you're not going to be able to come to me for advice, you know?"

Our debts—had been settled, too.

Oshino continued.

"It's been a while since I first started wandering from place to place, but this is the first time I've ever spoken this much with any one person. There is the fact that you've gotten yourself involved with one aberration after the next—but the thing that's a little odd about you is that you try to deal with every single one. Once you've experienced an aberration, you're more likely to attract them in the future—that much is true, but most people who encountered an aberration will then go out of their way to avoid them."

"……"

"That's how things balance themselves out. This relates to what I said about you being a tsundere, but you say all kinds of things about girls, don't you? That they're meddling, or that they're good at looking after others. But all of those traits apply to you, Araragi—not that it's a bad thing. I'm so envious of your personality that I keep saying nasty things to you, but I think you're good the way you are. But—what are you planning to do once I'm gone?"

"Er—well."

Well—I hadn't ever thought about that.

It went without saying that Oshino wouldn't reside in my town for the rest of his life, it was like a given—but the question of what I'd do once he was gone wasn't one I could answer on the spot.

Did we have to talk about this right now?

Oshino went on. "Aberrations exist as though it's natural for them to be there—they aren't something you should go out seeking. Do that and of course you might end up as the perp. I think you worry too much, Araragi. You're overprotective. You have a tendency to try to do something—even when you could just leave it alone."

"But..." But still. "Once I find out—what am I supposed to do? I know about these things whether I want to or not—so I can't look the other way or pretend not to know."

"Ha hah, so would it have been better if you'd forgotten it all, like missy class president? That just might be the best outcome for people like you, Araragi. Forgetting it all—little Shinobu too."

"How could I forget..."

Something like that?

Of course it wasn't possible.

It wasn't ever going to turn out like it had for Hanekawa.

"That's right," Oshino said, "little Shinobu, too—yes, right. You're going to have to look after her all by yourself once I'm gone. That was the choice you made—though you're of course free to abandon her, too."

"Come on—Oshino."

"You need to always be aware of the fact. Because Shinobu isn't human. You shouldn't allow yourself to get weirdly empathetic. She's a vampire. She can look like that now, but that doesn't change the fact—okay?"

"......"

"Sorry, was that a mean thing to say? There's no need to worry, though, we've gotten to know each other so well. I'm not going to disappear all of a sudden one day without even saying goodbye. I'm an adult, I do know my manners. But if you're thinking about what to do after graduating from high school—I think it wouldn't hurt to think about this while you're at it."

"So what you're trying to say is that it's irresponsible for me to attempt to save everyone I come across? That it's irresponsible to be kind to everyone—Hanekawa told me that one, too. But, Oshino, I can't become someone like you. Like you say, I'm about a tenth vampire—an actual aberration. I can't get on the human side and go around banishing aberrations."

If I did, the very first one I needed to banish was myself.

Then Shinobu.

And that—wasn't happening.

It wasn't something I could do.

"I wouldn't say that's true," Oshino told me. "This job is all knowledge and know-how anyway. A half-human, half-creature who hunts spirits? Sounds cool, like a manga character."

"Well…maybe it is possible, since there's even a Hawaiian-shirted specialist in the field…"

"And," Oshino reminded me, "*if ever in your life you feel like it, Araragi…you can abandon Shinobu and go back to being a full-fledged human*—I hope you don't forget that, either."

006

We were in the remains of the shrine.

That abandoned shrine atop the mountain.

It was the dead of the night, after we had been busy preparing for so long.

I considered waiting until the next day, but if we waited one more day, those scale marks, the Jagirinawa's grip, might reach up to her neck (she wouldn't be able to hide it if that happened since she couldn't walk around wearing a scarf in this season—even if regular people couldn't see those markings). The middle of the night or not, we decided to fight for every minute and second and do it as soon as possible. My family took a hands-off approach with me, and the same went without saying for Kanbaru. A slight issue arose regarding Sengoku's curfew as an active-duty middle schooler, but she asked one of her school friends to come up with an alibi for her (a sleepover or something like that). It seems obvious, but Sengoku apparently had friends other than the one who had cursed her.

Having a lot of friends.

A good thing, I thought.

While I was more than a little worried at first about doing this at the same shrine ruins where everything began, Oshino gave us his stamp of approval, telling us it was fine. I thought he said it because we had already placed the talisman on the main hall, but it was actually a matter of process. Even if we were dealing with *bad things*, all we had to do was get them on our side—according to him. The Jagirinawa's existence would be more conspicuous precisely because of the location—it would be easier to come in contact with—or something like that.

I didn't get it, to be honest.

But, I guessed, it was an expert's advice. I'd trust it.

Shinobu was in a room on the third floor so I gave her a casual greeting (She really had gotten in a fight with Oshino over Mister Donuts. He'd eaten all of her favorite flavors yet again. Mèmè Oshino, you're not even immature, you're just childish) before leaving the abandoned cram school and heading straight back home. Sure enough, Kanbaru hadn't laid a finger on Sengoku despite sharing a room with her the whole time, nor had she gone after my little sisters, both of whom were now home.

"Great job holding yourself back, Kanbaru!"

"Yes...and hearing the earnestness in your words of praise, for the first time I'm wondering if I'd joked around too much in your presence, and am regretting it..."

Kanbaru seemed depressed.

She not only hadn't tried to seduce Sengoku, but they'd been chatting.

"Miss Kanbaru was kind to me, Big Brother," the introverted Sengoku jumped in to stand up for her. "She let me borrow her volleyball shorts, too."

"That doesn't count as kindness," I played the straight man for Sengoku, a first.

A day for the history books.

In any case, talking to her was hard because our exchanges weren't punctuated with jokes unlike with the rest of the bunch. Thanks to those bastards, I couldn't have normal conversations anymore. Sadly for Sengoku, she'd have to go along with our style.

I had her and Kanbaru sneak out of my house while I kept my two little sisters busy, and then I stepped out, too, with nary an excuse. My sisters seemed suspicious (especially my youngest sister, perceptive girl), but I forced them away in the end and proceeded to the rendezvous point to meet up with the girls. We went to a general (and not a convenience) store that was open late to buy the needed tools (neither Kanbaru nor Sengoku had much money on them given how sudden this was, so I paid for it all) before heading to the mountains. We all walked.

"Sengoku."

"Uh, yes…Big Brother?"

She'd twitched.

Maybe she thought I was going to yell at her.

So delicate, like she was made of glass.

"Those marks on you—I heard they actually hurt. Are you okay?"

"Ah…" All the color drained from her face. "U-Um… Please don't be mad."

"No, I'm not trying to blame you for anything."

She probably thought I was about to scold her for lying. I didn't know if she was timid, or too quick to see herself as a victim… Every time a character like her appeared in a manga, I'd wonder how irritating someone like that would be in real life, but it actually wasn't that bad… I simply felt like protecting her, prior to whether or not I was a good person. Of course, the fact that she was quite a bit younger than me helped.

"I was just wondering if you were okay."

"W-Well." Sengoku tugged her hat far down her face. As if to hide it. As if she didn't want to be seen. "It hurts, like something is tightening down on me, but…I can still bear it."

Pulverizing the bones—to make it easier to eat.

Snake behavior.

"…Having to bear it is wrong to begin with. If something hurts—it's okay to say so."

"He's right," Kanbaru butted in. "Getting tied up is one thing, but staying tied up takes a surprising toll on your body. Whether it's a snake or ropes."

"Kanbaru, why you would gloss over getting tied up, and more subtly, the emotional toll of it, baffles me."

This woman didn't regret a thing.

Sengoku stifled a giggle at our back-and-forth.

Despite her timidity, maybe she was quick to laugh. In that case, talking about the thirteen-sign zodiac, which set off even Kanbaru, was absolutely off limits around Sengoku. She might laugh herself to death.

We sprayed each other with a bug repellent from the general store before going up the mountain. It was the middle of the night, which meant we needed to worry about bugs before any aberrations. While we were all fully protected in long sleeves and long pants, it was an additional safety measure for Kanbaru and me and could help Sengoku down along the line.

Once we finished, we got going.

It was pitch black, of course.

As we climbed the stairs, all three of us lit the way ahead with the flashlights we'd bought at the same general store. The wild animals and insects were horribly loud. It wasn't that way in the afternoon, and I felt like we were explorers on some expedition. I was almost deluded into thinking I was lost in a jungle.

"You know, Sengoku," I said.

"Yes?"

"I was wondering about something. Why did you turn that boy down? You didn't have any idea your friend had feelings for him, right? So there wasn't any reason for you to say no."

"Well…"

She fell silent.

Someone with so little mental fortitude, who went quiet over just that much, rejecting a confession of love was even more perplexing…

"I-I'm sorry," she apologized. For no reason.

"Um, it's not something you need to apologize for."

"Ah, y-yes, you're right. I-I'm sorry. I'm…well… I'm sorry."

She'd apologized twice between a single pair of quotation marks.

Three times in total.

She was over-apologizing.

"No, Sengoku—"

Kanbaru spoke up. "That was a rather insensitive question. It's unlike you. Be more considerate."

"Oh…really?"

"Yes, really. There are plenty of reasons to say no. In fact, why date someone you don't particularly love?"

"Hmm..."

It was a legitimate point.

I also realized that Kanbaru making one came to me as a surprise.

"Take me, for example," she said. "It's because I love you that—"

"We're not going out!"

"Huh...is that true?" asked Sengoku, puzzled. "You aren't dating Miss Kanbaru?"

"No!"

"O-Oh... You seemed to get along so well that...I was sure you two were."

"I'll admit that we get along."

About as well as I got along with Hachikuji.

Then again, unlike Hachikuji, at least Kanbaru never maligned me... In that sense, maybe I got along with her a little better.

...As for the girl I was actually dating, she only ever seemed to malign me...

"Kanbaru. Back me up and tell her no."

"Mm. He's right, we're not going out." She told Sengoku in an explanatory tone, "He and I are just having fun—we're playing around."

"That is very open to misinterpretation, isn't it!"

"We're such good friends that we could dismiss anything as a sort of accident."

"Are you just being straight-up pernicious?! I hate you!"

"Hey. That kind of hurt."

"Ack... Er, sorry. I love you."

Wasn't she going to receive anything I said with great joy? What a difficult girl.

Actually, I was the weak one here for apologizing.

Even as Kanbaru and I bickered, Sengoku mumbled, "Oh...so you're not going out," sounding relieved for some reason.

"I turned him down because there's someone else I like," she told us. Her apparent embarrassment was sweet. "But...that friend seems to have misunderstood me...and now this happened... I-I wonder if it was my fault…"

"Don't blame yourself. Then again, it wasn't supposed to end up this bad—it's because of that shrine."

Because of that shrine.

"Oh yeah, Kanbaru. You're probably going to start feeling sick again… A talisman's effect isn't immediate, or so I've been told."

"Fine with me. Plus, I can be ready for it if I know it's coming."

"I see."

What a jock.

All it took was guts, huh?

I'd normally refute it as unscientific but found myself believing it because it was Kanbaru. She was, after all, a formidable woman who'd gone from clumsy girl to national-level basketball player thanks to nothing but guts and the effort to go with it.

"Big Brother Koyomi, how much do you remember about before?"

"Uh…well, not much, to be honest. I don't have a very good memory."

"Oh…"

Sengoku was visibly disappointed.

"You, on the other hand," I hastily turned the subject to her, "remembered me. I'm impressed because we'd only played together a few times when you were little. And I was just your friend's older brother. You normally forget that stuff."

"I didn't get to play with people all that much," Sengoku said haltingly. "Back then, the only friend I had who'd play with me after school was Rara…"

Rara must have meant my youngest sister. Right, the friends she brought over used to call her that. Her grade-school nickname, Rara, excerpted from our family name, Araragi. Now, though, she and my other little sister combined were Tsuganoki Second Middle School's "Fire Sisters"…

How things change.

Of course people change.

But if we're going to talk about those days, back then I was annoyed when my little sisters brought over their friends and made me play with them…

I'd felt shy about playing with girls.

That's how it was at that age.

"Though Rara and I don't go to the same middle school…all the times I got to play with her, and you, are my precious memories."

"I see…"

That—made me feel better.

By the way, I hadn't told Sengoku about the aberrations that Kanbaru and I bore, only giving her a whiff of the fact that we had anything to do with them. I certainly could share that with her, and maybe I needed to in terms of building a relationship of trust, but after talking it over with Kanbaru, I paid heed to the possibility that it might only accelerate a mental breakdown. So Sengoku probably didn't understand why anyone would feel sick from going to the shrine, and perhaps thought that Kanbaru was spiritually sensitive, or something. Then again, that wasn't altogether wrong.

"I'm an only child," Sengoku said. "I was jealous—that she had an older brother."

"………"

It sounded like a case of wanting what you can't have.

Like someone without a little sister wanting a little sister.

At times I wished I had an older brother or sister, or a younger brother—and envied people who had them. But maybe it was different for someone like me, who had actual little sisters, and for Sengoku, who was an only child.

So—she was an only child.

"Hey, what about you, Kanbaru? You don't have any siblings—do you?"

"Nope. I'm an only child, too."

"I see."

And so was Senjogahara. And Hachikuji, and Hanekawa.

Huh, so they were all only children.

And—Shinobu?

Did vampires have siblings?

"Okay—we're here."

I was leading the way, so I was, of course, the first to arrive.

The ruins of a shrine.

A desolate, barren sight.

The talisman was still—stuck to the door.

"Are you feeling okay, Kanbaru?"

"Yes. Better than I thought."

"Try saying something stupid."

"I like reading books on the road and making myself carsick."

"Try saying something funny."

"I couldn't help it! He threatened not to pay me if I didn't!"

"Try saying something perverted."

"Just when I thought the girl I liked was a virgin, it turned out she was vermin."

"Okay."

That last one was a little weird, but she seemed fine.

Next to me, Sengoku was hugging herself and shaking. We'd tickled her funny bone.

She really was quick to laugh.

It seemed she was more amused by my interaction with Kanbaru than the actual content, but in fact that was a good audience reaction, so I couldn't complain.

"Okay," I said, "let's get ready now… Let's get ready already."

Kanbaru asked me, "Why did you bother to rephrase yourself?"

We found an appropriate spot…which is to say a location that wasn't too overgrown, then placed four flashlights, the three we held and one more in my bag, in each corner. They formed a square and illuminated the center.

The ground was dirt.

We drew lines in it next using a nearby tree branch and linked the flashlights into an actual square—a so-called spiritual boundary. It was pretty makeshift but would do, according to Oshino, because the simple fact that it was demarcated was what mattered most about these boundaries. We spread a plastic sheet on the ground to cover the square. Another purchase from the general store, naturally.

And then—Sengoku entered the square.

Alone.
In a school swimsuit.
"………"
The swimsuit wasn't from the general store (they don't sell them at general stores). Just like those volleyball shorts, Kanbaru had "happened" to have one ready.
I said to her, "You didn't have the money to buy a flashlight, so what are you doing carrying around volleyball shorts and school swimsuits?"
"There are some things in this world that money can't buy."
"I completely agree, but volleyball shorts and school swimsuits aren't among them."
"I was trying to play to your tastes."
"Well, don't."
"You're not denying it's to your taste?"
I checked to find that Sengoku was indeed chuckling to herself in the boundary… It was for the joke factor that she was wearing a school swimsuit in the middle of a decrepit shrine, but she found it funny too?
At any rate.
To see how the purification was proceeding, we needed to keep track of the scale marks on her skin, and Oshino's instructions were that she shouldn't stay in long sleeves and long pants, but we couldn't have her in nothing but a pair of volleyball shorts outdoors. While showing us the Jagirinawa's marks in my room, Sengoku had taken her hands off of her chest at one point, causing her to start crying all over again—a mishap that even an honest guy like me didn't share with Oshino—so this was particularly necessary.
And so, a school swimsuit.
Instead of changing at the shrine, she'd worn it under her long sleeves and long pants like an elementary schoolgirl might. Though we could see the scale markings on her legs, the swimsuit hid her torso, making it difficult to gauge the extent of her affliction—and maybe I was just imagining it, but they seemed to have climbed up to around her neck. Had its grip on her tightened since the evening?
If so, we needed to hurry.
We simply didn't see it.

But Sengoku's body—was still in the grip of a giant snake.

I handed her the amulet Oshino had given me.

"Now, sit in the center…on the sheet. Hold the amulet as tight as you can, close your eyes, calm your breathing—and all you need to do is pray."

"Pray…to what?" asked Sengoku.

"To something. In this case, probably to—"

The snake.

The snake god.

The Jagirinawa.

"Okay…I'll try my best."

"Alrighty."

"Big Brother Koyomi…you'll watch over me?"

"I will."

"You have to watch over me."

"…Yup, I will."

In any case—it was the only thing I could do.

Honestly, it was all up to Sengoku from here.

No matter—what happened.

People who get saved got saved on their own.

I exited the boundary, and together with Kanbaru, who had just finished lighting a mosquito coil, circled around at a distance to stand in front of Sengoku.

"Okay…"

Sengoku's eyes were already shut.

Both of her hands—were squeezed tight in front of her chest.

The ritual had already begun.

Not even Oshino knew how long it would take—he'd said to be prepared to stay here all night in the worst case. Kanbaru and I were one thing, but I didn't know if Sengoku's psyche could hold out for that long. We'd just have to try. There was no rehearsing this.

The glow of the flashlights.

They gently illuminated her—from four corners.

"Hey," Kanbaru spoke to me.

Her voice was so small I could have missed it, even though she stood right next to me. It must have been her way of being considerate to Sengoku, who was concentrating inside the boundary, but in that case, wasn't it best not to talk at all?

"What is it?" I said. "No more banter from here on out."

We couldn't afford to have Sengoku laugh during the ritual.

It would all be for naught then.

"Yes, I know... But there's something I was wondering about, now that we're here."

"What?"

"The serpent-slaying that she stoutly carried out on her own. What about all that?"

"That's one hell of a way to put it...but yeah. You mean chopping up those snakes."

"Yes. Wasn't doing that, only in the proper way, the correct measure, rather than this onerous ceremony?"

"Well, yes...and I said the same thing, but it sounds like that way would take even more time. According to Oshino, that is. Apparently, when it comes to snake-chopping, what's important is actually the locale."

"The locale... And since *bad things* are gathered here..."

"Well, this spot is the absolute worst, but that doesn't mean anywhere else would do. I didn't have enough time to ask for details, but he talked about it not being very effective unless you use snakes from Tohoku, or something."

"Regional differences?"

"Regional differences. Important when it comes to aberrations."

They had to be spoken about, and all.

Sengoku had chosen this mountain because she'd heard she could find snakes here, but she'd needed to do a better job picking her mountain and her snakes for a ritual—supposedly. Of course, as far as that went, it would have been best if Nadeko Sengoku hadn't done anything to begin with.

She chose this hangout, of all places.

This spot where *bad things* gathered.

But now, ironically enough—we needed to get those *bad things* on our side to help cleanse Sengoku of her aberration.

"Got it, makes sense," Kanbaru said. "Mister Oshino keeps some pretty handy things around, doesn't he? An amulet you can use to exorcise aberrations?"

"When I bothered him about it, he said it's not that handy of an item. It's useless except in cases like this one."

It only worked because the aberration had been sent by a human.

And only because it was a snake.

"So we're combating foul play with foul play," Kanbaru commented.

"He described it as one heterodoxy for another."

"I guess it's fine if it saves Sengoku… Still, you really do try to help out every person you come across, don't you?"

Kind to everyone.

Irresponsibly—kind to everyone.

"I wouldn't say every person, but I do whenever I can," I answered. "Especially if it's someone I know."

"I think that's part of what my dear senior loves about you, and I, too, think it's part of your charm. I—at this point, I'm glad that she's going out with someone like you. But I do hope—"

Kanbaru paused before continuing.

"If—the day ever comes when you have to choose just one person, I hope you'll choose her without a second thought."

"……"

"You're free to sacrifice yourself as much as you want, but please take good care of her… Not that I really have any right to be saying this."

Kanbaru's left arm.

It once tried to kill me.

Not because anyone shackled it.

With a firm will of its own, as an aberration.

"Kanbaru…I do think you have the right to say that. In fact—I think you're especially qualified."

"…Good to know."

"I'm just as glad that you're Senjogahara's junior as you're glad that I'm her boyfriend."

"Hearing that from you—really helps. Oh…"

There, Kanbaru pointed straight ahead.

At Sengoku, who was there praying with all her heart and soul.

And when I looked at her.

The scale markings on the parts of her body that weren't covered by the school swimsuit—those clear traces etched across every inch of her skin—were gradually fading. Oshino had said to be prepared to spend all night, but not even ten minutes had passed.

So—it was powerful.

It was going well, too.

The scale marks at the base of her neck—disappeared.

The scale marks around her collarbones—disappeared.

The Jagirinawa was leaving Sengoku.

"It looks like it's going forward—without a hitch."

"Yes," Kanbaru agreed.

"Neat."

Given my own presence, which tended to jinx everything, this state of affairs, quite honestly, could qualify as unexpected. Well, thank goodness. Now Sengoku needed to stay focused for another minute—

"Still," I said, "it's not like everything will be over once we rid her of the snake." To avoid sapping Sengoku's motivation, I hadn't told her this ahead of time, of course. "At the minimum, her relationship with that old friend is going to be irreparably broken."

"Well…you might be right." Kanbaru nodded. "There aren't too many people who could forgive such a thing. Nope… Not that Sengoku would want to mend the friendship, and the other party might not want to, either."

"So a breakdown—in their relationship."

Humans were scarier than aberrations.

No need to give voice to such a cliché, though.

"Romantic entanglements are so damn scary," I said. "But I wonder who Sengoku has a crush on. I'm a little jealous to know that someone out there is the object of that cute a girl's affections."

Were this a rom-com manga, the love interest would turn out to be none other than me, but I highly doubted that was the case here. I was her "big brother" and nothing more.

Brother and sister—

While I said I was jealous, I had a girlfriend, so of course, if Sengoku really did have feelings for me, it would just be a headache… But using this opportunity to revive our ties perhaps wasn't such a bad thing. It would be sweet, and she was precarious enough that someone needed to watch over her, though I had no idea what my little sisters would say…

"She is a girl, after all. And—she's fourteen? Heheh," Kanbaru chuckled. "Myself included, not every girl her age longs for a prince in a white coat to come in and swoop her away."

"Well yeah, I'm sure…"

Because, for one thing, it would be a prince on a white horse.

Sheesh, white coat… Like a doctor?

Ophiuchus.

"Come on, Kanbaru, didn't I tell you no idle talk? We're not done yet, so we can't risk breaking her concen—"

"Look!" Kanbaru suddenly yelled.

I was the one whose concentration had broken. Carelessly—I'd taken my eyes off of Sengoku. When I returned my gaze back at her—Nadeko Sengoku had collapsed face-up on the plastic sheet we'd laid on the ground—and was twitching freakishly, violently.

Her mouth.

It was open wide.

Her jaw was stretched as far as it would go.

Like a snake—swallowing an egg.

Like there could even be—a snake's head inside.

"Wh-What happened?!"

"I-I don't know—she suddenly…"

The scale markings on Sengoku's body—were disappearing.

They were *about halfway* gone.

But—the *other half* remained.

They hadn't disappeared.

And.

They were even on Sengoku's neck, where they didn't seem to be only moments ago. The snake—the Jagirinawa had her in its grip.

What happened…what went wrong?

Where had we gone wrong?

The illustration of the Jagirinawa that Oshino had said was in the *Compilation of Snake Curses*—of a man constricted by a snake that entered into his body through his mouth—not a deathly but a murderous, killing aberration.

A serpent god.

Possession by a serpent god.

"Did it fail?!" shouted Kanbaru. "Is that it?! It failed, and the purification ritual went out of control, ran amok—"

"No—this ritual isn't supposed to be a risky stunt… It isn't some powerful feat. That's why it's heterodox. It shouldn't be double-teaming her, there's no reason it would. Because *this is supposed to be like a negotiation with the aberration*—"

Ask it.

You need to ask it—Oshino had said.

Humble yourself before it.

And yet… Did Sengoku let herself get distracted, like in Senjogahara's case? Even then…the aberration suddenly reaching its final stage like this…

It was going so well until we were halfway in, too!

"…Halfway?"

Crap, I realized belatedly.

Sengoku was writhing on the plastic sheet.

Her legs, still yet to fill out, that extended from the school swimsuit—the scale markings were half gone from them as well.

Half gone—in only the crudest way.

The scale marks had completely disappeared from her right leg—but remained on every inch of her left leg, from her toes to her crotch.

Not a single one had disappeared.

I didn't know about her torso, but it was the same for her neck and collarbones, as clear as day once you noticed—

"Kanbaru…I had it all wrong. *If only we could see,* we'd have gotten it right away—"

"What do you mean?!"

"*The Jagirinawa—it wasn't just one of them. There were two.*"

"........kk!"

Even so—

There were hints we should have picked up on.

The traces covered *every inch of her skin* aside from her arms and her neck up. Her toes, her shins, her calves—and she had two legs. For one snake to *wind itself around every inch* of both of her legs was structurally impossible. If there'd been only one snake, *there couldn't have been markings on her inner thighs.*

From the tips of each leg's toes.

A Jagirinawa had its grip on her—one for each leg.

As if they were constricting Sengoku's body.

Two snakes.

"...Dammit!"

One of them—had been removed with the power of Oshino's amulet.

The Jagirinawa had gone away.

Gone away *here and there.*

But then the amulet's power was spent.

I hadn't said enough—had I realized that there were two Jagirinawa, Oshino would have come up with an appropriate plan. Unlike every other time, there was no limit to how much he would help. Nadeko Sengoku was a victim, and he was pulling out all the stops. But because we'd premised our discussion on one Jagirinawa, he'd prepared a strategy for just one—

Which is why the other—was running wild. Of course it was—the other giant snake with which it had shared its grip on Sengoku had been exorcised.

"Kanbaru! Stay there—no, get back!"

"Shouldn't we contact Mister Oshino—"

"He doesn't have a cell phone!"

Not on principle—but because he failed at modern gizmos.

So—our only choice was a hardline approach.

I rushed into the makeshift boundary—into the square illuminated by the flashlights. I grabbed onto Sengoku's body and sat her upright—she was hot to the touch. You could say burning. It was so bad I thought my hand might get scalded—

The scale markings at the base of her neck.

They were now digging so far into her skin that calling them traces would be ludicrous. They were eating into her to the point of altering her silhouette—gnawing in as if to pulverize bone and tear flesh.

As if to chop her up.

Eating into her.

I could almost hear her body—groan and creak.

"Sengoku…"

Her eyes had rolled back—she'd lost consciousness.

Swallowed whole—

"Nkk…!"

I laid her body, which I was holding, on the plastic sheet again. Then, I slowly reached my hands toward her.

No, not toward her.

Toward the Jagirinawa.

"*Even if I can't see it—I should be able to touch it.*"

He'd said so.

Ever since spring break—vampire blood ran through my veins. Blood. You could say I was an aberration myself—and an aberration should be able to touch another aberration.

If I could touch it, I could peel it off.

Right.

The key was to imagine it. To visualize the Jagirinawa through the traces that its scales etched into Sengoku's body—and to puzzle out the manner it exercised its grip. I couldn't afford to be wrong. Dammit… Like the younger of my two little sisters, and unlike the older, I was ever the indoorsy type…so this was my first time touching a snake. The first one ever was going to be an aberration…

Courage, me.

Even Sengoku, who used to play with that youngest sister of mine, caught more than ten snakes on her own—*what kind of big brother feared doing as much?*

"Agh…hkk!"

Slither—

An unpleasant sensation, in both of my hands.

A sensation like sticking my hands into mucus.

A sensation like spiked scales stabbing into them.

It was plain disgusting.

What made it disgusting was that I was touching something I couldn't see—I'd never thought that doing so would be as viscerally repulsive. I'd mustered such a strong will to touch it—but now wanted to take my hands off of the aberration as soon as I possibly could.

I tried to use its sliminess to my advantage by sliding my hands around it to get them in the right position. Grabbing its cylindrical body, about the size of what a musclehead's thigh must be, I then—pulled with all my might.

It wasn't like I had the physical prowess of a vampire as well.

Plus—it was slippery.

Because I was pulling in the same direction as its scales, I wasn't putting my strength to much use. I changed my approach and dug my nails into the giant snake's body (so soft it felt like my fingers sank into it) before pulling again—

To peel it off—!

"G…aaaaaagh!"

An unimaginable pain—ran through my right arm.

I looked at where the pain came from to see blood—spurting everywhere. My arm was *flattened* as if a machine press had gotten hold of everything from my wrist to my elbow, and two deep, deep holes had been bored into that flattened area.

"—A-Already?!"

The snake's head had already pulled out of Sengoku's mouth—my fingers burrowing into its torso had been understood as an attack, and it had exited her body to strike back at me. I didn't notice until it bit me because I couldn't see it—

"Oww…wwwww!!"

The overwhelming pain made me leap and roll away confused—meanwhile, Sengoku's body seemed to flap and flop at random around the plastic sheet in the square, likely as a result of the Jagirinawa undoing its grasp on her body. I could only guess since I couldn't see it, but it must have been the case, given the situation.

Which meant—that it was coming to grip and possess me next!

Before it could try, I slammed my flattened right arm on the ground. Even greater pain came over me—but a moment before my arm hit the ground, I could sense the buried fangs—the Jagirinawa's, no doubt—sliding out. Realizing that my plan was to pin its head between my arm and the ground, it had preempted me. As a result, all I managed to do was bang my injured arm against the earth.

It almost felt like my arm had torn off.

A moment later, it was my leg.

My left ankle.

Scrush—a flattening sound.

As with my arm—it seemed this snake could crush a human body just with its bite… What monstrous jaw strength. Well, it was a literal monster's jaw strength, but even so—

Estimating where the Jagirinawa's head would be based on the fang marks drilled into my ankle, I nevertheless stuck my fingers between its mouth and my foot and pried them apart—though it was biting down on me with an absurd amount of force, I used the small gap I created to twist my leg out. It was shot, down to the bones, but the nerves still seemed intact. It was fine, it still moved.

It would have been nice if I could hold on to the snake's mouth, but I reflexively let go when I felt a wet slap on my hand (the snake's long, forked tongue must have licked me).

"Nkk!"

Still, the blind, haphazard kick I sent the Jagirinawa's way with my other leg seemed to hit it, or at least it felt that way. It was the same sensation as kicking a rubber ball, so I doubted that I'd dealt any damage. I then rolled backward, two times, three times, to put some distance between myself and the Jagirinawa.

It was only the day before yesterday that I'd given Shinobu my blood.

That meant my body should have been able to heal itself even faster than normal—but my flattened right arm and left ankle weren't recovering so easily. They didn't even show signs of doing so. The pain wasn't going away, either… Wait…was the Jagirinawa a poisonous snake?

Even vampires are susceptible to poison. All the more so considering how minimally vampiric I was. Shinobu in her prime would have brushed off such a wound—

I hopped myself back up on one leg. My right arm dangled uselessly at my side… It hurt too much even to raise.

It wasn't as if I had no experience battling aberrations, and their kin and ilk, over the past few months. In fact, you could say I was fairly experienced for the short amount of time. But—I'd never fought an aberration that I couldn't see. I'd always thought of the invisible man as a ridiculous concept in this day and age, not even good for a joke. I never imagined that an invisible enemy could be this dreadful!

I was up against a snake.

I recalled that snakes had some tissue called pit organs that allowed them to sense infrared radiation and to find prey via heat—which meant our eye levels' height difference probably didn't work to my advantage. It went past trying not to be seen by your enemy while seeing him.

Ssszzzsss…

I could hear a sound.

Of something crawling, creeping my way.

"……kk! A-Ahh!"

While I was able to stand on my left leg, I couldn't use it for much else. My movement was now as inefficient as it could be, but—the Jagirinawa had *probably* tried to attack my upper body, and I *dare say* that I dodged it.

Turning around, I tried to guess where it landed.

The Jagirinawa's landing point—

Was clear to me.

"I—I might be able to do this."

I just might—be able to do it.

I stood on guard so I could confirm my guess.

I waited for the second strike, my eyes glued—I kept my eyes glued to the Jagirinawa's current position. To tell what your opponent is thinking—you look into their eyes. Not that I knew whether I should be looking into the snake's eyes or pit organs, not that the Jagirinawa was visible to begin with—

It moved!

I leapt aside and dodged it.

Clamp! came a noise from right beside me, as if a bear trap had been set off—no doubt the sound of the Jagirinawa's mouth closing as it missed. It gave me chills—if that thing ever got around my head, it was game over. It'd be bitten straight off.

But…

I saw a way for me to win.

This arena—was my ally.

A dirt ground.

Overgrown with grass.

And snakes—were creatures that crawled on the ground.

That was true even if the creature was an aberration.

I might not see the Jagirinawa itself, but it left behind a clear trail—just like the scale markings etched into Sengoku's body.

The churned ground sent up dust.

The grass parted like it was in the way.

On asphalt or concrete, I wouldn't be so lucky. If the serpent exorcism were taking place at the abandoned cram school where Oshino lived, like in Senjogahara or Kanbaru's case—I'd be toast. But wait.

Maybe this stage direction came courtesy of Oshino.

Right, come to think of it, this aberration could ignore clothes. It only made sense for it to be able to do the same for dirt or grass. Even its slithering *sszss* and the sound of its mouth snapping shut shouldn't have been audible. If the Jagirinawa couldn't ignore the field's physicality—that was the arena's doing. On these grounds, the serpent, too, merely invisible, existed.

Because it was an aberration.

Like me and Kanbaru.

Like a prank curse actually taking.

An air pocket—a hangout.

Where bad things—gathered.

Oshino had said *to make allies of the bad things*—which meant this must have been part of the measure. The basic stratagem was predicated on creating a boundary, but the abandoned cram school hadn't been designated as the stage, just in case something unexpected like this happened—and maybe it was all thanks to the enhanced field that I could hear and touch the aberration.

Mèmè Oshino.

It hurt to feel so powerless.

The upshot was that for Senjogahara and Kanbaru too, I'd turned it all in to Oshino—I relied on him from start to finish. He wasn't going to be in our town forever, and yet, in each and every case—this time too!

Maybe I was the one who wasn't regretting a thing.

I'd learned nothing from all my time with Oshino.

I didn't see—a thing.

"Nkk..."

I somehow dodged the Jagirinawa's next attack, too.

Still...it felt like I was getting nowhere. If I focused on just dodging its attacks, then thanks to the power of the *bad things* that gathered on the premises, I could gauge the Jagirinawa's position and movements with some degree of accuracy from how it disturbed the dirt and grass—but striking back was a pretty tall order. Attacking would require wild guesses, and my right arm and left leg were out of commission. How was I supposed to mount a proper attack?

It was like—my body wasn't healing at all.

The pain was only getting worse.

It might have been my imagination, but it seemed to be spreading.

Could it really have been—poison?

Neurotoxins, hemotoxins, cardiotoxins.

A serum was—indispensable.

Would my attacks work on an aberration to begin with? Even regular snakes had such vitality that they seemed to refuse to die. Could a half-assed thing like me, a human with a bit of residual vampirism, hope to oppose it? It didn't seem completely futile, given that the Jagirinawa started attacking me the moment I dug my fingers into its body—but at this rate, wasn't kiting it all I could ever hope to do?

What would count as defeating this aberration?

No.

There was a more fundamental question… *Was it even okay to defeat*—this aberration? If I defeated it, would that be the end? Was it the *handiest* solution—as Mèmè Oshino might say?

Demons, cats, crabs, snails, monkeys—

Snakes.

Some saw snakes as holy—

"*My senior Araragi!*"

It was Kanbaru.

Suruga Kanbaru—was dashing toward me.

At full speed.

As if she were using her no-mere-high-schooler legs to—kamikaze me.

Idiot, I told her to stay away—no, wait!

"……!"

Right…maybe Kanbaru could!

Kanbaru's left arm, the monkey's paw, the monkey's arm—had the terrifying attack power we needed to counter the Jagirinawa! Within her left arm—resided a catapult that could smash through concrete blocks unaided. The Jagirinawa could have a body of steel and still be helpless against Kanbaru's unbridled strength.

But—if there was a problem, it was that unlike me, Kanbaru didn't have any healing abilities. If the Jagirinawa dodged her attack and retaliated with a bite, there would be no way to undo the damage. It would be irreparable and irreversible—and if I was right and the Jagirinawa was a poisonous snake, her life would be in immediate danger under even the most optimistic of scenarios. How ironic. I had the ability to recover from attacks but couldn't deal any damage, while the opposite went for her. Another factor I needed to keep in mind was affinity. This field was a bane to Kanbaru. Even now, she must be feeling pretty sick—

In fact.

However.

"*—Forgive me!*"

Kanbaru's attack was aimed—at me.

Not the Jagirinawa. Me.

With that left arm, she grabbed me hard by the base of my neck and, drawing on her momentum, used her vaunted legs to all but leap—and shove me. I, with my one good leg, couldn't hope to stand firm. Like a speck of dust in a raging sandstorm—I was blown away. Her left hand, still planted on my neck, wouldn't let go. It didn't let go. It held on. We flew about fifteen feet in the air like that—

Before slamming into the ground.

It may have been a soft, dirt surface blanketed with foliage.

But the full-body impact was so stunning that I couldn't breathe for a moment.

Kanbaru had made good on her word and shoved me off my feet with her left arm alone—though it wasn't down onto a bed.

I yelled, "Wh-What was that for—Kanbaru!"

She silently lay on top of me, in a full mount in grappling terms, using not only her left arm but her entire body to restrain me. I couldn't begin to resist given the state of my right arm and left—no.

Not even if my body was in perfect condition.

Not even if Kanbaru's arm wasn't a monkey's arm.

If she really tried to pin me down, there was nothing I could do about it. A jock on the national level against a washout whose only extracurricular activity was biking home. Being a year older or a guy didn't matter one bit. Struggle as I might, I couldn't even budge. My body was pasted to the ground, and though Kanbaru couldn't be that heavy, I felt like she was crushing me.

"Kanbaru…you—"

"Stay still! Calm down!"

"Calm down?"

"The poison is going to spread through your blood if you don't!"

Kanbaru was close to me—our faces were practically touching, but she shouted so loud I thought she'd perforate my eardrums.

"*Snakes are savage but shy creatures—they won't do anything if you don't approach and assault them! Don't provoke it! Just stay still, and the snake will go away!*"

"………kk."

Snake—behavior.

It was the same—even for an aberration.

Be it gripping or the use of pit organs.

Which meant—

Kanbaru was exactly right.

Even I—knew that much.

If I stayed still—the Jagirinawa would leave.

I'd already peeled it off of Sengoku.

The snake—would go back.

"...B-But, Kanbaru! That—"

It would only go back.

It wouldn't be banished.

It would return.

Turning back on the caster of the curse—

When one is cursed, two holes are dug.

When one is cursed—two holes are dug.

Like a snake piercing the skin—two holes are dug.

"I beg you—" Kanbaru said in a pained voice. Like she was pleading with me. "Don't mistake who you're trying to save here."

Ssszzzsss.

Ssszzzsss.

Ssszzzsss.

I heard it.

The sound of the Jagirinawa crawling on the ground—I couldn't see the dust rising or the grass being parted from my angle. But—I could tell the sound was receding at a steady pace. The Jagirinawa—was trying to crawl away. Perhaps it had lost sight of me after Kanbaru's left arm had transported me fifteen feet away in one go. Or maybe—the Jagirinawa hadn't given a damn about me in the first place.

The snake—was going back.

Back to the one who had cast it.

Bringing back with it—its curse.

"........."

Slump—I could feel my strength leaving me. I wouldn't make it in time. I could give chase, but what hope did I have of following a snake I couldn't see? Its sound and its presence would vanish once it left the grounds. And, to begin with, there was no getting out from under Kanbaru.

Even if I could—I couldn't see myself doing it.

"My senior Araragi…"

Kanbaru must have felt me slump powerlessly—there was concern in her voice.

"I'm sorry," I apologized to her. I couldn't think of anything else to say. "I'm sorry I forced that role onto you."

"Please, don't apologize… I wouldn't know how to reply."

"Yeah…sorry."

"My senior Araragi."

"I'm sorry, Kanbaru… I'm really sorry…"

Sorry—was all I could say to her.

It felt like I was always apologizing to Kanbaru when it mattered the most. I really felt bad. Burdening her…for being such a pathetic senior, I really did—feel bad.

Kanbaru's decision was the right one. There was no denying it. I could have continued, but I had almost no chance of beating the Jagirinawa. How could I, a mock aberration, ever handle a real, live aberration? Frantically dodging the snake's biting attacks and collapsing from the poison rushing through my body as a result was the best outcome I could have hoped for.

But—I just hadn't been able to give up.

It was like I'd been throwing a tantrum.

That's why it hurt so much.

The pain in my right arm, the pain in my left leg—

They were nothing compared to this other pain.

I was flimsy.

I was feeble.

I was—utterly powerless.

"Big Brother Koyomi…"

The snake gone—

Sengoku approached Kanbaru and me with faltering steps, having regained consciousness. The boundary was pointless now that the aberration had departed—and the scale markings eating into her flesh had vanished from every inch of her skin visible on her swimsuit-clad body.

Not half-gone.

Fully gone.

Her skin was fair, smooth, beautiful.

She wasn't suffering anymore.

She wasn't hurting anymore.

She wasn't going to have to cry anymore—

"Big Brother Koyomi. Thank you for saving me."

Stop it.

Sengoku.

Please...don't mouth words like "thank you" that I can't bear to hear. I don't have any right to be thanked by you. Because of all things—I was trying to save even the person who cursed you.

007

The epilogue, or maybe, the punch line of this story.

I was roused awake the next day as usual by my little sisters Karen and Tsukihi and began getting ready to go to school. Tuesday, June thirteenth, a weekday. My right arm and my left leg seemed to have healed to the point where everyday tasks didn't pose an issue. With Kanbaru and Sengoku supporting me on both sides, pathetically enough, I had gone to the abandoned cram school afterwards to have Shinobu drink a bit of my blood so as to bolster my body's healing capabilities. However hands-off my parents, I couldn't come home with a crushed arm and foot. As ever, Shinobu didn't speak to me. Perhaps she was appalled, perhaps she wasn't thinking anything at all. Either way, she couldn't have minded a surprise opportunity to drink even more of my blood and must have been in one of her better moods. As a matter of proper procedure I did give a simple report of the events to Oshino, but he didn't say much either. Perhaps he was appalled—perhaps he wasn't thinking anything at all.

After that, I spent the night with everyone in one of the abandoned cram school's rooms. Sengoku had lied to her parents and said she was at a friend's sleepover party, so she had to be somewhere that night. With no other suitable locations available to us, we slept right there in the ruins. We were excited at first like kids on a school trip, but all three of us must have been tired and fell asleep in no time.

If it's winter, then spring isn't far behind.

Night is always followed by day.

Kanbaru and I walked Sengoku home, promised to meet again, then parted ways. After putting together some plans for Senjogahara's birthday party for a bit, I split up with Kanbaru too at a crosswalk. Then, once I finally got home and got to work falling back asleep in my own bed, I was roused awake by my little sisters. For no real reason, I asked Tsukihi, "Do you remember Sengoku?"

She replied saying she did.

Oh, you mean Sen?

When I heard that, I remembered—just as she'd called me Big Brother Koyomi, I'd called her Sen.

Even so—

I couldn't call her that now.

Changing into my school uniform, I began to think.

About why there had been two Jagirinawa.

Why two snakes—had possessed Sengoku.

There was that girl, her friend, with her misbegotten grudge—she resented how the boy she fancied confessed to Sengoku only to get turned down. The girl turned to occult charms, a fad at her school, and to a top-drawer curse at that. It was her way of venting steam, and she must not have thought that it would actually work...

That incident alone offered up one more person—another character who might have resented Sengoku. Yes, the boy whom Sengoku had given the cold shoulder. As with Sengoku's friend, I didn't know his name—but it wouldn't be shocking if he, too, held a misbegotten grudge against her. You could even call it reasonable, psychologically speaking. A simple case—of romantic entanglements. Of being head over heels. The girls didn't have an exclusive patent on those charms that were a fad at their school. It was entirely possible for someone to attempt a curse without informing the target like an honest fool. Placing a curse in earnest—also a possibility.

When one is cursed, two holes are dug.

Well, that's all just my conjecture. I don't have any firm evidence, and even if I'm right, who the Jagirinawa went back to, the girl or the boy, and how a returned curse works is something I can't hope to figure out.

Sengoku doesn't need to know, either.

However you look at it, that would be shoes on a snake.

ANIPLEX
傷物語
I 鉄血篇
-KIZUMONOGATARI-
PART 1: TEKKETSU
-Blu-ray Set-
NOW
AVAILABLE
-ORDER TODAY-
FOR MORE INFORMATION, VISIT:
WWW.KIZUMONOGATARI-USA.COM
© NISIOISIN/KODANSHA, ANIPLEX, SHAFT

DECAPITATION
KUBIKIRI CYCLE
The Blue Savant and the Nonsense User

A dropout from an elite Houston-based program for teens is on a visit to a private island. Its mistress, virtually marooned there, surrounds herself with geniuses, especially of the young and female kind—one of whom ends up headless one fine morning.

The top-selling novelist year by year in his native Japan, prolific palindromic phenomenon NISIOISIN made his debut when he was only twenty with this Mephisto Award winner, a whodunit and locked-room mystery at once old-school and eye-opening. Previously published stateside by Del Rey, the translation has been retitled and revised just in time for the long-requested animated series based on illustrator *take's* character concepts.

NOW ON SALE!